Waking THE Moon

Waking THE Moon

ELIZABETH HAND

HarperPrism

Grateful acknowledgment is made for permission to reprint excerpts from the following:

"The Hollow Men" in *Collected Poems 1909-1962* by T.S. Eliot, copyright 1936 by Harcourt Brace & Co., copyright © 1964, 1963 by T.S. Eliot, reprinted by permission of the publisher.

"In the Evening," "The City," and "Voices," in *The Complete Poems of Cavafy*, copyright © 1961 and renewed 1989 by Rae Dalven, reprinted by permission of Harcourt Brace & Co.

"Northern Sky" written by Nick Drake. Copyright © 1970 Warlock Music (BMI). Used by permission. All Rights Reserved.

"She Lives (in a Time of Her Own)" © 1981 by Roky Erickson, Tapier Music.

"I Have Always Been Here Before" © 1981 by Roky Erickson, Orb Music Co./Bleb Alien Saucer Publishing.

HarperPaperbacks *A Division of* HarperCollins*Publishers*
10 East 53rd Street, New York, N.Y. 10022

HarperPaperbacks may be purchased for educational, business, or sales promotional use. For information please write: Special Markets Department, HarperCollins*Publishers,* 10 East 53rd Street, New York, N.Y. 10022.

First printing: July 1995

Printed in the United States of America

HarperPrism is an imprint of HarperPaperbacks. HarperPaperbacks, HarperPrism, and colophon are trademarks of HarperCollins*Publishers*.

Library of Congress Cataloging-in-Publication Data

Hand, Elizabeth
Waking the moon / Elizabeth Hand.
p. cm.
ISBN 0-06-105214-0
I. Title.
PS3558.A4619W34 1995
813'.54—dc20 94-47085
CIP

---

95 96 97 98 99 v 10 9 8 7 6 5 4 3 2 1

Anyway those things would not have lasted long. The experience
of the years shows it to me. But Destiny arrived
in some haste and stopped them.
The beautiful life was brief.
But how potent were the perfumes,
on how splendid a bed we lay,
to what sensual delight we gave our bodies.

An echo of the days of pleasure,
an echo of the days drew near me,
a little of the fire of the youth of both of us;
again I took in my hands a letter,
and I read and reread till the light was gone.

And melancholy, I came out on the balcony—
came out to change my thoughts at least by looking at
a little of the city that I loved,
a little movement on the street, and in the shops.

C.P. CAVAFY, "IN THE EVENING," TRANSLATED BY RAE DALVEN

For Oscar John Long,
friend and voyager
with all my love

Contents

PART ONE: DEPARTURE

1. The Sign *5*
2. Raising the Naphaïm *20*
3. Oliver and Angelica *26*
4. The Lunula *38*
5. The Sound of Bones and Flutes *60*
6. The Reception *71*
7. Night of the Electric Insects *90*
8. Twilight at the Orphic Lodge *107*
9. The Harrowing *150*

PART TWO: ABSENCE

i. Pavana Lachrymæ *177*
ii. Threnody: Storm King *178*
iii. Lost Bells *187*
iv. Saranbanda de la Muerta Oscura *189*

PART THREE: RETURN

10. Ignoreland *193*
11. Ancient Voices *200*
12. The Priestess at *Huitica* *211*
13. Other Echoes *231*
14. Devil-Music *241*
15. Ancient Voices (Echo) *259*
16. Black Angels *271*
17. Falling *282*
18. A Meeting *293*
19. Fire from the Middle Kingdom *307*
20. Threnody and Breakdown *318*
21. Waking the Moon *358*

If all those young men were like hares on the mountain
Then all those pretty maidens would get guns, go a-hunting.

If all those young men were like fish in the water
Then all those pretty maidens would soon follow after.

If all those young men were like rushes a-growing
Then all those pretty maidens would get scythes, go a-mowing.

—Maying Song

Prologue

They never found her. Nothing at all: no clothes, no jewelry, no bones or teeth or locks of auburn hair. No lunula. Maybe that's why I never truly mourned Angelica. Oh, I *grieved*, of course, with that hopeless misery one reserves for lost youth or broken chances or a phantom limb. That was how I wept for Angelica; not the way I'd raged when I lost Oliver. Not even the muted anguish I'd felt during all those lost years in Dr. Dvorkin's carriage house.

This was a small grief, really: because how can I believe that Angelica is really *gone*, any more than a storm or hurricane is gone? The clouds pass over, the skies clear; but there are still the shattered homes and decapitated trees, the dunes given to the sea. And always there will be that clutch in the chest when you see a darkness on the horizon, a greening in the evening sky.

Like Oliver, she was beautiful; she was so beautiful. And she was kind and smart and funny, the sort of friend you dream of having. The kind of friend *I* dreamed of having, and somehow she found me, just as Oliver had. If she was a force of nature, she was still human; at least until the end. How can I believe she is gone?

But she *is* gone, and I have so little to remember her by. If only I had written more about my friends, or done something with my nearly empty college notebooks. If only I had taken pictures, or saved Oliver's funny crabbed drawings, and the delicately calligraphic notes Angelica pinned to the door of my room in Rossetti Hall with their faint musky scents of sandalwood and oranges!

But I kept nothing of Oliver and Angelica, not a single real photograph or letter or drawing. Only a black-and-white Polaroid that Oliver gave me shortly after we met, showing his shoe—a rather worn black wing tip—and part of his bare ankle; that and the sea urchin lamp Angelica sent me our first Christmas.

That's all. Though I have more of them within me now than they could ever know. Perhaps, that is almost enough.

PART ONE

Departure

CHAPTER 1

The Sign

I met them in Magic, Witchcraft, and Religion. A fitting place, that magician's grove within the enchanted forest that was the Divine, where Balthazar Warnick presided at his podium and wore a hand-painted paisley tie and three-piece Fergus Corméillean worsted suit to every session—even though there were only seven of us students, and the dyspeptic radiators hissed as though black winter gnawed at the stained glass windows, instead of the city's sultry Indian summer.

I had taken a seat at the very back of the room. It was my first day of classes, my first official day at the Divine. I had arrived the previous Friday, meekly following the Strong Suggestion listed in the Introductory Handbook—a slender volume printed by the University on heavy cream-colored paper meant to invoke the physical and intellectual weight of vellum.

> It is *strongly* suggested that underclassmen attending the university for the first time arrive during the week of September 1st, 1975, when Orientation and Introductory Sessions will be held for both students and those parents who wish to attend.

At the top of every page glowered the University's coat of arms, a Gryphon rampant and Pelican *gules*, the latter tearing at her own breast to feed her young. Beneath them was a motto—

> *Vita, sine literis, mors est.*
> *Life without learning is death.*

—and the school's name spelled out in glorious sweeps of gold and blue and crimson.

The University of the Archangels and Saint John the Divine.

The Divine, as I learned to call it within a few hours of my arrival. *School*, my mother called it, as when after the five-hour drive she stood with me in my dormitory room, surrounded by overstuffed boxes, and said, "Well, good luck at School, Katie."

The drive had been long and hot and anxious, my mother and father veering between elation and depression at seeing the last of their six children plummet from the nest. My parents had married for love, high school sweethearts from Astoria, Queens. My mother still had the accent—muted to be sure, but jarring, when you took in that delicate face beneath fiery curls. My mother was an Irish beauty of the old school. Not so my father, who stood six-foot-four in his bare and uncommonly ugly feet and—notwithstanding the degrees from Saint Bonaventure and Fordham and the elevated position at IBM—looked more like Victor McLaglen than Jack Kennedy. My two sisters were the beauties, my three brothers rebels who, as adults, made good.

Me? I was the smart one, the loner, the hapless rebel and youngest by many years. Katherine Sweeney Cassidy, named for my maternal grandmother Katherine Sweeney; with my mother's grey eyes and my father's feet, Katie to the family but Sweeney now to the world. Sweeney to the Divine.

After we carried my things into the dormitory we had a quick and uneasy lunch at the local Holiday Inn, where far jollier family groups yelled boisterously to new arrivals and where our waitress seemed to know every customer by name, except for us. Afterward, my parents departed almost immediately. My mother confessed years later that they had been too heart-stricken to stay, but I didn't know that at the time. They kissed me, my father still smelling slightly of ketchup, and then climbed into the blue Volvo wagon that would bear them north again. I waved as the car shot with nervous speed back into the stream of traffic on North Capitol Street. Then I ran my damp palms across the front of the maroon floral skirt my mother had laid out on my bed the night before (newly purchased from Lord & Taylor for the occasion, it was the first and only time I ever wore it) and slowly walked back to the dorm.

This was the first time it struck me that there might be disadvantages to a happy childhood. Everywhere I looked there were people who belonged here. Long-haired sunburned girls in puckered cotton sundresses, stretched out on the grass and smoking black cigarettes. Long-haired boys who pulled clinking green bottles from a cooler and toasted each other in sure, joyous cadences. In the near distance, beneath the shadows of the immense and baroque Shrine itself, the tiny white-clad figures of nuns in their summer habits walked with heads thrown back, diamond light sparkling on their sunglasses. A heavyset man in a yarmulka stood on a set of curved steps that spiraled down from one of the Shrine's promontories like a stairway in a Dr. Seuss book. As I watched he removed his yarmulka and absently patted his cheeks with it. The heat was intense. The oily scent of car exhaust wafting over from North Capitol Street vied with that of roses, which grew as profusely on the grounds of the Divine as within a public garden. My skirt hung limply about my knees, my long-sleeved cotton blouse felt heavy and moist as wet wool. As I dragged myself up the sidewalk to Rossetti Hall, a boy in a dashiki shirt bumped into me.

"Oops—sorry—" he mumbled, not even glancing aside as he hurried onto the lawn surrounding Rossetti Hall. Beneath one of its elaborate diamond-paned windows he stopped and bellowed "LINNNN—DDDDAA!" Above me windows flew open. Tanned faces stared down, laughing.

"Yo, Stephen," a blond girl called lazily. "Like, shut up."

No one took any notice of me at all. I flushed. My clothes burned against my skin. I looked away and ran up the steps and inside Rossetti Hall.

Somehow I got through that first weekend. My room turned out to be a surprisingly comforting haven, cool and quiet and mine alone. Like all of the buildings at the Divine, Rossetti Hall was a huge and Gothic edifice, vine-hung, sweet with the carnal scent of wisteria blossoms. Beneath its walls wandered a weird profusion of nuns and rabbis and sikhs and friars, and others of even more dubious spiritual provenance: Hare Krishnas, earnest Moonies, witches and druids nouveaux. The effect was superbly and spookily medieval, with color and comic relief thrown in by a small but noisy undergraduate population bearing the last battered standards of 1960s *gambado*. I was sorely aware of how drab I looked and felt.

My room was in a long corridor, cool and silent as an ice locker, even in these last weeks before autumn cast its phantom gold upon the city. I walked slowly down the hall, staring at my feet and trying to decipher the peculiar mosaic covering the floor. The tiles formed odd geometries in worn nursery colors, ducky yellow, little-boy blue, a nasty medicinal pink. The walls were a pale green that the years had treated more kindly, the plaster faded to a pleasant crème de menthe, with runnels of cream and chocolate where cracks had appeared. I spent a lot of time in that hall those first few days, waiting for someone to say hello, to invite me into another room. But the place remained strangely quiet. I was desperately lonely, my homesickness so intense I felt as though I'd been stabbed. Why hadn't I wanted a roommate? Worse, it seemed that in spite of the Strong Suggestion in the orientation manual, I had arrived several days too early. The hall's only other inhabitants were a trio of girls from Iran, distant relatives of the Shah, who were freshman engineering students. They spent their days brushing and plaiting one another's long black hair, and their evenings on the floor's single pay telephone, weeping and railing at the cruelty of their parents in sending them here.

I wished I could give myself over to such a luxury of grief. But when I called my parents I assured them all was well, school was great, my first class was Tuesday, Thanksgiving was not so far off, no really, everything was *fine*. Then I handed the phone back to the Iranians and returned to my room.

"Shit," I said, and slouched into a chair.

It was a long and narrow room, with old wooden furniture that smelled of lemons and chalk. I shrugged out of my skirt and blouse, stood shivering while I tried to remember which bag held my clothes. Then I pulled on ripped jeans and black T-shirt, punted the skirt beneath the bed, and turned to survey my kingdom.

At the end of the room a huge arched window glowed whitish blue in the afternoon light. I stepped over a tangle of stereo wires and peered outside. The mullioned panes were of heavy whorled glass. The casements opened by means of an ornate cast-iron crank that shrieked when I tried to turn it, until I found and released the latch holding it closed. The window began to open, very slowly. Air heavy and thick and sweet as cane syrup flowed into the room. I leaned forward, my hands resting on the broad granite sill.

My room faced east and looked out over the Strand, the long sward of grass and trees that ran down the center of the campus. All the campus was spread before me like a huge board game tricked out in gold and green and marble. Archaic grey buildings and great spreading elms formed a gauzy tapestry in the late-summer light. The horizon was bounded by a heavily wooded hill, where the pale dome of another building poked through the greenery like the top of an observatory or the ruin of some ancient temple. Rows of tourist buses were parked beneath the trees. Directly beneath my window the students I had seen earlier still lolled in the grass and passed each other joints, while dogs rolled laughing and barking between them. Above everything loomed the Shrine, that brooding sphinx, wavering in the heat. The whole scene had the unreal aura of a tinted postcard of the World's Fair. It never struck me that I could just have walked outside and been a part of it all.

But I *could* get a better look. I made certain the window was open as far as it would go. Then I swung out onto the ledge. For a perilous moment I crouched there like a gargoyle, until I caught my balance and scrunched up against one end of the window. My back butted up against something carved into uncomfortable points and angles. I wriggled until I felt more comfortable, then leaned forward to stare through the window and back into my room.

On the far wall hung a mirror. It showed me my reflection, a skinny figure like a goblin trapped in glass. Long legs in torn denim, bare ankles and feet betraying how unfashionably pale I was. Long arms with thin bony wrists, big hands, big feet, ragged fingernails. Limp shoulder-length black hair, straight and fine as a child's. A wide milk white pixie face, distinguished mostly by large pale grey eyes and star-tilted nose, a few freckles, an engaging little gap between my two front teeth. *Shanty Irish*, my high school English teacher had once described me. I liked the description. At eighteen I fancied myself a spiritual daughter of Brendan Behan and Flann O'Brien, an able drinker and quoter of melancholy verse. My nose even had a nearly undetectable list to one side, where my brother Kevin had broken it during a childhood rout over Matchbox cars.

"Hey!"

I turned and looked down. Two boys throwing a Frisbee waved up at me. Clutching the edge of the window frame, I waved back.

"Come on down!" one shouted. I shook my head, yelled, "Later!"

Near them a girl reading a magazine flopped onto her side, shading her eyes until she sighted me, then waved languidly and looked away. The boys laughed, skimmed the Frisbee between them, and loped off across the grass.

So they were friendly; so there was hope. I sat there for the rest of the afternoon, my face tipped to the sun, daydreaming about my classes, trying to figure out how many days were left before Columbus Day weekend.

But finally the heat got to me. My shoulders hurt, too, from whatever the hell I was leaning against. I stretched, carefully so as not to fall, and crept back to the window. At the opening I hesitated, and craned my neck to see what made that damn wall so uncomfortable.

There was an angel there. No—*two* angels. One to each side of my window. They were so lifelike that I started, the glass shuddering behind me. For a sickening moment I thought I'd fall; then I grabbed onto the window frame and caught my balance. After a moment I calmed down.

They're only angels, I thought, *stone angels*. Given the peculiar spiritual history of the Divine, not unusual at all. I just hadn't noticed them before. I blew down the front of my T-shirt, trying to cool off. Then I took another look.

There were angels everywhere. They seemed to flank each window of Rossetti Hall, and for all I knew they were everywhere across the entire campus. Ten feet high, wings folded in close against their sides, their long legs and flanks straight and smooth as pillars. It was the curling ends of a wing that I had been leaning against, its feathers swept up like the crest of a wave. Their long slender hands were posed in different attitudes—prayerful, admonitory, threatening, placating—their faces serene, eyes closed, mouths set in thin, unsmiling lines.

What was so startling about them was that they were naked, and had no genitals. Their thighs formed an inverted V and cast charcoal shadows against the wall. Stretching my hand, I could just barely touch the outline of sinew in the granite, the curve where a tendon bulged in a knee; the tiny details of muscle and lineament so lovingly rendered they must have been drawn from life. They didn't look desexed, or childlike, or like they were missing anything. They looked like they were *supposed* to look like that; like they were true androgynes. Real angels, turned to stone.

And staring up at the face of the one guarding my room, I thought that it had been very purposeful of the artist to depict it with eyes closed: because it would have been terrible to have one of those creatures gazing down at me.

Suddenly I felt cold. The blind faces were turned to where the Shrine's shadows had begun to creep across the Strand. I started to shiver uncontrollably, and realized I must have gotten sunstroke. I clambered back inside, kicked among my clothes until I found an old grey cross-country sweatshirt, and pulled it on. It was after five o'clock. I could find dinner in the dining hall, and maybe company.

That same afternoon, the afternoon of Sweeney Cassidy's arrival at the Divine, word of the Sign came to Balthazar Warnick.

He was in his study at the Orphic Lodge, the *Benandanti*'s retreat in the Blue Ridge Mountains, nursing a brandy and making a halfhearted effort to repair the miniature orrery that stood in one of the many recessed windows that lined the room. Outside, rain lashed against gables and dormers, and sent the limbs of great oak trees rapping threateningly upon the mansion's shingles and ancient panes of leaded glass. A late-summer storm had settled in during the night. While most of its fury was spent, frequent squalls and shrieks of wind still raged about the study's turret.

"Well," Balthazar said softly. The constant noise made it difficult to concentrate, but he wasn't overinvolved in his task. Squinting, he adjusted his eyeglasses and peered at the instrument. "Now then."

Between his long fingers the orrery looked like some giddily elaborate Christmas ornament, with its brass fittings and enameled representations of the planets dangling from orbits of gleaming wire, all of them rotating about the large golden image of the sun. Red, yellow, green, orange, white, blue, violet, black. His thumb and forefinger closed about the tiny whirling bead of emerald, pinched it until he could feel it grow hot beneath his touch.

And where is the world the Benandanti *occupy?* he thought, and Balthazar's unlined face grew grim. Where was the world Balthazar himself lived, with its eternal rounds of meetings and retreats, its endless days and hours and decades of *waiting*? Without thinking, he pinched his fingers more tightly together. Threads of smoke rose from the little emerald globe, and glittering tufts of fire. The green planet third from the sun was in flames. Balthazar's clouded expression suddenly grew calm. He leaned over the orrery, extinguishing the tiny blaze with a breath. The minute globe cooled, its smooth green surface uncharred, unchanged. Sighing, Balthazar set the orrery back upon its brass mount and turned to stare out the window.

Far below where the lodge perched atop Helstrom Mountain, the Agastronga River had flooded its banks. But above the line of mountains to the west the storm was finally starting to break up. On the easternmost rim of the horizon Balthazar gleamed a faint rind of gold, marking where the sun still shone. It would be unbearably hot in the capital today, at least until the storm moved in to cool things off. He winced at the thought. As though he had summoned it by this small action, a knock came at the door.

"Yes, Kirsten," Balthazar called. "Come in." For another moment he gazed out the window, then turned. "Yes, my dear?"

The Orphic Lodge's housekeeper strode into the room, a bit of white paper fluttering in her hand. Balthazar's heart sank.

"Excuse me, Professor Warnick. A telephone message."

Kirsten crossed to the window, picking up the silver tray with the remains of Balthazar's lunch, pickled herring and *cornichons* and a few crusts of pumpernickel bread. She handed him the slip of paper and took his brandy snifter, still half-full, and placed it on the tray. "Francis X. Connelly called. I wrote down the message."

"Oh!" Balthazar nodded. He removed his glasses and squinted, trying to make out Kirsten's spidery European hand.

Thursday 20 August 1:30 P.M.

Tell Professor Warnick to come at once and meet me on the steps in front of the Shrine.
Tell him there has been a Sign.
Francis X. Connelly

Balthazar started as a gust of wind sent the casements clattering. He read the note again.

Tell him there has been a Sign.

He rolled the paper into a little tube, carefully set it on the luncheon tray. He gazed wistfully out at the rain. "Well, I suppose I will be leaving, then."

The housekeeper took the note and slipped it into her apron pocket. "Will you be back for supper, Professor?"

A *Sign*. Balthazar felt his heart beating a little faster. He jangled the keys in his pocket. Kirsten repeated her question.

"Dinner? Oh, well, no. I mean, I expect not—not if—well, if Francis has really—if there's really something going on back at the Divine."

Kirsten's blue eyes narrowed very slightly. "I am making *kalve frikadeller*," she said, holding the tray straight out in front of her as though it bore a ritual offering. Balthazar thought of the heads of certain saints and smiled weakly. "Veal, and *chokoladebudding*."

His favorite dessert. Balthazar nodded, touched. "Yes. Well, I will certainly try to be back for dinner," he said, and stood. He reached for the brandy glass, slowly drained it, and replaced it on the tray. "Thank you very much, Kirsten. Lunch was excellent, as always. I will—I will call you later, when I know what my plans are."

The door groaned shut behind her. Kirsten's heavy footsteps echoed down the hall. Balthazar drew the keys from his pocket and gazed at the orrery on its brass stand.

"Well," he said, his voice thin and uneasy. "*Well*," he repeated, and crossed the room.

There was a small door set between the bookshelves on that side of the study. It was made of mountain ash, the wood burnished to the color of pale ale. It held a small, old-fashioned keyhole. The lintel was formed of graceful Art Nouveau arabesques, rubbed with gilt paint that had nearly all flaked away with age, and surmounted by threadlike, almost invisible crimson letters.

Omnia Bona Bonis. The Benandanti's motto.
All things are Good with Good Men.

Balthazar rested his palm upon the wood. For a moment he glanced over his shoulder, gazing longingly at the door leading into the hall. His car was still parked out front. It would take nearly four hours to drive back to Washington, by which time Francis would long since have lost all patience and stormed back to his room.

Or—what was far more likely—Francis would come bursting through this little ashwood door, and forcibly drag Balthazar back with him. At the thought Balthazar sighed. With one quick motion he slid the key into the keyhole and turned it. The door shuddered, then flew open.

There was nothing there. Not the dim interior of a closet; not the cool watery sky, greenish-cast and storming. Nothing but a formless emptiness, neither dark nor light but somehow *other*, cold and rent by a high keening wail.

A Sign.

Without looking up, Balthazar took a step into the void. His foot fell through empty air and his chest tightened as he felt himself start to tumble forward. The last thing he heard was, very faintly, the sound of the wind slamming shut the door behind him.

At the top of the main steps of the Shrine Francis Xavier Connelly waited, just as impatiently as Balthazar had imagined, for his mentor to arrive. Below, the daily flood of tourists poured from a seemingly endless stream of buses, the women fanning themselves with folded maps and brochures, the men loosening ties and cuffs and gazing back yearningly at the air-conditioned vehicles. People still got all dressed up to visit the Shrine, although some of them would get no farther than the gift shop.

Watching them Francis snorted in annoyance and glanced at his watch. Nearly two o'clock. Someone bumped his elbow, apologizing in a shrill voice. Francis looked down to see a group of tourists armed with fearsome-looking cameras, trying vainly to encompass the vast expanse of domes and minarets and bell towers that made up the Shrine.

They don't know the half of it, he thought. No one would ever know a fraction of what went on around and beneath—and above and below—the University of the Archangels and Saint John the Divine, and the Shrine that stood at its heart.

"Come *on*, Balthazar," he said beneath his breath.

He turned and looked out to the long white driveway that led from North Capitol Street into the Shrine parking lot. A tiny utility building stood near the entrance, plywood and molded blue plastic. A Gray Line Tours bus pulled in from North Capitol and careened past the shed, trailing exhaust. When the smoke cleared a slender dark-haired man stood on the curb in front of the shed, coughing and flapping his hands.

"About time," muttered Francis to himself. He leaned back on his heels and dug in his pockets for a cigarette. "About goddamn time."

In the parking lot, Balthazar Warnick tried to catch his breath. He groaned and smoothed the front of his shirt, already damp and heavy with sweat, then crossed the parking lot and headed for the steps.

"Balthazar! Kirsten gave you my message, then." Francis's Harvard-Yard voice rang out stridently as Balthazar staggered the last few feet toward him. "I was starting to worry . . ."

"Ye-es!" gasped Balthazar. He stopped and dabbed at his face with his handkerchief, then, catching his breath, added, "Sorry to take so long. So damn *hot*—"

Francis nodded and peered irritably into the hazy air, as though waiting for someone more interesting to arrive, perhaps by helicopter. Looking up at him, Balthazar smiled wryly. His protégé was exceptionally, almost grotesquely, tall, bigboned, and stooped, with an air of supercilious hauteur that Balthazar associated with certain breeds of camel. Like Balthazar, he was terribly nearsighted, but too vain to wear glasses. So Francis was always peering impatiently into thin air and complaining about inattentive companions. His cigarette twitched between nervous fingers with nails bitten to the quick. He was one of the youngest of the *Benandanti*, and Balthazar's most promising protégé—except for the archaeologist Magda Kurtz, who had first arrived at the Divine nearly a decade earlier and had long since left to pursue her career elsewhere. Though now Magda was back at the Divine for the summer, as a visiting scholar, and Francis had never left.

"It's *always* hot," Francis muttered, as though it were Balthazar's fault. "Diplomats used to get paid hardship wages for being posted here."

Balthazar smiled. As an undergraduate Francis had been Balthazar's golden boy and, like Magda, an archaeology student, though Francis had never strayed from his original love of classical Greece and Mycenae into the muddier territory of Old Europe.

"Anyway, it's not the heat that gets you," Francis added. "It's the humidity."

Balthazar nodded, sighing. In addition to being head of the Divine's renowned Department of Anthropology, his formal titles included that of Provost of Thaddeus College, as well as 144th Recipient of the Cape of the Living Flame of the Gjnarra of Transbaikalia in the Gobi Desert, a title that was less honorary than some of his colleagues in the Explorers' Club might think.

And, of course, he was the chief of the *Benandanti* at the Divine. Here his duties consisted of a certain type of surveillance, an eternity of watching and waiting for an enemy who never seemed to arrive. An enemy who might no longer exist at all. Balthazar did not in fact like everything about his job, but the *Benandanti* were in some ways like the military. You were often born to the job, and once indoctrinated you were indentured for life, and presumably beyond. For the last six years, Francis had been as close to family as Balthazar had here: a melancholy thought.

Francis took another quick drag on his cigarette. "Thank you for coming, Balthazar," he said. For the first time he grinned. "But wait till you *see*!" Turning, he gazed up at the bulk of the Shrine, his face shining. "It's incredible, Balthazar, incredible—"

Balthazar shook his head and followed Francis's gaze. "Well, perhaps you'd better show me," he said mildly.

Above them reared the heart of the University—the Shrine of the Archangels and Saint John the Divine. A fabulously immense Byzantine folly, completed early in the twentieth century after nearly two hundred years of construction. Minarets and mosaics and Gothic sandstone buttresses, crenellated parapets and winding stairways that led to no visible doors: all of it surmounted by a dome of gold and lapis lazuli that threw back to the sky its own gilded map of the heavens. Seven different architects had designed and built disparate aspects of the Shrine. Inside, no less than fifty-seven chapels, some no larger than a closet, others the size of bowling alleys, had been consecrated to saints of varying rank and degree of holiness. The upper level alone was so crowded with ghosts that in the predawn hours the nave was filled with their hollow whispers. In the crypt chapel near the catacombs, icons routinely wept blood, and in dim corners lustful teenagers lagging behind on class trips often glimpsed Victor Capobianco, known as *Damnatus*, the Doomed Bishop, kneeling on the granite floor and weeping as he recited the Stations of the Cross. Francis's Sign would have to be quite original to merit even this minor investigation.

For a moment Balthazar let his gaze rest upon the stone triad above the entryway. Callow undergraduates had christened the trio The Supremes. They actually represented Michael and Gabriel and Raphael, the Archangels who guarded the Divine. Balthazar waited, just in case they had a message for him, but there was nothing.

"Come on." Francis tugged at Balthazar's elbow and steered him past a noisy flock of nuns. "You've *got* to see this."

It was like stepping from a subway platform into the arcane circle of some immeasurable cavern. "I saw it in the Tahor Chapel," said Francis. His voice, always too loud, boomed so thunderously that a number of tourists turned to stare. Balthazar followed him down one of the wide side aisles, stepping in and out of spectral pools where light poured from stained glass windows onto the floor. Everywhere banks of candles shimmered behind kneeling figures. As they passed, Balthazar could hear the soft sounds of weeping and whispered invocations.

Saint John, pray for us. Saint Blaise, pray for us. Saint Lucia, pray for us . . .

Balthazar paused as Francis raced by a tiny chapel, with a solitary penitent and single guttering candle. A painted statue stood in an alcove, its plaster robes flecked with dust: the image of a young woman holding out a gilt tray from which a pair of eyeballs peered mournfully. For a moment Balthazar stared at the disembodied eyeballs, then hurried on.

Wilting flowers, donated by wealthy alumnae and the grateful beneficiaries of successful cardiac bypasses, filled other alcoves in front of more exotic images of marble and glass and wood, steel and plaster and humble plastic. The main altar was a glowing curtain of gold and silver rippling in the distance. Balthazar followed Francis down a narrow staircase, around and around and around until finally they came out into a dimly lit indoor plaza. Everywhere you looked you saw high stone archways opening onto other corridors or chapels. Some were closed off by iron grilles, others guarded by still more statues or the occasional noisy air-conditioning unit.

"Almost there," Francis sang out. "*Here* we *go*—"

Balthazar hoped there would be no one in the Tahor Chapel; and blessedly it was empty. They stepped inside. Francis pulled shut the high iron grille that served as door, and for good measure dragged out the CHAPEL CLOSED sign and set it behind the threatening spikes and bars. Then he fished a key from his pocket and locked the gate behind them.

"Okay," said Francis. "Okay okay okay."

His voice broke and he looked anxiously over his shoulder at Balthazar. "It's—well, I was here this morning, and I saw it then, but—well, I hope—"

Balthazar made a dismissive motion with his hand. "Not to worry, Francis." Smiling expectantly, he tilted his head. "Please—show me—"

The Tahor Chapel was a tiny L-shaped room, its walls of smooth black marble veined with gold and pale blue. Ambient light spilled from small recesses in the ceiling, but the prevailing illumination came from thick white candles set into crimson glass holders, dozens of them, flickering in front of a narrow stone altar. There was a faintly spicy smell, like scorched nutmeg. In spite of himself Balthazar felt his spine prickle.

"It was here this morning," Francis repeated as they approached the altar. "Jeez, I hope . . ."

Atop the stone altar rested the chapel's famous icon, the so-called "Black Madonna" of Tahor found in an Anatolian cave five centuries before. It was over a thousand years old, the image of its central figure dark and shiny as an eggplant. A halo of gold chips radiated from her head. Piled in front of the wooden likeness were heaps of rosary beads. Very carefully Francis removed them, the beads spilling from his fingers in jingling strands. Then, with exquisite caution, he took the icon itself and moved it to one side.

"Ahem," said Balthazar. He wondered what had driven Francis to move the icon in the first place. This was forbidden, of course, and anyone besides a *Benandanti* who tried such a thing would have been quickly and quietly dispensed with. "Francis, is that really—"

But before he could say anything else Francis grabbed him and pulled him closer. "Balthazar. *Look*—"

Inside the altar was a figure, thumb-sized and roughly thumb-shaped. Dull black and slightly gleaming, it appeared to be of stone, but it was not: it was carbonized wood smooth as a chunk of polished quartz. It had been discovered at the same time and in the same place as the Black Madonna, and from the first its significance was recognized by the *Benandanti*. For hundreds of years it had been closeted in Ravenna, and later in Avebury, in one of their countless holdings of rare and arcane objects. New initiates to the *Benandanti* often expressed amazement at the seemingly careless handling of such artifacts. But the *Benandanti* had many such secrets. And, as Balthazar had once told Francis, "These things have a way of looking after themselves."

It was the figure of a woman. The very crudeness of its execution told how ancient it was. An eyeless, mouthless face; twin inverted triangles for breasts; a slit to indicate the vulva. A Goddess image, precious as the Venus of Willendorf or the Paphian Aphrodite. The *Benandanti* called it the Tahor Venus.

"Look," Francis exclaimed. In the flickering light, the Venus cast an eerie shadow across the altar. From his breast pocket Balthazar withdrew his glasses. For a long moment he held them, as though unwilling to see what they might reveal; finally he slid them onto his nose. Beside him Francis pointed at the figure. *"Balthazar!"*

Balthazar nodded, his throat tight. He had seen the Venus before, had even handled it, for the sheer wonder of touching something that was twenty thousand years old. He would not touch it now.

From the breasts of the Tahor Venus, and from the nick between her stolid legs, sprigs of greenery protruded: brilliant as the first spears of hyacinths thrusting through the cold earth. At the end of each frond was a starburst of deep purple, tiny petals slender and frail as cilia. As Balthazar and Francis stared, the minute flower heads moved, so slightly they might have been stirred by their breathing. A moment later and a musky smell perfumed the air, the faintest breath of sandalwood and oranges.

"Francis," Balthazar whispered. "Did you—what did you—"

The young man shook his head and stepped backward. "It didn't do that this morning," he said, his voice shaking. "I mean, that smell—"

From behind them echoed a dull clang, so loud they both jumped.

"When will it be open? Father—Father—?"

Turning, Balthazar saw a young woman in a nurse's uniform peering at them through the locked gate.

"Damn," Francis breathed, but Balthazar quickly ducked behind him, moving the image of the Black Madonna back into place and sweeping the heap of rosary beads in front of it.

"Yes—right now, we'll be right out," he called, pushing Francis in front of him. Just before they reached the gate Balthazar glanced back at the altar. Then, smiling apologetically, he fumbled for his keys and opened the door.

"Cleaning," he explained, letting the young woman pass. She nodded, wiping her eyes with a tissue, and went inside. A moment later they heard a soft thump as she settled onto the kneeler in front of the altar.

"Well?"

They walked quickly, slowing only when they reached the main corridor. Balthazar stopped at a doorway and leaned against the wall, rubbing his forehead and trying to calm his thudding heart.

"It's a Sign, isn't it?" Francis was saying, his tone low and urgent. "I mean really, nobody will deny it— it's a Sign, a *real* Sign! When you show the others, they'll see—"

Balthazar took a deep breath, then nodded. "Yes. Of course: it's a Sign, you were right, Francis, it's a Sign. No doubt, no doubt at all."

"Right*o*!" Francis exclaimed, his voice exploding with relief. He clapped his hand to his shirt pocket, and nodded to where a placard announced that the cafeteria was now open. "So now, now something's happened, I mean all this time and now something, a Sign, they can't deny *that*—"

Balthazar let his breath out in a long sigh and shook his head. "No, Francis, of course not, no—"

"But then—Balthazar, what does it *mean*?"

The hallway funneled into another corridor. Balthazar felt a familiar dull throbbing behind his temple, saw at the corners of his eyes the blurred lightning that always presaged a migraine. He bit his lip.

"Anything," he said in a low voice, rubbing his temples. "It could mean anything."

Francis lowered his head to whisper conspiratorially.

"But really," he said. "We'll know, right? What it means? What's going to happen now?"

"We'll know," said Balthazar, plucking a tiny lozenge from the engraved silver pillbox he carried in his breast pocket, "when She—or Somebody—is ready for us to know."

And silently they joined the line snaking into the cafeteria.

Everything about the Divine was turning out to be stranger than I had expected. The dining hall itself was a bizarre affair, another grey Gothic ivy-clad building with rows of gargoyles glaring down from parapets and turrets and balconies. The building would not have looked out of place in fourteenth-century Nîmes; its gargoyles had been created by the same master carvers who spent years working on the National Cathedral. Unfortunately, inside the place was much more mundane. I found a table in the dim far corner, across from the coffee machine. I sat and ate quickly, embarrassed to be alone but also terrified that one of the other students might engage me in unwanted conversation. When I finished I fled to my room.

Outside, the sun had dipped below the Shrine. It was my first night in the city; my first night away from home. The sky was glorious, indigo and violet and gold, and there was a warmth and sweetness to the air that I could taste in the back of my throat, burnt honey and car exhaust, and the damp promise of a thunderstorm charging it all. I walked slowly across the Mall, alone save for one or two hooded figures I glimpsed pacing the chestnut allées beneath the Shrine's eastern tower. I finally halted atop a small hillock where a single oak sent shadows rippling across the grass.

From the Shrine's bell tower came the first deep tones of the carillon calling the hour. I turned, and saw in the distance the domes and columns of the Capitol glimmering in the twilight, bone-colored, ghostly; and behind it still more ghostly buildings, their columned porticoes and marble arches all seeming to melt into the haze of green and violet darkness that descended upon them like sleep. City of Trees, someone had named it long ago; and as I gazed upon the far-off buildings and green-girt streets my heart gave a sudden and unexpected heave, as though someone nudged it.

I felt something then that has proved to be true. You have a first city as you have a first lover, and this was mine. I had read about the traffic, the poverty, the riots; the people living in boxes, the Dupont Circle crazies and the encampments of bitter veterans at Lafayette Park.

But nothing had prepared me for the rest of it. The tropic heat and humidity, so alien to me that I felt as though my northern blood was too thin and my grey eyes too pale to bear the burning daylight. The purple-charged dusk cut by heat lightning; the faint and antique glow of marble buildings.

And everywhere, everywhere, the trees. Crepe myrtles and cherries and white oaks, princess trees and hornbeams and pawpaws, horse chestnuts and trees of heaven and the humble flowering crabs, and the scent of magnolias mingling with that of burning paper and the soft white dust of the streets. For all its petty bureaucrats and burned-out storefronts, decaying warehouses turned to discos and the first yawning caverns that would soon be the city's Underground: still it all had a queer febrile beauty, not haunting so much as haunted. As much as Delphi or Jerusalem or Ur, it was a consecrated place: its god had not yet come to claim it, that was all. And that first evening I was seeing it all for the first time. But I knew then, with that odd certainty that has come only a few times in my life—when I met Oliver, and years later when I first saw Dylan—that my life would change irrevocably when I walked away from the shadows of that tree and returned to my room. I recalled the words of the poet of another place—

> *You will find no new lands, you will find no other seas.*
> *The city will follow you. You will roam the same*
> *streets. And you will age in the same neighborhoods;*
> *and you will grow gray in these same houses.*
> *Always you will arrive in this city. Do not hope for any other—*

But at that moment I hoped for nothing else, nothing but stars blurring through the violet smog and the faint echoing laughter that rang in my ears as I watched the Shrine fall into darkness, as the first tentative cries of students and locusts rang out to greet the night.

I returned to my room, exhilarated, no longer deviled by fear and loneliness. I bought two beers at the Rathskellar and carried them in paper cups to the dorm, drank them while sitting on my bed. Then I peeled off my sweaty clothes and wrapped myself in one of the new cotton sheets my mother had bought for me. Almost immediately I was asleep. I had no clock set up, and so didn't know what time it was when I awoke in the middle of the night, too hot and terribly thirsty. I sat up, groggy and disoriented; then froze.

There was someone in the room with me. Two figures—I could see them standing by the door, tall black shadows with heads bowed and extraordinarily long arms raised to their chests, like praying mantids. They seemed to be hunched over. But even so they were tall, too tall to be anyone or anything even remotely human. They had been talking about me, their voices had awakened me. Now they were silent.

I was too terrified to move, only clutched the sheet to my breast and tried not to breathe. Behind me the window was open—I could feel a warm damp breeze stirring, and hear distant thunder—but I knew I had closed it before I went to bed. By the door the two figures remained still. I slitted my eyes, afraid that they would see that I was awake, be moved by the reflection of starlight in my pupils to reach for me with those horrible arms. Still they said nothing, only stood there unmoving, watching, waiting.

For hours I lay rigid, my breath coming hoarser and shallower as I tried not to breathe at all. Until finally I realized that somehow I must have fallen asleep again. I sat up, gasping, the sheet sliding through my fingers.

The figures were gone. Gone, gone; the window was closed, the hasp carefully in place as I had left it. From somewhere in the dorm came the smell of fresh coffee and the cheerful static of a radio. The night's storm had passed; already sunlight turned the Shrine's dome to flame. It had been a dream, of course. My first night alone, too much beer, not enough dinner. I shuddered, then began to move, very slowly, still holding the sheet close to my chest. My feet had barely grazed the cool floor when I stopped.

Beneath the window something moved. I bit my lip as I stared at it, knowing then that it was as I had thought: everything had changed, nothing would be the same again. Upon the grey tile floor lay a single feather, as long as my forearm and the color of blood. The downy vanes at its base trembled, as though something breathed upon them. Then very slowly it crept across the floor, borne by a silent breeze, until it rested cool and sharp as a blade against the side of my bare foot.

CHAPTER 2

Raising the Naphaïm

That same evening, in a tower room on the other side of campus, the noted archaeologist Magda Kurtz sat cross-legged upon a worn oriental rug chased with the ancient Pasquar pattern known as *Three Children*. The room was in a building set aside for visiting scholars. Magda, whose term as visiting professor of European Archaeology had been for the summer only, would be leaving the day after tomorrow. From the dark corners of the turret her few belongings—mostly books and reams of curling dissertations—sent shadows straggling across the floor. The odor of singed hair overpowered the scents of wax and musty wool and her own faint musk of Joy perfume.

She was still a young woman, though Sweeney Cassidy wouldn't have thought so. She had dark thoughtful eyes, a wry mouth, determined chin. Her brown hair was cut in a pageboy and was streaked with grey. She wore unfashionable clothes, baggy trousers of black linen and a Betsey Johnson blouse that had been *le plus ultra* when Magda herself was an undergraduate, but now was faded and somewhat shabby. More striking was Magda's necklace: a crescent-shaped collar of beaten silver. At its widest point it was engraved with a triskele composed of three interlocking moons. The workmanship was exquisite, in the Celtic style favored by metalworkers in Bronze Age Europe. The lunar curves joined to form an abstract pattern of still more crescent moons, smaller or larger depending on how they caught the light. There was a gap in the collar, a hole where another, smaller, curve should fit. But ancient treasuries and burial sites are often raided or despoiled, by grave robbers and disinherited relatives and greedy priests.

The necklace was a *lunula*, sacred to the lunar goddess Othiym. Magda knew of only a handful like it which had ever been found—one, a mere fragment, had been discovered by her mentor and was now among the holdings of the National Museum. It was an object of great power, especially in the hands of a *Benandanti* like herself. Had it been whole, and not missing that curved spar from its center, it would have been unimaginably so.

Magda knew where that missing fragment was, but she had long ago decided not to retrieve it. Her West Coast mentor, the great June Harrington, had found a fragment of a lunula during one of her own early excavations, and (to her later regret) donated it to the National Museum of Natural History. She told Magda of glimpsing it there many years later in the museum archives, a sliver of light in a dusty glass case.

"I often think of it," June had sighed, her gnarled hands opening and closing in her lap. "I could have just taken it back, you know. I could have just *taken* it, they never would have known.

"But I never did. And I never saw it again."

Magda did not show her lunula to June Harrington. She did not show it to Balthazar Warnick, who had sponsored her within the *Benandanti*, or indeed to anyone at all. Had the *Benandanti* known she possessed it, they would almost certainly have tried to wrest it from her. But until now it had remained safely in Magda's possession. The lunula—and its Mistress—protected its own.

"*In hoc signo spes mea*."

Magda recited the words softly, her fingers brushing the edge of the silver collar upon her breast.

"*Othiym, Anat, Innana, Kybele, Kali, Artemis, Athena, Hecate, Potnia, Othiym. In hoc signo vinces*." In this sign is my hope, in this sign thou shalt conquer. "*In hoc signo spes mea: Othiym. Haïyo Othiym Lunarsa.* "

Some years ago, Magda had been one of the first female students admitted to the Divine. She was still one of the few female *Benandanti*. Her career since then had been quietly triumphant. Early tenure at UC Berkeley, several major archaeological discoveries, a few token appearances on morning talk shows. She had written a work now commonly regarded as a classic text, the two-volume *Daughters of the Setting Sun: The Attic Mystery Tradition in Anatolia*, which her mentor, the eminent classicist June Harrington, had called "absolutely indispensable." This past summer, Professor Kurtz's lectures at the Divine had been crowded with undergraduates and doctoral students alike, and she had briefly considered staying on a little longer, to see the fall term begin. To see for herself the new crop of students and decide if there were any worth claiming.

But then she had learned of the Sign—learned just that morning, which left her precious little time for what she had to do. Because, while Magda had a long past history within the *Benandanti* and the Divine, her present loyalties lay elsewhere.

She knelt on the rough wool of the Pasquar rug. A round copper dish stood in front of her, and a tiny cloisonné casket filled with gold-tipped matches. Next to the casket gleamed a small silver bowl filled with water. Very carefully, Magda smoothed out a lock of her hair and plucked a single strand. She examined it, then placed it upon the surface of the silver bowl. She sat back, lips tight and eyes closed. After a moment she leaned forward.

In the copper dish was an object wrapped in newsprint. She began to unwrap it, until an untidy heap of old newspaper fluttered at her side and she held something slightly smaller than her own hand, swaddled in cloth. Magda grimaced as she unraveled the strands of rotting linen. Another smell overwhelmed the scent of burned hair: a smell of rot, but also of spices, acrid pepper and salt and the sweetish citric tang of vervain. She pushed aside the discarded wrappings, careful to keep the newspapers from coming too close to the candles in their heavy brass holders. Then she laid her prize upon the copper plate.

It was a hand. Perhaps three-quarters the size of her own, mummified and faintly green with mold, its flesh puckered and pocked with flecks of orange-and-white fungus. It had been dipped in wax, but much of that had cracked or turned to an oily scum upon the dried flesh. It sat upon the plate, fingers upcurled like the frozen appendages of a dead tarantula, fingernails furred with mold. Magda wiped her hands on a small towel and stared at it with distaste.

"Well." She reached behind her for an unlit candle. Taking one of the gold-tipped matches, she lit it, then very slowly touched it to each of the fingers on the dead hand. A spurt of bluish flame. Black smoke thick as rope uncoiled from the fingertips and settled onto the floor. The room filled with the putrid smell of spoiled meat. Magda held her breath. After a moment the fingers began to glow with a faint yellow flame.

"Yes," she murmured. She turned away, coughing delicately, and blew out the candle. The Hand of Glory burned with a steady, poisonous gleam, flames licking at its fingertips. Where the smoke touched the rug it left a heavy dark smear, like rancid fat.

She turned to the silver dish, where the single strand of hair floated, and spoke beneath her breath. The hair started to move. Magda Kurtz continued to murmur in the same quick, almost thoughtless manner; but her eyes were slitted with concentration.

Upon the surface of the water, patterns began to appear. Faint lines, dull red and black against the silvery surface. After a minute or so an image emerged. Blots of light and shadow that soon took on the contours of a face: a young man's face. Magda fell silent. For a long time she stared at the image, her mouth tight. Then she breathed upon the water. The face disappeared into cloudy ripples. From the Hand of Glory came a spattering sound as a drop congealed upon the tip of one finger and burned in a small greasy cloud. Magda glanced aside, finally began speaking again.

Her words sounded no different this time, but the hair moved more slowly in response to her voice. It grew thicker, until it might have been a nematode squirming there, or some bloated larva. The water roiled and churned, and suddenly was still.

Within seconds the second image appeared: the face of a young woman with huge slanted eyes, their color unguessable, but an unmistakably beautiful girl. Magda gazed at the image thoughtfully. Finally she nodded and whispered.

"I thought as much."

She held her hand above the bowl, touched the water with a finger. The hair writhed like a worm upon a hook, with a soft hiss disappeared into a thread of white smoke.

"So," said Magda.

So this was what the Sign portended. She almost laughed, thinking of her old friend and mentor Balthazar Warnick. "All for naught . . ."

For millennia the *Benandanti* had watched and waited for the awakening of their ancient enemy. For a resurgence of old ways, old deities; half-hoping that when their Sign finally came it might presage not Her return, but the arrival of a Champion, a Hero, a Second Coming of a Great Good Man. *Omnia Bona Bonis.*

But was this what the loathsome Francis X. Connelly had glimpsed in the Tahor Chapel?

Magda laughed aloud. She had seen for herself who was to come. Not one person, but two. Not a hero of the *Benandanti*—politician or diplomat, or even a sturdy tenured classics professor—but a couple of *kids*. A young man and a woman—boy and girl, really—the oldest story in the book, and not at all what the *Benandanti* had been expecting.

Not quite what Magda herself had been expecting, either.

She frowned. The boy had taken her by surprise. And yet the Sign had been unmistakable. She had scried his face in the basin, as clearly as she had seen that of the girl. Now it only remained for her to learn who they were.

Magda glanced at her watch. Past midnight already. She stretched, then crouched before the Hand of Glory. The flames had burned to the first knuckle of each finger. Melting fat coursed in dark runnels to form a small pool in its withered palm. Magda grimaced. She began to speak in a loud, impatient voice, as though calling an animal to her.

"*Eisheth. Eisheth. Eisheth.*"

As she spoke she very slowly began to stand, straightening until at last she stood with arms outstretched. Pronouncing the name one final time she took a step backward.

"*Eisheth*."

Directly in front of her, a shape like her own shadow rose in the darkness, arms outstretched, its back to her. Only this was a shadow filled with light. As Magda watched it slowly grew brighter, the lineaments and contours of its body so radiant that she had to shade her eyes. Her arms prickled with heat. Just when it seemed its intensity was such that she must burst into flame, the light dimmed. A figure stood there, taller by a foot than Magda. She gasped, as she always did. Its long black hair like marble coils upon its shoulders, the wings like sheaves of knives enfolded upon its back.

"Eisheth," Magda whispered hoarsely. "Eisheth, look at me."

The figure turned.

"Ah!—"

Her stomach knotted with rage and frustration at her weakness, but still she could not keep from crying out. The figure nodded. In spite of herself Magda started forward, her hands raised halfway between supplication and an embrace. But then she forced herself to stop. The figure continued to stare at her, its yellow eyes cold and unblinking as a tiger's. Magda took a few deep breaths.

"Eisheth—thank you—"

The figure inclined its head to her and smiled. It might have been a man, except for some feminine roundness to its mouth, the arch of its cheekbones and the sly way its eyes took her in, appraising her as another woman might. Its skin was golden, not tanned or ruddy but a pure pale gold, the color of fine marble rather than metal. It was naked, and you could see its muscles as clearly as though they had been sketched upon its skin. From its chest two breasts swelled, a young girl's breasts, tipped with pale roseate nipples. Its groin was hairless, its member engorged and erect; she had never seen it otherwise.

Magda forced a smile and stared boldly back into his eyes. She always thought of Eisheth as *him*, despite his breasts and coquettish smile, even as some of the other naphaïm she perceived as female despite their obviously masculine attributes, or the absence of genitals altogether.

"Yes?" The naphaïm never addressed her by name. "I have come."

His voice made her quiver, trapped between stark terror and the most abject desire. It was the voice of a young boy before the change, sweet yet resonant with a man's power. Magda clasped her hands tightly and indicated the silver basin on the floor.

"A few minutes ago I scried there in the water two faces. A young man and woman. I wish to know their names."

As she spoke she grew more confident. She glanced down at the Hand of Glory. The smallest digit, a shriveled grey knot, was already burned away, and the flesh of the palm itself had begun to char. She went on quickly, "I—I could not see them clearly. And I do not know their names. I need you to tell me who they are."

The naphaïm stared at her and smiled. At its back its wings rustled. "Last year, and the year before, and years before that: you who watch are always looking for a Sign, but one never comes."

A flicker of desperation licked at the woman's spine. She shook her head. "I am no longer among those who watch, Eisheth. I serve another now. And a Sign *has* come. I wish to know the names of those whose faces I scried in the water."

Eisheth's smile broke into a grin. He had very large, white teeth, and his tongue as it flicked between them was pointed, like an asp's. "And does not your mistress know their names?"

"My Mistress—my Mistress is—She is not mindful as you are, Eisheth." Magda's desperation fanned into panic even as her tone grew more wheedling. "She sleeps, but perhaps this girl is the one who will help me wake Her, if—"

If I can find this girl before the Benandanti *do.*

Eisheth laughed. At the sound the walls trembled, the candle flames leapt until they formed a fiery ring about the two figures. He stretched out his great hand until it enveloped hers, and took a step forward. Magda shuddered. Willing herself to stare up into his eyes, she choked, "Their names, Eisheth! Or I'll dismiss you and summon another—"

"Ahhh. A pity," he murmured, mockingly. Slowly he withdrew his hand. "As you will."

He stared down at the silver bowl, as though seeing something there beside the rippling reflections of candlelight and shadow. After a moment he spoke a name, and then a second name. He glanced at Magda and tilted his head.

"You will ask more of me?" His boy's voice sounded innocent, almost tearful. "Or will you dismiss me so soon?"

Magda's breath caught in her throat. "No more. *Go*—"

Quickly she repeated the rest of the incantation. Eisheth bowed his head, ebony locks spilling across his shoulders. From his wings smoke purled. Then, in a soundless conflagration, his entire body burst into flame. Magda stumbled backward, shielding her face. When she lowered her hand the naphaïm was gone. She drew a shuddering breath, looked down to see that the fingers of the Hand of Glory had burned away. A single ragged flame, brownish red like dried blood, scored the air above its clenched palm.

One last time she knelt before the copper dish. Almost frantically she began to whisper strings of words—Greek, Latin, Old Norse, and English, too, just to be sure. A simple cantrip, something to disrupt the meeting between those she had glimpsed.

Because almost certainly the girl could be turned to serve Her whom Magda served. But the boy was another matter. And the two of them were linked, Magda had seen that.

So now let them be torn apart.

And so Magda pronounced her cantrip. It was an ancient spell—Magda found such old folkways charming, and useful, too—and one that seldom failed to work. At the appropriate moment she whispered the boy's name. Let *him* bear the brunt of whatever danger might come from Magda's interference in the work of the *Benandanti*. She would trust her Mistress to see that the rest followed as it should.

". . . uia Othiym psinother theropsin nopsither nephthomaoth . . ."

When she finished Magda sighed and stood. She crossed to where a white ceramic pitcher waited upon a windowsill. She took the pitcher, returned to the Hand of Glory and poured a thin stream of milk onto it. The Hand of Glory, sizzled, sending up a sour, clotted smell, then gave a shrill whistle as steam escaped from its pores.

"There," Magda pronounced. She smiled with relief. So very simple, and also a little chastening, when one thought how it was that tiny acts such as these had kept their great and ancient feud alive for so many thousands of years. She moved cheerfully about the room, blowing out one candle after another, humming. She had been a promising student at the Divine herself once, before she joined the *Benandanti* and then betrayed them. It gave her a poignant thrill of nostalgia to think of those two attractive young people with all the world before them. With a final *pouff* like a kiss she blew out the last candle. Then, gathering her papers, she left the room, to spend the night at a friend's apartment.

As for the candles and bowls, and the smirched remains of the Hand of Glory—well, custodians at the Divine were accustomed to disposing of such things.

CHAPTER 3

Oliver and Angelica

I don't know what I was thinking when I dressed for my first day of class. Recalling September in New York, I guess, where the air would have the ringing chill of true autumn. Or else maybe it was some kind of magical thinking already at work inside my head, stirred by that terrible dream of angels in my room, the bizarre and inexplicable reality of the long crimson feather I had carefully wrapped and hidden in the bottom of my knapsack. For whatever reasons, I left my room poorly armed against the numbing heat outside. I wore black velvet trousers tucked into knee-high black leather boots and a white cotton poet's shirt, and a man's black satin vest, very old and with tarnished silver buttons. By the time I was halfway across the Mall the shirt clung damply to my back. A blister throbbed insistently on the side of my left ankle. The sun beat against my cheeks like hot fists, and for a few minutes I considered returning to my room to change, or just going back to bed.

But then I saw the boy who'd waved at me the day before, strolling across the parking lot with his Frisbee sticking out of a knapsack. When he saw me he smiled and waved.

A Sign, I thought. I was always looking for Signs. And so I went on.

The Department of Anthropology was at the far end of campus. Today all that part of the Divine has been built up, given over to the Bramwell Center for Dysfunctional Study and Thought. But then it was mostly trees, scraggly kudzu-hung locust trees and sumac bushes, with that nasty footing of broken bottles and tattered newsprint that you find in city woodlots.

I followed a narrow meandering path. All the tropic glamour that had clung to the city last night was gone, burned away by the remorseless sun. The air smelled faintly of garbage. I wiped my face, panting with relief when finally I saw my destination, rising from steaming sumac mounds like Atlantis from the sea.

I approached it slowly: an ancient building formed of blocks of granite so colossal they might have been stolen from some neglected menhir. Several students lolled on the steps. They had that ruddy heartiness I would soon associate with archaeology majors—sunburned and freckled, hair bleached by the sun, sturdy work boots and fatigues stained red with mud. They smiled but said nothing when I passed, feeling dandyish and stupid in my velvet pants and harlot's boots. At the door I paused to catch my breath. They didn't even glance at me as I went inside.

Edgar Hall was like all the buildings at the Divine. Cool and old and silent, even the loudest of voices hushed by the long high corridors with their aqueous light. I found my class on the second floor, the door propped open with a torn textbook. Like my room at Rossetti, the classroom had high arched windows, though these were of stained glass that formed uninspiring geometric patterns, blue, yellow, red, blue, yellow, red. After the soft green light of the corridor, the riotous colors were painful to look upon. For a moment I stood there, shy, embarrassed by my clothes. I nudged the textbook that held the door open. The spine crackled softly, and a signature of pages slipped to the floor.

Child Sacrifice in Edessa, A Study in Ritual Infanticide. I kicked the pages aside. When I entered the room, four faces in the front swiveled to look at me, then returned to staring at the runic words on a blackboard.

MAGIC, WITCHCRAFT & RELIGION
PROF. BALTHAZAR WARNICK

An unusually small wooden podium had been set beside the chalkboard, and in front of this a slight man stood sorting papers. Except for him and those four students, the place seemed empty. Some thirty-odd seats staggered toward the back of the room. In one of them someone slouched, head flung forward above the desk so that all I saw was a mass of long straight black hair, an arch of neck with a white crescent bitten out of sunburned skin. I had never sat in the front of a classroom in my life, but I didn't want to be alone amidst all those empty chairs. So I settled on an empty seat near the black-haired apparition, who didn't look up. I dug into my knapsack, grubbing among wadded tissue, leaky pens, three new notebooks already soiled with ink. For an instant I grazed something sharp: like running my fingers longways across a razor.

The feather.

I snatched my hand back, dug more deeply until I pulled out a heavy book. It fell open and I looked down at the curling pages, pretending to be engrossed. A much-worn copy of *Finnegans Wake* that I carried everywhere but never actually read. The room grew warmer, the other students whispered as I sweated and tried to focus my eyes.

O, O, her fairy setalite! Casting such shadows to Persia's blind! The man in the street can see the coming event. Photoflashing it far too wide. It will be known through all Urania soon.

"Hel*loo*."

I glanced aside. The apparition had moved. I saw streaming jet black hair above a field of white—white shirt, white pants, black wing tips with no socks—and large chapped hands swooping the hair from a sunburned face. When I lowered my gaze I saw the pants were not really white but baggy chinos, faded to the color of bone. The hands were large and nervous. After smoothing back all that hair they attacked a pair of spectacles with ugly black plastic frames, jamming them onto a hawkish face.

I started. Something—the hair, that delicately curved neck or perhaps just the suggestion of affected disarray—had made me think the figure was another girl.

But it wasn't. It was a boy. He glanced warily behind him, then at the front of the room, then back at me, staring at me so intensely I started to feel a little uneasy. Then he stood, looking around nervously, and slid into the chair next to me. His chinos rode up to display glossy muscular calves, pale in front, sunburned in back, and completely hairless. Later he told me that he shaved his legs, something to do with the aerodynamics of cycling. But at that moment all I could think of was those eerie sexless angels gazing blindly from their ramparts at Rossetti Hall. He smelled of sweat and sun and 3-IN-ONE oil.

"Well then."

He had a sweet voice, boyish, with that clipped prep school delivery that produces the faintest echo of an upper-crust British accent. Unexpectedly my heart was pounding. I closed my book and started to shove it back into my bag, when he leaned across his desk and peered up at me. His eyes were a piercing sea blue, startlingly bright against his sunburned cheeks. He had a sharp chin, a narrow, slightly upturned nose. The sort of handsome yet delicate face that you find in doomed matinee idols, James Dean or Rudolph Valentino. But his glasses were cheap and very dirty and seemed out of place. They might have been part of a bad disguise, Cary Grant as bumbling professor, or some ridiculous bit of stage business—*put these on and no one will know you're Superman!* With a flourish he shoved them against his face again. Then he took the copy of *Finnegans Wake* from my hand, glanced at the title, and placed it back on my desk. His head cocked as he gazed at me and asked, "*Why* is a raven like a writing desk?"

He was the most beautiful boy I had ever seen.

I rubbed the bridge of my nose and looked away.

Why is a raven like a writing desk?

It was the Mad Hatter's question to Alice, of course. I knew it because I had directed a children's production of the play at home that summer. And now this boy was sitting there like it was the secret password, waiting for me to come up with the right retort. I remembered the feather in my knapsack. I remembered the figures in my room the night before, the rows of angels flanking my window. I shivered.

Something truly weird was happening. Some kind of test, some bizarre initiation that I hadn't been warned of. My fingers tightened on the edge of my desk as I raised my head.

He was still staring at me. And suddenly, inexplicably, more than anything I had ever wanted before, I wanted him to like me. Wanted him to keep on looking at me like this: eyebrows raised, almost smiling—not snidely but gently, encouragingly, as though to say *Come now, you know the next line.*

And the crazy thing was, I did.

"'*Your hair wants cutting.*'"

The almost-smile disappeared. He removed his glasses and peered at me more closely. He looked dismayed, but also confused. All the glory faded from his beautiful face, the way the blue drains from a cornflower after it's been picked.

My heart sank. Something had gone wrong, his face showed it. He hadn't expected me to know the answer—and why should he? Still . . .

"That's right," he said. He folded his hands on his desk, frowning. I felt idiotic and about fifteen years old, as if I were waiting to hear I hadn't made the cut for the cheerleading squad. But I couldn't help it. Maybe it was just my homesickness, the terror that I would never make another friend in my life. That I would never wear the right clothes or say the right thing again. But somehow, it seemed that everything hung on whether he liked me or not.

There was a long moment when I could hear the soft conversation of the others at the front of the room, the sound of a pen scratching on paper. Then, abruptly, he stretched a hand toward me and grinned.

"Oliver Wilde Crawford."

I looked into those sea blue eyes and nodded slowly. As suddenly as it had appeared, his doubt was gone. We might have grown up together, played Ringolevio in the summer twilight, been betrothed as children. For a moment I could only stare, until he nudged me.

"Sweeney," I said. I took his outstretched hand. On his shirt cuff a watch had been drawn in blue ballpoint ink, the hands pointing to four o'clock. Always time for tea. "Sweeney Cassidy."

"Ah hah." Oliver slumped back into his chair. His eyes narrowed. "Sweeney. You're from someplace very cold. Maine?"

I shook my head. "New York. Why?"

He drew an imaginary line from my velvet-clad knees down to my boots. "It was cold in my room," I said defensively.

"Of course it was." He nodded, tugging at the collar of his oxford cloth shirt. "I rode my bike down from Newport," he went on. He spoke so quickly that I had to lean forward to make sure I didn't miss a word. "A 103 Vega, I traded my twelve-string for it—1964 Gibson, with that kind of marbled bakelite detailing around the frets? That guy from the Thirteenth Floor Elevators had one just like it. Everything else's coming in a trunk. Greyhound. I didn't get here till yesterday night, took me three days, no change of clothes, I washed these this morning."

He held out his arm and I touched the cuff above the ballpoint wristwatch. It was damp, but I barely had time to register that before his hand shot back, swooping the hair from his eyes, and he continued.

"So New York. Manhattan? Detour from the High School for Performing Arts? Or no, NYU film school but then you saw that Truffaut movie and—"

He cuffed my boot. "—here you are, Iphigenia in Northeast, our own Voila! And you're taking Warnick's class," he added approvingly, adjusting his glasses. "Have you seen the pre-Columbians yet?"

I blinked. I was sweating so heavily I was surprised there wasn't a pool at my feet. "Pre-Columbians?"

"At Dumbarton Oaks. We can go this afternoon. They open at two." He glanced down at his wrist. "Can you borrow a bike? Or the 63 bus goes there."

I felt a faint buzz at my temples, a thrumming sound that spread across my skull and down my spine. I felt stoned; at least, I couldn't make any sense out of what Oliver was saying, although he seemed to think he was carrying on a normal conversation.

"The bus," I said.

Oliver nodded. "Okay," he said, pleased. "Sweeney, huh? Mockingbirds outside your window last night, near the Convent of the Sacred Heart? O sacred head surrounded?" He tilted his head sideways, gazing at me with glittering eyes.

I stared back, nodding like I had some idea what he was talking about. If he wasn't so unabashedly beautiful, you'd think he was nuts. But this was Oliver's peculiar gift—one of them, at least—that if you didn't understand him, or were confused (and I usually was), or even just bored, you always felt like it was *your* fault.

"Tom O'Bedlam," he said, and gave my chair a little kick by way of urging me to join the fun. "*You* remember. Gloomy Orion and the Dog outside your window while your parents were arguing downstairs. Spread your knees and fly away. 'Sweeney Among the Nightingales.'"

I swallowed and riffled the pages of *Finnegans Wake*. This was worse than an oral exam. But then from outside came a faint burst of song: right on cue, a mockingbird in unwonted daytime concert. And suddenly I knew what he was talking about.

"Dumbarton Oaks," I said. "'Let us go and make our visit.'" It was the only line of Eliot I could remember.

Oliver nodded excitedly. "Right!" He removed his glasses, spun them by an earpiece. "Now, we'll have to eat first—"

He rattled on, more unfamiliar names. Blue mirrors and Georgetown and numbers, 330 and six-oh-five, but was that a time or a bus or an address? It was my first exposure to one of Oliver's odd monologues, composed equally of literary and private allusions and delivered at breakneck speed in his prep school voice, punctuated by dramatic tugs at his long hair and glasses. I nervously twirled a lock of my own hair and just kept nodding. *I* have a gift for looking and talking as though I know more than I really do.

But Oliver didn't care. Oliver just kept on talking, smiling that loopy grin that let you know he'd spent a lifetime being loved by everyone he'd ever met.

". . . so we'll hit the Blue Mirror, hardly worth the transfer anyway, save your quarters for the Rockola at Gunchers and some Pall Malls, excellent sort of sub-Deco architecture and—"

Behind us footsteps echoed down the hall and then stopped. I glanced away from Oliver to see a figure standing in the doorway. A somewhat hesitant figure, the carnival light from our classroom's windows broidering it with gold and red and green.

Now *what*? I thought.

It was a girl. Another of Dr. Warnick's students, of course—if you could conceive of a Piero de'Franceschi madonna showing up for class in a Bloomingdale's peasant dress and high-heeled Fiorucci sandals and Coach bag, trailing a cloud of perfume that smelled of sandalwood and oranges. She peered into the classroom doubtfully, turning until her gaze fell upon Oliver and me. Her eyebrows arched in a delicate show of disbelief.

"Is this Professor Warnick's class?"

She had a beautiful throaty voice, with a slight vibrato. Oliver fell silent. I could hear the students in the front of the room whispering.

"Balthazar S. Warnick. That is correct." Oliver found his voice and gestured at an empty seat next to him. The girl smiled, a rapturous smile that made you feel lucky just to have glimpsed it. I glanced at Oliver and could see that he was actually blushing, twiddling his glasses and staring at her, transfixed.

And suddenly all the cold misery that had overwhelmed me before rushed back. Because, of course, *this* was who was supposed to know the answer to Oliver's ridiculous opening question. *This* was who he was supposed to meet—not me. *Never* me. Though from his expression he seemed quite unnerved. He looked away, shoving his glasses back onto his nose. "Ummm—a seat?" he asked, and tentatively patted the empty chair.

The girl stared at Oliver. Her eyes narrowed, and a curious expression crept over her face. Mingled apprehension and longing, but also a sort of restrained *hauteur*, as though she waited for a servant to come show her to her chair. As though she, too, had been expecting someone different. It was an unsettling expression to see in someone my own age. I wished I had taken a seat in the front of the room, wished that I'd never come here at all.

Her gaze flicked from Oliver to the chair beside him, and then to me. I found myself staring right back at her—a cat may look at a queen, right? For a long moment her eyes held mine. Luminous eyes, bottle green and almond-shaped, with long curled lashes tinted a dusky green as improbable as her irises. At the front of the room the muted conversation had stopped.

"We-ell," the girl said softly. She shifted her bag to her other shoulder and stepped into the room. Then, to my surprise, she spun on her heel and sank into an empty chair.

The chair next to *me*.

"I am Angelica di Rienzi," she said, and smiled.

"Wow." An explosive breath from someone in the front of the room. "Daddy, buy me one of *those*."

She was like a pre-Raphaelite Venus. Those enormous slanted eyes, cheekbones so high and sharp you'd cut your lip if you tried to kiss them. A wide curved mouth carefully shaped and colored with pale violet lip-gloss, hiding perfectly white teeth and just the slightest hint of an overbite. Her hair was a gorgon's tangle of bronze curls, pulled back loosely with a thick purple velvet ribbon and hanging halfway down her back. Between soft tendrils glinted a pair of gold hoop earrings set with amethyst beads, and around her long neck hung a fine gold chain set with another, single tear-shaped amethyst. She wore a flowing cotton peasant dress, with short gathered sleeves and a scoop neck and little violet ribbons trailing from the bodice. Your basic trust fund hippie look, and just about anyone who affected it—me, for instance—would look infantile or perhaps, if they were fortunate, engagingly girlish.

But not Angelica di Rienzi. Angelica looked *regal*. How can I describe what it was like, seeing her in a university classroom? A classroom at the Divine, to be sure, but still just a classroom, smelling of chalk and cigarettes, floor wax and earnest fear. It was like glimpsing a peacock on a lawn in New Rochelle; like hearing someone sing the *Magnificat* in Grand Central Station. No one could look at her and not believe that the world would give her whatever she wanted. Not even Oliver. Not even me.

She tilted her head. "And you must be—?"

"Sweeney," I said, my voice cracking. "Sweeney Cassidy."

"Angelica." Oliver repeated her name slowly, unconsciously aping Angelica's theatrical diction. He moved his desk and chair closer to hers and extended his hand. "Oliver Wilde Crawford."

Angelica nodded graciously. She pulled a notebook from her bag and let the purse slide to the floor, then, with another dazzling smile, took his hand.

In the front of the room someone giggled. I twisted around to see a heavyset young man in mirrored sunglasses staring at Angelica, his face expressionless, a cigarette dangling from one hand. I had a glimpse of dark eyes and a handsome, broad face with Asian features. Then with deliberate slowness he turned away.

"Are you related to *the* Wilde?" Angelica was asking Oliver. Her innocent emerald gaze made me kiss the pre-Columbians good-bye.

"Ah, yes. *'The old somdomite,'*" he said, giving her one of his vulpine smiles. "As a matter of fact Vyvyan—his son, Vyvyan—"

But at that moment Professor Warnick cleared his throat.

"Good morning, gentlemen and ladies. Welcome to the University of the Archangels and Saint John the Divine."

One of the other students called back, "Good *morning*!" and another laughed. Professor Warnick gave a small tight smile, more like a stoat baring its teeth, and glanced at the papers in his hand. He was a diminutive man, his longish black hair touched with grey, but with a young, rosy face and blue eyes that blazed almost angrily beneath thick black eyebrows. He looked comfortable at his podium, despite clothes as ill suited to the weather as my own: a stylish and expensively tailored suit of charcoal black worsted, cream-colored shirt, and an expansive paisley tie of purple and poison green. The podium he leaned against had been specially designed for him. Its brass fittings were set into richly gleaming wood—rowan, I was to learn, and ancient oak imported from Aylesbury— the whole thing set upon polished casters that squeaked malevolently when it was wheeled from classroom to classroom. It might have been all of four feet tall, and Professor Warnick himself perhaps a foot taller.

"Ahem." He inclined his head toward the back of the room. "Perhaps the Ghostly Trio would like to join the rest of us—?"

A titter from the other students. I gathered my things, abashed. Oliver stumbled noisily from his chair and took my elbow, looking past me at Angelica. She stared at Professor Warnick before giving him a small smile. His own cool gaze remained fixed as Oliver led me through the maze of empty chairs to the front of the room, Angelica behind us.

"Will this be sufficient, sir?" Oliver asked. He paused beside three seats and cocked his head. Professor Warnick smiled slightly.

"That will be fine," he murmured, and began handing out sheaves of Xeroxes.

We settled into our chairs. Oliver looked at Angelica. He whispered, "Have you a writing implement? And some paper?"

She fumbled in her bag and came up with a gold Cross pen, tried to tear a sheet of paper silently from one of her pristine notebooks. Professor Warnick looked up as she hurriedly passed the contraband to Oliver. Immediately he began sketching cartoonish figures in the margins. I glanced back at Angelica. She had opened a notebook with marbled cover and endpapers, and was writing carefully at the top of the first page with a Rapidograph pen, drawing elegant cursives in peacock blue ink. I looked at my own battered notebook and my pen: leaky Bic ballpoint, black ink, cap missing. I decided not to take notes.

Professor Warnick's class was strange. He began by dismissing other methods of teaching the subject at hand—

"Anthropology is very good as far as it goes, which is not very, since the discipline itself is only as old as *The Golden Bough*. And archaeology you will find is *more*, rather than less, problematical. Ah! you think, but how can that be so, since with archaeology we have, at least, the physical evidence in hand, it is only up to us to apprehend the culprit! But, I ask you, how many of you, looking upon a truly ancient artifact from a truly unknown culture, would have the slightest idea of *what it was*?"

Professor Warnick's clear tenor rang through the room's musty air. Dead silence from his students. Only from Oliver's desk came faint scratchings and squeakings as he continued to sketch. Professor Warnick swept us all with a dismissive gaze. Then from somewhere (but where? it seemed too bulky to have fit in his pocket) he swept forth an object consisting of a straight upright metal rod with crossbars and several dangling narrow strips of metal. Although cleaned and burnished to a warm bronze color, it still looked stained and worn and undeniably ancient.

"What is this?" he asked. When no one answered he pointed to the heavyset Asian boy in the front row. "Mister"—craning his neck to read a computerized class list—"José Malabar?"

Mr. José Malabar removed his sunglasses and squinted, stretched a hand to touch one of the dangling bits.

"Uh uh uh," scolded Professor Warnick. "No touching. Quick!—"

"A cattle prod?"

Laughter. The girl beside José Malabar suggested a hair curler. Professor Warnick stalked with quick small steps around the room, holding the rod aloft like a torch. Finally he stopped, turning all the way around once, like a dancer. I was terrified he would call on me. But no, his mouth was opening to say something, obviously he was about to reveal the true purpose of his toy, when . . .

"It's a sistrum," said Oliver. He didn't raise his head. His glasses balanced precariously on the very tip of his nose as he scribbled away. Angelica drew her breath in sharply and glanced at me. I slid lower in my seat and watched Professor Warnick.

At Oliver's words our teacher had frozen. Now he pivoted neatly, turning until he faced Oliver.

"That's *right*," Professor Warnick said in a soft voice. "And what is a *sistrum*, Mister Crawford—?"

"An Egyptian instrument used in the worship of Isis." Oliver narrowed his eyes pensively. "Fourth Dynasty, I believe."

"Ha!" exclaimed Professor Warnick. *"Third!"*

He raised the instrument and shook it. It made a harsh jangling, the sound of nails slowly being dropped onto glass. My scalp prickled. The sound died away, but for an instant I thought I heard something else. Another sound, like the distant sawing of cicadas in long grass, hot and tremulous and anxious.

Then it was gone. I lifted my head, chagrined to find myself yawning, and Professor Warnick staring at me with an odd smile.

"I will see you all on Wednesday," he said, and minced back to the front of the room. "Please have read *The Golden Ass* by then—don't complain, you'll find it goes very quickly! The Adlington translation, I believe the bookstore should have it in by now. Oh—"

He looked up from piling papers and sistrum and the end of his tie into a cracked leather briefcase. "I am supposed to mention that there is a reception tonight for Molyneux scholars, at Garvey House. At—"

He peered at a stack of papers rustling between his fingers. "Oh, I don't know. Seven, I think. Are there any Molyneux scholars here?"

Students paused in their flight to the door. I stood uncertainly between Oliver stumbling to his feet and Angelica carefully inscribing *Golden Ass, Adlington Trans.* into her notebook.

"None?" Professor Warnick said. His gaze flicked across the room. "Mister Crawford? Your friends?"

Angelica looked up, then slowly raised her hand. In the front of the room José Malabar did the same.

And so did Oliver.

"Ah," said Professor Warnick, and returned to gathering his things.

In the hallway I tried to get a better look at José Malabar, but he hurried off, fingers twitching around a cigarette.

"What's a Molyneux scholar?" I wondered aloud, but Oliver had already swept past. Angelica halted in the middle of the corridor, poring over a burgundy leather datebook.

"Damn," she muttered. "Can you tell me what that says? Is it 102 or 202 Reardon?"

I read the fine italicized print as 102. Angelica nodded absently, digging in her bag until she came up with a pair of eyeglasses. "It's my contacts," she explained, holding the glasses to her face and staring at her miniscule handwriting. "I've got those new tinted lenses and I really can't see out of them. Okay. 102. You were right."

Tinted lenses! Well, that would account for the eyes, at least. Angelica flashed me a smile and closed her bag. "Thanks, Sweeney. He's a little strange, isn't he?"

I thought she was talking about Professor Warnick, but then I saw her gaze dart to where Oliver leaned against the wall. "Java?" he called, snapping his fingers.

Angelica shook her head. "I have a class at Reardon."

"We'll walk you over." Oliver waited for us to catch up with him. "Sweeney looks half-asleep, anyway."

"I can't—I've got Medieval History—"

Oliver gave me a smug grin. "Me too: kid stuff. Lecture. Origins of civilization, conversion of Constantine. Pseudo-Ambrose and the Avicennian heresy. Got the notes from a guy on my floor who took it last year. We can catch up on the reading tomorrow."

I laughed, then saw he was serious. "We-ell—"

Behind us footsteps echoed. I caught a faint whiff of sweetly scented pipe tobacco. "So! You're this year's crop of scholars."

It was Professor Warnick. He walked beside us with small neat steps, his blue eyes glittering. "You, of course, Angelica."

Angelica gave me a queer, almost apologetic look, then nodded.

Professor Warnick smiled. "And you?" He raised his eyebrows at Oliver, who clicked his heels and bowed. "What a silly question! Yet another scion of the Crawford clan. And you?" He looked up at me roguishly.

"N—no—"

"No?" There was a world of disappointment in the word. I flushed, started to stammer some excuse but stopped.

Because from somewhere down the hall came that sound again, the droning noise that had seemed an echo of the sistrum's graceless note. For a moment the hallway seemed to vibrate, as though we all stood inside some huge drum that had been struck. Then silence. I was staring into Professor Warnick's bright feral eyes, and he was staring back at me with pity and what might have been relief.

"I see," he said softly. "Well, I think you will all enjoy *The Golden Ass*, and *I* will enjoy meeting with you again on Wednesday." A mocking smile as he tilted his head in farewell. "And some of you I may see tonight at the reception."

We watched him march off, his silhouette growing smaller and more gnomelike as he approached the end of the hallway. Abruptly he disappeared, leaving us alone and at a loss for words.

"Well," Angelica said at last, "I don't want to be late."

We clattered down the steps without talking. I felt overwhelmed and a little shaken. At first I was afraid to say anything, but then the heat began to work at me like a drug. Relief flooded me, and exhilaration, and fear: as though I had just escaped some terrible accident.

"God," I said as we finally burst out into daylight. "Is it just me, or was that, like, the weirdest class you've ever seen?"

Angelica and Oliver looked at me curiously. "Guess not," I said, and shut up.

The campus had come alive since last night. There were students everywhere, and enough anachronistically dressed clerical types to cast *The Greatest Story Ever Told*. As we headed toward the Strand, Oliver pointed out things of interest—

"Dutch elm trees, planted in 1689 by Goodman Prater and Arthur Simons. They've died of blight everywhere else in the United States, except on the seventh fairway of the back nine at Winged Foot. "

Or, "That's Brother Taylor Messingthwaite. He was ethical consultant on the Manhattan Project, teaches postgrad Confucian Ethics and Modern Christian Problems. Last year he got a Pemslip Grant for five hundred thousand dollars."

Or, "That's the *Ma es-Sáma* mosque. This sheik donated a million dollars to build it, so Islamic students here would have a place to worship. No one else's allowed inside. It's got a sixty-foot lap pool underneath."

Or, "Wild Bill! He's on my floor, grows psilocybin mushrooms in a terrarium, plus he has this hash oil factory with Martin Sedgewick—yo, *Bill*!"

Angelica laughed at each pronouncement. I said nothing. The effort of trying to maintain my poise had given me a headache. And it seemed like a bad omen, to be skipping class on my first day at college. The heat blurred my vision. My velvet pants felt as though they'd been dipped in hot wax. In the nether distance, the soaring towers of the Shrine shone like glimpses of some watched-for shore. It all made me light-headed. Not giddy, but a cheerless dizziness, as though I had opened my front door at home and somehow found myself at the edge of some windswept chasm.

"Reardon Hall. Designed by Emmet Thorson, the pedophile—he hanged himself in the foyer after it was completed," Oliver announced as we approached a small Palladian-style building. "Same architect as designed Rossetti—"

"What's a Molyneux scholar?"

Oliver halted, teetering on the curb with one grimy wing tip toeing into the grass. He stared at me nonplussed.

"I mean, is it some secret thing?" I went on. "Like I'm not supposed to ask?"

Oliver and Angelica exchanged a look. After a moment Angelica said, "Well, yes, it is. It's a—it's something they test you for, before admitting you here."

"But I never—I mean, they didn't ask *me*. I don't think. Is it like an advanced placement thing?"

Oliver pursed his lips. "You sacrifice some accuracy in describing it that way."

I tried not to sound petulant. "So what's the big deal? I mean, Warnick was talking about it in class. It can't be *that* secret."

"It's not that kind of thing," Angelica said slowly. The warm wind stirred her tangle of curls. She brushed the hair from her face and turned, sighing, to stare at Reardon's neoclassical facade. "Some of it's hereditary, a legacy—I mean if your father went here or something. It's more like—well, like Skull and Bones. Have you ever heard of that? At Yale?"

"Sure. If you're a member and somebody asks you about it, you have to leave the room."

"Right. It's more *that* kind of secret—"

"But what do they test you for?"

Angelica smiled wryly and shrugged. A few yards away, students lolling on the steps of Reardon were starting to gather their books and knapsacks, extinguishing spent cigarettes or lighting new ones. "I have to go. You're in Rossetti, aren't you? I saw your name on a dorm list. I'm on the third floor. You want to meet for dinner?"

"I guess. But—"

"The reception's at seven," said Oliver. He ducked his head, making agreeable noises as three white-clad friars rushed past us. "If we get separated, we'll all meet there."

Angelica laughed—a surprisingly loud and heartfelt laugh, not at all what you expected from such a carefully assembled beauty. She shook her finger at me and said, "Well, Sweeney, let's you and me *not* get separated. I'll wait for you outside the dining hall—"

She turned and hurried off, head bowed so that all I could see was her flag of shining curls.

"Come on," Oliver said. He was staring after Angelica with a hungry expression, but he sounded relieved. "The coffee's pretty good at the Shrine cafeteria. Then we can hit Dumbarton Oaks."

"Let me make sure I got my wallet—"

Oliver drew a wad of bills from his shirt pocket. "Don't worry about it."

He spun around, like Puck in a play, and added, "Don't sweat this Molyneux thing. Nothing but legacies. Alumni stuff, old school tie, *you* know. Another Old Boy Network—they're just *Very* Old Boys, that's all. Come tonight and you can see for yourself, okay?"

His blue eyes were intensely earnest, almost pleading. I smiled gratefully and nodded.

"Sure," I said, and flapped the front of my shirt to cool myself. "Whatever you say, boss."

Oliver grinned, walking backward and gesturing wildly as he began once more to lecture me on the plight of the city's Dutch elms. I was so busy watching him that I almost didn't notice the two figures that stood watching us from the curb. A diminutive man in black and, behind him, an almost grotesquely tall figure in an ankle-length black monsignor's cape, the hood pulled so close around its face that its features were lost to sight, except for the malevolent glitter of a pair of huge and watchful eyes.

CHAPTER 4

The Lunula

Magda found the lunula on her first dig—not her first archaeological foray, but the first one she supervised. Not coincidentally, it was the first excavation she had carried out without any direct regulation by the *Benandanti*. She was twenty-six years old at the time, in the postgrad program at UC Berkeley, heavily involved with her doctorate and the work that a few years later would become *Daughters of the Setting Sun*. She had gotten some funding through UC Berkeley, but most of it was to come from a wealthy patron named Michael Haring.

He was the CEO of an American automobile corporation: forty-two years old, Harvard-educated, never married. Magda met him at the Divine, at a reception in his honor. Michael Haring was one of the *Benandanti*, though his provenance was industry rather than the more rarefied realms of the university. Still, he had donated funds for several expeditions and financed the renovation of the reading room at Colum Library. He collected Neolithic art, concentrating on those tiny bronze figures of animals that were often found in Celtic graves and burial pits. He also collected young women, and was especially partial to the dark-haired Ivy League types who reminded him of his own youthful dreams of a career in classics.

"That's him?" Magda was still young enough to be impressed by someone whose picture had appeared on the cover of *Time* magazine. "Michael Haring?"

The man next to her nodded. "Sure is. They put a little plaque in the reading room with his name on it. But hell, he could have rebuilt the whole building."

"No kidding." Magda moved away, thoughtfully sipping her Tanqueray and tonic.

For almost two years now she had been seeking financial support for an excavation in northern Estavia. She had received the promise of small grants from the Divine and UCLA, and even a tiny stipend from the National Science Foundation.

But both her supporters at the Divine and those at UCLA's Department of European Archaeology felt that her proposed work was not important enough, dealing as it did with a site associated with a minor European goddess cult.

"Why don't you go with Harold Mosreich to Yaxchilán?" That had been Balthazar Warnick's suggestion. "He thinks that one of the stelæ there has a connection with the main pyramid at Chichén Itzá. Plus he has that National Geographic film crew—you know, 'Mayan Adventure!' or something like that."

Magda shook her head. "The Mayans are overdone. This is something *new*, Balthazar," she said fervently. "We both know that. Why won't you back me?"

Balthazar had been her advisor since her freshman year. Even then she'd wondered what someone like Balthazar Warnick—a world-renowned antiquities scholar, the man responsible for cataloging the Metropolitan Museum's Widdecombe Collection of Cycladic Art—was doing teaching an introductory anthropology course, even at a place like the Divine. *Especially* at a place like the Divine.

She'd found out, of course, when he'd tapped her for the *Benandanti*. Since then she and Balthazar had butted heads more than once, most recently over her decision to leave the Divine for UC.

"*Not* the place for a scholar of your rank." Balthazar never raised his voice, but his mouth had been tight as he rifled through a stack of photographs, the most recent mailing from the Chichén Itzá site. "California! Jesus, Magda, you tilt this country on its side and everything loose rolls into California! There's nothing out there but hopheads and surfers and rioting students. How are you going to get any work done?"

She'd gone anyway. She never told Balthazar that part of Berkeley's appeal—part of the appeal of the entire West Coast—was precisely that open-mindedness that Balthazar and many of the *Benandanti* dismissed as quackery or, at its worst, a threat to their ancient ways. But she remained on good terms with her old mentor. Remained an active member of the *Benandanti*, even when her own work began to diverge from what they felt was important.

What they did *not* feel was important was the small but growing body of evidence that Magda, and June Harrington before her, had uncovered: all of it pointing to the existence of a matrilineal culture in ancient Europe. Balthazar at least had been courteous, reading preliminary drafts of her articles for *Antiquities*, but he did not feel that Magda's theories were worth pursuing into the field.

"It's small potatoes, Magda." He turned and stared out the window of his office, to where the Shrine's blue dome glistened in the sun. "Sure, you'll find something there, but it's not going to ever *amount* to anything. I mean, look at Catal Huyuk: there's one of your goddess sites, a big one, too, but it doesn't really add up to much, does it?"

Magda had listened, her foot tracing Xs on the expensive kilim that covered Balthazar's floor.

Doesn't add up to what you're *looking for*, she thought furiously. But she said nothing. She hadn't expected him to agree with her. Balthazar was after much bigger fish than her modest research had discovered. The *Benandanti* had financed digs in Jerusalem, Sardinia, Luxor; at Karbala' in Iraq, and Katta-Kurgan near Samarkand; in Niger and Jamshedpur and the Hentiyn Mountains in Mongolia. Anyplace where the *Benandanti* had ever built a temple or cathedral of clay or gold or marble was suitable for resurrection. As was anyplace where their ancient enemy had once been worshiped: Athens, Knossos, Ur.

But a minor Balkan river goddess in a Soviet backwater was not exactly the powerful and vengeful deity they had been set to guard against. And so there was no funding for Magda's project.

Fortunately, there was at least one other person willing to entertain her ideas.

"It's lovely, isn't it?" She smiled brightly at her host. It was a few days after the Divine's reception for Michael Haring, a few days after Magda had finagled the invitation to visit Haring at his Georgetown town house. "It's a helmet crest, first century B.C.."

Michael Haring turned the figure over in his hand. A little bronze boar, no longer than his middle finger, its raised dorsal spine worked with an intricate pattern of whorls that ended in the tiny beaked heads of cranes. He whistled softly. "It's absolutely stunning. Where'd you find it, Magda?"

"It was June Harrington's. She gave it to me a few years ago, for a birthday present."

"And it came from your proposed site?"

She nodded. "The American Museum mounted an expedition there in 1923, with June and her first husband, Lowell Ackroyd. She's given me her field notes, and some of the pictures he took. They're not very good—the photos, I mean, her notebooks are superb—but I can tell, Michael, I can just tell! June says they found three burial pits with evidence of ritual animal sacrifices, and that—"

She gestured at the bronze figurine. "—*that* came from the last one they uncovered, Eleven-A. The neighboring valleys show signs of having very advanced Bronze Age settlements—we're talking collective burials, hypogea with detailed wall paintings, and heating from thermal springs, maybe even some kind of linear script on some of the pottery fragments. The whole valley's a potential gold mine. The surrounding heath is pretty marshy, which means there's a good chance that whatever we come up with could be well preserved."

Michael nodded, turning the bronze boar between his fingers. "Why did they stop the dig?"

"Winter. The valley becomes completely impassable in winter. The first storm came in early October; June and Lowell and the crew barely got out before the snows blocked off the pass."

"I see." Carefully Michael set the boar back into its nest of yellowed newsprint. He reached for the bottle of claret beside it and raised an eyebrow. "More?"

"Please. It's wonderful." Magda held out her glass, smiling brilliantly and hoping he wouldn't notice how nervous she was. "So!" She toasted him and let the first rich mouthful of wine slide down her throat. "What do you think?"

Michael Haring looked around his living room. There were glass cabinets everywhere, some arranged against the wall, others floating like huge crystal pendants amidst the expanse of black leather furniture and white shag carpeting. The cabinets were filled with figures very like the one that rested on his table, and with silver torques, beaked masks, bronze armor in the shape of wings, plaques inlaid with bone and silver and crudely polished stones. He surveyed them all, not with pride but with a certain wistfulness that gave his dark eyes a mournful cast. An Iron Age prince's ransom in artifacts and metalwork: nearly all of it obtained on the black market, spirited from original holdings in Britain and Czechoslovakia and Turkey and Greece. He was tied up in litigation right now with the embassy of a small country in Eastern Europe, fighting over the disposition of his most-prized treasure: the mummified head of a Bronze Age man found in a peat bog, and now displayed within a tall glass case like a casket stood upon its end.

"I think," he said carefully, staring at the tea-colored head in its crystal chamber. "I *think* that this could be a very important adventure you're planning, Miss Magda. For both of us." And turning, he let his hand rest upon her thigh.

Six months later Magda and her crew were in Çaril Kytur. The site was in a desolate corner of northern Estavia, deep within the Psalgÿuk Mountains—tall, needle-thin spars of quartz and flint that shot up against leaden skies that rarely showed the sun. Like something out of a Dürer etching of Hell, Magda thought, or Murnau's *Nosferatu*. Even the trees were stunted, crippled pines and alders whose roots poked through the thin acid soil where they sought footing.

It was late July. In the three days it took Magda and her companions to drive from the Estavian capital to Çaril Kytur, they passed only two other vehicles: an empty Intourist bus with Moscow plates, and an ancient grey jitney piled high with wooden cartons, live chickens and ducks tied to its extremities with red twine. The bone-jarring trip was enough to make Magda wish that she'd left Janine, at least, back in Washington.

"This is *not*, like, what my faculty advisor told me to expect," Janine announced after their second night in the Jeep. "I thought I was going to get to practice my Russian, but there's nobody *here*."

"Well, we're stuck with each other now," Magda said grimly. "So if you want to bail out, start walking."

No one did. A few hours later they'd reached their destination.

"Oh man," breathed Nicky D'Amato, another of the triumvirate who'd signed on from the Divine. "Are you sure you read that map right?"

Magda sighed. "I'm sure."

They stumbled from the Jeep and looked down into the valley of Çaril Kytur, a long narrow spit of land crosshatched with streams that fed into a huge marshy area to the south. It was a dispiriting landscape. The stones dun-colored, pleached with lichen and moss; the few trees hunched against the wind that whistled down through a gap in the mountains to the north. Lowell Ackroyd's theory had been that a band of Paleolithic hunters was stranded here during one of the minor ice ages, surviving to found the ancient encampment known as Çaril Kytur, Belly of the Moon. Certainly it was hard to imagine why anyone would *choose* to live here. The surrounding mountains were sparsely populated, mostly by shepherds who eked out a living from the barren hillsides and more temperate valleys. Magda had thought the natives would be eager to supplement their meager incomes with what they could earn from assisting on the dig, but that wasn't the case at all.

"He says they're not interested."

George Wayford, the last of the three grad students who had accompanied Magda from D.C., shook his head. They were sitting in front of Magda's tent—Magda, George, Nicky, Janine—the entire Çaril Kytur crew. Overhead the sky was grey and skinned-looking. A cold wind blew down from the mountain pass to the north, sending skeins of mist racing across the encampment. Magda shivered in her heavy Icelandic wool sweater and wondered why she'd thought this was a better idea than the Yucatán. "He says the whole valley is *stantikic't*—"

"What? Haunted?" Janine interrupted derisively.

George squatted in front of the hissing campfire and lit a cigarette. "No," he said, and tossed his match into the flames. George had majored in Slavic languages at Georgetown, and was hoping to find linguistic links between the Estavians of the Psalgÿuk range and the neighboring Cuclterinyi culture in the Transylvanian Alps, and even modern Crete. "*Isch'raval*, that would be haunted. This is more like *tainted*."

"But they're not coming. That's what you're telling us, right? That we are *it* as far as personnel goes—" Nicky looked balefully at his three companions, then picked up a stone and shied it at the Jeep. "Fuckin' A, I *knew* we should have called first."

"Called?" Magda laughed in spite of herself. "Christ, Nicky, there's not a phone for seventy miles!" She got to her feet, rubbing her hands and doing a mental inventory. "Look, we don't need anyone else, not really. We'll start right in with the shaft at Eleven-A. That's the one June said they'd just opened when they had to leave. It's where they found that boar helmet crest—"

(now part of Michael Haring's collection)

"—and it won't be as much work as digging out a totally new site. We should be able to handle it on our own."

Janine and Nicky shot her dark looks, but George was already heading for the makeshift lean-to where their tools were stored. "All right then," Magda said, and started after him.

It took them four days just to dig through the accumulated debris and soil that had silted over the old site. But once they'd cleared away the dirt and rotting shrubs, the excavation that June Harrington had named Eleven-A proved to be remarkably well preserved. Nearly fifty years had passed since the original team from the American Museum had set up scaffolding around the burial shaft. But when they reached the first level, Magda and her students found that the timbers placed by Lowell Ackroyd were still holding back the chamber's earthen walls.

"I'd feel better if we had some new beams there," George announced, staring dubiously at the sagging timbers.

"I'm not climbing down otherwise," Janine said flatly, peering into the dim reaches of the pit.

Magda nodded and took the shovel from Janine's hands. "Well, then, I guess you and Nicky can start cutting down trees."

By the end of the first week they had erected a second scaffold around the first, the whole shaky edifice sunk twenty feet into the earth. Curiosity and greed had gotten the better of the natives in the nearest village. Now Magda had a half dozen laborers helping to pull up buckets of soil and gravel. Janine carried these to a system of seines and screens set up nearby, and sifted through the debris for anything that might hold a clue to the nature of the shaft. So far they'd found potsherds, and a few bones that were probably a dog's, but nothing more dramatic—no figurines, no human remains, nothing to make this site worth much more time and effort.

"I *know* it's a burial pit," Magda said stubbornly. She was balanced precariously atop a ladder sunk into the soft marshy ground at the bottom of the site, sipping her morning brew from a battered tin mug. She grimaced and stared at the cup's murky contents, a concoction made from powdered beetroot that was the locals' answer to coffee. "God, this is awful—no wonder they're all so surly."

"You're gonna need something besides dog bones and a little bronze boar to determine that," George replied mildly from a few steps below her on the ladder. "Chasar—" Chasar was the spokesman for the locals. "—Chasar says this hole is *fancr'ted*—unholy, you know, profane. *Not* a sacred site—"

"Or it could mean it was a pre-Christian site, which obviously it *is*," Magda retorted. "And if the locals have some vague memory of *that*, they'd think it was profane, meaning pagan, meaning bad juju. *Unholy*," she added, frowning for emphasis.

"Nah. This could've been a midden, someone might have pitched that ol' boar in here—" George flicked at the wall and sent a miniature avalanche of pebbles and dirt flying to the bottom of the shaft. "Or it could have fallen out of somebody's Neolithic pocket—"

"Do you *mind?*"

From the belly of the pit Nicky shouted amidst the hail of stones, brandishing a shovel. He wore waders and a totally useless plastic Soviet-made hard hat, and was covered with mud from head to toe. "Dammit, George!"

"Sorry, man." George waved apologetically, shifting his weight on the ladder. Magda realigned herself to keep from falling. "But it's been over a week, Magda—I really, *really* think we should abandon this site and check out that mound by the marsh. There could be human remains there, and the chances of preservation are so much better—"

"One more day," said Magda. She and George had been having this argument for almost a week now. "June said she thought it was a burial site, and she wouldn't—"

"June is *senile*, Magda! That was fifty years ago; they still believed in *Piltdown* Man—"

"One more day," Magda said stubbornly. Without looking, she turned her mug upside down and dumped its contents. "Okay? Just—"

"Goddammit, Magda!" Nicky shrieked from below.

George and Magda burst out laughing. Magda shook the hair from her eyes and smiled. "Let that be a warning, Wayford."

"Okay, okay," George said, and grinned. The ladder shimmied as he climbed back to the top. "One more day."

That night she couldn't sleep. Part of it was anxiety over abandoning June Harrington's site. George was right, of course. The shaft at Eleven-A had yielded little in the way of data, a few bits of bone and fired clay that might have been found anywhere—nothing remarkable at all. The mound near the swampy end of the valley might well hold more interesting material, and there was always the hope of finding human or animal remains preserved by the bog.

"Damn," Magda swore aloud. She lay inside her tent, arms folded behind her head, and stared at the canvas ceiling. Outside the moon must be nearly full. The tent's worn green fabric glowed so that she felt as though she were floating in a phosphorescent sea, the cool breeze carrying the scent of the tiny night-blooming stonecrops that were the only flowers that grew in the valley.

One more day.

There must have been some reason why June Harrington had been convinced of the site's importance, something besides a little bronze boar and a few canine tibiae. It was the fragment of the lunula, of course: such a small thing to build a life's work on, and lost now in the Museum. Magda wished she had questioned her mentor more carefully, but June had been so certain, her usually restrained site notes so exuberant—

> *. . . Yesterday at Eleven-A I uncovered an artifact of hammered silver, a luniform pendant the size of my little finger. Of course it is only a fragment remaining of what must have been an extensive burial site; but judging by the workmanship the pendant came not from anywhere near here but from the Sea of Crete. There is a marked similarity between the devices inscribed upon it and the record of those figures engraved upon the so-called "Lost Ring of Minos"—this curvilinear charm might well prove the authenticity of the lost Ring, if only it could be found again! Quite beside myself with excitement and trying not to read too much into this single artifact but Lowell agrees, there is a good chance the entire valley was sacred to Inachus; that is, Leucothea, or the White Goddess, herself an avatar of the Great Goddess of the ancient Minoans. Which would, of course, prove my theory that trade routes existed between the Hittite and Minoan cultures. And Harold Sternham (bless him! he seemed a stick at first, but I am grateful now of his patronage!), dear Harold may be correct in his assertion that the minor nymph called by the natives Othiym, affiliated as she is with the river of that name which once ran through here, is related to that same river-goddess Ino or Inachus who was worshiped in Crete . . .*

There had been a curious addendum to this entry. Curious because June so seldom revised her first impressions—she was in the habit of being right. And so Magda had been surprised to see something scrawled in the margin, a quotation that had obviously been recorded decades after the original entry.

I should never have taken the lunular fragment from the site. "The dark aspect of the antique mother-goddess has not yet reappeared in our civilization."

And after this, the words:

No: She Lives.

Magda started as a sudden gust sent the tent's flaps and lines humming, and an eddy of dust flying up from the door panels.

"The hell with it," she said aloud, and scrambled from her sleeping bag.

Outside the night air struck her like a clapper to a bell, making the blood sing inside her head and her ears throb painfully. She shivered in her heavy sweater and held the flashlight close to her chest, as though its pale beam might give some warmth. In front of George's tent she hesitated. Even with the shrill wind she could hear his breathing, loud and measured as the pulse of a metronome. For a long moment she stood there, as though waiting for him to rise and come out to join her. But of course he didn't wake, didn't stir at all. She turned away.

She walked carefully between the other tents, her work boots sending gravel flying as she tried to tiptoe through the loose scree of pebbles and sandy soil that covered the valley floor. She paused again after she passed Janine's flimsy little Sears Roebuck shelter, with its absurd red-striped awning and Janine's wool socks hung out to dry.

"Janine?" Magda called softly, tilting her head. "Nicky?"

She saw no one: only the shadows of tents and stones, unnaturally large and black in the brilliant moonlight. But she *had* heard something, a faint noise like the tiniest of footsteps, or pattering rain. She waited, holding her breath; but the sound died away into the breeze. Finally she took another step. And stopped.

"Ohh!—get away, *no*—!"

It was as though she had walked into a whirlwind. All around her were falling leaves, hundreds of them: livid grey-green in the cold light, rushing up from the ground in a whirring explosion of dirt and dusty foliage. Magda shrieked and struck at them as they whirled and fell, brushing against her cheeks as they fluttered everywhere, tangling in her hair and slithering between her fingers. A scent of damp earth came with them, a smell like bitter chocolate. When she struck one with her open palm it exploded in a damp burst, as though she had crushed a rotten fruit.

"Jesus!—ugh, go away!"

She stumbled forward, beating at the air and whimpering, as the leaves covered the ground in a rippling carpet. For a moment the air was still. Then to her horror they rose once more from the rocky earth, fluttering and rustling, their fragile stems and tattered fronds beating against her like tiny living things as they climbed the legs of her jeans and clung to her sweater.

And suddenly Magda realized what they were—not leaves but *insects*, hundreds, *thousands* of them—wings crinkled and mottled in uncanny imitation of dying foliage, their legs and bodies elongated to resemble twigs. They filled the sky, blotting out the moon. She choked on the scent of bitter chocolate. Her legs felt bound as the insects clung to her jeans; she felt something brush against her throat, the soft impression of legs ticking slowly across her cheek.

"God damn it!" she yelled, and fled.

She ran for a few yards, wielding her flashlight like a bat. Then she had to stop, panting as she tried to catch her breath, hands raised protectively to her face. Her cheek felt wet. When she lowered her hands she gasped.

"What the *hell*?"

The insects were gone. Magda was so startled she shrieked again and jumped backward, caught herself and turned slowly, holding her flashlight at arm's length as she swept its beam up and down her body.

Nothing. On her sweater, her jeans, her face: nothing at all. When she looked back she saw only the empty gravel in front of Janine's tent. A single leaf twirled beneath the canvas awning and disappeared. She heard no sound except for the wind rattling distant branches. Her own tent stood off by itself. From a makeshift tripod her mud-stained rugby shirts and jeans hung drying, and moved like her own shadow in the breeze.

Magda let her breath out with a shudder. She might have dreamed it all. Only, as she brushed furtively at her sweater, her hand scraped against a tiny leg caught like a splinter in the coarse wool. As she walked away from the camp, she smelled the rich odor of bitter chocolate.

After a few minutes she quit trembling. Her heart slowed, she relaxed her grip on the flashlight and even grinned a little, imagining what June Harrington would have had to say about *that*.

> *Tonight at the moon's full we were set upon by a swarm of leaf insects,* Phasmida luridium. *Harold has noted that at Mount Ida these are sacred to the Bee-goddess Melissa, and representations have been found on kraters from the so-called Dark Age . . .*

She kept walking, not paying attention to where she was going, intent only on calming herself and trying to remember enough details of the swarm to relate convincingly to George in the morning. So it was that when she stumbled on the sharp edge of a boulder she looked up in surprise, and saw that she was heading for Eleven-A.

"Huh," she murmured, and laughed.

Overhead the sky was clear, the color of a mussel shell and nearly starless. The moon had risen above the eastern edge of the valley. Where its light fell upon Çaril Kytur, it was as though someone had streaked the valley with chalk. Magda switched off her flashlight and tilted her head back until all she saw was the swollen moon. When she looked away pearly swabs of light still clung to her vision. The wind whistled down the channels it had found in the ragged bluffs. A fresh icy scent filled Magda's nostrils, like rain on clean stone, and washed away the bitter odor of the swarm. She slid her hands inside the sleeves of her sweater and shivered.

It must be long after midnight; that cold thin hour when the dreaded *keres* of ancient Greece moved freely between their own dark world and this one. Magda smiled again, thinking of June Harrington and her endless ranking of specters and demons and harpies, all the nightmare eidolons that haunted the past. She would love hearing about the leaf insects. Magda shook her head ruefully. A hundred yards or so from where she stood, the rickety scaffolding of Eleven-A rose from the barren landscape.

"All right." Her voice sounded shaky, so she repeated the words, louder this time. "Let's have a *smoke*."

She felt in the pocket of her jeans until she found the cello-wrapped packet of cigarettes she had gotten from Chasar a few days earlier. She'd traded him a half dozen of her Old Golds for three times as many of the local smoke—stubby hand-rolled cigarillos heavily laced with soft amber chunks of Turkish hashish. She lit one and smoked slowly, standing with one hand resting against the trunk of a wizened tree as she stared at the shadows in the lunar valley before her.

It was weird, how different the place looked by moonlight. Not just the normal difference you would expect between day and night, or between the night of a full moon and any other. It was much stranger than that, stranger and more unsettling. And, of course, the hash made it all even more intense, and the memory of the swarm.

Magda shuddered and took another long drag on her cigarette. As the moon rose higher, the chalky outlines of things grew burnished, until stones and withered trees and rocky outcroppings all took on an October glow. In the hollows, the tiny stonecrops covered the thin soil in a pale yellow carpet. Above Eleven-A hung the moon, placid, ripe as a pear about to fall. From an unseen roost a bulbul sang, its bubbling voice as improbably lovely as the night-blooming flowers.

"Wow," Magda breathed. Smoke hung in a pall about her face as her eyes widened. "Too fucking much."

The bulbul's impassioned song rose and fell and rose again. A sweet smoky scent hung over everything, and Magda had one of those mind-jarring stoned moments when she wondered if she had somehow wandered far from the camp, far from Çaril Kytur itself, and come somehow to another country, the landscape in a dream.

But that was stupid; that was just the hash. She took a final drag from her cigarette and tossed it into the shadows. Then she headed for Eleven-A.

Even through the heavy soles of her work boots she could feel the bite of stones and thorns. She had no idea what time it was. Probably no more than an hour or two until dawn, judging from the moon. She thought of returning to bed, but in spite of the hashish she wasn't tired—fear and adrenaline and wonder had purged all the sleep from her body. She stared balefully at the scrim of canvas and two-by-fours that hid the excavation.

One more day.

At the thought of abandoning the site she felt a twinge of guilt and disappointment. Guilt on June Harrington's behalf—Magda had promised to finish the excavation her mentor had begun so long ago. And disappointment to think that, really,

George was right. There never had been anything to Eleven-A to begin with. It was only another mismanaged and uncompleted excavation, from an age when archaeologists relied on *The Golden Bough* and dreams of Troy instead of dendronic rings and radioactive isotopes. She sighed and walked to the edge of the pit.

It was no different than it had been that afternoon. The same piles of rocky earth banked around the entrance to the dig. Nicky's red flannel shirt still hung from a shovel stuck into a mound of gravel. Janine's panniers and makeshift seines were where she'd left them, beside the carefully sorted and labeled boxes of bones and potsherds. An empty bottle of the local brew leaned against another pile of Janine's painstakingly organized fragments.

Red Dot A. Red Dot C. Lightning Patterns. Canines. Auroch? Misc.

It was all innocent and bland as an abandoned sandbox, and as interesting.

"Damn it," Magda whispered. She thought of June Harrington and the bronze boar, of the fragment of a lunula long since lost in the Museum. The single eidolon on which June had hung so many hopes. Then she climbed into the pit.

When she lowered herself onto the ladder it shuddered. Silently she cursed Chasar and the co-op where they'd been forced to get all their supplies. The ladder was old and had obviously been retired, for good reason. Now she could feel the soft wood buckling beneath her foot and creaking loudly as she hurried to the next step. Loose earth and stone flew into her face as she made her way down, and once the entire wall seemed to ripple. Magda had a horrifying vision of herself buried beneath a ton of earth and Nicky's flannel shirt. For a few minutes she gripped the flashlight between her teeth and trusted to blind luck that she'd get safely to the bottom. But finally her foot rested gingerly against something soft yet solid. With a gasp Magda stepped onto the ground.

It was like being at the bottom of a grave. Far above a ragged violet hole opened into the night. Its perimeter glowed faintly where moonlight touched the edges of things, wooden pilings and stones banked up to form a rough retaining wall. But in the pit itself there was no light at all, nothing except the feeble gleam of Magda's flashlight. She stepped forward, stumbled against a tin pail that gave an echoing *clank* when she struck it. She raised her flashlight and leaned back against the earthen wall, careful not to disturb the rough system of beams and joists that kept the whole ancient structure from caving in on her.

In daylight Eleven-A was dank and dim and uninspiring. At night it was downright creepy. Magda nearly choked on the pit's earthy scent: not just dirt, but the heavy moldering smell of thousands of years of decay, shrubs and leaves and rotting timbers, the decomposing bodies of all the dogs and cattle whose remains they had already unearthed, and god knows how many other animals that had been sacrificed or merely tossed into the shaft, before the pit itself was abandoned. Magda tightened her grip on the flashlight. She coughed and covered her mouth and nose with her sleeve.

She'd never noticed it before, but an awful putrefying smell seemed to cling to the bottom of the shaft. There should be nothing, of course, only the ripe but relatively innocuous scent of decaying vegetable matter. But this was awful, as though something, squirrel or rat or vole, had fallen into the pit and died there. Magda grimaced, peering more closely at the floor. The flashlight revealed nothing, just the normal accumulation of stones and twigs, the gritty reddish sand that formed this stratum of the excavation.

She paced the bottom of the shaft. Five steps north, five steps south, six steps east and west. In a battered red plastic bucket someone had heaped a grouping of larger stones with uniformly pointed edges. Evidence perhaps of some kind of toolmaking, or—more likely—nothing but pedolites, naturally occurring rocks that appeared to have man-made characteristics. She squatted beside the pail, picking out a few stones and examining them in the flashlight's watery glare. One of them had the sharp edges associated with knapped stone, but it was feldspar—not good for toolmaking, merely a type of rock prone to breaking in this particular pattern. In disgust Magda tossed it across the shaft, wincing as dirt rained down where it struck the wall.

"Well, shit. I'm just wasting my time."

The earthen walls swallowed her voice, made it sound thin and childish. The putrid odor was so strong she breathed through her mouth. All at once she felt exhausted. She stood and leaned back against the wall again, sighing. Her high had worn off. The odd things she had glimpsed, or thought she had glimpsed, suddenly seemed embarrassingly commonplace. The kind of things a careless site manager might run into, if she was the sort of person who got stoned in the middle of the night and went wandering around in a godforsaken place like this. Bugs and moonshine and bad smells, that was all.

She twisted her head and stared up into the shaft. Far overhead the sky had paled from violet to pinkish grey. The moonlight that had touched things with faerie gold was gone. In an hour it would be sunup. By this time tomorrow the site would be abandoned, for the second time this century, and probably forever.

At the thought anger welled up in Magda: at George and Nicky and Janine, for refusing to believe Eleven-A might hold anything of historic value; at June Harrington, for encouraging her to believe that it did. The flashlight's beam wavered fitfully—after this moonlight outing the damn thing would need new batteries again. She thought of Balthazar Warnick's persistent urging that she give up this crazy plan and join Harold Mosreich in Mexico. At this very moment she could have been perched atop the main pyramid at Chichén Itzá, waiting for moonrise.

Damn June Harrington!

Magda kicked furiously at the sandy ground in front of her. Her boot hit a rock. In a sudden rage she kicked again, hard enough to send the stone flying. With surprising force it struck one of the support beams in the wall opposite her. There was a soft hollow *klunk*. Then, with mesmerizing slowness, the beam started to buckle forward, and with it the entire earthen wall. Eleven-A was foundering.

Magda stared in horror as the timber split, its rusty splints groaning as they separated. From the surrounding wall soil and stones tumbled, not in an avalanche but with creeping slowness, like lava overtaking a mountainside. Earth like dark foam boiled across the floor, small stones and flecks of gravel flying everywhere. Magda cried out and tried to protect her face. Beams collapsed upon themselves in slow motion, soil covering them. Bit by bit the sandy floor disappeared. There was a soft mumbling sound, like voices heard from another room. When Magda craned her neck to stare upward she could see where other support timbers had begun to bulge outward. Her breath came in sharp gasps; she felt as though earth already filled her lungs, pressed upon her chest with numbing force. Too late she tried to scramble onto the ladder, felt the wall shivering behind it like boggy ground. When she opened her mouth to shout for help, dirt splattered her tongue like rain. Tears of rage and horror filled her eyes as she crouched and stared at the encroaching wall.

She could have extended her arms and touched it, a solid mound of darkness blotting out the little light that remained. The reek of decay was overpowering. Her mouth was filled with sand, dirt covered her boot as she tried desperately to pull her foot from the moving path.

Make it stop, make it stop, oh please . . .

And then, as abruptly as it had begun, the earthen flow ceased. Not a foot from where she crouched a dark and softly rounded hummock rose to meet the other side of the shaft. The mumbling undercurrent of sound grew still. Magda waited, not daring to move or breathe. Then, very slowly, she stood, with one hand retrieved the half-buried flashlight. She switched it on and trained its feeble beam on the opposite wall.

It was like looking into an empty well. Where timbers and support beams had been, there was now a hole big enough to drive the Jeep through. A dank breeze crept from its mouth. The choking scent of decay faded. Magda didn't have time to wonder what the breeze might portend, or where the rotting odor had come from in the first place. Before she could turn and flee back up the ladder, a final solid chunk of earth dropped, like a great slice of cake sliding from a knife. When it struck the ground, Magda froze and stared openmouthed at the wall.

Suspended in the motionless waterfall of soil and rock was a skeleton. Perfectly formed, it lay curled upon its side, ribs, humerus, femur enmeshed in delicate bands of sepia and white. Even seeing it in the wake of that nearly silent avalanche, Magda knew its posture was not accidental. It was the same carefully arranged stance that she had seen in photographs of countless burials, from the famous Neanderthal remains of Shanidar to dozens of Celtic graves throughout Britain and western Europe. The exact same pose: body carefully set upon its side, legs drawn up, arms tightly folded as though they held something.

And in this case, the arms *did* hold something: a skull. The long curving spine ended above the shoulders in a twist of vertebrae like heavy ivory beads. The skull was gone. Decapitated—the edge of the first vertebra sliced cleanly away. She shone her flashlight back upon the rib cage and there it was, a pale globe clutched within a cage of fingerbones and slender femurs. Its eye sockets gave back a hollow glow where the beam touched them.

"Sweet Jesus," Magda breathed, and tears sprang to her eyes. "June was right. She was *right*."

She half walked, half swam through earth and stone, heedless now of further danger. Enough light leaked from where the sun was starting to rise overhead that she could see it all clearly. Notched and shattered vertebrae like bits of broken chalk. Around one slender wrist a bronze cuff, chased in a pattern of curves and dots. A dusting of rust-colored powder—red ocher—on several ribs, staining the soil beneath like blood. Something glittered from the skull, and she caught glints of gold and silver where bits of metal had fallen into the rib cage as the corpse decayed. Peering into the hole left by the collapsed wall, she glimpsed another array of bones and a very faint glimmering.

More artifacts. When she withdrew, her heart was pounding so hard she thought she might faint. She gazed back at the skeleton. Nothing, no ancient hoard of gold or bronze, could be as precious to her as that human form. She wept openly to look upon it.

"Jesus God. June, June, June."

Somehow it had not been crushed by the weight of millennia. Perhaps the slow withdrawal of the River Othiym from the valley had eased its passage, providing a protective boggy medium until the harsher weather of modern times overtook Çaril Kytur. Or maybe it was as June Harrington had told her once—

"They look after their own, you know. It doesn't matter how long—they don't sleep, and they don't forget."

June had been speaking of the *Benandanti*, but Magda had used the anecdote with her own students, referring to the remarkable preservation of the Shanidar site.

"They don't sleep . . ."

This one hadn't been sleeping when they killed him. Or perhaps he had been. Perhaps among the shattered remains of pottery and ornament she would find a ritual cup, a cauldron with pollen still adhering to its rim, chemical traces of psylocibin spores or *papaver rhoeas*, corn poppy. She extended one hand, her fingers trembling as they brushed the fragile-looking arch of ribs. She half expected the bones to crumble into ash at her touch, but they did not. They felt cool and solid as polished wood, their slightly rough pitted surface giving them a softer edge than she would have expected, like the velvet covering a yearling stag's antlers. If she struck one, she was certain it would ring sweetly, like a bell.

It was bright enough now that she switched off her flashlight and stuck it into a soft mound of earth. She turned and lovingly ran both hands across the long femur, her fingertips catching on the raised lip of a scar, the rounded knob of its pelvis gleaming softly in the silvery dawn. Not just a burial, but a sacrificial burial: a ritual murder dating back some three thousand years. A major, *major* find.

June Harrington would be vindicated. Michael Haring would recoup his small investment. And Magda Kurtz's reputation would be made.

Somewhere far above a warbler let loose a thin ribbon of song. She should go and wake the others, get cameras and notebooks and plaster of Paris down here, some kind of sandbags to keep the shaft from eroding further. Automatically she noted all the things she would write up later. Width of pelvis indicated a male. The clean edges along the damaged vertebrae suggested that a very sharp blade had been used for the sacrifice. A broken rib had healed unevenly; perhaps he had been a warrior. Teeth in surprisingly good condition, which meant a good diet. Probably quite young by modern standards, maybe eighteen years old. Most striking of all the positioning of the skull: carefully placed within the hands so that it faced outward, its empty eyes watching, waiting . . .

Nowhere had she ever read of a ritual slaying even remotely similar to this. She thought of George's linguistic research, of how it pointed to heretofore unproven links with the Aegean. Together with the skeleton, this find would give weight to his work, and to all the hours of research that Magda herself had put into proving her mentor right. The welter of objects buried with the victim might at last provide conclusive evidence for June's theories of a matrilineal culture in central Europe, undeniable proof of human sacrifice to a lunar goddess.

Magda took a deep breath. She pressed her clenched fists to her breast to keep them from shaking. This wasn't just another find to be written up in *Archaeology* or *Science*. Not with women burning their bras and someone like Valerie Solanas shooting Andy Warhol. This would mean coverage in the *Times* and a mention on national news, early tenure, maybe even her own film crew . . .

She let her breath out in a long gasp and reluctantly forced herself back to the task at hand. There was still a considerable danger that the entire shaft might collapse. She should set as many details to memory as she could, and get the hell out. She thought of removing some of the jewelry for Michael Haring. This, after all, was what she had been hoping to find; this was why Haring had underwritten the spiraling costs of the entire odyssey.

But for once Magda Kurtz the scientist won out over raw ambition. If the site's integrity was destroyed, any future speculation regarding the nature of Çaril Kytur would be compromised. There would be plenty of time to pocket some precious toy for her patron; this afternoon, perhaps, while the others were shoring up the excavation, or even sooner. She smiled and started to turn back to the skeleton.

Before she could, her gaze fell upon a small mound. Dun-colored and coarse with dirt, the mound had been easy for her to overlook. But now Magda whistled softly. The pile held tiny figurines, dozens of them, carved of bone and ivory and stone and clay. No bigger than a knuckle or forefinger, although Magda glimpsed one cylinder of dark green stone the length of her arm. Most of the figurines were simple, pendant-shaped, with tiny protrusions representing arms, legs, breasts; others were more elaborate and showed the figure of a woman extravagantly garbed with swirling drapery and ornate headgear.

"No," breathed Magda.

Goddess figurines. There might be a hundred of them, spanning thousands of years of worship: Lascaux to the Parthenon, the Venus of Willendorf to Persephone. Magda's hand hovered above them, and almost she could feel heat rising, the dust and earth turned to ashes as flames licked at sculpted azurite and carven bone.

Oh, June, if only you could see this! She gazed down, filing it all away in her head, and prayed that nothing would happen before she could get George and Nicky down here with shovels and sandbags.

Slowly she turned from the figurines, and back to the human skeleton. She stooped to examine the bones more closely. The corpse had been painted with red ocher, same as at Shanidar. Or perhaps it was left to decompose and be picked clean by vultures—there were ancient paintings of such a ritual in Anatolia—and then the bones were colored in another ceremony. Gently Magda ran a finger along a blunt curve of vertebra rusted with the powdered mineral. Clay and hydrated ferric oxide, dark red, almost brown. They'd have to run an analysis on the pigment, see if it was local or not. She could smell the pigment, a faint tang like scorched metal. She drew a little X on her wrist and watched as the ocher seeped into her skin, a stain like old blood. Amazing. To think of such a ritual surviving for tens of thousands of years, from Neanderthals to proto-Celts! The thought made her feel exhilarated and a little nauseated. It was like doing really good acid, this whole night had been like some horrible and wonderful drug—

But then from somewhere overhead she heard a dull clinking sound. She looked up. Someone was awake in the camp. George, probably. He liked to drink his ersatz coffee while going over the previous day's field notes, and he didn't trust anyone else to fire up the recalcitrant little oil-burning stove. Her mouth opened and she almost called up to him, but thought better of it. Instead she bent over the skeleton once more.

How had it been aligned? The bodies found in Celtic burials at Lindow and Gournay had pointed east. She looked up at the small rosy mouth of the shaft. After making adjustments for the burial site shifting over time, and for the sudden collapse of the wall, she decided that the corpse had originally been aligned with its head facing east. To the rising sun, as in the Shanidar burials.

Or the rising moon.

"The moon." She said the words aloud and bit her lip.

Othiym, a minor lunar goddess with possible links to the great female deities of Knossos and Boeotia and Nippur in Sumeria . . .

The moon. As she raised her hand to brush the hair from her eyes, her nostrils filled with the sweet incense of hashish that still stained her fingers. With sudden clarity she recalled her walk, the eerie flood of moonlight and swarming insects. It was as though it had all been meant to lead her here, to this. For a moment she felt again the icy breath coming from the opening behind her, a chill that seemed to freeze her thoughts as well; but she quickly shook it off. She turned a last thorough gaze upon the burial victim, its arms clenched to its barren chest, its skull cupped within clawlike hands like a scryer's globe.

And then, for the first time she saw something glittering upon the skull's smooth surface. She had missed it in the darkness, but now dawn touched it with a rosy glow. It hung from the skull's jutting brow in a gleaming curve, like a scythe or grinning mouth made of silver. She leaned forward until she could touch it, her fingertips grazing its edge so lightly they might have caressed nothing at all.

But it was there. It was real. Beneath her hands she felt metal, so cold it was as though she had plunged her hands into icy water, as though she had received an electrical shock. A jolt of pure energy bombarded her, shoving her back onto her heels. With a cry Magda reached forward again, though gingerly this time: because all she could think of was touching it, holding it. All she could think of was possessing it.

Upon the skull's brow gleamed a crescent of pure light, so brilliant she had to shade her eyes. When she lowered her hand she could see it clearly: a span of smooth silver, like a little moon. At its widest point it was engraved with a triskelion that formed three moons, their intersecting crescents making a pattern as breathtakingly lovely as it was simple. Where the moons overlapped, there was a small crescent-shaped perforation, a grinning aperture. Very faint lines showed where once it had been touched with gold.

A sacrificial amulet, buried as an offering to the moon goddess. A talisman meant to guide the victim to his waiting and eternal mistress.

A lunula.

Magda hardly dared to breathe. Over the centuries only a handful of them had been recovered. Two from Artemis's temple in Boeotia, where the *Arktoi* danced, bear-virgins sacred to the huntress. One from an Etruscan tomb, where no doubt it had been preserved as a curious relic of an even more ancient day. One or two others had been scattered across the Roman Empire, and now were locked within the holdings of the Vatican.

And then, of course, there was the fragment that June herself had found and given to the National Museum. With trembling fingers Magda touched the crescent-shaped hole in the pendant. This had to be it: the original of June's lunula, the necklace from which the missing piece had been lost or stolen millennia before. Her breath caught in her throat. Michael Haring would give a fortune for it; any number of museums or collectors would give a fortune for it . . .

Magda pushed these thoughts aside, focused on the lunula itself. As she drew it from the skull, the hasp caught on a rounded plate of bone. Gently she tugged it free, and turned it slowly to catch the sunlight. The incised lines of its interlocking figures flickered from black to silver as it moved. The crescents seemed to burgeon from shining spindles to swollen orbs as she watched, new moon, half-moon, full, the missing crescent a bitter black mouth that twisted into darkness.

"Magda!" She jumped, the lunula swinging so that it struck her wrist. When she looked at her hand she saw a red blister there, faint as an old scar. "Magda! My lighter's dead, I need some matches—"

In the glowing gap of the shaft's entrance she saw George's silhouette, his long hair a frizzy aureole.

"Hey! Thought you might be down here. You got matches?"

Magda stared up at him in panic. Her hand tightened around the lunula and she took a step backward, her feet sinking into the soft new fallen earth. "George," she whispered.

"Couldn't wait, huh?" he called cheerfully. He swung his legs over the edge of the shaft, one foot nudging at the air until it found the top of the ladder. "Last day's a thirty-six-hour day, huh?"

She watched him slowly descend. Pebbles and clods of dirt fell in a dark rain as he came down. "Hey, you should be careful, you know? I mean, coming down alone like this in the middle of the night. This whole thing could collapse."

She stood with her back pressed against the shaft's wall. Panic boiled inside her. She was going to show it to him, to all of them; but so soon, so soon? A few feet away from her the skeleton lay streaked with light. In her hand the lunula was a burning arc, a star, a scythe. She clutched it against her breast and raised her face to where George stood midway down the ladder. His head turned this way and that as he squinted, trying to find her in the near-darkness. When he called out again his voice sounded muffled, confused.

"Magda?"

He shouldn't be here.

The thought was another flaming arc. He shouldn't be here. It was wrong, it was profane, *stantikic't*. Not just tainted but forbidden. Against her back the earthen wall pressed, a moist enveloping weight. She could feel the lunula burning through her sweater, through her T-shirt, the smell of scorching metal and a raw red pain as the crescent bit into her hands, her fingers seared until nothing but blackened bone gripped the moon's two horns and pressed them to her breast. Smoke filled the bottom of the shaft, smoke and the sound of her own anguished voice as she shrieked. Pain worse than any she could have imagined as the lunula branded her, its grinning livid mouth burning against her breast to leave its imprint, a pucker of moon-shaped scar tissue and just a trace of blood.

"Magda?"

She opened her eyes and he was there. His frizzy hair was pulled back sloppily with a leather thong and he wore a stained red T-shirt and jeans. He was staring at her, concern clouding his eyes as he stepped from the ladder and tried to find firm footing on the soft uprooted soil. He blinked in the dimness and pushed his steel-rimmed glasses firmly into place. He brought with him the scent of the open air, new morning and cold ashes and a faint smell of rain.

"Magda? You okay? You look a little—"

She tried to back away from him but she could go no farther, there was nothing but darkness now surrounding her, and earth. But George didn't notice. He no longer seemed to see her at all. There was a quick sharp sound as he sucked in his breath. Behind their steel frames his eyes widened. Very slowly he raised one hand, pointing to the pale mound of bones glistening in the darkness. Before she could say or do anything, he lunged forward, shouting in amazement.

"What the *hell*? Magda, what did you *find*, that's a, there's a—"

Othiym.

She didn't know if she said the name aloud or merely thought it. But she must have said something, done something. Because George froze, one hand reaching for the skeleton, his head turned to stare at her.

"Magda?"

It *was* a moon, a star, a scythe. Glittering in the darkness of the shaft as she swung it, a band of quicksilver slicing through the fetid air. She could feel its weight in her hand, a solid comforting thing like a smooth round stone, and feel how easily it sliced through his throat. Like a river swollen by the spring rain, erupting from its frozen prison to pierce and gouge its way through rocky soil; it was so easy, she brought her hand back and struck at him again, this time hearing a small *pop* as the lunula severed his windpipe.

"*Maaaa . . .*"

His voice was a child's, soft, whimpering, the sound fading into a hiss as air leaked from his throat. He staggered and fell at her feet, and she stared down to see where the blood ran in a bright shining stream from the dark cleft left by the lunula. Her hand remained upraised, the silver crescent an eye peering into the shaft. Along its curved edge blood gathered in small black beads. Like water on an iron grill the beads danced and ran one into another, until they vanished and only fine white wisps of smoke remained. A metallic smell filled the air. Magda's tongue grew swollen, dry and with the taste of something ferrous, flaking rust or dried blood clinging to the back of her throat until she retched and pitched forward onto the ground.

When she came to she was lying with her face pressed into the soft earth. Bits of dirt and gravel stuck to her lips. Her hair was matted with soil. She pushed herself onto her elbows, coughing. Her right hand still clutched the lunula, a leaden curl of metal now, all its glory gone; but her hands bore a fine red cross-hatching of fresh scars and she could feel a dull ache opposite her heart, as though she had been punched.

She got to her feet, brushed the dirt from her clothes and turned to look for her flashlight. That was when she saw George Wayford. He was lying on his side, his body twisted into a grotesquely fetal position: arms curled inward, legs bunched up against his solar plexus.

"George?"

She bent over his corpse, her fingers stretching until they stroked the curve of his jaw. Gingerly she cupped her hand beneath his chin, tilting it until his head moved and she could see the wound beneath, as clean and smooth as though it had been executed with a razor. The blood made a stiff crimson sheet of his T-shirt, crumpled into hard folds like lava or ice; but the flesh of his throat was smooth and white, almost translucent. She marveled at the concentric rings inside, flesh and cartilage and sinew. She reached to touch it, then recoiled. From the corner of her eyes she had glimpsed his, dull and speckled with dirt. He had fallen so that his glasses were mashed into his face, and she could see the fine network of broken capillaries radiating from the shattered glass like twin spider's webs.

"Oh, *god*."

She stumbled to her feet, frantically wiping her hands on her legs. She turned and ran the few steps to the ladder, stopped and tried to calm herself, tried to keep the nausea from overwhelming her. She mounted the ladder, then looked back.

In the dimness the two bodies lay just a few feet apart, their posture nearly identical. It was like two stages in a time-lapsed sequence showing decay: before and much, much after. There would be feasting and song, exultant wailing from sisters and wives and mothers; but then the scarab beetles would come, and the elegantly segmented worms and ivory-billed vultures, and smooth-skinned boys with their arms full of asphodel and handfuls of red dust to be rubbed into the bones . . .

No.

She whimpered. This was crazy; she'd gone insane; it was the hash or something worse, some hallucinogenic poison percolating in her brain all these years. *Acid is Groovy, Kill the Pigs*! But even as she clutched at the worn ladder she heard something, a low moaning that rapidly grew louder and louder, filling the chamber like a torrent of black water pouring down. It wasn't until something struck her cheek that she looked up and saw that the circle of light at the mouth of the shaft had been eclipsed, tongues of shadow licking fiercely at its sides as gravel and rusted tools began falling everywhere. Eleven-A was collapsing.

"No!"

Her voice was swallowed as she scrambled upward, the ladder bouncing against the earthen wall as huge chunks of compacted soil slid and fell away to either side. All she could see was the shaft above her and far away its opening, a small dead moon. She screamed, choking on dirt and debris; but still she went on, forcing her way out, until finally she could feel the top of the ladder; there were no more rungs, no more darkness, only grass-strewn earth and light and air. She scrambled from the pit and rolled away, heedless of her torn clothes, a place on her right arm that ached as though it had been caught between hammer and anvil. Behind her the rumbling grew to a thunderous roar, so loud her entire body shook. Then, abruptly, silence.

She lay on the ground, weeping softly. The echo of that final explosive surge died away. She could hear other sounds— Nicky's shouts, Janine yelling her name in a shrill, panicked tone. When she tried to wipe the crust of dirt and leaf mold from her face, her hand grew sticky with blood.

"Magda! Oh my god, Magda, what's happening, where's George, *where's George*?"

Nicky helped her to her feet. "Magda? Can you hear me? *Magda?"*

She pushed him away and barreled past the hysterical Janine, looking wildly for the excavation site.

It was gone. Anything that had ever been recognizable as the result of human engineering had vanished. There was only a great concave declivity like a sinkhole, fresh earth and stones strewn across its surface. From the soft dirt protruded two small nubbins of wood like fingers or horns: the top of Chasar's ladder. Magda stared at them in stunned disbelief. They were all that remained of Eleven-A.

". . . you were down there? Goddammit, Magda, I can't *believe* you were down there!" Now Nicky was hysterical, his voice rising shrilly as he ran around the perimeter of the site, searching futilely for some way down, a passage, an air chimney, anything. "George! Can you hear me? *George*—"

"Of course he can't hear you," Magda said dully. She turned to where the sun hung above the horizon, the violet edges of the mountains in bold relief against the thin gold light.

"We have to get help—the Jeep, drive into town, someone to dig him out—"

She nodded mutely as Janine screamed on and on and Nicky shouted at her: as though his rage might somehow make things different. But after a few more minutes she let the two of them hurry her to the Jeep and help her into the back, where she lay on a heap of burlap. She tried not to cry out as the vehicle leapt forward, jouncing over rocks and gulleys as Janine's voice rang desperately through the chilly morning air.

"We'll find Chasar, right, he's always there this time of day, why the *hell* don't we have a goddamn shortwave—"

Magda bit her lip, wincing from pain and the effort of keeping silent. She knew they'd never find George. Chasar wouldn't take on the job, and neither would anyone else. There was no way she and Nicky and Janine could get down there alone. The Çaril Kytur dig was finished. A thousand years from now someone else would discover George lying beside that other skeleton and marvel at the eerie symmetry, two victims in identical posture buried millennia apart in this desolate European wasteland.

At the thought Magda began to weep again. The ache in her breast grew stronger with each shuddering breath she took. She turned onto her side, still crying, and drew her hands upward. She grabbed at the damp weight of her sweater, kneading the wool as she tried to find some way to make the pain stop.

And then she felt it, cold and sharp as glass. The twin spurs of the crescent had been jammed into her, with enough force that they sliced through the heavy wool of her sweater and T-shirt before piercing her right breast. Magda closed her eyes. Her fingers ticked along its edge, feeling the cool bite of silver against her skin and the curve of her breast rising beside it, a solid aching mass. She expected the metal to cut her fingers but it did not; it lay there like something that had been planted in her, watered with her blood and waiting to bear fruit.

For a long moment she lay with eyes closed. The Jeep coughed and rattled, mercifully drowning out Janine's voice. Magda wondered vaguely if she would lose consciousness, but it seemed that she hurt too much for that. Her entire body shimmered with pain.

Finally she couldn't stand it anymore. She pulled herself up slightly, bracing herself with her feet against the floor and trying not to go flying as the Jeep made another precarious turn. With both hands she grabbed the edge of the lunula and, with a choking gasp, pulled it free. Agony exploded within her and she shouted, but neither Janine nor Nicky could hear her over the engine. With a grinding roar the Jeep lurched forward and began its treacherous ascent of the valley's mouth. Magda pressed her hand to her breast, trying to staunch the wound. There was an incredible amount of blood—her T-shirt was soaked, her sweater bright crimson from collar to cuff—but she knew she'd be all right. She withdrew her hand, her fingers gloved with blood and dirt, and turned to look down into Çaril Kytur.

A shimmer of mist lay across the valley, softening the harsh edges of rocks and crippled trees. For an instant she had a glimpse of the ancient riverbed, the shadowy outlines of bawns and temples rising from its banks. Then it was gone, burned to nothing by the sun. She turned away, squinting in the painful light, and looked at what she held.

It was still there; it was real. She had been wrong—something besides Chasar's ladder had survived the devastation of Eleven-A. As she raised her hand the Jeep's groaning roar faded, and with it the dull buzzing of the others' voices. A thin shaft of sunlight pierced the back of the vehicle. There was a smell of rain. Very faintly, as from some immense distance, she could hear the high plaintive cry of a bulbul seeking shelter from the day. Magda tilted her head and slowly drew her hand to her face.

Against her ruddy palm the lunula gleamed, the sun igniting its etched surface so that she could see all the moons there at once, new moon, full moon, dark, and within its curving bands of light the contours of a face, shuttered eyes and mouth half-open to the dawn, a sheen of blood staining her cheeks and lip and chin: Artemis, Durga, Cybele, Hecate, Inachus, Kali, Hel . . .

The Great Mother, lover and slayer of Her faithful son.

Othiym Lunarsa. The Woman in the Moon.

CHAPTER 5

The Sound of Bones and Flutes

We never made it to Dumbarton Oaks.

"Actually," Oliver said, steam from his coffee clouding his glasses, "I think they're closed on Mondays and Tuesdays."

I tilted my cup until I could see my face reflected in it. "That's okay. I don't know where I would've gotten a bike."

Medieval History had come and gone, then Introduction to Archaeology, followed by Oliver's Early Greek Drama and my Philosophy 101. We hadn't moved from our booth in the Shrine cafeteria, except to help ourselves to unlimited refills from a pair of battered plastic thermoses on a side table along the wall. Oliver took great interest in the endless stream of tour groups that filed through.

"Now watch them," Oliver announced, tilting his nose toward a claque of grey-haired women. "Fill their plates because it's an all-you-can-eat thing, but they won't eat any of it, except the salad. Just watch."

Ten minutes later, the women left. Oliver leapt from his seat and sidled up to their empty booth. He returned a moment later with two laden plates.

"See?" he said triumphantly, setting one of them before me. "You like shrimp creole? She didn't even touch it."

I stared at my plate. The shrimp creole did indeed look untouched. Only a fastidious bite taken from a biscuit, and a smear of lipstick on the water glass showed that he hadn't just filled the plate himself. Looking at it made me feel ill.

"Uh—no thanks," I said, standing. "More coffee?"

Oliver shook his head. He reached into his pocket and withdrew a small object roughly the shape and length of his forefinger. When he held it up I saw that it was a little silver pocketknife tarnished almost black. On one side an elegant monogram spelled OFOW in extravagant arabesques. Oliver flicked it open and a glittering blade appeared, like a minnow leaping from dark water. He speared a triangle of overdone meat. "Would you like some liver?"

He polished off three plates. I couldn't bring myself to eat anything, and I was so nervous I drank coffee till my ears rang. But I didn't care. I felt the way you do when you wake up in the morning and, before you even get out of bed, remember it's the first day of summer vacation. Here I was, on my own for the first time, with all the Gothic mysteries of the Divine to be explored and an entire city to discover. The sickening loneliness that had haunted my first days was abating, but that wasn't what made me feel light-headed, so giddy I laughed at everything.

What it was, was Oliver.

He was so beautiful, and so odd, and so utterly unself-conscious. If I'd been older, I might have found him insufferable, with his fey affectations and prep school jargon; but I'd never met anyone like him. He smoked hand-rolled cigarettes made of dried flowers from England that smelled sweet as rain. He claimed secret knowledge of IRA gun-running operations and military experiments using LSD. He showed me a tiny scar on his right hand, beside his pinkie, where he said a useless sixth finger had been amuptated hours after his birth. And there was his beauty, and the way he made me feel that I was in on a secret. Most of all, I guess, it was how he seemed to take for granted that I was his confidante, that I would always understand what he was talking about.

"Here," he said, after finishing his last plate of liver. He took my hand, placed a neatly folded paper triangle in the palm, and closed my fingers around it. I opened it: the page that Angelica had given him during class, now covered with spidery drawings.

"Hey!" I smoothed the paper on the table. "These are really *good*."

They were funny, rather wistful caricatures of Oliver and Angelica and myself, with Professor Warnick a Nijinsky faun dancing in the foreground, sistrum upheld, sparks shooting from his little horns.

Oliver grinned. "You'll like *The Golden Ass*," he said, leaning back in his chair.

"Actually, I've read it." I hadn't, of course, but figured by tomorrow I would have.

"We-ell." Oliver's chair thumped forward. "I thought so," he said softly, and began telling me his history.

He was from Newport, from an old, old money family that had its roots in County Meath in Ireland. Oliver claimed some character in a Fitzgerald story was based on his grandfather, and that Booth Tarkington had written *The Magnificent Ambersons* after the tragic death of Oliver's great-great-aunt. His parents were famous (and famously wealthy) anthropologists, now estranged.

"Sort of," Oliver explained. "Mom lives in the carriage house and does her pottery. Dad's still in the main house, because of all his America's Cup stuff."

Oliver himself was the youngest of six brothers. The two oldest had enlisted to fight in Vietnam. Osgood died there. Vance returned a junkie and now lived in San Francisco. Another brother, Leopold, was a well-known female impersonator in

London. Cooper played piano in Newport jazz clubs; Waldo had become a Buddhist monk.

That left Oliver.

"So what are *you* doing here?"

He shrugged. "I'm a legacy. We Crawfords all attend the Divine. I didn't really have a choice. They tapped me a long time ago. I went to Fairchild Abbey—"

A preparatory school in Vermont's Northeast Kingdom, run by an obscure order of brothers. *Not* Jesuits, Oliver was quick to explain; not Benedictines either.

I laughed. "So what's left? Capuchins? Franciscans? Cathars?"

"No." He frowned so fiercely that I looked into my coffee cup, abashed.

"There'll probably be some there tonight," he said a minute later, and sighed. "At that damn reception, I mean."

I waited for him to go on. When he said nothing, I took a deep breath and asked, "So what are they? The Molyneux scholars, I mean?"

Oliver only gazed at the ceiling again. When I glanced up I saw squares of petrified Jell-O arrayed across the acoustical tile, like Mah-Jongg pieces. I decided to save face by getting more coffee. But then—

"Magicians," he pronounced as I slid my chair back.

"What?"

"They're magicians."

For a moment I caught the full force of his eyes: so improbably brilliant and defiant he looked slightly deranged. Before I could say anything he glanced at his wrist.

"Uh-oh! Four o'clock, time for tea!" He stumbled to his feet.

"But it's—I mean, it can't be more than three—"

Oliver gulped the last of his coffee, held up his wrist so I could see the faded timepiece drawn there. "Wild Bill—harvesting the psylocibin—paid him last night—*got* to get back to the dorm. See you at seven—"

I watched him lope down the aisle, waving distractedly at a table of guys in fraternity sweatshirts. On the wall above them a dusty-faced clock showed it was nearly four.

"Damn!" I grabbed my knapsack. If I hurried, I might make my last class of the day.

When I finally got back to my room, there was a note on the door from Angelica, elegant lettering in peacock blue ink.

> Sweeney—
> We're going to dinner early but it won't be the same without you! Meet us out front!
> Angelica

I drew the note to my face and smelled the woodsy odor of sandalwood and a sweet scent like mandarin oranges. I went inside and changed, throwing my velvet pants and sweat-soaked shirt on the floor and flinging on a T-shirt and black jeans. I pulled off my lace-up boots, thought of putting on sneakers but decided on my old, battered cowboy boots. They were of worn black cowhide with faded crimson stitching and pointed steel toes, still lethal enough to punch holes in drywall. I tugged them on and thumped back downstairs.

Angelica was waiting outside the dining hall, another girl beside her. I felt a jolt of disappointment that we wouldn't be dining alone.

"Sweeney! Do you know Annie Harmon? She's my roommate, she's in the Music School—"

"No. Hi—"

Annie stuck out a small sticky hand. "Pleased to meet you. Nice boots."

Her throaty voice was totally incongruous with her appearance: a weary old whore's voice coming out of this little girl. She only came up to my chin, a slight figure in old green fatigues and a moth-eaten flannel shirt and very small red tennis shoes. Her thin brown hair was cut short and stuck up in a ragged cowlick. Next to Angelica, with her bird-of-paradise hair and exquisite makeup and expensive clothes, Annie Harmon looked like an inquisitive quail. But she had beautiful woeful eyes, deep brown touched with violet, and I was certain she was not wearing tinted lenses.

"Thanks," I said. "Nice to meet *you*."

Annie nodded solemnly. "Charmed."

We walked into the fake medieval Dining Hall, Annie and I first. Angelica followed, smiling and nodding as other students passed. I felt as though we were in a procession, clearing the way for the Queen. Angelica had changed into a tight black dress that ended just above her knees, the bodice inset with a revealing panel of black lace, and replaced her Coach bag with a tiny lozenge-shaped purse covered with jet and lapis beads.

"Kinda dressed up for dinner, huh?" Annie remarked, cocking a thumb at her roommate.

"You never have a second chance to make a first impression," Angelica said primly. She let loose with that improbable laugh, and pointed to something bubbling on a steam table. "What do you suppose *that* is?"

We found a table in a corner. Angelica was quiet, picking at her salad and sipping ice water. I was so tired I was happy to let Annie do all the talking. She rambled on in her throaty voice, eating whatever we left on our plates.

"So they didn't let me in the first time I applied," she said, taking the crust of my apple pie and eating it with her fingers, "So I tried again in the spring. Zilch. But then I tried again in July, and *bin*-go! Third time's the charm, and they accepted me."

Angelica smiled fondly, as though this had all been her doing. For all I knew, it had been.

We left when we heard the Shrine's bells ringing 6:45, faint tolling beneath the clatter of silverware and eager conversation. Angelica went first this time, and more heads turned as she passed. A few people called to her by name. She smiled and waved, but didn't stop.

"Get used to it." Annie nudged me. "Living with Angelica is an amazing experience. I walk into a room with her and *poof*! I'm invisible."

Outside, the sultry afternoon had faded into a glowing early evening. The sky had deepened to a pure lacquered blue. A few supernaturally bright stars defied the jaundiced glow of the campus crimelights. We walked without speaking, Annie noisily scuffling her sneakers through the damp grass. The air smelled of mud and marijuana smoke and roses. It was so warm that I felt as though I had no skin; as though my blood flowed directly from my veins into the soft blue light. From off in the distance a percussive beat echoed from a stereo, melody and vocals smelted away by the heat. Angels looked down upon us from the stone facades of dorms and classroom buildings, and a skein of friars in their white summer habits strolled across the green lawn, silent but somehow companionable as they watched a few students playing Frisbee and hackeysack. From the onion-shaped dome of the *Ma es-Sáma* mosque came a ululating cry, and the echoing croon of sleepy mourning doves settling in the elms. It was all improbably lovely and strange. We approached Reardon Hall, and the great white porticoes of the Colum Library, and finally crossed onto the Strand.

"So you had lunch with Oliver, huh?" Annie asked. She paused and removed her sneakers, wiggling her bare toes in the grass.

"Yeah," I said. "How'd you know?"

Annie pointed at Angelica. I shook my head. "I mean, how do you know Oliver?"

"Oliver? Hey, *everybody* knows Oliver." Annie yawned and wiped a bead of sweat from her lip. "I mean, look at him. He's like the E-ticket guy for the whole freshman class. Someone in my Composition Seminar saw him at the Vigilant last night with Maxwell Rheining."

"Who's he? What's the Vigilant?"

Annie glanced at Angelica, who said nothing. "It's a gay bar in Southeast," Annie said at last. "Max Rheining's artist-in-residence at the Pater Theater this semester. You'd recognize him if you saw him."

"A transvestite bar," Angelica corrected her. "On a houseboat in the Potomac. Rheining does a lot of work Off-Broadway. He's pretty famous."

I tried not to look impressed. "So how does Oliver know him? I thought he just got here last night."

"Oliver is a very busy young person," said Annie.

"So how do *you* guys know all this?" I persisted.

Angelica gave me a sly smile. "See what you miss when you skip class?"

Annie laughed. I slung my hands in my jeans pockets and turned to look at the Shrine. "Oh." I felt a sudden hollowness inside me. "Well, that's cool, I guess."

"So, Sweeney." Angelica adjusted her earrings and smoothed the bodice of her dress. "What did you and Oliver talk about at lunch?" Her tone was casual, but her eyes fixed on me like two searchlights.

"I dunno. Just stuff. Where he grew up, his family, stuff like that."

"That's all?" Angelica's eyes grew even wider, and her voice rose in an exaggerated schoolgirl squeak. "Nothing else? He didn't ask about *me*?" She laughed.

"I don't think so." I was starting to get pissed off. I glared at the Shrine and tried to think of some excuse to leave. I'd left my knapsack and all my books back in my room, so I couldn't really go to the library. But I didn't feel like returning alone to the dorm, either. Before I could say anything Annie's hoarse voice broke in.

"Well, I hate to miss all the fun, but I got to hit the stacks for a while." She raised an eyebrow at Angelica. "You gonna be home tonight?"

"*Eh sì, bella*."

"Okay." Annie stood on one foot, arms outstretched like a bird taking flight. "Wish I could go with you to your pah-tay, Angel, but . . ."

"Oh, man . . ." I gazed in dismay at my T-shirt and black jeans, the patina of dried mud on my cowboy boots. "I forgot all about the reception! I can't go like *this* . . ."

Annie poised in mid-flight and eyed me quizzically. "But *you* can't go. You're not one of them, are you?"

"Huh?"

"A Molyneux scholar." She glanced at Angelica and then at me again, her face expectant: as though in those intervening seconds I might have changed into someone else. "Naaaah . . ."

I felt myself blushing. From the Shrine came the first notes of the carillon. "I don't—"

"Of course she can come." Angelica's tone was offhand. "She's my *guest*; I mean, they're not going to say I can't bring a *guest*, are they?"

Annie sniffed. "That's not what you told *me*—"

"This is different, Annie." Even as Angelica smiled, there was a soft threat in her voice: *don't argue with me*. "Sweeney and Oliver and I are in the same class."

Annie started to protest, then shrugged and looked away. "Whatever you say, Angel."

And that was that. With a satisfied smile, Angelica turned to stare at the Shrine: the great Byzantine folly silhouetted against the darkening sky, a few stars salted across its dome. Suddenly, as though it had been strafed by an invisible enemy, the entire huge edifice burst into flame. I gasped, and Annie's hand shot out to steady me.

"Hey! Relax, girl—it's just a light show—"

It was, but like nothing I'd ever seen. There were spotlights, footlights, rays of gold and silver and blue streaming from hidden recesses. The bell tower tolled seven o'clock.

Bong. Bong. Bong . . .

I looked up with a growing sense of unease. I felt as though some strange game was being played out by everyone I met, and I hadn't been cued in to the rules. But when I glanced at Annie, my own anxiety sharpened into a blade driving deep into me. Because she was staring at Angelica, and her eyes were bright with fear.

"Do you really have to go?" she whispered. "Do you, Angelica?"

Angelica seemed not to hear. "*Do* you?" Annie asked again.

Now *I* was getting freaked. "Hey, Annie—you okay?" But when I tried to touch her, she shook me off.

"*I* never heard that they had a guests policy," she said coolly.

"Oh, come on!" Angelica gestured dramatically at the floodlit Shrine. "That's for us! I mean for the reception—all of us, the alumnae and everybody. They do it at Homecoming too—"

"And when we win a field hockey game," Annie snapped. "Keep it in perspective, Angel." She spun on her heel. "Bring her home by midnight, will you, Sweeney? I don't want her waking me up at dawn."

"*Ciao*, Annie," Angelica called.

"Chow chow chow," echoed Annie, and headed for the library.

"They really *do* light it up for us," Angelica said as we started away from the Shrine. The last echoes of the carillon hung in the sultry air. "It costs a thousand dollars a night. This reception is going to be *great*."

I sighed. "I don't know, Angelica. I've got all this work to do, and—" I gestured at my T-shirt and scuffed my boots in the grass. "I just don't know if I really feel up to it."

Angelica took my hand. She pulled me after her into a narrow drive that led up a tree-covered hill to where a single domed building gleamed in the darkness. The breeze brought me the sweet musky scent of her perfume, sandalwood and oranges. "Oh, for Christ's sake, Sweeney, come *on*. And don't worry, you look fine, very *gamine*.

"Besides," she added, giving one of her odd clear laughs. "No one will give you a hard time. You're with *me*."

Garvey Hall stood at the far end of the campus, atop the hill known as the Mound. The broken concrete drive wound through white oaks and tangles of sumac, with a row of ancient iron lampposts casting a bleary yellow glare through the leaves. We saw a few other people straggling up the path—middle-aged couples in evening dress; students in thrift shop finery, stained velvets and satins; a tall black woman wearing elaborate African tribal robes. One young man in a dusty tuxedo did a double take when he saw Angelica, turning to stare at her so that he ran into a tree. Angelica pretended not to notice, but when we rounded a curve in the path she burst out laughing.

"They really do think with their dicks, don't they?"

"*That* one was walking with his."

She giggled, tilted her head to regard me with pursed lips.

"May I?" she asked, and gently smoothed the hair from my temples. "You know, you should cut your hair, Sweeney." Her touch gave me goose bumps. "Really. You have such beautiful eyes, they'd really stand out if your hair was shorter. I'll do it for you if you'd like."

I laughed uneasily. "Yeah, well, maybe. Maybe over the weekend. I'll think about it."

Angelica continued to stare at me, her gaze intense and yet somehow oblique. I glanced away, finally said lamely, "Look, about this party—I just feel a little underdressed, that's all."

"I told you, you're with me." Her voice took on that same tone it had earlier with Annie: impatient, subtly threatening. "Look, Sweeney—do you want to go to this thing or not?"

She grabbed me, not roughly but with unmistakable insistence. *"Do you?"*

I swallowed but didn't pull away. A few inches from mine her eyes were huge, their color washed to topaz in the sulfurous light. I tensed, resisting her. If she let go of me, I was certain I would fall.

"Do you?"

Her words lingered in the air. But then I heard another sound, a faint jangling echo as of a glass harmonium shattering, its brittle notes fading into Angelica's voice.

"Do you?"

It was a real choice she was offering me: a deal of some sort. Like Oliver's opening parry, this was a kind of acid test—but what the hell was I being tested *for*?

The jangling grew louder. In counterpoint to it rose another sound, the tremulous sigh of wind in dry reeds. Angelica's grip on my arm tightened as she pulled me to her, until her body's warmth enveloped my own. Her perfume was everywhere, musky and sweet. The sound of our breathing faded into the wind.

"Sweeney," she whispered. "Will you come with me?"

I wanted to reply but I felt too sleepy to talk, too sleepy to do anything but lean into her arms. My head lolled back until I was staring at the sky, the afterlight of sunset gone now, given over to a glowing purple the color of hyacinths. The moon was there, just barely—a slender crescent with a silvery ridge of cloud banked against its curving tines, and a single pallid star beside it. The crimelights gave a weird sepia tinge to everything. Moon and falling leaves and even our own shadows seemed to be strewn across the faded dusty plane of an old photograph—everything except Angelica.

She was so much brighter and *realer* than everything else. I could feel her arms around me, feel her hair blown against my cheeks and smell her perfume mingling with the scent of decaying leaves and moist earth. The rattling of the wind in the trees grew louder, the scent of sandalwood and oranges filled my nostrils until it all blurred together: the moon sweeping across my vision, Angelica's warm breath and the soft pressure of her hands upon mine, the beauty and strangeness of the Divine itself joining to claim me as the night grew deeper around us.

Will you come with me?

I closed my eyes. A faint earthy sweetness lay upon my tongue, and almost I imagined I could smell woodsmoke, the scent of burning leaves. I opened my eyes and smiled, half-turning my head to look up into Angelica's face. I could feel her there, just as I could feel the chill wind.

But I did not see Angelica. What I *did* see made me gasp.

There was a woman in the moon. I could see her as distinctly as though she were my own reflection. Her face calm, with the ageless features of a Toltec image—heavy lips, long slanted eyes, high rounded cheekbones. Her eyes were half-shut, and the curve of her mouth mirrored the moon's bow glittering upon her brow. Milky light washed across her, so that it was as though I gazed at a face in deep water, a shattered caryatid waiting to be pulled from the depths. It was a beautiful face, but what made it beautiful was its utter calm, the overwhelming sense that in aeons and aeons she alone had never bowed before the wrath and fury of time and lust and death. I could have stared upon her forever, I felt, and myself turn to stone and ash and never even care.

But then the woman began to change. Her hair first, its cloudy mass dispersing into darkness until only a few bright threads remained. Then the rounded contours of her face hardened. Her mouth grew thin and taut. A row of teeth protruded from beneath her upper lip—teeth white and glittering as ice, grotesquely long and needle-sharp. Very slowly her mouth parted in a smile. Behind the row of teeth loomed a darkness more complete than any I had ever seen: starless, formless, not even a mote of light glimmering within it.

And then the moon began to burn, not brightly but with dull red clouds swelling above it, as though it had been set upon a smoldering pyre. I watched in horror as those bloody clouds grew and finally burst into a poisonous black haze. The fragile arc of moon collapsed. Where it had shone moments before was—*nothing*—only that immense face with its shuttered eyes, and the sighing wind.

I was shivering uncontrollably. I could feel the hammering pulse of blood in my temples, feel Angelica's arms around me, cold and unyielding as iron, and hear her breathing. But my vision was filled with the dreadful visage that took up the entire sky: eyes like charred holes, her mouth a howling void. I was filled with a terror so intense, so sharp and pure and cold, that it was almost like joy. For a long moment everything was so still I thought we might stay this way forever, frozen beneath that implacable sleeping face. And then its eyes began to open.

I screamed; at least I tried to. But Angelica gripped me so hard the sound was choked out of me. Above us floated that gorgon's face, vast and ravenous and patient. Once more the moon burned upon her brow with a hard silver gleam. Her hair flowed across the sky, her mouth gaped wider and wider until I thought it would swallow us. But what was most terrible was her eyes.

Because they were not a gorgon's eyes. Instead, when the heavy lids lifted, there in that dreadful white face shone eyes warm and blue and brilliant as the heart of summer. Looking at them my knees buckled. Even Angelica gasped. She let go of me and I dropped to the ground, weeping.

Because I could have borne the gorgon's stare, shuddered and kicked and fought some nightmarish vision of Hecate or Kali or Circe. But not this. Never this.

Because this was my *mother. Her* summer eyes staring down at me as she woke me in the morning, met me after school, waved a sad farewell in front of Rossetti Hall. But at the same time it was also *Angelica* I saw there. Angelica as I had first glimpsed her, poised in the doorway of a stifling classroom, Angelica staring at the Shrine as it burst into flame. I wept, overwhelmed by the most primal surge of yearning that I have ever felt.

And the Woman in the Moon gazed back down upon me. Her eyes, too, welled with tears, her lashes drooped even as her mouth yawned wider and I felt myself falling into Her. All around me was heat and flames, the stench of charred wood and cloth and cinders. My hair burned, my clothes turned to ashes and my hands to sizzling bone as I reached for Her, crying aloud. Because She was my mother, She was whispering my name, the only name my mother ever called me, even as She devoured me—

"*Katie—Katie—Katie—*"

—and in Her burning embrace my tears hissed upon my cheeks, my hair and skin were nothing but smoke—

"—Sweeney! Sweeney—*please*!"

I opened my eyes and blinked painfully. "What . . . ?"

"Sweeney! Are you all right? Sweeney?"

In front of me crouched Angelica. Her face looked greenish in the crimelights. I coughed, waved unseen smoke from my bleary eyes. "Yeah, I'm okay. But Angelica—did you—did you see—?"

Her eyes widened as she shook her head. "I thought you were having a *seizure*," she said. "You're not—well, epileptic or something?"

I stared at her in disbelief. "No, I'm *not* epileptic. Didn't you—I mean, Angelica, *what the fuck was that*?"

Angelica said nothing. Above us the night was clear; at least it was clear once you got above the scrim of heat and exhaust that hung above us like the ghost of some other, older place.

"What was what?" Angelica asked softly. "I mean—you just seemed—well, a little out of it."

I glanced at her sideways: her pale face, the way she looked away from me and then back again, her gaze skipping from mine like a stone over cold water.

A little out of it.

She was lying. *Something* had happened, but who knew what? Not me; but then maybe not Angelica, either. I took a deep breath and forced myself to stare into the sky again, looking for the face I had seen there before, the moon like a bright reflection of my own deepest fears and longing.

It was gone. Oh, the moon was there, all right, but not *The Moon*: only a whitish blur hanging above the trees. There were no stars, no eyes; nothing but that pale scar in the bruised sky. As I stared, a thick brown haze encroached upon it, slow but relentless, until at last the moon was gone. Where it had been a smudged cloud gave forth a dull incendiary glow against the lowering darkness.

"No," I whispered. When I looked at Angelica I saw that she was watching me, her gaze intent and not a little frightened. She opened her mouth and for an instant I thought she would explain, or at least apologize. But she only looked away again.

A moment later her voice came to me softly, more imploringly than before. She drew close to me, rested her hands upon my shoulders, and whispered, "Do you still want to come?"

I said nothing. Instead I tilted my head to the sky, eyes shut, and listened, wondering how I could ever have thought the night was silent. Distant traffic, far-off laughter, and voices not so far, the pleading whine of a siren fading into the tossing leaves.

And once more I felt that faint eerie music, truly *felt* rather than heard it—a deep wild note that hummed through me, resonating within my chest as though I were a drum that had been struck. I trembled, with fear and expectation and yearning. All the exhiliration and uncertainty I had felt over the last few days hardened into a single thought, a small cold nugget that might some day crack and yield an explanation for what was going on. I had had a glimpse of what might be behind all of this, an intuitive flash that told me *Yes, something really is happening here*, and *Yes, you can leave now if you're afraid*, and *Yes, this really isn't your life anymore.*

Because in my life the moon did not call out my name. Angels didn't appear in my room at night and leave their plumage upon the floor. Eerily beautiful boys and girls didn't befriend me, and I didn't hear distant music like bones and flutes. In my life I would gently take Angelica's hands from my shoulders, then turn and walk away from the Mound. I would go to call my parents, or return to my room to study and maybe make some other new friends, misfits like Annie or myself who had been let into the Divine by mistake.

But this wasn't my life anymore. I knew that. Because I only nodded, and raised my hands until they closed around Angelica's.

"Yes," I whispered, my fingers tightening about her wrists. The sound of bones and flutes died away into the laughter of others coming up behind us on the path. "I'll come with you, Angelica. Of course, you know I will."

CHAPTER 6

The Reception

Garvey Hall was a domed Italianate villa dating from the mid-1800s, with kudzu-wound porticoes and twisted cedars hunched against the crumbling walls.

"Look at that." Angelica sighed rapturously. "It's like a set from *Les Enfants du Paradis*."

I thought it looked more like Tara on bad acid, but Angelica didn't waste time discussing the architecture. Instead she swept past the dozen or so people scattered about the patio and on into the crowded reception.

I hesitated. Inside all seemed to be smoke and scarlet and gold, with touches of black and white where groups of tuxedoed men bowed their heads.

I can't go in there, I thought. But Angelica was already *in* there, smiling and nodding. So I hurried to catch up, my bootheels echoing loudly on the parquet floor. I was sure that someone would stop me, question me, ask to see my invitation.

But Annie's comment about Angelica conferring invisibility was borne out. No one noticed me at all.

"Just act like you belong here," whispered Angelica as I clunked past an aged monsignor chatting with a young man in a kilt.

"Oh, *sure*," I muttered, but Angelica only grinned. The monsignor started in annoyance as we elbowed our way past, only to beam when he saw Angelica smiling down at him.

"Hello, dear," he murmured. The boy in the kilt eyed her appraisingly before turning to his companion. Angelica and I went on.

It was an enormous round room, with faux marble walls and columns, parquet floors, a frieze of fanciful creatures circling the high ceiling around the dome's perimeter. From somewhere rose the sweet strains of a string quartet. There was no air-conditioning, and the heat and humidity were intensified by the smoke. I felt as though I were swimming through some warm grey pool, washed by currents of expensive pipe tobacco and perfume and the fumes of about seventeen different kinds of exotic cigarettes, including clove, camphor, and what could only be hashish. Everyone smiled at Angelica, one or two of them greeting her by name. A few people even smiled at *me*. I smiled back, trying to put all of my charm and energy into my teeth, so they wouldn't notice my clothes.

And everywhere I looked in vain for Oliver. I remembered what he had said about the Molyneux scholars—

"What are they?"

"Magicians—"

Though if anything, this looked like an assemblage of some very wealthy if eccentric alumnae, with a few flushed undergraduates and faculty members thrown in for good measure. And, whatever the Molyneux scholars were, they gave a loose interpretation to the term *Formal Attire*. I saw tuxedos of every vintage, as well as morning coats, evening gowns, beaded miniskirts, tribal robes, kimonos, velvet yarmulkas, and every kind of ecclesiastical attire, including a woman who appeared to be wearing a cardinal's biretta and dalmatic. What I did not see was anyone else wearing a Blue Cheer T-shirt and black stovepipe jeans tucked into battered cowboy boots.

"I'm dying of thirst," Angelica announced. She paused, smoothing her dress against her thighs, and peered through the smoke. "Come on—"

The bar was a long mahogany-and-brass affair that might have been imported from a 1920s cruise ship. Behind it a phalanx of harried undergraduates in ill-fitting white jackets poured drinks and opened bottles of champagne. I got a vodka tonic; Angelica took a fluted glass of mineral water. Then we walked to the end of the bar and staked out a spot by the wall. Angelica leaned back so that her dress rode up her legs, her stockings and high heels stark black against the creamy painted marble. I stood beside her and knocked back my vodka tonic.

"Nice bunch of folks," I said, crunching ice cubes. "You think Oliver's coming?"

Angelica shrugged, but I noticed how her gaze kept darting about the room. I was thinking of getting another drink when I spied a stocky figure off by himself, smoking a cigarette as he leaned against a medieval-looking tapestry.

"Hey! There's that guy from Warnick's class—what's-his-name, you know—"

Angelica turned quickly, then nodded, disappointed. "Oh, *him*. José Malabar. He kept hitting up on me at orientation. He's a commuter, lives here in D.C. with his parents."

"And *he's* a Molyneux scholar?"

"Yes—one of his brothers was, too. He's an English major. Writes poetry. He showed me some of it."

I rattled the last ice cube in my glass. "Any good?"

Angelica grimaced. "Not really my taste. Sort of raw. But it was okay."

I looked back at the dark figure. He nodded and lifted his cigarette in greeting.

"Listen, I'm getting another drink," I said. "You want something?"

"Maybe in a minute. But I'll get it myself."

At the bar I smiled gamely at the guys pouring drinks.

"You know her?" one asked, pointing his thumb at Angelica.

I took my vodka tonic and downed most of it in a gulp. "Yeah."

"Huh." He stared admiringly at Angelica, then flashed me a grin. "Well, you're shitting in some high cotton, sister. Have another." I traded my empty glass for a full one and stepped away. Angelica had floated toward the center of the room, deep in conversation with a white-haired man who could have been her grandfather. I turned and walked to the tapestried wall.

"Hi," I said. José Malabar looked startled. "You're José. You're in Warnick's class with me, right?"

He took a long drag of his cigarette and regarded me warily. He was my own age, heavyset and olive-skinned, with dark straight hair falling unevenly about his ears and small, almond-shaped eyes. He wore an ancient black suit over an open white shirt, flocked with burn holes and a dusting of ash.

"Joe," he said at last, in a low voice. He had an accent that I couldn't place. "Baby Joe."

"Baby Joe." I nodded and raised my drink to him. "I'm Sweeney Cassidy."

He stared at me through a halo of grey smoke. "Yeah," he said at last. "Sweeney. I know you. You're the one got tagged by Beauty and the Beast this morning." He began to laugh, a childlike wheezing giggle, and reached for my glass. I smiled uneasily and gave it to him. He took a sip, raising it in mock salute. "What're you doing here?"

"I came with Angelica."

"Huh." Baby Joe frowned, then finished my drink. He handed me the empty glass and shook his head. "Yeah, I know her too. She's okay. But you're not one of *them*."

"Who's 'them'?"

Baby Joe's voice was derisive. "You know. The *Benandanti. Brujos*."

"No." I looked around uncomfortably, then set my empty glass on the floor. "I mean, I guess not. I never even heard of them until today."

"That's good." He dropped his cigarette. "Because I hate them."

He stared at the floor, waiting till his cigarette had burned a tiny black hole in the wood; then ground it out with a filthy high-top sneaker bound with electrical tape. The sneakers matched his shapeless suit, which was baggy even on his ungainly form. On the lapel was a small red button. I squinted as I read the tiny letters.

IT'S NONE OF YOUR FUCKING BUSINESS WHAT IT SAYS.

I laughed, but Baby Joe's expression remained enigmatic. He tapped another cigarette from a pack of Pall Malls, then began to speak with exaggerated slowness.

"Let me tell you something, Sweeney Cassidy." He spoke so loudly that several people turned to frown in our direction. "You shouldn't be here. This scholar shit is dangerous, *di ba*?"

I grew hot with embarrassment and stared at the tips of my boots, but Baby Joe seemed to enjoy the glares we were getting.

"You think you're getting in for some nice schoolgirl fun, you and Barbie Doll over there, but you're gonna get fucked."

He paused and turned an insolent stare upon two elderly women who regarded us with tight frowns. "YOU—ARE *GOING*—TO *GET*—*FUCKED*."

The women moved off in disgust. Baby Joe smiled, then looked at me and added, "And your friend Oliver? *Talagang sirang ulo*—fucking crazy bitch! He'll be pushing a shopping cart down Fourteenth Street one of these days. He's crazy, that whole family is crazy. My brother was here with his brother, Walter—"

"Waldo."

"Whatever. He was nuts, fucking nuts, *di ba*? Tried to poison some teacher that failed him. With *rat* poison. Once he shot at my brother with a bow and arrow."

"He's a Buddhist monk now."

"Figures. These guys—" He gestured disdainfully at the well-dressed crowd surrounding us. "—these guys tapped my brother years ago, *di ba*? When we were in Manila my mother was a *bruja*, you know, a—a midwife and—well, some other shit—but then she had a run-in with President Marcos's chauffeur and they made things tough for us. My father died of *bangungot*—you know what that is? Bad juju, Schoolgirl, very bad stuff—and we had to leave Manila, leave the whole fucking country. My uncle lives in D.C. so we came here, but then he's got like some weird connection with *this* place and my mom gets plugged into all *that* shit. And my brother Nestor, they think he's *brujo* like my mother, they give him some tests and finally he gets a scholarship."

He shook his head and giggled softly. "'Religious Studies.' But, like, this is the only way we get to go to college, *di ba*, so who's going to say no?"

I nodded as though this was all perfectly normal. "What's your brother doing now?"

"He's got this band, Euthanasia. They play at the Atlantis sometimes." He sighed. "Me, I'm only here 'cause they gave me a full scholarship. *Nobody* gives scholarships to poets."

He raised his eyes thoughtfully. "But what are *you* doing here, *hija*? How'd you hook up with those two?"

I shrugged, stabbed at the floor with the metal toe of one boot. "I don't know. They just started talking to me in Warnick's class."

"Huh. *Talking*."

Baby Joe looked disgusted, as though this was an obvious setup. But he said nothing more, only gazed through hooded eyes at the room in front of us.

I fell silent. I stared at my feet and wondered if I should cut my losses and just sneak out now. It seemed clear to everyone I met that I didn't belong at this reception; didn't belong with Angelica, and probably didn't belong at the Divine. The three vodka tonics made me feel weepy and hopeless. I thought of my parents and how much it was costing them to send me here, how much they'd save if I returned home and commuted to SUNY Purchase. I thought of the classes I'd skipped, and the copy of *The Golden Ass* I wasn't reading.

"Shit," I said under my breath. I glanced up, hoping I might see Angelica, or maybe even Oliver. But there was only Baby Joe, smoking and brooding like an extra in a bad French movie. Angelica seemed to have disappeared, and Oliver, I was starting to suspect, wasn't going to show at all.

So I turned back to the party going on without me; and who I saw was Professor Warnick. Amidst all that extravagant finery he looked absurdly small and demure in a pearl grey morning suit and striped ascot, his dark hair swept back from his face. He was watching the crowd with a bland expression, his blue eyes guarded but calm.

It was the figure standing behind him that made my neck prickle: the same extraordinarily tall figure I'd glimpsed outside of Reardon Hall that morning. Only now, instead of a simple cape, he wore robes that evoked some bizarre liturgy. Cloth of a purple so deep and rich it was almost black, but with a sheen that picked up the light and shot forth a phosphorescent glow. They swept about his emaciated form, cuffs and hem trimmed with golden ropes and cords and tassels. The effect should have been ludicrous, *Duchess of Malfi* meets *Star Trek*; but it wasn't. It was terrifying.

"Hey, Baby Joe," I said hoarsely.

My voice died in my throat as the figure turned. Its hooded face bobbed, like a blind hound trying to pick up a scent, and I shrank against the wall. I was ridiculously certain that he was looking for *me*. I recalled the figures in my room last night. This could have been one of them, only even more frightening, because no one else took any notice of him at all. He towered a good three heads above Professor Warnick—cadaverously thin, head weaving from side to side, the robes looped about his frame like winding sheets.

"Baby Joe," I hissed, but still Baby Joe didn't hear. He was staring absently into space, nodding in time to some private music. Between his fingers the cigarette had burned out. I started to reach for him, then stopped.

This was crazy. Whether it was the vodka or nerves or just bad vibes, I was acting like I'd lost my mind, or at least the part of it that should tell me how to behave at a party I'd crashed. I took a deep breath and forced myself to look up.

Professor Warnick and his companion were gone. In their place stood a group of boisterous undergraduates who seemed to have all just come from the same boozy pregame show. I glanced around, certain that I'd be able to find that towering emaciated figure; but it was gone. It might never have been there at all.

My fear faded into drunken ennui. I watched the laughing students and tried not to feel envious and stupid and headachy. Finally I turned to Baby Joe and asked, "So. You live in D.C.?"

"Huh?" Baby Joe started, gazing in surprise at his dead cigarette and then looking suspiciously at the crowd. "Hey, *hija*—isn't that Barbie Doll? Over there with that famous lady professor—?"

I turned. For a moment I glimpsed Angelica between waves of black tie and silk, her auburn hair shimmering. She was talking excitedly to a woman who kept glancing over her shoulder and motioning Angelica closer to her.

"Her?"

Baby Joe nodded. "Yeah—you know, that archaeologist. I forget her name."

I tried to get a better look at the famous lady professor archaeologist. She was maybe in her forties, brown-haired and sexy in a scholarly kind of way. Not exactly pretty but *interesting*-looking, with intense dark eyes and a Mary Quant haircut and probably the same frosted lipstick she'd been wearing since grad school. The same minidress too: a sleeveless black-and-white sheath with big eyes on it. A little weird, but the sort of thing I could imagine an archaeologist might think was appropriate formal wear. Whoever she was, Angelica looked more excited than I'd seen her all day. I thought of joining them, but another wave of partiers swept through and I lost sight of them.

"You want a drink, *hija*?" Baby Joe pulled at his shirt collar to expose where it had been repaired with black thread. "Sweeney? You look like you need one."

"Yeah, I guess I do. Thanks."

He started for the bar, pausing to stare at my T-shirt and boots. "Blue Cheer. Well, fuck me. *Di ba*, okay, maybe you'll be okay . . ."

I walked with him, this time accepting the Pall Mall he offered me, and for good measure ordered two vodka tonics.

Magda Kurtz, the famous lady professor of European Archaeology, had come tonight against her better judgment. It meant canceling her flight back to the West Coast, which was an expensive indulgence, and now she wouldn't get enough sleep, which was always annoying.

But mostly, it was dangerous. All summer she'd been playing fox and hounds with the *Benandanti*, tiptoeing around the Divine like the renegade student she still felt like. While her own students here treated her like the prophet of a new age, the other teachers were more circumspect. Distant, at best, like Balthazar Warnick—and *why* were so many of them at the Divine still *men*? You'd think they'd at least make some recruitment effort!—at worst, cavalier or disdainful or even suspicious of her work. So different from Berkeley, where her theories were already part of the core curriculum.

But then the Divine had always been like that—so far ahead of its time in many ways, positively medieval in others. The Anthropology Department especially seemed hardly to have changed at all since she'd left. Sometimes, she thought wryly, it seemed like it hadn't changed since Malinowski's day.

A lot of that was Balthazar's doing, of course. He'd been the one to approve her summer term here—it had been his suggestion, in fact, and Magda still wasn't sure why the invitation had come. But once offered the chance to return, she'd been surprised at how strong her feelings were for the place, how very much she wanted to be here again, even in the middle of the summer.

So Magda had come. She hadn't been back since the disastrous Çaril Kytur expedition. That was how they all still referred to it, even Magda herself. As in the words of the *Washington Post* article that had heralded her return this summer—

". . . that disastrous Çaril Kytur expedition from which, like a phoenix from the ashes, Magda Kurtz arose with her landmark theories of the matristic cultures of ancient Europe."

Here at the Divine the students loved her. Professor Kurtz, with her wry, rather droll teaching style. And, of course, her theories, and her books—the trade paperback edition of *Daughters of the Setting Sun* had recently become a campus best-seller. And the legendary parties she held in her tower room on campus, where a few of the chosen would pass around Magda's ancient ivory opium pipe with its embellishment of tiny grinning evil-eyed lions, and smoke opium—*Real opium! from Nepal! She was* **Too Much**!—and where, as the night burned to dawn, one (and sometimes two) of the more comely undergraduate boys might be discreetly steered toward the little back room, while the rest of her admirers were directed to the door. Oh yes: Professor Kurtz was famous.

But always she was aware of how the other, older members of the *Benandanti* regarded her. Not quite, not *necessarily*, as a traitor. Certainly there had been others before Magda Kurtz who left the Divine, to carry on the *Benandanti*'s work in the government and the arts and even at other places of learning. But Magda's work had reawakened an old, old feud, perhaps the very oldest one of all.

So this summer she had kept to her students, and to her tower room. Her little romances and necromancies helped pass the time, and the Divine's extraordinary library, and of course all the other pleasures of the City on the Hill. She avoided the other faculty members as much as she could, especially Balthazar Warnick; but it had been difficult. As always she found herself falling under the diminutive Balthazar's spell, his peculiar blend of wistfulness and melancholy and biting wit.

I might have fallen in love with him, she thought, slightly wistful herself now as she sipped her champagne and gazed absently across the crowded reception room of Garvey Hall. *It might have all been different then, it might have—*

But really it could never have been anything but the way it was.

"We serve at different temples now. Different temples, different gods," Balthazar had said a few weeks earlier, over lunch in one of the sunlit upper rooms of the Old Ebbitt Grill. It had always been one of Magda's favorite places in the city. Balthazar had taken her there when they first met, awkward student and ageless mentor, and ordered her a Clyde's omelet—bacon and spinach and sour cream—and *kir* in a round goblet. It was the most sophisticated meal she had ever eaten, and the first time she'd drunk wine from a wineglass.

"Different gods," he repeated, and his voice sounded sad.

Outside the afternoon traffic strained past, inching toward the Old Executive Office Building and the White House. Magda sipped her *kir*. Balthazar continued to stare at her with those piercing electric blue eyes.

"Perhaps we always have," he added.

Magda answered smoothly, pretending to misunderstand.

"Oh, but it's always the same old ivory tower, Balthazar, you know that! And you'll see, I've been right all along. Soon every student at the Divine will have read *Tristes Tropiques* and *Of Grammatology*—"

Balthazar made a face, and Magda laughed. "Well, I'm still very grateful *you* let me teach here this summer, Balthazar."

He smiled. "But who could turn away the lovely and brilliant Magda Kurtz?"

"You refused Paul de Man."

"You're much better looking."

Magda stared at him, amused, but then she saw how Balthazar's eyes had clouded, blue shivering to grey.

"It's nothing but *theory*, Balthazar. Just another way of looking at the world."

"Theories can be dangerous things," said Balthazar. His tone was light, but she saw how his eyes were cold and parlous as fast-moving water. "Remember Rousseau and romanticism."

"I can't sleep for thinking about them," Magda said, laughing; but that gaze had stayed with her for a long time, like a bad chill.

She shivered at the memory, quickly composing herself as a passing couple greeted her. It was exhausting, keeping up the pretense of being just another Molyneux scholar made good in the ivory tower. She knew there'd been talk. Within the legions of *Benandanti* there was always talk. Conspirators wormed through its long history, brazen or retiring or deadly, but always *there*. In this the *Benandanti* were like the Vatican, only far more ancient. Like the Inquisitors of old they had their little ways, their probings and inquests, scrutators and catechists, their spies and delators and indagations. Cabals of old men—the *oldest* of old men—and they gabbled and gossiped like crones. Women had gotten a bad rap for being gossips, Magda thought bitterly. She had never known a group more eager to snipe and speculate than old Catholic priests and the *Benandanti*. No better place than the Divine (or the Vatican) for that.

Though, unlike the Vatican, the *Benandanti* left no histories for the world to read. Most of their cadastrals and cartularies had perished with the libraries of Alexandria, after which time the *Benandanti* became a nomadic sect. They maintained their eternal vigilance from behind the marble clerestories of the Eternal City, and the Kaaba in Mecca; from the Maharajah's pavilion at Varanasi, and Italy's octagonal Castel del Monte and even, very briefly, the Old Map and Print Room on the fourth floor of Harrods. It was not until the colonization of the Americas that the *Benandanti* found at last a permanent home, a place where all the old wise men of the Indo-European steppes could settle to grow even older and wiser, and from the dusty classrooms of the Divine watch their protégés make their way into this brave new world.

And now that an unmistakable Sign had come, those at the Divine would be especially watchful against traitors. Without thinking, Magda touched the amulet at her throat.

In hoc signo vinces. Othiym Lunarsa, Othiym, Anat, Innana, Othiym evohe! Othiym haïyo.

The ancient tongues ran together but she knew them all. *In this sign we shall conquer, Othiym. We exult! We praise you.*

She'd been recklessly stupid the other evening, leaving her room with the spent Hand of Glory and the other remnants of her craft in it. That was what happened when you toyed with the naphaïm—they made you feel indestructible, made you forget that while they could soar above it, you were likely to plunge into the inferno and burn. Her fingers played along the smooth edge of the silver crescent, the half-conscious refrain still echoing in her head.

Othiym, Anat, Innana . . .

But she should watch her thoughts here—*especially* here—shroud them in nonsense or dull mental chatter. She closed her eyes and dredged up one of George's dopey verses, composed on that endless flight to Estavia—

Magda is so very mean
She's a Ramapithecene
When she hangs around with us
She's Australopithecus.

Someone touched her elbow and she started. One of her students, holding a bottle of Heineken and peering at her in concern.

"You okay, Professor Kurtz? You want a beer or something?"

She smiled and shook her head. "No thanks. Just tired. I have an early flight."

He nodded sympathetically. "Oh, yeah, man, I can relate. Jet lag. Have a few drinks first, it really helps."

She grimaced. "At 7:00 A.M.? Maybe not."

He grinned and left her, weaving slightly.

Magda took another sip from her champagne. All these drunk kids, thrilled to be drinking Heineken when there was Veuve Clicquot and Tattinger Brut for the asking. She sighed.

Because of course it was the kids who had brought her here tonight. Knowing it was foolish, knowing it might mean dangerous questions from Balthazar or his toady Francis—still she hadn't been able to resist the notion of seeing in the flesh one or both of the faces she'd scried in her room the night before. She wondered if the *Benandanti* had yet determined who they were, those two innocents doomed to be pawns in this latest skirmish between ancient enemies. She couldn't imagine Balthazar not knowing, if only because she couldn't imagine Balthazar not knowing anything.

She finished her champagne and handed the empty glass to a passing busboy. Over the years she had attended dozens of receptions like this, and some far more strange. *Benandanti* in full evening dress gathered in a derelict warehouse beside the Potomac; a seventeen-course dinner at the Gaslight Club served by naked young women; *Benandanti* mingling with career diplomats and Balinesian hierodules at Dumbarton Oaks. She had seen Michael Haring's disconcertment turn to awe when he first viewed the collection of Iron Age cauldrons in the library of Saint Vespuccia's College at the Divine. She had seen Balthazar Warnick walk through the door of a custodial closet in the Shrine, thence to disappear among the flower-strewn monuments on the island necropolis of San Michele in Venice. Compared to some of those other gatherings, the annual reception for new Molyneux scholars was nothing but a glorified frat party.

But tonight Magda felt uneasy. Perhaps it was her knowledge that the two innocents she had glimpsed last night were here, somewhere, ready to meet and ignite. Or perhaps Magda felt a small share of guilt over having doomed some poor fool to walk into the resulting conflagration. She took a deep breath and once more fingered the pendant around her neck.

Othiym, haïyo.

This, too, was a risk. But she always felt stronger when she wore it, and she often did so despite the danger. A number of the guests here might recognize it for what it was: a real, a true *lunula,* sacred to the ancient European Goddess, she who in the northern lands was called *Kalma*, "corpse-eater," and in Greece the White Goddess; in Sumeria *Lamasthu*, "daughter of heaven," and in certain remote valleys of the Balkans Othiym Lunarsa, Teeth of the Moon. She who is both Mother and Devourer, whose breath is plague, who suckles serpents and devours children. She who had made Magda's reputation.

Because in the end the Çaril Kytur expedition hadn't been a disaster for Magda Kurtz. George's death had been a tragedy, of course, but a minor one. There had been an inquiry, and a grief-stricken family mad for justice, but in the end it had been like that *I Ching* hexagram Magda had always favored: K'uei, *Opposition* but also *No Blame*. Michael Haring had been disappointed that she had not returned with illicit artifacts, but he soon found solace in another archaeologist.

In the wake of the Çaril Kytur investigation, with its threats of lawsuits and damaged reputations, Balthazar Warnick had not refrained from saying *I told you so*. Yet Magda herself had been surprisingly cool about the whole thing. Her colleagues chalked it up to the general unpleasantness of the experience, another good reason to avoid the Soviet-controlled Balkan states like the plague.

And eventually the whole thing blew over. George Wayford's family settled for a scholarship endowed in his name. And Magda wrote the landmark paper that was published in *Antiquities*, the monograph that became the framework for *Daughters of the Setting Sun*. From what should have been a career disaster, Magda Kurtz emerged not only unscathed, but triumphant.

Some of her colleagues remarked how obviously nobody knew the whole story; and of course they were right. Because Magda told no one about the lunula. Not Haring, not Balthazar Warnick, not even June Harrington.

You are the secret mouth of the world
You are the word not uttered
Othiym Lunarsa, haïyo.

In the wake of the failed expedition came long months when she researched her secret treasure. She traded her dimly lit carrel in the Colum Library stacks for a battered wooden desk in the upper reaches of the Museum of Natural History, then went to the American Museum of Natural History in New York. Finally she made her way to London, for two weeks' study in the dusty cool recesses of the British Museum. This was followed by a week of visiting private collections in the Scottish countryside, including a sojourn at Dalkeith Palace outside of Edinburgh, where she viewed the legendary skulls owned by the Dukes of Buccleuchs.

What she learned there sent her to Athens. In a cafe shadowed by the Acropolis she met with Christos Eugenides, an eminent archaeologist friend of Michael Haring's whose involvement in the thriving black market trade between the Aegean countries and the rest of the world had long been supported by the *Benandanti*.

"These are very good, you should try them." Christos speared a prickly star the size and color of a tarnished nickle. "Baby octopus. Quite wonderful. Or the *bekri meze*—you might like that."

Magda's smile was more of a grimace. The sun and heat and effort of translation and travel had given her a permanent headache. She felt feverish and disoriented. The scent of olive oil and fried fish was nauseating. As a panacea, she sipped grimly and steadily at a glass of fiery *tsipoura*.

"No thank you. Michael said you might tell me more about an object I found—"

She could feel it nestled at her throat, cool as a blade for all the numbing heat. She parted her collar and let her fingers rest upon the crescent's smooth edge. Christos Eugenides leaned forward.

"Ah—*ah*." His voice rose sharply, as though he had been kicked.

"You know it, then."

Christos Eugenides had already drawn back into his plastic chair. "This is not within my provenance," he said curtly. "I'm quite sorry. Michael must have misunderstood—"

"He said you knew about Cycladic figurines—"

"This is not remotely Cycladic."

"—and other things."

He removed a bill and several coins from his pocket and set them on the marble surface. "I have an acquisitions meeting at the university at six o'clock. I'm quite sorry not to have been more helpful." He rose.

"Then can you recommend someone else?" The lunula slid back into the folds of her blouse. "I've come all this way . . ."

"Surely the Museum Library is quite—"

"I've *read* enough. I need to talk to someone who's *seen* one of these—"

"There is no one."

She waited for him to go on but he said nothing more, only stared fixedly at her throat. Yet despite his tone and words, he seemed reluctant to leave. After a moment he turned to face the endless parade of automobiles, the sand-colored shadow of the mountain looming above them. Exhaust fumes mingled with the stench of fried fish, and Magda raised her glass to her face, breathing in the harsh smell of *tsipoura*. For a long moment they stood there, silent. Finally Christos sighed.

"Spyridon Marinatos."

"Who?"

"Spyridon Marinatos. In Akrotiri on Thera—that is, Santorini. He is excavating a city on the south shore of the island, beneath the village of Akrotiri. It is a Bronze Age city . . ."

His voice drifted off into the drone of traffic and the carnival sound of a radio blaring bouzouki music.

"Marinatos?" Furiously Magda scribbled the name into her battered notebook. "Spiro Marinatos?"

Christos shook his head very slightly, as though hearing some more distant music. "Spyridon. *Nea Kameni*," he said softly.

"Nea—what?"

"*Nea Kameni*. 'The New Burnt Land.' It is a fabulous city, buried like Pompeii or Herculaneum beneath the volcanic ash from the great cataclysm of 1450 B.C. He believes it was the capital of the great lost Minoan culture."

For an instant the roar and rush of traffic, of blazing wind, died away. His next words sounded unnaturally loud in the abrupt silence. "He believes he has found Atlantis."

Magda put her pen down and rubbed her throbbing temples. "Oh, *please*—"

Christos Eugenides shot her an angry glance. "This is all quite true, Miss Kurtz. The site is thousands of years old and I assure you more spectacular than anything you have ever seen. It is a more important archaeological find than Pompeii or Tutankhamen's grave. "

He paused, his gaze lingering upon her neck, then added in a very low voice, "You are aware, I am quite certain, that the Minoan culture is at the very heart of worship of the great goddess. Perhaps the most ancient culture of the Mediterranean. And we know next to nothing about it at all."

At the word *goddess* Magda's mouth grew dry. "Of—of course," she said, and gulped the rest of her *tsipoura*. The raw liquor scorched the back of her throat. "Yes, of course—and this Marinatos will see me? I can catch a plane to Santorini?"

Christos Eugenides shook his head. "I do not know if he will see you or not. You will have to find someone with a boat. It may be difficult; Spyridon is not a popular man right now. His political views are considered reactionary and dangerous."

"Can you give me the name of someone with a boat?"

He turned and walked to the edge of the patio. "I can give you nothing, Miss Kurtz. I am quite sorry." But as he stepped down onto the sidewalk he hesitated, then said, "Santorini—that is not the correct name. In Greek it is called Thera."

He walked quickly toward the corner, his last words hanging in the sullen air before the wind and dust swallowed them.

Thera: Fear.

She had not gone to the island. Instead she returned to her room in the cheap *pensione* she'd found in Monastiraki, the old Turkish quarter near the site of the ancient Agora. There she finished another bottle of *tsipoura* and tried vainly to find some English-language news on the ancient radio. She knew she shouldn't be drinking. She felt sick and frightened and exhausted, ready to give up this entire crazy quest to learn something about her stolen artifact. She wished she could leave tonight, but she'd booked a return flight for two days hence and couldn't afford to change it.

"Ahhh, hell."

With a groan she collapsed onto the mattress, flattening a pile of books and papers. The sheets were damp and reeked of bug spray. Her notes looked as disheveled and forlorn as Magda herself. She reached for the *tsipoura*.

"Hair of the dogma," she said, frowning. The bottle was empty. She couldn't remember finishing it. "Well, enough already."

She dropped the bottle onto the cracked cement floor. With a satisfying crash it shattered. "Goddamn waste of time," Magda swore.

From the room next door came the endless percussive thud of music. The same song, the same tape played over and over until she could feel it in her spine as she writhed on her foul-smelling bed, trying vainly to sleep. Her neighbor wailed along with it, his voice hoarse and giddy.

She lives, no fear, doubtless in everything She knows
Through time, unchecked, the sureness of Her grows
She leaves Herself inside you when She goes.

She lives in a time of her own.

"Goddammit!" she yelled, but the noise drowned her words. "Turn it DOWN!"

Drumbeats and a fadeout; then the song began again. Magda rubbed her temples and moaned.

"Oh, Peter, *please*."

She'd run into him when she had arrived two days earlier, a young hippie taking a year off from Swarthmore. A sweet kid, actually, stoned every time she saw him, his head bobbing to music real or imagined, it didn't seem to matter. But she just couldn't stand it anymore.

You have always heard Her speaking
She's been always in your ear
Her voice sounds a tone within you
Listen to the words you hear
Her time has no past or future
She lives everything She sees
Her time doesn't stand outside Her
It's in every breath She breathes.

Magda stumbled into the hallway, its stained white walls pocked with dead silverfish and faded blue handprints, talismans against *ker*, the spirits of the dead. From a small recessed window came the muted noise of traffic. When Magda pounded her neighbor's door, the cheap wood paneling felt frail enough to break.

"Peter!"

Abruptly the door swung inward. Music and smoke poured into the hallway, the smells of sweat and burning wax. And there was her neighbor, blinking sleepily and holding a cotton kimono closed at his chest.

"Peter," she repeated, striving to be heard above the din. "Look, could you turn it down a little? I—I'm not feeling well."

He stared at her curiously, then backed into the room. She could glimpse a small tape player atop a heap of dashiki shirts and frayed jeans. In one corner a tiny old-fashioned oscillating fan turned listlessly back and forth, back and forth. He'd dragged his mattress onto the floor and covered it with an Indian print batiked in lurid shades of purple and orange. When he reached the mattress he stopped, kicking it idly with a dirty bare foot. He made no move to turn down the music.

"Peter?"

He was young, nineteen or twenty. Young enough that even after days, maybe weeks, without shaving he had only the faintest gold stubble on his chin. Thin but broad-shouldered, with long unwashed blond hair spilling down the back of his kimono. Where his robe hung open she could see his chest, hairless and tanned, and the smooth slope to the top of his narrow hips, the jutting edge of his hipbone and a flash of white where the sun hadn't touched him. He nodded and cocked his head.

"Hey, Magda," he said in a thick honeyed drawl. "How you doing?" His brow furrowed. "Um, maybe you better come in."

She took a step after him, stopped as the warm wind from the fan tickled her legs.

No wonder he was staring: she'd stormed out barely dressed. Her jeans were still on the floor where she'd flung them after she'd returned from her unhappy meeting with Eugenides. She was wearing nothing but her blouse and white cotton underwear.

"Oh, shit." She clutched foolishly at her collar and started to leave, but Peter was already at the door, peering outside before closing it with exaggerated courtliness.

"Hey, it's okay," he said, then, miracle of miracles, crossed to the tape player and turned it down. Without looking back he tossed her a dashiki shirt. "You want to get high?"

High? With no way to get to Thera, no hope of learning more about the lunula, only fifty-three dollars (American) in her pocket and no credit left on her American Express card?

"*No*—" She shrugged into his shirt, then laughed. "Oh, what the hell. Sure, why not."

The shirt hung almost to her knees. It had a strong powdery smell of jasmine incense. "Looks nice," said Peter. He settled cross-legged on the mattress, reached beneath a lumpy pillow, and pulled out a small agate pipe. "Here—"

They smoked in silence. Peter's head bobbed in time to the soft music, the small blue candle flame shivered with each pass of the ancient fan. After a few minutes Peter set aside the pipe.

"Is that the only song on this tape?" Her voice was hoarse, her tongue felt thick and sweet, as though she's been eating jam.

He nodded, eyes slitted. "Yeah. Isn't it great?"

"For the first million or so times."

He only smiled and tapped out a rhythm on his thighs. Magda sat across from him, her headache still throbbing gently somewhere far beneath the soft buzz of hashish. She was so tired, she should get up and leave, thank him for the hash. She thought about moving, might even have stretched one leg toward the edge of the mattress; but when she looked up she saw that Peter was staring at her, his eyes gilded to gold coins by the candlelight.

"That's really beautiful." He moved until he sat on his knees facing her. He put one hand on her shoulder and gently touched her throat. She felt the weight of the lunula there, rising and falling with the pulse of her blood. "*You're* really beautiful."

She laughed again, softly. "Yeah, sure," she murmured, but she didn't draw away.

"No, really, I mean it." One of his hands moved to stroke her breastbone beneath the crescent; the other brushed the hair from her face. "You really are. You look like a—" He shook his head, smiling, and made an extravagant gesture.

She could feel herself blushing: she'd been called *beautiful* about three times in her life. As he gazed at her Peter's brown eyes were luminous, but also a little surprised, as though his own words confused him. He rested his palm against her cheek, staring at her with his lips parted, his eyes narrowed as though he was trying to remember something, like where or who he was, how she'd gotten into his room. Magda stared back at him. Her own breath was coming faster now and her heart was pounding. There was something about the flickering light, the way the shadows coursed across the boy kneeling in front of her—as though she was watching him from some impossible height, with webs of cloud and mist between them and blue waves smashing against cliffs far far below. She shut her eyes and the vision became even clearer, a barren mountaintop where small purplish flowers clung to the stones, their star-shaped petals hanging from a lax head nodding in the wind. Their scent was overpoweringly sweet, the smell of hyacinths. At cliff's edge flames scored the rim of a blackened brazier. The air was full of sound, keening wind and gulls, the wail of an ibis. She heard voices, faint music and the sound of drums. Her bare skin burned from sun and salt water and she could smell something burning, a pungent leafy scent. Not wax or hashish but something else: yarrow sticks, dittany of-Crete, crushed bay leaves; and this mingled with the musky odor of Peter's sweat, the faint scent of jasmine that clung to his hair, and the wind-borne sweetness of hyacinths. He was so near to her that his breath was warm against her skin, her throat. Nearly as warm as the metal crescent upon her breast, as the flames leaping behind them. She opened her eyes. A few inches from hers, Peter's face was flushed, his eyes half-closed as though he was dreaming it all: the music, Greece, Magda herself.

She lives . . .

Magda shook her head, tried to blink away the flares of grey and gold and blue that streamed at the edges of her vision. *What the hell is this?* But she could see nothing clearly save the boy in front of her. He was impossibly beautiful, his hair unbound and his throat and face and eyes all turned to gold, his robe fallen open so that she could see his skin, smooth, the color of expensive oil. Like a bronze *kouros*, one of those sacred images dredged from the Aegean, his blank eyes fixed on some point in the unfathomable distance. He was unbuttoning her shirt, his fingers cupping her breast, his weight pressing the lunula into her flesh as he kissed her.

She . . .

She pushed him back against the mattress, pulling off his robe until he lay there, naked. For a long moment she looked at him, stroking the tops of his thighs, tracing the long curve of his waist and then cupping his ass in her hands as she lowered her head and took his engorged cock into her mouth. His flesh tasted salty, bitter; she could smell the sea and feel the wind cold upon her back, his hands hot as metal as they crushed her breasts and he groaned. A few bitter drops burned against her tongue. She drew back quickly before he could come. He groaned louder; she straddled his legs, took his cock in her hands.

"Oh—hey, don't stop—"

His voice cracked as he stared up at her, his eyes no longer soft but imploring, almost desperate. She smiled, a thin smile, and mounted him.

It was too fast for him, she could hear him begging her to slow down but she didn't care. Her fingers raked his chest, her nails left red streaks as she pulled him harder into her. Blood welled from beneath his bottom rib; she brought her finger to her mouth and sucked it, then lowered her face and kissed him. He moaned and tried to grab her, but she pulled back again, still holding him inside her.

When she came she gasped and let her breath out explosively. She could hear him crying out, a high thin sound carried away by the wind, felt the faint pulse and throb of him beneath her as she drew away. Her head pounded so that it drowned out everything else.

"God—ah, god—" Peter murmured where he lay beside her. "That was amazing . . ."

There was a sound. A lingering echo as of the voices she had heard earlier, far-off and indistinct. She sat with her knees sinking into the mattress, naked except for the silver crescent upon her breast. From its twin spars candlelight glinted, gold and red. The voices grew louder.

Strabloe hathaneatidas druei tanaous kolabreusomena
Kirkotokous athroize te mani Grogopa Gnathoi ruseis itoa

As though she were reading them in the air in front of her, the meaning of the words became clear. She had always known them, had heard them before a hundred times, a thousand.

Gather your immortal sons, ready them for your wild embrace
Ravage Circe's children beneath the binding Moon
Bare to them your dreadful face, inviolable Goddess, your clashing teeth

The voices died into the rush of wind and the sea. Magda shook her head, trying to recall just where she was, why her knees seemed to be digging into rough dirt instead of cloth. She could smell the musty thick odors of Peter's room, incense and semen and unwashed clothes, and see a small blue flame beneath its spiral of grey smoke. But the outlines of walls and floor and ceiling had grown blurred, lost in a growing haze. Then the sun was gone, and the candle flame. Everywhere about her was night save for a fine thread of silver drawn across the sky and the pale form of the *kouros* in front of her. In her hands she felt the lunula's weight, no longer warm but icy cold. As she drew it over her head she felt the bite of metal, a tugging pain as it raked her temple.

Then it was free. Between her fingers she held the shining reflection of the new moon that burned high overhead. The face of Cybele, *Brimo Hagne*, Terrible Pure One. The sleeping moon, the fasting goddess: Othiym. She could feel eyes upon her, could see them now in the dark. But not Peter's eyes.

No: *Her* eyes, cold and bright and full of yearning. She was there, standing before Magda on the mountaintop, the moon upon Her brow like an arc of flame, Her mouth curved into a smile. Magda could see Her white teeth and Her hands outstretched as though to gather Magda to Her breast; but Her breasts were withered and shrunken as an ape's, Her hands knotted into clumps of bone. From Her mouth flowed a blackness so immense that Magda swooned; but before she could lose consciousness something grabbed her, she felt stony fingers pulling at her arms and that cold foul breath filling her nostrils like fetid water. Magda opened her eyes and She was still there, more immense and terrifying than anything Magda had ever seen.

"No!" Magda cried; but as she sought to wrench away she could feel herself bowing, even as her mind cried *Worship! Worship!*

And then She was gone. Magda gasped, blinked and raised her hands protectively, expecting to see that monstrous face. Instead she saw the boy, one arm flung across his face so that his eyes were hidden. His throat was pale, smooth, showing only the smallest bulge of Adam's apple beneath his childish face. His breathing was soft. Across his mouth spilled a slender bow of moonlight. He stirred, murmuring, then lay still again. Without a word she raised the lunula, grasping its spurs so that the curved glittering blade faced outward, and fell upon him.

Long after she woke. She lay upon the pallet, the lunula still in her hand. The room was dark. From the sliver of bluish light that crept from beneath the door she guessed that it was morning. A foul smell hung in the air, excrement and bile and blood. There was blood on the sharpened edge of the lunula, still damp, and blood on the first three fingers of her right hand. On her knees was the crumpled mass of the shirt he'd given her. When she bunched the cloth between her fingers it crinkled, as though it had been starched. A tangle of something soft tugged at her fingers and she looked down to see a long matted plait of blond hair, at one end stuck with a felted blackish mass. Flies lifted from it in a lazy droning spiral, like the lingering ghost of the boy's stoned chatter, and disappeared.

She drew her head up slowly. A few inches from where she sat, Peter's corpse sprawled on the mattress. His head sagged backward; it had been nearly severed from his neck. He was so white he looked as though he had been frozen. She had never seen a body so purely albescent, like a figure carved of quartz or crystal. His hands were curled into rigid talons. His hair had fallen across his face, so that all she could really see was his mouth; his lips had drawn back in a snarl. One of his front teeth was missing.

"Aaahhhhh . . ."

With a moan she backed away from the corpse. When she bumped into the door she shrieked softly, covered her mouth with her hand. She stood there for a long time, staring. Finally she gazed down at the lunula dangling from her fingers.

In the dim light it looked almost black. The spots where the blood had dried were like jagged bites in the soft metal. As she stared, the blood staining the silver began to glow. The metal grew hot, so hot she cried aloud, but just as she moved to fling it away, the crescent cooled, as rapidly as a hot poker stuck in the snow. She saw where lines began to stand out on the smooth silver, the full curves and swells of its moons so brilliant they looked molten. Magda thought it would begin to drip, spattering liquescent metal upon the floor.

But then the lines faded, red to black to grey. The lunula's surface gleamed as before, pure and smooth as though it had been cast anew.

She waited more than an hour before leaving his room. When she did, she saw no one. Not then; not when she bolted into the filthy bathroom at the end of the hall to wash. Not when she left the next day, her duffel bag stuffed with books and clothes, a small newspaper-wrapped bundle beneath her arm. She had paid for her room in advance; there was no one who cared when she departed, as long as it was before Friday. She had spent the intervening hours curled in a ball on her mattress, feverish, nearly delirious, waiting for the sound of footsteps that never came. When she finally left the *pensione* she walked quickly. She crossed several streets until she came to an empty alley. Without stopping, without even hesitating, she dropped the bundle containing Peter's bloodstained shirt into the gutter.

Her flight left Athens as scheduled. While the customs officials spent twenty minutes going through her bag, and confiscated a model of a water clock that she had purchased in a shop near the old Agora, they took no notice of the crescent moon that hung pale and lucent as a tear against her throat.

"Excuse me—oh!"

Someone bumped into her and Magda winced. She ducked her head and let the lunula slip behind the silken folds of her dress.

"Well, well! Professor Kurtz! We're sorry to be losing you again, Magda."

It was Harold Mosreich, he who had attained such success with his work in the Yucatán and was now a fully tenured professor of Central American Archaeology at the Divine. He smiled at her, genuinely forlorn: whether because he had bumped her or because she was leaving, she had no idea. Magda smiled and leaned over to kiss his cheek, catching a whiff of talc and Lilac Vegetal.

"Oh, Harold. You're the only one."

He shook his head. "Not at all. Only yesterday I heard Balthazar Warnick say how sorry he was you were leaving us so soon."

"So soon?"

At mention of Balthazar's name she grew cold. She thought of the naphaïm in her room; of the faces she had glimpsed in the silver basin, the boy and girl she had come in search of tonight. She stammered, "I was actually supposed to leave earlier, but I stayed on a few extra days. Bind up a couple of loose ends. You know . . ."

Her voice trailed off. She wished she'd gotten another drink, or a canapé, something to use as a prop and distract Harold, keep him from looking at her face. She felt the lunula like a brand burning at her throat. *How* could she have been so stupid as to wear it here?

"Oh. Well, maybe he was sorry you hadn't left sooner, then."

She glanced at him sharply, but Harold's expression was without irony. He was gazing across the room at a drift of white-clad nuns blocking one of the service doors.

"You don't suppose they're all going to the bathroom together, do you?" he asked. When Magda raised her eyebrows he went on, "It's just that Balthazar particularly asked that we don't have a lot of traffic upstairs tonight—they were supposed to cordon off that end, but then the loo by the kitchen backed up, and—well, you don't want to hear all this, do you?"

He took her hand and shook it affectionately. "Good luck, Magda. Have a safe flight back."

"'Thank you, Harold."

She smiled as she watched him make his way through the crowd, his bald head gleaming beneath the gently swaying chandeliers. Before Harold reached the doors leading upstairs, she turned to snare more champagne from a passing waiter.

And so she didn't see Balthazar Warnick step from behind the cluster of nuns to greet Harold Mosreich, with Francis Xavier Connelly looming behind him. By then Magda Kurtz was much too far away to hear Harold's words to her former mentor, or to see how the tenured professor of Central American Archaeology sketched a half circle in the air, his melancholy eyes even sadder than they had been a few minutes earlier. She did not see how Balthazar Warnick nodded as she took her champagne flute, or how he marked the tenebrous halo about her like a cloud's passing, the glint of silver at her breast.

CHAPTER 7

Night of the Electric Insects

I always wonder what would have happened if I hadn't gone with Baby Joe for those two vodka tonics. If instead, I'd gone over there to stand with Angelica and Professor Kurtz. In my head that's always been the moment when everything changed, the stone tossed into the stream that changes its course. If I'd been there talking to them, maybe the others would have left them alone. Maybe my entire life would have been different.

Probably I couldn't have done anything at all. But I would have saved them if I could.

Her conversation with Harold Mosreich left Magda uneasy.

Only yesterday I heard Balthazar Warnick say how sorry he was you were leaving us so soon.

But she hadn't told Balthazar, or anyone else, that she was going. He could have easily figured it out, of course: the summer session was over, the fall term had already started; but it was still unsettling. She had interfered with *Benandanti* matters; she had stolen knowledge of their Sign, cast a pebble into the clear water where they went to scry their secrets.

Time to go, she thought. But as she started for the door a voice cried out to her.

Wait!

The command was so loud and clear that she stopped, glancing around furtively. She saw only the same crowd of well-dressed men and women, nothing else. But when she took another step it came again—

Wait!

—a man's voice, low and insistent. She smoothed her damp palms against the front of her dress, closed her eyes as she tried to summon whom- or whatever had called to her.

Nothing. She heard scattered bits of conversation—classes, football, something about incunabula at the Library of Congress—the sweet sad notes of the string quartet. *Tod und der Mädchen*. She opened her eyes.

All was as it should be. There was Harold Mosreich, chatting with a blue-haired matron. There was one of her students, a boy who had been her partner in a brief and intense liaison over the Fourth of July weekend. Near Harold was another boy, stocky and dressed in an ill-fitting suit, who leaned over to light the cigarette of a pale, dark-haired girl, with a freckled, waifish face and nervous hands. Nothing more.

Magda let her breath out. Nerves and fatigue, that was all. She had forgotten how the effort of summoning the naphaïm exhausted her. By this time tomorrow she'd be back in her apartment at Berkeley, readying herself for her own fall term. She'd done what she could to intervene on behalf of her Mistress. Now it was out of her hands. She finished her glass of champagne and was turning to leave when the girl approached her.

"Professor Kurtz?"

Magda froze.

"I'm Angelica di Rienzi."

It was the girl Magda had scried in her room. In sudden panic Magda took a step backward, then caught herself and tried to smile. The girl smiled back and went on breathlessly.

"I wish I'd been able to take one of your classes this summer—I wanted to audit one but they wouldn't let me. I'm just starting here," she added. "But I wanted you to know how much I loved *Daughters of the Setting Sun*—"

She was *such* a beautiful girl! Magda nodded, stunned. "Angelica, how—how nice of you—"

She winced as Angelica took her hand and shook it vigorously. The girl had incongruously large strong hands, a peasant's hands despite their long polished nails, with broad, slightly callused fingers.

"Oh, I mean it, Professor Kurtz, it was *wonderful*—"

That smile! It was ravishing, and Angelica was probably not as unconscious of its effect as she tried to appear. When Magda wanly smiled back, she felt that her own mouth was too small and meager to project anything remotely worthy of this girl's radiant good will.

"—I did a paper on it at school. It really, *really* changed my life."

Magda arched an eyebrow. "Really *really*?"

"Oh, *yes*! I loved that story about the Greeks—the fight between the men and women, and how when the women lost, the men said their children would no longer be allowed to keep their mothers' names. That was the *first time* I ever thought about the whole notion of a matriarchy. It was like a *door* opening, and you opened it for me."

"Saint Augustine."

"Excuse me?"

"The story's from Saint Augustine. You know, the proto-feminist," Magda said drily. "So I guess you should thank *him* for opening the door."

"Oh. Well, anyway . . ."

When you took them apart Angelica's features were almost *too* exotic, at least to someone accustomed to California, where girls were polled neatly and expensively as *bonsai* evergreens. And, of course, she was wearing green contacts. *No* one had eyes that color, Magda thought, like the virent flash of some Amazonian butterfly's wing.

". . . made me want to become an archaeologist. Before that I was planning to go into the theater—a friend of mine from Sarah Lawrence said she could set me up with an audition for 'Dark Shadows' . . ."

Magda nodded. The girl definitely had *something*. The unusual features projected a striking, almost disturbing, beauty—Magda thought of the famous bust of Nefertiti, or the heavy-lipped face of the hermaphroditic Akhenaton. Exquisite, but in a way that wasn't quite human. She wondered why the *Benandanti* had brought her here. Perhaps they had known, somehow, that she was to be chosen for some great work. But Magda was fairly certain that even the *Benandanti* had not known until a few days ago that a Sign was to appear.

No, something else would have driven them to Angelica; the world was full of beautiful girls who were not marked for the *Benandanti*. What Magda sensed in her was an overwhelming determination, a great and terrible *will*.

Will toward *what*, Magda had no idea. Probably the girl herself didn't even know—not yet, at least. But when she found out, all hell would break loose. Magda stared at her thoughtfully as Angelica went on.

". . . spent some time with my cousins in Florence and then . . ."

It wasn't just her beauty: she projected such raw pure *energy*. Nearly everyone stared at her. A few, men and women both, quite literally stopped in their tracks to stare. As though some great icon—the Sphinx, Venus de Milo, Greta Garbo—had strolled into a cocktail party and mixed herself a drink.

And, while she seemed to pay no heed to this constantly changing backdrop of admirers, Angelica di Rienzi noted every single one of them. Magda was sure of it.

"And then one night I got a phone call from Balthazar . . ."

Balthazar? Since when did undergraduates call him Balthazar? Angelica reached out to stroke Magda's bare arm, the girl's touch like warm oil poured across her skin. Magda shivered.

". . . and I love it, I just *love* it . . ."

Magda closed her eyes. The girl's perfume enveloped her, a sweet warm fragrance like sandalwood and oranges. Like the sun burning down upon those tiny wild hyacinths that grow beneath endless blue Aegean skies—

Kirkotokous athroize te mani Grogopa Gnathoi ruseis itoa

—like the sweet smoke drifting up from the mountaintop, the *kouroi* gathered there and harrowed in the dusk like grain . . .

"So I like, really think that I'll *find* myself here." Angelica laughed and let go of Magda's arm. "I'm sorry to go on like this! But your work really has meant so much to me."

. . . Othiym haïyo . . .

Magda drew back as though she had been slapped.

What the hell is going on?

But Angelica had noticed nothing. Her huge emerald eyes were fixed on Magda. She opened her hands and held them palms upward as she recited in a low voice, "'*I have made you a lioness among women, and given you leave to kill any at your pleasure.*'"

"What?" demanded Magda. *"What did you say?"*

Angelica dropped her hands. "From your book." She looked confused. "I mean, I *think* that's where it's from. I'm sorry—was it, was I—did I remember it wrong?"

Magda drew her clenched fists to her breast.

"No," she said, trying to keep her voice from shaking. *Who* is *this girl?* "It's—it's not from my book. It's from the Mysteries of Eleusis—I mentioned them in there, but I never quoted that verse. I never quoted it anywhere."

"Oh. Eleusis. The corn thing." Angelica gave a self-deprecating laugh. "I must have read it somewhere else, then."

Her voice trailed off and Angelica suddenly looked away. Magda followed her gaze.

On the other side of the reception room there was a stir, as people turned and craned their necks, to watch someone arguing with a gentleman by the front door. Magda heard tittering, a single raucous shout. Several students cheered drunkenly. Magda stood on tiptoe, trying to see over the crowd.

In the smoke-filled entrance to Garvey Hall stood a tall unsteady figure, wearing what appeared to be white robes—no, a *sheet*—no, *two* sheets, and one of them patterned with lurid purple daisies—draped around his torso and across his head like a hood. As she stared the figure straightened and pulled a small white rectangle from somewhere within his makeshift toga. Magda recognized the same heavy embossed card that had been issued as invitation to every Molyneux reception she had ever attended. With a flourish the sheet-clad figure presented it to the man at the door. The guard peered at it suspiciously, then waved the newcomer through. The boy walked into the main room with his head bowed, face still hidden by white and purple folds. Whistles and catcalls filled the air.

"Check it out!"

"Hey, Ah—lee—*VER*!"

"Ah—lee—*VER*!" chanted a group by the bar. "Ah—lee—*VER*!"

The boy in the toga drew himself up. He gave one shoulder an exaggerated shake, like a stripper shedding her costume, and threw his head back. A flurry of long ebony hair fell around his shoulders. Angelica gasped.

"Friend of yours?" asked Magda.

Angelica nodded, covering her mouth and then exploding into laughter. "I—I can't *believe* it—"

"Very nice," Magda remarked.

It was a clumsy effort at drag, but credible. Just a raw gash of lipstick and two streaks of rouge and some kind of bright blue eye shadow. But even this crude effort could not hide how good-looking he was—indeed, the makeup gave him an eerie, almost otherwordly, prettiness, as off-putting in its way as Angelica's beauty. He walked with great dignity through the cheering students who gathered around him. No mincing or prancing, no sheepish grin. He looked like the biblical harlot from some early Cecil B. deMille epic, and while a few of the older guests were scowling, most laughed, or at least pretended to.

"Who is he, Angelica? Do you—"

Magda abruptly shut up. The girl's lips were parted, her eyes glowing. Whoever this boy was, Angelica was staring at *him* the way everyone had been gazing at *her* all evening. Magda touched the lunula at her throat and bit her lip.

Of course. This was the *other* one, the boy she'd glimpsed last night. *Oliver*, the naphaïm had named him; and now across the parquet floors snaked a conga line led by a half-dozen drunken boys in evening dress, yelping, "Ah—*lee*—VER! Ah—*lee*—VER!"

"He's—very good-looking," said Magda. But Angelica only smiled, a look of perfect seigniory, and continued to stare.

And that was when Magda saw the pattern, the secret behind the Sign. That beautiful boy, this beautiful prescient girl; all of Angelica's pure fiery will turned onto nothing but *him*. The oldest story in the book, that was all it came down to. Nothing more.

Magda turned. As quickly as they had gathered to lionize him, Oliver's admirers had fallen away. Now he stood by himself, holding the crumpled sheet to his chest in a surprisingly delicate manner. He was gazing abstractedly at the ceiling, where the Venetian glass chandelier swayed slightly. Oliver moved with it, arm raised. His eyes were closed and he was singing to himself. He appeared to be stoned out of his mind.

". . . so I better go now. It was wonderful meeting you."

With an apologetic smile, Angelica started to walk toward Oliver. Magda watched her go. From a hidden recess, the string quartet began to play an austere arrangement of "Pavane pour une enfant defunte." In spite of herself Magda felt her eyes well with tears.

Through our great good fortune, in our youth our hearts were touched with fire.

Sudden fury lanced her. All of her hopes for the Sign, all the divided energies of the *Benandanti* and her Mistress—and they came down to *this*, some adolescent passion! She stared at Angelica and thought of all that golden energy, just waiting to be released in a dorm room with some horny zonked-out *kid*. It was insane! Almost without thinking, Magda darted forward and grabbed the girl by the shoulder.

"Angelica! Wait—"

Angelica stopped, taken aback.

"Angelica—I—I just wanted to—"

That was when Magda saw them: Balthazar Warnick and his young stooge Francis. Even from here she could see Warnick's sapphire eyes glittering, his fixed smile as he nodded to a passing colleague. Then he turned, and his gaze locked with hers. In an instant she realized what her recklessness had cost her.

They knew.

Magda could tell by Balthazar's eyes, and by something else: an abrupt though subtle shift in the air, as though a window had been opened to let a freezing wind vent through the smoke and laughter. The names of the two innocents were no longer a secret. The *Benandanti* had learned of her betrayal.

"Angelica! Wait—" Magda put every ounce of her will into the command. The girl gazed at her, puzzled. Around Magda's neck the lunula burned like a heated coil.

"Tell—tell me your name again," she ordered. Angelica frowned. "Please! *Tell me your name*."

Angelica glanced over her shoulder, looking for the boy in the makeshift toga; but beneath the chandelier the floor was empty. She turned back to Magda. "Angelica di Rienzi."

"Angelica—"

The lunula was a white-hot collar about Magda's throat. She could scarcely breathe, scarcely find the energy to speak. The air buzzed with static electricity; she felt a burst of nausea as before her everything spun into a sudden tumultuous brilliance, jagged rays of white and crimson distorting her view: a terrifying prismatic radiance that did not illuminate but disturbed the outlines of everything about her. Light and color pulsed and throbbed and even seemed to produce a *sound,* an anguished shriek like a razor drawn across a whetstone. A few yards away, two shimmering forms moved through the luminous maelstorm.

"That's right. Angelica di Rienzi," the girl said softly.

Magda summoned all her strength. "Angelica di Rienzi." She could hear Francis's heavy tread. Quickly Magda reached for a stray curl upon the girl's forehead, plucked a single bronze strand and snatched her hand back.

"*Angelica Di Rienzi: In hoc signo vinces. Othiym, haïyo*!" She opened her fingers: the hair flickered into a wisp of flame and white ash. "I would like you to have this, Angelica."

With one smooth motion Magda pulled off the lunula. She held it in front of her and gazed upon it for the last time.

All the brilliance that had filled the room now seemed to radiate from the shimmering crescent, so that nothing but shadows surrounded herself and Angelica. From somewhere very far away she heard murmuring, a woman's voice raised in lamentation. The shadows grew thicker. For an instant Magda had a glimpse of the new moon rising above a stony outcropping, the scarlet arc of George Wayford's throat against the earth. Before the vision could fade she slid the lunula over Angelica's head.

"I'm very glad you enjoyed the lecture," Magda said loudly as Balthazar and Francis Connelly swept up behind her.

"What?" exclaimed Angelica; then "*Ow*!—it's *hot*!"

"But now you'd better *go*—"

Magda pushed the girl toward the bar. In a daze Angelica stumbled past Professor Warnick and his companion, then on through the diminishing crowd, her fingers splayed across her throat. For once no one took any notice of her.

"Magda."

Magda could smell Balthazar before she turned to greet him: that deceptively serene mixture of Borkum Riff and chalk and moldering books. "Balthazar," she whispered.

The small slender man shook his head. In his pearl grey morning suit and ascot of pale green satin, he looked like a darkly elegant cricket.

"I was so—*surprised*—to learn you were still among us. I thought your flight was today." His tone was mocking but also wistful.

"I changed it."

He took her right arm, Francis her left. "You changed a few other things as well," Balthazar murmured as they assisted her through the crowd. "News of your recent fieldwork reached me only this morning. I had no idea your interests had—expanded—so far beyond ours."

Gently but irresistibly they steered her toward the same door where Harold Mosreich's nuns had gathered earlier. Magda looked away so they couldn't see the fear in her eyes. Her throat and breast felt scorched. Without the lunula she felt utterly exposed, as in a nightmare of facing a lecture hall naked, her students gaping in disbelief. As Balthazar and Francis led her through the darkened doorway she whimpered.

Here the sounds of the reception were abruptly silenced. They were in one of the service wings of Garvey Hall. The narrow passage was dark and cool, the floors smelling of disinfectant and neglect and giving a hollow echoing tone to their footsteps. A chill wind moaned querulously as it plucked at Magda's bare arms. When they turned a corner her captors' hold on her grew tighter.

"Where are you taking me?" she whispered.

They faced a wide stairway that curved upward through several stories until it disappeared into utter darkness. From far overhead came the rattle of an unlatched window. As Warnick and Francis dragged her up the steps she pulled back with all her strength.

"*Where are you taking me?*"

"Forget it, Magda," spat Francis. "We know all about you, we—"

"Francis!" Warnick's commanding voice rang out. Francis fell silent and glared sullenly at Magda. Balthazar shook his head.

"Forgive me if our methods seem a little crude, Magda. But we just can't afford to let you go."

"Where—" she began; but Balthazar hushed her.

"I was terribly, terribly sorry to lose you to Berkeley," he said, his voice so regretful that she glanced at him hopefully, half-expecting to see tears in his eyes. There were none, but the look he gave her was immeasurably sad. "And now this—losing you twice . . . Oh, Magda—"

They stopped, halfway up the stairs. Francis stared pointedly into the darkness and glowered. But Balthazar gazed at Magda, his handsome features disarmingly youthful as ever. To her amazement she saw that now his eyes *were* brilliant with tears. She could feel his hand trembling even as he held her unyieldingly. For a moment she thought he was going to stand on tiptoe to kiss her. Instead he turned away.

"This is a great disappointment," he said, and pulled her after him.

"Please, Balthazar, can't you tell me—"

Her words broke off as she stumbled onto a landing. They stood at the entrance of another dim hallway. Seemingly endless ranks of closed doors lined each side of the corridor. There was a smell of stagnant water, the faintest whiff of gasoline.

"A safe place," Balthazar said softly. "No people to bother you—"

"Balthazar, listen to me—"

"—no people at all—"

"Balthazar, please!"

No one heard as they dragged her into the silent passage.

The string quartet had packed their instruments and were lined up at the bar, ordering shots of tequila. A tape of the opening strains of *Carmina Burana* wafted above the dying smoke and laughter. At my feet a little army of empty glasses glinted, as I finished another vodka tonic. I was already totally wasted, but I had some stupid idea that the more messed up I got, the safer I would be here.

"They *always* play this as a sign-off," Baby Joe said in disgust. "It's like the fucking national anthem at midnight." He shifted against the wall, pointed with his drink. "Uh-oh. Here comes Barbie."

I looked up to see Angelica.

"The weirdest thing just happened to me." She raised an eyebrow at the rows of empty glasses and the cigarette in my hand. "Have you seen Oliver? Sweeney . . . ?"

"Angelica." I grabbed Baby Joe's arm. "This is Baby Joe—remember, you said you'd met him—"

Angelica flashed him a distracted smile. "Sure. Hi. Look, Sweeney, this is *very strange*—do you know who Magda Kurtz is?"

"Uh-uh. No, wait—" I looked at Baby Joe. "Wasn't that who you were telling me about? "

"Visiting Marcellien Professor in European Studies." Baby Joe regarded Angelica through slitted eyes. He looked like Peter Lorre sizing up a little girl for the kill. "Saw you talking to her."

"Well, look—she gave me this—"

I leaned forward to see what she pointed at: a crescent-shaped silver necklace, like a Celtic torque.

"Wow. It looks expensive. She *gave* it to you?"

Angelica nodded earnestly. "Isn't that weird?"

"Beware of geeks bearing gifts." Angelica looked annoyed as Baby Joe pointed across the room. "There's one now. Your friend Oliver."

Angelica whirled. I made a show of casualness and turned slowly, taking another drag on my cigarette. When I saw him I started coughing uncontrollably. Baby Joe snickered.

"Maybe he heard the calla lilies are in bloom. *Talagang sirang ulo*."

In the middle of the room Oliver stood gazing at the dome as if he were reading something there, his horoscope maybe, or the name of a good psychiatrist. A few feet away two middle-aged couples were trying very hard to ignore him. He was wearing makeup—at least what was left of it, most seemed to have come off on some kind of sheet wrapped around his neck. What remained was a red hole of a mouth and two bruised eyes, and of course all that disheveled hair and a flowered Marimekko sheet. He looked like the survivor of some terrible crash on a fashion runway, beautiful and wrecked.

Angelica stared at him transfixed. When I finally stopped coughing I wheezed, "He's got to be totally wasted—he told me he was getting some mushrooms—"

"Mushrooms?" Baby Joe perked up. "Maybe I'll go see how he's doing."

He rambled off, trailed by a grey cloud of ash. I started to follow when Angelica grabbed my arm.

"Come with me?" she pleaded, glancing back at Oliver. "I wanted to find the ladies' room—I feel so grubby, all this smoke—"

I nodded reluctantly. When I looked back I saw Baby Joe standing a few feet from Oliver, smoking and staring at him pensively, as though he were on display in a museum. Oliver didn't seem to know he was there.

We went to the bar. I shouted "Ladies' room?" and the bartender yelled something about Doors, Right, Upstairs, gesturing vaguely with one hand as he poured scotch with the other.

"I think he said this way," I said. We elbowed through an uproarious claque of young men who parted like the Red Sea when they saw Angelica. A minute later we walked through an open doorway and out of the reception area.

"God. *This* is an improvement. At least we can *breathe*." Angelica started to laugh. "Did you see Oliver? He must be *wasted*."

I grinned, reached over to finger her necklace. It was cool to the touch and surprisingly heavy. "She really gave that to you, huh? Wow."

Angelica sighed. "Probably I should give it back. Maybe she was drunk or something."

"Maybe she meant to give it to Oliver."

"Maybe *I'll* give it to him."

I leaned in to get a better look, and noticed where a crescent shape had been cut out of the metal. "You know, it looks like part of it's missing—" I poked my finger through and tapped her breastbone. "—see? Here."

"Maybe that's why she got rid of it. Damaged goods."

I drew back and let the pendant fall from my hand. "Yeah, maybe. Let's go. I want to get back and find out what's happening with Oliver."

We padded down the narrow corridor. After a minute or two the hall branched. To the right stretched an even darker, narrower passage; to the left stairs curving up and up through several floors.

I frowned. "He must have meant this way," I said, and turned to the right. We walked for a few minutes but saw nothing—no doors, no windows, not even a painting on the dim walls—until finally we found ourselves in an empty utilitarian kitchen thick with the smells of steam and stale cooking.

"This can't be right." Angelica wrinkled her nose. "This is like, the servants' quarters or something."

"So maybe we're supposed to use the servants' bathroom."

She shook her head. "No. It must have been back there. "

We retraced our steps until once again we stood at the foot of the broad staircase. Angelica started up, but I remained at the bottom, my hand clutching the banister.

Above me the stairway twisted into darkness, ominous and silent. I shuddered. From the hall behind me came a sudden gust of laughter from the reception. I had only to turn back, walk a few steps, and I would be safe again. I could get another vodka tonic, find Baby Joe, and Oliver . . .

"Sweeney? You coming?"

I looked up and saw Angelica's face suspended between the banister's curves, the silver pendant at her throat glistening. She looked like the figure I had seen earlier: those terrible eyes floating above me, hair streaming into the night while all about her whirled into chaos. The woman in the moon.

"Sweeney?" Her exasperated voice floated down. "Come *on*. They'll all still be there when we get back."

"Okay," I said, defeated. "I'm coming." Moments later I stood beside her on the landing.

"What's the matter, Sweeney? You look awful." She ran her hand across my cheek. "Sweeney! You're burning up!"

Her fragrance clung to my skin, the faint musk of sandalwood and oranges like rain washing over me. I closed my eyes and breathed in deeply, until that other, sickening odor was gone.

"I'm okay. I guess I drank too much."

Angelica smiled wryly. "I guess so. Well, I've got some aspirin in my bag. Let's find some water."

She took my hand—firmly but companionably, like a determined English schoolgirl—and led me down the hall. After a few minutes I felt better.

"Well, *this* sure isn't the servants' quarters," I said.

It was like being inside a landscape by Moreau. Against a shadowy black background all was painted or upholstered in dark jeweled colors, bloodred and purple and blue, shot with gold like spasms of daylight. A subdued ruddy light suffused everything, burnishing the oak wainscoting and worn oriental carpets that muffled our footsteps.

"Who the hell *lives* here? The second Mrs. de Winter?"

"No," Angelica replied absently. "This is where visiting *Benandanti* stay."

On the walls there were ornate brass fixtures shaped like griffins and gargoyles and beautiful women, and on the heavy closed doors brass plates engraved with simple legends—*The Red Room, The Luxor Room, The Tuscan Room*. Everything had the air of being made ready for guests, but at the same time it all smelled musty and closed-in, as though there had been no visitors here for months, maybe years.

"How do you know?" My voice was too loud. "I mean about the *Benandanti*. How do you know they stay here?"

"My father."

"Your father." I rolled my eyes. "Oh, sure."

Angelica didn't seem to hear. She continued on down the hall, not even looking to see if I was following her.

I wasn't. I stood there, my hands clenched, and asked, "So who are the *Benandanti*?"

Silence.

"I *said*, who are the—"

"Ssshh!" She stopped and glared. "I thought you were *sick*, Sweeney. Come *on*—"

"I'm not your fucking sidekick! And I'd feel *better* if *someone* would *tell* me—"

Suddenly she was there in front of me, her hand on my waist, the silver necklace glowing against her black lace bodice.

"Sweeney," she said softly. She touched one finger to my chin and tilted my head back, until all I could see were her eyes, huge and slanted and that impossible green. "It's okay, Sweeney. Really, it's okay—"

She kissed me, not a schoolgirl's peck on the cheek but a real kiss; and I let her, though I had never kissed another girl before or even really thought about it. Her hair spilled across my face and I felt lace like dry leaves crinkling beneath my fingertips; her breasts spilling into my hands like warm water, and the hard smooth weight of her thighs where they pressed against me. But all I could think was that it wasn't that different really, there was nothing soft about her at all, not her hands or her skin or anything except her mouth, so small and so hot I gasped, then moaned as she pulled me closer.

"Don't be afraid," she whispered, and though she didn't say it aloud I could hear what came next—

You're with me.

I tried to kiss her again, but she only smiled, drawing away from me and twisting a lock of my hair around one finger. "Come on, *kemosabe*—let's get you that aspirin."

I followed her in silence. I didn't feel embarrassed or angry or even all that confused—just a little turned on, and very, very tired. She was so matter-of-fact, it was all so matter-of-fact that I was starting to think maybe this was what it was like for everyone on their first day of college. Angels at dawn, visions in the afternoon, succubæ at night. It was like a dream, like the best high you ever had; but I knew it was all a mistake.

Angelica had stopped where the corridor ended, at the top of yet another flight of stairs. She looked at me and frowned.

"*Now* what?"

I peered down the stairwell. A freezing draft shot up from it, and an oily smell.

"Maybe we just walked right past it," I said weakly. "All those doors . . ."

We turned back, but only took a few steps before I saw something we'd missed—a narrow passage extending out from the hall. At the end of it I could see a greyish blur that might have been a doorway left ajar. I grabbed Angelica and pulled her into the passage. "I bet this is it."

"Great." Angelica stopped to fumble with her little beaded purse. "Okay. I *know* I've got some aspirin, I just—"

She stopped and looked at me. From the main corridor came the hollow echo of voices and muffled footsteps. Before I knew what was happening, she yanked me further down the passage, until we stood in a small recessed alcove facing a door.

Angelica rattled the knob. "Damn! It's *locked*—"

"Jeez, who cares? We're just looking for a—"

"Shhh!" Angelica crouched on the floor. "Get *down*."

"What?" This was ridiculous. The worst that could happen was that we'd be reprimanded for snooping around, maybe asked to leave. But then I remembered that cold, black stairwell. I shivered. The voices grew louder as Angelica pulled me down beside her.

"I can't—" I whispered.

"Shut up." Angelica moved her hand in a small tight gesture and leaned back, as though trying to fold herself into the wall. I crouched beside her in the darkness.

Shadows blotted out the entrance to the tiny passageway. Men: two of them, I thought at first. But then the taller one moved, and I saw that they carried a third between them, a limp figure who kicked halfheartedly at the floor.

I felt a warm rush of relief. Just a drunk being walked around by his friends. But still Angelica didn't move or say anything. Her sweat had overwhelmed the musk of her perfume, its fragrance now rank and sour, like the smell inside a small room where a child has been locked and forgotten.

Footsteps. The figures passed us, silent except for a faint wheezing from the man supported in the middle. I could see the trouser cuffs of the closest figure, a tall lanky young man wearing tennis shoes and no socks; I could have reached out and grabbed his bare ankle. Next to him slumped his drunken friend, and behind them I could barely glimpse the third figure, so small he was like the shadow of the other two. They stopped in front of the doorway across from us. The figure in the middle suddenly jerked upright, head thrown back, and let out a short strangled cry.

"No!"

Beside me Angelica stiffened.

"Let me go!"

It was a woman's voice. Not a drunken man, not some frat boy being carried around by his friends, but a woman. I stared in horror as she cried out.

"Please."

The taller figure twisted her arms behind her so that she couldn't move. He was holding her so tightly I could hear her bones creak.

Oh, shit, I thought as the woman's voice rang out again.

"You can't do this, Balthazar. It's against the charter, to strike someone within the boundaries of the Divine—" Beside me I could feel Angelica shaking. "—you *can't*, Balthazar, you know you can't . . ."

It was the woman who had spoken to Angelica at the reception. The one who'd given her the necklace: Magda Kurtz, the famous professor of European Archaeology. The man she spoke to, the smaller of the two others, shifted without loosening his hold on her. It was Professor Warnick, his face utterly impassive as he stared at her, not saying a word, just watching and listening. Her voice rose desperately.

"*Please*, Balthazar."

Warnick took a step closer to her. "*You* broke the charter, Magda. A long, long time ago, it seems."

Even in the darkness I could see how his face was twisted, not with lust or hatred or anything else I had expected but with longing, the purest distillation of desire and sorrow I had ever seen. "You found it and never told us. You never told *me*."

"Only part of it," Kurtz whispered. "It's still incomplete, I only found part—"

For the first time the other man spoke. "You *stole* it! How else could you have—"

"Shut up, Francis!" Warnick's voice cracked. Looking at Magda Kurtz he suddenly cried out, "I wish you'd left yesterday. Why didn't you just *leave*?"

At the sound of his anguished voice I trembled. Beside me Angelica was absolutely rigid, her eyes huge and horrified. Professor Warnick pulled away from Magda Kurtz, pushing her toward the other man. Warnick's hand made a slashing motion as he turned and took two quick steps that brought him within inches of the door in the passageway.

"You should have told me," he whispered, and bowed his head.

I had thought the door was ajar. In fact it was tightly shut. Whatever light it held leaked from its seams, grey-blue, dull as ashes—not sunlight or even moonlight but some other kind of glow, with no warmth and scarcely any color to it at all.

"Balthazar." Magda Kurtz's voice died. Slowly she drew her hands to her throat.

Warnick traced his fingers across the wood, murmuring. I couldn't understand the words, they were in a strange language, not Latin, not anything I recognized. As he spoke I began to feel a dull buzzing in my ears. An overpowering drowsiness filled me. It was like the hottest longest afternoon of summer, like falling asleep on the screened porch while the cicadas droned outside. I could hear their persistent burr, soft at first but growing louder and louder. The sound filled my ears, filled me until my bones rang with it and I could hear nothing else, not Professor Warnick's voice, not Angelica's breathing, not my own heart. The locusts' cries rose to a mindless shrieking that wasn't the sound of any insect or machine or human I could imagine. It wasn't the sound of anything I had ever heard at all.

And then came another noise—an echoing rattle and thump, the sound of countless large objects being thrown against the door. In front of us the wall shuddered. The door bulged outward as the shrieking grew to a howl, a clamor nearly drowned by furious scratching. I could hear wood creaking and splintering. The steely light grew brighter, but there was no warmth in it, nothing of sun or candle glow or embers. It was utterly cold, grey-blue and stark as bone. The three figures standing before it were like people trapped in a video screen. The tumult became a roar, the howl of metal grinding against stone.

"Balthazar, *no*!"

Professor Warnick stepped back. The door flew open. I started to scream, but Angelica's hand closed over my mouth. She pulled me to her breast, trying to shield me so I wouldn't see what was there. But I tore away from her, and I did see.

There was a world beyond the door. It was the world that went with that howling, mindless noise, with that blinding leaden glow. An endless expanse of dead plain, colorless, treeless, a horrible lifeless steppe pocked with shadowy hollows and spurs of jagged stone. Overhead stretched the sky, purplish black and starless. On the horizon monstrous shadows rose and ebbed like clouds, and smaller blackened objects fell like hail or a rain of stone. It was a landscape bereft as the moon: no stars to light it, no aqueous Earth casting its blue glow upon the horizon. Only bare ground and stones and freezing air, and a faint foul smell like gasoline. Above it all the deafening roar continued, relentless, as those bulbous black shapes dropped from the sky onto the ravaged plain.

I moaned. In front of us the three others stood, their faces bluish white, their shadows stretching across the floorboards. Angelica's hand tightened over mine, and as it did the horrifying clamor seemed to die. A sudden vast silence engulfed us, and a darkness more profound than any I have known.

"Angelica," I wanted to whisper. But the name would not come.

Then out of nowhere I heard a thin monotonous voice; a voice chanting inside my head from a million years before.

Shape without form, shade without color . . .

Scratched and faint: an old man's voice that struggled with the words even as I struggled to recall where I had heard them.

Remember us—if at all—not as lost
Violent souls, but only
as . . .

And I remembered. I was slumped in a chair in a darkened auditorium, a dim spotlight fixed on the stage where a horrible grey-faced rector chanted.

There are no eyes here
In this valley of dying stars
In this hollow valley
This broken jaw of our lost kingdoms

—or no, I was crouched before a leaping flame, fighting to keep my eyes open as a small figure clad in furs and leather tapped out a monotonous rhythm on a skin tabor.

Here we go round the prickly pear
Prickly pear prickly pear
Here we go round the prickly pear
At five o'clock in the morning. . . .

Abruptly the voice rose to a scream and faded into a chittering wail. Once again I heard that buzzing roar, softer now though more distinct, a sound punctuated by thumps, the hollow impact of empty pods on gravel. And I almost laughed—*would* have laughed, deliriously, if Angelica hadn't caught me and held me close.

Because when I first saw that charred landscape I thought that there could be nothing more horrible than that utterly barren place where nothing had ever grown or died, not scarab nor vulture nor thorn tree nor worm. But now I knew there was something infinitely worse.

Because in all that colorless formless desert, something was alive. *Many* things. What I had at first perceived as monstrous shadows, as clouds or mountains or fog, were not shadows at all. *They were the monstrous things themselves*. Huge, at least twice man-high and skeletally thin, with the outlines of ribs and thorax and skull gleaming in the silvery light.

But they were not skeletons, or cadavers. They were not even remotely human. They were immense arthropods, like praying mantids or walkingsticks or leaf insects. Many-jointed, silvery grey as the scar they danced across, their long, jointed legs trailing behind them like matches spilling from a box. They had huge round eyes, smooth and curved as glass, with a tiny black spot marking the pupil. Some of them had wings that retracted when they struck the ground. They filled the black sky of the world beyond the door, a vast horde growing nearer and nearer. I saw a blurred flutter as one fell to earth and then exploded into the air again, wings beating furiously as it propelled itself toward us. Above its twitching mandibles its eyes glittered like steel bearings.

"Balthazar! Balthazar, no—"

Magda Kurtz's scream was silenced as, with a single thrust, her captors pushed her through the door. I struggled in Angelica's arms, then pulled free.

For a final instant I glimpsed Magda Kurtz. She was on the other side of the door now, and she staggered as though blinded, arms flailing, before falling to the ground. Grey dust puffed up around her knees. I heard pebbles rattling against the wooden portal, wind buffeting the wall behind us. The air pouring from the doorway was so cold my teeth chattered. The smell of gasoline choked me. I could no longer feel Angelica's hands clasping mine. I could no longer see anything, except what lay beyond the door.

Above Magda Kurtz hovered an immense black shape. Its dangling limbs moved slowly up and down, its huge witless eyes were fixed on what lay beneath it. For perhaps a minute it hung there, wings beating in silent rhythm. Then without warning it dropped to the ground. A cloud of glittering dust rose as it extended one long, jointed leg like the metal shank of a tripod.

In its shadow crouched Magda Kurtz. She looked impossibly small, a doll-woman or the spindly figure from a cave painting. She drew her arm up to shield her face and turned to look back at the doorway. But I could tell by her blank expression and gaping mouth, by the way her head weaved back and forth, that she could no longer see the door or what lay beyond it, that our world had closed upon her forever. The last thing I heard was her scream, a rising wail sliced off as the door slammed shut.

"Jesus fucking Christ!"

Before Angelica could grab me I was gone, stumbling out into the main passage. From behind me came shouts; then Angelica's desperate voice.

"Sweeney, no!—the stairs—!"

She pointed and I sprinted down the hall to where that horrible back stairway yawned. Behind me footsteps clattered like hooves; I heard Professor Warnick's deceptively calm voice echoing through the darkness.

"*Kids, it's some students, that's all—*"

Then Angelica's scream.

"No!—let go of me—*Swee-nee*!—"

I whirled. Francis Connelly had her by the wrist. He twisted it as he pulled her toward him and Balthazar watched impassively.

"Let *go*, you bastard, let me *go*—"

I could hear Angelica panting, could see the dark welts where he gripped her cruelly. An arm's length from them, Professor Warnick crouched against the wall like a goblin fearing sunlight. And then Francis began to drag Angelica toward the alcove where they had taken Magda Kurtz.

"NO!" Angelica shouted, scratching at his face.

"God *damn* it, you stupid—"

Francis's voice broke off as I darted toward him. I grabbed Angelica, then, with all my strength, kicked him in the shin. A satisfying instant when I felt my boot's worn metal toe smash into bone. With an anguished howl Francis collapsed onto the rug.

"Oh dear," murmured Balthazar Warnick.

"Come on!" I gasped, and pulled the half-sobbing Angelica after me.

Around us all was a blur of scarlet and black and gold. I thought I heard voices, the muted sound of vast wings. Then we were at the end of the corridor. Below us the staircase unfurled. From behind us came the rattle of bone, a shrieking wind rank with the smell of gasoline and burning leaves. I couldn't think, couldn't move . . .

"Sweeney, *go*!"

Angelica shoved me. I grabbed the railing and lunged down, two and three and five steps at a time. When I saw the floor only a few feet below I clambered over the banister and jumped. Then I bolted, toward a screen door gaping open onto the night. Beyond it lay the comforting yellow glow of the campus crimelights, a few half-shadowed figures gathered atop the Mound. When I reached the door I slammed my fists against the screen and, gasping, looked around for my friend.

"Angelica?"

She stood at the foot of the stairs, her hair wild, her breast heaving as she steadied herself against the rail. Her dress was torn, so that I could see her skin dead white against black lace and satin. In one hand she brandished a high-heeled shoe like a club. She was staring up to where the others gazed down: Francis, white-faced with rage; Professor Warnick, tight-lipped, his gaze steady as he stared back at her disheveled hair and blazing green eyes. She looked like a wolf brought to bay, like a maenad unrepentant on the mountaintop. No longer frightened but nearly incandescent with rage: if you held a match to her she would burst into flame.

"Angelica," I whispered.

Around her neck the silver crescent was glowing. Not with any reflected light but with a hard cold brilliance, brighter than any star I had ever seen, so bright that I had to shield my eyes. As I stared Angelica's hand crept to her throat, until it touched the edge of the pendant. Light streamed around her fingers in spectral rays, blue and white and silver. Her expression changed from fury to wonder as Professor Warnick's voice rang out, clear and bitter as gin.

"She has the lunula."

"The lunula?" shouted Francis. "How did *she*—"

With a cry Angelica turned and fled. An instant later she flung herself at me and together we stumbled outside. Professor Warnick's soft voice drifted down behind us.

"It's too late, Francis."

I looked back to see the two men trapped in the banister's curve as in an embrace. Francis looked sick with fury, but Professor Warnick's expression was subdued, almost tranquil—except for his eyes, which were the deep burning blue of the winter sky showing through a storm. A hungry, almost expectant, expression, but also somewhat dazed, like a fierce well-fed dog that has had its supper snatched away.

"Swee-ney!"

Angelica's nails dug into my arm. With a very slight, ironic smile, Balthazar Warnick waggled his finger at me scoldingly. Then I lost sight of him. Angelica and I were running, running down the hillside, stones flying up around us and branches slashing at our cheeks. There was the sound of distant traffic and sulfurous light everywhere, light and drunken laughter and people crying out as we raced like mad things away from Garvey House.

CHAPTER 8

Twilight at the Orphic Lodge

I slept with Angelica that night. Lying in her bed with my arms tight around her, not saying anything, hardly even moving except when a bolt of fear would tear her from some feverish half dream. Then I would gently stroke her hair, and let my tongue linger upon the sweet-scented arch of her neck. Once I felt the curved amulet that lay there against her skin, its smooth curve icy beneath my lips, and cried out softly as its keen edge bit into me. At last I must have dozed off. Much later I woke to Angelica's muttering in her sleep. Nonsense words, or perhaps not, perhaps only something I could not understand. I kissed her, my hands cradling her face. Her pale eyes opened, widening in fear, then grew soft as the mumbled words became my name.

Near dawn I woke again, to find that she had slipped from my arms. On the other side of the narrow bed she sat with her back to me, her tangled hair massed about her shoulders. Violet light from the room's high arched window made her look like a woman made of amethyst. In the night sky hung the new moon, its crescent distorted by the window's greenish panes so that it appeared to be a globe floating in deep water, one of those bubbles of rainbow-colored glass escaped from a fishing boat a thousand miles away and tossed about like a stray thought by the waves. Angelica had a globe like that on her desk, alongside an erubescent sea urchin twice the size of my fist and a small wooden *garuda* with a lizard's crest and baleful onyx eyes. Her room's guardians, she told me, to keep her safe from demons.

But in that room there was another moon, too, a slivered crescent nestled in Angelica's throat, rising and falling as she breathed, lost on another sea. She sat and stared up at the sky, arms extended before her with her hands curled upward, the fingers opening as though to receive some benison. When the sky grew light she turned to me, not smiling, not saying anything at all, her hair falling across her shoulders in a dark stream, and drew me to her. Afterward I slept again, fitfully as before, and dreamed of angels with the wings of locusts, of hail and hammered silver blades clashing against stone in the night.

It was almost evening when I woke, *really* woke, with a hangover and raging headache and the ominous feeling of having slept with someone when I was too drunk to know better.

"Wait! Don't move, I want to take a picture: you can be this year's AA poster girl."

I groaned and sat up, blinking, and saw Annie Harmon perched on a chair. She was barefoot, still wearing the same plaid flannel shirt and fatigues. She smiled at my rueful expression, but her brown eyes were humorless. She looked pale and tired, and when I glanced over at her bed I saw it was neatly made with a worn log cabin quilt and Snoopy pillow.

"I slept at the library," she said in her husky voice. "I didn't want to *intrude*—"

I groaned. "Oh, shit, Annie, it wasn't like that—"

"Oh no?" Her eyes narrowed. " Well, then, please tell me what it *was* like."

"Annie. Give me a break." I ran my hands through my hair, grimacing. I was still wearing my rank T-shirt; my hands smelled faintly of sandalwood. "Where's Angelica?"

"At class. You didn't think she was going to wait for *you*, did you? She never misses a beat, our girl. You got to get up pretty early in the morning to fly with the angels. Pretty fucking early." She glowered and slapped the edge of her chair.

I sighed. "Look, I didn't mean to cause some kind of thing with your girlfriend. I didn't even know she *was* your girlfriend—"

"*And*, speaking of early, it is now five o'clock. *P.M.* And Angelica, just in case you're wondering, is meeting Oliver Wilde Crawford for dinner."

"Oliver?" I felt as though I had been poisoned. Of course! The two of them had just taken off, leaving me here to deal with the murderously jealous lesbian roommate. I rubbed my throbbing forehead. "Ah, come on, Annie! It was a mistake, all right? Forget about it. Where're my boots?"

It wasn't until I stood, my bare feet smacking against the chilly floor, that everything *else* about the previous night rushed back to me.

"Oh, man."

Annie tilted her head. "Feeling a wee bit foolish, are we—"

"Shut up, Annie, just shut up." My voice was shaking; I thought I might throw up. I looked beneath the bed, saw my jeans and cowboy boots atop the torn remnants of Angelica's dress. I grabbed my things and pulled them on hurriedly, hoping Annie couldn't see how sick I felt, then headed for the door.

"Sweeney. Wait."

I hesitated and looked back.

"Sit down," she said in a softer voice, and patted the neat coverlet on her bed. "We have to talk."

"Look, Annie—if this is about you and Angelica, I'm, uh, *really* not—"

"Will you just close the door and *listen* to me?"

I put down the urge to storm into the hall. Instead I shut the door and leaned sullenly against Angelica's desk. "I'm sorry, okay? I was drunk, and there was all this—well, this *crazy* shit—"

Annie crossed to the door, drew the bolt, and pulled the chain tight. "I know," she said. "I mean I know about the crazy shit. That's what I want to talk to you about, Sweeney. Listen—

"Angelica told me about what happened last night—don't look at me like that, I'm her roommate, okay? *You* were passed out—"

"I was *exhausted*—"

Annie rolled her eyes. "Well, when I came back this morning you were making like the living dead over there, and Angie had to talk to someone. So she told me."

"What did she tell you?" I asked guardedly.

"About that necklace. And Magda Kurtz—"

Her face was so pale that her freckles stood out like soot. "Sweeney, you guys are in big trouble. I told Angelica, but she never listens to me. I told her she oughta ditch that thing and get the hell out of Dodge—"

"Did she? Did she give it back?"

"Give it back? To who? No, Angelica didn't give it back. She's never gonna take it *off*. She's wearing it right now. Like a fucking sign around her neck—"

"Shut up, Annie." I sank to the floor with my head in my hands. I felt sick and angry and embarrassed, and totally, totally screwed up. What was I *doing*, sleeping with someone I hardly knew, sleeping with a *girl* I hardly knew; and at the same time mooning over some guy I'd just met the day before? "Please, shut up."

"No! Listen to me, Sweeney—I don't know what you think is going on, but you're way out of your league here. So's Angelica, and your friend Oliver—"

"What are you *talking* about?"

"I'm talking about all *this*—"

She stalked to the window and gestured furiously toward the Shrine, the neat white paths winding along the Strand. "And if you really don't know what's going on, you better start learning. *Fast*—"

She paced over to her desk and picked up a folded newspaper, stared broodingly at it before handing it to me. "Here."

It was that afternoon's *Washington Star*, opened to the Metro section. I glanced at it and frowned: the usual accounts of petty theft, local politics, urban renaissance, and decay. But then Annie jammed a finger at a small item on the bottom of the page.

"Check it out," she said, and I began to read.

6 KILLED WHEN PLANE CRASHES
IN W. VA. MOUNTAINS

A chartered Beechcraft 640 bound for Philadelphia crashed in the West Virginia wilderness today, killing all on board. Two crew

> members and four passengers died when the aircraft plowed into a mountainside in dense fog. Bad weather hampered rescue efforts until early this morning. Among the dead was renowned archaeologist Magda Whitehead Kurtz, who had been returning from a summer appointment at the University of the Archangels and Saint John the Divine. In an official statement, FAA officials said that . . .

I read the story again, and again. At last I folded it back up and returned it to Annie.

"I don't understand." I gazed up at Angelica's desk, the bulging red eyes of her little carven *garuda*. "How did Magda Kurtz get away?"

Annie slapped my arm with the newspaper. "You idiot! She *didn't*. Don't you get it? It's a setup—all those other people died, just so there'd be an alibi for why Magda Kurtz is missing!"

"No."

"*Yes*! Sweeney, you have have to listen to me—I know about this stuff, *I've seen it all before*."

I said nothing, just stared at the desk. Angelica's sea urchin, Angelica's neat stack of marbleized stationery. A little Art Nouveau perfume flask, its blue crystal stopper shaped like a dolphin. Angelica's scent. Angelica and Oliver . . .

". . . told her when we met that . . ."

My head pounded, there was a roaring in my ears that nearly drowned out Annie's voice.

". . . *Benandanti*, the whole thing all over again, your scholars and people like Oliver—*that's* who killed Lisa."

"Lisa?" Groggily I got to my feet. "Who's Lisa? I thought we were talking about Magda Kurtz—"

Annie smacked me again with the newspaper. "My *cousin*. Aren't you listening?"

"Ouch! Well, yeah, but—" I rubbed my arm and wished I didn't feel like throwing up. "Your *cousin?* Jeez, Annie, this is all a little too weird for me . . ."

"No shit, Sherlock! But that's what happens when you crash the wrong party." She strode back to her own desk and pulled open a drawer. I had a glimpse of papers rolled up with rubber bands, sheet music, some old magazines. Then, very carefully, she withdrew from the mess of pages a manila envelope and gave it to me.

"Okay, look at this—be careful, it's starting to fall apart."

I peered warily into the envelope and pulled out a wadded newspaper clipping. When I pried it open flecks of yellowed paper spilled down the front of my T-shirt.

CENTRAL PLAINS ADVOCATE

Weekly News from the Five Towns

I saw a small, badly reproduced yearbook photo of a misty-eyed girl smiling into the distance, her long straight hair parted in the middle and barely brushing her shoulders. Around her neck glinted a tiny cross on a chain.

"Lisa Harmon," said Annie bitterly. "Lisa Nobody, now. My cousin."

"Your cousin."

She nodded, and carefully I smoothed out the page.

COLLEGE STUDENT A SUICIDE
University Denies Involvement with Satanists, Blames Drugs

Surprise, Nebraska April 11—19-year-old Lisa Marie Harmon, home from college on spring break, was found dead in her parents' house here Friday evening after apparently taking a deadly overdose of sleeping pills. Grief-stricken relatives and friends expressed shock, stating that the popular student had never been involved with drugs and had "every reason to live."

Harmon was a sophomore at the University of the Archangels and Saint John the Divine in Washington, D.C., where she was studying Comparative Religion and Music Therapy. Parents and guidance counselors at Raymond Jollie High School remembered a girl who was treasurer of the SERVE Club and played guitar at folk masses at Our Lady of Good Hope.

But a high school friend of Harmon's, who refused to be identified, alleged that at college the former A-student had gotten involved with "some kind of coven." University officials, however, denied all charges of occult activity at the school. A fellow student there recalled another girl, one who had taken to dabbling in narcotics and who over the course of several months had repeatedly sought help from the school's counseling program.

This afternoon, relatives from across the county gathered to mourn and . . .

I stared at the girl in the yearbook photo, then glanced at Annie. There was the same determined chin and dark eyes, though the pixie smile was conspicuously absent from Annie's face.

"I'm sorry, Annie. When did it—"

"Two years ago."

I continued to stare stupidly at the page. Finally Annie took it back. I coughed and turned to look out the window. Beneath a cloudless twilit sky the Shrine's dome glowed blue as the heart of a flame, and the golden stars painted upon it seemed to flicker and burn. At the foot of one of its narrow stairways a boy and a girl sat with their arms around each other and stared up at the gleaming monolith. A terrible longing swept over me: to be that girl; to have Oliver be that boy; to have that huge and lovely presence overseeing my life . . .

Behind me a drawer slammed shut, and Annie thumped onto her bed. I sighed and left the window to join her, moving her Snoopy pillow out of the way.

"Really, Annie. I'm sorry about your cousin." I patted her back awkwardly, wondering when Angelica would return, and if Oliver would be with her. "It—it must have been horrible for you."

She drew her knees up to her chin. "It's a fucking *lie*, is what it is. Lisa didn't kill herself. She was a saint, she would *never* kill herself. And she would never take *any* kind of drugs. You know what they found in her room when she died?"

I shook my head.

"Dilaudid. You know what that is? No? Well, it sure isn't *sleeping pills*—

"Dilaudid is like, synthetic heroin. Now you tell me how an altar girl in Nebraska gets her hands on that. The local police had never even *seen* it before—they had to bring in someone from the hospital in Lincoln to identify it. And Lisa was doing this stuff?" Her voice rose incredulously. "No way."

"But then—"

But then why are you telling me this? I thought. Instead I leaned back on her pillow and asked, "But then how did it happen? How did she die?"

"They killed her. *Them*. Professor Warnick and his pals."

I groaned. "Oh, come on—"

"They did. They planted it there. In the house, in her room. I don't know how they got that shit into her, but they did." Her brown eyes had gone quite wild. "Look, I know this sounds crazy, Sweeney, but it's *true*. With Lisa it was just like with you. She made these friends, Molyneux scholars, they'd been chosen for that secret society of theirs. Then she and Frank started sleeping together and I guess he must have violated some vow of silence or something, because somebody decided she got too close. She told me about it when she was home at Christmas. All this weird shit . . ."

"What kind of weird shit?"

"Oh, man, things you wouldn't believe! Visions and witchcraft, all this stuff about the Second Coming—"

"The Second Coming?"

"*You* know," Annie said impatiently. "Like that poem. Weird things being reborn—"

"I know what it is! But—you really think Professor Warnick—"

"They got rid of Magda Kurtz, didn't they? And Warnick didn't do it alone. He had the *Benandanti*." When I said nothing, she added disdainfully, "The Good Walkers. Those Who Do Well."

I thought of Angelica's casual mention of them upstairs at Garvey House, and Baby Joe— "*Benandanti. Brujos. The Golden Ones. . .*"

What are the Molyneux scholars?

They're magicians.

I took in Annie's grim look, and decided that this was not one of those times when pretending I knew about something would do me any good. "Okay. *Benandanti*. So what's that?"

"I'm not sure. But I bet Oliver would be able to tell you."

"Oliver?"

"Listen, Sweeney, I know what all this sounds like. But you saw yourself—well, whatever it was that you and Angelica saw last night. It was real, right?"

I nodded reluctantly.

"Well, you should have seen what I had to go through to get accepted here. It was like I was applying to the CIA or something. They know I'm related to Lisa, it wasn't like it would be hard to find that out. And they didn't want me here. For all I know they've got some kind of file on me or something . . ."

"But then why'd you come here? I mean, isn't it dangerous? And why'd they let you in?"

She knotted her hands in her lap. "I don't know why they let me in. Probably they need a few normal people to round out the campus profile. You know, so it's not all people like Angie and Oliver. But Lisa was my cousin; she was my best friend. And they murdered her and got away with it. And I don't want that to happen to Angelica. Or you."

I swallowed nervously. "So what *do* we do?"

"I don't know." Elbows on her knees, chin in hand, she looked more like a bemused kid than ever. "I guess we stay in touch." She glanced at me sideways and, for the first time, gave me a crooked grin. "I guess we're all kinda stuck together now, huh?"

I stood and walked to the window. For a last long moment I stared down at the Strand, trying to find Oliver among the tiny figures wandering across the darkening lawns. Finally, "I guess we are," I said, and left.

I went back to my room and locked myself inside, pushed a chair against the door, and bolted the window shut. Then I prised the wooden curtain rod from the closet and leaned it against my bed, beside every hardcover textbook I could find and my electric typewriter in its heavy melamite case. It crossed my mind that people who slipped Dilaudid to nosy college students and fed archaeologists to gigantic insects might not be too put off by someone beaning them with the third edition of the *Prolegomena to the Study of Greek Religion*, but I didn't care. I fell asleep with all the lights on, and slept for thirteen hours.

Next morning I found Angelica at the dining hall. I sat beside her and she said nothing, absolutely *nothing*, about what had happened. I might have dreamed it all—everything except for sleeping with her. Angelica's knowing smile told me that, at least, had been real. Her smile and the way she said good-bye, kissing me on the cheek and letting her hand surreptitiously brush against my breast for just a moment. Her fingers stroked my nipple until it hardened beneath my shirt, and then she drew away.

"*Ciao*, Sweeney. See you at dinner?"

I stammered some reply and nodded. As I watched her leave I noted that she still wore the moon-shaped necklace Magda Kurtz had given her, and like a talisman beneath her arm carried a copy of Magda Kurtz's book.

And so began my new life. My *real* life, I thought then. Meeting Angelica and Oliver for breakfast at seven-thirty, Annie following her roommate like a grim conscience in cutoff fatigues and worn flannel shirts. Me drinking too much coffee in a feeble effort to kill what had become a near-constant hangover. Angelica picking fastidiously at slices of cantaloupe and grapefruit. Annie wolfing down petrified scrambled eggs with ketchup and ersatz home fries, while Oliver sat across from the three of us, kicking at the table legs, his hands never still as he swept back his hair and scribbled his odd ballpoint sketches on paper napkins.

"Very nice," Annie would remark thoughtfully, peering at the pile of napkins fluttering in front of him. "That looks just like me. Except for the antennae, of course."

Then she'd gather her books, give Angelica a soulful look, and leave. Annie never hung around after breakfast. She had an eight o'clock Music Composition class, and I sometimes thought the only reason she joined us was to keep an eye on Angelica.

Though Angelica seemed infinitely able to take care of herself. I knew she wore that crescent-shaped necklace everywhere, although she was careful to keep it hidden. A few days after the reception at Garvey House, I dropped by her room and found her reading by the light of a small banker's lamp with a green glass shade. On one knee she balanced a steaming mug of tea. The air smelled warmly of vanilla and chamomile.

"Sweeney!" Angelica looked up, smiling. "We missed you at lunch today."

At her throat nestled the lunula, its bright lines softened to grey in the dim light. *Sans* makeup, with her robe and glasses and white china mug, she looked solemn and a little silly, like a diva costumed to play the student in an operetta. Silly, but still beautiful enough to make my heart start rattling around my chest like a stone.

"Where's Annie?"

"Library," replied Angelica without glancing up again. She was painstakingly copying something into a notebook.

"What're you doing?"

"Stuff."

I made a face. As usual, she was poring over stacks of old books and anthropological journals from the Colum Library. She flashed me an earnest look. "This is fascinating, Sweeney. Really—you should check it out."

I leaned over to pick up a volume slightly smaller than my hand, bound in calfskin faded to the color of old ivory.

Lucian Samosata: De Dea Syria

One of the texts listed in the handout that Balthazar Warnick had given us the first day of class, along with *The Golden Ass* and "The Bacchae" and "The Hymn to Demeter"—

> *DE SEA SYRIA/THE SYRIAN GODDESS: Evocative contemporaneous account of the ancient rites associated with the worship of Aphrodite/Astarte and the cult of Adonis in Phoenicia . . .*

Gingerly I turned the pages. They seemed to be printed in Latin. When I reached the end of the book, a slip of loose-leaf fluttered out, covered front and back with Angelica's fine cursive hand. I caught it and held it up to the light.

> *"There is another great sanctuary in Phoenicia, which the Sidonians possess,"*

I read.

> *According to them it belongs to Astarte, but I think that Astarte is Selene. One of the priests, however, told me that it is a sanctuary of Europa . . . Zeus desired her since she was beautiful, he assumed the form of a bull, seized her, and carried the girl off with him to Crete . . .*

I turned over the scrap of paper.

> *There is another form of sacrifice here. After putting a garland on the sacrificial animals, they hurl them down alive from the gateway and the animals die from the fall. Some even throw their children off the place, but not in the same manner as the animals . . .*

"Gee, Angelica, that's really nice."

"Be careful!" Angelica picked up the volume, cradling it as though it had been a puppy. "It's really old, and it doesn't belong to me."

"You can read Latin?" I asked sarcastically.

"Yes, Sweeney, I can read Latin. And Italian, and French." She settled back on the bed. "Why haven't you been to Warnick's class all week?"

I felt like shouting, *You know damn well why I haven't been to class*! Instead I just shrugged. "Listen, me and Oliver and Baby Joe are going down to the Cellar Door to see Patti Smith. You want to come?"

"I can't. Professor Warnick lent me his own copy of that—"

She inclined her head toward the small leather-bound book. "—and I promised I'd give it back after class tomorrow."

"Angelica! *What* are you—"

"*Sweeney*. Please."

"Fine. Forget it." I waited to see if she'd say anything else, if she'd bother looking up; but I had been dismissed. "Well, I guess I'll see you later."

She flipped through the pages of a monograph and nodded absently. "Tell Oliver to drop by after the show."

"Sure. Whatever."

I stalked outside, angry and embarrassed. To be commanded to carry a message to Oliver, as though I was nothing but her go-between! Still, I gave him the message. I'd do anything for Oliver, and almost anything for Angelica.

Each morning at a few minutes before nine, Oliver and I would escort her to Magic, Witchcraft and Religion. We'd walk to the foot of the Mound and watch Angelica stride up its path alone, her long legs flashing between the gauzy folds of a flowered skirt. Then we would turn away, and the real business of the day would begin.

We would go to the Shrine to drink more coffee and then wander around the gaudy chapels, occasionally pilfering the collection boxes for bus change. Sometime before noon we'd catch an 80 bus downtown. We'd get off at Dupont Circle, find a bench, and watch the boy hustlers at work. Oliver knew a lot of them from the bars; they'd wander over to bum cigarettes and tell us where to find the party that night, before sauntering off to lean on the hoods of big cars with diplomatic license tags and dark windows. As the afternoon wore on we'd head over to Meridian Hill Park. There Oliver would score marijuana or some very dubious acid from one of the starved-looking rastas—*blottah barrels hemp two bucks too bucks*—and then it would be time to head back to the Divine and figure out our evening agenda.

I would *never* have dared to do any of this on my own. But with Oliver I felt invulnerable. His beauty, his air of *noblesse décharge*, even his very obvious lack of judgment, seemed to protect us from the stunningly real dangers of the city. He'd lope through the city's worst—and best—neighborhoods, his long hair streaming behind him, wearing his standard uniform of white button-down shirt and faded chinos and black wing tips with no socks, mad blue eyes agleam, arms waving as he told me some hair-raising story. And somehow we never got mugged, or arrested, or even lost. This despite the fact that much of the time Oliver was flying high and loose and pretty as a grinning dragon kite, tripping on acid or mushrooms or god knows what.

Though the truth was, I could never really tell if he was stoned or sober. With Oliver everything seemed strange. I think that in some bizarre way he could *make* strange things appear. A bald eagle landing in Lafayette Park to prey on feeding pigeons; a red fox skulking outside the entrance to a K Street law firm. Blind nuns, transsexual punks. An armless legless man on a skateboard who sang the Irish national anthem in a bone-freezing tenor, and then rolled a cigarette with his tongue and greeted us by name. It got so that if something peculiar *didn't* happen on one of our outings, I'd feel disappointed and a little wary.

Nights we would take a Yellow Cab to Southeast and go dancing inside a warehouse where I was the only girl among hundreds, maybe thousands, of boys and men. When everyone spilled back outside at dawn, the same Yellow Cab would be waiting for us on the narrow dark street beneath the dusty trees of heaven. Cab Number 393, with its driver Handsome Brown, a former prizefighter who by that hour was as drunk as we were.

"Where to, children?" he'd rumble, his face filling the rearview mirror. Usually we'd go back to the Divine, to stagger off to bed. But some mornings Oliver would have him drive us to the Tidal Basin to watch the sun rise, or to some all-night place where we could sober up over bad coffee and greasy sausage sandwiches.

Some of these places weren't safe, according to Handsome Brown; but "I'll take care of things, my man." And leaning over with one hand on the wheel, he'd pop open his glove compartment, to show us the gun in there—to show me, actually, Oliver usually choosing these cab rides to nap—and occasionally remove it and brandish it as he drove.

Through it all Oliver walked with me like my demon familiar. I got a weird buzz from going with him to the discos, where no one seemed to know I was a girl. Oliver usually seemed happy enough to forget. He knew I was in love with him. I told him, many times, when I was sloppy drunk, but he only grinned that crooked canine grin and threw his arm around me.

"Oh Sweeney. Why ask for the moon when we have the bars?" And he'd drag me to another club.

Angelica was in love with him too, of course. I knew that from the beginning. It seemed that there could be no way they wouldn't end up together. Sometimes after dinner the two of them would rise from the dining hall table and go off alone. Or else Oliver and I might return from our evening's debauch and he would walk me to my door, then continue, singing softly to himself, up the stairs to Angelica's room. I would throw myself on my bed, feverish with jealousy and yearning and something else, something worse: the fear of having been befriended by mistake, of being found out as an impostor. I tried to console myself by thinking that, even if Angelica slept with Oliver, *I* understood him.

But now I know better. No one understood Oliver although Annie, perhaps, came closest.

"Forget him. He's a nutjob," she pronounced one night in a vain effort to comfort me. "Really, Sweeney. Haven't you ever read *Brideshead Revisited*?"

I sniffed. "No."

"Well, it turns out *very badly* for boys like Oliver."

I didn't care. Hanging out with Oliver was like being attached to some dense yet glittering, rapidly spinning object. By virtue of his speed and beauty he attracted all sorts of things—middle-aged professors, exotic cigarettes, postcards from Tunisia, psychotropic drugs—and now by association many of those things were becoming attached to *me*, chief among them Angelica di Rienzi and Oliver's habit of increasingly sporadic class attendance and casual narcotics use.

So the semester passed. October's acid glory burned into November ash; and one day the Xeroxed flyers appeared across the campus.

AUTUMN RETREAT

AT

AGASTRONGA RIVER ORPHIC LODGE

Friday, Saturday, return Sunday night

For Details See Balthazar Warnick, Provost, Thaddeus College

At dawn I woke to someone calling my name from outside my window. No angels, no creatures from the other side of the Door; only Oliver. His long hair was dirty and when I let him in the front door I could tell he hadn't showered since we'd last met: he had a not-unpleasant musty smell of Tide-scented clothes, cigarette smoke, and boyish sweat.

"Oliver," I croaked as I let him in.

Outside dew sparkled on the grass. The Divine's domed and turreted buildings and dusty oaks seemed to float untethered above us, like the city's dream of itself.

"Oliver," I repeated, rubbing my eyes. "You're up so early."

"Didn't go to sleep." He bounced past me into the dorm, squeezing my shoulder and grinning. "Went back and had a little taste from Wild Bill's terrarium." I shuddered and pulled the door closed after him.

In the hall he paused to read one of Balthazar Warnick's flyers. "Well!" he said cheerfully, "It's the day after tomorrow, so I guess we still have time to pack."

I yawned. "Pack?"

Oliver nodded. Carefully he detached the flyer, rolling it into a little cylinder and sticking it in a pocket. "There's only a limited amount of space for these things, we should sign up now." He turned and began walking back to the front door.

"Oliver, it's 5:00 A.M.! And the retreat's not till Friday—"

He stopped and regarded me thoughtfully. I had on another pair of ripped jeans, but I hadn't washed off my makeup, and I was wearing the same T-shirt I'd had on for three days now. "Then perhaps you'll have time to do your laundry," he said mildly, and grabbed my arm. "*Come* on—"

The nightmarish thought of a weekend under Professor Warnick's tutelage was eased by the notion that I might finally have some time alone, really alone, with Oliver. We found a sign-up sheet in the empty foyer of Thaddeus College, and he was right—only a few spaces were left, and my heart jumped to see that Angelica's name was not there. But after fastidiously writing his name and mine in spidery letters, Oliver added *Angelica de Rienzi* to one of the remaining lines.

"Wait," I said, and wrote *Anne Harmon*. "There—"

Two days later, Annie and Angelica and I were in the parking lot of Thaddeus College. I was wearing one of Oliver's shirts, too big for me and infused with the musty marjiuana scent of his room. Annie had on a red flannel shirt and beat-up tweed jacket that Baby Joe had given her. She was so small and compact that her guitar case looked incongruously large, like a cello carried by an earnest mouse. Angelica wore yet another gauzy flowered dress under a light woolen cape, her hair tied back with a green velvet ribbon.

"*A weekend in the country . . .*" she sang. Annie rolled her eyes.

A small crowd milled outside Thaddeus College. Beside a battered Volvo wagon Balthazar Warnick stood and read aloud from a list of names. I slunk behind Angelica and Annie and did my best to avoid catching his eye. Angelica checked us in and we waited for instructions. I dropped my knapsack and peered into the Volvo. Mounds of boxes and coolers rose from its back compartment, and I was relieved to see a number of gallon jugs of red wine. Several other vehicles arrived and were poised for flight, motors running, drivers cranking up tape players and radios. I saw Baby Joe and his friend Hasel Bright leaning on Hasel's ancient Volkswagen bug. When they saw us, Hasel saluted Angelica with a Jack Daniels bottle.

"Avanti, Angelica! I want you to have my love child—"

Angelica smiled indulgently and blew him a kiss. People began tossing last bits of luggage into trunks and clambering into cars. The caravan was ready to go, but there was still no sign of Oliver. Angelica walked over to Balthazar Warnick, Annie and I trailing reluctantly behind her.

"Professor Warnick, someone else is coming," said Angelica. "Oliver Crawford—"

Balthazar Warnick lifted his head to regard her coolly.

"Mr. Crawford seems to be carrying on a family tradition of holding everyone up," he began, when Oliver came loping across the parking lot.

"Oliver!" cried Angelica. "We almost left without you!"

Oliver shoved his hands into his pockets. "Oh surely not." He bowed, then draped his arm over Angelica's shoulder. "Here I am."

"All right. That's everyone, then—" Professor Warnick folded his list and stuck it into his jacket. "Mr. Crawford, perhaps you would give me the great honor of riding with me—I want to hear how your brothers are doing, and how you have been spending your time away from my class—"

Oliver smoothed his hair back and tugged at his shirt collar.

"Yes, Professor," he said, bowing. He was so loose-limbed, his pupils so dilated, that he looked like an Oliver rag doll with black-button eyes. "I'll give a—uh—full report."

"Come on, then." Professor Warnick opened the front door of the Volvo and shooed Oliver inside. "You too, my dear—" He gestured for Angelica to follow.

"Don't forget our bags!" Angelica called to Annie. I watched in chagrined disbelief as Oliver kissed her cheek.

Annie nodded in disgust. "Yes, Mistress! Igor obeys—" She turned to me and cocked a thumb at Angelica's bags. "Mind giving me a hand?"

I sighed. "Yeah, sure." With a sick feeling I watched Balthazar Warnick climb into the car with Oliver and Angelica. Then I hefted one of Angelica's leather suitcases, grunting.

"Jeez, what's *in* here? The True Cross?"

"Books on witchcraft," said Annie, "and the entire fall line of Mary Quant makeup."

I stared at the bag despairingly, "Why are we *doing* this, Annie? I mean, there's Warnick, and—"

Annie actually went white. "Why are we *doing* this? We are doing this because for some *insane* reason you and Oliver *signed us up*—"

"I signed *me* up! I wanted to be *alone* with him for once, without—"

"Last train for Debarksville, girls," someone shouted.

"Forget it," fumed Annie. "Let's go."

We found two empty seats in the back of a Dodge Dart piloted by a dour young seminarian. I slumped in my seat and stared disconsolately out to where Oliver and Angelica sat laughing in the front of the lead car. Behind them Hasel's VW rocked dangerously back and forth. Then there was a break in the traffic, and the two cars careened out of sight in a cloud of exhaust and dust.

"Hey, get over it, Sweeney, okay?" Annie looked at me and shook her head. "I've been wanting to ask you—did something really *special* happen the first time you put on that shirt? Or are you just waiting for Oliver to notice you've been wearing his clothes for three days?"

"Oliver and I are just friends," I said loftily.

"Hey, don't think I'm, like, *jealous*. I don't *like* icky boys. Although I personally think your friend Oliver may be a member of the He-Man Women-Haters Club. *Uno amigo de Dorothy*, if you take my meaning."

She dropped her voice. "I tell you, Sweeney, you oughta be selling time-shares in that boy. I mean if *you're* not sleeping with him. 'Cause I know that Angelica—"

I turned to her, furious, but Annie backed off. "Ex-cu-use me!"

We sat in silence as the car inched through rush hour traffic. Outside, all the sultry glamour of the city had vanished. The Washington Monument looked smudged and worn against the dirty white sky, the distant shape of the Jefferson Memorial like a great cracked egg hidden among dusty trees. Above Haines Point an endless line of aircraft roared into National Airport. Between the noise and exhaust fumes, the Lysol stench of Brother John's car deodorizer and all the beer I'd drunk, I felt distinctly queasy.

"You know where we're going, don't you?"

Annie nudged me, but I refused to look at her. "You know what this is, right?" she persisted. "This Orphic Lodge?"

I waited a long moment before shaking my head. "No."

"It's their headquarters. Summer camp for your boy Balthazar and all the rest of them. Home base. Ground Zero. Your retreat business is a trap, Sweeney—"

Her words were like a window slamming shut behind me.

"—a fucking trap, and we've walked right into it."

If the retreat house *was* a trap, it was a very nice one.

It took us nearly three hours to get there. I dozed, an achy hung-over nap that brought little in the way of real repose and gave me uneasy dreams of pursuit and flight. When I woke it was just past nightfall. Outside all was dim and softly moving, painted in shades of green and black and violet. The little car wheezed and bucked as it made one hairpin turn after another, climbing higher and higher. Suddenly we made a sharp turn, veering onto an even narrower road. The car jounced over stones and fallen branches, abruptly came out into a wide space where the trees fell back and the sky opened above us, black and studded with stars.

"Well, we're here," said Brother John, and we piled out.

The Orphic Lodge was the sort of place where you spend one enchanted August as a child, and devote all of your adult life to finding again. A sprawling Craftsman-style mansion, its pillared verandas and balconies and gabled windows thrusting out in bewildering profusion. When we stepped onto the front porch the wooden flooring boomed and creaked beneath our feet, as though we were walking on ice. Upside-down Adirondack chairs and wicker sofas were pushed against the walls. There was an air of genteel desolation about it all—the grey limbs of an espaliered pear tree; drifts of dead leaves everywhere; the echoing of ghostly voices from upstairs rooms where windows had been flung open to the chill night air.

But inside, the Lodge looked more like the first day of vacation. Students running up and down steps, back and forth between cars and the kitchen, carrying duffel bags and knapsacks and boom boxes, cartons and bags of food, paper towels, beer, wine. A fat, friendly-looking grey cat sat on a windowsill and regarded us all with mild yellow eyes. On a wider windowsill in the main foyer Balthazar Warnick did the same, though with a more feral gaze. Beside him stood a tall stern-featured woman, with black hair and very black straight eyebrows, wearing a paisley dress and old-fashioned chef's apron.

". . . said thirteen and I have made dinner for thirteen. *Gravadlaks* and *salat*, and the *gravadlaks*, the salmon, will not keep well. And those boys are spilling something on the stairs."

"Thirty, Kirsten, I said there would be *thirty*. Mr. Bright, would you please assist Mr. Malabar with the cooler?" Balthazar looked distractedly at the tall woman. "We brought spaghetti for dinner tonight, Kirsten. We *always* have spaghetti the first night of retreat. You know, lots of water boiling, many eager hands at work. A sort of icebreaker."

The housekeeper gazed suspiciously at the many eager hands now reaching for the cooler Hasel Bright had opened in the middle of the floor.

"Good night, Professor Warnick, they deserve their spaghetti," she announced. "I am going to bed."

"Our housekeeper does not approve of undergraduates drinking in the lodge." Professor Warnick frowned at Hasel, who sheepishly replaced his bottle and closed the cooler. "Let's get unpacked and get dinner going before she changes her mind and comes back to supervise the kitchen, eh Mr. Bright?"

Warnick turned to where Annie and I were standing, somewhat at a loss, by the front door. He regarded me measuredly before saying, "The girls' rooms are in the east wing on the second floor. To the right."

We straggled upstairs, yelling greetings back to the others, who'd already unpacked or were still arriving below.

"Where do you think Angelica is?" I panted. "She's got to be here; they were in the lead car with Warnick."

Annie shrugged, pausing red-faced to swing her guitar and one of Angelica's bags to the other arm. "Who knows? She and Oliver are probably settled in the honeymoon suite already."

The rooms in the east wing all seemed pretty much the same. A few simple camp-style beds lined up against the pine walls, unmatched curtains at the windows, maybe a worn rag rug on the floor. Annie stopped wearily in front of an open door.

"The view from this room is *really terrific*, Sweeney, I read about it in the promotional literature downstairs; this is like the *best room* in the whole place, okay?"

"Okay," I said, and then Angelica appeared in the dim hallway.

"Sweeney! Annie! I got a room for us—down here, the third door on the left."

"Hooray," said Annie. She dumped Angelica's stuff on the floor and took off down the hall with her guitar.

Angelica picked up her bags and smiled. "Thanks for bringing my bags, Sweeney."

"Sure." I rubbed my shoulder. "Where's Oliver?"

"Oh, he's around." She smiled, a secretive delighted smile, and started after Annie. "I helped him get settled upstairs. I think he went down to help with dinner. Okay, this is it—isn't it great?"

It actually didn't look much different from any of the other rooms—bigger, maybe, with four beds extending from the far wall, and it did have its own bathroom with shower stall and ancient rust-stained pedestal sink where Annie was already noisily washing up. But the long far wall was filled with windows, and even in the darkness I could make out the shadowed hump of the mountains and the velvety star-filled sky.

"Yeah. Yeah, really, it's nice." I dropped my knapsack on one of the beds and flopped onto it. "Yow. Nice mattresses, too."

"Mine is stuffed with corncobs," announced Annie from the bathroom. "I sure do hope Oliver's not sleeping in that other bed, Angelica."

Angelica shook her head. "No, he's not. Corn*husks*, Annie; I don't think anyone ever stuffed a mattress with corncobs. Come on, Sweeney, I told Oliver we'd help them out downstairs. We'll see you later, Annie."

Annie watched us go, nonplussed. In the hall Angelica took my hand. "God, this is so great here! Isn't this great?"

I shrugged and tried to smile. We still hadn't talked about what happened that night after the Molyneux reception, but obviously Angelica wasn't the type to discuss such things. And I was burning to hear about Oliver, and to find out what room he was staying in.

But Angelica only laughed, pausing to pull her hair back into its loose ponytail. "Oliver says from his room you can lie in bed and watch Orion progress across the western horizon."

I smiled ruefully. "Progress, huh? How does he know? He hasn't been here before—"

"No." Angelica started down the corridor. "He's never been here, but his brothers have. I guess they told him which room was the best one . . ." Her voice trailed off.

"So—I guess you guys are really like, involved, huh?"

I laughed as I said it, but I knew I sounded lame and jealous. Though probably I couldn't even have told you what, exactly, I was jealous *of*. Angelica, I suppose, but it was stupid to be jealous of Angelica—like being jealous of the Mona Lisa. And really, what could be better? My two best friends were in love with each other. Only that left *me* somewhere in between, running back and forth like a stupid yappy little dog; because I was in love with both of them.

"Oh, you know Oliver . . ." She sighed. "I can tell you one thing, though. My father would hate him."

"How come?"

We started down a wide stairway. "Oh, everything. The drugs, the partying all the time. Just the way he *is*. Okay, I think the kitchen's over there—"

We found the kitchen, large and brightly lit and filled with huge gleaming stainless steel stoves and sinks and refrigerators. Small hand-lettered signs admonished everyone to wash their hands and put things back where they'd found them. Balthazar Warnick was nowhere in sight, but Hasel Bright was bent over a sink by the wall, pumping furiously at an old-fashioned hand pump and shouting excitedly as water gushed out.

"Look at this! It's amazing—" yelled Hasel.

I peered into the deep slate sink, the water sluicing down a small hole in the middle. "Isn't there running water?"

Hasel looked at me, red-faced and grinning. "Yeah, sure there is, but isn't this *amazing*? I've been doing this for fifteen minutes, and it *never stops*!"

I laughed. "Wow. That really is great, Hasel. Maybe later you'll invent the wheel."

I crossed to where Oliver and Baby Joe and Angelica stood before one of the big gas ranges. Oliver was poking thoughtfully at an immense steaming pot with a wooden spoon. Baby Joe was smoking a cigarette, occasionally leaning over to tap his ashes into the pot. Angelica was watching Oliver, her brow furrowed.

"You want it to be just barely *al dente*," she said primly. "Do you know how to tell when it's done?"

"Yes." Oliver leaned forward on the balls of his feet and dipped his utensil into the roiling water. He backed up, shaking his head to clear the steam from his glasses, then dramatically flicked the wooden spoon and sent several long streamers of spaghetti sailing toward the ceiling. Baby Joe and Angelica ducked as a few of them sailed back down, but Oliver nodded.

"It's done when it sticks," he said. I looked up and saw the ceiling mapped with dozens of darkened threads of dried pasta, and among them several fresh and glistening strands. "And it's done."

We ate in the dining room, a big open space with raftered ceiling and chandeliers made of antlers. I counted thirty-two of us, students and grad students and Balthazar Warnick, the only genuine adult present although I assumed the housekeeper was brooding elsewhere. The room was dark and drafty. There were citronella candles in little red glasses at every table, and spongy Italian bread from the Safeway back in D.C., and gallon bottles of Gallo Burgundy. I sat at a long table with Annie and Angelica and Oliver. Behind us Baby Joe and Hasel talked and laughed loudly, watching the rest of us, but especially Angelica, as they passed around bowls of spaghetti and iceberg lettuce drenched with bottled dressing.

"Hey, we're having a party later. You want to come?"

"Keep it down, man." Hasel tilted his head across the room to where Balthazar Warnick sat with half a dozen well-behaved graduate students.

Baby Joe lowered his voice. "Upstairs. Oliver knows which room it is."

Angelica smiled and looked at Oliver. "Oliver knows where *everything* is."

Annie stuck her finger in her throat and made a gagging noise. "I'm out of here. It's either help with the dishes tonight or do breakfast in the morning." She grabbed her plate and stood. "Later, guys."

Oliver grinned as he watched her leave. He leaned back in his chair, and Angelica turned sideways in her seat so that she could lean against him. "There goes Jiminy Cricket," he said.

Angelica closed her eyes and nestled closer to him. "This is wonderful. Isn't it wonderful, Sweeney?"

"Absolutely, it's wonderful." I stacked our dishes and left them what remained of the bottle of wine. "I guess I'll see you later, then."

"I'll find you," Angelica called. "Oliver says they'll make a fire later in the big room down here."

In the kitchen I dumped the dishes into the sink and hoisted myself onto a counter. "I'm a morning person," I said to Annie. "I'll watch you clean and I'll do breakfast tomorrow."

A few other people straggled in, dropping off plates, drying a few glasses and dishes before wandering off again. Hasel bounded through, eyeing the slate sink and pump longingly, but Annie yelled at him to leave. He stuck his hands in the pockets of his torn jeans and sauntered out the door.

"Now don't you all forget to come to our party," he yelled.

"Maybe if he had two brain cells to rub together, he could start a fire," Annie said, and sighed. "You know, the only reason I came along was to keep an eye on Angelica. And now look at me."

"It seems kind of laid-back," I said at last. "I mean, nothing weird is going on. It all seems pretty quiet. Kind of boring, actually."

Annie swiped at her sweating face with a dish towel and nodded. "Yeah, I know. Maybe I was wrong. Maybe I'm just paranoid."

"Well, you've got some reason to be paranoid. I mean we all do, I guess, you and me and Angelica, at least."

"If I were you, I'd be worried about Oliver."

"Oliver? How come?"

Annie stared out one of the black windows. "Look at him! He's wasted *all the time*. And he hangs out at those places in Southeast—"

"So do I."

"Yeah, but it's different for you, Sweeney. I mean, no offense, but underneath all that black eye makeup and stuff, you're kind of—well, kind of *normal*. But Oliver just seems to be too unstable to be doing all this stuff—"

"Oliver is *brilliant*," I said hotly. "He says he wants to be a visionary, a—"

Annie put on her best long-suffering expression. "Boy, no one can tell you anything, can they?" She squeezed a stream of grungy water from her sponge and wiped her hands on her fatigues. "Well, I'm done. Tell Hasel Bright he can come back now and pump all he wants."

After she left I sat there for a long time, chatting with whoever happened through. Somebody brought in a half-empty bottle of red wine and I drank most of that, filling and discarding paper cups as they disintegrated into a soggy red mass. After an hour or so I left, taking the rest of the wine with me. When I got to our room the light was on. Angelica stood in front of the bathroom mirror, curling her eyelashes. She smiled at me and waved her mascara wand.

"Hi! I was hoping you'd come back up—I couldn't find you downstairs."

I flopped onto the bed nearest her, the wine bottle at my feet. It was dark. She hadn't turned on the lights in the rest of the room, but I saw a hurricane lantern on the windowsill behind me. I picked it up and slid open the metal hatch on the side, where a box of matches was stored. "I figured you and O wanted some time alone together."

"Well, we did." She turned back to the mirror and wiped a smudge of mascara from beneath one eye. "But you could have come with us, Sweeney . . .

"I kind of felt like a third wheel."

"Fifth wheel."

"Whatever. I felt like a wheel." I cupped the hurricane lantern in my hands, and asked, "Listen, Angelica—you mind telling me a little bit about what's going on here?"

She dotted carmine gloss on her lower lip and rubbed it in very slowly. When she was finished she looked at me. "You mean with Oliver and me?"

"I mean with everything."

"Sweeney." She tilted her head and smiled with maddening sweetness. "My dear soul mate. Are you jealous?"

"No, I'm not jealous. I'm just—I guess I don't know *what* I am," I sighed. I gulped a mouthful of wine from the bottle and grimaced. "Gah. This stuff is awful."

Angelica regarded me shrewdly. "Perhaps it would taste better if you didn't drink so much of it. But okay. Twenty questions. What do you want to know?"

"The *Benandanti*."

She said nothing.

"Who they are," I said. "*What* they are."

"We—ell." She took a deep breath. "They're sort of a sacred priesthood." She said it matter-of-factly, as though she'd announced "They all went to Harvard" or "They play in a foursome every weekend at Burning Tree."

"What does it mean?"

"Benandanti." The word slid off her tongue. "It means 'The Good Walkers,' or sometimes 'Those Who Do Well.' They started in the Middle Ages, in Italy—I mean their whole sort of organized way of doing things dates back that far, to the eighth century, I think. You can find accounts of them in records from the

Inquisition. But really they're much, *much* older. They go back thousands and thousands of years, my father told me once."

She stopped and reached for the wine bottle, as though she was going to take a sip, but then thought better of it. I took another swig and asked, "But what do they do? I mean, is it like the Masons or something, that you can't talk about?"

"No—well, yes, some of it is. Most of it, I suppose; at least there are things my father has never told me, and I guess he never will. Because I'm a woman, and women are—well, they're not exactly forbidden, I mean there've always been a few women—Magda Kurtz was one—but as far as the *Benandanti* are concerned, women are just sort of beside the point."

I frowned and let this sink in. "Is it part of the Church, then? I mean, there they all are at the Divine, all these priests and rabbis and ministers running around—"

Angelica shook her head emphatically. "No. It's not a religious thing—at least, it's not *just* a religious thing. It's more like the Church is part of the *Benandanti*—like *all* these churches and religions and things are part of it. There are members everywhere, all over the world. The Masons, the Vatican, Bohemian Grove, Skull and Bones . . . It's like the ultimate Old Boys' Network."

"But then why doesn't anyone *else* know about them? I mean, even if it's such a huge secret, wouldn't this have popped up on 'Sixty Minutes' or something?"

"It's not a secret."

In the glow of the hurricane lamp Angelica's face looked lovelier and more serene than ever, but also strangely remote: her voice detached, a little strained. As though she was reciting something she'd learned long before and was having difficulty remembering. "'Hide in plain sight,' that's one of their maxims. So, we all know about *parts* of the *Benandanti*—but nobody knows about *all* of it, unless you're in the very center; and that's where people like Balthazar Warnick are."

"So what do they do?"

"Research, mostly. Very obscure, totally useless research." She began to enumerate. "Sacrificial rituals of the ancient Scythians. The secret meaning of the Book of Genesis. Trying to find a pattern in NYSE figures between April and June of 1957." She laughed. "I mean, can you imagine wasting your whole life on something like that?"

I thought of Balthazar Warnick running his fingers across a door, letting it fall open upon the landscape from a nightmare. "Yeah," I said at last. "Yeah, as a matter of fact, I can see how it might come in pretty fucking useful."

I moved closer to her.

"Angelica," I said, my voice low but urgent, "if what you're telling me is true—and, I mean, it *is* true, I *saw* what they did to Magda Kurtz!—if this is all true, it means the world is completely different from what we think it is. It means—it means there's, like, *magic*, or something—

"It means that everything I know is *wrong*."

"No." Her eyes were huge and luminous. "It just means that you didn't know everything. That's all."

"But what happens now? Are they going to kill me because I saw them? Because I found out about this big awful secret?"

She looked at me pensively. "I don't think so. I think if they were going to kill you, they would have done it already. I mean, I found out about them when *I* was young, and nothing happened to me."

"But you said your father is one of them."

"He is. But my father always said that no one ever really learned about the *Benandanti* unless they were supposed to, unless there was some reason for it. No, I don't think they'll kill you, Sweeney."

I leaned back and gazed at the ceiling. "Tell me this, then. What's the point? Why are they doing all this research, if it's so useless? I assume they get their weird books and monographs published, and they all get tenure, but *why*? What are they trying to find out?"

Angelica hugged her pillow to her. "It's not so much that they're trying to *learn* things. It's more that they're trying not to forget, trying to make sure they remember—

"Someone like Professor Warnick . . . he knows the words to all the *Vedas*, he knows a language they spoke in eastern Europe *ten thousand years ago*. Not the whole language, maybe, but words, phrases, stories: this whole incredibly ancient oral tradition that's been carried on since the Ice Age. Maybe even before then; maybe so far back that the people who spoke it, we'd hardly even recognize as human at all. But the *Benandanti* remember. That's their job."

I felt chilled, by what lay behind her words: thousands of years unrolling in the darkness before me like a vast eternal plain, endless steppes where tiny figures could just barely be discerned, crouched around a single flame or dancing with arms outflung beneath the starless sky.

"So," I said at last. "They go out and find these old primitive priests, these witch doctors, and take their pictures and film them and stuff. Like they're an endangered species. They're just into saving all these old shamans."

"No, Sweeney," Angelica said softly. "You don't get it. The *Benandanti* aren't into saving the shamans. They *are* the shamans."

She walked over to the lantern on the floor, squatted before it, and held her hands out, so that black smoke licked at her fingers. "Thousands of years ago they came out of the northern steppes and *boom*! everything changed. The way people lived, the way they talked and dressed, how they divided property, how they determined parentage. There was this sort of cultural explosion, and we're still feeling the aftershocks; we'll go on feeling them forever. *That's* what the *Benandanti* are for: to make sure we keep on hearing the echo of a bomb that went off seven thousand years ago.

"The men in my father's family have been *Benandanti* since the fifteenth century, when the sultan Mehmed helped create the *Laurenziana*, the de' Medicis' library in Florence. So my ancestors were librarians. Balthazar Warnick goes back to the Dark Ages, to those monasteries in Ireland that were the only place in western Europe where they still could read and speak Greek, until the Renaissance. And Oliver's family goes back even further than that, to the first wave of Milesians in Ireland."

I stared at her for a long time, the lunula a faint gleam upon her breast. Finally I said, "This is crazy."

Angelica looked up, her face composed. "No, it's not," she said calmly. "When it starts to get crazy is when you find out that underneath this whole Indo-European tradition is an even *older* tradition. One that goes back twenty, thirty thousand years; and *that's* what the *Benandanti* are afraid of.

"Because the people who were there before the *Benandanti* knew things that make my father and Balthazar Warnick look like Boy Scouts putting on a magic show. The *Benandanti* did their best to stamp them out, but old things survive. Old religions survive. And the *Benandanti* are afraid that someday the old ways will truly return. If you know anything at all about history, you can see the signs: there'll be these little isolated outbreaks, like the old religions that were persecuted as witchcraft during the Middle Ages, and again in Salem. The whole hippie movement in the 1960s, and some of this pagan revival stuff that's going on now.

"All that stuff scares the *Benandanti*, and they do their best to put a stop to it. You want conspiracy theories? Well, this one beats them all, Sweeney. The *Benandanti* are so powerful that, for the most part, they've succeeded in keeping any resurgence of this other ancient tradition from gaining anywhere in the world. Probably the smartest thing they ever did was to infiltrate the Church; although the earlier religion got a toehold in there as well, with all those holdovers from Isis and Dionysos grafted onto Christianity.

"But mostly the *Benandanti* have just made sure that *their* guys are always in charge. That's how they've managed to carry on in this unbroken line for all these aeons, all of them: presidents and generals and priests and monks and scholars and regular guys, witch-hunters and that guy pumping gas at the Sunoco station who thinks Batman is a real person. He's not as dumb as he looks; and my father and Balthazar Warnick and some of their friends are a whole lot smarter."

"Okay," I sighed. "So your old man and Richard Nixon and the de' Medicis and I guess the Dalai Lama are all in on this together. So what're they so afraid of? What are they trying to keep us from finding out about? What is the big fucking *secret*?"

Angelica turned to stare out the window. A shaft of light from the hurricane lamp speared her crescent necklace so that it flared into a burst of gold and crimson.

"The Goddess," she whispered.

I flung myself upon the bed. "Oh, *man* . . .

Angelica looked at me furiously. "I'm not kidding, Sweeney! Haven't you read Magda Kurtz's books? Don't you remember what happened to her?"

"Okay." I ran my hand through my hair and wished I was someplace else. "Magda Kurtz. You're right, obviously something totally weird was going on with her. So tell me about your crazy goddess stuff."

She began to declaim in her theatrical voice. "Well, in a way we just don't know all that much. I mean, there're these cave paintings and carven images that go back tens of thousands of years. The Venus of Willendorf, the Snake Goddess. And then later there's Isis, and all these other Mediterranean goddesses; and Innana in Babylon, and the Great Goddess of Crete, whose name we don't know. And the

Roman Laverna and Satine in Indonesia and Skadi in Scandinavia. And the Virgin Mary, of course—she's sort of the Sears knockoff of Isis—"

"I read *The White Goddess*," I snapped. "I know how it turns out. Here's all your goddesses, this nice big *kaffee klatsch*, and *you're* saying that along came the *Benandanti*—okay, okay, the Scythian horde or the Hittites or Hyperboreans—that your basic group of patriarchal sky-god worshipers swept down and wiped them from the face of the earth. And for some reason Balthazar Warnick and his friends are doing whatever they can to keep them gone. Is that what you're trying to tell me?"

"Yes. That's what I'm trying to tell you. I've been reading about it—you'd be amazed at some of the stuff Colum has in the stacks. I think these matrilineal cultures must have had some pretty dramatic type of social control. Their goddess religions were probably *much* more intense than we like to imagine. Almost certainly there was some form of recurrent human sacrifice. Magda Kurtz thought so; otherwise, why are there all these survivals of incredibly violent rituals? Even the ancient Greeks—we think of them as being so civilized, but originally the Greeks took most of their religious notions from places where the Goddess was worshiped, from Crete, and Anatolia, and probably other places we'll never know about. When *we* read about Theseus and the minotaur, it's just a fairy tale. But to the classical Greeks it was a memory of something almost unimaginably ancient, the remnant of some kind of human sacrifice to the Goddess. A tribute of young men and boys brought from the mainland to Crete at the end of every lunar cycle . . .

"And so for twenty thousand years we had these relatively peaceful matristic societies. No wars, no warriors. If we bought that peace at the price of a few men or boys a year, well so what?"

I stared at her as though her hair was on fire. "You're kidding, right?"

"No, I'm not kidding," she said haughtily. "I've been thinking about it a lot lately."

"But it's insane! You're saying that human sacrifice is acceptable as some weird kind of social control!"

"No, that's *not* what I'm saying! It's just a theory, anyway—but why would that have been such a terrible thing? I mean, what about Christianity and the crucifixion? *That's* a kind of human sacrifice, and nobody thinks *it's* weird. Why is it okay if a *man* does it?"

I wanted to laugh, but Angelica's piercing glare shut me up. "Angelica, I hate to say this, but—but isn't this all kind of—well, *paranoid*?"

For the first time in the nine weeks I'd known her, Angelica got mad: really, really mad.

"Listen, Sweeney! Maybe I don't know *everything* about the way the world works, but I know enough not to buy into every idea my father taught me. Or Balthazar Warnick. I mean, look at this—"

She crossed the room to her bed, dug into one of her bags and withdrew a book: Magda Kurtz's *Daughters of the Setting Sun*. She flipped through it, walked back, and shoved it at me.

"What's that a picture of?" She pointed to a print showing a pattern of intersecting lines and Vs. I squinted at the page and shrugged.

"Swords."

"Guess again."

"I dunno. Spears, I guess. Some kind of weapon."

"Why not leaves? Why not fish, or birds, or fir trees?"

I shrugged again. "I don't know. They just look like spears to me."

"They look like spears because you've been *taught* to see spears. Or swords, or javelins. What about this?" Her finger jabbed at another image.

"Easy. Some kind of phallic symbol."

She shook her head. "Doesn't it look a little top-heavy for a phallic symbol? Look again—"

I peered at it more closely; and this time I saw that there were incised lines on the top of the little image, forming a crude face, and lines along its body marking a vulva. I nodded and handed the book back to her.

"You're right," I said, a little surprised. "It's a face—"

"It's a *woman*. A goddess figurine. And yet for a hundred years people were digging these things up and insisting they were phallic objects, when they could just as easily have been *mushrooms*! Just like they were insisting every circle or delta was a shield or sun, when they were found surrounded by millions of these goddess figures, and were probably supposed to be vulvas, or moons. Just like you said all these patterns of lines represented some kind of weapon, when they could have been any number of other things."

"Then why can't they just be *nothing*?" I asked stubbornly. "I mean, these people didn't have notebooks to doodle in. Maybe they were just scribbling on the walls."

"That's not the way the world works, Sweeney."

"Oh yeah? Who died and made you hierophant?"

Suddenly she looked exhausted. Small lines showed at the sides of her mouth and eyes as she leaned to cup her hands above the hurricane lamp.

"Look, maybe I *don't* know what I'm talking about," she said wearily. "What I do know is, I read Dr. Kurtz's book in high school, and it was like a bell went off in my head. All of a sudden all these things made sense—why they used to burn witches at the stake, why women aren't allowed to be priests or rabbis, why Christmas is a big deal, but Halloween is just for little kids—all these things that had always just seemed to be the result of some weird random decision on somebody's part.

"And Dr. Kurtz's book *explained* all this stuff. Okay, so maybe a lot of it isn't even true—but maybe it doesn't all *have* to be true. Maybe just *some* of it is true, and maybe for me that's enough. Because when I read her book, for the first time I felt like I *understood* things. Things that had to do with my father and the *Benandanti*, with everything I'd been brought up to believe in . . .

"And so I came here to the Divine, because my father went here, and I met you and Oliver and Annie, and Daddy's old friend Balthazar Warnick, and Magda Kurtz—this woman I *idolize*!—and out of nowhere she gives me *this*—"

Her fingers clutched at the silver crescent hanging around her neck.

"—she gives me this, and then she's *gone*. The paper says she was in a plane crash but *I* know she wasn't and *you* know—and there has to be a reason, Sweeney. Otherwise, she wouldn't have given it to me. *There has to be a reason*."

I was quiet. Finally I said, "Sure there's a reason, Angelica. Magda knew someone was going to kill her. She knew someone wanted that thing, and she was trying to get rid of it. And if *you* were smart, you'd get rid of it, too.

"No." Angelica crossed her arms. "The only reason Warnick got to her at all was that she took it off. The lunula was protecting her. As long as she wore it, she was safe.

"And then she gave it to me . . ."

Her voice faded. When she spoke again it was in a whisper so soft I could barely hear her.

"That's why I have to learn about it. If I was meant to have it, I have to know *why*. There are no accidents—that's what my father says. Nothing ever happens without a reason."

"Yeah, and when God closes a door, He opens a whole new can of worms. Well, you better be careful, that's all," I said darkly, and pointed at her throat. "I don't know what that thing is, but it's bad juju, I can tell you that."

Suddenly the door to our room flew open. We both jumped; but it was only Annie.

"Hey, what's this? You guys having a séance?" She flopped down beside Angelica and beamed. Her face was bright red and sweaty, and her hair stuck up in little tufts across her forehead. "Anyone I know?"

"Annie, have you been *drinking*?" Angelica raised her eyebrows in astonishment.

"Hell, no. I've been *dancing*, with Baby Joe and Hasel and those other guys. I just came back to get my sweater. You should come back with me. And listen: they're having another party tomorrow night—"

She started throwing clothes out of her knapsack, finally held up a moth-eaten cardigan. "Eureka."

"I think tomorrow's supposed to be an evening of quiet contemplation, Annie," said Angelica.

"Yeah, well, after vespers there's gonna be some party over in Hasel's room. I said you'd come, Angelica—oh, you too, Sweeney, don't look at me like that!—they've got a boom box and a bunch of tapes, it'll be great."

"Sounds wonderful," Angelica said doubtfully. "Is Oliver there now?"

"Oh, lighten up, di Rienzi! No, he's not. I don't know where he is—probably outside communing with Jupiter. Probably he's *on* Jupiter." Annie pulled on her sweater and whirled out the door again.

Angelica turned to me. "You can go if you want."

"I don't think so. Maybe tomorrow."

"Are you tired?"

"Not really. I'm kind of buzzed, actually."

"Would you like to take a walk? Outside, I mean."

"Sure."

We found a door that led out onto a rolling lawn. Beneath our feet the grass was brittle with frost and crackled noisily, like a match set to pine boughs. On the horizon, above the black tips of the trees, stars burned with a cold brilliance. There was no moon. We walked without speaking, and for once silence didn't seem awkward to me. It was amazing how quickly we left the Orphic Lodge behind, neither light nor sound nor anything but the smell of woodsmoke hinting that it was there at all, sweet applewood and cedar, and an occasional flurry of red embers streaking the darkness overhead.

"I'm glad I met you, Sweeney," Angelica said after a long while. The lawn had finally surrendered to tangled vetch and tall stalks of milkweed and yarrow. The night was utterly still; it was too late in the year for crickets, and even the night birds seemed to have fled. There was only wind rustling in dead weeds, and the crackling of leaves underfoot. "I don't know, now, what I would have done if I hadn't. I love Annie, but she's different from you—you *understand* things about me, I don't have to explain everything."

I smiled ruefully and shook my head. *I don't understand anything!* I wanted to yell, but didn't.

"You really are my soul mate. You and Oliver." Very tentatively her fingers brushed against the glimmer of light at her throat. Then she reached to take my hand. "Oh, Sweeney."

I froze, my mouth suddenly dry as I waited for her to pull me closer. But she didn't, only looked at me for a long moment with those uncanny green eyes. Finally she dropped my hand and continued down the hillside, picking her way carefully among weeds and brambles and stones.

In front of us the field dipped into a tiny hollow and rose again, ending in a grove of birches and sapling pines. In the moonless night the woods looked ominously black. Behind the timid growth of birches and young oaks, the evergreens formed a solid impenetrable wall, with thatched masses of dead ferns and leaves beneath.

"Maybe we should head on back now." I was afraid that Angelica wanted to plunge on into those woods, and that as her soul mate I would be expected to follow. "I'm kind of cold."

"Sure." But abruptly she drew up short. "Sweeney!" she whispered. "There's somebody there!"

I peered into the darkness, my heart pounding. I could just make out a pale figure sitting in a patch of dried milkweed. I took a few cautious steps forward, then laughed with relief.

"It's Oliver!"

The night seemed to fall away. I turned giddily and grabbed Angelica. "Oliver!" I shouted.

"Oliver," repeated Angelica.

He was all alone at the very edge of the field. He had a guitar in his lap and was holding it awkwardly yet lovingly, as though it were a baby. When he saw us, his mouth crooked into that odd canine grin. But he said nothing; only tipped his head so that his face was hidden.

"Oliver," Angelica called again in a low voice. Her fingers closed about the lunula, so that its gleam was lost to me. Oliver did not raise his eyes. In the cold breeze his long hair rippled, as though some muscular impatient animal waited beneath. And then suddenly he looked up, not focusing on either of us but on some point far far away, between the ghostly shapes of the trees and the diamond-studded sky. In a thin clear plaintive voice—a boy's voice, slightly off-key but so sweet and earnest it gave me goose bumps—he began to sing.

Seems like a bell rings, time for déjà vu
Everything is familiar now, being here with you
All you've ever had before you had to understand
Now all you have to do is want to have at your command.
I have always been here before . . .

His guitar playing was like his voice—edgy, a little too fast, his fingers stumbling over the chord changes. But there was something about it all—the moonless sky, the trees bereft of leaves, even the wind stirring the dried stalks of milkweed and Queen Anne's lace—something that was lovelier and lonelier and more fragile than anything I had ever experienced before. I leaned forward until I stood on the balls of my feet, poised for flight, though I didn't know that then, and as I listened I felt Angelica's hand slip into mine.

That that is pleasing; that that is real,
That that is forever keeps filling, never filled.
That that snuck up upon you in the night,
That that you remember in an early childhood light
That that was supposed to have frightened you,
But somehow you never took to flight:
I have always been here before . . .

I began to cry. You have to remember I was so young, and drunk, as full of raw wet emotion as I was of bad wine; but even so there really was something there, I felt it then and years later I knew that I had been right, there really was something about Oliver, and Angelica, and maybe even me; but mostly it was Oliver. Even after all the rest of it, even now, when I think of Oliver that night is what comes to me first: standing in the cold dying grass, with the faint tang of woodsmoke wind-borne from the Orphic Lodge, the stars like cracks in the sky through which I might have peeked and seen all that was to come, if only I had known to look. And Oliver himself, the shadow of the song, singing as though they were the only words he knew.

From the gargoyles to Stonehenge
From the Sphinx to the pyramids
From Lucifer's temples praising the Devil right,
To the Devil's clock as it strikes midnight—
I have always been here before.

He fell silent, strummed the guitar a few more times, and then cocked his head to listen to the sound die into the wind.

"Oh," whispered Angelica. "That was wonderful—what is it, that's the most beautiful song . . ."

"No, it's not," cried someone behind us. I whirled and saw a pale face peering from a tangle of seedpods and dead grass: Annie, the front of her holey cardigan covered with burdock. "Who said you could use my guitar?"

Oliver stood. He brushed himself off and extended the instrument to her. "I'm sorry, Annie. I didn't think you'd mind." Glaring, she took the guitar from him and hugged it to her chest. After a moment she plucked at it tentatively.

"Huh," she said, wincing as the strings jangled. She looked up and for the first time seemed to notice Angelica and me. "*There* you are. They're asking for you up at the council fire."

"I thought you were with Hasel."

Annie yawned. "I was. But we went down to get something to eat and got caught up in this other stuff. You should come back in, it's kind of fun."

"We will—" I started to say, but then saw that Angelica had stepped over to join Oliver. The loose folds of her dress hiked up on a patch of burdock, but she didn't notice. She had her arms around Oliver and was pulling him to her and he was kissing her, his hands sliding down her back slowly at first, then tugging at the thin folds of cotton until I could hear a faint *shirring* noise as the fabric pulled from the weeds and tore.

"Hey." Annie nudged me with the neck of her guitar. "Come on, Sweeney," she said softly but kindly. "Let's go inside."

I stood for another moment, staring, then quickly followed her up the hill. When we reached the Orphic Lodge I turned to look back, but everything behind us had been swallowed by the night.

I woke very early the next morning. It was still dark outside, the windows pewter-colored and edged with a tracery of frost. In her narrow camp bed Annie was a small snoring mound of blankets. Angelica's bed was empty. I lay on my side and stared at the neatly made rectangle with its quilt and cotton comforter and pillow, Angelica's blue silk makeup case, and the little black box that held all her contact lens equipment. At last I got up. I dressed in the dark and ducked into the bathroom.

Even without the black eye makeup, the face staring at me from the mirror didn't look sensible at all. At night, dancing in a dark club with gaudy lights arcing through the smoke, I could pass for androgynous and sinister: cropped black hair, gashed mouth, bruised eyes. But the act didn't play well by daylight. I looked burned out and exhausted and younger than I liked to admit. I threw some water on my face, trying to pretend that made me feel better. I decided to forgo a shower because I didn't want to wake Annie, and went downstairs.

The lodge was silent and cold and dark. I tiptoed into the kitchen, found some instant coffee and boiled water and drank the awful stuff black. Then I went outside for a long walk, down the hillside and to the edge of the woods where we'd been the night before. I smoked most of a pack of cigarettes and looked for signs of Angelica and Oliver's passing. Crushed bracken, stray bits of clothing, the lingering smells of sandalwood and smoke. But, of course, I found nothing. Whatever the night might have known of them, the day held nothing—nothing, at least, that it would share with me. Where the overgrown meadow ended I slumped against a birch tree with my head bowed and eyes closed, the cold wind gnawing at my back and the empty windows of the Orphic Lodge gazing down upon me, and smoked my last cigarette.

I spent the rest of the day alone. The whole morning and most of the afternoon skidded by, and I never saw Angelica or Oliver. As dusk fell, I went down to a cheerfully airheaded ecumenical service in the living room, in front of the empty ash-streaked fireplace. The dreaded acoustic guitars were brought out, and a boy played "Embryonic Journey." Two grad students sang an Elton John song that I hated. Everyone clapped politely, and then to my surprise, Annie Harmon rose and carried her guitar to the front of the room, climbing atop a wooden stool and perching her slender frame there. She fiddled with her guitar until she got the tuning right, pushed up the sleeves of her plaid shirt, and nodded.

"Okay," she said. She gave a quick nervous laugh, and then began to sing.

She did "Chelsea Morning" and "Been Too Long at the Fair" and "Afterhours"—

If you close the door, the night could last forever

—tapping the sounding board of her guitar so that it boomed as she sang in a deep scary voice scarcely above a whisper.

Remember hallways, you're seeking always
To see behind the door
You've never seen her, you want to meet her
The first time's so unsure . . .

Her voice filled the room like smoke and we breathed it in, its rich dark menace, the simple words suddenly becoming a warning.

Oh, she is still a mystery to me . . .

All too soon her voice died away. There was an instant of silence in which I could feel the last cold notes dissolving on my skin; then everyone began yelping and cheering.

"Whoa, Harmon!"

"Bravo!"

"Brava, bella!"

I looked over my shoulder and saw Angelica and Oliver leaning against the wall. Oliver was wearing the same clothes he wore last night, and Angelica had on her same dress, with a faded maroon sweatshirt that read *Northeast Kingdom Abbey* pulled on over it. She was red-cheeked and smiling, applauding wildly. She looked younger than I had ever seen her, more like a freshman college student and less the mysterious *femme fatale*. Her hair was loose and uncombed and, without its exquisite *maquillage*, her face was sweet and girlish.

But Oliver: Oliver looked awful. Chalk white, his blue eyes shadowed and so dark they looked like raw holes. His hair hung lank about his cheeks and he stared fixedly at his hands, flexing and unflexing his fingers. Every now and then his mouth twitched, as though he were trying to keep from laughing or crying aloud.

If I were you, I'd be worried about Oliver . . .

I stared at him, as drawn as I had been by my first vision of his fey prep school beauty. But now something truly terrible hung about Oliver: no more that casual aura of adolescent abandon, but a palpable air of ravagement and decay. His expression was vacant yet at the same time almost demonically intense. He rocked back and forth, back and forth, shifting his weight as though it hurt him to rest too long on one foot. Abruptly he moved away from Angelica with a queer shambling gait, more like a wounded animal than a person.

"Oliver—" Angelica called after him. But instead of turning to her, Oliver stopped and looked at me.

I froze. I was overwhelmed by dread—that he would say something to me, that he would call my name, and so doom me to whatever horror had consumed him.

Instead Oliver only smiled, his own sweet crooked smile. He shook his head, as though seeing me had awakened him from his stupor, and looked down at his feet. He was wearing his customary black wing tips without any socks, but there was a nasty gash on one ankle, the wound black and the flesh around it grossly swollen. I cried out and started toward him, but someone grabbed my arm.

"Sweeney!—" Annie popped up beside me, grinning. "What'd you think?"

"Hmm?"

"My singing. Didn't you like it?"

"Huh? Oh sure, Annie—sure," I said absently, then turned to see Oliver and Angelica near the door. She was holding his hand, talking and gazing at him with worried eyes; but Oliver ignored her. He was staring straight ahead, his eyes fixed on something I couldn't see. Angelica lifted his hand to her lips and kissed his knuckles—they were scraped raw and black with dirt—but he never looked up. I tried to catch his eyes, willing him to notice me, but Oliver's gaze never wavered from whatever dreamscape had captivated him. "Annie, look at Oliver—do you think he's okay?"

Annie shook her head, her dark eyes troubled. "I don't know." She shifted her guitar case and shrugged. "But those Molyneux scholars—somebody always keeps 'em from falling. Come on—"

We walked in silence to our room. Once again, Angelica had somehow gotten there first.

"Sweeney! Annie! What's up?" She still had on Oliver's sweatshirt, and there were burrs in her softly curling hair. "You know, I think I *will* go to that thing tonight in Hasel's room. You guys up for it?"

"Sure." I glanced at Annie, cleared my throat, and asked awkwardly, "Is—what's Oliver up to?"

For a moment Angelica's smile looked strained. Then, "Oliver will be there. Don't you worry. *Ciao*, Sweeney—"

She slipped into the bathroom. I sat on my bed and turned to Annie. She pursed her lips, wriggling her fingers as she blew a kiss at me.

"*Ciao*, Sweeney," she said.

When we got to Hasel's room, things seemed ominously silent.

"Hey! The girls are here!" Annie yelled. She frowned, kicking aside an empty beer bottle. "What's going on, Hasel? Is this a wake, or what?"

"Warnick gave me a hard time about all the noise last night," explained Hasel. "So we figure we'll just go outside. You guys have warm clothes on?"

"Angie doesn't," Annie said.

"That's okay," murmured Baby Joe. "She's got her *love* to keep her warm." He giggled soundlessly and tossed me a beer.

For a few minutes we sat around and made desultory conversation. I sipped my beer, Annie swung her feet restlessly and kicked at the rungs of her chair, Hasel and Baby Joe smoked in near-silence. Angelica stood by the window and gazed out at the night. The spectacular sunset had faded to a tattered fringe of black and red above the mountains. Elsewhere the sky was already black, save where the first stars clove through the darkness. Hasel finished his beer and stared at Angelica, after a moment said softly, "You sure look beautiful tonight, Angelica."

She did, too: wearing a long-sleeved cobalt blue dress of champagne velvet, with a shirred bodice and silver embroidery and silver tassels hanging from the cuffs and hem. She had on the same half-moon earrings she'd worn the first time I met her. Against her throat hung the lunula. Every now and then she'd touch it, as though for reassurance.

"What? This old thing?" Angelica laughed, but her voice sounded odd: as though she were acting at being Angelica, pretending to be more self-assured than she really felt. "He should be here any minute—"

"I *think*," Annie broke in, her eyes widening, "I *think* he's here now."

We all turned as a shadow filled the doorway—a shadow in stained tuxedo shirt and moth-eaten trousers and dirty black wing tips with filthy laces trailing behind them. The bare foot shoved into one of them was so swollen and bruised it looked black.

"Oh, Oliver," whispered Angelica.

It was Oliver, all right; but his hair was gone. All that beautiful long hair, sheared away until there was nothing left but coarse black stubble. He must have tried to shave his skull—there were bald patches, and angry-looking cuts left by a razor.

I have never seen anyone so appallingly changed. His face was still beautiful, and with his shorn head, the high cheekbones and shadowed eyes gave him a monkish look. But his eyes were wild, and all Oliver's sweetness, all his sly humor and intelligence were gone from them. He looked sinister and frighteningly out of place, like the victim of some terrible accident who has crawled for miles and miles, finally to collapse on the lawn at a wedding.

For a minute we were all silent. Then Hasel started to clap.

"Way to go, man!" Hasel crossed to the door and drew Oliver into the room, laughing. "'Bout time you got rid of that hippie hair!"

"Oliver," cried Angelica. I thought she was going to burst into tears. "How *could* you?"

Still Oliver said nothing. He looked dazed, and let Hasel lead him to where the rest of us watched in awkward silence. Beside me Baby Joe cringed, and Annie for once was speechless.

"Hope you brought a hat, man," Hasel went on heedlessly. "It's *cold* out there—"

Oliver lifted his shorn head and stared at me, his eyes black and huge.

"Sweeney," he whispered. "Save me, Sweeney."

Hasel laughed. "*Shave* you? Man, there's nothing left to shave—"

I walked over to him. "Oliver," I murmured, and touched his poor ravished scalp. I thought it would feel prickly and rough, but it was soft, the little hairs like velvet. "Jesus. Looks like you got a haircut the hard way."

Oliver tilted his head. Unexpectedly he flashed one of his crazy smiles, then grabbed me and hugged me to him, held me so tight I couldn't breathe, so tight I could feel his heart slamming against his chest as though it would fly out and into my body like a bird seeking shelter. I could smell the drugs seeping from his pores, a falsely sweet smell like vitamins, the fresh scents of lavender soap and shaving cream and beneath it all a meaty odor that I knew must come from his swollen foot.

"Sweeney?"

The smell filled my nostrils until I couldn't breathe, he was dragging me underwater and I was drowning, drowning. I tried to move, I needed to get away, though at the same time I wanted to stay there in his embrace, could feel how he was *willing* me to stay—

Save me, Sweeney . . .

Abruptly he let go. I fell back, gasping. When I looked up Angelica stood beside him, frowning as she ran her fingers across his head.

"Oh, Oliver. What a mess." She made a face. "Well, you're definitely making a *statement*." She peered behind her, looking for the rest of us. "Should we meet you guys outside?"

Baby Joe shrugged. "I guess we're ready." He and Hasel headed for the door. I started after them, then paused.

"Annie?"

Annie shook her head. "I—I don't think I'm in for this one," she said slowly, adding in a low voice, "This is starting to look too weird, Sweeney. I'm going back downstairs."

"You sure?" I said anxiously. Because it *was* looking a little too weird, even for me. There was Hasel, eerily oblivious to Oliver's misery, and beer-sodden Baby Joe in his ragged suit, ashes trailing him like a bad reputation. And me in my old cowboy boots and Oliver's shirt; and finally Angelica and Oliver. Angelica radiant as ever; Oliver in his skewed formal wear. We really did look like some deranged wedding party; though whether Oliver was lunatic preacher or runaway groom, I couldn't guess.

"I'm sure." Annie squeezed my arm. "And Sweeney—if things get too out of hand, promise you'll come back inside, okay? Promise you'll come get me?"

I nodded and watched her leave, then went to help Baby Joe with the beer.

"Okay," said Hasel. "We're on the buddy system: everybody got a beer? Let's go—"

Hasel had discovered a set of ancient rusted fire stairs that cascaded down the outside of the lodge. Probably we could have just gone right out the front door and no one would have bothered us, or even noticed, but something made us furtive. One by one we went down the zigzag steps until we reached the lawn. A faint wind stirred the upper branches of the trees and sent a few dead leaves spinning drunkenly to the ground. I sat down for a few minutes, and tried to calm myself by looking at the stars. The chill air magnified them until they seemed huge, brittle flowers waiting to be torn apart by the wind. Finally I stood.

A few yards downhill waited Hasel and Baby Joe, their heads craned to stare at the sky. We were on the far side of the lodge, facing the woods. Without a sound, Angelica appeared beside me.

"Let's go that way—" Her voice rang out as she pointed to where the silvery grey lawn flowed into darkness. "Someone told me there's a pond there."

"Kinda cold for skinny-dipping," called Hasel. "But I'll keep you company!"

He laughed and gave Baby Joe a shove. The two of them loped on down the hill. Angelica nudged me and I looked back to see Oliver. I started to call out to him, but he hurried after Hasel and Baby Joe.

Angelica gave an angry sigh. "I *hate* the way he looks. Why'd he *do* that to his beautiful hair?" She spun on her heel and started down the hill. "Sometimes I really think he's crazy."

It was a cold, nearly windless night. What breeze there was smelled of rain-washed stone and mud. When it shifted it brought with it the tang of woodsmoke from the lodge, the harsh scent of marijuana smoke. There was still no moon. I understood nothing of lunar phases, else I would have known it was the darkest quarter, the fourth of four nights when the moon is absent from the sky. But that only meant the stars shone all the brighter.

We turned before we reached the trees. We were in rank pasture now, bordered by a tumbledown stone wall covered with matted clumps of kudzu and wild grapevines.

I slowed my steps, wondering how Angelica could walk so surely and quickly among the stones and clumps of burdock. But she merely lifted her long skirt and went on. Occasionally Hasel's slow stoned laugh floated back to us, or Baby Joe's. Angelica walked alone, mad at Oliver, I thought, or maybe she just wanted to be by herself.

Suddenly she stopped. She lifted her arms and let go of the ends of her skirt. A few yards away Oliver and Hasel and Baby Joe halted and stared at her. Angelica turned to me, smiling.

"Here we are, Sweeney."

We were at the top of a wide shallow depression, a sort of bowl in the surrounding meadowland. The ground was covered with very short dry grass, as though it had been mowed or heavily grazed. Everywhere myriad tiny stones were strewn like the stones in a gravel pit, and the fragile stalks of burdock and milkweed rustled softly where we walked.

At the center of the hollow was a small perfectly round man-made pond, what in farm country they call a tank. It was like a hole cut in the fabric of the night, and so black that I was surprised to see stars floating in it, innocent as lilies. Certainly it had been put there for watering cattle, though there were no cows anywhere that I could see, and the Euclidean symmetry of the pool gave it a strange, almost supernatural appearance. It seemed unlikely that it would be spring-fed, and I saw no streams running into it. But it didn't have that neglected-fishbowl smell I associated with small ponds. Instead the water smelled sweet, wonderfully sweet: like spring rain and apple blossom and oranges, charged like a storm ready to break. It smelled so insanely wonderful that I jumped back from its edge as though I'd seen moray eels there waiting to tear me into ribbons.

"Sweeney? What's the matter?"

Angelica stood on the bank and watched me. She had removed her sandals and was probing the black water with a toe. The sweet fragrance was so strong that my hair stood on end—not just the hair on my scalp or neck but *everywhere*—every filament of my being a wick ready to burst into flame.

"Sweeney?"

About her head runnels of violet light streamed like water. I stared at her, as frightened by her matter-of-fact tone as by everything else. "What's wrong, Sweeney?"

"Hey, ladies. Wait for us!"

Behind me I heard shuffling footsteps, Hasel's soft drawling laugh. Out of nowhere rose a strong wind. The cropped grass at my feet rippled, and dust rose and wheeled in grey clouds.

"Sweeney—could you help me with this?"

In front of me Angelica stood with her back to the pool. She was pulling up her dress, but it had caught on a spike of dried milkweed. "Sweeney—?"

She was only inches away from me, her arms upraised, hair a long tangle of dark gold. In the starlight her skin was so pale it was as though her body was a rift in the night.

"Sweeney: please. Take the dress."

Her voice was a whisper but also a command. I gathered her hem between my fingers and raised it. Warm velvet spilled over my knuckles like foam, and with it her scent, sweet oranges and sandalwood rushing into me like a drug. I fell to my knees, leaned forward until my lips brushed the skin just below her thigh. I kissed her, pressed my mouth against her flesh until I could taste sweet salt and oranges, the soft pressure of her skin giving way beneath my teeth and the velvet of her skin softer than anything. The folds of her dress slipped from my fingers and I started to fall forward, pulling her down with me. But then her voice rang out sharply.

"Sweeney."

I stumbled to my feet, cringing as though I had been struck.

"My dress."

This time I pulled it up and over her—thighs, groin, belly, breasts, chin—all in one swift motion. Before I could drop it Angelica snatched the dress from me and tossed it aside.

"There now," she murmured.

I crouched at her feet, my hands clutching at dead grass. Above me Angelica cast no shadow in the pale starlight. She was naked, her skin smooth as molten silver, nothing to show that she'd ever worn any clothes at all. Save only this:

A crescent like the sleeping moon above her breasts, its spars reaching toward her shoulders and the whole thing glowing as though it had just been drawn from the flame. I heard a sharp intake of breath and Baby Joe's nervous giggle, then Hasel's awed voice.

"Fucking A. A fucking *goddess*, man—"

But from Oliver, nothing. Not a sound, not a breath. I wanted to look back at them, to reassure myself I wasn't alone; but I couldn't. I couldn't do anything but stare up at Angelica, my hands crushing the dead grass against my palms.

For a long time she stood, utterly silent, her slanted green eyes glowing. It was as though the rest of us weren't even there. As if, like Magda Kurtz, she had walked or been pushed through some gap in the world and now breathed a different air than we did, finer, rarer, infinitely more precious. About her face her long hair lifted and flowed in dark coils. Her eyes were serene, her lips parted so that I could glimpse her even white teeth. Upon her breast the lunula sent shafts of pure white light streaming into the darkness.

Without a word she turned from us, the slope of her hips and buttocks catching a glint of starlight before they faded into shadow again. Very slowly she paced to the water's edge, and, as we watched, she walked right into it, not even hesitating at its brink, walked straight and slow as though drawn by an invisible rope toward the center of the pool. With each step the water rose higher and higher, lapping at her ankles, then her thighs and flanks, finally sliding up across her rib cage to touch her breasts with shadow. Her body was swallowed by black water like the moon in eclipse, until at last only her head remained, her hair flowing 'round her. I had a glimpse of her eyes, hard and cold and shining, and a softly glowing core of light where the lunula lay upon her breast.

Then she was gone. Ripples spread from the center of the pool, expanded until they touched its shallow banks and disappeared, one by one; and all was still again.

I heard a whimper, tentative footsteps. I turned and saw Baby Joe and Hasel huddled together, their awestruck gaze fixed on the placid water. A few paces behind them stood Oliver. His face was utterly implacable. I could have read anything I wanted in his staring eyes—terror, relief, amazement, even complete indifference.

"Oliver," I called hoarsely, not caring that he'd hear how scared I was. I stood, my feet scrabbling against pebbles and dead grass. "Oliver, let's go—"

His expression changed. Like water flowing into a glass, some of the old Oliver seemed to fill him. He blinked and, for the first time, noticed me.

"Sweeney." His voice was frail and tremulous, an old woman's voice. "Thanks for coming." He stepped toward me, and there was something ghastly about his smile, as though it, too, had been stolen from someone else. "I didn't think they'd let you come, I didn't know you were here—"

He reached for me, and when his hand closed about mine, I cried out: the flesh was so dry and loose it was like bark shifting beneath my touch.

"Don't fear me, Sweeney." His voice rose as I pulled away from him. "It's still me, Sweeney, it's still me, *please don't leave me*—"

An explosive sound ripped the night. The air shattered; shards of glass rained upon us, filling the night with a sound like bells. I screamed, drawing my hands to my face; but when the splinters struck me they were not glass at all but freezing water.

"*—with her.*"

At pool's edge stood a tall slender figure. Angelica, shaking her head so that her hair spun out in long black tendrils and more icy rain scattered everywhere. She was laughing. Water streamed from her uplifted hands to spill upon her breasts and thighs, and when she moved atoms of light shot from her, like sparks from a glowing forge. Upon her breast the lunula still gleamed, but its glory seemed to have been swallowed by her eyes, treacherous fox fire eyes. She turned and all their fatal splendor focused upon me.

"Oh Beloved. It is time."

Her voice, sweet as rainwater falling upon stone. I stepped toward her, my arms opening to her embrace: what else could I do? But then I saw that she was not looking at me; nor at Baby Joe or Hasel or Oliver.

She was not looking at any of us. She walked right past me, past the others, and never said a word. It was so still that I could hear Hasel swallow when she swept by him, the dead grasses rustling beneath her bare feet. After she had passed we all turned in her wake, peering through the darkness to see what drew her.

In the overgrown meadow crouched a hulking form. At first I thought it was an immense boulder, or maybe some abandoned farm equipment.

But as Angelica approached it, her arms flung open in greeting, I saw that it was not a machine. It was a cow—no, a bull, a huge dun-colored creature with arching horns and a ponderous dewlap that hung down between its legs. When it sighted Angelica it snorted and shook its head. Its dewlap shuddered. It pawed nervously at the ground and a cloud of vapor enveloped its nostrils. It seemed merely huge, until

Angelica stopped only two or three paces from where it watched her with rolling black eyes. Then it became monstrous, unimaginably vast.

My breath was coming fast and shallow. I glanced over to see Hasel staring transfixed and Baby Joe wide-eyed and motionless, a dead cigarette caught between his fingers. Beside them, Oliver was a brooding shadow, silent and minatory. In the field Angelica and the bull stared at each other, their breath fogging the chilly air. And then, very slowly, they began to move.

She took a step; it took a step. She slid sideways, it raised its front legs and came down in a furious explosion of dust. Now and then the bull would lower its head and charge her, and Angelica would drop to the ground and roll away, darting to her feet again quick as thought. She was still naked; where the dirt and grass touched her, her skin was streaked black and grey, her long legs mottled with tiny seed heads. On one breast a smudge like a handprint showed as though she had been struck.

But the patina of dust and grime didn't make her look less beautiful. In some perverse way it made her *more* so, made her more arousing, gave some earthy taint of straw pallet and byre to her unearthly beauty. She ducked and darted, reaching now to strike the bull's flanks with the flat of her hand, now to tug at the heavy curtain of flesh dangling from its throat, then leaping away to flick at its ears; once even grabbing a long stick and making a sudden lunge between its legs, striking at its shadowy member and rolling away seconds before its hooves thundered back down. With each flashing motion the bull snorted and gamboled, tossing its head and rolling its eyes in a sort of ecstasy of fear and fury, its black hooves sending up a steady rain of stones and dirt.

And still she came at it, tireless, relentless, crying out in low sharp bursts, a wordless, teasing song that was the perfect music for that dance. And dance it was, not crude or stumbling but fluid as the mad rush of water raging down a ravine, beautiful and awful and horribly, infinitely perilous.

Suddenly she stopped. She was panting, I could hear her and see how her ribs rose and fell, see how her entire body was flushed and smell her sweat mingled with that of the bull and the pungent odor of the trodden grass. When she turned I caught a flash of light at her breast, a gleam like the sun on water.

In front of her the bull was still as well. Its nostrils flared and it shook its head, no longer furiously but slowly, as though exhausted. It pawed clumsily at the ground with one foot. Every now and then a shiver would run across its entire body and its skin would ripple with a long single tremor. Its ears lay flat against its huge skull. Two long strands of spittle dangled from its mouth. Darker patches stood out against its greyish hide. On its rear right fetlock there was a small gash that bled when it moved.

And now, oh so slowly, Angelica began to walk toward it. She would take one step and halt, wait and then take another. When the bull shuddered and lowered its head, eyes madly rolling, she would become motionless and remain so for a minute, two minutes, three. Then she would step forward again. Overhead the moonless sky stretched black and boundless. The stars threw down a pale bitter light that cast no shadows, illuminated nothing but the things themselves: a beautiful girl and a bull.

Finally she stopped. The bull's head was inches from hers, its horns reaching to embrace her. Above her breasts the lunula glowed, its raised prongs deadly as the bull's horns, its gleaming curve radiant beneath Angelica's face. So slowly that she scarcely seemed to move at all, she lowered herself to the ground, never taking her eyes from the bull's; until she sat cross-legged at its feet, her head thrown back. Its dewlap hung above her upturned face. It shook its head, tail flicking at the air as though to drive away an insect. Slowly it raised its head, its huge eyes fixed upon the frozen stars, and lowed: a chilling desperate cry.

As it did, Angelica brought her hands to her throat and then snatched them upward, so quickly that all I saw was a flash of white. I gasped. In her hands she held the lunula, grasping it so that it formed a curved blade like a scythe. Without a word she lunged, slashing at the bull's throat. She drew back and lunged again, and this time when the animal bellowed the sound was a screaming roar, so loud I covered my ears.

But I couldn't look away. She struck at it again, and again, and it kept on roaring, its legs buckling as it sank and kicked out at Angelica, frantic with rage and pain. Once it nearly struck her but she pulled away just in time. It staggered toward her, moaning, its head lowered so that its horns formed a dull moon to her glittering crescent. All the while its blood poured from its throat in a dark torrent.

The bull stood weaving slightly as it stared at her, its black eyes no longer bright but shrouded with blood and grit. With a coughing roar it fell onto its side. Its flanks heaved as, with a last strangled bellow, it struggled to lift its head. Finally it was still.

In front of it Angelica was frozen in a half crouch. When it was clear that the animal was dead she stood, her arms held stiffly in front of her. Slowly she turned to face us.

She was all but unrecognizable. Her long hair was clotted with blood, her face and hands and breast covered with it, a black syrup I could smell even from here. A stench that I had never known before but which was somehow, impossibly, familiar. Bile and heat and shit, the faint green fragrance of crushed grass and spring rain. But also the cloying sweetness of spoiled meat, and that unmistakable musky odor that was Angelica, sandalwood and oranges and something else, the salt smells of sweat and the sea. I stared at her in horror, as terrified and repelled as when we had watched Magda Kurtz given to the hollow land. But Angelica only smiled, her teeth red-streaked, and raised the lunula above her head.

She held it by its slender spars, so that it formed a silver arc above her. As I watched it began to glow, until it was not just a piece of glowing metal but something else, something *real*, its edge still black with blood, but so dazzling, so *pure* that I couldn't bear to look upon it; I tried to tear away my gaze but could not. Angelica's lips were moving although I could hear nothing, only my own breathing and the faint desperate knocking of my heart. From the small curved opening in the pendant flames danced, higher and higher, until they wreathed the entire crescent, until Angelica herself was ablaze.

And then I saw what it was, saw what *She* was—

The Moon: the *real* Moon, not the dead stone that whirls blindly in Earth's shadow but Hecate, Selene, Artemis: the pure and terrible One. She hung above us like a dream, like a doom waiting to fall and crush us—myself, Oliver, Hasel, Baby Joe—all of us frozen. All of us waiting to be chosen. Waiting to be destroyed.

But not me.

I started to run. Someone grabbed my arm—Hasel, though he held me without looking at me, his eyes still riveted on what was before us.

And then, what was before us spoke.

"Come to me."

It was only a whisper, but the night shivered with it, each dried blade of grass trembling as though a hot wind roared down from the sky.

"Come to me," she said again, and every bone inside me strained toward her. But it was not to me she called.

As though he were walking through deep water, Hasel turned and stepped toward her. She opened her arms to him and he walked straight into them, heedless of the filth and gore that clung to her, the clots of blood thick and black as flies. Behind her the bull lay upon the earth like some fallen monument: black, its horns the color of bone.

She drew Hasel to her and he grabbed her furiously, moaning as her hands moved across his body. He was like a candle flame, small and pale, shining more brightly in the moment before it is extinguished. I could see the lunula, dangling from her right hand. Her fingers tightened and drew the bright crescent across his shoulder. Hasel cried out, his voice torn between longing and pain, and pulled away.

For an instant they stood apart. Hasel reached to touch his shirt, parted the slitted cloth and probed there. His eyes widened when he saw his fingers slick with blood.

"Hey," he said. *"Hey . . ."*

Angelica cupped a hand beneath Hasel's chin. Her lips parted as though to kiss him, but her free hand moved toward his breast, her fingers taut around a blade of light—

"No!"

Oliver darted between them, pushing Hasel aside. With a moan Hasel staggered away from Angelica, clutching his chest. The front of his shirt had been ripped from shoulder to hem, and where the cloth flapped open blood oozed from a long shallow gash across his sternum.

"Oh—*God!*—Sweet Jesus, I'm fucking *bleeding*—"

I moved to help him, but fell back as another voice rent the air.

"You said it was me!"

In front of Angelica, Oliver stood with hands clenched at his sides. His eyes were wide and maddened, his face contorted with rage.

"You wanted *me*!" he shouted. *"You said it had to be me!"*

Angelica stared at him, the lunula dangling loosely from her fingers. For the first time she seemed uneasy, and her gaze darted from Oliver to Hasel. Suddenly she nodded.

"Yes," she said in a low voice. Quickly she draped the lunula back around her neck, awkwardly brushed a matted strand of hair from her eyes. Before she could move, Oliver grabbed her, his hands stark white against her bloodied arms. For a moment I thought she would pull away from him, but he pushed her roughly to the ground. She did not cry out or try to flee. Instead she stared up at him, her mouth a hard line curving slowly into defiance and a sort of grim joy. Oliver stared down at her, his hands fumbling at his belt. His trousers slid down his legs. Like a clumsy schoolboy he fell onto her, pulling her beneath him as her arms closed around his back.

"No."

I covered my eyes but still I could hear them, their bodies thrashing against the dead stalks and Angelica's low moaning whimper, Oliver making a deep grunting *ah! ah! ah!* as though he were being struck over and over again. In a way it was more horrible than all that had gone before, if only because it was so banal and so joyless, like listening to some machine echo the most precious remembered words of a lover long dead. But there was also something maddening about it: truly maddening. I was seized by a dreadful terror that if I stayed there I would lose my mind, as Angelica and Oliver seemed to have lost theirs.

So I turned to run—and froze.

On the rise behind me stood Balthazar Warnick and Francis Connelly. They might have been two stones set there as sentinels to guard the scene below. In the cold starlight they looked grey and stern: Francis's mouth curled in disgust, Professor Warnick grim-eyed as he gazed down upon Oliver and Angelica moving in the dust.

As I stared, other things began to appear in the darkness to either side of them. Shapes tall and thin and white as birch trees, and others huge as menhirs, with great upswept wings; and still others the forms of ordinary men and women, seeming frail as porcelain beside those monstrous shadows. From horizon to horizon they stretched in an unbroken line, demons and angels and human men and women. Though they were mostly men. Men old and young and middle-aged, men of every race imaginable, their faces drawn and silent as Balthazar Warnick's.

I began to shiver uncontrollably. There was no mistaking who they were. They were the *Benandanti*: Those Who Do Well, The Good Walkers. The chosen ones who for millennia had watched over mankind, benevolent sentries but also jailers, who meted out punishment and torment and death with as much care as they preserved a way of life. As the Furies were known as the Eumenides, The Kindly Ones, so the *Benandanti* saw themselves as benevolent; but to me they were dreadful even in their stillness.

I turned to look back down upon Oliver and Angelica; and now it seemed that they were not a man and a woman rutting in the dirt but two grasping dwarfish figures, struggling as they fought, the dead bull behind them. And then again they were not two *people* at all but mere shapes; and then not even that but formless things grappling beneath another, greater darkness. One white, the other black. Not the black that soothes and brings sleep but a chthonic darkness, a vast supplanting emptiness that was both maw and womb, whirling maelstorm and the storm's calm fixed eye.

And as I watched a cry rent the air, a howl so anguished that I dropped to my knees. To hear such despair and horror given voice! I would be deafened, rather than hear such a sound again. As it died I cowered and prayed that whatever had cried out was lifeless now, or fled.

Behind me something moved. I cringed and flung one arm out to protect myself. But when I looked up I saw that it was only Baby Joe and Hasel, and behind them Balthazar and Francis, all staring at where Angelica and Oliver lay motionless in the grass.

"Ohh . . ."

I whirled and saw Oliver stumble to his feet, yanking at his trousers until they hitched up around his waist. He moved clumsily, the loose cuffs of his pants billowing around his calves. His fly was still open; his shirt was blotched with dirt and blood. A poisonous-looking crimson line tracked up the side of his leg. With his shambling gait and shaven head he looked like an old drunk. He kept putting his hands into his pockets and drawing them out again, like a nervous boy or pantomime beggar, and I could hear him mumbling—

> *"—bulbul, bulbulone! I will shally. Though shalt willy. You wouldnt should as youd remesmer. I hypnot. 'Tis golden sickle's hour. Holy moon priestess, we'd love our grappes of mistellose! Moths the matter? Pschttt! Tabarins comes. To fell out fairest . . ."*

Suddenly he saw me staring at him. He raised his hand; for a moment I couldn't see what he was doing, waving or mimicking a swimmer crawling to shore or showing me something, something bright and glittering between his fingers . . .

Then my gaze was drawn downward, to where Angelica lay at his feet. She was smiling, her eyes closed. Behind her the dead bull had shrunk from primitive icon to a grotesque and pathetic corpse, its legs stiffly crooked like broken planks, its eyes shuttered with dust. Angelica blinked, then slowly drew herself up, like a cat stretching. She opened her eyes and extended a languid arm to her consort.

"Oliver," she said.

Oliver looked down at her. If before his face had been twisted with rage, now it was contorted into something almost impossible for me to fathom. Loathing, yes. But also love, and perhaps even admiration, but most of all, fear. One hand dropped to fumble with the buttons of his trousers. The other tightened into a fist. Whatever shining thing he had grasped was gone. Then he was staring not at Angelica but at me, though not at me really but at something else. Very slowly the familiar crooked canine grin spread across his face. His head fell back, and he raised his hand. For a dizzying instant I thought he was going to strike Angelica. I caught a flash of something lucifer-bright as his hand swept down: a slender shining blade. It fell, not upon Angelica but upon his own groin.

"Oliver, no!" I shouted.

If the bull's dying bellow had been thunderous, then Oliver's scream was lightning: a blast of pure agony. I sprang forward and struck his hand, sending the knife skidding across the dirt. I heard Angelica screaming, Baby Joe and Hasel shouting. Oliver howled as I pushed him to the ground and tried to hold him still. Damp warmth spread across my jeans as I yelled for help. His legs thrashed, his eyes were open and staring blindly at the sky as he still gave forth that unending anguished howl.

"Enough."

A low voice commanded me. I looked up and saw Balthazar and Francis. Francis grabbed me roughly, but Balthazar shouted and he let me go. Then Balthazar knelt beside me, tearing off his shirt and trying to staunch Oliver's bleeding. With one hand he pushed me away. "Leave him to us now."

Oliver's howl cut off and he began to scream. I stared mutely at Professor Warnick. Exhaustion fogged his blue eyes, and a terrible, terrible weariness. "Go now," he said.

As I stumbled to my feet someone grabbed me.

"*Hija*, come on—" It was Baby Joe, and Hasel at his side.

"No!—let me go, damn it, *help* him, we have to *save* him!—"

"Stop it, *hija*!"

"No—you don't understand, they'll kill him—let me *go*—"

I shouted and pulled free from Baby Joe. "I'm not leaving him!" I yelled, then looked around frantically. "Where is she, where's—

"Angelica!"

As though echoing me Francis stood. "She's gone!" His gaze fixed on the distant woods, and he started sprinting toward the trees when Balthazar shouted.

"Leave her, Francis!"

Francis glanced back, took another step as Balthazar commanded him.

"I said, *leave her*."

Francis nodded and returned to Balthazar's side. Professor Warnick looked up at Baby Joe and Hasel and me. "Get back to the house. Go, all of you!"

"Come *on*!" cried Hasel. He and Baby Joe began running up the long rise to the Orphic Lodge, dragging me between them. After a few steps I turned to look back.

In the darkened hollow they waited: the dead bull; the fallen boy; the silent guardian; the fool. Of Angelica I saw nothing. Balthazar Warnick crouched above Oliver, his hands moving quickly across the boy's groin. Oliver's face was so white that I feared he was dead. But then he moved his head slightly from side to side. He opened his eyes very wide and stared straight up into the sky, as though he saw something there, something glorious and terrible. Even from here I could see how angry Francis was: almost literally hopping with rage.

"But she's *got* it!" His words sounded thin and clear, as though plucked from wires. "We can't let her go, she's—"

Warnick turned to him, his eyes burning. "It's too late, Francis. Go to the lodge and call an ambulance. Get my car ready in case it doesn't come right away."

"But—"

Warnick's voice shook as he shouted, "It's been *done*, Francis. It's too late now—"

He staggered to his feet. Oliver made a noise like gurgling laughter, his eyes still fixed on the horizon. Baby Joe and Hasel halted. Without speaking we all turned to where Balthazar Warnick pointed at the eastern sky.

There, above the unbroken line of leafless birch and sturdy conifers, above the tumbled stones and dying ferns, a pale light glimmered. As we watched, the frailest, most delicate arc of a crescent moon rose above the trees. A new moon where no moon should be; a new moon when the heavens should hold only its darkest quarter. Balthazar's voice rang out, taut with wonder and dread.

"—She's not sleeping anymore."

CHAPTER 9

The Harrowing

By the time I reached our room, the entire lodge was in an uproar. Lights were flicking on everywhere, yawning students peered out their doors while the housekeeper Kirsten waited grimly by the front door like the old mansion's Cerberus, glaring at anyone who ventured down the steps. Annie stood in the corridor, white-faced, her hair sticking up like a porcupine's.

"Sweeney! What happened? Where's Angelica?"

I shoved past her into the room and raced from one window to the next, yanking each open and leaning out, desperately scanning the night for what I needed to see: Angelica and Oliver laughing together as they walked back up to the lodge.

But instead there was only darkness, the sweeping shadows of the mountains and a few faint stars blinking wanly beneath the sickle moon. I pulled my head away from the open casement and stared at Annie. My breast ached with fear and hopeless longing, a palpable throbbing pain as acute as though I had been stabbed.

"She's gone."

"Gone? What do you mean, gone?"

"I mean I don't know where she is." I went from the window to Angelica's bed and stared down at the neat worn coverlet, her bulging cosmetics bag, the little case that held her contact lens solution.

She won't get far, Sheriff. She rode off without her eyeliner.

"You don't know where she *is*?" Annie's voice rose to a hysterical pitch. "Jesus! What happened—"

Through the open windows came a sudden high wailing. It grew louder and louder, perfect counterpoint to my anguished thoughts. Crimson light streaked the trees, strobing from red to black to red.

"No!" I ran into the hall, but Annie stopped me.

"Sweeney, what happened? You have to tell me, you can't just take off like this—*where is she?*"

"I don't know!" I yelled. "She took off! Something—something happened, something with her and Oliver—"

"Drugs? Was it drugs?"

"No, it wasn't *drugs*, I *wish* it was drugs! Angelica split and Oliver, he tried to—he—"

"Goddamn it!" Annie tore across the room to her bed and started throwing clothes into a knapsack. "I knew it, I *knew* I should have gone with you." The ambulance's siren went dead, although its ghoulish light show continued. "Where's my stuff? Did you do something with my other bag? Oh, *god*, why'd I stay here—"

Grief and fear exploded inside me. "Christ, Annie, what do you think you could have done? Some kind of, of *witchcraft*, what could you have done about that! These people are crazy; *Angelica* is crazy and you think you could have *stopped* her?"

"I *would* have stopped her! I would never have let her go—"

"There was nothing you could have done."

We whirled to face the door. There stood Balthazar Warnick, one delicate hand resting upon the wooden jamb. On his forehead a vein throbbed, and he brushed distractedly at it, as though it were a fly. His sweater was covered with dirt and leaves and blood.

"You shouldn't have interfered," he added wearily; though I was unsure if he was talking to me, or Annie, or himself. "Katherine Cassidy, I want you to come with me."

I stiffened. "I'm not going anywhere with you."

Professor Warnick shook his head. "No one will hurt you. We're sending you back to the city, that's all."

"Why can't we stay here?" Annie's voice cracked and she clutched her knapsack protectively to her chest. "Why can't we leave in the morning?"

"You can leave in the morning with the others. Miss Cassidy has to leave now."

"Why?" I started to cry. I hated myself but couldn't help it. "What's going on? Where's Oliver—"

"They're taking him to the hospital. I think he's all right, just a bad cut although he did lose some blood." He ran his hand across the front of his sweater and winced. "Come on, Katherine. Pack your things."

"No. I'm not going with you."

"Do yourself a favor," snapped a nasal voice, and Francis Connelly loomed behind Balthazar. He looked more shaken than I would have expected, but his eyes were cold. "Just shut up and come with us, okay?"

"Francis." Professor Warnick turned to him angrily. "It's under control. I told you to go to the hospital—"

"But it looks like—"

"I will meet you there," Professor Warnick went on smoothly, but his voice had a dangerous edge. Francis stared at him, as though waiting for him to change his mind, finally nodded, and shot me a last disdainful glance. When he was gone Balthazar looked at me sorrowfully.

"Sweeney." He'd never called me that before; his tone was so gentle that my silent tears gave way to sobs. "You have to come with me."

"What are you *doing?*" Annie flung her arm protectively around my shoulders. In her too-long Snoopy T-shirt she looked like a kid fighting bedtime. "You can't just take her—"

Professor Warnick sighed. "We've found drug paraphernalia in Miss Cassidy's dorm room. Marijuana, some kind of mushrooms—"

"Hey! You didn't have—" said Annie, but I cut her off.

"You were in my room? Who let you in my *room*—"

"I don't believe it!" yelled Annie. "This is a setup, it's a fucking—"

"I have a responsibility to the University," Balthazar said coolly. "The penalty for drug possession is mandatory expulsion."

"Expulsion!"

His voice rose impatiently. "Consider yourself fortunate, Miss Cassidy! We *could* call the police."

"But—you didn't have a warrant! Isn't there some kind of appeal, can't I—"

"There's also the matter of missed classes—I haven't seen you in *my* class for over a month, and there have been complaints from your other teachers as well.

"I think," he said, putting a hand on my shoulder and starting to steer me toward the door, "I *think* that it will be best for all concerned if you are removed from the University immediately. We could have you arrested, you know: it wouldn't be at all difficult to obtain a search warrant. But at the Divine we prefer to deal with these things in our own way. You have had an unfortunate influence on some very promising students, Miss Cassidy. Enough is enough." He pushed me into the hall.

"You bastard. Where the hell are you taking her?" I looked over my shoulder to see Annie staring after me in a rage.

Balthazar Warnick shook his head. "I'm sorry, Annie. It's not just that she broke school policy. Drug possession is against the law—"

"The law! This has nothing to do with the law, and you know it, you—"

Professor Warnick pulled the door shut behind us.

"Are you going to expel her, too?" I demanded. "Are you going to expel everyone who's here tonight?"

"Not unless they interfere." Balthazar Warnick tugged at a greying forelock. He was breathing heavily, and his face was flushed. "Katherine Cassidy. Come with me, please."

His hand shot into his trouser pocket and withdrew an old-fashioned key ring.

"Where are we going?"

He said nothing, only kept his hand on my shoulder and guided me down the corridor, up a small flight of stairs and through a narrow hall, up another stairway and finally into a wide passage carpeted with thick oriental rugs woven in somber hues of black and crimson. We were in a part of the Orphic Lodge I'd never seen. The sounds of urgent voices died. I could hear nothing but our echoing footsteps and the falsely cheerful jangle of Professor Warnick's keys.

"This way, if you will."

Professor Warnick dropped his hand and walked briskly down the hall. I walked beside him, resigned to whatever horror was in store for me. It seemed futile to try to run. And in truth, at that moment I was more afraid of being alone than of anything else. There was something about the passage that reminded me of that darkly ornate upstairs corridor at Garvey House: the same queer aura of readiness and neglect, the same brooding strangeness that was not assuaged by the gleaming brass fixtures and resiny smell of cedar. The passage was lined with doors, but unlike those in other parts of the lodge, they were all closed.

And now we were nearing the end of the corridor. There was a heavy oaken door with a brass handle, a little brass plaque that read *Please Knock*.

"Here," murmured Professor Warnick.

I stopped and shook my head. "No. I mean, *no*. I'm not going in there."

Professor Warnick slid a key into the lock, turned it, and listened for the clicking of hidden tumblers.

"I didn't *do* anything," I pleaded. "I mean, *everyone* keeps some pot in their rooms, you can't just—"

"This isn't about your drugs," he said, grasping the doorknob. "It's—"

"No!" I cried; but at that moment the door creaked open.

"—it's just my study," said Professor Warnick gently, raising an eyebrow. "Please, come inside."

I went inside.

It was a large room, very dark until Balthazar switched on a tall floor lamp. A fringed maroon paisley throw had been tossed over the shade, and its rosy glow did a lot to make the place look less threatening, more like an eccentric scholar's homely lair. Bookshelves lined the walls, full of flaking leather volumes and curling manuscripts, sheaves of computer printouts and encyclopedias and something that looked very much like papyrus.

"I won't keep you very long, Katherine. Have a seat."

I remained standing. Balthazar had crossed to the far wall, a wall taken up by an enormous bay window with many small, mullioned panes. On the window's wide sill there was a small brightly colored model of the solar system. Balthazar stared at it thoughtfully. The orbs representing the planets were enameled in bright, almost violent, colors—scarlet, cyan, Tyrian purple—and embellished with odd symbols and curlicues. The sun was sheathed in gold with a network of black wires across its surface. After a moment he picked up the orrery and stared at it, brow furrowed.

"It is changing," he murmured.

Balthazar raised the model to his face and poked one of the glowing beads with a finger—the ball that was enameled emerald green and blue, the orb that was third from the sun. It turned languidly, a marble in slow motion. With a sigh Balthazar pinched it between his thumb and forefinger.

"Worlds within worlds," he began, and stopped.

In his hand the planets in their shining orbits trembled. A thin sound filled the air. The hair on the back of my neck prickled. A sound like shattering crystal; a sound I had heard before.

Balthazar's eyes widened and he raised the orrery, as he had done with the sistrum all those weeks before. In the air before him the globes began to spin: slowly at first, but more and more quickly, until it seemed he was beset by a cloud of bees. Tendrils of grey smoke rose from their blurred circuits. Balthazar's ruddy face grew pale.

"No," he whispered, then grimaced in pain. He swore and snatched his hands from the model, as though it burned his fingers; but instead of falling the orrery remained in the air before him. With a crackling sound, flames erupted from the dizzying vortex. Professor Warnick fell back against the window.

"No!—"

There was a roar, a sound as though somewhere miles beneath us the earth was collapsing. The floor lamp swayed perilously back and forth before it crashed to the floor, plunging the room into darkness—save where the orrery burned in the empty air. Its brightness terrified me: as though waves of liquid flame poured forth from some depthless fiery sea. Yet the flaming globe gave off no heat. And while the roar continued it was muted now, a pervasive vibration that made my bones and blood hum.

"Get back, Katherine!"

The orrery candled into a single glowing mass, not the warm gold of any fire I have ever seen but a blinding silvery white, with a black core. It pulsed like a swimming medusa, and then suddenly, soundlessly, its dark heart exploded outward. I was staring at a spherical void, a black hole crowned by a fiery white corona. At its center glowed a bloody-looking crescent. Dark liquid streamed from it onto the floor.

"Professor Warnick!" I cried. I could barely see him behind the luminous apparition, but I lunged across the room, knocking aside a chair as I tried to reach him. "Professor Warnick, can you hear me?"

"Stay back—don't come near—"

His voice sounded faint and thin; it might have been the sound of branches scraping at the window. Behind the dazzling crescent he was all but invisible, enveloped by the black heart of that flaming mass.

"Get away—" His voice echoed faintly. "—warn them—!"

An anguished shout came from behind the glowing sigil, then a scraping sound, a sort of *gnawing*. My boots grew unbearably hot, as though I'd been kicking at live coals. Balthazar's voice grew fainter still, and more desperate, as frantically I tried to get closer to the pulsing spectral orb. But it was futile: like trying to force my way through a wall of flame.

By now I had all but lost sight of him. The gnawing sound gave way to avid lapping. To my horror I realized that the luminous sphere was moving. This was no illusion of darkness and radiance: the spectral moon was *devouring him*. Bit by bit Balthazar Warnick was being eaten away by the utter blackness, a man in eclipse; and all the while sparks and dazzling rays of white and silver-blue shot from the half-moon above him. For an instant I was paralyzed. Then I dived at him through the moon's penumbra.

Silence. The fluid lapping sound faded. I could see nothing, *feel* nothing but cold, a cold so penetrating the breath froze in my throat. I choked, unable to breathe or move or cry out, and crashed to the floor.

The rug beneath me was soaked through with warm liquid. I stumbled back to my feet, straining to see something in the clouded darkness. I drew my hands in front of me; I could barely discern that they were stained black. I could smell something hot and bitter-rich, and realized that I was soaked with blood. Desperately I looked around for Balthazar.

He was there, a few feet away, shielding his eyes from the terrible radiance that surrounded us. He looked tiny and wizened, and unbelievably ancient. Like one of those mummified cadavers dragged from the bottom of a peat bog, his skin turned to friable leather, his hair a few damp strands across his skull. His hands were drawn before his face and his mouth was open as though he were screaming in agony, but he made no sound.

Around us that awful light billowed and pulsed. On the nap of the worn rug in front of me I could see the tiny star-bright image of the moon, its body black and swollen, capped by a shining crescent like the indentation left by a fingernail. Like one of those images you make of the solar eclipse, using a piece of cardboard with a pinhole in it. I took a deep breath, my throat still raw with cold, and reached for Balthazar, then, with all my strength, crushed the image of the moon beneath my boot.

A shriek pierced the air—a woman's voice. At that moment my arms closed around Balthazar. Beneath his heavy sweater his bones were like bundled twigs. The shriek grew into a roar. But worst of all, worst of any of the things I could have imagined, there came a cry so faint it was scarce a sound at all—

"Sweeney—"

"Angelica!" I gasped.

She was there. Dazzling flames flowed from her, and upon her breast the moon shone like a beacon—only it was not the moon but the lunula, brighter than any moon, brighter than the sun. Her face was like the face I had seen that night upon the Mound, terrible and beautiful, her hair a streaming darkness as she reached for me, her sweet voice begging me to come to her. And I would have gone, would have embraced her as eagerly and heedlessly as I had done before, had not Balthazar Warnick pulled me away.

"Sweeney, no!"

For an instant we strained against each other: me striving to flee into Angelica's arms, Balthazar holding me back.

"Swee—ney!"

She wailed my name as though her heart would break, and I felt my own heart torn inside me. I lunged forward, trying to shake Balthazar from me.

"Come to me!" cried Angelica, her voice piercing me with sorrow and longing as her fingers grasped at mine. *"Swee—ney—"*

She was aflame, the tendrils of her hair whipped about me but I didn't care, didn't care about anything save that this was Angelica and at last I would be hers. I felt myself tumbling forward, falling into her arms, into her open mouth, and suddenly my boot skidded across the floor. It was enough for me to lose my balance, enough for my hand to slip from hers so that Balthazar could drag me away.

"Close your eyes!" he shouted. "Don't look at her, come this way—*now*!"

I shut my eyes and turned. Balthazar clutched me as we staggered through the darkness. From behind us came a sound that made my entire body shudder, a horrible freezing cry.

"Sweeney, nooo—"

Her voice cut off. I pulled away from Balthazar, shaded my eyes; but whatever had been there was gone. I was on the floor, Balthazar sprawled beside me. In front of the window, the oriental carpeting was bunched up in a blackened heap. I could smell the coppery hot stench of blood. Against the edge of the ruined carpet, a small twisted mass of wires smoldered.

"The orrery," said Balthazar. He got to his feet and stumbled to the window. I stayed where I was, feeling as though I'd been beaten black-and-blue. My clothes were stiff with blood, my arms scored with raw red lines, as though someone had gone at me with a razor. I thought of the lunula's glistening edge raised above Hasel, and felt sick.

"She destroyed it." Balthazar nudged the smoking clump of wires with his foot. His tone was more awestruck than angry, but when I looked at him I was shocked to see his face wet with tears. He pulled his bloodstained sweater over his head and wrapped it around his hand. Then he bent over the charred ruin and picked it up, holding it at arm's length.

"See what your friend has done," he whispered. "As above, so below."

All the shining globes had melted and congealed into a single corroded mass. At one side there was a crescent-shaped hole, like a gaping mouth.

"It is a warning—an unnecessary one—that She has the lunula now; without it She would never have dared attack me here. But it is not whole."

His finger probed warily at the opening, and I shuddered, absurdly afraid that the smoking moon would *bite* him. "And *that* might be what saves us—perhaps, perhaps . . ."

He stepped to a corner of the window and opened a casement. Leaning out into the night he flung the ruined orrery in the direction of the river, far below. I held my breath, waiting to hear a faint splash or crash upon the rocks. Balthazar seemed to be listening, too; but there was nothing but the sound of wind tugging at the trees. He waited a moment, then with a grimace pitched his sweater out as well.

"There," he said as to himself. He turned back into the room, wiping his hands on his trousers. When he saw me watching him he started, as though he had forgotten I was there.

I stood, my legs still weak. "Is it—is it over? Is she—is Angelica dead?"

"Dead?" Balthazar's voice hardened. *"Dead?* She has never been more alive—not for centuries, not for over two thousand years—"

"We knew that She would return, and so we watched for Her—in all the old familiar places, as the song goes." He laughed sharply, a fox's bark. "But I did not think She would be so bold as to come *here*. And so I have spent a lifetime waiting for Her—*many* lifetimes—and it all comes down to this—a meddling child's *foolishness*—

"No, Katherine, Angelica isn't dead. But she isn't *Angelica* anymore, either." His eyes were livid with fury and disdain. "Your friend has been chosen for a very important task, but the work demands some alterations—"

"What did you do to her?" I whispered. "You bastard, what did you do to Oliver and Angelica?"

"What did I do to them?" Balthazar's face darkened. "What did I *do?*"

"Tell me!"

"I did nothing, you stupid girl! Angelica has been *claimed*—by She who has a dozen names in every tongue, by the one we call Othiym—

"For aeons She has been waiting—for the lunula to be found; for the right woman to be born; for the moment when Her talisman and Her chosen daughter would be brought together. And for all those aeons we too have watched, and waited, and searched. We have prepared, as well, in each generation making certain that there would be one young man who might be strong and beautiful enough to win Her, to seduce Her and so weaken Her—and for nothing! Because in the end we have been betrayed. Betrayed by Magda Kurtz, whom I loved as my own—"

He looked away from me. "—as my own daughter. Betrayed by the daughter of one of our most trusted members, and by Oliver's weakness, and *your* own meddling in things you cannot possibly understand."

His hand tightened into a fist as he snarled, "I might have had the lunula, Katherine. I *would* have had it, there in Garvey House, had you not pulled your friend Angelica from my hands. Just as you pulled me from *Her* hands a few minutes ago—"

The vulpine snarl cooled to an icy smile. He stepped delicately across the floor, once more composed and elegant, and glanced over his shoulder at me.

"Come here, Katherine."

I stayed where I was, tensed and shaking. "No."

He stopped and drew himself to his full height. If I had been standing beside him, he would have come barely to my chin. But his face was so ravaged, his eyes so brilliant, that I might have been staring into the terrible visage of some ancient sphinx, might have been looking upon the dark Goddess Herself.

"Come here."

There was a threat to the words, but more than that, a command; a Power. Even as I willed myself to run, I found that I was walking toward Balthazar Warnick, until I stood beside him at the far end of the room.

"I know everything there is to know about you, Katherine Cassidy," he said softly. "And that is very little: because to us you are a little thing. Do you understand that? A little, little thing—"

His white teeth glittered as he pinched together his thumb and forefinger to show how insignificant I was, how small and stupid and clumsy, but not useless, oh no! Not that—

"But somehow—" His face tilted to look up into mine, his eyes bleak. "Somehow you have come between those two Chosen Ones—"

The disdain in his voice melted, and while there was no warmth to his words they were no longer hateful. "—and somehow, somehow you saved me, when She would have devoured me."

He turned to look at the ruined carpet beneath the window, the blackened place where the orrery had been consumed. "And I don't understand it." He gazed at me and I shifted uneasily.

"Me neither," I said.

"I know." Balthazar gave a low laugh. "That is why I am going to show you something. Something that might help you to—"

He walked away from me and gestured meaningfully. "—better understand *us*."

He stopped. Set into the paneled wall was a door. A very old door, fashioned of pale wood and surmounted by an ornate lintel where a motto had been painted in now-faded letters.

OMNIA BONA BONIS

I stared at it in horror, remembering Magda Kurtz, the hellish landscape where she had been thrust by the same man who now held me captive.

"What does that mean?"

"It doesn't matter."

"Where—where does it go?"

From a pocket in his stained trousers he withdrew an old-fashioned skeleton key the length of my hand. He stared at it, his eyes slitted, then turned and slid it into the door.

"Go?" he echoed. A raging wind ripped the word from him, as before us the door swung open. "It goes where I will it to go—"

Streamers of mist rushed past me into the room. I began shivering uncontrollably, and scarcely felt it when Balthazar put one hand upon my shoulder and with the other pointed at the doorway.

"Behold the world She would give you!—"

All was darkness: total, engulfing darkness, so empty and vast even the memory of dawn was swallowed by it. But what was most horrible about the abyss was that *I knew it*. Knew its enveloping airless heat and flow; knew the all-encompassing void in which I floated like a lightless star, the pulsing mass of black matter that surrounded me, swallowed me, imprisoned me within its maw. I tasted rather than smelled a hot rich odor, the stench of blood and excrement and earth. The stink of the grave but also that of the incunabulum; of the gutter, the birthing room, the byre . . .

The beginning place.

"It is Othiym," Balthazar's voice echoed through my thoughts. "She who is the mouth of the world . . .

". . . She who is the word unspoken. Othiym Lunarsa."

His words fell away. Then,

"Look now." Balthazar's breath was warm in my ear. "Can you see them?"

In the wasteland a flare appeared, crimson and faintly blue.

"There," murmured Balthazar.

Another flame; then another, and another, and another, until everywhere I looked I saw small bursts of gold and yellow and scarlet, numerous small bonfires spread across the darkness.

"Watch," said Balthazar Warnick. "Now they will make the night their own."

Shadows appeared before the flames. Without a sound they began to crouch and leap around the bonfires in a sort of grotesque hobbling dance, until each small circle of flame had its lumbering cavalcade. The bonfires blazed up suddenly. I glimpsed flame-gilded antlers and hairy pelts, a leather priapus and cloven hooves, a pinioned mask formed of a screech owl's fell. The pungent incense was overwhelmed by an earthier stink. Trampled mud; singed hair; the putrescent reek of an ill-cured hide. And sweat, *real* sweat, with no sweet undertones of soap or perfume, and the hot ripe smell of women, like brine and yeast and blood.

"Ahhh . . ."

A whine escaped me and I bit down, hard, to keep my teeth from chattering. The splayed black bodies and antlered heads, the shrieking ragged voices that rang out like birds of prey—they were all somehow both more and less than human. Like that awful ancient figure painted upon the wall of a cavern in the Pyrenees—antlered but with a lion's paws, wolf's tail and cat's genitals and human feet, and terrible staring owlish eyes. *Le Sorcier*: The Sorceror.

"Animals," whispered Balthazar, his disgust tinged with fear. "Always, they would be nothing more than animals . . ."

I recalled Angelica's words—

The Benandanti *aren't into saving the shamans. They* are *the shamans.*

But then why was he afraid? I hugged my arms to my chest and forced myself to gaze more closely into that empty darkness.

And I saw what Balthazar saw.

The figures leaping and shambling around the blaze were women. All of them—shadows crowned with horns and leaves, feathered dwarfs and limping cranes—all, all were women. Dark gold–skinned women tall as men, long-necked and proud; women small and somber as badgers, beating the earth with blackened hands; girls no higher than my thighs, who tripped in and out amongst the others and shrieked like hunting kestrels. And mothers with nurslings, and grey-faced women who must be carried, and cold-eyed laughing girls who bore antlered crowns and flaming brands, goading the pelted shadows that humped along before them.

"Beasts," whispered Balthazar with loathing. "Nothing but beasts."

I knew then what he feared.

Women's magic.

That's *where the real power lies*, Angelica had said.

And it was true. Because I sensed the power of blood and milk, of flesh and sinew drawn together in the potent darkness. Of spittle rounding out a lump of clay, shaping it into the squatting figure of a Mother vast enough to embrace us all; of colored powder and kohl and rouge, shaping a mask to entice and enthrall; of a lone stern figure stooped over a fiery alembic, drawing forth a glowing wire like an arrow to spear the night.

And Angelica herself, her lap full of timeworn folios and crackling tomes; Angelica in bed beside me, her breath warm upon my neck; Angelica rising slowly from black water, her breasts silvered with light, her green eyes glowing and her hair streaming behind her: Angelica in all I could imagine.

From the night country rose a wind, warm and redolent of spices. Coriander and sandalwood and galingale, and sweet as their fragrance a childish voice, chanting.

I am eldest daughter of Kronos.
I am wife and sister of Osiris.
I am she who findeth fruit for men.
I am mother of Horus.
I am she that riseth in the Dog Star.
I am she that is called Goddess by women.

Bone upon bone and the thumping of cloven staves, fingers tapping upon a hollow skull and a sudden chorus of keening voices—

Othiym haïyo!
You who rule the gates of Hell in the earth's black heart,
golden Praxidike, first blossom of Deo,
Mother of Furies, Queen of the netherworld—
Othiym haïyo! Othiym Lunarsa!

"You see how they are," Balthazar murmured. "Rooting in the dirt, smearing their faces with soot and filth. And there is worse than that—"

A scream ripped the night. The fires flickered out. All was utter darkness, save only this—

Upon the rim of the world a sliver of moon perched, a tiny crescent like the memory of magic. After a moment it faded. From the abyss a wind rose, cold and insistent.

"So it will always be," whispered Balthazar as he pulled me from the edge of the portal. "She forgets that chaos begets only chaos, and cannot prevail."

I clasped my arms to my breast, shuddering. "No."

"No?" Balthazar's tone was unforgiving as the wind. "Are you a fool like Mr. Crawford, then?"

"N-not a f-fool—" I said through chattering teeth. With a grunt I pulled away. Two quick steps and I stood within the portal.

Dimly I was aware of the room, a shadowy place where outlines of walls, furnishings, windows hung ghostly in the darkness. But the *real* world lay before me—eternal and empty and torn by wind.

"Listen to me, Katherine!" shouted Balthazar. "Oliver is weak! He believes that we have no power left—that our time has ended—and so he sought to align himself with our Enemy. He thought She had changed, he thought She would not destroy him; but he is wrong! We are the only ones who can save him! You *know* that—"

I hesitated, thinking of Angelica wielding the lunula as a weapon, of Balthazar rushing to Oliver's side in the field.

"We are always the strongest, Katherine! *Force majeur*; and we always prevail. Even in this darkness—"

He swept up behind me. "Even now, we will prevail—"

In the wasteland a light appeared. Not the carnal blaze of a bonfire, but a steady glow, deep blue and shot with sparks of living green. The glow took shape, grew into a single pillar—then two—then four; until I was gazing upon the spires of a cathedral, tiny and perfect as though carved of crystal. Upon the horizon a second light appeared, and another edifice arose—a mosque this time, its dome a cobalt tear.

"Witness *our* legacy," cried Balthazar.

As though he had sown them, more and more structures sprang up, each more intricate than the one before. Pyramids of glass and steel, glittering alcazars and raised tombs of stone, pavilions and columned temples and immense black slabs of polished jet: all shining like gems, like prisms of flame. A stone had been hurled into the abyss and the darkness shattered, and each shard shone as brightly as a sun. A chorus of voices rose from them—voices now sweet and high and clear, now deep and tolling like those drowned bells that ring the changes beneath the sea. I could not make out their words, but I understood them well enough. They were singing joy and pride and courage in the day, singing long and loud against the dark.

"Do you understand now, Katherine?" Balthazar's laughter sounded close beside me. "There *is* no choice, really—not unless you would choose darkness and ignorance over light and order."

I felt his hand rest lightly upon my shoulder as he went on.

"Though it does not matter—not for you, at least. I show you these things just so that you will not forget—so that you will have something to take away with you from the Divine. Something to remember us by, if you will."

I felt a tightening in my throat. "What are you going to do with me?"

"Nothing." Before us the lights winked out, one by one. The glorious singing faded into the wind. "I will take you downstairs, and Francis will drive you back to the city—"

"Francis!"

He made a dismissive gesture. "I have much to do now. This has taken too much time already. Someone will be contacting you about forwarding your transcripts to your parents. I have no doubt but that you will do much better at your next school."

He turned and began to walk away from the door. I watched him, stunned, then looked back at the portal.

Beyond it loomed the abyss. As I stared the outlines of the doorway became more distinct. The wood's grain and the faint glister of light upon the doorknob grew brighter and brighter, until what lay behind them was all but lost to view.

"*Behold the world She would give you . . .*"

Yet could that truly be the world Angelica's Goddess would bring?

I know enough not to buy into every idea my father taught me. Or Balthazar Warnick . . .

Why should the darkness be seen as evil and bleak and nullifying? Why women's magic nothing more than rutting in the cinders? Why chaos and the end of all things?

Why is a raven like a writing desk?

"Katherine," Balthazar said, gently but insistently, "it's time to go."

"No."

Before he could stop me, I darted to the edge of the portal.

"Katherine! Get away from there—!"

Behind me lay Balthazar's study. Somewhere in the lodge beneath us Annie slept, and Baby Joe. Somewhere Oliver slept as well, swept into the night on a tide of Demerol and hospital sheets; and perhaps even Angelica, perched on the cusp between earth and sky, dreams and waking.

That left me and Balthazar Warnick. His hands clenched as I edged away from him.

"If you step through there you will be destroyed!" he cried. "It is nothing!—"

"I don't believe you, Professor Warnick!"

I took another step. The wooden lintel disappeared into fog. I stood upon a precipice hanging out above the abyss. "Nothing is that simple—maybe Angelica is wrong, but you're wrong too! Or maybe you're both partly right—"

The freezing wind howled up from the wasteland. Behind me Balthazar shouted, but his words were lost to me. Suddenly I laughed.

Because if it was a choice between the void and what lay behind me—the loss of my friends, the loss of the Divine and all its promise—then I would take my chances with whatever was down there rooting in the night. I turned to look at Balthazar—and jumped.

For an instant he was frozen in the air before me: hands outstretched, his mouth open in a wordless cry. Then it was as he said—

A raging wind, ice and darkness and the freezing air tearing my clothes from me, my flesh and hair and voice—

Nothing.

I came to in some kind of shed. Eerie blue light resolved into a wintry glare filtered through walls of translucent corrugated plastic. There was a strong sweet smell.

Lemons, but *chemical* lemons. I rubbed my eyes, looked down, and saw that I was sitting on a nearly empty plastic container. Greenish liquid spilled on my boots. My stomach churned; I put one hand in front of my face and with the other pushed forward, until I felt the thin plastic give way. A door opened and I fell out onto the driveway in front of the Shrine.

"Ow."

I got to my feet unsteadily. I felt light-headed and a little sick to my stomach, but otherwise okay. Above me the Shrine was booming the quarter hour; but which hour? Seven, I guessed, by the grey thin light and the scattering of cars across the parking lot. Seven-fifteen on a Sunday morning. At seven-thirty the first Mass of the day would begin.

I wiped my gritty hands on my shirt and hunched my shoulders against the cold. As I headed for my dorm I glanced over my shoulder at the utility building I'd stumbled from. Its cheap plastic door flapped open, but then the wind slammed it shut again, and I glimpsed the sign there—

Members Only.

I went to Rossetti Hall. My key still opened the front door, but when I got upstairs to my own room the lock had been changed. It was so early there was no one in the hall or lounge to ask about it, but I didn't want to stick around and risk running into Francis Connelly or something worse.

I hurried up another flight to Angelica's room. I banged on the door, but there was no answer. It was too soon for them to have returned from West Virginia; at least that's what I hoped. I slunk outside through the back door, feeling like I had a big black X on my forehead.

It was just like my first day at the Divine, that first awful day before I met Oliver and Angelica. The few people I saw paid no attention to me at all. I might have wondered if they even actually *saw* me, except that an immaculately dressed family hurrying past on their way to the Shrine gave me disapproving looks. I must have looked exactly like what they were praying to be delivered from. I dug into my pockets, fished around until I found a few wadded bills and some change, and went to the Shrine to scavenge breakfast.

I ended up spending most of the day there. I was afraid to venture back out onto the Strand. I hid in a corner booth and drank endless cups of coffee, bought a pack of cigarettes and rationed them, one every twenty minutes. I even slept for a little while, my head pillowed on the Formica tabletop, until the clatter of dishes and silverware woke me. When I looked up I saw the old round schoolhouse clock at the end of the room, its red second hand sweeping briskly along. Four o'clock: time for tea. I shoved my cigarettes into my pocket and went in search of Baby Joe.

Dusk was already falling, barren trees throwing long shadows beneath the streetlamps. In Baby Joe's room a light was on. I was afraid to go to the front door, so I threw pebbles at his window until he peered out. He mimed surprise and relief, raising his hands and shaking his head, then motioned for me to go around to the back of the building. I crept through a hedge of overgrown box trees until I saw Baby Joe leaning against the dorm's ivy-covered wall, holding open a fire door with one hand. In the other he held my battered knapsack.

"Hey, *hija*. I was starting to worry when I found this in your room but no Sweeney. You in trouble?"

"Something like that."

I followed him to his room. He shut and locked the door, and I groaned with relief. Baby Joe hugged me awkwardly, his stolid face creased with concern.

"What happened, *hija*? Me and Hasel went looking for you, but you were gone."

I perched myself on the edge of his bed. Except for the fine layer of ash over everything, Baby Joe's room was disturbingly neat. A Royal Upright typewriter sat on the old wooden desk, surrounded by carefully arranged stacks of paper and textbooks. Issues of *Punk Magazine* and *New York Rocker* and *The Paris Review* were lined up against one wall, and I knew if I opened one of his bureau drawers I'd see his tired white T-shirts and black nylon socks stored with just as much solicitude. It all made me feel incredibly disgusting.

Baby Joe didn't notice or didn't care. He cracked open the window, reached out onto the sill, and withdrew two bottles of Old Bohemian. "Here, *hija*. Where the hell'd you go?"

I told him everything that had happened since we fled back to the Orphic Lodge. Baby Joe leaned against his desk, giggling softly in disbelief and laughing out loud when I told him about the *Benandanti*'s portal.

"No shit? One of their *puertas*? You got *cojones*, Sweeney!"

But when I mentioned Francis Connelly he shook his head.

"Francis X. Connelly. Someday I'm gonna take him out—" He pointed a finger at me and cocked his thumb. "*Bang*. I'd do it now, but they might revoke my scholarship."

I told him about watching Magda Kurtz being shoved through the door in Garvey Hall, about Angelica's crescent-shaped necklace and how I wasn't sure if she was working with Balthazar Warnick and the *Benandanti* or against them.

"Probably against them. Angie, you know Angie is smart but not that kind of smart," said Baby Joe. "These student *brujos*, they get kind of cocky. I've seen it with my brother's friends; they think because they're tapped for the *Benandanti* they can do anything. Fly, walk on water, kill a big cow with a charm bracelet. But Warnick? I wouldn't fuck with Warnick, I tell you that."

At last I finished. My beer was still half-full, but all of a sudden I couldn't stomach any more. I buried my face in my hands, and started to cry.

"Hey. It's okay—" Baby Joe sat on the bed next to me and patted my back. "You can stay here tonight, you can move all your stuff here if you want, *hija*, it's okay—"

"It's *not* okay! They're kicking me out, my parents are gonna kill me, and Christ, Baby Joe, what is going *on* here? Where's Angelica? Where's Oliver? What—"

I swallowed, my voice fading to a whisper. "What we saw in the field—what the hell was *that*?"

Baby Joe shrugged. "You tell me," he said softly. "But these *Benandanti*, they do a lot of crazy shit—"

"But *that* didn't have anything to do with the *Benandanti*. *That* was something else. Angelica's gotten all hyped up about some weird goddess cult; she's been reading all these books and talking about the second coming of Kali or Ishtar, or—"

I punched the mattress furiously. "It's fucking *nuts*."

"Ishtar, huh?" Baby Joe reached for my beer, drank it thoughtfully. "Well, at least she fits the job description."

"It's not funny."

"Who's laughing?" He finished the beer and leaned back on the bed. "But man, you are right, this is some crazy shit Barbie-girl has gotten herself into. And you don't know where she is?"

"I don't think anyone knows where she is. She must have taken off into the woods. And unless she wants to end up with Magda Kurtz, she better stay there."

For a few minutes we sat in silence. Outside, the Shrine bells tolled five-thirty. It was already full dark. All around us, people would be getting ready for the start of another week. I took a deep breath, then asked the question I'd been waiting to ask.

"What happened to Oliver?"

"Oliver?" Baby Joe regarded me through slitted black eyes. "Oliver's here."

"Here?" I looked around quickly, but Baby Joe went on, "Not here in my room—I mean he's back here in D.C. They brought him to the ER in West Virginia last night, but I guess he was okay 'cause they just looked him over and discharged him. He came back with Warnick this morning. Hasel heard them talking, they were supposed to take him to Providence for observation—"

"Providence Hospital?"

He nodded. "To the psychiatric wing."

"Don't they have to get the family's permission before they do that?"

"*Hija*, Warnick *is* his family. All the *Benandanti*—they come first, they take care of their own—"

"But Oliver's not crazy."

"Normal people don't try to cut their dicks off with a Swiss Army knife."

"Okay, okay."

He lit a cigarette and smoked pensively for a moment before saying, "You know, that's what they used to do."

"Who? The *Benandanti*?"

"No. Your goddess-worshipers. In Iran or someplace. Turkey, maybe. The priests would go into some kind of ecstatic frenzy and castrate themselves." He gave a wheezing laugh. "We read about it in Warnick's class. You can see how church attendance might drop off after a while."

"But—why would *Oliver* do that? I mean, how would he even know about it. He hasn't been to Warnick's class in two months."

Baby Joe shrugged. "It's not like it's a big secret. It's history, man, anyone can read about it. Maybe he and Angie, you know—she's playing Ishtar, he's gonna be Adonis. *Talagang sirang ulo*."

I got to my feet. "I know, I know: *crazy fucking bitch*." I ran my fingers through my hair. "God, I just wish I could have a decent meal and a bath and sleep for a week—"

Baby Joe put a hand on my shoulder. "Stay here, Sweeney. Really—you can have the bed, I'll crash on the floor—"

"Oh, Baby Joe—thanks, really, thanks a lot. But I can't. I think—I think I better go see Oliver. How far is Providence?"

"Maybe five, ten minutes on the bus."

"Okay. Do me a favor, then. Will you call Annie and tell her where I am, and find out if she's heard from Angelica? She's got to come back, she can't be out there running around the woods without her clothes—"

Baby Joe grinned. "Nice for the trees, though, huh? Yeah, I'll call Annie."

"Thanks."

He followed me to the door. "You too, you know. You're a fucking crazy bitch too, but you're not *nuts*."

He drew circles in the air beside his temple, then cocked his finger at me. "Be careful, *hija*. It's the 84 bus, stops at North Cap and goes right to Providence. Five minutes."

He leaned against the door and watched me go. "Tell Oliver I hope he feels better." With a soft, nervous giggle he turned away.

Oliver's room was on the second floor of the hospital. Down the hall a woman wailed in an eerie childish voice. A family composed of father, mother, little girl sat in a dreary waiting area, holding magazines in their laps and staring out the window at the parking lot. When I peered through the door of Room 114 I saw Oliver on the bed, reading *The Ginger Man*, a copy of the *Washington Post Book World* atop his pillow. There were bars on the window behind him but no shades or blinds, no curtain pulls or chains or cords. On one pale green wall an unadorned wooden cross hung above a wooden chair. Oliver was very pale. His right foot had been bandaged and was propped awkwardly before him on the bed, like a superfluous piece of luggage. The bandage and green hospital robe, coupled with his shaved head and blanched face, made him look like someone terribly, perhaps fatally, ill.

Seeing him like that terrified me—how long had he looked like this, why hadn't I noticed before?

Because you were too fucked up yourself, I thought. *Too fucked up, too selfish, too fucking stupid to stop him!*

Anger and self-loathing flooded me. How could I just have let him go like this? The drugs, of course it was the drugs: he'd been eating acid and mescaline and hashish and god knows what else, eating it like candy for months, maybe years. And this is what it came to—

For one awful moment I thought of turning around and leaving, before he could look up to see me. But then I remembered how he had hugged me the night before, holding me so desperately I almost wept to think of it.

Save me, Sweeney. Don't fear me . . .

"Oliver." I forced a smile as I stepped into the room. "What's shaking?"

He glanced up. When he saw it was me he grinned and tossed his book onto the pillow. "Smelly O'Keefe! What took you so long?"

I plucked at the sleeve of my shirt and made a face. "Stinky Cassidy, more like it. They let you read that stuff in here?"

He pulled me onto the bed next to him. "Ow. Watch the gam."

I nodded sympathetically. "Looks pretty gross."

"Septic poisoning. How'd you get up here?"

"Just walked."

"Did you sign in?"

"Was I supposed to?"

Right on cue a nurse popped his head through the door. "Somebody at the station said you have a visitor? Oh, hi there—did you sign in? No? Well, don't get up, what's your name, I'll do it, I've got to give him meds anyway. Right back."

"That's Joe," explained Oliver. "He's my keeper—"

Before he could finish Joe was back. "All right, six o'clock, time for these." He handed Oliver a paper cup of water and another little cup containing two tiny red pills. Oliver waved away the water, tapped the pills into his hand, and swallowed them.

"Ugh. How can you do that, I could never do that." Joe gave me a measured look, checking me out, I guess to determine if I had a hacksaw stuck down my jeans. "More friends," he said after a moment. "This boy has *more friends*. Oh, and Oliver, another one of your brothers called, he said he'd try again tonight. Do you want dinner, sweetheart?"

This to me. I shook my head. "No, thanks."

"All right, then. Visiting hours on this floor are *officially* over at seven, but I won't do a bed check till eight." He grinned, took the little plastic cup from Oliver's hand, and left.

When he was gone Oliver got up and crossed the room to the door. He moved slowly, like a gunfighter in an old Western, and I tried not to think about what the hospital robe must be hiding. He closed the door and stayed there for a long moment with his back to me. A moment later I heard him gagging.

"Oliver! Are you okay—"

He turned and nodded, eyes watering, and opened his hand. His palm was wet, streaked with crimson; but before I could cry out he shook his head.

"Thorazine." He automatically reached for a pocket; then remembered he was wearing a hospital robe. He turned to get a tissue from his nightstand. He wiped his hand and went into the bathroom and flushed the toilet, then walked over to the chair beneath the little wooden cross. "They gave it to me in the ER last night. I was under restraint so I couldn't do anything about it. It made me hallucinate; I thought I was totally brain damaged. So now I cough them up."

He kicked absently at the chair, then turned and crossed to the narrow bed, motioning me to join him. "I guess I could save them for you."

"No thanks." I smiled. "First time I've ever seen you turn down drugs."

His pale blue eyes were sharp and guileless as he gazed at me. "I'm not crazy, Sweeney."

"I know you're not crazy. You don't *look* crazy," I lied. "But . . ."

But normal people don't try to cut off their dicks with a Swiss Army knife.

"I don't look crazy because I'm *not* crazy."

I said nothing. After a moment I raised my head to look at him: the dark stubble covering his skull, the crimson web where he'd cut himself with the razor; his cheeks and chin still smooth as a boy's though I was certain he hadn't shaved in days.

It was like gazing at someone who had been consumed by fire, a lovely porcelain figurine left too long in the kiln; and now all that remained was this human ash, frail and white and cold. Except for his eyes, those madly burning blue eyes that still might without warning burst into flame.

He covered my hand with his—so cold, surely he shouldn't be this cold?

"I'm not crazy, Sweeney. I'm just not what they wanted," he said softly. "Angelica and my father, Warnick and all the rest of them—they all wanted different things, they all wanted something from me I can't give. They wanted me to be strong, they wanted me to give them a champion. But I can't, Sweeney. They don't understand. I'm not like that.

"I wanted to—"

He stopped, stared at his hands with their bitten-down nails.

"I wanted to mend things," he said at last. He looked at me and sighed. "I know it sounds stupid, but I thought—all this bullshit about darkness, and light, and different powers for men and women—all this *fighting*, all this, this *hatred* the *Benandanti* and the rest of them have—I thought I could make it different, somehow. At least I thought I could *escape* it," he added with a grim smile. "But I was wrong, Sweeney. I can't. No one can. We'll never understand each other, any of us. Not ever."

I nodded like *I* understood, although of course I didn't. After a moment I asked, "But—if you're not what the *Benandanti* want you to be, or Angelica—what *are* you?"

He tipped his head and smiled.

"*I'm lovely*," he sang in his sweet quavering voice. "*All I am is lovely . . .*"

I laughed even as my eyes filled with tears, and touched his poor ugly scalp. "Well, you'll be lovely again, Oliver. It'll grow back."

With sudden vehemence he shook his head. "*No*. Does the reed once cut return? Will the trees now barren turn again to greet the spring? What name did Achilles take among the women? Does the Eagle know what is in the pit?"

His hand shot out to grab my wrist, tightening like a wire as he pulled me to him. "*Why is a raven like a writing desk?*"

"O-Oliver," I stammered. His face had twisted into a bitter mask, still smiling, but it was a contorted smile now, and his eyes were no longer laughing.

"Sweeney? Surely you remember? It was the first thing we ever talked about. *Why is a raven like a writing desk*? Tell me the next line—"

He gripped me so hard that pins and needles darted from my wrist into my arm. "*Tell me*!" he hissed.

"I—I don't—"

"Say it!"

"Your—your hair wants cutting."

"There!" He cried out triumphantly and let go of my hand. I rubbed it gingerly, and moved a fraction of an inch away from him. "See, Sweeney? You remembered."

With some effort he stood, moving slowly. He grabbed the hem of his robe and tossed it flamboyantly behind him, as though it were a flowing train. "I knew you would. Sweeney."

He stopped and stared at me. The front of his robe gaped open and I had a glimpse of white bandages beneath, although maybe it was just his underclothes. "I know about you," he said very softly. Once more his voice was gentle. He was gazing at me with pity, but also with great tenderness. "You're in this by mistake—"

I shook my head desperately, but he went on. "It's okay, Sweeney. Because even after I figured it all out, that you weren't in on any of this—I mean, you're not a Molyneux scholar, and obviously you're not a *Benandanti*, and you're not with Angelica, wherever the fuck *she* is—but, well, you're still great, Sweeney. Anybody else would have run away screaming from all this, but you stayed, you were my friend and you stuck with me. And you're great; you're just so great to have done that. You know that, right?"

I bowed my head, mumbling something about *No, well, maybe* . . .

He knelt in front of me. It must have hurt, because he grimaced as he took my hands. He held them very tenderly, his fingertips barely grazing mine.

"Sweeney." His blue eyes were clear as water. "I'll love you next time. I promise."

I bit my lip. Tears stung my eyes, and I shook my head furiously. "Why not *this* time? Why her and not me? I mean, I *know* you better, Oliver, I *know* you—"

He smiled and leaned forward to kiss my cheek.

"—and *I love you*. Even if I'm not one of them! I could be better, I could be good for you, I could help you out of this—"

I gestured at the pale green walls, that humble little wooden cross, the crooked chair near the door.

"Oh, my stars! Goodness had nothing to do with it, kiddo. Listen—"

He dropped my hands and got to his feet again, pulling his robe tight. "This isn't new for my family. It isn't new to me, not really. The *Benandanti* waited a long time for me, but in the meantime they used my brothers for target practice. Firing off a few rounds of firecrackers while they're waiting for the *Bearna Beill*. I saw what happened to Osgood and Vance and Waldo, just like you saw what happened to Magda Kurtz. These guys take no prisoners, Sweeney, especially now. They've been expecting me for a long time—but they've been expecting Angelica even longer. Waiting for Electra, or someone like her."

I laughed uneasily, but Oliver shook his head. "I mean it! You read all this stuff about the Second Coming, but no one really expects it to happen, maybe not even the *Benandanti*. Especially when you consider that when the Second Coming actually *Comes*, it's not a He but a She, and *she's* taking even fewer prisoners than *they* are."

He went on bitterly. "They had me all picked out, you know, they *bred* me for this. And I was supposed to just kind of go along with them, be the sacred cow, be this sort of *lure* for Her when She arrived. Like this crazy arranged marriage or something, like once She got hold of me She might just roll over for them and play dead."

His voice rose to a desperate pitch. "But I'm not going for it, Sweeney. Maybe Angelica doesn't understand what's going on, but I do. I'm not the right guy for the job. And if you're not the right kind of person, if you're not what they expect, if you don't do *exactly what they want*, they throw you away, they use you up and throw you out and that's it. And I'm not going to let them do it to me."

"Oliver, this really *is* crazy, it doesn't make any sense—"

He slashed at the air in a rage. "No! You *saw* what happened to Magda Kurtz; Angelica told me. You know what I'm taking about—"

"But, Oliver—you can't *hurt* yourself! I mean, you're playing right into their hands—"

"No, I'm not, I'm not, I'm not." His voice cracked as he paced to the bathroom. His hands kept fluttering around his forehead, making quick nervous motions as though to keep phantom hair from falling into his eyes. At the bathroom door he stopped, and asked suddenly, "Have you seen Angelica?"

"No. She's gone. Nobody knows where she is."

He made an anguished face. "Ahh—she's really gone, then, it's too late anyway—" He stopped, ran a hand across his forehead. "Jesus."

"Do you—do you think she'll be all right?"

"All right? Angelica?" He laughed incredulously. "She'll be fine! I mean, probably every guy she ever meets will end up like this—"

He cocked his head, rolling his eyes with his tongue hanging out and gabbling *Ngah ngah ngah*—

"Maybe we'll *all* end up like that, but *She'll* be fine. Blessed art Thou among women and all that shit. Listen, Sweeney, don't you worry about her: Angelica is destined for Big Things." His voice dropped to a conspiratory whisper. "Very, very Big Things."

I decided to change the subject. "I got kicked out."

His eyebrows arched in amazement. "You did? My little Sweeney, expelled from the Divine all by herself? Congratulations!"

"Jeez, Oliver, I'm not *happy* about it."

"You should be," he said quickly. "Oh yes very yes, you should get out of here as fast as your little bunny legs can take you, before this thing starts to blow. Oh yes."

He fell silent, staring thoughtfully into the empty space between us. After a moment he took a few steps, until he stood in front of the wooden chair beneath the cross. He reached up and took the cross in one hand, lifted it carefully from the wall, and turned it over thoughtfully.

He looked up at me and said, "There is nothing for me but misery."

I started to protest but he went on as though he hadn't heard.

"There is nothing for me but misery,
What shape is there that I have not had?
A woman now, I have been man, youth and boy;
I was an athlete, a wrestler,
There were crowds around my door, my fans slept on the doorstep.
There were flowers all over the house
When I left my bed at sunrise.
Shall I be a waiting maid to the gods, the slave of Cybele?"

He lifted the cross in front of him. Around its crossbar tiny green vines moved, twining up and over the dull wood, their leaves so pale at first they were nearly white, but then quickening to yellow and gold and finally a rich deep green. As I watched in horror the vines spread, crept along the spars of the cross and then twisted around Oliver's fingers, writhing and creeping like elvers or tiny serpents. They covered his arm in a tracery of gold and green and brown, leaves springing out so quickly that his white flesh was completely buried beneath them and I could see a few places where his veins had burst, sea green and crimson and the pale lavender of a new bruise, and the vines fed there and swelled to the thickness of a finger, a wrist, a thigh; then burst into scarlet blossom.

"Oliver!"

Now they began to trace the outlines of his torso, his shoulders and neck and face crumbling like old stones beneath a mantle of ivy and honeysuckle, his bald scalp covered with a frail yellow filigree that quivered and darkened to emerald. From within all that greenery only his eyes still glowed, twin flashes of blue as though some bright clever jay nested there, and his voice rang out like a blade slashing through the curling vines—

"'I regret now what I have done, too late I repent of it!
Oh dear gods, let me go free!—'

But Cybele only looks down with her red mouth parted.
Her hands close around the barrel of the whip as she cries:
'No! Be merciless, drive him mad!
He has had the impertinence to refuse me—
Drive him insane, let the woods shake with his shrieks and lamentations!'"

I screamed. But the sound choked within my throat, as all around me there was green, a horrible livid glory of green and living things, vines coiling about my breasts and ivy everywhere, bitter leaves thrusting themselves into my mouth and their stems pulling taut around my wrists and neck and ankles; but even as I struggled to free myself suddenly all fell away, leaves and vines turning into whirling ropes and arabesques that flared blindingly and then died into grey ash and disappeared. There were no vines, no leaves, no ivy. Only Oliver standing in front of me with his twisted smile, holding a simple wooden rood.

"He that has no cross deserves no crown," he said lightly, and tossed it to me. I shrieked and jumped back. But the cross only struck the floor and lay there, a dull brown thing as lifeless as a pencil.

"What is going on?"

Behind us the door swung open to reveal the nurse, Joe. He frowned and strode inside, glancing around quickly.

"You're not supposed to have the door shut," he said. He stooped to pick up the cross. "Maybe we better cut this short, okay, Oliver? You seem a little overstimulated."

Oliver said nothing.

"I've kind of got to go anyway," I said stiffly. "But could we, like, say good-bye first?"

Joe went to the wall, moved aside the chair, and placed the cross back upon its hook. "All right. But they're starting to bring dinner around, and your friend's had a long day—"

He turned to me so I could read the message in his eyes: *so give him a break, okay?*

"—so maybe you and he could catch up some more tomorrow."

We waited until he left, the door hanging open behind him like an unanswered question. When Oliver took my hand and led me to the bed I was shaking uncontrollably. I wanted to scream, to ask him a million things; but I said nothing, only clung to him as though he really were a tree and I was in danger of plunging to my death.

We sat together in silence for a long time. From outside the barred window I could hear faint sounds of traffic and machinery; the steady hum of the hospital's air-conditioning system; and the rustle of voices, distant and muted as though heard from underwater.

"You won't forget me, will you?"

At the sound of Oliver's tremulous voice I looked up, shaking my head fiercely. "Never! I love you, you know I'll be back tomorrow—"

"I know," he said. He put his arm around me and hugged me close. "But in the meantime you have to be careful. Don't sleep in the subway, button up your overcoat, hang on to your head. Don't forget your friends, Sweeney."

I looked down so he wouldn't see that I was crying. "My—my friends?"

"Oh, Sweeney." His voice was low and solemn as he tilted my head back up. He touched my cheek, drew away a finger with a tiny droplet on it, and brought it to his mouth. He touched his finger to his tongue and smiled, the same sweet crazy knowing smile I'd seen so many times before when he was out there skimming across some private sea. "You remember . . ."

His eyes gleamed, blue and strange as scallops' eyes, and I knew he was looking at me from some great distance.

"You remember . . . you were little and you woke up on Sunday morning before your parents did and your brothers were still asleep, and outside there was that kind of golden rain that comes sometimes in the spring and the air smelled like roses and bacon, and when you looked over the side of your bed you saw him there, a little green lizard with hands like a baby, and he looked up at you and you fed him limes."

He cupped his hands as though to receive an offering, and smiled.

"Oh, Oliver," I whispered, and, weeping, buried my face in the folds of his robe.

A few minutes later the nurse arrived with Oliver's dinner tray. Under his watchful gaze Oliver escorted me to the door. There he smiled and kissed me, then stood in the hall waving cheerfully as I walked to the elevator.

"My brother Leo's coming to take me back to Newport," he called after me. "Come stay with me over Thanksgiving, we'll go hear Cooper play the Limelight—" He flexed his fingers and mimed playing a piano.

"Okay," I said. My heart leapt at the thought of visiting him at home, of meeting his family for a holiday. "But I'll see you tomorrow."

He grinned and crooked a finger. "Next time, Sweeney. Bye."

I got a bus back to North Capitol Street, got out and wandered around the campus. For some reason I was no longer afraid. I knew I could stay with Baby Joe but that would mean more talking, more discussion of what had happened the night before, and I was too tired to think about that right now. I didn't want to think about bulls or blood or ivy or trees, about any of the things miraculous or terrible that I had seen. I wanted only to think about Oliver; about how his eyes had glowed and the way he had smiled at me; about taking the train up to Newport and staying with him and hearing his brother play stride piano in a barrelhouse; about what he had meant when he said *You're great, Sweeney* and *I'll love you next time. I promise.*

So I waited a few hours, walking across the Strand and thinking of all the things we'd do together, thinking of all the things we'd done, Oliver and I: lying there beneath that tree, sitting there talking in the Shrine's shadow, drinking coffee and rum there while we waited for Angelica to get out of class. When I finally went to Baby Joe's room it was late, after midnight. I threw pebbles at the window until he came down yawning to let me in the fire door. He refused to let me sleep on the floor.

"Forget it, *hija*. My grandmother would kill me."

So Baby Joe curled up in the room's single worn armchair and I curled up in his bed, still thinking about Oliver, willing myself to dream of him, his crooked smile, his mad blue eyes.

That night I dreamed I was swimming in the ocean, a hundred yards or more from shore. Oliver stood on the sand in the blazing sun, and with him Angelica and Annie and Hasel and Baby Joe. They were all holding beer bottles and laughing and talking, and every now and then one of them would look up, shading his eyes until he or she saw me. Then they'd wave, absently but still happy to see me, and maybe raise a bottle in greeting. They didn't know that I was being pulled away from them, that I could feel something black and cold clawing at my feet and dragging me; they didn't know I was going under when, a minute later, they glanced up again and vainly searched the horizon, looking for me. They just kept on looking at the ocean, certain that I was swimming there somewhere, safe among the green and dancing waves. They never knew about the riptide or how dangerous the currents were. They never knew at all.

When I woke up someone was pounding on the door to Baby Joe's room. My watch read twenty-five after five. Baby Joe was snoring loudly in his armchair. The window was pearled with first light. I stood groggily and walked to the door, not totally conscious that I wasn't still in my room at Rossetti Hall, and pulled it open.

In the darkened hallway stood Annie Harmon, grey-faced and shivering in her red flannel shirt and fatigues, her hands shaking as she pushed past me through the door. She had come to tell me that, sometime around four o'clock that morning, Oliver had walked out of his room at Providence Hospital and climbed the fire stairs to the Oncology Unit. There he found a utility closet with a window that opened onto the parking lot. He jumped out, plunging five stories before he went through a metal awning and the roof of an oxygen truck parked near the entrance to the Emergency Room. There had been no signs of distress, there was no suicide letter. Nothing but a scrawled note in the margin of last Sunday's *Washington Post Book World.*

It said, *I'll be right back.*

PART TWO

Absence

i

Pavana Lachrymæ

When I learned of Oliver's death it was as though a door had slammed shut upon me. In the sudden darkness and echoing clang of its closing, I was blinded, deafened. The wonders of the Divine were as lost to me as though they had existed only in a book I had once glimpsed, a book taken from me and put into the safekeeping of people wiser and lovelier than myself, people who would never again make the mistake of allowing it to fall into such careless hands. I would never be permitted to return to the sculpted lawns or allées of the Divine. Never again would I glimpse an angel in my room, terrible and fatal; only in dreams. Years afterward I might pass on the street someone I had known as a student, and once on a crowded subway platform glimpse Balthazar Warnick wrapped in his moth-singed chesterfield; but they did not see me, or greet me when I called out to them.

ii

Threnody: Storm King

After Annie left Baby Joe's room I went out and bought a liter of vodka and a six-pack of Orange Crush. I didn't try to follow her, didn't even wake up Baby Joe. I drank all that day and into the evening, returning at last to Baby Joe's dorm. There I passed out behind the overgrown box tree hedge. When I woke up I did it all over again. I didn't try to locate Oliver's family or find out about funeral arrangements. I stumbled to the front of the dorm in search of Baby Joe, but no one answered when I knocked. Finally I went to the Shrine cafeteria and found a pay phone. I tried to call Annie, but her phone had been cut off.

I stumbled back outside. I looked up and saw pale shining spires and lapis domes rising from the grey autumn mist, the small cloaked figures of scholars and a few brave tourists on the steps of the Shrine. The immense sandstone building seemed more Sphinx-like than ever. I could feel its will bearing down on me, saying, *There is nothing for you here.* I turned, shivering, and walked away.

I had 107 dollars in my checking account, enough money to buy an Amtrak ticket home. I could only assume that Balthazar or someone else had taken care of the things in my room—thrown them out or burned them or shipped them back to New York. I still hadn't called my parents. Except for trying to reach Annie, I hadn't called anyone at all. I wandered across campus, thinking of Oliver, and it was as though I had died too. I saw no one I recognized, no one at all. When I tried to get back into Rossetti Hall my key didn't work. For what seemed like hours I waited for someone to leave or enter the dorm, so that I could slip in behind them, but no one ever came. When I waited outside Baby Joe's dorm the same thing happened. I tried calling his room, but he never answered; tried finding Hasel Bright and Annie, but I never did. Finally I returned to the Shrine cafeteria, half-expecting to be turned away from there, too, but I wasn't.

I stayed there for three days: washing up in the rest room, sleeping in chilly alcoves of the Crypt Church when the cafeteria closed, my head pillowed on my knapsack, warming my hands by the feeble light of votive candles. I left only to buy more vodka and to check my mail at the campus post office. Nothing there but the *New Yorker* and a formal computer-generated notice of permanent suspension from the Dean's Office.

And then, on the fourth day after Oliver's suicide, I received a letter. A heavy cream-colored envelope addressed in an elegant calligraphic hand. My fingers trembled: I was certain it was from Angelica, but when I inspected it more closely I saw that the letters were smaller, the cursives more controlled. And it was written in dark blue ink, and I had never seen Angelica use anything but peacock blue. I fled back to the warmth of the Shrine cafeteria, bought a cup of coffee, and found a corner booth.

"Oh man," I said beneath my breath. My hands were shaking so much I could hardly open it. "Please, god, please . . ."

The inside of the envelope was lined with marbled paper, blue and violet and green. The edges of the heavy rag stationery were gilt, as was a tiny monogram stamped at the top of the page.

L d R

I drew it to my face, breathing in Pelican ink and the sharp medicinal tang of eucalyptus, and began to read.

November 12, 1975
Storm King, New York

Dear Ms. Cassidy,

Angelica gave me your address; I hope that you will not find it presumptuous of me to write to you.

My daughter spoke very warmly of her time with you at the Divine. I have just learned of the unfortunate events that have befallen your little circle of friends, and also of your own academic situation. As an alumnus and trustee of the University, I feel that I may be able to be of some help to you in making your future plans, and so have taken the liberty of enclosing a round-trip plane ticket for you to come visit me at our home here in Storm King. Alas! my daughter will not be able to join us, but it is at her urging that I am writing to you, and I know that she very much would like for you to come.

If there is any scheduling problem, please let me know. Otherwise, I will arrange for a car to meet you at the airport and deliver you here on this Friday evening.

With warm regards,
Luciano di Rienzi

Wrapped in a second sheet of the same heavy smooth paper were two airplane tickets.

I went; of course I went. I was afraid not to, but even more afraid of what I might do or what I might become if I stayed at the Divine, drinking and hiding in the Shrine and slowly going insane. It felt strange, to be flying into Westchester without my parents' knowledge. At the airport I was seized by the absurd terror that they would be there, that somehow they had found out about everything and had come to collect me and bring me in disgrace back home. But there was hardly anyone at the airport at all, besides a few weary wives come to collect their weary husbands, and a young man in a cable-knit sweater and salmon-colored golf pants, holding a sign that said SWEENEY CASSIDY.

"That's me," I said. He took my bag and I followed him to the waiting car, a navy blue Oldsmobile with MERCURY SKYLINE LIVERY stenciled on the side. I was a little disappointed but mostly relieved it wasn't a limousine.

"Do you work for Mr. di Rienzi?" I asked after we had left the parking lot.

"Nope. He just hired me for tonight, and to take you back in the morning. Mind if I listen to the news?"

I shook my head. He clicked on the radio, and that was all the conversation we had. We drove north on the interstate. After an hour we pulled off Route 684 and crossed the Bear Mountain Bridge. Forty-five minutes later we arrived at Storm King.

I was expecting something grand, after the plane tickets and mysterious letter and the liveried car, something along the lines of the Orphic Lodge.

Instead, the di Rienzis' house was at the end of a cul-de-sac in a small woodsy development, high up on the Palisades overlooking the Hudson. STORM KING ESTATES, said a wrought-iron sign, but there was nothing quite so dramatic as an estate anywhere in sight. The other houses were pleasantly suburban, set amidst plenty of trees now bare and stark against the backdrop of browning lawns and neatly raked piles of leaves. The di Rienzis' house stood apart from all of these, on a small rise planted with huge old rhododendrons and mountain laurels and a slender, pampered-looking Japanese maple. Behind the trees and shrubs rose a sprawling Queen Anne Victorian, a real dowager dating to the turn of the century, with grey weathered shingles and a wide porch sweeping around it on all sides. It was certainly the oldest house on the street, and it commanded a marvelous view of the river and Storm King Mountain and even the George Washington Bridge, glittering like a string of glass beads in the distance. But it was a surprisingly comforting-looking house, nothing grand or intimidating about it at all, until Angelica's father appeared at the door.

"You must be Sweeney."

"Yes, sir," I said, shaking his hand. It was the first time I had ever called anyone *sir* in my life. "You are—it was very, very kind of you to send me the tickets to come here."

He smiled. "Well, I am very, very happy that you came. Please, come inside."

I was shocked to see how old he was. Older than my parents, older even than my grandparents. Had Angelica ever mentioned that to me? But there was nothing frail about him—he was over six feet tall, big-boned and broad-shouldered, with an exaggerated, almost military, bearing, and his hand, while bony and blue-veined, was so strong my fingers cracked in his grasp. I protested when he bent to take my knapsack, but he ignored me and went inside, waving offhandedly to the Oldsmobile as it drove off.

"Did you have a pleasant flight? I wasn't certain if you would have time to eat, so I have dinner ready for you." I followed him down the hallway, too nervous to say anything but *Yes sir* over and over, like a new recruit. "At any rate airplane food is appalling, isn't it? Let's take this upstairs to your room, so that you can wash up if you'd like."

He had a beautiful sonorous voice, with just the slightest Mediterranean warmth to it, and such extravagantly pronounced diction that he sounded like an exotic bird that has been trained to speak. I followed him upstairs, and then down a long hallway, where a number of photographs of Angelica hung in expensive, heavy frames. Angelica as an infant, innocent and self-contained as an egg; Angelica in a white dress for First Communion; Angelica graduating from elementary school, high school; Angelica at summer camp. Camp! I could as easily imagine her at camp as distributing alms to the poor in Calcutta; but there she was, tanned and squinting into the sun in her khaki shorts and white short-sleeved shirt with WENAHKEE OWLS embroidered on it. Between the photos were doors, all of them shut tight. I tried to guess which hid Angelica's room.

"This is the guest room, here—you don't have your own bath but it's only a few steps down the hall. And there's plenty of hot water."

My room was large and cozy, the walls papered with a pattern of ivy squills and the floor covered with bright rag rugs. There was a large canopied spindle bed piled high with a feather comforter in a green duvet, and a small night table, where a vase of chrysanthemums and marigolds dropped petals onto a stack of magazines. On the wall hung a watercolor of gold hills and blue water and feluccas sailing in the distance.

"It's wonderful," I said. "This is so kind, Mr. di Rienzi—"

"Not at all, not at all." He waved me away, setting my knapsack on the floor. "Now you'll probably want to freshen up. When you're comfortable, come downstairs. We'll have dinner on the porch—I think it's still warm enough for that, don't you?"

On the porch it was barely warm enough, but Mr. di Rienzi got me one of Angelica's cable-knit sweaters and draped it over my shoulders. It smelled so strongly of her perfume that I felt dizzy; but it helped keep off the lingering chill.

The veranda overlooked a long wooded hillside that sloped down to the Hudson. Over the white wooden railings I could glimpse the tops of trees, a few still brushed with scarlet and brown, and the river itself, dark and shimmering faintly beneath the stars. On the far shore glowed the lights of Beacon and, a few miles north, Poughkeepsie. Two symmetrical rows of red lights showed where a barge was being towed toward the locks upstate.

"Will you have some wine, Sweeney?"

It was odd to have an adult call me Sweeney rather than Katherine or Kate. But then Mr. di Rienzi only knew of me through his daughter, and Angelica wouldn't have called me anything else.

"Yes, please." I had changed into a white cotton shirt and chinos, faded but clean. At first I was afraid this would seem too casual, but now in the friendly darkness, the brisk air softened by the faint smell of Angelica's perfume rising from her sweater, it all seemed just right. "Thank you very much."

We drank a bottle of chardonnay, and ate warm crusty bread and fried potatoes drizzled with golden olive oil and fresh rosemary, and chicken and arugula brightened with pimiento. Mr. di Rienzi did not grill me about what had happened at school. When I asked after Angelica, he said that she was visiting her cousins in Florence, at the University there. He would join her for the Christmas holidays, but she would probably remain even after he returned to New York, to begin classes in the spring term.

"It is so beautiful there in the spring, it would be a shame for her to have gone all that way and then miss it. But already *I* miss her so terribly, it is painful for me to talk of her. I hope you understand."

He stared at me with huge eyes pale and luminous as Angelica's own. There was a faint flicker in them, a gentle threat that might almost have been amusement; but I knew better.

"Yes," I said. "I understand."

So we spoke of other things. He gently but insistently drew me out to talk about my family, where my father had gone to school, how my parents had met, how many older siblings I had and what their careers were. We finished the bottle of wine, toasting the slow dark coursing of the Hudson with our last glass. For dessert he brought out a little orange-enameled tin of *biscòtti* wrapped in colored tissue, and showed me how to twist the discarded papers and loose them above a candle flame, so that they danced and spun and finally flared into ash. He would not let me help with the dishes—

"No, leave them. I have my own ways of taking care of them; it gives me something to do in my retirement. Now, I think it is getting too cold out here for you. Let's go inside to my study. Will you join me for a Sambuca?"

I was very impressed by all of this. In my family we did not eat outside or have wine at meals. We never ate after seven in the evening, and we certainly never had cordials after dinner. It was the first time I had Sambuca, and the sweet licorice taste reminded me of drinking Pernod with Oliver. Mr. di Rienzi served it in a tiny glass, like a lily blown of crystal, igniting it for an instant to send blue flame rippling across the surface.

"Very nice," he said. "It takes the chill off the liqueur, and dissipates some of the volatile spirits. So you will not have a headache in the morning." We were in his study, a small book-lined room. He smiled, motioning for me to sit in an enormous chair upholstered in slippery oxblood leather. "Now then—

"I understand that there were some very unfortunate things that happened to you, and to some of my daughter's other friends at school this semester. Now, I don't want to hear any more about it—it was quite unpleasant, hearing about it once from Angelica—so you don't need to tell me or try to explain. I certainly do not blame *you* for any of it, Sweeney," he went on in a gentler tone. "It is very, very common for young people to find themselves in—difficult circumstances—especially, perhaps, young people from good families. Coming from a sheltered background, being on your own for the first time, all that sudden freedom! Though I will say, I told Balthazar Warnick I think the University should have been much more circumspect in its dealings with the students, especially as regards that retreat. In my day we had parietals. It just would not have been permitted for young ladies and gentlemen to be unchaperoned for the weekend. But anyway," he sighed, and went on.

"Anyway, Angelica has spoken very, very highly of you. Of how fond she is of you, and how much fun you had together. I know that young people today do things I don't approve of, very dangerous things, and I don't care to know what you may or may not have done with my daughter. But I *do* feel, in light of what has happened to your young friend Oliver, that you, Sweeney, have experienced quite enough punishment for one school term.

"I can't do anything about your grades. I'm afraid they will follow you, and I hope serve as a reminder to you of what can happen if you don't tread the straight and narrow path. But I have spoken to Balthazar Warnick and asked him to adjust the terms of your departure from the Divine.

"He has agreed to remand your suspension, under the condition that you submit a formal request to withdraw from the University and transfer to another school. At my request he has not mailed notice of your dismissal to your parents. It seemed to me that if they have successfully raised all those children, it would be an unnecessary heartbreak for them to deal with the academic failure of their youngest daughter.

"I know from Angelica that you are an exceptionally bright young lady, Sweeney, and have a wonderful future ahead of you. Now, there are several excellent schools in the D.C. area, and I know people at all of them. But the Dean of Students at George Washington University is an old friend of mine. They have a very fine Anthropology Department—slanted toward physical anthropology and archaeology, but very highly regarded. Now, if you would like, I would be very happy to contact Dr. Cohen and speak to him about your case. Your grades are shaky, but I'm sure it's nothing he hasn't seen before. Certainly the fact that you were accepted at the Divine will make a difference. And I know, of course, that you will *throw* yourself into your studies, and someday make us all proud with some marvelous discovery!"

He threw his arms open, laughing, and smiled at me.

What could I say? Of course it was a bribe, an effort to buy my silence; but I had no doubts but that the *Benandanti* could have ensured my silence as easily as they had arranged for Magda Kurtz's, and perhaps Oliver's.

No, it was truly a kind gesture that Mr. di Rienzi was making, and a very generous one: it meant that I was still under Angelica's protection, though perhaps for only a very little while longer.

"It's—that would be wonderful," I said. "Really. I'm overwhelmed—I can never thank you enough."

Mr. di Rienzi looked pleased. "Well then—a toast to your new life!" He refilled my glass, and said, "Now I know you're aware that GW doesn't have the same cachet as the University of the Archangels and Saint John the Divine. But it's a *very good school*, and I think that there you'll have a chance to shine, Sweeney. There are advantages to being a big fish in a little pond, although GW is a challenging place, don't get me wrong about that. It's in the heart of downtown, you can walk into Georgetown, I believe, and in a year or so there'll be a subway stop right there. And of course the wonderful hospital affiliated with their medical school—"

I winced at the word *hospital,* but he didn't notice.

"—although there is limited dormitory space, but if you wanted to live on campus, I'm sure arrangements could be made."

I thanked him again and told him I'd figure something out. All this *largesse* was starting to make me feel uneasy and a little prickly. Unworthy of such kindness, and perhaps liable to start acting unworthy. I decided I'd better go to bed. I got to my feet, thanking him, and hoped I didn't sound like I'd had too much to drink.

"It—it was a wonderful dinner, sir. This is all sort of too much—"

He waved his hand, as though dispersing a cloud of unpleasant smoke. "Of course, dear, of course. You don't need to make a decision right away. I don't imagine you could really start as a matriculating student anywhere until the spring term; but if you'd like to sit in on classes at GW . . ."

I told him I'd think about it. He gestured toward the door of his study.

"Angelica still feels very close to you, Sweeney," he said. His gaze softened and his hand held mine for a long moment. "My daughter has always had wonderful judgment in her choice of friends. Nearly always," he corrected himself. His eyes took on a keen look; I knew he was thinking of Oliver. "Now, you scamper up there and take a nice long bath, help yourself to any books you see, and tomorrow morning you sleep as late as you please. I get up early but don't you worry about that. I think your flight is at two in the afternoon? The driver should be here by noon, to make sure you get there in plenty of time. Here, now I'll see you to the steps—"

He placed his hand on my back and steered me out the door. At the foot of the stairs he smiled down at me.

"It will all work out for the best, Sweeney," he said softly. "It always does."

Impulsively I leaned up to kiss his cheek. "Good night, Mr. di Rienzi. And thank you again—"

"Good night, dear. Sweet dreams."

The guest bathroom was small. A huge claw-footed tub took up most of the space, but after my four days of exile it seemed like a royal bath at Pompeii. A willow basket held seashell soaps from France, and muslin sachets of dried lavender and chamomile, and there were blue-and-white striped cotton towels thick and soft enough that I could have spread them on the floor and slept there. I almost wept at all this homey luxury, but instead I clambered into the steaming tub and stayed there for an hour. When I got out my fingers were puckered and pink as boiled shrimp. I felt thoroughly serene, calmer than I had been in weeks. Everything suddenly seemed manageable again. I had a new life waiting for me, new friends, a new school. Though of course GW wasn't the Divine, and there would never be anyone like Angelica or Oliver.

I went back to my room, and found the covers turned down, a white plate with two foil-wrapped Perugina chocolates on the night table beside a carafe of water and a glass. To the pile of *Vogue*s and *New Yorkers* a few books had been added: *The Thirty-nine Steps*, *Anne of Windy Poplars*, Margaret Mead's *Blackberry Winter*. But I was much too tired to read. I ate the chocolates, drank a glass of water, and fell into dreamless untroubled sleep.

The next morning I slept until nearly nine o'clock. After showering and changing I went downstairs. There was a note on the kitchen table saying that Mr. di Rienzi had unexpected business to attend to and probably would not be back before my departure. He wished me well and told me that someone from George Washington University would be contacting me soon, and left the number for Mercury Skyline Livery, in the unlikely event that my car didn't show by noon. There was coffee set up in the coffeemaker, cream and milk in the fridge, and a basket of pastries and fresh fruit.

I ate and went back upstairs. I lay on the bed in the guest room, thinking about my dinner the night before, and flipped through the stack of magazines. There was a recent issue of *Paris Vogue* addressed to Angelica, and the copy of *Blackberry Winter* had her name in it, written in that familiar swooping hand with peacock blue ink. I looked around the guest room for other signs of her presence but found none. Only that watercolor of a Mediterranean scene, which she must have brought back from some long-ago visit to the Aegean.

At last I gathered my things and went to wait for the car. As I walked slowly down the hallway I stopped in front of a closed door and tested the knob. I was curious to see Angelica's room, just for one moment. But the door was locked. So was the next one, and the next, and the one after that. All the doors were locked. When I got downstairs I put my knapsack by the front door and walked very quietly down the hall, calling out softly for Mr. di Rienzi. There was no answer. When I reached his study, it was locked. Everything, locked. I returned to the front door, and waited with a mixture of melancholy and resignation and relief for the car that would bear me from Storm King.

I did not hear from Angelica. No letters, no phone calls; nothing save a small package that arrived a few days before Christmas, posted to my parents' house in Armonk. The box was neatly wrapped in brown paper, and covered with brightly colored airmail stamps and the word FIRENZE stamped in red ink. When I opened it, there was another box inside, and inside that a nest of Italian newspapers and shredded bits of wrapping. I dug my fingers into the nest and withdrew something round and pocked with myriad tiny raised bumps, trailing an electrical cord.

It was a sea urchin. Like the one Angelica had on her desk at the Divine, its swollen sides striated in shades of pale rose and lavender and white. A sea urchin lamp, actually—it had been fitted with a tiny Christmas-tree bulb. It glowed a wonderfully soft, twilit purple, like a globe representing some lost and secret place. There was a little card with it, of marbled paper, and Angelica's swirling peacock blue handwriting.

For my darling Sweeney,
A Gift from the Sea—
With all my love,

Angelica

iii

Lost Bells

Four years later I graduated from college with a respectable grade point average and a bachelor's degree in sociocultural anthropology. As if by magic, the week before my graduation I received a letter from Luciano di Rienzi. It was written on the same rich paper and with the same royal blue ink as his earlier missive, and in the same controlled yet flamboyant hand. Inside he congratulated me on my matriculation, and hoped that I would not think it presumptuous that he had contacted an old friend of his at the National Museum of Natural History, Dr. Robert Dvorkin, and informed him of my interest in native studies. Dr. Dvorkin had agreed to set up an interview with me at my earliest convenience. Mr. di Rienzi wished me well in all my endeavors and remained, with warm regards, Luciano di Rienzi. There was no mention of Angelica.

My job at the museum consisted of cataloging all the photographs in the Larkin Archives, a collection of fifty thousand photographic images dating from the late 1800s to the present. Pictures of Native Americans, of every tribe imaginable, recorded in every shade of sepia and ocher and grey and black and white, and every kind of image: old silver nitrate negs, Polaroids, daguerreotypes, official government photos, Brownie snapshots, Kodak slides, Hasselblad 8x11s, even a strip of Imax film taken from one of the space shuttles.

Actually, there were 63,492 photos, but no one knew that until I had finished logging every one. That took three years. I was very lucky to have a job in my discipline, any job. If I'd been an archaeologist, I might have fared better. As it was, I was an armchair anthropologist, as distant from the objects of my study as James

Frazer had been from his. Destined (doomed, I secretly believed) to a lifetime career at the museum.

Over the years we acquired other photographic collections, all of which needed to be archived. I had no advanced degree, and no money to go to graduate school, and indeed no burning desire to do so. But Dr. Dvorkin was exceptionally kind to me, almost a surrogate uncle. I was certain that he was a *Benandante*, but I never dared to ask. If I had, I'm sure he would not have given me an answer.

And then another small bolt of lightning struck, in the form of a grant from the estate of Josepha Larkin, she of the 63,492 photos. There was a very new technology, almost completely untried, which utilized laser-read videodiscs as a means of storing archival information: fifty thousand still-frame images per side of a two-sided disc. Would the museum be interested in developing this technology as a method of storing and sharing its photographic collection?

Since there was no one in the federal jobs system who had the precise requirements for a Videodisc Project Manager, Cultural Anthropology, BA or MA required, the job fell to me. Almost overnight I got a promotion and a raise and my own office and my own telephone and even my own staff, consisting of one part-time employee who worked nights at Popeye's. It wasn't the fast track that everyone else was following in those years, but it was security, a paycheck every two weeks and a pension when I retired. And while I was pretty much doing the same job as before, there was that office, with a door that closed when I wanted to put my head on my desk and nap, and my name on the door in neat green letters. And most of the time, that seemed to be enough.

iv

Saranbanda de la Muerta Oscura

Years went by, many years. When I met Oliver I was only eighteen. At that age, privilege and latent schizophrenia can look an awful lot like genius. Now I was more than twice as old, and had made up for missing his funeral by attending many others. The plague years were upon us. I watched people I loved die and with each death something more of beauty drained away not only from the world but from me. I do not mean just that my life was lessened by their dying—though it was—or that I was not fortunate to be alive and grateful for it. I only mean that I had always felt that it was others who made me beautiful, by choosing to love me. This sounds like the sober admission of a dysfunctional woman, I know. But unless you had seen Oliver and Angelica together, laughing, or been as heartsick and lonely as I was when Oliver first greeted me that morning in Professor Warnick's classroom: unless you had been *me*, enthralled but willing servitor, knowing I was unworthy of such friends, and so grateful to have been chosen—you could not know how I felt, how beautiful they were, how beautiful I was, on what a sweet bed we lay.

But now it was all to start anew. *Finnegan begin again . . .*

It was early morning of the first of May, a clear unseasonably cool morning for the city. I was hurrying from a cab to the sliding glass doors of the Emergency Room of Providence Hospital. A friend had gone into acute pulmonary distress, the last time it was to happen but I did not know that yet. I had not forgotten Oliver's suicide, of course, but this hospital had long since become the scene of other dramas for me. I walked quickly to the ER doors with my head down, staring at the cracked concrete, the carnival detritus of shivered glass and metal. An ambulance was backing up from the doorway. Just outside the entrance a heavyset raw-faced woman was standing numbly, tears streaming down her cheeks. I did not want to look at her. So I looked down, tightening my grip on my briefcase. On the pavement were shattered crack vials and flattened cans, the ruby lens of a smashed headlight. You might have been able to trace the history of all the unfortunates inside of Providence, if you only knew where to look.

Then something else caught my eye. I hesitated, stopped, and bent to look more closely.

Overhead a metal awning thrust above the entrance to the Emergency Room, so that the rectangle of broken tarmac beneath stood in perpetual shade. There were small filthy pools of scummy water that never dried, and large black beetles with knobbed antennae that crawled across a liquefying red-and-white box from Popeye's.

And there was something else as well: pushing up through a crack in the concrete, not frail or etiolated as one might have expected but strong, its stem thick around as my forefinger, its curved leaves the deep nitrogen-rich green of leaves that bask in the sun all day.

A flower. A hyacinth.

Not the bulbous heavy-scented bloom known as a hyacinth in this country, but *Scilla non-scripta*, the wood hyacinth, Homer's *huakinthos.* Its blossoms so rich a violet-blue they seemed to have been cut and folded from velvet, their yellow stamens as vivid and startling as eyes glimpsed from between the lappets of a heavy cloak. An amazing thing! I knew they did not grow anywhere outside of the Mediterranean, and even there only in wild lonely places, crags and mountainsides sacred to Artemis and her twin Apollo, and to the memory of the slain lover who gave his name to the flower.

Impossible; but there it was. As I brought my face closer I could just barely discern beneath the scents of car fumes and creosote its fragrance: sweet but very very faint, as though borne to me across mountains and rivers and stony plains, across an entire ocean, across a night country whose steppes I had seen only once but never forgotten. As from a past that was not my own but was somehow laying claim to me from an unthinkable, almost unbearable, distance.

PART THREE

Return

CHAPTER 10

Ignoreland

I didn't really change all that much. I didn't turn grey. I didn't get fat, I didn't get married, I didn't have children, I didn't die. When I wasn't at work I wore the same T-shirts and jeans and battered cowboy boots, although I drew the line at buying a black leather jacket at thirty-seven and pretending I was still twenty-two. I listened to the same music I always had, although Baby Joe did his best to educate me beyond the tastes I'd formed when I was still in college. It wasn't exactly like I'd sold out on my life and dreams and all that other bullshit, because the truth was I'd never actually had anything to *sell*. It was more like I slowly froze in place, inside my little office at the museum; more like some part of me just fell asleep one day and never woke up. Everything that had happened to me all those years before gradually disintegrated into a kind of dream.

There was nothing to tether me to my memories of the Divine. Oliver was dead, Angelica might as well be. I had invested everything in two stocks that failed. Baby Joe remained my only real contact from that single semester. He had graduated *summa cum laude*, with a degree in English, and was now the beleagured Alternative Arts & Music critic for the beleagured New York *Beacon*, from whence he waged an ongoing war against his rivals and detractors in the Manhattan print media. Every few months he'd send me a compilation tape of music he thought I should be listening to. Baby Joe's idea of must-hear stuff included the Ramayana Monkey Chant as well as the entire and surprisingly extensive catalog of a dreadful band called Boink. His scant free time he devoted to writing a novel, but he did a good job of keeping in touch. He called me every couple of months, telling me about people from the Divine I'd never had the chance to know—famous people, a lot of them, anthropologists and theologians and actresses and fledgling politicians—as well as Hasel Bright and Annie Harmon.

I thought of Annie often. Baby Joe gave me her number, but I never called. What do you *say* after nearly twenty years? But I was also embarrassed: like Baby Joe, Annie Harmon had gone out there and *done* something. Annie had become a cult figure.

She'd come out of the closet shortly after I left the Divine, spent a bunch of years knocking around the whole coffeehouse/nouveau folkie scene, and then, *mirabilis!* she'd become a star.

"'Silver-tongued dyke with a gold-plated mike,'" said Baby Joe dryly, reading to me over the phone from an article in *On Our Backs!* "Huh. But she's great, you should hear her."

That spring it was impossible *not* to hear her. The video of her version of "She Is Still a Mystery," with its Georgia O'Keeffe backgrounds and the waltzing figure of Annie herself in full George Sand drag, had been getting heavy rotation on MTV. Then there was the notorious cover for *Our Magazine*, Annie dressed as Nijinsky in "L'Après-midi d'un Faun," simulating orgasm with an Hermes scarf before an audience of captivated bluestockings. I couldn't walk into a club or Galleria without Annie's husky contralto seeping into my thoughts like fragrant oil. Baby Joe said she lived somewhere in the Berkshires with her lover, and although she had changed her name to Annie Harmony, that was the only cute thing about her.

"She looks dangerous, man. Shaved head and all these piercings. I hear she has a gold ring through her clit. I *know* she has one in her nipple." He laughed. "Maybe you should try it, *hija*. Get you out on a date with something besides a lawyer."

Baby Joe regarded my social life (or lack of it) with even more horror than my musical taste. About once a year he'd come to D.C. to visit old friends from the Divine and to see me. We'd go to small, pleasingly gritty clubs to hear bands with monosyllabic names that were easy to remember, though their music was hard to dance to.

Anyway, by then I wasn't dancing much anymore. I'd kept up with the times: turning off, drying up, straightening out. I worked out three days at week. I lived in a rented carriage house on Capitol Hill and walked to work. I had a VCR, PC, and an aging VW Rabbit, though I resisted getting a CD player. It seemed an unnecessary expense, since I wasn't buying much new music. And I didn't care for CDs—they looked too much like the videodiscs I'd given my life to, they looked too much like what had happened to everything around me, people and things all getting sleeker, shinier, harder, bright reflective surfaces that put a spectral gloss on the world, but it was no longer the world I wanted to see.

That spring I learned that Hasel Bright had died.

"Bad juju, *hija*. I mean, real bad shit."

Baby Joe called me at home one evening, his voice slurred. In the background I could hear distorted music and laughter, someone yelling for a Kamakazi shooter.

"You at Frankie's?" That was the local dive where Baby Joe spent his few nights off.

"Yeah. Uh, Sweeney—something bad happened."

I sucked my breath in. "You okay? What—"

"Not me, *hija*. Hasel. Very bad." A pause. I heard ice clattering in a glass. "Shit. Listen, Sweeney—I gotta go. It's bad. But tomorrow—"

"For god's sake, *what happened?*"

Another pause. Finally, "I can't now. I got a flight out of LaGuardia, I'm going to Charlottesville for the funeral. His wife called me. But I got a letter for you from him—"

"From Hasel? To *me?*"

"No. I mean, he wrote it to me, but I'm sending it to you. A copy. I have to go. I'll call you when I get back. Be careful, okay, *hija?*"

The line went dead.

"Shit," I said. I paced into the kitchen and pulled out the bottle of Jack Daniels. I did a shot for myself, and another one for Hasel.

Two days later I got the letter, a bulky envelope so swathed in packing tape I had to open it with a steak knife. When I turned it upside down, out slid a wad of paper, along with a note scrawled on a Frankie's cocktail napkin.

Sweeney—
don't tell anyone.
Joe

The Xeroxed pages that followed were on letterhead from Hasel's law firm, neatly laser-printed and justified left and right, amended here and there with Hasel's precise tiny printing.

June 25

Dear Joe,

Thanx for the Gibby Hayes interview, pretty funny. Sorry I couldn't get into this on the phone the other night but I felt so weird talking about it I figured I'd be better off writing. Only chance I get to *write* these days anyway other than briefs and memos to Ron Scala. Forgive the typos and stuff, obviously I can't have the paralegals do this for me.

Ok, so this is weird, but I think for obvious reasons you might make sense of it after you finish reading this. I didn't tell Laurie, because she's heard me talk about Angie and might take it the wrong way, so don't mention it to her on the phone or something, ok?

Remember that place we went a few years? Out in the country, a few guys from UVA went with us and we went fishing? I go fishing there a lot, usually later in the season. This year I haven't even got my license yet but I went out anyway. I never catch much though one of the partners here says there's some good-sized bass, the stream gets all clogged up in the winter with brush and stuff and makes a little pond. Anyway I usually leave my house about three a.m., it takes about forty-five minutes to get there and slog through the woods and all that, so it's just about dawn when I finally reach the stream.

I went there last Saturday. Laurie pulled a double shift otherwise she would have come and the girls have dance class Saturday morning, so I went alone. It was a very clear night and there were a lot of stars out. I got off a little late so it was closer to dawn than I would have liked but anyway I got there. Afterwards Laurie reminded me that it was the summer solstice. *That* kind of made my hair stand on end. (I told you this was weird.)

But I didn't know that then. It was a real pretty early morning or late night, however you want it. Listened to that bluegrass station out of Warrenton til the signal faded past Crozet, pulled the van over and got my stuff and walked in.

There were a few mayflies left and the fish were definitely biting. I don't use flies so I went for a popper, didn't get anything so I dug around and finally found a couple of worms. That's illegal, to use live bait right now, but who's going to check, right? Anyway it didn't matter because I didn't catch anything. I mean I didn't catch any *fish*—it was still pretty dark and I snagged a *bat*, that happens sometimes cause they hear the line I guess and they go for the bait, they think it's an insect. Usually happens to fly fishermen but this time it was me.

Now, bats don't bother me really but you don't necessarily want to be there in the dark with a bat flopping around on your line. I couldn't tell if I snagged its wing or what, but I don't think the hook was in its mouth. It fell in the water a few feet in front of me, pretty shallow mucky water and thrashed around. Weirdest thing was how you're not supposed to be able to hear bats, but honest to god I could hear this one—a very strange high-pitched crying sound. Like wires or something, you know when you pluck a wire? And then I could start to hear *other* bats, Joe, it was creepy as hell. They were looking for it I guess and calling out and it was answering them. The poor little bat's just struggling in the water, I guess I could've found the hook but I was afraid it would bite me. Plus, it's a goddamn *bat*.

So I got my penknife and cut the line. I needed some more coffee, I could feel it was going to be hot and the bugs started coming out and it was definitely time to go. That poor little bat's still flopping around in the water, so before I left I got my rod and leaned over and pitched it onto the shore. I didn't want it to drown. Lot of trouble for a stupid bat, right? But I think it was just a baby, it was so tiny, not even big as a mouse. It stopped struggling but I could still hear it crying and no kidding, it was like fingernails on a blackboard, gave me the chills.

So I turned around and got my stuff, started to head back out of the woods when behind me I heard a noise. Not the bat but something splashing in the water. Otter I thought first but it sounded pretty big and I stiffened because you know there's a lot of bear down here, see them up on Skyline Drive all the time. Just little black bears but my daddy didn't raise no damn fool, you don't turn your back on a bear! Wished I had my camera, but I didn't. It was still splashing around back there, didn't see me or didn't care. So I turn around very slowly and damn straight, Joe, I *wish* I brought my camera!

It was *Angie*. No damn bear and I know you'll think I'm nuts, but it was *her*. I know you remember the same things I do, so I don't have to tell you: I wasn't drunk, I wasn't stoned. *It was her*.

She was in the stream—the pool, actually, the open space where the stream had swelled after the rain and snowmelt. I didn't think it could be deep enough in there to swim but that's what she was doing, stroking through the water and her hair floating all behind her.

I just about had a heart attack. She was naked and I swear to god she didn't look any different than she did that other time, remember that weekend in W. Va? This was like that, she was swimming and she'd stand and the water would just slide off her and still she didn't see me. I just stood and stared, I mean what would *you* do? Wanted to say something but I was so shocked I couldn't. Couldn't even move.

Then she turned around. Sort of holding her wet hair up off her neck and her eyes closed and then I really *did* think I was going to have a heart attack. Because her eyes popped open and she was staring right at me. Those amazing eyes and her face just like it always was, not any older *at all*, and you know I might have been hallucinating except I knew I wasn't. She stared right at me and I wanted to say something but she wasn't smiling. Looked right at me and I could tell she recognized me, I almost thought she was going to say my name but she didn't. She had a funny look on her face, not a very nice look to tell you the truth, and I thought maybe she was pissed I was there watching her without her clothes on but hell, this was *Angie*—I mean, when did she care about that?

You tell me, Joe. Next thing I know my rod fell on my foot and when I grabbed it and looked up again she was gone. She was gone and that little bat was, too. I looked for it, swept the tip of my rod through the muck and waded out a little but I couldn't find it. Guess it rolled back into the water and drowned after all.

So there it is. A weird story, and I don't know who else I could tell it to. "A Current Affair" maybe, huh? Jesus. Let me know what you think.

And let me know when you're heading down this way—we'll go fishing.

Hasel

I put the last page of Hasel's letter on the side table. There was one more page: a Xerox of two newspaper items, with arrows scrawled by Baby Joe. I didn't want to read but of course I did. *What would you do, Joe?*

It was a short article from the Charlottesville paper, about the death by drowning of a local attorney. The date was June 27.

"Tragic and almost inexplicable," the paper said; he had been fishing in the Branch Creek near Crozet, and somehow had fallen into the stream and drowned in a few inches of muddy water. There was no evidence of foul play.

The other item was his obituary: Hasel Atkins Bright, attorney. Age 36, drowning accident; survived by his wife and two young daughters. In lieu of flowers, contributions could be made to a scholarship fund in Hasel's name at the English Department of the University of the Archangels and Saint John the Divine.

So.

Hasel was dead, Oliver was dead. Baby Joe was drinking heavily but otherwise okay in New York. Annie was famous, and Angelica—unless one was to believe Hasel's account of seeing her bathing in the Branch Creek near Crozet, Virginia—Angelica was still unaccounted for.

And me? At 38, I was a GS-11 and holding, just barely holding on.

Once, I'd dismissed Angelica's account of the *Benandanti* as craziness. But during the years following my expulsion from the Divine, I often thought that she had been right. That whatever opportunity for change or expiation or revolution the dark goddess and Magda Kurtz and Angelica herself might have represented was now gone forever. The *Benandanti* had not relinquished their control over the world. They never would. If anything, their hold was stronger now than it ever had been. Fourteen years earlier, the day after the presidential inauguration, I stood at the entrance to the Dupont Circle Metro subway and watched as workmen hauled away the newspaper racks selling the *Atlanta Constitution* and *Village Voice* and *Mother Jones*, binding the flimsy metal-and-plastic machines in heavy link chains and dragging them down Pennsylvania Avenue to a waiting garbage truck. The next day, shiny new dispensers appeared, holding the *L.A. Times* and *Wall Street Journal*. What Angelica had told me of the *Benandanti* made it all sound mystical and darkly glamorous, secret shamans ruling the world from behind a scrim of smoke and leaping flames.

But the truth was as banal and everyday as the headlines of the *Washington Post* and the endless parade of silver-haired men frequenting new restaurants in the corridor between K Street and Georgetown, lobbyists and lawmakers trailing in their wake like remoras. And like everyone else I knew in the city, I just got used to it. My life never stopped, I had a few casual friends and occasionally lovers, and through it all I was lucky enough to have a fairly decent job and a nice place to live.

But I knew that my heart had gone to sleep at the Divine. When it woke nearly two decades later, I started to emerge from Ignoreland, just like everybody else. It was going to take a teenage riot to get me out of bed, but that's just what I got.

CHAPTER 11

Ancient Voices

To reach the Anthropology Department, you ascended a series of grand curving marble staircases, up through Plant Life and Vertebrates and Paleontology, past the enclaves of Man and the Higher Mammals, skirting the secret temples of Egyptology and the Ancient World and stopping short of Gems and Minerals and the breeding cells for the Living Coral Reef and the Insect Zoo. Each marble step held a shallow depression worn into the stone by more than a century of thoughtful treading by scientists and receptionists and cleaning personnel. Slender grooves showed where hundreds of fingers had absently traced the edge of the marble banisters; if you knew where to look you could see a faint rusty stain, like the shadow of a raven's wing, that marked the exact spot where Othniel Marsh and Edward Cope had grappled during an argument concerning the use of the name *Titanosaurus* for an immense herbivore. The steps to Calvary or Mount Olympus could not have been more resonant with ancient secret power than those of the Museum of Natural History.

My office was on the south side of the building, overlooking the Mall. Each morning I walked down the long dim corridor, past Invertebrates and Arthropods and Ungulates (which had migrated here because of lack of space in Mammals), the Department of Worms (where department chief Vic Danhke had a sign on his door that read HEAD WORM), and so into the Department of Anthropology. The entire floor had a faint rainy scent, punctuated by occasional bursts of formaldehyde and the woodsy odor of the beetles Molly Merino used to clean the occasional shipment of tapir or wildebeest pelts. There were boxes and cartons and shelves everywhere, spiring up into the dark recesses of the ceiling, lit by dangling tubes of fluorescent lights and the occasional blinding nova of a halogen lamp trained upon a fragile human femur or mummy restoration-in-progress. Here and there the pale green light of a computer monitor glowed in the darkness, or you might glimpse the flickering opalescent lozenge of a laptop exiled with its curator to some dank corner.

Nothing looked as though it had been cleaned since at least the Bicentennial. An overzealous expedition by the building's custodial crew had once resulted in the loss of a pipe used by the Yanomano to blow psychoactive residue into each other's nostrils. Barry Hornick claimed his work on the Yanomano diorama was set back three weeks, and the entire South American Peoples division traced the late opening of their new gallery to this same housekeeping error. Since then, cleaning was done sporadically if at all. A rich yellowing patina covered everything, composed of bone dust and pollen and beeswax, varnish and plaster of Paris and the odorous cabbagey residue from the *kim chee* Robert Dvorkin bought at a little Korean place in Alexandria and ate every day for lunch. A fine silvery net of webs from the Insect Zoo's runaway golden orb weavers hung from the rafters and kept the cockroach and silverfish population at bay. In the summer most office doors remained shut, not out of any burning need for privacy but because that was the only way to retain some slight breath of cool air from the museum's balky central a/c system. The closed doors formed a kind of informal gallery of Gary Larson cartoons clipped from the *Post,* along with amusing postcards from colleagues in distant places (HAVING a GREAT TIME in *CAIRO* DIGGING UP some *OLD FRIENDS!* CHANUKAH GREETINGS from OLDUVAI GORGE!) and the occasional announcement of an honorary degree or new publication in *Antiquities*. In the fall, the doors flew open again so that the heat blasting from the museum's ancient furnaces could find its way into cubbyholes full of carven masks and heaps of moldering newspapers and damp *papier-mâché* replicas of Breton menhirs.

In contrast to all this nearly Victorian splendor and decay, my office was compact and bright and sterile as a hypodermic needle. A sleek steel display case held video monitors and television sets and the assorted VCRs and incidental equipment necessary for running the archival videodisc system. A network of multicolored cables connected these to computers and still more monitors and CD ROMs on my desk. The desk itself was a battered wooden contraption tunneled with pigeonholes and drawers in varying states of disorder. It looked as uncomfortable with its glittering satellites as a dowager aunt with her skinhead niece, but I liked it. It had been my first desk at the museum, and had traveled with me from my first little cubicle next to the Department of Worms to what would probably be its final home here. My window had an unobstructed view of the brick turrets of the Castle across the Mall. On sunny days the ghostly sound of calliope music echoed up from the ancient carousel outside the Arts and Industries Building, and sometimes stray balloons tapped plaintively against the glass before drifting off to float above the Tidal Basin and the Pentagon.

After so many years, my job had become more of a PR position than anything else. New technicians handled the eternal sorting and cleaning and labeling of photos in the ever-expanding Larkin Collection. None of the actual production was done in-house, and three years earlier the museum had cut a deal with Jack "Jolly"

Rogers of Winesap Computers to write, manufacture, and distribute the accompanying software for the system. The videodiscs weren't exactly best-selling items, but we almost managed to break even. And it was a nice tax write-off for everyone concerned, since the museum, of course, was an educational not-for-profit institution, and good PR for Winesap.

Jack liked me. He'd grown up in Yonkers, dropped out of high school in his junior year to play around with the earliest generations of personal computers, writing accountability programs for the mainframes at ConEd. He'd made his first million while still a teenager. We were the same age, and the yawning rift between our income brackets was bridged by a mutual distaste for Republican politics and a fondness for cheap beer and noisy proto-punk music. Once or twice a year he dropped in on one of his lobbying circuits of Capitol Hill, and we'd sit around my office with a smuggled six-pack of PBR to reminisce about seeing the Ramones and the Cramps in high school gyms and lament the failure of great unknown bands like the Shades (once of Trenton) and D.C.'s own Velvet Monkeys.

"Kids today, they don't know what it was like." Jack shook his head, his thinning blond hair slipping from its ponytail. He wore Doc Martens and white painter's pants and a faded blue T-shirt depicting Officer Joe Bolton and the Three Stooges. "They rip off someone else's riffs and go on MTV and jump around and—"

He made a rude noise, then consoled himself with a mouthful of chicken vindaloo. It was the last day of June and we were sitting in my office, gazing out the window at the crowds below. That morning, there'd been a Senate hearing, something to do with the Communicopia Bill. Jack had blown in and out of the Senate chambers, making the appropriate noises for C-SPAN and the national news, then ducked over here to check up on things. "Hey, this is pretty good curry, huh?"

I nodded, my eyes watering. "No lie."

Outside on the Mall a month-long carnival was in progress: the Aditi, the Festival of India, sponsored by the Museum and the Indian government and SOMA Software (publisher of the fabulously successful GEOQUEST! and a division of Winesap Computers, Inc.). For weeks workmen shouting in Hindi and Urdu and English had been constructing stages and booths, staking out tent sites and laying wooden walkways across the trampled yellowing grass. Now most of the Mall, from the old west wing of the National Gallery of Art all the way down to the Museum of American History, had been transformed into an idealized Indian village, like something from a soundstage for Kim. Gaudy paisley pennants hung from booths selling wooden toys and *puri*, lime pickle and vegetable *samosas* and edible effigies of Durga with spun sugar skulls dangling from her neck. From a small tent echoed the eerie wavering cry of a bone flute, along with the shrill voices of children shouting in Hindi as they practiced their tumbling, clambering onto each other's backs to form pyramids three- or four-high, then leaping off with outflung arms, graceful as flying squirrels. Even from here I could smell frying *ghee* and the overly sweet scents of jasmine incense and sandalwood, and hear an occasional burst of raga music from one of the wooden platform stages in front of the Hirshhorn's sculpture garden.

"Quite a little show you got on down there." Jack stood and crossed to the window, holding his paper plate and spooning yellow rice into his mouth. "We should be drinking Pink Pelican beer. You ever had that, Sweeney? It's all I drank when I was in Bombay last year, trying to get visas for those fire-eaters I told you about. Brewed from water from the sacred Ganges. Pink Pelican." He sighed and shook his head. "Great stuff."

"How long will you be in town, Jack?"

"I've got a four o'clock this afternoon from Dulles. Shareholders meeting in Bel Air tomorrow. Hey, any of those things get C-SPAN?" He pointed at the bank of video monitors, spilling sauce on his T-shirt. "I wanna see if I'm on yet."

I put down my plate and slid my chair over to the steel display case. "Sure. Hang on—"

I turned on the newest monitor we had, a thirty-two-inch HDRTV (Jack told me he had a two-inch Sony SuperHDR in his Range Rover). I fiddled with the remote, scanning through dozens of channels until I found the right one.

"Live Coverage of the House Subcommittee Hearings on Census Statistics and Postal Personnel," read Jack in disgust. "They preempted me for *that?*"

"Maybe you were on live. Or maybe they're saving it for tonight—"

"Nah. They bumped me, that's all. Screw 'em. I'll have Maggie Gibson loose her Stinkbomb virus on their system. Ever hear of that one? Replaces all your data with the screenplay of *Ishtar*."

He cackled, then snatched the remote from my hand. "Give me that, let's see what else is on—"

Random images flickered across the screen: Bugs Bunny, "Bonanza," soaps, "Reading Rainbow," vintage PeeWee, Windex, the Stephen King Network, what looked like a live broadcast of an assassination attempt on the president but turned out to be the new Slush video, Pepsi, Astroboy, Hoji Fries. It was impossible to tell what you were supposed to buy and what you were supposed to actually watch—Brando, Datsun, IBM—Jack made another rude sound—Donahue, McDonald's, "Mormon Matters," Sally, Oprah, Geraldo, Angelica—

Angelica?

"Stop!" I shouted. The screen froze on "This Old House."

"Here in Lubec, Maine," Bob Vila was saying as he tapped a coil of glittering blue foil, "you need an R-value of +47 to provide even the most basic insulation—"

"This?" said Jack in disbelief.

"No! Go back—wherever you were a second ago—no, slow it down, I can't—There! That's it, stop!"

"Opal Purlstein?" Jack was incredulous. "You watch Opal Purlstein?"

On the screen, talk show hostess Opal Purlstein was curled at one end of her cozy *aubergine* couch, staring raptly at this afternoon's guest.

". . . when you think of it, it's really just a return to the natural world order. In the grand scheme of things, the last few thousand years of history—well, let's be overly generous, and say the *last* ten thousand years—why, in geologic time, that's *nothing*! Just a blip—"

Opal nodded earnestly. At the other end of the couch, a stunning bronze-haired woman in an elegant crimson sheath extended her hand, delicately spreading her fingers as though they were the petals of some rare desert flower.

"—pfff! That's all," the woman said in a lilting voice. She looked as out of place on Opal's show as Brooke Astor at McDonald's. "That's what our civilization is worth."

Opal nodded, wide-eyed, and the audience burst into applause. On the couch the bronze-haired woman smiled demurely. Behind her stood two raven-haired Amazons, easily topping six feet, their arms crossed on their chests. They were lean and muscular and lethal as a pair of cheetahs, and stared with oblique black eyes into the camera. Both wore sleeveless black tank tops; silver armillas shaped like serpents coiled around their biceps. Their hair was cropped short as a boxer's, but the effect wasn't butch so much as purely androgynous: their faces were too serene, their eyes as carefully made up as Angelica's own. The girl on the left looked very young, maybe eighteen or nineteen, her face for all its grim expression surprisingly childlike. Her partner had a tattoo of a crescent moon on her cheek.

"It is *very important* to understand this," the bronze-haired woman said in a low, urgent voice. From the audience came murmurs and scattered clapping. "We are only trying to reclaim what originally belonged to us. We are only trying to bring back the world that was ours, the world that *is* ours."

The audience roared. Opal opened her mouth, closed it again, and nodded. The bronze-haired woman turned so that she directly faced the camera, her eyes huge, almost imploring. Then she smiled, lifting her hands slightly to acknowledge the applause. From her ears dangled two delicate silver crescents; on the breast of her ruby sheath lay another silver crescent, dazzlingly bright where the spotlights struck it. Her hair was still long and thick and curling, its ruddy highlights silvered here and there as though touched with ice. A faint web of lines radiated from the corners of her eyes, and there were laugh lines around her mouth, as delicate as though drawn with a *sumi* brush. She didn't look as Hasel Bright had described her in his letter: still a girl, young as when we had last seen her at the Orphic Lodge. But her eyes were the same as ever, that unnaturally brilliant emerald, and her smile could melt enough ice caps to cause major coastal flooding along the entire Eastern seaboard.

Letters flashed across the bottom of the screen.

ANGELICA FURIANO, AUTHOR.

"But I know her!" I leaned forward to stab at the screen. For a moment my finger pinned her there, then the station cut to a commercial. "That's Angelica!"

Jack took another bite of chicken vindaloo and nodded. "Yeah, I know her. She was at my birthday party—did I tell you Erica threw a surprise party for me at Morton's last year? A bunch of people came, like big Hollywood types. Tom Hanks, that woman with the hair. I mean, Erica knew *everyone*. Did *you* know Erica?" He shook his head remorsefully. "Kind of a kook, but boy, she had great legs. We're not together anymore."

"No, I mean I *really* know Angelica—we were at the Divine together, she was my best friend!"

Jack raised an eyebrow. "No kidding?"

"Really! She was—well, if you met her, you know what she's like. We were best friends, before—well, before I left. I lost touch with her, I haven't heard from her in, jeez, it must be nineteen or tewnty years now."

"I thought she said she went to some school in Italy, Rome or Florence or something."

"That was later—I met her here, at the University of the Archangels and Saint John the Divine. We were both anthropology majors." I continued to stare at the TV, shaking my head. "I can't *believe* it—"

Jack nodded. "Yeah, that would be her—she was talking about some place she was at, in Sardinia or Sicily or somewhere like that, she had a villa there that was built above some tomb that's three thousand years old. She married an Italian duke, Rinaldo somebody, Rinaldo Furiano, I guess, Erica knew him because he used to help produce Fellini's early stuff and Erica is a very big Fellini fan. But he died, he was a lot older than she is. She's very big on the West Coast. Your friend, I mean." He pointed at the television with his fork.

"*Big*? Big for what?"

He shrugged. "Like this cult or something. Well, no, not a cult—she's got this sort of self-help group, I guess it is. Only it's religious, kind of crackpot stuff but women out there just go crazy for it. *Whoo-whoo* at the moon, raise your consciousness, all that kind of shit. Plus she's written all these books. Like what's-her-name with the legs, you know. Shirley MacLaine."

"You're kidding."

"No—she's really popular. I think it's a boatload of crap, all this New Age stuff. But Erica was totally into it, that's how come she invited her to my surprise party. Geena Davis was there. Did I tell you I met Geena Davis? That girl could eat apples off the top of my head."

The screen cut back to Opal and her guest.

"Let's see what the audience has to say," Opal announced. She stood and marched into the rows of seats, waving her cordless mike like it was a censer. On the couch Angelica uncurled her legs and smiled beguilingly at the camera. Behind her the two tall black-haired women shifted. Their arms rippled with muscle, smooth and powerful as anacondas. The one with the moon tattoo smiled slightly, her thin mouth opening to flash very white teeth.

"Who are *they*?"

"Oh, those are her bodyguards—"

"Bodyguards?"

Jack laughed. "Yeah, her Amazons, she calls 'em. Cloud and Kendra. They're kickboxers. They were at the party too—"

"Angelica needs *bodyguards*?"

"Oh, sure," said Jack. "She gets death threats all the time. Guys are always trying to jump her bones or else trying to cut her up. I gather her views are a little extreme—well, here, listen—"

"My name is Amanda Jeffries, from Port Lavaca, Texas," a round-faced, heavyset woman was saying. "I was married for seventeen years to a man—"

Her voice broke. Beside her Opal jockeyed with the mike so it would catch every breath.

"—My husband used to beat on me, so bad sometimes I couldn't go to work. And our children, too. I threatened to leave him but he always said he'd change but he never did. Then I heard you talk at Victoria Community College—"

She inclined her head and the camera angle jumped to show Angelica listening intently, her brow furrowed and her green eyes glowing with concern.

"—I heard you talk about the Warrior Goddess inside of us and I went home, I signed up for a self-defense class at the Victoria YWCA and filed for divorce."

Opal nodded. "And your husband let you go?"

"Oh, no." Amanda Jeffries shook her head. "He came at me with a baseball bat—"

Gasps from the audience. "What did you do?" urged Opal.

"Well, I ran outside and threw the kids in the Pontiac and tried to drive off, but he smashed the windshield—"

Another cut to Angelica, her perfect eyebrows arched, the two women behind her silent and brooding.

"And?" said Opal.

"And so I ran him over. I—I—killed him. In reverse."

More gasps; scattered applause and one deep *boo*. Amanda Jeffries wiped her eyes. "I—I didn't want to do it, I loved him but—the jury said it was self-defense and the Women's Defense Fund helped me and my children while the trial was pending—"

"Let's hear another point of view." Opal walked deftly through the rows of seats until she reached a burly young man scowling near the back of the room. "What do *you* think of Angelica Furiano's—"

"I think she oughta be *locked up*—"

The camera focused on the man's face, his brown eyes darting from Opal back to the stage. "My wife and her friend went to one of her workshops in San Diego and this woman—"

His arm jabbed out as he pointed toward Angelica.

"This—" *bleeep!* "—is advocating overthrowing the government—"

Boos and catcalls, so loud the man looked startled and fell silent.

"I *think*," Opal said gently, "I *think* that she's calling for a change in the patriarchal system in this country, not overthrowing the government." She whirled to face the stage. "Am I correct, Angelica?"

"Yes," Angelica's clear voice rang out. "And—"

"Can I finish?" The man broke in angrily. "These women, they get together and they all bitch about how their husbands abuse them and they can't get decent jobs and I'm a rapist and everything comes down to Men Suck, but I work fifty-hour weeks to support my family, I never lifted a finger against my wife or children, I supported the Equal Rights Amendment and what do I get? My wife left me, she says I was *condescending* to her, she says I—"

"Well, perhaps she did not correctly perceive your concern," Angelica suggested smoothly. "Very often men are not aware that they treat their wives in a childlike fashion. You see, we're still trained to see women in only certain ways—and other countries are worse than the United States in this, when I was in Italy it was *very* pronounced—the whole Madonna-Whore syndrome. Or you have this whole way of looking at women as either nurturers or as children who need constant protection. Many of the world's ancient Goddess religions represent the Goddess as having three faces: those of the Mother, Daughter, and Crone or Destroyer. And a number of recent books help women focus on two of those aspects: Gaea, the nurturing Mother, and her daughter Kore. And that's wonderful. I truly think these books are wonderful and I think that they've helped women a great deal; but it's not enough."

The camera moved in slowly for a close-up on Angelica's face. Shafts of light from the silver crescent on her breast flickered across her cheeks and jaw; she looked as though she were rising up from deep clear water. Her voice grew softer, more intense. Beside me Jack leaned closer to the television set, and I could imagine everyone in that audience shifting in their seats, everyone straining to get closer to Angelica.

"—Because we can't just ignore that other face of the Goddess. For thousands of years we've pretended that She doesn't exist, that human history begins and ends with the Old Testament. But now, for the first time in millennia, women are starting to embrace Her again. And that's marvelous, but we can't just pick and choose which of Her aspects to honor. We have to deal with *all* of them. With the Full Moon and the New Moon but also with the Dark of the Moon, Hecate's realm. We have to acknowledge the Mother *and* the Avenger. We must embrace She Who Mourns and She Who Creates, but we must also honor She Who Destroys.

"Because otherwise we will never be whole. In traditional patriarchal societies, men have always acknowledged their own aggressive tendencies—that's why they've always been the warriors and the football players, the generals and bank presidents and—"

"The serial killers!" a shrill voice shouted. Uneasy laughter from the audience; but Angelica only nodded seriously.

"—and yes, the serial killers—but also the great artists and writers and composers. But until we as women acknowledge our own personal need for power and our own capabilities for aggression and independence, we will never be whole. We'll continue to be good mothers and daughters, we'll continue to be muses, we'll continue to be *victims*—but we won't be whole and strong. We won't be the Supreme Goddess that we can be. We need to acknowledge all the aspects of the Goddess within us; we need to *embrace* the chthonic darkness, to welcome and awaken the Moon; and then we will be whole again. Then we will be strong, unconquerable, sovereigns of the Sacred Earth.

"Then we will be One with Her."

Riotous applause and a few enraged shouts from the audience. A quick cut to the burly young man shaking his head and mouthing something obscene. But Opal had already abandoned him and was walking briskly back to the stage.

"Well, thank you, Angelica! I know *I've* read your books and found them incredibly empowering, and I took your Dark of the Moon workshop up in Vancouver last summer and—well, it was wonderful, absolutely wonderful! Thank you *so much*—

"Angelica Furiano, on a cross-country tour promoting her new best-selling book *Waking the Moon: Toward a Supreme Spirituality of Women.*"

Opal held up a book: I could just glimpse its title, in bright gold letters against a black background, and the glinting foil crescent that surmounted Angelica's name. Cheers and excited yelps. Angelica stood. The studio lights made a golden aureole of her hair, and while she should have looked like a thousand other talk show guests, sheepish or giddy or simply inane, she did not. She looked as she always had, beautiful and poised and utterly regal. Very slowly, as though performing in a Noh drama, she rested one hand upon her breast, her fingers spreading to cover the lunula, and then raised the other hand to the audience as though in benediction. Once again glittering letters flashed across the screen.

ANGELICA FURIANO: WAKING THE MOON.

I stared at her and shivered.

"Boy, she is a looker, huh? And she looks just like that in real life, I mean in L.A., some of these girls you see on TV or in the movies, you see 'em in real life and pffft—" Jack made a disgusted sound, his eyes still fixed on the screen. "But she's the real thing, I tell you."

"Her eyes aren't real," I said.

"Huh?"

"Her eyes—those are green contacts; her eyes aren't really that color."

Jack stared at the screen, then shrugged. "Well, whose are? You think she's a dyke?"

"Angelica?" I said softly. "I don't think so—I mean, I don't think she used to be. I always sort of thought of her as pansexual."

Jack snorted. "Yeah, sure. Her and what's-his-name. And I'm the Ludovicher Rebbi."

From behind the couch strode Angelica's two bodyguards. The black tank tops flowed into army-style khaki shorts, and they wore lace-up black leather boots with thick clunky toes and nasty-looking metal spurs. The one with the crescent moon tattoo had a long thin braid falling down her back, its end tied with a leather thong hung with crimson feathers and what appeared to be bones. Jack stared at her admiringly, then sighed and wiped the corner of his mouth with a paper towel.

"Well, listen, kiddo, I got to go."

The two Amazons flanked Angelica, their heads held high like pro wrestlers. I had to admit it made a striking tableau, those two black-haired beauties guarding their golden idol. Angelica smiled and nodded as her guardians looked around the room, eyes glittering. As Opal's theme music surged Angelica turned. Her bodyguards smiled, thin mirthless smiles like those of a dreaming cat, and escorted their mistress offstage.

"Wow. I still can't believe that was Angelica."

Jack grinned. "What a piece of work. 'Angelica Furiano.' The Avenging Angel. Sounds like she made it up."

"When I knew her, her name was Angelica di Rienzi." I sighed and shook my head. "God, I can't believe it's been that long. I completely lost touch with her, you know? For a couple of months it was like we were bonded at the hip, and then—" I stared sadly at the TV screen. "I never heard from her again. Christ, I'd love to see her."

Jack took a last bite of his chicken vindaloo and shoved the paper plate beside a video monitor. "Well, like I told you, she married this count guy from Italy. Erica said he was like one of the three richest guys in the country. When he died it all went to Angelica, and I can tell you his first three wives weren't happy about that *at all*. Ah well, gotta fly."

He stood and picked up his bag, a worn Guatemalan rucksack. "Have fun at the festival. I'll have one of my boys see if they can track down a local distributor for Pink Pelican and send you a case."

I walked him to the door. "When will you be back in D.C.?"

Jack hugged me to him, gave the top of my head a swiping kiss. "Shit, I dunno. Christmas I'll be visiting my dad in Florida, maybe I'll be through then. We're test-marketing this new software program in the fall, a tie-in with the big dinosaur exhibit reopening at that other museum in New York. Maybe I'll be out then. We can check out the mosh pits downtown."

We walked down the hall, Jack stopping at every door to read the cartoons posted there and hooting with laughter. Finally we reached the end of the corridor. At the head of the broad curving stairway he stopped.

"Well, listen, Sweeney, it's been a slice, like always."

He took a few steps, then turned to look back at me. "And listen—I was going to call Erica when I get back, she's still got all my Arvo Pärt CDs. You want me to see if I can get your friend Angelica's number from her? She and Erica have mutual friends or something, they used to run into each other a lot."

I nodded eagerly. "That would be great, Jack! I mean it—I'm sure Angelica remembers me, tell Erica—"

He waved me away. "Sure, sure. See you, kiddo."

I watched him descend the steps, taking them two at a time like a kid eager to get out of class. Then I went back to my office.

The little room smelled of cumin and fenugreek. From outside came the high skirling wail of flutes, the carousel's ghostly fanfare. Billowing smoke from the Aditi's outdoor grills mingled with the yellow dust of the Mall's wide walkways. I turned from the window and for a long moment stared at the TV screen. The credits for Opal's show were still running—*This program was previously recorded in front of a live audience*—the music soaring until it was rudely cut off by a commercial for tooth powder. I turned off the TV and closed my door, settled into my chair, and for a few minutes rocked thoughtfully back and forth.

Angelica Furiano. The Avenging Angel. I thought of those two Amazons, of Opal Purlstein and women across the country crowding her workshops, listening to her talk about the rights of women and becoming empowered. Kickboxers and former nuns and slacker dykes, New Age hausfraus and *fin de siècle* suffragettes.

"What a crock," I said out loud.

But then I thought of when I had last seen Angelica, nearly two decades ago: a beautiful young girl rising naked from the water in the shadow of the Orphic Lodge, a young girl striding through the dust, dancing around a lowing bull in a dark field. I thought of her lying in the grass with Oliver; I thought of Oliver himself with his poor mutilated scalp and his mad blue eyes, making that last leap of faith from the window of a closet at Providence Hospital. I thought of all these things; and of Balthazar Warnick staring at me from atop a curving staircase; of Francis Xavier Connelly helping to push Magda Kurtz into the wasteland; of a boy's reedy voice cutting through the darkness like a heated wire through black glass.

From the gargoyles to Stonehenge
From the Sphinx to the pyramids
From Lucifer's temples praising the Devil right,
To the Devil's clock as it strikes midnight—
I have always been here before . . .

I thought of them all, and of Hasel Bright lying facedown in a pond in the Virginia woods. And Angelica so rich and famous that she had homes in Los Angeles and Italy and god knows where else; of Angelica writing best-selling books and having a following that could number in the thousands, maybe in the tens or hundreds of thousands for all I knew. I had no idea at all what she'd been doing all those years—writing books, I guess; teaching people to go *whoo-whoo* at the moon. Above the haunted strains of the carousel and the faint cries of children, I heard Oliver's voice the last time I had seen him alive—

"*. . . don't you worry about her: Angelica is destined for Big Things. Very, very Big Things—*"

I thought of Hasel's letter. After a few more minutes I got out of my chair. I walked to the door and made certain it was shut, then reached for my phone and called Baby Joe in New York.

CHAPTER 12

The Priestess at Huitaca

Why don't you all take the night off? I don't think you've had a day off since Opal."

Angelica di Rienzi Furiano reached for her glass of chardonnay. She raised it, toasting the sun where it struck bolts of violet and gold from the edge of the butte that rose above her home. In its delicate goblet the wine glowed. A tiny bee with green eyes hovered above the lip of the glass. Angelica flicked at it with a carefully sculpted fingernail. The bee spun off and disappeared into the late afternoon light. Angelica sipped thoughtfully at her wine, suddenly smiled. "I know! *Dr. Adder*'s playing in Flagstaff, you could go see that. It's supposed to be pretty good."

In the pool, Cloud and Kendra and Martin lay on inflatable plastic floating chairs. The two bodyguards wore plain back one-piece bathing suits; Martin an ancient pair of surfer's baggies appliquéd with yellow smiley-faces sewn on by Kendra. Cloud's dark pigtail drifted across the turquoise surface behind her like a dozing water moccasin. A few feet away Kendra and Martin held hands, their floats bumping noses every now and then in a companionable way. They were all three burnished copper by the sun, though Martin's hair was white-blond, straight and fine as a baby's. He was Angelica's personal trainer, and lived in a casual ménage with the two girls in the adobe gardener's cottage down the hill from the main house.

"Girls?" Angelica inquired softly.

"You sure?" Kendra lifted her head drowsily, shading her eyes as she squinted up at their employer. She was only eighteen, taking a year off between high school and Bennington. She had a black belt in karate and for the last two years had won the Idaho State Martial Arts Competition. "Cloud said she heard something outside last night—"

Angelica shook her head. "I saw it later—a coyote, looked like it had a jackrabbit. No, you all go on; I think the early show's at seven."

"A coyote?" Cloud repeated dubiously.

Angelica nodded. She tipped her head to gaze at Cloud from above the rim of her sunglasses. "Isn't that amazing? It came right up to the house. They've never done that before."

Damn straight they've never done it before, thought Cloud. *They haven't done it yet*. The night before she'd been up late, reading a new Pasolini biography, when she'd heard it. Something was struggling on the path that led from the cottage to the pool, something too large for any animal, and besides, she'd distinctly heard a voice, a boy's voice, she thought. She hadn't been able to make out any words; she hadn't waited around to hear more. By the time she got outside, arms and legs taut and ready to strike, whatever had been there was gone.

"You really should put the surveillance system back on, Angelica," said Kendra. "I mean, someone could walk right up to the house—"

Angelica shook her head, her hair escaping from beneath a huge sun hat. "That's why I have *you,* bambina. Besides, the animals would set it off every night—I told you, it was a coyote."

Her tone was light, but Cloud heard the soft threat in it: the topic was closed. "Listen, Artie down at the Soaring Eagle said he was getting in a shipment of Dungeness crabs today—you all should go there for dinner, check it out for me. Elspeth"—Elspeth was her agent—"Elspeth will be coming out next week and I've got to figure out where to take her."

Cloud grimaced but said nothing. She *loathed* the Soaring Eagle. The others were more cheerful.

"Aw *right*," Martin sang. He slid from his float into the pool. "Man, I *need* a night off." He yawned and absently flexed his arms. "Thanks, Angelica. We'll bring you back some Ben & Jerry's."

Angelica smiled. "Pomegranate sorbet, if they have it."

"Cha, boss." Martin gave her a thumbs-up, turned to pull Kendra from her float. She slid into the pool silently and smoothly as an otter. Then she and Martin swam to the steps and climbed out, Martin squeezing water from his long hair, Kendra shaking her feet off like a cat before they gathered towels and sandals and sunscreen and began to pick their way across the terra-cotta-tiled patio to the path that led to their cottage. In their wake a string of tiny garnet butterflies rose from the tiles, and fluttered tipsily about Kendra's closely shorn head.

"You coming, Cloud?"

Cloud raised her head from her float, her pigtail slithering between her shoulder blades. On one cheek was a tattoo of a crescent moon, its dark curve outlined faintly in red. Three gold rings pierced the web of skin that stretched between her thumb and forefinger, and her upper arm was tattooed with zigzag bands of black and deep blue.

"In a minute. Go on ahead, I'll catch up." She turned onto her stomach and stared at Angelica, her golden eyes slanted and wary. "Leave me some hot water in the shower."

"Take the Porsche," Angelica called as the other two disappeared around a tumbled pile of sandstone. "You know where the keys are—"

She leaned back into her chair, a banana yellow Italian chaise that she had had shipped here from her villa on Santorini. It was elegant and simple and sleek as a driving glove. Its curves fit those of Angelica's body, and she liked the feel of the warm kidskin against her own bare flesh, the musky scent the leather released in the heat. She was wearing only a simple black maillot, cut high to show off her long legs and the taut abdomen Martin worked so hard to maintain. "Cloud, don't you want to go?"

Cloud gazed at Angelica, her eyes heavy-lidded. Lines of sweat had gathered around the outlines of her moon tattoo, giving a silvery gleam to the dark crescent. She smiled, a thin smile that showed her small white teeth and the pink tip of her tongue.

"In a minute."

Angelica stared back at her, her wineglass balanced between two perfect fingers. Cloud had been difficult lately—nothing major, just small annoyances like this: her refusal to leave when she'd been dismissed, her insistence on having heard something last night when it was clear that Angelica wanted that something to have gone unheard. Cloud was smarter than Kendra and Martin, a few years older as well—she'd graduated from UCLA film school, worked for a while as an apprentice foley artist before getting bored and taking off on her own. Two years ago in October, she'd attended Angelica's Samhain workshop in Minneapolis, the one where Angelica had been heckled by a guy who kept calling her a castrating bitch and a bull dyke. Afterward he'd slimed his way through the crush of autograph seekers and hauled off and hit Angelica in the face. Cloud had felled him with a single kick to the solar plexus, holding him down until security arrived. Angelica had hired her on the spot. A year or so later, when they were back in Los Angeles, she hired Kendra.

"So you won't get too lonely on the road," she'd told Cloud.

"You mean so *you* won't get too lonely," Cloud had replied with a smirk. Cloud preferred men, serious ironworkers when she could meet them at the gym, which wasn't often when you were on the road, and besides, you had to be real careful whom you went out with these days. But she'd had a brief fling with a girl at UCLA; she figured Angelica must be a lesbian, one of those older lipstick dykes with the clothes and the heels and Opium perfume, although Cloud had already decided she wasn't going to go to bed with her. It was bad karma to sleep with people you had to work with. But, somewhat to Cloud's disappointment, Angelica didn't put the make on her. She never seemed to put the make on anyone. Although sometimes when her son was visiting, Angelica might go out to dinner with him and a few of his friends, and afterward Cloud suspected that some of the young boys spent the night at the glass house in the desert.

Yes, Cloud was sharp. If she'd been a *real* cloud, she would have been one of those brilliant crimson flares you saw sometimes above the buttes just after sunset, a cloud like flame and not a gentle rainbringer. Angelica gazed across the turquoise pool, caught the glint of Cloud's golden eyes staring back at her, measuring, unafraid. She took another mouthful of wine, letting its sweetness fade, the faint tang of raspberries and smoke dissolving on her tongue.

Angelica had her own reasons for wanting her staff gone this evening. Her housekeeper, Sunday, came to work during the day, spending the night only when Angelica gave one of her rare parties. So she was never a problem. Cloud and Kendra and Martin usually had one free night a week together, when they drove Martin's Jeep up to Flagstaff or Sedona. The three alternated their other days off, but once a month, at the dark of the moon, Angelica had to make up excuses to get them away from the compound. This had never been a problem at her place in Los Angeles, where so many clubs and bright lights beckoned, or in Santorini, where Martin had a legion of admirers among the sloe-eyed girls who worked as waitresses at the waterfront restaurants, and where Kendra and Cloud liked to go night-diving for octopus with Sabe, the old fisherman who cared for the Furiano estate when Angelica was away.

But when they were here in the desert, the girls and Martin didn't like to leave Huitaca. Martin complained about the flaky old women in Sedona (Angelica laughed, most of the tourists were younger than she was), and Cloud thought the food in the local restaurants was disgusting. As for Kendra: well, Kendra was just plain lazy. Left to her own devices, Kendra would lie outside by the pool with her +87 factor sunscreen and a pile of *Sandman* comics, and read and doze until she dried up into a little heap of brown dust and blew off into the Mazatzal Mountains.

Although really, Angelica couldn't blame her for wanting to do just that. Huitaca was a glorious place. She had bought the land a year after Rinaldo died. She had just sold her first book—*Into the Nysean Fields: Empowered Dreaming for Women Who Have Suffered Enough*—for a modest five-figure advance. She'd visited Sedona on the tour promoting *Nysean Fields*, fallen in love with the buttes and vast lonely expanse of the desert, the blue sky like wet enamel paint and the wonderful midnight incense of piñon pine burning in fieldstone fireplaces. She'd found this place for sale and closed on it a month later, hired a brace of architects and contractors and carpenters. A year later she moved in.

She named the spot *Huitaca* for the Chibcha moon-goddess, a deity known for her love of indolence and intoxication; one of Her more easygoing incarnations. The compound was tucked between sandstone crags and a piñon-topped bluff where ravens and vultures nested. In the chaparral roadrunners and chachalacas rustled, hunting snakes and the little spiny lizards that hid among the stones. On spring mornings she could hear the chachalacas screaming raucously from the tops of huisache and scrubby pines. The cloudless air smelled of hot dust and pine resin; on summer evenings she could see prayers for rain rising like blue smoke from the distant belfry of the little church in Cottonwood.

Huicata was a few miles from Sedona, with its crystal wavers and wealthy pilgrims seeking enlightenment at overpriced restaurants that served blue corn chips and free range lamb *fajitas*. Every now and then a gaggle of tourists would find its way through the hills to Huitaca. Then Cloud and Kendra would get to do their stuff, politely but firmly directing the disappointed women back into their rented four-wheel-drive vehicles, watching until they jounced down the dusty gravel road, and out onto the main highway. Huitaca was an enchanted place, almost as beautiful as the Furiano villa on Santorini. Outsiders were only welcomed on special occasions.

The main house was dazzling, three thousand square feet of low-E glass and adobe and two-hundred-year-old beams salvaged from a deconsecrated church in Phoenix. The walls were hung with Navajo sand paintings and an entire steer's skeleton had been reassembled above the massive fieldstone fireplace, its bleached bones threaded with beads and feathers and rattles made from the shells of tortoises. The floors were covered with hand-painted tiles imported from Tuscany, and small dried bundles of sage burned day and night in front of a tiny altar near Angelica's bedroom.

But it was outside that Angelica did much of her work. The pool and its surrounding patio were set in a sort of natural amphitheater. On clear nights it afforded an unobstructed view of the eastern sky, with the violet-tinged buttes and hillsides erupting like frozen geysers of stone above the desert. On the patio, there were studiedly naturalistic plantings of native grasses and succulents: lecheguillas, the thorny leafless wands of ocotillo; rock nettles and prickly pear. Collared lizards slept upon the tiles; horned toads crept into the crevices where tiles had cracked, and laid their eggs among shards of terra-cotta. A colony of sidewinders visited there as well. Once Martin had tried to kill one, but Angelica stopped him—

"They only come here to drink," she said. To his horror and amazement she stooped above a snake as long as Martin's arm and thick around as his wrist, its head a raised fist, the dry husk of its rattle a blur.

"Here now," murmured Angelica. Before the rattler could strike, she grabbed it behind its head. It dangled from her hand, writhing and twisting into improbable loops, its tail slapping her thigh hard enough to leave a red streak like the mark of a belt. Angelica held it at arm's length and gently squeezed its jaws, so that Martin could watch the venom stream in milky strands from its hollow fangs onto the tiles. Then she let it go. Martin jumped onto a chair as the rattler made its crazy sideways flight across the patio and finally disappeared into a stand of prickly pear.

"Let them drink if they want to," Angelica commanded. "And don't you *ever* kill one."

Martin had never threatened another snake, but he and the girls were much more careful about swimming after dark. That was fine with Angelica: she preferred swimming alone. The pool itself was a good twenty feet deep, designed to resemble a natural spring-fed mere. And it was small—three good strokes and Cloud was across it. Angelica had been concerned about its impact here in the desert, although not enough to forgo its construction, or to curtail the steady trickle of water that coursed from a hidden spigot into the narrow end of the pool. In its depths flecks of gold and silver glittered from a mosaic, done in the style of the women's apodyterium in the Forum Baths at Herculaneum. It depicted the phases of the moon, with a triumphant female figure at center, the full moon held like an offering in her cupped hands.

Now, Angelica toyed with the idea of taking a swim. It was the twenty-ninth of

June, and hot enough that your spit would sizzle on a rock. But Cloud was still there.

"I guess I'll go on in," Angelica said at last. She finished her wine, setting the empty goblet on the table beside her chaise. "Don't miss your ride into town," she called out, and went inside.

Cloud waited till she was gone, lying on her stomach and letting her hands trail through the blood-warm water. *My ride*, she thought. She flexed her hand, the hand with the three gold rings piercing it, feeling the water lap against the sensitive delta of flesh. Near her float, a beetle flailed against the surface of the pool, a small dun-colored atom of the desert. It had probably never seen this much water in its life. Cloud slid her hand beneath it, lifted it so that the beetle was marooned on one of her knuckles. For a moment it remained there; she watched as the film of water on its mottled carapace dried. Then its wings lifted and it flicked off into the heated air.

My ride, thought Cloud, and dived beneath the turquoise water. Maybe Kendra and Martin were too brain-dead to notice, but Cloud had figured out a pattern. One night a month Angelica got rid of them, with excuses mundane or byzantine by turns. Tonight, Cloud would peer a little more closely at that pattern, and find out just what was really going on at Huitaca.

I'll have a fucking ride, all right. And she swam to shore.

Angelica's preparations were, as always, simple. She waited until she saw Cloud saunter back to the gardener's cottage. Then she turned from the window. She walked down the hall into the bedroom wing, went into the bathroom with its imported coralite marble floors and the frieze of ecstatic maenads she'd had smuggled into the country from Turkey, and stepped into the shower, a tall cubicle of green industrial glass.

Inside the light was diffuse: like showering beneath a hurricane sky. An alabaster dish held natural sponges and soaps scented with wild lavender and catmint; there was also a small canister of sea salt. Angelica poured a tiny mound into her palm, touched her tongue to the bitter crystals, and then let the water sluice it away. The smells of salt and lavender made her think of the Sea of Crete off the coast of Santorini; made her think of the Aegean, of narcissus nodding on stony hillsides and wind marbling the waves to whorls of white and midnight blue.

Afterward she changed into a plain white linen shift, sleeveless, knee-length, belted with a cord that only Angelica knew was made with real gold thread. She pulled her wet hair back into a ponytail, fastening it with a strip of leather. Then she sat at the battered Mission-style table she used as a vanity, the unstained wood so old and weathered it was soft to the touch, like suede. A small round mirror rested against a piece of lava from Akrotiri. Pots and tubes of expensive cosmetics were strewn everywhere, but Angelica ignored them. Instead, she reached for a terra-cotta vial stoppered with a cork, and tapped a little heap of coriander seeds into a marble pestle. She ground these, together with a piece of red sandalwood and a few slivers of dried blood orange peel, carefully rubbed the powder onto her breasts, wrists, thighs, neck.

All this while Angelica stared into the mirror before her. It was ancient, of polished metal that had corroded with time, so that her reflection was pocked with darkened spots and craters. Around its border were painted arabesques of dark green and umber, the fluid pattern broken here and there by a pair of eyes. *Scungilli*, her uncle had told her when he had given it to her, nearly twenty years before in Florence. *Octopus*.

"It was your mother's," he had said. There was a little break in his voice. Not of sorrow, Angelica knew that now. Remorse, perhaps, or apprehension. "Your father has forgotten I have it."

"My mother?"

Her uncle nodded. He was older even than her father, for all that his youngest child was only seven. She had been with him and her cousins for only a short while; she had visited them often before, of course, but this was different. This was like an exile. "I found it. Afterward . . ."

"But I thought my mother died!"

She was amazed. Close as she was to her father, he had never spoken of her mother: it was a forbidden topic. Cousins and aunts here in Florence had told her that she died in childbirth. Angelica herself suspected something less dramatic. Her father and one of the hired girls, or a wealthy student, or . . . These things happened; so Angelica let it be. No one in Florence cared, and no one at home in the States knew.

But on that late-winter afternoon her uncle had only shrugged, and avoided looking at her eyes. "Perhaps she did," he said after a long moment. Outside silver wands of rain tapped at the high windows overlooking the piazza. "We do not know."

"Wh—what do you mean?" Angelica reached for her glass of *aquavit*—her young aunt claimed it stimulated the appetite—and without wincing downed it in a gulp. "Tell me."

"You must never tell your father that I did so." Her uncle poured himself another glass. "But it is not right, that you do not know. Especially now," he added softly.

"It was years ago—well, *you* know how long it has been." Her uncle leaned across the divan to stroke her hair. "My sweet girl—it is so difficult to remember you have already been to university! Nineteen," he murmured, then went on.

"Your father was traveling to Rhodes, to meet with some of his friends—the university professor and some others, I do not recall. Their plan had been to rendezvous at Athens and depart from there on your father's boat—*Cefalû*, the same boat he has now—but their flight from London was delayed, and there was some confusion regarding how long it would take them to get to Rome. Luciano has always been impatient: he decided to go on alone, and await them at Mandraki Harbor. That is a fine yacht harbor on Rhodes, but it is a dangerous passage in the summer. He went from Cape Sidhero on Crete to Kasos, and thence to Scarpanto—Karpathos. His plan was to continue on to Mandraki and meet his friends.

"He stayed overnight on Karpathos, and early in the morning decided to leave for Mandraki. He should have had a relatively safe passage—the Karpathos Strait is not dangerous, once you leave the shadow of the mountains—but at midday a storm came up. From nowhere, your father said. The sky was without clouds, and in the near distance he could see that the waves were unruffled; but the *Cefalû* was hard beset. He was forced to make landfall on an island. A godforsaken place, no larger than our villa near Poggibonsi. It was without water or any living thing, no trees or grasses; only a tiny beach surrounded by lava stones. It was fortunate for your father that the *Cefalû* was well provisioned, because he was marooned there for two days. He tried to radio for help, but the storm kept up, and he was unable to reach anyone. By daylight he explored the islet, but there was little enough there, and he was afraid the winds might swamp the boat. But the second night it was calm enough that he left *Cefalû* where she was moored and took the Zodiac to shore, to sleep there. He had so little sleep, I think that it affected his wits, but your father is angry when I say that.

"So he camped on the little spar of rock. A charred place, he told me; but when he returned with his friends a few weeks later they found gold and skeletons in the waters there—they brought divers, in hopes of finding treasure, and they did. I believe it was one of those islands burned up by a volcano long ago, but you know I do not pay much attention to your father's work.

"That night he had only a driftwood fire, and his blankets against the wind, and a bottle of Tocai he found on *Cefalû*—still, not an ugly picture, eh? The storm had died and there was a full moon, which made the sea look like blue snow—that is how your father described it. Blue snow."

Her uncle fell silent, staring at the windows. The panes shuddered as water cascaded from a gutter overhead. After a moment he turned to her once more.

"She came to him in the night. He woke and she was there—not with him on the island, but in the water. Swimming. He wondered how she could swim, the bottom was so sharp with rocks, but she swam well. It was still dark but he could see her quite clearly from the beach, and he told me that he knew immediately she was a woman and not a dolphin or other fish—or a man.

"He watched her for some time, and then she came onto the shore. She was naked—no bathing costume, no bathing shoes, nothing to protect her from the wind or the stones. Only in her hand she carried a very old mirror made of polished metal. He thought she must have stolen it from some ancient tomb or grave, because he knew by looking at it that it was very old, not a thing a young girl swimming alone off the coast of Rhodes would have!

"She knew he was there watching her—and when she came ashore she walked directly toward him. The water behind her like blue snow and the full moon in the sky. She was beautiful—of *course* she was beautiful! An hallucination, they are always lovely! Young, and very slender, and though she had long legs she was not tall. So *that* you inherited from Luciano. And she had wide hips and high breasts and long hair that was very dark and curled, and huge golden eyes, though how he could see the color of her eyes I do not know because it was dark. Even in the moonlight it is dark. He said she was not like any woman he had ever seen before—not because of her beauty, but because of how she was put together. Such small bones, and so delicate but very very strong.

"And so he lay with her, and in the morning she was gone. He never saw her again."

Angelica stared at him. "But what about *me*! He *must* have seen her again, if she was—if she was really my *mother*!"

"Luciano says he did not." Her uncle gave her a piercing look. "Perhaps he never saw her in the first place, eh? But some months later he was in London, staying with friends, and in the middle of the afternoon there came a knock at the door and when they opened it—pfff! There was a very nice basket from Harrods, and a blanket, and inside the blanket was a baby—and with the baby there was *that*—"

He pointed to the tarnished-looking mirror on the table before her: a round mirror the size of her two hands, carefully wrapped in chamois leather, and decorated with an octopus's elegant dark coils. "A fairy story, eh? I do not believe all of it, but you are here, so—" With a heavy sigh he settled back upon the divan beside her, and raised his glass in a toast. *"Cede Deo."*

"But who *was* she? What was her name?"

Her uncle smiled sadly. "I do not know, my darling. We none of us know. Not even your father—"

"But he must—you said—"

"Perhaps he *does* know. But he has never told *me*. He said only what I have told you already—that she was beautiful, and also that she sang, and he found her songs very interesting. They were old songs, he told me, very old songs. I am only a financier and so I do not know about these romantic things! But he said they were in a language we no longer remember."

"But isn't there a picture? Or a birth certificate? Somebody has to have *something*—"

Her uncle's eyes widened. "My dear! You must not be so distressed—here, I will have Giuletta bring you some warm milk and *biscòtti*—"

Angelica looked stricken. "No—I mean, isn't there anything else? A photo, *something*—"

Her uncle pursed his lips, frowning. "I can show you what your father showed me," he said at last, and went over to the tiers of bookshelves that covered one wall. "Here—"

He pulled a heavy volume from the wall. Angelica craned her neck to read the title.

Kretisch-mykenische Siegelbilder.

Lavender-smelling dust rose when her uncle blew upon the cracked binding. "One of his books. See?"

She glimpsed a brightly colored plate of a vase, the pink clay fragments carefully repaired and painted with a wide-eyed octopus.

"Like yours, eh?" Her uncle cocked his head at the mirror on the table. "*Scungilli*. But *this* is what I want to show you—"

Beckoning Angelica closer he held up the book to display another illustrated plate. "He showed me this, afterward. Many years later. He said it reminded him of his woman from the seashore."

It was part of a fresco showing the profile of a woman's face. A woman in a blue-and-white-striped dress bedecked with scarlet ribbons, her long hair elaborately arranged; her huge eyes accented with kohl, bee-stung lips brightly rouged. In her hand was a sort of axe, double-bladed, the heads crescent-shaped. At the bottom of the plate were words printed in German. Beneath them Angelica recognized her father's casually elegant script—

MINOAN PRIESTESS CA 1650 B.C. PALACE AT KNOSSOS

"She is lovely, eh?" her uncle murmured.

"Y—yes."

The image had none of the inhuman coldness of Egyptian paintings. Angelica could easily imagine this girl laughing, eating bread, dancing; smoking too much and drinking too much wine and falling into bed and—

"Yes, she's very lovely," whispered Angelica—

Very lovely, and she looks just like me.

"So you have seen her," her uncle said after a long silence. Angelica could feel him staring at her, but she refused to look up. What remained of her energy she was saving to keep tears of outrage and fear and disbelief from spilling down her cheeks. With a sigh her uncle closed the book and set it back upon the shelf. "But in your studies, Angelica, your archaeology—such a famous image, you would have seen her someday and noticed the resemblance, even without me."

Downstairs in the main kitchen she could hear footsteps, Giulleta giving orders to one of the maids to bring *mostaccioli* and a glass of marsala to Signorina. Her uncle finished his *aquavit*. He wiped his mouth with a napkin and carefully folded the metal mirror back into its chamois. "But perhaps I should not have spoken of this now. Forgive me, Angelica—"

He kissed her cheek, his breath smelling of *Sen-sen* and spirits, and pressed the soft packet holding the mirror into her hands. "But you do have this, and your mother's necklace—" He inclined his head delicately toward her throat.

"What do you mean?" One of her hands closed tightly about the mirror in its chamois wrapping; the other touched the lunula beneath her scarf.

"Your necklace." Her uncle leaned back against the divan and closed his eyes. "Eh! This rain is exhausting."

"My necklace?"

He opened his eyes and nodded. "Yes—the other thing she had, besides the mirror. Your father said she wore a silver necklace, like the new moon—like the labrys the priestess carries—"

He glanced at the bookshelf. "—the double axe. I am glad he gave the necklace to you; I cannot stand these family secrets. Ah! Your aunt has sent us some wine and *biscòtti di cioccolata*! She knows we must make you fat!"

"But he didn't—I didn't—" Angelica stammered, then grew silent as a maid entered the dim room. She had not told her father of the lunula. She had worn it casually here in her uncle's house, because she had been certain no one would recognize it; but now . . .

"Thank you," her uncle said to the maid. "Here, Angelica—"

And he had handed her a crisp dark crescent on a tiny silver plate, a little smiling mouth like the new moon. "Now, my darling—eat."

Now, nearly twenty years later at Huitaca, Angelica gazed into the same mirror. When she turned her head, the metal's blurred surface showed her the same profile she had glimpsed so many times since then: on postcards at Knossos and Iraklion; in art histories and volumes of mythology; in the publicity photographs that adorned her books. The bull-priestess, the moon-priestess, the author at home. Angelica Furiano.

"Haïyo Othiym," she murmured, and brushed her fingertips against the mirror's pitted surface. Then she took the lunula from where it lay in a carved sandalwood box. For an instant the lunula's reflection gleamed in the window, like a glimpse of the moon rising above the chaparral. She slid it over her head, being careful not to snag her hair, and fingered its cool edge as though she were testing a blade. She gazed another moment at her image in the bronze mirror, then left.

She went back out into the main house. Sunday waited there as she always did, standing by the window and staring out at the chaparral—she had seen a puma there once, and Angelica knew she was hoping to see it again. She gave her housekeeper a little white envelope—Sunday liked to be paid in cash, and she liked to be paid every day—thanked her and walked her to the front door. Angelica watched her housekeeper climb into her new red Chevy pickup and take off down the rutted drive. She waited half an hour later, until she saw the Porsche disappear in a haze of dust. Angelica was alone at Huitaca.

Well, almost alone.

It was the hour after sunset, when you could feel the desert heat seep back into the earth. She went to the back of the room and drew open the sliding doors, opening the entire rear of the house to the night.

"Well now," she murmured, and breathed in luxuriously.

Overhead the sky was violet. The horizon paled to green where the buttes reared: immense pillars of sandstone, so huge and strange and silent they were like living things, vast watchful manticores or sphinxes waiting to descend upon the sleeping plain. Heat lightning stabbed fiercely at the tallest crags, and though Angelica knew there would be no rain, the scent of water filled the air, sweet as incense. Angelica smiled to see what awaited her outside.

At the pool's edge, myriad small things had gathered to drink. Desert crickets, kangaroo rats, fat golden-eyed toads, and tiny sleepy-looking owls. Nighthawks and shrikes swooped above the water, and crimson bees like strings of beads spilled across the tiles. And rattlesnakes that paid no attention at all to the furtive kangaroo rats and nervous mice, but drank and then slithered back across the patio with a sound like the rustle of a wooden rosary.

Angelica watched them all, her smile a benediction. Then she slipped outside.

Beneath her bare feet the tiles felt warm, but the air touching her arms was cool enough to raise goose bumps and make her nipples harden beneath the thin fabric of her chiton. A few of the animals looked up, but none fled. A kit fox froze, water dripping from its jaws, then lowered its head once more. As Angelica watched it, she felt something tickle her foot. She looked down to see a tarantula, three of its legs extended so they brushed against her instep, a fourth raised to tap tentatively at her little toe. She stooped and opened her hand. The tarantula stiffened, then relaxed, its legs unfolding like miniature landing gear, and crept onto her hand. The hairs on its legs and abdomen were soft as those on a mullein leaf. It crawled onto her wrist and crouched there, its eyes bright and intelligent as a magpie's.

"Ah, little sister." Angelica walked toward the pool, stooped, and rested her hand against the warm tiles. The tarantula jumped from her palm to the ground. Angelica laughed, then stood and stretched her arms toward the sky.

Bats swept down to skim the surface of the pool and ricocheted back into the night. A few stars pricked the darkness. Angelica lowered her hands and pulled her dress over her head. She untied the suede ribbon that bound her hair, so that the thick curls fell in a damp mass down her back. She was naked, save for the glint of the lunula above her breasts. As she moved, the animals moved as well. Not fearfully but with care, as they would move to accommodate some great beast, bull or elk or antelope.

But someone else froze at the sight of the woman in the dark. Staring at Angelica from the shadows, Cloud felt her breath catch in her throat. She'd been hanging furtively around the edges of the patio, trying to come up with some kind of MO for the evening, when without warning Angelica appeared at the bank of sliding doors. With a muffled cry Cloud darted into a thick stand of underbrush.

Immediately she wished she'd worn something other than her usual uniform of tank top and hiking shorts and Doc Martens. Thorns tore at her bare legs and arms. Cloud muttered a curse, crouching among snaky wands of ocotillo and agave blades. She felt giddy from the rush of adrenaline. A stupid overreaction. She shouldn't be this stoked about hiding in the bushes and peeking at Angelica, but here she was.

And there *she* was—

Cloud held her breath. This was, like, definitely Out There. She had always thought her employer was beautiful—*everyone* thought Angelica was beautiful—but seeing her like this Cloud finally understood the fanatical, almost worshipful reaction of Angelica's fans.

Cloud had read a few of Angelica's books, but it was hard for her to take them seriously. All that crap about the Goddess, about atavistic beauty and power. A power that would fill *any* woman, if only she would open herself up to it. Angelica had designed an entire ritual for this: Waking the Moon, she called it. Cloud had watched the ritual plenty of times. To tell the truth, it was not very impressive, at least to Cloud. A lot of incense and chiming bells and chanting, a certain amount of Camp Fire girl rowdiness and restrained nudity. Cloud usually dozed through most of it, leaving Kendra to watch in case any crazies showed up.

So maybe Cloud was missing out on something. Certainly afterward the women appeared to be ecstatic enough. Chattering about the Goddess, and how empowering it was to know Her true names. About what it was like to *feel* that power and to see Her beauty, a terrible beauty that She held within Her very bones, a beauty that would burn like flame and consume anyone foolish enough to come too near.

In Angelica's workshops—and these were very special workshops, participants were carefully screened, and to further ensure that only the very serious-minded took part, the experience would set you back two grand and change—in her workshops, Angelica even hinted that she, Angelica di Rienzi Furiano, was the final and supreme incarnation of the Goddess. Cloud had always thought this was a little presumptuous of Angelica, to say the least.

Now she wasn't so sure. Now, it seemed that maybe Angelica was onto something. Because *this* was different. *This* looked like the Real Thing.

In front of the pool Angelica stood, arms upraised, bathed in a cold bluish glow like moonlight. But when Cloud tilted her head back, she could see no moon, only a black-and-grey chiaroscuro of thorns and scrubby leaves. She moved gingerly, trying to get more comfortable, snagged her arm and swore beneath her breath.

When she looked up again Angelica was at the very edge of the pool. Light rippled across her bare flesh, mirroring the lightning overhead. About her throat she wore the same moon-shaped pendant she always wore for her rituals. The necklace must have been catching the light in some weird way: it glittered and sparked as though it were white-hot and had been struck with a hammer. The eerie light made Angelica look as though she were made of some semiprecious stone, fluorite or azurite or agate, something that filled her veins so that she glowed like phosphorous. Her hair streamed across her shoulders and over her breasts, tangling with the ends of her necklace. Angelica was a good ten or twelve years older than Cloud, but you couldn't tell by looking at her now. Her breasts were high and full, her waist small above wide hips, her legs long and muscular.

Gazing at her Cloud's mouth went dry. Her head was pounding, as though she'd had too much to drink; but Cloud never drank. She tried to take a step forward, felt her head yanked back sharply.

"Ow!"

Her pigtail was caught on a thorn. She sucked her breath in, terrified. But a few yards away Angelica stood oblivious, her hands rising and falling as she chanted.

> *Hail Hecate, Nemesis, Athena, Anahita! Hail Anat, Lyssa, Al-Lat, Kalika. Great Sow, Ravener of the Dead, Mistess of the Beasts, Blind Owl and Ravening Justice. Hail Mouth of the World, Hail All-Sister, Othiym Lunarsa, haïyo! Othiym.*

Cloud teased her pigtail free. She brushed a line of sweat from her upper lip, glanced back up at Angelica, and froze.

Angelica had fallen silent. For the first time Cloud noticed the myriad small creatures at her feet. Squirrels, or maybe rats, something that must be a horned toad and a ponderously moving creature with a tail squat and thick as its body. A gila monster, gaudy as a beaded clutch.

Ugh! Cloud grimaced, but Angelica paid no attention to the lizard. Instead, her hands were poised above something that Cloud couldn't see. Faster than Cloud would have thought possible, Angelica snatched at the ground. An instant later she raised her arms triumphantly. From each one dangled a snake—sidewinders, Cloud could hear their rattles as they whipped the air, and the whistling noise of their bodies writhing frantically to escape.

She's gone nuts! Cloud swallowed, her mouth gone sour with fear and disgust. *Time to check out, Sister Cloud—*

She wanted to run; but Cloud had chosen her hiding spot too well. She couldn't move without dislodging something or getting stabbed by thorns.

She moved anyway. Immediately a branch snared her tank top. An overhanging limb snagged her pigtail. Cloud yanked the ocotillo from her shirt; the fabric ripped as she lurched away. A small burst of pain as hair pulled from her scalp; then she was free again. She staggered forward, falling to her knees. Holding her breath, she raised her eyes to look out onto the patio.

Angelica was still there, her body shimmering in the violet dusk. In her hands the snakes flailed. Her voice rose, nonsense syllables that Cloud did not recognize.

> *Beryth, Eisheth, Zenunim, Lilith, Rahab, Naamah, Ashtaroth, Cammael, Dommiel, Exael . . .*

Within the darkness a light appeared, a tiny flicker like a spark fallen from a burning log. As Cloud gaped the light grew stronger, until a flame leapt there, higher than Angelica's head, high enough almost to lick at the stars. The flame spread, grew into a wall of fire that obscured utterly the serene surface of the pool. Cloud raised one arm before her eyes.

Like an earthbound aurora the wall of light flickered. In front of it stood Angelica, the two frantic serpents coiling and uncoiling in her hands, like living question marks. Like some terrible question themselves, and that awful heatless flame the answer.

> *. . . Beryth, Eisheth, Zenunim, Lilith, Rahab, Naamah, Ashtaroth, Cammael, Dommiel, Exael. Oye Eisheth, haïyo Othiym, oye haïyo, Othiym Lunarsa!*

There was a figure within the flames. It was as tall as Angelica, and like her it faced the eastern sky with arms raised. Save that it bore no serpents, it might almost have been her shadow—a shadow limned in flame, almost too brilliant to look upon. Angelica lifted her hands. The snakes squirmed furiously as with a cry she flung them from her.

For an instant Cloud saw them, curling and hissing like two hairs held above a lit candle. Then the sidewinders burst into flame. A searing blast, a smell like burning leather—and they were gone, vaporized as cleanly as though they'd been tossed into a furnace.

"Oh, *man*." Cloud shivered helplessly. "This is some shit."

Angelica brought her hands to her face. She clapped, just once, and took a single backward step.

"Eisheth!"

A hissing, as when hot metal plunges into water. Then the thing that stood within the flames walked toward Angelica. Cloud made a groaning sound deep within her throat.

It was like a man or woman made of fire. Light rippled about it like leaves thick upon a tree, but as it moved from the flames its bright skin faded to ruddy bronze. Its hair fell about its broad shoulders in tangled brassy strands. From its shoulders sprang two immense folded wings. While it made no sound, there was a heaviness to its tread—it moved like a creature formed of the same stone as the buttes and mesas. Its hands were crossed tenderly upon its breast. It held something there, but Cloud could not see what it was.

"Eisheth," whispered Angelica.

The creature lifted its head, and Cloud nearly cried aloud for the sheer mad beauty of it. It had a long angular face, with high, planed cheekbones and slanted eyes, a strong jaw and jutting chin. But there was something feminine about it as well, something soft in the wide mouth and rosebud lips, the enormous eyes and arching brows. Its pupils were almost without color, pale and icily prescient, like those of a malamute. Its skin was the color of thick cream, ivory tinged with yellow, its body smooth and hairless as an infant's.

It had wings.

"Eisheth," Angelica repeated.

"Yes," the thing replied, its voice a whisper. A girl's voice, or a boy's before the change. Its arms remained crossed; whatever it held neither struggled nor cried out.

"Do you know me, Eisheth?"

The thing bowed its head very slightly. "I do, Mistress."

"And you have brought what I commanded you to bring me?"

"I have, Othiym."

Othiym, thought Cloud. She dug her nails into her thighs to keep from crying out. *Othiym, it called her Othiym—what* is *this shit?*

"And the other naphaïm: they have done as I asked? They are heeding when they are called?"

"They are."

"And they do as my priestesses bid them?"

"They do, Othiym."

Cloud's knees shook uncontrollably.

Othiym. Angelica was calling herself *Othiym*. And this other—*thing*, whatever the fuck *it* was—*it* was calling her Othiym, too!

The two of them were barely fifteen feet from where Cloud squatted. Behind her, past more ocotillo and the deactivated electric fence, stretched the gravel road that led to the highway and open desert. If she took off now, she could be out of sight in moments. Cloud knew she could outrun Angelica—all that personal trainer stuff was great for keeping your stomach flat and your thighs taut, but it didn't do shit for your stamina.

But *was* this Angelica? And could she outrun something with *wings*?

"Let me see him, then." Angelica's voice was impatient. Cloud forced herself to look up again.

Behind the naphaïm, the fiery wall had died away. There was only the pool, still and calm as before, though streaks of lavender and green occasionally flickered across its surface.

"Now!" demanded Angelica.

The naphaïm's wings spread into a shimmering tent of gold and bronze and black. It opened its arms. From them something staggered, something pathetically small and frail-looking. It took a few steps, stumbled, and clumsily got to its feet again.

"Hey." The figure looked around slowly. "This isn't the bus station."

Oh, shit, thought Cloud.

It was a kid. A boy, no more than sixteen or seventeen. He wore standard street gear—baggy pants cut off at the knees, a paisley shirt once brightly colored but now faded to grey tears. Busted-out boots with no socks, filthy bandanna, bruised knees. Kind of a sweet face, sunburned pink where it wasn't grey with dirt. Blue eyes, freckles: basic Midwest issue. Probably hadn't seen a shower in a month. His hair was blond and very dirty, hanging limply to his shoulders. What Cloud could see of the rest of him was dirty as well.

"Hello," murmured Angelica. Almost imperceptibly she gestured at the naphaïm. "Eisheth—go now."

The boy lifted his head, blinking. Behind him the naphaïm took a step backward. Its wings shuddered, beating the air. There was a sound like thunder. For an instant the air grew darker, as though a cloud had swept before the moon; but of course there was no moon. The boy covered his head, like he expected to see something bearing down on him, crazed eagle or renegade jumpjet or some other desert weirdness. After a moment he lowered his arms, gazing stupidly into the empty air and then at the ground, where a single feather trembled, as long as the boy's arm and the deep crimson of fresh blood.

"Hello," Angelica said again.

The boy's eyes widened and his mouth dropped open.

"Who—oa," he breathed.

Angelica smiled. One hand flicked playfully at a lock of hair falling into her eyes, a fleeting motion that for an instant made her look more human. So that, Cloud thought, maybe—like if you were this kid and hadn't had a hot meal in a week and were homesick and heartsick and probably sick with other things as well—just *maybe* you could imagine she was something like a normal woman. He was gaping like a gigged frog, running one hand nervously through his stringy hair and staring at Angelica—beautiful, unearthly, *naked* Angelica—like he didn't know whether she was real or just some hemp-fueled vision.

"What's your name?"

Angelica stepped toward him, still smiling. It was all so crazy and horrible and yet so *real*, and of course the only sane thing for Cloud to do was to *run*, get the hell away from there as fast as she could. But Cloud was paralyzed.

"Russell," said the boy, his voice cracking.

"Russell," repeated Angelica. "How old are you, Russell?"

"Uh—seventeen."

Her necklace cast a delicate silvery glow across his face, so that for a moment you could see that he really was a nice-looking kid, but definitely younger than seventeen—Cloud thought fifteen, tops. He closed his mouth and swallowed, unable to tear his gaze from Angelica. The amazement in his eyes flickered into something else. Confusion, a certain wariness.

Fear.

"You must be awfully hot—would you like to go swimming?"

Angelica's hand rested lightly on his shoulder. Cloud hadn't seen her move to touch him, and apparently the boy hadn't either. He jumped, then shook his head.

"Uh—no—I mean, I don't have like, a bathing suit or anything? I was trying—I was *trying* to get to the bus station . . ."

He frowned, looking up at Angelica, then peered into the darkness behind her as though searching for someone. Cloud's heat pounded. Surely he must see her crouching there amidst the thorny scrub, he'd point and say something and Angelica would turn and then—

"No?" Suddenly Angelica's voice was exasperated: she might have wasted hours talking with him, instead of minutes.

One hand lay upon her breastbone, fingers spread to cover the silver crescent. Bluish light streamed between her fingers. As Cloud stared Angelica's hand tightened about the pendant. "*Well* then, Russell—"

She pulled the necklace over her head, held it with both hands, her fingers curling over its curved points. The boy stared at her, his expression frozen between surprise and disbelief. Before he could move she was upon him.

A streak like the moon through a shuttered window. The boy's hair fell across his face. His mouth yawned hideously. Cloud saw Angelica's hand snatched backward, the silver crescent a swath of darkness, blood flowing in its wake. The boy's head flopped onto his chest. Cloud glimpsed his eyes, wide and startled, his mouth brightly crimson as though lipsticked.

"Ah," he said.

There was a glistening darkness where his throat had been cut, a net of red covering his face and hands. Very slowly his body crumpled, until he lay on his side like a sick child, his dirty hair fallen across his face.

Above him stood Angelica. She held the crescent before her, its silver tarnished black and crimson. Smoke threaded between its two prongs. Her upturned gaze was beseeching yet triumphant, her voice like hail hammering against the desert floor.

Haïyo Othiym! Othiym Lunarsa!

From distant hills and canyons her voice was thrown back—

Haïyo Othiym! haïyo haïyo haïyo . . .

—voices dying, dying, dying . . .

With a yelp Cloud bolted from the underbrush. Thorns tore at her legs, she could feel blood spurting onto her thigh but she didn't care, she didn't give a fuck about anything as long as she was *gone*. Beneath her soles stones scattered like marbles. She slipped, catching herself on a barrel cactus and crying out as the thorns pierced her hand. From the corner of her eyes she glimpsed Angelica standing above the corpse of the boy she'd killed, her face twisted with rage.

"*Mellisæ agevahe! Oye Mellisæ!*"

"Fuck you!" gasped Cloud. She leapt over a prickly pear and landed on the smooth surface of the drive. *And fuck Melissa, too!*

She hurtled up the driveway. Ahead of her, she could just make out the tall posts with their sagging loops of electrified wire strung between, the crossties of the weathered gate that opened out onto Fire Road 53. Her heart was like a brick slung inside her chest, her shins ached from pounding the rough ground, but it was only a few more yards, she could feel where wild grass and sedge were poking up through the loose dirt beneath her feet and all she had to do was reach the gate and she could—

"Shit!"

Pain erupted from a spot above her knee. She slapped at her leg, felt another agonizing stab at her palm. Still running, she drew her hand up, saw a glistening red spot on the fleshy part of her thumb. Blood.

She shook her hand, trying to dislodge the shining droplet. But then the drop upon her thumb *moved*, coalesced into a gleaming bead of crimson with black legs and two bright black beads for eyes. Its jointed antennae twitched furiously, its swollen body thrust upward so for an instant she glimpsed what protruded from its abdomen, a black splinter like another thorn. Before she could slap it away another burst of pain lanced her shoulder, her leg, her breast; then another, and another. She glanced down and screamed.

She was covered with bees: a living shroud of bees, so many she could hear the pattering of their legs as they crawled over each other, trying to find purchase on her exposed skin. Thousands of them, each with its blaze of agony like a tiny blade drawn through her flesh. She shrieked and slapped at them, lurching across the stony ground, but it was like trying to outrun the rain. Her mouth opened and one darted inside; she gagged as she felt its legs, and then a horrible bolt of pain as it stung the back of her throat. She fell to the ground, clawing at her tongue.

Her throat was swollen shut; she couldn't see for the bodies swarming across her eyes. They were crawling into her nostrils, she could feel them burrowing into her ears, their spent stingers a pelt of soft black hairs across her tongue and cheek and lips.

A few more minutes, and you could not tell that there had ever been a person there at all. The swarm covered a mound that could have been a large stone or dead animal, vaguely human-shaped. The bees crawled atop each other, coupling, feeding, moving their abdomens in vicious thrusts, squeezing their eggs from their bodies to lie beneath the girl's skin, before it grew too stiff. When nearly an hour had passed, they departed. In long skeins like thread spun from a spindle, they lifted and sang off into the night, their humming growing fainter and fainter until it died.

From a few yards away a figure watched, silent, unmoving. Upon her breast glowed a swollen moon. It gave forth beams of splintered light as she raised her arms and chanted in a clear strong voice.

Oye Mellisae! Haïyo Othiym, oye Thriae . . .

I have crowned you, Bride of the thunder:
Your breath is on all that hath life, you who float in the air
Beelike, deathlike, a wonder . . .

And now that the bees had gone she summoned their sisters:

Oye myrmidon, oye!

—and the ants came, the voracious red driver ants named *eciton* that lay waste to vast areas of the rain forest, devouring anything in their path. They were like a shadow creeping down the hillside, like a ragged hem of darkness falling across that small still form. As quickly as the bees had found Cloud, the ants foamed across the barren desert and onto her corpse. Their feet made a whispering sound as they climbed upon her, her limbs and face bloated with venom. They darkened her skin like a bruise, crept beneath her loose clothing so that the fabric moved with a soft undercurrent of sound, a rustling that grew into a sort of tearing noise, like shears being drawn through thick canvas.

The noise continued for a long time. An acrid smell filled the air, released from glands near the ants' mandibles. As they fed, other creatures crept up from the tiled veranda to watch: a pair of soft slow tarantulas and the elfin kit fox. But when they detected that bitter smell the tarantulas raised their front legs defensively and stalked back into the darkness. The kit fox's ears flattened against its skull as it whined, then fled into the shadows. Only the bats whistled overhead, now and then sweeping down to carry off one of the winged sentries that hovered above the corpse.

When finally they had fed, the ants moved on. Like water poured onto the desert floor, the dark cloud spread; then disappeared into countless unseen cracks and crevices. Only their scent remained, a smell like bitter melons, and a glistening assemblage of bones and skull, a torn black shirt and khaki shorts like the flag of a fallen army sunk between loops of ivory.

It was Martin who found her early the next morning, out on his dawn run. He recognized her clothes, and also the three tiny gold rings he found caught in the curve of a finger bone, alongside the shivering crystal wedge of an insect's wing.

"Oh, my god," he whispered, and raced back to the house.

"What is it?" demanded Angelica, as she met him at the door.

"Stay inside, just stay in here," commanded Martin, and he dialed 911 with shaking hands.

A short while later the police and ambulance arrived, but of course there was nothing they could do. The dogs they brought, sturdy cheerful German shepherds trained in tracking lost children and hikers, sniffed at the sad array of bones and then bellied miserably onto the ground, pawing at their muzzles and whining.

"The coroner's on his way, and Dr. Sorrell from up at Flagstaff," the chief of police told Angelica. He was pale as he scratched a few notes onto his clipboard. By the pool Martin was comforting the hysterical Kendra, who had, despite orders from Angelica, run to the top of the ridge and seen what was there. Sunday was talking excitedly to a reporter, telling him about the puma she'd seen months before. "He says fire ants have killed folks in South Texas but that was more of an allergic reaction. This just seems like some kinda crazy freakish thing—"

"I can't believe it, I just can't believe it," murmured Angelica. She shook her head and stared out the open front door. Three police cars and the coroner's car and an ambulance were in the drive, along with the pickup trucks of two local reporters, all parked every which way, some with their doors still hanging open. As she stared a plume of yellowish dust rose from between the jaws of the wooden gate at the top of the hill. A moment later a Jeep came bouncing down the drive.

"Who's this?" asked the chief of police.

"My son," Angelica said softly. "He's been driving back from college—"

The Jeep slammed to a stop. Its door flew open and a tall figure jumped out. He paused and stared at Martin and Kendra on the patio, turned to gaze in disbelief at the policemen and ambulance and the howling brace of dogs caged in a police car.

"Mom?" he yelled, running up the sidewalk. He ducked through the front door, glancing around frantically until he saw her. "Mom!"

"Dylan," she said, and opened her arms to embrace him. "Dylan—"

"What happened, Mom, what's—"

"Shhh," she said, raising her hand to stroke the long hair from his eyes. "Shhh, don't worry, it's okay—

"Just something bad, that's all. Something bad that happened to Cloud."

CHAPTER 13

Other Echoes

When I called the *Beacon* I got Baby Joe's voice mail, his soft sleepy voice followed by a few bars of the Bernard Herrmann score for *Jason and the Argonauts*. I left a message, then went to clear my head.

Outside on the Mall, the Aditi was in full swing. Raga music, wailing flutes, fire-eaters and magicians and puppet masters, all obscured by the thick smoke of frying *samosas* and the dust raised by thousands of passing feet. Already the grass had been trampled into a dirty greenish mat pleached with cigarette butts and trampled hot dogs and broken balloons. You could see the heat shimmering from the sidewalks and the flow of traffic on Constitution Avenue. In front of the National Gallery of Art, water arced from a line of sprinklers and children ran shrieking in and out of the rainbow spray. A woman in a stained sundress rummaged through a trash bin.

It was the second of July. Tens of thousands of tourists had descended on the city, and they all seemed to be *right here*, mingling with the dancers and fakirs and weavers imported from India at the expense of Winesap, Inc. I watched a family in full American tourist drag staring at a Bengali mother in tissue-silk sari and gold bracelets and her children, as *they* watched two young men angle a pair of fighter kites across the sky. In the background the Capitol glowed like a huge white cloud, its perimeter ringed with flags and the concrete bulwarks set up over the last few years to guard against terrorist attacks. The kites swooped and dipped, delta chips of green and yellow. Their strings had been coated with broken glass, so that when one suddenly dived at the other, the tail of the second kite was severed. It went into a stall and crashed. The victor reeled in his kite, smiling; then the two warriors gathered their reels and arm in arm walked to a Good Humor wagon.

It was all a little too weird for me. I went to a booth with a yellow-and-white awning and bought a lemonade. I crossed the Mall to the Freer, always an oasis of calm amidst the summer storm of tourists and children. I sat on a bench and sipped my lemonade and mused on what I had seen on TV.

Angelica a cult figure.

I shook my head and took another sip, getting a grainy mouthful of sour sugar. Although, really, it wasn't totally unexpected. If I really thought about it, I would have been surprised if Angelica *hadn't* turned out to be somehow extraordinary. If instead of an Italian count, she'd married a chemical engineer from Houston and settled there to raise their children. I wondered if she *had* children, dismissed the notion as ridiculous, maybe even a little grotesque. I could imagine Angelica hiring someone else to bear a daughter for her, and then engaging an army of nannies and tutors and linguists to raise her, a serenely beautiful child playing by herself in a Florentine garden.

But Angelica pregnant, Angelica in labor; Angelica changing diapers and making Play-Doh and watching *The Brave Little Toaster*? Not in a thousand years.

I finished my lemonade, dropped the empty cup atop a trash can already filled to overflowing. I walked slowly back across the Mall. A murky breeze carried the greasy smells of hot dogs and egg rolls from the lines of roach coaches parked in front of the museums. A bunch of marines in summer whites posed on the museum steps with a cardboard cutout of the president and his wife. Two museum guards watched, laughing, and saluted.

Too weird. I let the heavy revolving doors bear me inside, breathing gratefully the cool recycled air, the heady scents of tourism and scholarship, and returned to my office.

A little while later Baby Joe called.

"What's shaking, *hija*?"

"Baby Joe!" I was unexpectedly relieved to hear his voice. "You okay?"

Silence. It had been only a week since Hasel's death. "Yeah, I guess. Why?"

"Well—I just saw the weirdest thing on TV. On Opal Purlstein—"

"You watch Opal Purlstein?"

"*Angelica* was on! I saw her, she was promoting some new book—"

"Oh, yeah. *Waking the Moon*. It's supposed to hit the best-seller list this Sunday."

I was flabbergasted. "I have a friend at the *Times Book Review*," said Baby Joe tentatively, "he says—"

"You *knew*?" I exploded. "You *knew* about Angelica and didn't *tell* me?"

"Hey, Sweeney, it's not like it's some kind of state secret—"

"I know that! But all that stuff about Hasel, and you never even *mentioned*—"

"I didn't even *know* until a few months ago. I mean about her," he said, aggrieved. "And—well, with Hasel and everything, I kind of forgot—"

"How could you *forget*?"

"Cut me some slack, Sweeney! My best friend fucking died!"

"But *Angelica*—Hasel said he saw—"

I could hear a soft intake of breath as he dragged on his cigarette. "Maybe we shouldn't talk about Hasel right now," he said finally.

"Fine," I snapped. "Can we talk about Angelica?"

Another long silence, followed by a sigh. "Yeah. But listen, Sweeney—there's something weird going on. I mean with Angelica—"

"So that's news?"

"Back off, huh? Okay, this is what I know: someone here interviewed Angelica for the Leisure section a little while ago. She's got some kind of cult following out on the West Coast, feminist grad students, something like that . . ."

"You could have *told* me, Baby Joe. Jeez, I almost had a heart attack when I saw her—"

"How'd she look?"

"Fantastic. I mean, she doesn't look different at all, she looks just like—"

I thought of how she had looked the last time I'd seen her: crouched over Oliver, as though she were a wolf and he her prey. I felt a clutching in my chest, the same awful disjointed feeling I'd had when Baby Joe told me Hasel died.

"—she looked just like always," I ended lamely.

"Yeah." Baby Joe sighed again. "Okay, I guess I should have told you when I first found out. But I kept thinking of Oliver, and well, you and Angie had all that weird history—"

"We did?"

"Hey, *hija*, you tell me. But Oliver, you know, I thought it would just make you feel bad . . ."

His voice drifted off. I imagined him sitting at his computer, hazed with blue smoke and a dusting of ash. My anger melted—because seeing Angelica *did* make me think of Oliver, and that *did* make me feel bad.

"It was a long time ago," I said at last.

"A long time ago, in a university far, far away," Baby Joe giggled softly. "Hey, you didn't videotape her or anything, did you?"

"No. I guess I should have. But I was so—well, I was kind of *shocked*. It was like *The Picture of Dorian Gray* or something."

"Yeah. And somewhere there's a *very bad* photo of Angelica, with her mascara running and no lipstick. Very scary."

I laughed. "So she's a best-seller now, huh? I had no idea. I'll have to get her book. You know anything about it?"

"Not really. But I'll fax you that interview."

We exchanged a few scurrilous remarks, and I told him about the Aditi.

"Sounds pretty wild. I bet the food's good—"

"It's great. You should come down and check it out."

"Do they have *baluts*?"

"What's *baluts*?"

"Filipino specialty. You take these embryonic chickens and bury 'em in the dirt for a couple months, and then—"

"That's *enough*. No, I'm pretty sure there's no *baluts*."

"Too bad. Don't you ever do any work down there?"

"Nah. This is the government. Mostly we just take turns answering the phone and going to lunch."

I heard someone calling to Baby Joe in the background. "Listen, *hija*, I gotta go. I may have something else for you later. You gonna be there?"

"I guess—"

"Okay."

He hung up. I sat for several minutes staring at my desk.

"Katherine?"

I turned to see Dr. Dvorkin framed in the doorway. "Robert! Come on in."

"Thanks—I can't stay, Jack left me some paperwork I've got to fill out for his fire-eaters."

He grimaced: a small round man, with white hair and a neatly trimmed white goatee, wrinkled and kindly and smartly dressed as an F.A.O. Schwarz Santa doing time in a fancy law firm. Even now, in D.C.'s broiling summer, he wore an immaculate grey three-piece suit, complete with testosterone yellow tie and matching pocket handkerchief.

"Katherine, I have to attend a Regent's Supper at the Castle tonight. Would you mind checking in on the cats for me?"

In addition to being my boss at the museum, Dr. Dvorkin was my landlord. For the last eight years I'd rented the tiny brick carriage house in his back garden on the Hill. It was the most wonderful place I'd ever lived. The only place I could even imagine might be nicer was Dr. Dvorkin's own town house.

"Of course not. Should I be looking for white smoke rising from the tower?"

Dr. Dvorkin sighed. For several months now the search had been on for a new Regent; three months earlier one had died at the age of ninety-seven and his replacement had yet to be named. "Not yet, I'm afraid. We're meeting someone else this evening. I hope to god this thing doesn't take all night. I think there's some basil in my refrigerator, you should take it when you come over, it's about to go bad."

"Thanks, Robert."

"Thank *you*." He turned to go, then stopped. "I almost forgot—you got a fax."

I took the pages, tossed away the cover sheet, and settled back into my chair to read.

ANGELICA FURIANO: WAKING THE GODDESS WITHIN US ALL

It wasn't what you'd call an in-depth piece—the New York *Beacon* wasn't exactly noted for its coverage of Nobel Prize winners—but it seemed like a pretty decent matching of journal and subject. While there wasn't a photo of Angelica accompanying the interview (and *that* seemed a mistake), there was a loving description of one of her homes, in the canyons north of Hollywood, and a rather breathless listing of the original artwork hanging there: Frida Khalo, Mary Cassatt, Cindy

Sherman, Robert Mapplethorpe's polaroids of Patti Smith, an ancient vase fragment depicting Sappho's lament for the virgin Gorgo.

The (female) interviewer was obviously bewitched by Angelica. It was easy to see why—Angelica was so charming, her answers to even personal questions funny and self-deprecating. I could just imagine her, lounging on her white leather sofa with the picture windows overlooking the canyon. She wore expensively tasteful clothes: Italian sandals, pleated cream-colored skirt, jade green silk blouse. The interviewer noted that she wore simple jewelry, silver earrings shaped like crescent moons, and a moon-shaped silver pendant around her neck.

I learned that her husband the duke had been eighteen years her senior, and had died during a sailing trip in the Aegean five years ago. Following his death, Angelica returned to the States and began writing in earnest. Her first two books, *The Nysean Fields* and *Amazons in America*, had been published as trade paperbacks by a small New Age press. The books had become surprise best-sellers, and a *cause célèbre* in both New Age and small press circles. After *Amazons in America* turned up on the *New York Times* best-seller list, Angelica started giving workshops stressing the same things she invoked in her books: how women should avoid becoming victims, how they should take responsibility for their own failures as well as successes; how they should learn to recognize the Goddess within themselves. There was a strong occult slant to all of this, with the Goddess (whom Angelica called Othiym) standing in for that ubiquitous Greater Power favored by adherents of AA and its ilk.

And, unlike any Twelve-Step program or women's self-help group that *I'd* ever heard of, there were some genuinely disturbing elements in Angelica's Goddess-worship. The emphasis on the division between the sexes, rather than their union; a certain disregard for the importance of family or any other ties except for those between the Goddess and her followers. In the little I'd read of other, similar, female gurus—Shirley MacLaine, Lynn Andrews, Marianne Williamson—there was always an emphasis on the powers of love and forgiveness, of the importance of loving yourself so you could better love someone else.

Angelica didn't buy it.

> "That's condescending to women." Furiano's brilliant green eyes narrowed as she reached for her Limoges teacup. "For thousands of years, women have wasted their lives taking care of men—tending their homes and their children and their castles and their farms, tending their offices and corporations and schools, making sure they look young enough and beautiful enough to keep a man—and why? Because we have been brainwashed into thinking that men are necessary for our happiness and self-esteem—"

The reporter gently suggested that perhaps it wasn't as bad as all that. Dr. Furiano bristled.

[*Dr*. Furiano: I was impressed.]

> "Come now—you're a woman, you know what it's like! *I* say, *"Enough."* We've all put in our time being Aphrodite and Hera"—the goddesses of Love and the Hearth respectively—"we've all been the dutiful daughters and good mothers and noble prostitutes and loyal secretaries. It's time to acknowledge that there are *other* roles for us to play. That we can be warriors, not just in the skies and in the armed services, but on the home front, where most of the battles are fought anyway. That we can be lovers but also leaders; that we are not victims! Everybody *knows* that women really are the stronger sex—you read accounts of shipwrecks and accidents, the journals from the Donner Party . . . it's the *men* who go down whimpering, and the women who walk out of the jungle alive. If men had menstrual periods, they'd have ten paid sick days a month! And can you imagine a *man* having a baby? Why, we would have discovered a cure for childbirth a hundred years ago!

I laughed. This sounded like the old Angelica.

> Dr. Furiano offered me more tea; a young man (a graduate student in cultural anthropology, Dr. Furiano told me later, working for her as a summer intern) came out bearing a silver tray of tiny butter cookies shaped like horns. I asked her if her next book was going to be an extension of her earlier work, or if she had done away with men altogether.
>
> "Not yet! You see, I still find uses for them—" She laughed, and her grad student grinned. "No, truly, I have many men in my life, I always have. My father raised me after my mother died when I was an infant, and he was probably the greatest single influence on me. I absolutely *do not* have a vendetta against men.
>
> "My new book—my new book is called *Waking the Moon* and will be published this summer. I always try to have my publication dates coincide with one of the Goddess's ancient holidays—though this one will be out before Lammas, which is a celebration of the harvest that used to end with the sacrifice of beautiful young men to the great Goddess. When people think of human sacrifices, they think of the Carthaginians tossing children into the flames, or beautiful virgin women tied to the stake. But actually the first and greatest sacrifices in human history were nearly always of men, in an effort to appease the Goddess. So it is easy to

understand how men might have gotten a little *concerned*, and ended up seizing control of things out of desperation—"

And, this reporter thought, *you can see why Dr. Furiano's own work is met with controversy wherever she goes.*

"But, of course, we really can't really do that anymore, I mean at least not *legally*, and so . . ."

There was more of this sort of talk; then,

Dr. Furiano leaned closer to me. Through the window behind her, I could just glimpse the crescent moon gleaming above the Hollywood Hills.

"You know," she said, "all I've really done is follow in the footsteps of those who went before me. The great female archaeologists of our time, June Harrington and Magda Kurtz and Marijta Gimbutas, women who discovered so much about the Goddess cultures of ancient Europe, and who inspired people like me to go searching for more answers.

"I found *my* answers in the ruins of ancient temples in Estavia and Crete and Turkey. I found them in what I discovered there about the goddess Othiym, and now I want to share my knowledge with women everywhere."

She pointed to the window behind her. "*Waking the Moon* isn't just about personal empowerment. It's really about something much, much bigger, about all of us—women *and* men—reaching *outside* of ourselves and using that chthonic aspect of our own natures to change the world. To take a world and a race on the brink of self-destruction and shake it back to life again. I truly believe that very drastic measures will be needed to change things, if we are to survive. There is a quote from Robert Graves which I find quite interesting, considering he wrote it nearly fifty years ago, in *The White Goddess*—

The longer Her hour is postponed, and therefore the more exhausted by man's irreligious improvidence the natural resources of the soil and sea become, the less merciful will Her five-fold mask be, and the narrower the scope of action that She grants to whichever demigod She chooses to take as Her temporary consort in godhead. Let us placate Her in advance by assuming the cannibalistic worst . . .

> Dr. Furiano's hand remained poised in the air. Beyond it the moon rose slowly above the hillsides.
>
> "But I think change is coming," she said softly. "I think it is coming very, very soon. And I very much want to be a part of it."

I put the fax paper down on my desk, smoothed it with my hand.

Othiym. *Waking the Moon*.

It was all crazy, of course, but exactly what I would have expected from Angelica. The part about saving the world made it sound like maybe she'd tripped off the line somewhere, but the rest seemed pretty much in character with the girl I'd known nineteen years before. And at least she'd given credit to June Harrington and Marija Gimbutas and . . .

At the thought of Magda Kurtz I shivered, reached instinctively for the cardigan I kept hanging on the back of my chair all winter. But it was July now. The sweater was stuffed in a drawer at home, and I doubt if it would have offered much comfort anyhow.

"Katherine?"

I started, turned, and saw Laurie Driscoll, our department secetary. "Another fax for you." She handed me a piece of paper. "And Alice said to tell you that your intern will be here tomorrow morning—I guess a whole batch of them arrived this morning, they've got orientation and then some kind of lunch at the Castle. So *finally* we'll have some help getting that new stuff organized."

"About time." I took the fax, glanced down, and recognized Baby Joe's signature. After she left, I read Baby Joe's addendum.

> Sweeney—
>
> This just in, I thought you should see it. Also, I talked to Annie Harmon and she said she'd call you.
>
> I'll be in touch.
>
> B. Joe

It was a copy of a brief article from that morning's *New York Times*.

> FLAGSTAFF, AZ July 2 Police stated that yesterday morning the skeletal remains of Cloud Benson, professional bodyguard to noted feminist archaeologist and author Angelica Furiano, were discovered on the grounds of Furiano's home in Sedona.
>
> In what appears to have been a grisly freak accident, Benson's corpse was completely devoured by wild animals—probably some

> type of fire ant, says County Medical Examiner Warren Schaner—so that only her skeleton and remnants of clothing remained. Benson, 19, had been a member of Dr. Furiano's entourage since the fall of 1993. She was last seen alive the previous evening, when her colleagues Kendra Wilson and Martin Eisling left her in the cottage they shared on Furiano's 200-acre ranch. Furiano speculates that Benson, who liked to run every evening along the ridge that marks her property line, may have tripped and injured herself, and so fallen prey to some kind of predator. Sunday Jimenez, Furiano's housekeeper, reported seeing a puma on the property some months earlier.
>
> Flagstaff Police Chief Robert Morales has voiced concern that whatever attacked Benson may also be responsible for a string of unsolved disappearances in the Southwest. Since last October, seventeen young men between the ages of 15 and 27 have been reported missing in Arizona alone. Several of the men were known to be prostitutes and runaways, and authorities are concerned that the numbers may actually be higher.
>
> "It's a definite longshot that killer ants could be responsible for these disappearances, but we're not ruling out any possibilities," Chief Morales said.

I stared at the paper, unsure whether to laugh or not. At first I thought it was another one of Baby Joe's practical jokes—killer *ants*?

Then I remembered the things I had glimpsed behind the door in Garvey Hall so long ago.

I had spent the last nineteen years trying to forget what I had seen in my few months at the Divine; trying to forget Oliver. Because Oliver was dead, and Magda Kurtz, and now Hasel Bright . . .

But *I* was alive, and so were Baby Joe and Annie and Angelica. Even if part of the unspoken deal I had made with Luciano di Rienzi and the *Benandanti* was to cut myself off from my friends, it had been almost enough, during all those years, to know my friends were out there still. To know that *they* were thriving, even if I was not. Even if my head and heart had remained under some kind of house arrest ever since.

And there was always Baby Joe, who had stayed in touch with me in apparent defiance of the *Benandanti*. Who had struck out on his own into the tabloid jungle, rather than become the *brujo* the *Benandanti* wanted him to be.

But now it seemed that all the unfinished business of my life that I had thought safely interred in the past was waking, moving slowly beneath the dry earth and starting to break through. I thought of the words of the poet of another city—

Ideal and dearly beloved voices
of those who are dead, or of those
who are lost to us like the dead.

Sometimes they speak to us in our dreams;
sometimes in thought the mind hears them.

And for a moment with their echo other echoes
return from the first poetry of our lives—
like music that extinguishes the far-off night.

I stared at the pages Baby Joe had sent me.

> *"But I think change is coming,"* I read once more. *"I think it is coming very, very soon. And I very much want to be a part of it."*

I took the pages, folded them as neatly as I could, and put them in the top drawer of my desk. I made sure all the monitors and VD players were turned off, checked the latches on my windows, and left.

C H A P T E R 1 4

Devil-Music

Her encore was always the samc. She walked offstage, got doused with Evian water by Patrick and Helen, tore off her sweat-soaked tuxedo shirt and replaced it with a sleeveless black Labrys T-shirt showing the double axe and her label's motto. She gulped down a second bottle of Evian, smoothed her buzz cut with one hand and exchanged her acoustic Martin for a shocking pink electric Gibson.

"Good house," said Patrick. He was her manager. They'd known each other for thirteen years, since Annie first began singing in campus bars and rathskellers and then coffeehouses when the drinking age was raised to twenty-one.

"*Great* fucking house," retorted Annie. She reached over to get Helen's head in a hammerlock, kissed her scalp, and turned to run back out onstage.

"Provincetown, we love you!" she yelled, raising her fist.

A wave of screaming applause from the audience. The band stepped from the shadows where they'd hidden all night, giving the occasional muted nuance to Annie's acoustic work. Annie kicked away the chair where she'd sat with her acoustic guitar. A droning bass line roared out, a few tentative drumbeats; then the opening bars, transformed into something ominous and brooding. Annie stepped up to the mike, standing on tiptoe to readjust it. She grinned, tossing her head back. Her smoky voice rang out, twisting around the odd rythmns of desire and rage and nostalgia: her first real hit, Number 2 on the alternative charts: not bad at all for a thirty-seven-year-old lesbian folksinger from Nebraska.

She is still a mystery to me . . .

The audience shouted out the chorus, several hundred women and a few guys singing and swaying, raising their margaritas and Bellinis and Amstel Lights to the diminutive figure on the small raised stage. The music raged on, the chorus repeated again and again as the audience refused to let her leave. Annie grinned, dipping her head so the sweat flew off in tiny droplets and turned to mist in the heat of the spotlight.

She is still a mystery to me . . .

Then, Annie heard it. The now-familiar chant rising from a half dozen people at a table in the very front, their voices at first keeping time with the music but gradually growing stronger and louder, running counterpoint to her own husky voice and guitar—

Othiym Lunarsa, Othiym, Anat, Innana, Othiym evohe! Othiym haïyo!

Annie's smile froze. She glanced up and saw her bassist Linga staring at her in concern.

She is still a mystery to me . . .

Still those other words rang out, loud enough now to drown her own.

Hail Artemis, Britomartis, Ishtar, Astarte, Ashtorath, Athena, Potnia, Bellona, More, Kali, Durga, Khon-Ma, Kore. Othiym Lunarsa. Othiym haïyo!

Annie glared down into the front row of tables with their flailing figures, trying to turn the tiny space into a mosh pit. She shouted the last lines of her song, heard the crash of echoing feedback from the band behind her. She bowed, trying to look as exhilarated as the women screaming a few yards away from her on the club floor. Then she walked offstage. The band followed her into the tiny dressing room, grinning and raising their fists.

Patrick met her there with more bottled water, a paperback book, and a huge sheaf of flowers.

"An admirer," he said, handing her the book: *Journal of a Solitude*. "And I don't know who these are from—"

He waved the flowers at her, but Annie turned away.

"Boy, they're really noisy tonight," said Helen. "Must be a full moon."

"Fucking amateurs," snarled Annie Harmony. She gulped her Evian water and tossed the book onto a table. "Dark of the moon."

"What?" Helen stepped behind her partner.

"Dark of the moon, they come out at the *dark* of the moon. Black angels," she added ominously. "Fucking cultists."

Patrick raised an eyebrow, gazing at her over the fragrant cloud of blossoms he still held. "I would have thought you'd be into all that stuff, Annie," he said in surprise. "You know, women's spirituality, awakening the goddess within, that kind of thing."

Annie scowled. She grabbed a towel from Helen and mopped her face.

"Annie went to college with Angelica Furiano," Helen explained. "They were roommates."

"No lie?" Patrick's eyes widened. "Was this in Italy or something?"

"D.C.," said Annie brusquely. "It was only a semester. I haven't seen her since."

She crossed the cramped room to gather her bag and a plastic quart bottle of Diet Pepsi, looked back at Helen. "I've got to go to the hotel; I forgot my filofax and I'd like to take a shower. Martha's supposed to meet us at the inn at eleven-thirty. Please don't make us late again."

Patrick and Helen watched as she swept out of the dressing room, the little swaggering figure shoving open the fire door and disappearing into a small crowd of fans waiting in the street.

"She doesn't like to talk about Angelica," Helen explained.

"Duh," said Patrick. He rubbed his earcuff gingerly. "So they were really roommates?"

Helen nodded. She was slender and dark, her hair braided into elaborate patterns spliced with red and yellow beads and brightly colored strands of *kente* cloth. "Yeah. Supposedly even back then, Angelica was really something."

"She and Annie have a thing?"

Helen shrugged. "Who knows? It's ancient history now. I know Angelica was involved with some friend of theirs, this guy who killed himself after she dumped him. I guess Annie must have taken it pretty hard. She doesn't like to talk about her *at all*."

Patrick regarded the flowers thoughtfully. "Well, I guess I can relate to that. You want to take these back to the hotel?"

Helen grabbed the bouquet, sniffed it tentatively. "Nice. Hey, these are pretty exotic. What are they?"

Patrick touched one delicately crumpled scarlet blossom. "Well, that looks like some kind of poppy, and these—"

He breathed on a handful of soft pale blue petals, "—these are anemones."

"And that's a jonquil." Helen's pinkie brushed a tiny pale orange flute surrounded by flaring white petals. "We used to grow them in Vermont."

"Narcissus, I think little ones like that are called narcissus, and this looks like some kind of hybrid hyacinth."

Helen breathed in deeply. "God, they really do smell wonderful, don't they? All these fragrant things. But what a bizarre arrangement—I've never even *seen* some of these before. Who'd you say brought them?"

Patrick shrugged. "I don't know. Some woman. She had on this cowled dress, *très mystérieuse*. She just kind of blew in and out before I could say anything. But wait—you know what, there was a card with them, let me look—"

He shuffled through the crumpled newspapers and plastic containers from the take-out Thai place next door, triumphantly held up a piece of paper.

"Ta da!"

"Let me see." Helen took it, a small white rectangle, expensive cotton rag paper with tiny letters written on it in black ink. A cryptic but very careful hand—the script looked as though it had been typed. Patrick stood behind her to read over her shoulder.

> *Utcunque placurit Dea verus*
> *for Annie, with much love*

Helen shook her head. "How bizarre. *Dea*, that means goddess, I bet. Well, that makes sense, there were a bunch of those girls out there tonight. But the rest's in Latin. You were an altar boy, what's it mean?"

Patrick took the note and puzzled over it. "'*Utcunque placurit*.' I think that's something like, *As it pleases you* or *May it please you*. And *verus*, that means truth. So this would mean, *As it pleases the true Goddess*. Weird with a beard."

"Weird with a merkin." Helen dropped the card onto the table and handed the flowers back to Patrick. "Here, go find some nice young man and give these to him."

"You don't think Annie wants them?"

"I think Annie would be a little freaked, Patrick. Those girls give her the creeps. Me too. Look, I gotta fly; if I'm late again, she'll have a fit."

"Yup. See you later. I'll clean up—"

He poured the rest of the Evian water into a jar and set the flowers in it, then went to meet the club manager to discuss the evening's take.

They met Martha in the bar at the Tides Inn, a small, pleasantly dim room cooled by several softly whirring ceiling fans. Air-conditioning would have been more useful—it was seventy-nine degrees outside, at midnight—but Annie had to admit the fans looked nice, big old brass-bladed things slicing through the darkness and making a gentle *whick-whick* sound. For once Helen hadn't been late. But Martha was, and so Annie and her lover sat alone at a small table by the window, silently holding hands. There was no one else in the place. The owner served them, a taciturn man with long white hair in a braid down his back. Helen got a Hurricane, Annie a club soda with lime. Through an open window wafted the brisk salt smell of the ocean, the reek of patchouli and joss sticks from the crystal emporium next door. They sipped their drinks and stared outside, watching the twinkling lights of boats bobbing in the water, the steady parade of sunburned couples on Commercial Street—men and men, women and women, women and men—laughing and talking, relishing the night.

Annie stared at them enviously. Everyone looked so bouncy and cheerful, as though they'd all just come out of the same Frank Capra movie. She always felt slightly dazed and suspicious when she visited P-town, just as she did in Key West and Palm Springs and the Berkshires, any place where gay couples could act just like everybody else. Any place, really, where people made being happy look so easy.

Face it: you'd feel like this in Disneyland, she thought. *Too many years in Nebraska, too many years singing and starving; too much time spent being afraid, remembering Lisa and Oliver and Angelica and now Hasel—*

She stiffened, and her fingers tightened around Helen's.

"Those girls tonight?" asked Helen softly. Annie looked up at her, shaking her head as though awakening from a dream.

"How'd you know?"

Helen smiled. "I have magical powers and the gift of sarcasm."

"That's *my* line, girlfriend. But yeah, I was thinking about them."

"It's not such a terrible thing." Helen twisted one of her braids around a finger, playing with the rows of striped trade beads. "How bad can it be, for women to learn how to stick up for themselves, to be assertive and all that stuff? I think your friend Angelica is onto something—I mean, there really *is* this dark aspect to goddess-worship that everyone has ignored for all these centuries. It's like being a Christian and refusing to acknowledge the Inquisition."

"She's not my friend."

Helen smiled wryly. "Boy, you must have had it bad, to still get so worked up over her."

"I'm *not* worked up over her, this has *nothing* to do with my feelings for—"

"Hi, guys! Sorry I'm late, I had to go home and feed the dogs. I brought a couple of friends—I hope you don't mind, Annie—"

They looked up to see Martha, resplendent in an African-print dress, her hennaed hair looped in extravagant braids and her ears hung with gold circlets. Around her throat she wore a thin gold chain heavy with little charms: a lambda, a dolphin, a crescent moon, a tiny silver image of the faience Cretan snake-goddess, serpents like two lightning bolts dangling from her raised arms. "This is Lyla, and this is Virgie—they were just at your show, Annie, I turned them on to you years ago and promised I'd introduce you to them someday—" Martha sank into a chair and reached for Helen's drink, took a sip. "Oooh, that's good. I'll try one of those."

At the sight of the two strangers Annie stiffened.

Moon-girls. She recognized them from the club earlier, shouting their goddamn mantra while she was trying to sing. Young, in their early twenties—so many of Angelica's girls were young, it must have something to do with having missed that whole first wave of feminism and liberation, of growing up under the conservative cloud of the eighties, of being desperate and cynical and incredibly naive all at the same time. Virgie was coffee-skinned, with long thick black hair and tilted black eyes and a *Hothead Paisan* T-shirt. She wore crescent-shaped earrings and a crescent-shaped pendant around her neck, a bad copy of Angelica's necklace made of cheap Mexican silver. Her companion was slight and short, wiry as a young girl, with auburn hair clipped close to her skull and a small tattoo of a crescent moon on her left cheek. When she extended her hand in greeting, Annie saw that she had another tattoo on the ball of her thumb, the tiny perfectly rendered image of a honeybee.

"That must have hurt," said Helen. She pulled two extra chairs from another table and scooted over to make room.

"Not really," said Lyla. She slid into a chair, her grey eyes never leaving Annie. "You let yourself flow into the pain. It's over pretty quick."

"I always thought body mutilation was the sin against the Holy Ghost," said Annie.

"What?" asked Virgie.

"Nothing. Obsolete cultural reference." Annie reached for her club soda and sipped, staring warily at the newcomers. "Enjoying your vacation?"

"Your show was fantastic, as always," said Martha. She inclined her head toward her two friends. "It was the first time they've seen you—"

"First time we've seen you *live*. Your video is great," broke in Lyla.

"Your music is *so* fantastic," gushed Virgie. "It cuts so close to the bone, I mean it's really amazing how you get so much out of your own pain and sense of loss, how you've managed to heal yourself and turn it all into those intense songs—"

"It's a living." Annie crunched an ice cube. She leaned back in her chair, staring at Virgie's throat with narrowed eyes. "Nice necklace."

"Thanks! I got it at one of Angelica Furiano's *Waking the Moon* workshops. Have you ever been—"

"No."

"Oh, but you *must*! I mean, she is *so* incredible, you can just feel the power emanating from her, I mean it was just the most incredibly intense experience of my *life*—"

"Wow," said Annie dryly.

"It *was* pretty intense," said Lyla. "We live in Northampton and we've started a group there, there's a lot of us who took the workshops and were awakened. We get together every week and the energy level is just amazing, and—well, you just wouldn't believe it, that's all. You really should check it out."

"Annie's pretty busy touring these days," Helen said. "We don't have a lot of free time—"

"Angelica really is rather remarkable," said Martha. She gave Annie an apologetic look. "I know you think it's all kind of dumb—"

"I don't think it's dumb. I'm not a separatist, that's all."

"Oh, but *all* kinds of people are into Angelica!" Virgie leaned across the table to stare earnestly at Annie. "I've even met *guys* there. I mean, most of the women at our workshop were straight, and it was so amazing to see how they blossomed! Most of *us*—"

She fluttered her hands, indicating the women at the table, the crowds outside. "We're *used* to feeling outside the mainstream, but for *them* it was like the first time they ever truly realized just how marginalized women are, how totally dependent on this archaic obsolete patriarchal system that enslaves us—"

Annie was silent. Martha and Helen exchanged a glance; then Martha said quickly, "I don't think she really meant that women were literally enslaved—"

"Oh, but she *did*!" exclaimed Virgie. Lyla nodded; the crescent moon on her cheek caught a stray mote of candlelight and seemed to flicker. "That's her whole thing, how we've been so incredibly conditioned we don't even *know* that we're nothing more than chattel, I mean look at the way they want to control our *bodies*—"

"The way they want to control our minds," added Lyla.

"But Othiym—I mean Angelica—I mean, she just makes you aware of this whole new way of looking at the world. A whole *old* way, really—"

She pointed at Annie's Labrys T-shirt. "Like that thing there, the double axe—that's a symbol that goes back to ancient Crete, to the Great Goddess religion there—"

Annie gazed at Virgie coolly. "I know what it means."

"Well, you should come to one of her gatherings and see for yourself, Annie." Virgie's sloe eyes widened as she spread her hands imploringly. "Angelica Furiano gives you a whole new way of looking at the world! And there's so *many* of us now! Somebody's even making a *documentary* about her—"

"Oh yeah? Who? Leni Riefenstahl?"

Virgie frowned. "Is she the one who did that Bikini Kill video?"

Annie moaned and looked away.

"You have to admit, Annie, at least it's a change," said Martha. "I mean, she really *does* make you think about things."

Annie stared broodingly out the window.

"I prefer to think of things on my own," she said at last.

"Annie's had some bad experiences with organized religion." Helen looked at her lover fondly. "You know, that whole lapsed Catholic trip—"

"Othiym says the reason conventional Western religions have failed is that they don't take into account the notion of sacrifice." Lyla's prim expression was at odds with her tattoo and cropped hair. "*She* says the problem with Catholics is that they don't take the idea of sacrifice far *enough*."

"We have to break away from all that," agreed Virgie in a childish voice. "'The New Woman will only emerge when she learns to commit every horror and violence that till now society has denied her as foreign to her temperament.'"

Everyone was silent.

"Gee, I never thought of that," said Annie.

"It's from the Marquis de Sade," Virgie confessed. "I read it in one of Angelica's books."

Annie's eyes flashed. "I think you're all playing with fire," she said, casting a poisonous look at Virgie and Lyla. "And I think it's incredibly rude of you and your friends to interrupt my show yelling your stupid slogans—"

"They're not slogans," Lyla said. "It's an incantation. Because all great music invokes the Goddess."

"You should be *flattered*." Virgie looked as though she might burst into tears. "I mean, that your music could invoke such *feelings* from us—"

"I don't think—" Martha stammered, but Annie was already getting to her feet.

"That's your whole problem, Martha. You *don't* think—*none* of you think, you're letting some rich crazy egotistical New Age bitch do it for you. Haven't you ever heard of *cults*, girls? Don't any of you know how to read a newspaper? The name Manson mean anything to you? David Koresh? Bhagwan Rajneesh? Jim Jones?"

Helen rolled her eyes. "Oh, come *on*, Annie—"

"It's not like that *at all*! This is something *beautiful*, something totally *new*—"

Annie snorted. "Oh, *give* me a fucking *break*! How much enlightenment can you get in a fucking weekend? And am I wrong, or are you *paying* for this transcendence?"

"Actually, Angelica's practically giving it away these days," said Martha. "She's got all these priestesses teaching new initiates—"

"Priestesses?" howled Annie. "Now she's got *priestesses*? Man, are you getting *hosed*! Do you all *dress* like her, too? Do you spend fifteen minutes with your eyeliner and—"

"Annie," growled Helen.

"Priestesses! I bet she passes the collection basket, too! Man, what a crock! Meet the new boss, same as the old boss. This one's got tits and a twat, that's all."

Helen raised her voice above Virgie and Lyla's angry protests. "Annie, you are being *totally* ridiculous!—"

"Oh yeah? Well, maybe you should just go with them and get in touch with your secret lunar self. I'm leaving."

Annie stormed from the table. She paused to stare disdainfully at the crescent moon on Lyla's cheek. "Hey, that's pretty cutting edge—only you and ninety thousand other girls have one of those." She headed for the door.

"It's a sensitive topic," said Helen, sighing. Martha put her arm around Virgie. Lyla just looked mad. "Look, I'll go calm her down—but let's not talk about religion anymore, okay?"

"I thought she'd *understand*," wailed Virgie. "She seemed so in touch with her own inner *cycles*—"

"Hush," said Martha.

Helen found Annie just outside the front door of the Inn, leaning against the wall. Down the street the usual nighttime crowd was starting to gather in front of Spiritus. A few yards away, a streetlamp's shining globe cast a rippling silver reflection on the dark surface of the water, the bright circle breaking into fluid coils when the breeze stirred it. From a sailboat at anchor echoed laughter and the strains of dance music.

"If you think I'm going back in there, you are out of your fucking mind."

Helen smiled in spite of herself, reached to stroke Annie's neck. "Don't you think you were overreacting a little?"

"No."

"Oh, come on—Charles *Manson*?"

"Angelica di Rienzi could eat Charles Manson for breakfast. Probably she already has," Annie added darkly.

"I think you're carrying around just a teensy bit of personal baggage, Annie. I know you said you never wanted to talk about Angelica, and I've always respected that, but this has kind of gotten out of hand. I mean, they're just a couple of dopey kids, that's all! Virgie's crying, Martha is totally bummed, and Lyla the Bee Queen looks like she is getting in touch with a very pissed-off inner goddess."

"Good," snapped Annie, but her mouth twisted into a half smile. "Maybe next time they won't ruin my show."

Helen sighed. "Well, I don't think you're going to get much repeat business from those two. Listen, Martha says there's some kind of dance party out at Herring Cove tonight—"

"Yeah," said Annie, nodding. From here you could just glimpse where the narrow spit of land curved to face the Atlantic, a hazy darkness spangled with a few bobbing lights. "In the old boathouse there. Patrick told me about it; he knows one of the guys who've put it together. They're supposed to have a fabulous sound and light show."

"So let's go and dance. Come on, it'll be fun."

"Oh, sure! A bunch of kids on X and vitamins—"

"You used to *love* to dance! Jeez, girlfriend, loosen up a little—"

Annie shook her head stubbornly. "If I ever loosen up, the world will come to an end. You know that. I'm the only thing standing between you and the dark of Mordor—"

"Hey. You know what, Annie? *Shut up*—"

Helen took Annie's chin in her hand, stared into her dark eyes, and then kissed her, long and slow, her hand dropping to stroke her lover's breast beneath the thin black T-shirt. After a minute she drew back and there was Annie, her face slightly flushed, the blazing light in her eyes somewhat softened. "You remember how to dance, don't you?"

Annie nodded, her mouth breaking into a slow grin. "Sure. You just put your lips together, and *flow*—"

And drawing Helen close, she kissed her again.

When they got to Herring Cove Beach the party was in high gear, the rickety old boathouse shaking dangerously as music throbbed inside and the party spilled out onto the sand, hundreds of bodies thrashing and moving ecstatically.

"Now I know why the bar was empty," Annie shouted.

"It's been going on since this morning," Martha yelled back. "I'm surprised they haven't gotten busted."

"They will if they stay out on the beach like that." Annie handed the boy at the door a ten-dollar bill. He glanced at her and did a double take.

"Yo, Annie Harmony! Great time inside—"

He stamped her palm with a little smiling Goofy face in purple ink.

"What, no change?" Annie looked down at the zippered cash bag that sat in the lap of the huge bodybuilder helping guard the door. "Ten dollars so I can get sand in my drink?"

"Ten bucks, ten bucks," he yelled, his head nodding up and down. "Chem free, smart drinks at the other door, no drinking inside—"

"Oh, yeah, *right*—"

"Enough, Annie!" Martha and Helen pulled her through the door.

She felt like she was inside a fireworks display, all explosive sound and color and motion. The boathouse was the only structure on this stretch of the protected seashore, a place curiously ignored by the local constabulary, most of the time. You could drink or cruise or engage in just about any carnal pastime you wanted there. Its piers had been bored by sea worms and salt, the roof was missing most of its shingles, the whole thing flooded whenever it stormed. There were ragged holes in walls and ceiling. Annie's sneaker got stuck in the gap between two floorboards. When she bent to yank it out, she could see through the hole to where black water lapped at the rocks and pilings below. She straightened and found herself alone on a patch of empty floor. The DJ had shoved a new song into the sound system, and everyone seemed to have rushed to the far wall. She could just make out Helen and Martha dancing a few yards away. Of Virgie and Lyla she saw nothing; they had stalked off as soon as they got here, whispering and casting baleful stares in Annie's direction.

Forget them, she thought. It was easy enough. The music was so loud it drove anything like a coherent thought from her brain, so fast it was like the steady rumble of an aircraft taking off, a mad stuttering sound that sent her blood hammering so hard her vision blurred. Everywhere she looked she saw people dancing, such a mass of indistinguishable bodies that it was like watching footage of bizarre underwater creatures, all waving tentacles and gasping mouths and teeth. Nearly all the boys and men were shirtless, a number of them completely naked except for plastic water bottles taped to a thigh or forearm. A lot of the women were naked too, their breasts flashing white in the steamy air. And of course she saw people humping, too. Not just in pairs, but in threes and fours and fives and serpentine lines too long to count, although there was something oddly sexless about their motion: it was like they were just another part of the machine, this vast human engine thundering through the old boathouse like a juggernaut.

It was too much to hope that she'd be able to hold out against it. Within minutes she was moving too, and if she'd worried about being recognized she soon forgot—hers was just another shining face, another pair of arms and legs flickering in the blinding strobe lights. She let the river of light flow across her closed eyelids, a spectral wash of purple and black. When she opened her eyes a moment later she saw a strange tableau against the far wall, frozen in the brilliant glare of the strobes.

It was Virgie and Lyla and several other women and young men. They stood together, not moving, not even engaging in the incessant nervous gestures of drinking and mopping sweat that, as far as Annie could see, was the closest anyone here came to actually standing still.

This crowd was standing still. They were utterly motionless, and they were staring at Annie. In the center of the little group was one figure that really stood out—quite literally, since he or she was head and shoulders taller than the rest. Annie slowed her dancing to a sort of halfhearted swaying, staring boldly at the others, daring them to keep looking at her.

They did. Virgie and Lyla stood by the figure in the middle, their faces stern and watchful. The others formed a half circle around them. Most of the women were young, their bodies taut and muscular as Lyla's; though one was much older, with greying hair pulled into a coil on the nape of her neck. Boys and girls alike, they all had tattoos. Like a brand, grinning crescents on cheeks and shoulders and swelling biceps.

Hah! real *Moonies,* thought Annie. She tried to keep her gaze fearless and disdainful, tried to keep moving. But those watchful eyes made her shudder. Like the multiple eyes of some patient spider, the way they just kept staring, like they had all the time in the world to wait for her to tire and weaken. And the frenzied crowd roiling about her only made it worse—she could scream and thrash all she wanted out here, and they'd only think she was having a good time. And for sure nobody was going to call the cops.

She glanced around uneasily, looking for Helen. Probably went out onto the beach to cool off. Annie turned back to her motionless sentries.

They hadn't stirred. They were still in their silent half circle, staring. It was the one in the center that made Annie's blood freeze. Tall, almost seven feet tall, with broad naked shoulders rippling with muscle. Yet it had breasts, too, small swelling breasts each tipped with a dark nipple. It had a narrow waist and hips, shadowed so that Annie couldn't tell what it wore, or even if it was a girl or a guy. It had no body hair at all that she could see; nothing except for a pair of breasts more suited to a thirteen-year-old girl, and beautiful long auburn hair. A wingless watchful angel struck down from its pediment. A fallen seraphim.

A black angel.

Annie swallowed. *So what the fucking hell is she—or he, or* it*—doing here, and why is it watching* me*?*

As if in answer to her thoughts, the tall figure looked away. Lyla and the others turned as well, as though they were all bound to it by invisible cords. Before they could look back and see her, Annie darted to where a bank of speakers rose above the dance floor.

"Whoa, Nellie." She caught her breath and leaned backward, until she was hidden between the speakers. From there she could watch them without being seen; from here they looked like just another group of partygoers.

So maybe that's all it is, she thought, a little desperately. *Just some of Angie's girls from Brown, and their friend the Incredible Miss Hulk.*

Then, in the darkness, someone begin to sing.

All that is holy is thine
All that is meat
All that flowers and gives birth
All that is fecund.

Darkness is thine
The stealth of the hunter
That strikes in the field . . .

A frail, quavering, voice—an old man's, or a woman's?—impossible to tell; but hearing it Annie shivered.

All that rots in the earth
All that is lovely
All that decays
Is thine, Devourer!
Is thine, Great Sow.
Haïyo! Othiym!
Othiym Lunarsa

The song flowed through Annie and she trembled.

All that is beauty,
All that is bone
Is thine, Ravaging Mother
All You have loved
All that is best
Is thine, O Beautiful One.
Haïyo! Othiym!
Othiym Lunarsa

As abruptly as it had begun, the song died away. Annie stood motionless with dread—it had *done* something to her, devil-music, she had been turned to ice or stone! Then across the room a screen door banged open. A gust of sharp salt-smelling wind raked her face. She sneezed, clapped a hand over her mouth, and shrank against the speakers. The spell was broken; she could move.

And so could the black angel.

Annie gasped. It really *was* as though a statue had come alive, some beautiful malefic creature, half-gargoyle and half-gigantic child. From here she could watch it striding through the crowd, pulses of crimson and white marbling its bare arms and chest. Now and then it paused, one foot poised above the floor, its great head swaying back and forth like a mastiff's. Annie was too far to see all that clearly, and she was certainly too far away to hear, but she had a horrible certainty that it was *sniffing* for something.

Once it stopped, and slowly turned. Annie almost fainted—it was staring right at her, it *saw* her where she crouched in the shadows. The tip of its tongue flicked between its lips, a tongue white and fat as a mealworm; but abruptly it looked away again, as though it had scented bigger prey, and strode off.

Behind it, Lyla and Virgie and the rest trailed in alert silence. Annie let her breath out, shuddering. Whatever it was hunting, it wasn't her—yet. She dared another peek out onto the dance floor.

Obviously it was going to take more than a murderous seven-foot androgyne to get the attention of this crowd: no one gave it a second glance. Hell, no one gave it a *first* glance. Its black eyes stared fixedly at something just out of Annie's range of vision, and as she watched she could see how the attention of its followers was turned as well.

It was staring at a boy. Like Annie he was by himself.

Just a stupid kid! Annie thought in a sort of bitter panic. Probably taking a few days off from his family vacationing down at Wellfleet or Chatham or Rock Harbor. Tanned and muscular, his short dark hair given ruddy highlights by the sun. He wore a pair of baggy tie-dyed shorts and a pair of sunglasses hanging from a cord against his chest. And he was wasted—that was obvious, he was laughing and talking to himself, his eyes shining, sweat glistening on his cheeks and brow. A little psychedelic fun in the shade, that was all; another harmless mindfuck.

All that is beauty,
All that is bone . . .

"Hey." Annie's mouth was so dry it hurt to whisper. "Hey, wait—*no*—"

She wanted to yell, to throw herself across the floor, *anything* to warn him. But fear flowed through her like a drug, so deadening it was a relief not to move. She could only watch as the silent angel crossed the floor, until it loomed above him.

Still the boy was oblivious. He kept talking to himself and giggling; now and then he'd feint and punch out at the air, then fall back laughing. The black angel's harriers sauntered toward him.

Darkness is thine
The stealth of the hunter
That strikes in the field
The joy of the archer
Who brings thee his kill
All this is thine
Othiym Lunarsa . . .

Suddenly the boy stiffened. He stared at the floor, for the first time noticed the shadow there. He raised his head.

The angel was gazing down at him with unblinking onyx eyes. The boy stared back, his smile gone now, his fists hanging loosely at his sides. Annie could hear the throbbing roar of music as Virgie and the others circled the boy.

His eyes widened, his mouth parted, and he tried to move, but someone grabbed him. Lyla; Annie recognized her lithe body and the dark crescent upon her cheek. When he tried to cry out, Lyla wrenched his arms back, whispering a warning into his ear.

Above them the tall figure smiled. Something huge and shadowy billowed behind it, a deeper darkness that furled and unfurled like great black wings. The dance music faded, until there was nothing but a persistent thudding backbeat, like waves against the shore. The sound grew louder. The dull percussive thud became words, a string of names that rolled across Annie's mind in an endless tide.

Othiym, Anat, Innana.
Hail Artemis, Britomartis,
Ishtar, Astarte, Ashtorath,
Bellona, More, Kali,
Durga, Khon-Ma, Kore.
Othiym Lunarsa, Othiym haïyo!

Like the slow soothing blood of poppies the words seeped into her, and as the music had faded, so now did the boathouse, dissolving into a colorless mist. Another room held her. A claustral space, dimly lit by smoking tapers and thick with the smells of flesh and wine. She was lying on her back on a wide stone table. A few feet away, someone else lay as well, sleeping soundly. Dream-logic told her that this was an altar; but it was unlike any church or cathedral Annie had ever been in. And, dazed as she was, she knew this wasn't a dream. Sweet smoke filled her nostrils, the scents of coriander seed and heated amber, sandalwood and oranges; and why was that so familiar? The fumes clouded her thoughts and she yawned. She wanted only to sleep, like her companion upon the altar—sleep and forget.

You are the secret mouth of the world
You are the word not uttered
Othiym Lunarsa, haïyo!

But sleep wouldn't come. This was all was too strange, and part of her wouldn't stop trying to make sense of it—had she been slipped a drug back at the boathouse? But this was more like a movie than an hallucination, albeit a movie with myriad smells and the acute discomfort of lying on a cold stone slab. Flowers were everywhere: orange lilies, cyclamen, purple morning glories already fading to grey. Tiny golden bees crawled over them, and gathered thickly upon the lip of a rhyton smeared with honey, sipped at a shallow salver of wine and one of soured milk.

Annie grimaced and tried to move, discovered that she was bound with cords—strands of vines and dried grasses that smelled sweet but were surprisingly strong. Several bees crawled toward her, drawn, it seemed, by her struggle. Annie stiffened, then sighed with relief as the insects stopped, too drunk on honey and fermented milk to go on.

She tilted her head to get a better look at the other figure on the altar. A boy, she thought at first—he was slight and curly-headed, his mouth open as though he were asleep. But then she noted that his fair hair was tinged with grey, and the torso beneath the hempen ropes was slack and pale—the skin white and translucent as ice, blue-tinged and with a faint damp sheen.

Annie whimpered. Dizziness swept over her: this was all wrong, she didn't belong here, and neither did that man, whoever he was. Whoever he had *been.* She tried to struggle but the ropes were too tight. She could hear faint voices somewhere just out of sight, the pad of bare feet upon stone floors. And there was that sweet smoke . . .

Don't breathe, try not to breathe!

She exhaled, with all her strength raised one elbow and rammed it against the stone.

She gasped. Her vision wavered; the pain curdled into nausea and a blade of fire jabbing through her arm.

Now! she thought. Because with the pain came a split second of clarity. She recognized the figure beside her on the altar.

Hasel Bright.

"No!" Annie shouted, but her voice was lost among the others singing.

All You have loved
All that is best
Is thine, O Beautiful One.

They emerged from the shadows, nine priestesses forming a half circle before the raised stone table. Behind them three male acolytes carried rhytons shaped like the heads of bulls. The women were tall, breasts exposed above long shirred skirts that swept to their ankles. The skirts were striped black and gold, bold and surprisingly modern in such an archaic-seeming place. They might have been wasps given women's form, moving in a slow measured dance. In their arms they carried a boy, a boy with very white teeth and tanned skin and sun-streaked hair.

Annie stared, entranced. They were so close that she could smell the boy's sweat, coconut oil, and the faint chloroform odor of XTC. When the priestesses raised their arms she could see silver crescents gleaming between their breasts. She could hear the papery rustling of their skirts, their low voices—

Strabloe hathaneatidas druei tanaous kolabreusomena
Kirkotokous athroize te mani Grogopa Gnathoi ruseis itoa

Each word with its echo of threat and fear—

Gather your immortal sons, ready them for your wild dance
Harrow Circe's children beneath the binding Moon
Bare to them your dreadful face, inviolable Goddess, your clashing teeth

The male acolytes approached the altar, gathered Hasel's limp form, and bore it away. Annie fought the panic boiling up inside her, but for the moment it seemed she was forgotten. The priestesses came forward, and gently placed the boy upon the altar. He lay upon his side, naked, his mouth stained from the libation. They had painted his lips and eyes with ocher, and drawn a half-moon upon his smooth chest. Against his honey-colored skin strands of ivy gleamed. He looked like a child at rest, eyes closed, his mouth in a sweet half smile; a child dreaming of his Mother. And his Mother came.

Without a sound she approached the altar, passing through the ranks of chanting women. Taller than any of them, and naked, her bronzy hair unbound and flowing past her shoulders, her lovely face calm, unsmiling. Between her bare breasts the lunula shone. Her priestesses fell silent as she stepped between them.

When she reached the altar she stopped. As Annie watched through a haze of smoke, Othiym's fingers tightened around the lunula. She moved until she stood directly above the boy. She raised the lunula over her head. Before Annie could flinch, the glowing crescent fell to strike the boy beside her. Sudden warmth splashed onto her face.

Othiym, haïyo!

Annie screamed. When she blinked her eyelids felt sticky. A salt-scorched taste burned her mouth. Through the roaring in her ears she heard Othiym's voice crying *Eisheth!* And Eisheth came.

It was no longer the black angel she had seen earlier. It was a vulture, so vast the shadow of its wings blotted out everything behind it. The stench of rotting flesh flowed from it, and she could see white grubs and blowflies rooting in the wattled flesh of its neck. It made a soft gurgling sound, like laughter, then pecked at the boy's eyes.

Annie gagged. The acolytes darted to the altar, vying with each other to catch the boy's blood in their rhytons. The vulture stared at them balefully, its black tongue clicking against its beak.

"Eisheth!"

A thunderous flapping as the vulture rose into the air. Annie tuned her head.

"Angelica," she whispered. It was almost a relief to say it.

The woman smiled. She looked improbably youthful and lovely as ever, with her tawny skin and hair, her slanted eyes. But her breasts were stippled with blood, and blood ran from her nipples to streak her belly. In her strong peasant's hands she held a rhyton shaped like a bull's head. Steam threaded the air above the vessel's opening as she lifted it, tilting it until a dark stream flowed from the bull's open mouth and into her own.

"All I have loved is mine," she said. Her mouth and tongue and teeth were black with blood.

Annie broke into hysterical gabbling. Beneath her the cold stone altar disappeared. The smoke dispersed, and with it the vulture's carrion stench. Once again she was crouching upon the wooden floor of the boathouse.

On the other side of the room people danced, oblivious. A few yards from Annie, Lyla and the others stood above a limp form. Annie's voice became a sob. Virgie glanced at her, then back down at the dead boy.

His eyes were gone, and his tongue. His torso had been split, the twin arches of his rib cage pried apart and his organs removed. In the empty cavity there was only a black-and-crimson feather, like a blossom sprung from his heart.

Annie shook convulsively. A single maddening thought raced through her mind—there should be *more blood,* she had *seen* how he'd died, there should be blood everywhere . . .

Without warning they were upon her, clawing at her arms and face as they dragged her to her feet. Annie screamed, she kicked and fought and yelled but they were everywhere, a mindless hive tearing at her clothes, pinning her arms behind her back.

"Be careful, be careful!—

Annie saw Virgie looking at her with round black eyes.

"*Agape,* Annie—you're *so* lucky you've been chosen—"

Annie moaned, closed her eyes against the pain. When she opened them again she saw a crescent flashing in the darkness. A few inches from her face someone held a battered silver vessel. She smelled blood: that choking thick smell, its ferrous taste as they prised her jaws open and it scalded her gums, blinded her where it splashed into her eyes. She couldn't scream, there was blood everywhere, filling her nostrils and ears and mouth. Through a film of red she saw the lunula, the Moon poised to rise and blot the sun from the sky . . .

"Let her go!"

A voice cried out. The hands upon her tightened; then the same voice cried again.

"Ne Othiym anahta, Ne Othiym—praetorne!"

Annie blinked. The others turned, gazing at a screen door that had blown open behind them.

"Ne Othiym anahta, Ne Othiym—praetorne!"

Her captors let go. Annie staggered across the floor.

"You fucking amateurs," she spat, and started to cry.

A few feet away Othiym's followers stared at the door, their faces angry and bewildered. Virgie let out a wail.

"Ohh—she's ruined *everything*—"

Like insects they scattered, and disappeared among the crowd. Annie tried vainly to stop sobbing.

"You better call someone. I mean like 911—" she choked, wiping her eyes and staring repelled at her blood-streaked fingers. "*God,* I don't fucking *believe* this—"

From the doorway came a muffled laugh.

"Funny?" Annie whirled, hoarse with rage. "You think this is *funny?*"

For the first time Annie saw her savior: a striking long-haired woman in a purple dress.

"Funny ha-ha or funny strange?" the woman asked.

Annie gasped. "B-but you—you were—"

The woman only smiled. Not with mockery or amusement, but with the purest joy and longing Annie had ever seen. Smiled and nodded, just once, whispering—

"Oh, Annie—I've missed you so—"

—before the wind sent sand like rain rattling against the floorboards, and without a sound she melted into the darkness.

CHAPTER 15

Ancient Voices (Echo)

I decided to walk home. The Metro would have been quicker and cooler, but the mere thought of all those thousands of happy tourists exhausted me. I stopped at a bookstore to order a copy of *Waking the Moon*, then headed back out.

More than ever I felt like a failure. Compared to Angelica—beautiful, eternally youthful Angelica, with her gorgeous hair, her string of books and villa in Santorini and bewitching (if false) green eyes—I *was* a failure. Here I was, thirty-eight years old, never married, no kids, no serious love affairs, still renting a house because I didn't make enough money to get a mortgage. The most interesting thing that had ever happened to me occurred half a lifetime ago, but even that didn't really count because whom could I tell about it? Who would believe it?

Or—and this was worse—who, after all this time, would even *care*? The only *real* friend I had was Baby Joe, because he was the only person who remembered me the way I was at eighteen.

And that was the way I still liked to think of myself. Not as Katherine Cassidy, the loyal civil servant who'd paid her dues at the National Museum of Natural History and after thirteen sober years had an office with a view, a government pension, five weeks of annual vacation and the occasional professional junket to New York or Chicago; but *Sweeney,* who had dreamed of discovering buried pyramids and sacred tombs, who could drink and dance all night and all day and still find her way home in one piece; whose friends were beautiful and magical and who for some reason, however briefly, seemed to find Sweeney enchanting too. Sweeney, who read poetry and saw angels and had glimpsed the *Benandanti*'s wasteland behind a hidden door; Sweeney, who had known the answer to the magic question when it was asked of her, and who had tried to remain loyal, courageous, and true till the end. Sweeney, whose one great love had taken a swan dive from the loony ward at Providence Hospital.

But Sweeney was gone, as surely as Oliver was. And to the rest of the world, to everyone except for Baby Joe and maybe Angelica or Annie Harmon, she had never even existed at all.

Dr. Dvorkin's house was on one of the myriad little cross streets that make up the residential blocks of Capitol Hill. From the street, the house looked much like its neighbors, a wide three-storied century-old brick town house, the walls painted a dark red that had faded nicely over the years and went well with the butter-yellow roses tumbling across the black wrought-iron fence.

The real wonder of Dr. Dvorkin's house could not be seen from the street. Because, for all the loneliness and boredom I'd lived with since leaving the Divine, the *Benandanti* had granted me this: a secret garden, my own hidden cottage in the woods. The garden itself was so lovely I was surprised it had never been written up in *Washingtonian* Magazine or one of the national shelter rags. But then I learned that Dr. Dvorkin had, indeed, been besieged with requests to photograph the garden, and always gently refused them.

"It's my secret place. And yours now, too, of course. And I would like to keep it that way."

The garden was behind the town house. It was bound on all sides by high brick walls overgrown with Virginia creeper, climbing yellow roses and morning glory and wisteria. There were flagstone paths winding through hostas and astilbes and a low dark green mantle of pachysandra, and around its perimeter all kinds of gorgeously exotic lilies. At the back of the garden, pressed up against one of the crumbling walls, was the carriage house, a nearly perfect square with a flat roof interrupted by a small belfry. It was made of red brick that had weathered to a soft rose that was nearly white. Ivy covered it, and wisteria that twined above the flagstone path that linked it to the main house.

Inside, the carriage house was cool as the hidden recesses of my own heart. From the rafters hung bunches of herbs I had bought at Eastern Market—valerian, lemon balm, mint. I inhaled gratefully, kicked my shoes off, and let my bare feet slide across the cool slate floor. I was home.

Downstairs the carriage house consisted of only one largish room, with a tiny bathroom tucked beneath the stairs and a miniature kitchen like an afterthought added on to one side. The main room had slate floors and the original exposed oak beams and joists. One entire wall was filled with bookshelves, and there was a small harvest table that held a lamp and a few domestic artifacts: a shadow puppet, a vase of oriental lilies, the sea urchin lamp that Angelica had sent me for Christmas so many years before.

Like the carriage house itself, most of its furnishings were borrowed from Dr. Dvorkin. He had more money than I did, I liked his taste, and so for all these years

I'd just lived with his things. Against the back wall was a sagging Castro Convertible sofa bed, draped with a heavy kilim rug. Shaker chairs hung from hooks in the beams, and there was an abandoned hornet's nest perched on a rafter in the corner. The tiny bedroom upstairs held a beautifully carved wooden bed from Sweden, a heavy armoire from Java, another kilim on the floor. Outside there were a couple of deck chairs and an old wicker table I'd salvaged from the curb.

Right now it was too hot to sit outside. I changed into an old T-shirt and turned on the radio. "All Things Considered" was starting, but I felt like I'd had enough news for one day. I fiddled with the dial until I found something more soothing—some nice madrigals, very dull, very pretty—then checked my answering machine for messages. There was only one, from Dr. Dvorkin, saying that he'd forgotten to tell me someone was staying in the main house, so I shouldn't worry if I saw lights there later in the evening. I reset the machine and went into the kitchen and poured myself some wine, then flopped onto the couch.

"Well, here's to Angelica," I said. I finished one glass and poured another, then another. I didn't usually make such a dent in a bottle of wine, especially on a work night, but this seemed like a special occasion, an evening for elegies and repining. The sad strains of the madrigals filled the little room, the slate floors cooled beneath my bare feet as the sun died and violet shadows crept across the deck and into the carriage house. From Ninth Street came the occasional hushed sound of a passing car, and I heard soft laughter from one of the neighboring houses. One or two stars glimmered in the darkness, and fireflies moved in a drowsy waltz above the hostas outside. I watched for lights to go on in the main house, trying to guess who Dr. Dvorkin's newest guest might be—someone connected with the Aditi, probably, a visiting curator or diplomat. Maybe even one of Jack Rogers's fire-eaters.

"Ah, well," I sighed. I leaned forward to refill my glass one last time, stood a little shakily, and put the bottle on a side table beside the vase of oriental lilies. A little water slopped out of the vase and I wiped it up with the hem of my T-shirt.

"Messy, messy," I said thickly.

By now it was full dark. I switched on the sea urchin lamp, the tiny bulb inside casting a rosy glow through the curved shell. A pink haze hung above the table, a lovely soft globe like a fairy lantern floating in the darkened room. I returned to the couch and lay back with my head resting against the kilim's rough wool, the wine-glass held between my hands, the sweet clear voices of the madrigal singers rising and falling in the room about me like the wind. Like the sea, like waves rushing and receding while I rested there, dreaming and untroubled in the sultry tropic night, while in the garden a single mockingbird sang.

Much later I awoke. The madrigal singers had been replaced by a man speaking in a very soft urgent voice about the need for a more efficient Capitol police force. I sat up, blinking, and put my empty glass on the floor. My watch said ten-thirty. Time for bed.

I hadn't eaten dinner, but I wasn't hungry, or even thirsty. The wine had left me with a feeling of drowsy well-being, as though I'd eaten that fairy fruit that eases all hunger and thirst and slows the passage of time. I yawned and started to get up, wondering if to was too late to call Baby Joe.

But at the edge of the couch I stopped.

The room was on fire. Shadows leapt across the walls, black and red and white, the air was thick with smoke, and I heard a persistent frantic sound like flames crackling. I stumbled to my feet and sent my wineglass spinning across the slate floor. I looked around, flushed with fear and wine: but there was no smoke, only the thick steamy mist that often appeared on the hottest summer nights. In the background the man's voice droned on and the wind rustled in the leaves, a sound like rushing water. Weirdly colored shadows moved upon the walls, rose red, velvety black, amber. Tentatively I crossed the room, until I stood beside the harvest table.

Something was trapped inside the sea urchin lamp. Its shadow darted across the room's walls as it beat frantically against the curved interior of its prison. The sound I had thought to be flames was its wings banging against the bulb. There was an unpleasant smell, as of scorched cloth.

I took the globe in my hand. It was quite hot, and I nearly dropped it. Very carefully I lifted it, holding it away from me so whatever was inside would fly out toward the open front door. For a moment or two it continued to thrash around. Then suddenly it emerged—very slowly, as though exhausted by its battle.

Antennae first, long as my forefinger and extravagantly feathered; then its long jointed legs, its thick brown-furred body and finally its wings. *Huge* wings, I was amazed there had been room for them inside. And how could it have gotten in there, surely the opening at the bottom was too small?

For a moment it poised on the sea urchin. Then it fluttered onto the table, landing beside an oblong drop of water spilled from the vase. I fixed the lamp, then squatted beside the table to watch it, marveling.

It was an enormous butterfly, a beautiful creature like a swallowtail, patterned with black-and-yellow stripes and dots. But the coloring was all wrong for a swallowtail—more orange than yellow, and the border around its wings was not black but a deep, rich purple. The edges of its wings were frayed from battering at the inside of the lamp. It opened and closed them slowly, as though trying to gather the strength to fly again. Then it fluttered up to perch on the lip of a yellow lily. After another minute it spread its wings again, and fluttered back down to the tabletop.

"Well," I said, yawning, "enough 'Wild Kingdom' for tonight. I'm going to bed."

I turned to close the front door, when something zoomed from the corner of the ceiling where the hornet's nest was perched.

"Shit!"

I scrambled backward as an angry buzzing filled the room. An enormous yellow jacket, big as my thumb and striped black and red, dived through the air to land on the table. The butterfly quivered, but before it could move the yellow jacket seized it, crawling atop it with wings beating so fast they were a dark blur.

I yelled and grabbed a magazine, slammed it against the table. The butterfly dropped to its side, the yellow jacket still clinging to it. Shouting I banged the table again. This time the wasp fell from its prey. Before it could move I smashed it flat, hitting it so hard I had to grab the sea urchin lamp before it could crash to the floor. When I finally stopped the yellow jacket was a reddish smear on the table top, its legs still feebly twitching. The butterfly had wafted to the floor and lay there, dazed.

Shuddering I scraped the dead wasp from my table and shook it outside, then got a broom and very, *very* gently prodded the football-sized nest hanging in the corner, terrified that a cloud of yellow jackets would come pouring out. When the nest toppled and fell to the floor I shrieked and ran outside.

But there were no wasps. The nest lay there like a softly deflated grey balloon, its white honeycombed innards spilling onto the floor. When I was certain it wasn't going to give birth to any more insects, I swept it outside, got some matches, and set it aflame. I watched it burn, the papery fragments disappearing before my eyes into the humid night air. Finally I went back inside.

The butterfly had flitted to one of the bookshelves. It was quite still, its wings stirring slightly in the draft. I left it and went to the harvest table to turn off the lamp.

"God damn it," I swore beneath my breath.

Where the wasp had been crushed, the wood was puckered and blistered, as though something caustic had been spilled there. I moved the vase to cover the spot, turned to salute the valiant little butterfly, and stumbled off to bed.

When I went downstairs the next morning the butterfly was still there. On a whim I got out a Ball mason jar, punched a few holes in its lid, and went outside to pick a tiger lily. For good measure I threw in a frond of wisteria, sprinkling a few drops of water onto the greenery.

The butterfly didn't move when I approached it. I was afraid it was dead, but its wings fluttered feebly as I slid it into the jar. When I got to the museum, instead of going directly to my floor, I went to see Maggie Lucas in her office by the Insect Zoo.

"Hi, Katherine. Care for a dead hissing cockroach?" Maggie held up an insect almost as large as her hand. "We've got plenty."

"No thanks." I moved a stack of magazines from a chair, plunked my jar on her desk, and sat down. "I want to make a donation."

"Oooh, a *butterfly*! A *pretty* bug." Maggie slipped the giant cockroach into a Baggie. She was a plump matronly woman in her fifties, a lepidopterist and assistant curator of the Insect Zoo, where in addition to the giant hissing cockroaches she watched over a beehive, a worm tank, numerous ant farms, bottles of pupating moths, an aquarium swimming with giant carnivorous water bugs, and a terrarium full of scarab beetles. "Now, what have we here?"

"I don't know. It was in my house last night." I told her about finding it inside the sea urchin lamp, and also about the yellow jacket that had attacked it. "I never saw anything so vicious—"

"Oh, that's pretty common. Some kinds of wasps are carnivorous, you know, and some of them even lay their eggs on caterpillars. Now, let's see what you've got—"

She opened the jar and gently shook the butterfly onto her hand. It fell into her palm and lay on its side.

"Did I kill it?" I asked in dismay.

"I doubt it. Sometimes these things only live for a day or two. Now this is interesting—"

She prodded it with a pencil, examining its wing markings.

"I thought it looked like some kind of swallowtail."

She shook her head. "It's not—wrong kind of tail hairs. Now this will sound kind of strange, but I don't think this is a native species at all."

"You mean not native to D.C.?"

"I mean not native to this continent. Unless I'm mistaken, this is some sort of festoon—"

She put the jar and the butterfly on her desk, crossed to a bookshelf, and pulled out an oversize volume. "Okay, let's see—"

She rifled the pages and stopped, pointed triumphantly. "Yup, here it is! *Zerynthia cerisyi keftiu. Zerynthia cerisyi,* that's the eastern festoon, and *keftiu*—that would be the subspecies from Crete."

"Crete?"

She looked puzzled. "That's in Greece, isn't it? Can that be right? Here, look at this and tell me what *you* think—"

She put the book down beside the butterfly and pointed to a colored plate, and yes, there it was: the same insect, the same pied wings and extravagantly feathered antennae.

"It—it sure looks the same," I said slowly.

"I wonder how it got here?" she mused. "Did someone just send you this lamp as a present?"

"No—I got it ages ago. I mean really long ago, almost twenty years."

"I was thinking maybe it had pupated inside—"

"Could it have been doing that for all this time?"

Maggie shook her head. "Beats me. I guess it could have, but I've sure never heard of anything like it before."

I looked back down at the illustration. On the facing page, there were plates showing several Greek amphorae, a small round seal like an irregularly shaped coin. I drew closer to the page and read.

In Mycenae and ancient Crete, butterflies often represented rebirth and the souls of the dead . . .

Maggie's voice made me jump. "Do you mind if I keep this? I'd like to study it—"

I pushed away from her desk, my heart pounding. "S—Sure," I stammered. "Listen, thanks, Maggie, but I've got to get to my office."

"Anytime! Hey, better stop and get a soda—I hear the air-conditioning's down in the west wing."

"Oh, *great.*"

"Let me know if you change your mind about the cockroach."

I fled upstairs. Maggie was right: the a/c was down. When I reached the third floor the heat was like a solid red wall. I stumbled past the security guard at the west desk and continued on down the corridor with my head bowed, so that I almost bumped into Laurie Driscoll.

"Katherine! Your intern's here—"

I groaned and slapped my forehead. "Oh, god, I *completely* forgot! Has she been here long?"

"Not really. Twenty minutes, maybe, they all had breakfast at the Commons but—"

"Okay, well thanks, I'll take care of her—"

I swept into my office, tossing my briefcase onto the desk and pausing to run my hand across my forehead. Then I put on my best formal expression and took a step toward the figure gazing out the window. She was tall for a woman, leaning on the sill to stare out at the Aditi already in full swing even in the sweltering heat.

"I am *so* sorry," I began, holding out my hand. "I had to drop something off on my way in here and I just—"

Slowly the figure turned to me. A lock of dark hair slipped across his forehead, his mouth curled into a crooked smile as he gazed at me and I stopped, paralyzed with the purest coldest terror I have ever known.

"Hi," he said softly, and brushed the hair from his eyes. "I hope you got my message."

"I—ah—ah—" I staggered back until I bumped my chair. *"No!—"*

It was Oliver.

He stared at me with wide blue eyes, holding his hand out in greeting. When I didn't move he frowned, glanced down at his extended hand, and then at me again.

"I'm sorry?" he said anxiously. "Is this—I mean, I called your voice mail and Dr. Dvorkin said this was—"

I slumped into my chair, clenching my hands to keep them from shaking. *"Who are you?"* I hissed.

"I'm Dylan Furiano. My mom says she knows you—Angelica Furiano, she says you'd remember her maiden name, Angelica di Rienzi—"

"Angelica?"

"Uh, yeah. I'm your intern—I wasn't on the original list because I was doing a semester abroad, in London. I'm at UCLA, studying film ethnography. My mom says to tell you hi."

"Angelica." There was a roaring in my ears. "Angelica is your mother."

He nodded. "See, originally I thought I had this summer fellowship at Sundance, but when that fell through my mom pulled some strings—my grandfather was good friends with Dr. Dvorkin, so Mom called him and they set this up—"

"Your grandfather." I seized on the notion like it was all that stood between myself and the abyss. I took a deep breath and nodded, my words spilling out breathlessly. "Your grandfather, *I* knew your grandfather—"

Dylan looked at the floor. "Yeah. He died a few years ago—"

So the *Benandanti* could die. "I'm sorry," I said softly, and meant it. "He was—I only met him once, but he was very kind to me."

"He and my father—they were out sailing together, there was this freak storm and the boat went down. They never recovered the bodies."

"God, how awful. I—your *father?*"

"Rinaldo Furiano. He was sort of this entrepreneur—well, it's kind of hard to explain what he did. We lived in Italy until he died. After that my mother and I moved here, to California. I guess probably you didn't know him."

"No," I whispered. "I—I don't think so."

But of course his father wasn't Rinaldo Furiano! I thought of that night at the Orphic Lodge, of Oliver and Angelica coupling in the shadow of the dead bull. No wonder she disappeared, ran off to Florence or Rome or god knows where, to hide from us all and have her baby and . . .

And here he was.

"Dylan," I murmured.

"Yes?"

I shook my head. "I'm sorry, I was just saying your name." I laughed, a little shakily. "So, are you named for Bob or Thomas?"

He looked at me blankly.

"Bob Dylan or Dylan Thomas."

"Oh! Neither, actually—it's Welsh, it means 'Son of the Wave.' I was born on this island and my mom was reading about some myth or something and there was this guy named Dylan, and so—"

He waved his hands: *pouff!*

"—here I am. She's into all this sort of weird stuff, my mom is." He smiled wryly, tilting his head to gaze at me. "But I guess probably you know that already."

Yeah, no shit, I thought. Now that I'd had a few minutes to calm down and look at him more closely, I could see how different he was from Oliver. His voice, for one thing—like Angelica's, it was musical and slightly accented, though the accent was more British than Italian, no doubt smoothed out by a few years in California. And he was much more handsome than Pretty Boy Oliver, with an underlying shyness that contributed to his almost feral beauty, like someone unaccustomed to wearing clothes or shoes.

Maybe that comes from growing up in Italy. Maybe in Angelica's house no one ever wears clothes.

The thought of this particular kid not wearing clothes made me dizzy. I swallowed, forced a smile, and said, "Yeah, your mom is a piece of work."

He laughed. He was not as tall as Oliver, but more muscular—he wore neatly pressed tan chinos and a white oxford cloth shirt, its sleeves neatly rolled to show smoothly muscled arms. A tie was loosely knotted at his throat and I could see the muscles bunched at his neck, flaring smoothly out onto his shoulders. He wore clunky black shoes like combat boots, with worn knotted laces. He was broad-shouldered, long-legged, slim-hipped—probably a bodybuilder, and god knows I had never seen Oliver lift anything heavier than a hash pipe. But he had Oliver's nose, Oliver's high cheekbones and piercing blue eyes, though Dylan's were flecked with green. One of his ears had multiple gold studs in a little line, gold and malachite and a single tiny silver crescent. And his long hair, though jet black, cascaded in loose curls like his mother's. He wore it pulled into a ponytail, but it kept escaping to fall into his eyes. His mouth too was Angelica's, full-lipped and sensual. When he smiled, it twisted into Oliver's canine grin.

He was smiling now. "My mom told me a lot about you. About how close you two were at school, and how much she always envied you and your boyfriend—"

"My boyfriend?"

"Yeah. That Oliver guy. My mom said that everybody was just, like, insanely jealous of you."

"Angelica told you *that*?"

He nodded. "She said you were so pretty, everyone was in love with you—" He tilted his head and added shyly, "She was right."

"Uh—*whoa.*"

I stared at the ceiling, bewildered and embarrassed. Angelica had told him some crazy story about Oliver and *me*? But it made a bizarre kind of sense, it was just the kind of thing I could imagine her doing; and maybe it made her feel less guilty about what had happened to all of us.

And it certainly seemed to have piqued Dylan's interest. He was gazing at me so boldly that I blushed, although there was something innocent about his expression, almost childlike. As though he'd never been told it was rude to stare.

But then why should I be surprised? Shouldn't I *expect* Angelica's kid to act like this? Not even in the room for five minutes and already he was turning up the heat; not that we needed any more heat. I groaned and wished I was back home asleep in bed.

Maybe this is what they're like in Italy, they're much more open there, such earthy colorful people . . .

I felt myself flush. This was ridiculous, and dangerous, too: the museum had truly draconian rules against sexual harassment. Although at the moment I had no idea where I stood in this jungle, whether I was predator or prey; whether this was even Real Life at all, or some twisted hallucination brought on by the heat and a mild hangover.

Because all of a sudden I was eighteen years old again, sitting in a stifling classroom and gazing at the most beautiful boy I had ever seen, the only person I had ever loved, waiting with my mouth parted for him to ask me a question only I knew the answer to . . .

I took a deep breath and stumbled to my feet. I pushed the hair from my eyes and smoothed my skirt—a short linen skirt; I had long legs and wasn't above flashing them around in the summer, not that anyone ever seemed to notice.

Dylan noticed.

I glanced up and there he was, staring at me like I was something in the downtown window of Victoria's Secret. When he saw me looking at him he smiled.

Slowly this time, a smile utterly without guile, sweet as a child's and so completely, unabashedly carnal that my legs buckled and I sank back into my chair.

"Hey," he said, and tugged at his shirt collar. "It sure is hot in here, isn't it?"

I decided we should go for a walk. Outside my office a steady stream of people hurried through the corridor, all of them heading for the steps or service elevator.

"Mayday, mayday." Laurie stuck her head through the door. "Hey, Katherine. They've put the Liberal Leave policy into effect, because of the heat. Everybody's taking off—"

"What an *excellent* idea," I exclaimed. "Thanks, Laurie—"

I started from my chair, and a wave of dizziness crashed over me. Before I could catch myself Dylan grabbed my arm and was helping me to my feet.

"Oh, that's all right, Dylan, I'm fine, *really*—"

I shrugged him away and put my hand up, trying not to sound rude. "Thanks, thanks, I'm okay—I just stood up too fast, that's all."

I tried to catch my breath, wondering if I looked and sounded ridiculous: an aging proto-punk Baby Boomer having a heart attack while getting out of an ergonomic chair. "Look, let me go tell Dr. Dvorkin that we're leaving—"

Dylan followed me into the hall. Dr. Dvorkin stood outside his office, his face bright red. He was wearing a short-sleeved shirt and no tie, practically unheard of for him.

"Oh, Katherine! I see you found my houseguest."

I stopped. "Your houseguest?"

"Yes—Dylan's grandfather was a very dear friend of mine—but of course you knew that, didn't you?" He mopped his face with a handkerchief, looked up at me and shook his head. "You know, I'd completely forgotten you knew the di Rienzis. You were friends with Angelica, weren't you?"

His questioning eyes were mild but I could see something else in them—a spark, a quiet intensity that I had never glimpsed before. A look like desperation, desperation or fear.

I waited a beat before replying. "Yes. But we haven't talked in almost twenty years."

"Then you and young Dylan here have a lot of catching up to do." He smiled, that familiar ironic melancholy smile, and suddenly was the man I had always known. "I think they're sending all the staff home. Apparently the heat and ozone levels up here are dangerous. Central Engineering's diverting all our power so they can keep the public areas open downstairs." He turned to Dylan. "We curators are always the scapegoats when something like this happens. Little lambs to the slaughter."

Through all this Dylan stood beside me, his boyish face composed into a serious mask, the good scout on his best behavior. And that's all he was, really, just a kid, for all the sculpted torso and earrings and scary shoes.

"Dylan, would you mind waiting for me by the steps? We can talk outside, but I've just got to grab some paperwork first—"

"Sure." He ducked his head in farewell, but before he could go Dr. Dvorkin put a hand on his shoulder.

"You have your key, don't you, Dylan? I'm so sorry I wasn't there to greet you last night, but we'll have dinner together this evening, how would that be?"

Dylan nodded earnestly, then walked slowly down the hall, glancing back once or twice. Dr. Dvorkin turned to me. "Did you need something, Katherine?"

"Uhh—well, Dylan's internship application, I never saw any of the paperwork that came through on him. I thought I was getting that girl, Lydorah Kelly . . ."

Dr. Dvorkin dabbed at his cheeks with his handkerchief. "Yes, well, Lydorah put in a request to go out to Silver Hill, to work in the forensics lab. It seems that's more what she's suited for than photo archiving. And then Angelica called me about her son, and, well I'm sure you understand how *that* works; and then of course *you* were without an intern, and *he's* studying film ethnography, and so it seemed like a good idea to place him on the videodisc project. But he's a very bright young man, Katherine. I think he'll contribute a good deal to your work."

I tried not to roll my eyes. Whatever was going on here, it seemed like a whole lot more than just some kind of insane coincidence. "I'm sure he will. Is there a 171 on him, though? Anything at all that'll give me some idea what he's done, what he's studying?"

"Oh, absolutely. Come on in, if you can bear it—"

He rifled through a heap of 171s, finally pulled one out.

"Here it is! If you'll excuse me, Katherine, I'm supposed to be at some kind of emergency powwow, and I'm already late."

I trudged back out into the hall, dragging my briefcase. The 171 form he'd given me was green and white, limp as wet lettuce. It was the standard government employment form, with a cover sheet detailing the particulars of the summer internship program. The empty spaces had been filled in neatly with a slightly italicized European hand.

Dylan W. Furiano.

I flipped through the Xeroxed pages. UCLA film school, majoring in film-and-video ethnograhy. Four years at the Lawrenceville School. Elementary education, the Cathedral School in London and private tutors, Florence, Italy. Reads and writes English, Italian, German, French. In case of emergency notify Angelica Furiano, Los Angeles, California, and Sedona, Arizona. I stared at the page for a long moment, then slipped it into my briefcase.

"Ms. Cassidy?"

I started, turned, and saw Dylan. His cheeks were pink and the knot in his tie had slipped halfway down his chest. "Someone fainted! They're sending everybody down the back fire stairs, but I wasn't sure where they were—"

I laughed. "Well, *you're* certainly having an exciting first day, aren't you?" I raised my briefcase to point down the hall. "Thataway."

"I figured you'd know."

The fire door had been wedged open with a chair. Squeezing past it I looked up at Dylan, his long hair falling into his eyes and his hands swooping to pull his hair back into its ponytail, his face red and glowing as with uncontained excitement. When he'd gotten his hair out of the way he stared down at me, his blue eyes so brilliant it was like the sky reflected there, or the ocean; like some wonderful dream of a warm blue place, some secret haven by the sea and for the first time in almost twenty years I was waking, waking—

"Hey, Ms. Cassidy—?"

I shook my head, dazed.

"Ms. *what?*" Suddenly I grinned, and nudged him with my briefcase. "Please, Dylan, do me one favor, okay—"

I swept past him, taking the steps two at a time, heedless of the heat or the blood singing in my ears, heedless of anything at all except the sound of him bounding after me, the metal banisters clamoring as he tugged at them. When I reached the landing I paused and looked back, out of breath and panting, laughing, *really* laughing, for the first time it seemed in decades.

"—Call me Sweeney."

CHAPTER 16

Black Angels

At the desk in her room at Huitaca, Angelica Furiano sat writing a letter. It was evening, hot enough that the petals of the oriental lilies in their Waterford vase had crisped into brittle orange tongues, and their leaves all fallen to the floor. In spite of the heat she had turned off the air-conditioning. She liked to hear the night come alive, she liked to hear the sound of small creatures splashing in the shallows of the pool outside, the muted voices of Kendra and Martin wafting up from the gardener's cottage and the radio behind her playing the Kronos Quartet.

Through the French doors she could see the tiled patio, and beyond that twisted spires of stone still flushed with sunset. Above the nearest rocky tower, named the Devil's Clock by the locals, the full moon dangled like a lantern hung there by a tired deity. Angelica stared at it, then sighed and looked away.

A small brass tray sat on her worn desk. Balanced on its edge like a cigarette was a smudge-stick of dried sage and coriander leaf bound with hemp, smoke rising from it. Beside it was the lunula. Angelica took a deep breath of the pungent smoke, then picked the necklace up idly. She rubbed the smooth surface with her thumb, feeling the faint impressions of the pattern etched there, the small gaping mouth where the lost portion of the triskelion was missing.

Four weeks from now would be Lammas; four weeks from now she would be Waking the Moon. She stared out at the evening sky, the limbs of the crippled piñon pines stirring gently in the hot breeze; then looked down to read over her letter.

July 2, 1995

Dearest Dylan,

I was so happy to hear your voice last night and know that you arrived safely! I sent the package with your T-shirt and your sandals, also you forgot your glasses case. Don't worry, I'm sure Sunday will find your notebook.

I got confirmation of my tickets to D.C. for your birthday next month. A limo is supposed to meet me at Dulles, but maybe we can arrange it so you can be there too—I'd love that!

I know you won't have had the opportunity yet to look for the lunula, but it's probably a good idea not to wait too long, in case it's more difficult to track down than I think. I can't imagine that it's been moved since June Harrington's time. Her notebook said it had been misplaced among artifacts from Indonesia and Malaysia, so that would still probably be the best place to start. Please be sure to eat this letter when you've finished reading it.

Only kidding! But remember what I said about being careful.

I know you'll have a wonderful time out there, even though I'll miss you horribly. Andy Ludwig called, also Serena, and I gave them your number at Dr. Dvorkin's house. Please be *sure* to use your calling card, we don't want him to have to pay for your phone calls! Of course you should always call me collect.

Give my love to Dr. Dvorkin. I love you!

Mom

As she reread the letter, the strings in the background soared into a sweet motet. *Spem in Alium*, Sing and Glorify, Judith seducing and then beheading Holofernes to save her people. Today, men would judge her actions as a crime, but three thousand years ago *Diis aliter visum:* it seemed otherwise to the gods.

Angelica pushed aside the letter, listening to the immeasurably sad music, the violin straining like a lover bidding a last farewell. She knew it was foolish, writing to her son like this—he never wrote back, preferring the telephone—but it made her feel close to him; alleviated some of the loneliness she felt. Her eyes filled with tears as she stared at a photo of Dylan on her desk. Dylan at four, playing on the rock-strewn beach near Akrotiri on Thera. He was naked, his dark hair burned to copper by the sun, wind-tossed as the waves behind him. His tiny fist held something, shell or stone, he was holding it above his head and laughing. In the background Rinaldo stood knee-deep in the water and smiled, his grey hair a bright aureole. It had been the first time Angelica had visited Thera and seen the excavations at Akrotiri. They had left the island the next day, to return to the villa near Florence, and had not returned for two years.

That was the only other time she had ever used Dylan to smuggle something for her: a thumb-sized seal of the Cretan bee-goddess that she had sewn into the waistband of his training pants. He had been as innocent of the seal's power as he was of the missing piece of the lunula.

"Oh, Dylan," she whispered. She moved the photo so that she could see the others behind it. An old Lucite frame held a picture of Hasel Bright, looking so young it almost took her breath away—he'd been a child, really, they'd all been little more than children! Hasel had given her the framed photo after they slept together that once, over Columbus Day weekend.

"It can't happen again, you know," she'd told him. Hasel so serious he looked like a cartoon owl, with those enormous blue eyes and a blinded, stricken look.

"Never?"

Angelica laughed. "I'm sorry, Hasel. But those are the rules."

He sat up on her bed—they were in her dorm room, Annie having gone to stay with friends for the holiday weekend—and took her hand in his, raised it to his mouth, and kissed the little cleft between her first and second fingers. "Rules? What rules? Do you, like, turn into a pumpkin or something?"

Angelica had laughed softly, drawing her hand away and leaning forward to kiss the top of his head. "No, sweetie—*you* do."

She pursed her lips, tracing the edge of the frame with a fingernail. It had been Hasel's destiny to die for Othiym. She leaned forward to blow a little thread of ash from the burning sage, then pushed aside Hasel's picture, moved several others where she could see them better. Frames of heavy darkened silver; frames of real tortoiseshell and delicate coral. Within them were more photographs: faded Polaroids, amber-tinted Kodachrome, crisp black-and white.

Mostly they were pictures of Dylan and her late husband, taken during her long Mediterranean exile. But here was her beloved uncle, at his villa near Poggibonsi, and there was her father, and there her beautiful cousin Rafael—her first cousin, twice-removed, ah! he had been so handsome, she was truly sad when he died—and here was another of poor sweet Hasel.

And one of Annie Harmon, taken by Angelica herself during one of their afternoon interludes. Annie looking very cross but also rather stunned, her worn old quilt pulled up around her breasts. And here was the young Sweeney Cassidy—not caught *in flagranti delicto* like Hasel or Annie, but looking quite gamine with her cowboy boots and cropped hair. And here was a more recent picture of Annie, clipped from an issue of the *Advocate* and stuck in the corner of a large framed picture of Dylan's graduation.

"Come here, you," murmured Angelica. Gingerly she teased the newspaper photo of Annie from the frame. She had been focusing all her will on Annie lately. She did not dare confront Annie as she had Hasel—Annie was another woman, after all, and had a better understanding of Angelica's true nature. She would be wary of a meeting with Angelica.

And rightfully so! Angelica thought, her mouth curving in a smile. But even Annie Harmony could not escape the naphaïm. She took Annie's photo in one hand, and with the other picked up the lunula. For a moment a pang of real sorrow made Angelica's eyes fill with tears.

Because while each sacrifice was holy, and each one made her stronger and stronger still, it was only those who had *loved* her who made the Goddess real, who made Her epiphany complete. *That* was the bridge between the worlds of Othiym and Angelica di Rienzi Furiano—a bridge formed of all those who had truly loved her, those who had died for her over the centuries. And for each of them she had wept, as she had wept for Hasel and Rafael and Oliver; as she would weep for Annie, and Dylan. As Ishtar, Au-Set, Isis, Artemis or Cybele, as the thuggees' Kali or Wilde's Salome, she had always received a tribute of souls—and blood. The bridegroom who lay with her but one night a year, and died before sunrise; the man who served as her consort for twelve lunar cycles and then was slain within her sacred grove. Even in modern times her ancient worship was not utterly forgotten. All those nineteenth-century artists who had painted her as sphinx and panther and vampire sensed the truth of it: Woman was a perilous country.

Angelica blinked her tears back, and ruefully smiled. In the tarnished mirror nestling between the photos, her reflection smiled back. Oh, men had feared her then, and women too—they had always feared her! But they had *loved* her as well, and perished for her willingly.

And so they would again. And each death, each loving offering, would be another stone in the bridge that swept from Angelica to the Queen of Heaven. Already she had received so many, nameless men and boys. But then there had been Hasel, an ardent sacrifice if ever there was one. And Oliver . . .

Her heart beat too fast, thinking of Oliver. She forced herself to stare at Annie's photo again, Annie with her freckles and her cowlick and her soft white skin. Tonight, perhaps, Angelica would finally see Annie again. When the Goddess came to her, when Othiym would *be* her. And someday soon, she would see Dylan, too, would cradle him within her as she had all those millions of others . . .

She took another deep breath, the scent of coriander and sage making her think of temples made of clay and earth and dung, of malachite and mammoth ivory. She raised her head to stare at the swollen globe in the eastern sky.

"For I so love the world that I will give unto You my only Son," she whispered.

With Dylan's death it would be done. Her epiphany would be complete: Othiym would awaken from her aeons-long sleep.

I am wife and mother and sister of Osiris
I am mother of Horus
I am She that riseth in the Dog Star
I am she that is called Goddess by women!

For me was the city of Bubastis built
For me was raised the City on the Hill

I divided the earth from heaven
I put the stars in their courses
With me doth true justice prevail!

I am the Queen of rivers and winds and the sea
I am the Queen of war
I am Queen of the thunderbolt
I raise the sea and I calm it
I am Queen of the storm
I overcome Fate
I am the secret mouth of the world
I am the word not spoken
Othiym haïyo, Othiym Lunarsa!

Her words faded into the plaintive strains of the string quartet. Her reverie ended when the telephone chimed. Angelica smiled, that would be Dylan, calling to tell her how his first day at the museum had gone.

"Hello?"

"Angelica?"

A woman's disembodied voice rang hollowly from the speaker. Not Dylan after all but Elspeth, her agent, calling from New York. Angelica heard traffic noises in the background: she'd be on her car phone. "I'm sorry to call so late, but there's been some trouble."

Angelica's heart stopped. "Dylan? Is he all right? What—"

"He's fine, Angelica. It's not him, it's—"

A pause. "Last night. A bunch of your girls were at some kind of party at an abandoned house in Cape Cod. Some big gay hangout on the beach up there. I just saw it on the news. A boy was murdered, a bunch of kids found the body and—"

"Who was it?"

"They don't know, the body was so mutilated—"

"No! The girls, which girls?"

Elspeth's voice rose edgily. "I have no idea, Angelica. But the way they described it, I'm certain—"

Angelica twisted her pen between her fingers, heedless of the ink spilling from its seams to stain her nails peacock blue. "Did they bring any of them in for questioning?"

"No, of course not." Elspeth gave a sharp laugh. She had been one of Angelica's earliest initiates, and was now at the center of a Circle in Manhattan's publishing district. "But they did note similarities between this death and that boy in Lubbock. *And* the New York *Beacon* mentioned Cloud."

"Cloud's death was a—a *horrible* accident." Angelica let her voice catch, so Elspeth could hear how the memory stll upset her.

"This kid's death was a pretty bad accident too, " Elspeth said dryly. "Apparently the body was so mutilated they had to use dental records to identify him." Another pause. "Do you know someone named Annie Harmony?"

Angelica was silent. "Did you hear me?" Elspeth asked after a moment.

"Yes, I heard you," said Angelica carefully. "I knew someone named Annie *Harmon.* She was my roommate for a semester at college. Why?"

"Well, someone named Annie Harmony may have seen what happened. She's a singer with a big gay following; my son says she's on cable all the time. She did a show in Provincetown last night and according to the club's owner there were a number of your girls in the audience, he said they disrupted her encore and she was pretty pissed off. Afterward she apparently went to this party and saw something."

Angelica's voice was tight. "Did she go to the police?"

"No. But I guess she's enough of a local celebrity that the news is all over the place—she was hysterical, screaming about black angels and some woman who saved her. Now the police want her for questioning but she's disappeared."

Annie! She couldn't lose Annie, not now! Not after so long—

"Angelica?" Elspeth's voice came through in an angry burst of static. "Are you listening?"

"Of course—it's just, well, a *surprise,* that's all."

Elspeth snorted. "Yes, I would say a murder in the middle of a crowded party is a pretty big surprise! Pretty careless, too—a lot of people noticed your girls and boys there, and even though the gay press is trying to make this out to be some kind of queer-bashing, the local media *and* the national news are talking about ritual murder. They're talking covens, they're talking witches, Satanic rites . . ."

Angelica finally gave in to exasperation. "Well, let them talk. Remember Freedom of Religion, Elspeth? Remember the Santeria decision?"

The distorted scream of a bus's brakes tore through the room. "This isn't about freedom of *religion,* Angelica! This is ritual *murder*—"

"One man's mass murder is another man's high mass, Elspeth. If they summoned the naphaïm no one will find anything." Her fingers drummed at the phone's speaker. "I'm expecting a call from my son—"

"Maybe you can suggest to everyone that they cut back on the Circles for a few weeks—"

"Elspeth, I'm not their Mother Superior—there are women all over the world acting on their own now! You know what it's like—all those splinter groups. I couldn't possibly contact them all."

Elspeth's voice rang out warningly. "This is *really* bad timing, Angelica! You have a new book out, and the tabloids *love* this kind of stuff, especially in the middle of summer—tomorrow it'll be on 'A Current Affair' and then you'll have Laurie Cabot and NPR and everyone else in the country shoving microphones in your face!"

"It won't be a problem, Elspeth." Angelica's voice was disarmingly calm. "All right?"

For a moment she heard only the drone of traffic, and faint music rising from the radio behind her. Finally Elspeth said, "I just thought you should know. Whether or not they can prove anything, the media and the public are starting to link these murders—"

"*Offerings,* Elspeth, *offerings,*" Angelica said gently.

"—to link these *offerings,* with *your* name. Your publisher is *not* happy about this *at all,* not one little bit."

Angelica reached for the disconnect button. "Thank you for letting me know, Elspeth. I have to go now."

For a few minutes she sat at her desk, staring at the moon outside. It was high above the cliffs now, its light falling in a shimmering curtain to cover everything, stones and tiles and pool, the twisted limbs of yucca and ocotillo and huisache.

"Four more weeks," she said softly, and picked up the lunula. It had grown so heavy over the last few months. It drew strength from the waxing moon; as the moon waned, the offerings made by her followers would fatten it once more, until a month from now it would be heavy as though it had been wreathed with the tiny carven images that had been buried with the bodies of the faithful so many centuries before. By then Dylan would have found the missing crescent, the little moon's lost dark quarter. The lunula and its Mistress would be whole again at last.

Now she felt the gravid curve heavy upon her breast. She ran her fingers across it, thinking of her beautiful son playing in the waves. She began to recite softly to herself, his favorite bedtime verse.

They dined on mince and slices of quince
Which they ate with a runcible spoon
And hand in hand, on the edge of the sand
They danced by the light of the Moon, the Moon, the Moon:

They danced by the light of the Moon.

Very early the next morning, Annie Harmon sat on the tiny balcony of the room she and Helen had rented at a B&B in Wilmington, Vermont. To the west stretched the Green Mountains, their peaks gilded with sunrise. Above Haystack Mountain the moon was poised to set, just a few hours past its full. Phoebes and titmice sang from birch trees in the yard below, and from Lake Whittingham echoed the wailing of a loon and its mate's anguished reply.

"We'll have to let Vicki and Ed know if we want the room for another night," Helen said gently. She took her coffee cup from the breakfast tray that had been left outside their door. "It's the Fourth of July weekend; they'll want to rent it to someone else."

Annie continued to stare at the western sky. She'd showered seven times since she and Helen had fled the rave on Herring Cove Beach, trying to rid herself of the smell and taste and feel of blood. Now her skin felt as though it had been rubbed with sand, so raw and sore it hurt to move.

"Annie?"

"I can't go on with the tour."

"You have to, Annie." Helen's voice was soft but annoyed; in the last twenty-four hours they'd had this conversation fifty times, at least. "You'll be in breach of contract, besides which we still haven't paid the mortgage—"

"There's money in my private savings account in Burlington. I'll write you a withdrawal; take it and pay all the bills."

"You have a private savings account?" Helen sounded aggrieved. "You never told me."

"Now you know."

"But *why*? I mean, aren't you going with me?"

"I can't. I can't go on with this tour, and I can't go back home with you. I told you, it's too dangerous."

"Dammit, Annie, why don't you just go to the police! This is ridiculous, you can't just—"

"The police won't be able to help me. The police won't be able to help *anyone* if this keeps up . . ."

"And you can?" Helen asked incredulously.

"No, I'm sure I can't. But maybe—maybe I can think of someone who can."

"Who? Your mystery woman back in Provincetown? All of a sudden you've got to run off and play Sherlock Holmes?"

"Helen, you *know* that's not what I'm doing."

"So tell me what you're doing."

"I can't."

"Always a fucking mystery. Always the fucking heroine," Helen fumed, gulping her coffee.

"Oh, stuff it!" But a moment later Annie was kneeling, clutching at Helen's knee. "Oh, *god*—"

Helen bent down to hug her, her eyes filling with tears. "Hush—it's all right, sweetheart, don't worry, it'll be okay . . ."

"It *won't* be okay. Something terrible is happening, something horrible and now *I'm* in it but I'll be damned if I'm gonna drag *you* into it with me—"

She closed her eyes to keep from crying, but that was when the visions came: those shadowy figures looming around the boy's ravaged corpse, darkness behind them and overhead the ghostly blurred face of the moon . . .

Annie moaned, and stumbled to her feet. Overhead the sun broke over the mountain. "I can't stay here. It's *Angelica*, Helen, if you only knew what she was *like*!"

"Try me."

"She's just so used to getting her own way—I mean everything she wants! Men, women, boys, girls—"

"Beauty," Helen suggested. "Eternal youth."

"It's not funny!"

Helen finished her coffee and reached for a croissant. "So, does she bathe in the blood of virgins, or what?"

"*Helen*. They killed that kid last night. And now—now she *wants* me. I don't know why—I mean, after all this time—but she *wants me*—"

Helen forced a laugh. "Don't flatter yourself, sweetheart."

From the bedroom came the sudden hoarse shout of a telephone: an old-fashioned rotary phone to go with the inn's 1930s decor. Two short rings and then a longer one. Annie stiffened and looked at Helen.

"Don't answer it."

"Don't be silly. I *have* to answer it; it's probably just Vicki or Ed checking to see if we want the room for another night." Helen got to her feet.

Briiing briiing.

"Helen. Don't."

Briiing.

"*Don't*! Nobody knows we're here, nobody should be calling, Helen, *PLEASE*!—"

"And *do* we want the room?" Helen glanced back as she picked up the heavy black Bakelite handset. "Hello?"

From the porch Annie watched her. Helen's sweet round face, the edges of her braids fuzzed from sleeping on them and her kimono falling open around her wide hips, that dark cleft and Annie's heart aching because they hadn't fucked, they'd fought, and now it was too late.

This is the last time I'll ever see her, she thought with a sort of greedy desperation. *This is it, make the best of it, Annie-girl, because—*

"Annie?" In the bedroom Helen's expression folded into fear, as quickly and neatly as a deck chair collapsing. She sank onto the bed, holding the phone out to Annie with wide eyes. Her voice faded to a whisper as she said, "It's Fiona. From Labrys. She says . . ."

. . . because . . .

"Fiona? It's only three A.M. out there, how the *hell* did she find—"

. . . because . . .

Helen stared at her in a daze, shaking her head. "I—I don't understand. She says she just got off the phone with Angelica Furiano and she wanted you to know right away—the bad publicity, for some reason Angelica called and threatened them with a lawsuit, something about that boy, and you being there, and—well, they're canceling the tour—"

Annie yanked the phone from her lover.

—because this is where things fall apart.

Angelica stood before her bedroom window, watching the moon disappear behind the black rim of the world. It had been a long night. After talking to Elspeth she had called Fiona from Labrys Music, dragged her out of bed and would not let her go until she'd promised to call Annie Harmon immediately. Let Annie wonder how she'd tracked her down; let her twist in the wind for a few weeks. By then it would be too late, and no one would be talking about the police, or anything else for that matter; not unless Othiym wanted them too. Her hand rested upon the lunula at her throat, felt its warmth seeping into her fingers.

You are the secret mouth of the world
You are the word not uttered
Othiym Lunarsa, haïyo!

Already first light was striking the Devil's Clock. Her fingers slipped from the lunula to pluck at the sleeve of her kimono, wipe a drop of sweat from her wrist.

Dylan had never called. She knew better than to worry about that—did eighteen-year-old boys *ever* call their mothers? Still, it was enough to spark a small *frisson* of fear and unease; enough to keep her from going to bed.

Though in truth she did not really sleep anymore. As the power of the lunula waxed, as Othiym Herself grew stronger and Angelica waned, she found that she had little need of sleep. Instead of dreaming, her waking mind burned with random images. Annie in the shower, her face raw from crying. The black angel Eisheth rising into the darkness above the Atlantic Ocean, huge and ravenous, its mouth a flaming hole, its fiery wings billowing until they were swallowed by the clouds. A Circle in a Kansas wheatfield, adolescent girls and boys with knives raised above the cowering figure of a young boy scarcely more than a child; another Circle in the old growth forest of the Pacific Northwest. Older women here, the last ragged edge of the failed separatist movement, their prey older as well, and the sound of invisible wings beating fiercely at the air. Angelica saw all these things and more; they chased sleep from her mind as though it were a gnat.

But of Dylan she saw nothing, and that was strange. And try as she might, she could not find Sweeney Cassidy.

From the room behind her static crackled softly. Angelica turned. She had forgotten about the radio. Whatever station it had been tuned to had gone off the air hours ago. The hissing of white noise had become part of the ambient fabric of the night. She crossed the room slowly, to the neat array of stereo equipment stacked atop an antique secretary. Her finger was poised above the OFF switch, when abruptly the static cleared.

"Now what?" she murmured, frowning. There was a moment of silence. Then the radio picked up some distant signal. Music caught in mid-song, a sonic blur of feedback and echoing synthesizers; then a voice. An unfamiliar voice, repeating unfamiliar words in a near-monotone.

But there was a thread of melody there as well—a familiar melody, it nagged at her, tugged at the carefully woven tapestry of memories she had cloaked herself in.

From the long barrows of Wilshire to the Pyramids
From the stone circles that challenged the scientists
And the Neolithics that tread the ancient avenues
Your children that died forevermore exist

"Enough," whispered Angelica. She stabbed at the OFF button. There was a gentle click, an electronic sigh; but the music did not stop.

I have always been here before . . .

The sound filled the room. Everywhere around her, the voice overdubbed so that it formed its own echoing chorus, the same voice ringing in her ears like the aftermath of an explosion.

The childish man comes back from the unknown world
And the grown man is threatened by sacrifice
Whosoever protects himself from what is new and strange
Is as the man who's running from the past

I have always been here before

The song ended. As though someone had dropped a bottle of perfume, a thick fragrance filled the room, a cloying scent that made her head ache. The smell of the festival games, when great armfuls of flowers were strewn upon the graves of all the golden athletes given to her in tribute. The smell of hyacinths.

She could hear her own heart, her breath coming in shallow gasps. Then another sound, so soft she thought at first she'd imagined it. A ticking noise like fingers rapping at a glass.

Angelica whirled, hands clenched at her sides. In the arch of the Palladian window, something beat against the panes. The shadow of its wings ballooned across the floor and up onto the wall behind her, but when she darted to the window she saw that it was actually quite small, no larger than her hand. She flung open the casement but before she could thrust her head outside it flew into the room. The smell of hyacinths grew overpowering, the syrupy odor so strong her tongue felt coated with it, she felt as though she were drowning in petals, stamens showering her with pollen until she could hardly breathe. She staggered back and it flew toward her, its wings slowly rising and falling, sending the faintest of currents through the warm air.

It was a butterfly, purple and yellow, its glittering eyes fixed upon her, its antennae wafting back and forth like sea hair. It hovered mere inches from her face. When she extended one hand it floated down, gentle and hapless as a falling leaf, until it rested upon her palm.

Angelica stared at it, the dusting of gold and violet scales thick as ash upon its wings, the tiny hairs upon its legs brushing the ball of her thumb. Its wings fluttered languidly, and the smell of hyacinths flowed into something else. The smell of rain-washed earth, of burning sand and the sea at Karpathos, of coriander and red sandalwood; the smell of autumn leaves and applewood burning in the chimneys at the Orphic Lodge.

"Oliver," she whispered, as she drew the butterfly to her face; then crushed it between her hands.

CHAPTER 17

Falling

We walked outside on the Mall, pausing to watch a magician who made a boy sharp-eyed and brown as a weasel disappear. The boy crawled beneath a rattan laundry basket scarcely large enough to hide him. The magician, a toothless man younger than I was, uttered some words in Hindi; when he lifted the basket, the boy was gone. Dylan and I inspected the packed earth, the laundry basket, the fringed edges of the silk tent: nothing.

"The Mysterious East," I said at last. We wandered on. After the airless inferno inside the museum, the Mall felt comfortable, although the temperature was well into the nineties. Dylan removed his tie and slung it around his neck; I took off my linen jacket and was glad that I'd gone bare-legged that day. Our museum IDs still were clipped to our breast pockets; apart from that, we might have been any two tourists goggling at the acrobats and sitar players and contortionists at play in the shadow of the Washington Monument.

"So, Boss," Dylan finally asked, "what do I do to earn my keep?"

I shrugged. "Not much." Summer interns weren't actually paid at all; the exceptional experience of working at the museum was supposed to be worth far more than any one person could possibly earn in the space of six short weeks. "To tell you the truth, interns don't actually *do* very much. At least mine never do. Laurie'll show you around the archives, I'll show you how the videodisc system works. I'm sure we can find some stuff to keep you busy. There's a new collection of photos that came in last week that needs to be cataloged; I'll get you started on that. But mostly just have a good time, take advantage of being here."

"I'm already doing that."

I blushed, glanced over to see if he was being smarmy. But no, Dylan had the same earnest open look as before. As a matter of fact, the way he was staring at me was pretty dopey: like a kid longing for a new skateboard or the latest Boink CD.

"So," I asked hurriedly, ducking into the shade of a great oak tree. "How's your mom?"

"My mom." Dylan kicked up a cloud of dust, flicked a strand of hair from his intense blue eyes. "Well, you know my mom."

"Actually, I don't. I haven't seen Angelica since—well, since before you were born. I really only knew her for a couple of months."

He stared at his feet. "I guess she's okay." He flashed me a crooked grin, a look that was so much like Oliver's I felt a stabbing at my breast. "To tell you the truth, *I* haven't seen her much since I've been born. My dad and I, we used to do a lot of stuff together. Riding, sailing, flying—my dad had a Cessna 150, he was gonna teach me to fly. But my mother—well, you know she's always been into all this strange stuff. Like digging up our place on Santorini, looking for tombs and artifacts. She's a real field archaeologist, at least she was until my father died and she started getting more into her books. I mean, she's a great mom and all. But I've always gone away to school, I *liked* going away to school; and so I didn't see her much except at vacations. And summertime she was always off on her digs, and Christmas we'd go see my grandfather . . ."

He leaned against the oak tree, staring across the long downward slope of green leading to the Tidal Basin, where little paddleboats like fat blue beetles swam through the water. "She's just one of these driven professional women you read about," he said at last with a sigh. "Over here, at least. In Italy you don't read much about them, because there aren't any. Not as many, at least." He fell silent again, gazing into the hazy distance.

"So," I said. So maybe it wasn't such a great idea to talk about Angelica. "So you like UCLA?"

He shrugged. "It's okay. It's a lot of driven professional students. I guess I'm just not as motivated as I should be, I dunno." He looked at me sideways and smiled. "I actually wanted to take the summer off and go cross-country with these friends of mine to Nantucket, but my mother had other plans. It was her idea to apply for this internship."

"Well, I'm glad you did," I said, and grinned. "Really."

"Me too."

His voice was sweet, with that hint of an accent and Angelica's theatrical phrasing. His glittering green-flecked eyes remained fixed on me. I wiped a bead of sweat from my nose.

This is insane, I thought. *I've known this kid for, what? an hour? ninety minutes? and already I'm totally wiped out by him.*

Although he is *incredibly fantastic-looking,* I told myself, like that was a good excuse.

Although he is exactly half my age, and I am his supervisor, and old enough to be his mother.

Shit, if I'd had my way with Oliver, I *would* have been his mother. I shook my head, feeling slightly delirious.

"You okay?"

I started. Dylan was just inches from my face, his sea blue eyes wide with concern. "Sweeney? You look a little—I dunno, sunstroked maybe. Maybe we should go inside—"

Gently he pushed the hair from my eyes. I felt as though I might faint.

I am losing my mind, I thought. *Or else this kid is losing his.*

"Uh, sure," I stammered. "We could duck in there—" I cocked my thumb at the Museum of American History. "—it's air-conditioned, we could just kind of cool off and decide what to do next."

"Sure. Here, let me take your bag—"

He reached for my briefcase but I tugged it from his hand. "That's okay, it's not heavy—"

"Really, I don't mind—"

"No, it's—"

I clutched my briefcase like it was the only thing keeping me from falling. "Right in here," I babbled, hurrying up the steps.

Inside we wandered through throngs of tourists gaping at the first ladies' gowns, Stanley Steamers, Fonzi's leather jacket, the nation's largest ball of string. We walked to where the doors opened onto Constitution Avenue and tourists crowded the gift shop and water fountains. All of a sudden I was noticing young girls—high school girls, college girls, mere children of twenty-five and -seven and thirty. All of them antic and colorful as guppies.

All of them younger than me.

The girls of summer everywhere and this poor kid was stuck with *me*, Electra on a coffee break.

But Dylan had inherited his mother's ability to confer invisibility upon his companions: no one noticed *me* at all. The girls saw only Dylan. He ignored them, doing his best to carry on a serious conversation with me, which was difficult since what we were trying to talk about was what the floors were made of:

"Marble, you think?"

"Maybe just marble-colored linoleum."

"Congoleum?"

"No, not linoleum, this is—"

This was nuts. We were acting like two people who were nervous because they were thinking about going to bed together, and I for one had always made it a policy not to sleep with someone until I had known him for at least twenty-four hours. Actually, in the last decade I hadn't had much cause to implement that policy, or any of the others I'd made up over the years. And yet here I was, stumbling along in a daze beside someone half my age, who, to his credit, seemed to be equally nonplussed by the situation.

Probably he's just embarrassed, I suddenly thought. The notion made my heart sink; but I knew it had to be true. He wanted to take off, meet some friends, *make* some friends, nice young people with tattoos and multiple body piercings; not hang around with a woman wearing sensible white tennis shoes and a Donna Karan suit.

"Listen, Dylan, do you want to go?"

We were outside now, balancing on the curb and feeling the last atoms of cool air plummet from our bodies onto the sweltering concrete. "There's really no reason for us to go back to the museum today, they won't get the a/c fixed till this evening and there's no way to work there without it. And I know you probably have stuff to do . . ."

Dylan stared at the sidewalk, his long hair draping one side of his face. When he glanced up at me a moment later he looked crushed.

"Well, no," he said. "I mean no, actually I don't. I don't know anyone here." He rubbed his nose and coughed self-consciously. "Actually, can I take you to dinner?"

"Dinner? It's only eleven *o'clock*."

"Lunch, then, can I take you to lunch?"

"Uh—"

"Coffee, we could get espresso somewhere?"

I started to say no, but then there was that earnest face—that earnest, *beautiful* face—and the earnest, beautiful body it was attached to, now leaning rather precariously from the curb into Constitution Avenue.

"Listen, you don't have to pay," he said, a desperate edge creeping into his voice. "I have my own Visa—"

I started to laugh. Trust Angelica to send her only child into the big scary world with his own Visa.

"Or we could—"

"Okay, okay!—let's go have lunch. Or espresso, or something. Only, no, you *can't* pay for me—even though you have your own Visa. *Christ*, Dylan, get out of the road, you're gonna get flattened by a Winnebago!"

I grabbed his arm as a land yacht roared past. For a moment we teetered on the edge of the curb, dust and smoke curling around us. He was tall enough to look down at me, he gripped my arm and held me tightly and I still hadn't let go of his hand. Very dimly I could hear the distant skirling of a sitar fading into the drone of traffic. Then Dylan was pulling me closer to him, and before I could yank away he had dipped his head to graze my cheek with his lips. He smelled of car exhaust and sweat, and the faintest breath of sandalwood.

"Wow! Sweeney. Thanks. But you'll have to tell me where we're going."

"Where we're going?" I swallowed, my mouth dry and my heart pounding like I'd just run a mile. "I guess—we'll go—well, somewhere that's *not* around here."

I looked over my shoulder at the museum. I unsnapped my ID and shoved it into a pocket, turned to Dylan and did the same to his. "Let's see. Uh, we'll go to—"

I frowned, staring out at the traffic, the tourists running to make the light. Then like a swallow lighting upon my shoulder it came to me.

Of course! Where else?!

I laughed. "We'll go," I said, grabbing his hand and pulling him after me into the crosswalk, "to Dumbarton Oaks."

———

We spent the entire afternoon there, until the gates closed at five. We wandered across the lawns and through the boxwood labyrinth; gazed into the shallow pool with its mosaic of Bacchus and the grape arbor nearby; shook our heads at the grim remains of the bamboo garden that had flourished for so many years and had finally flowered, as bamboos do once a century, and then died. We ended at the *trompe l'oeil* wooden gate depicting a fountain, its splashing waters done in precious stones and mother-of-pearl, then found our way back up a narrow flagstoned path. We stopped to watch a small girl dart beneath a grove of miniature fruit trees, plucking kumquats and running to give them to her mother, a very proper Georgetown matron who promptly hid them in her Coach bag.

We wound up on the stone ramparts overlooking the pool. Dylan gazed longingly into its depths: a lozenge of purest turquoise shot with glints of gold, like the pool in the garden of the Hesperides, like the pool in a dream.

"Does anyone ever swim in it?"

"Maybe visiting Harvard horticultural fellows. I've never seen anyone."

"It's so beautiful. It reminds me of the pool at Keftiu—"

Keftiu. I gazed across to where wisteria bearded the high stone walls opposite. Where had I heard that before?

"What's Keftiu?"

"My mother's house on Crete. She always says it's her favorite place in the world. I think sometimes that's why she married my father," he added softly. He rested his chin against the stone, his blue eyes wistful.

Keftiu. And I remembered the butterfly I had shown to Maggie that morning. The word had been part of its name.

"What does it mean?"

"It's what the Egyptians called ancient Crete. *Keftiu*, or sometimes just *Kefti*."

I was silent. Then I asked, "Why do you think it's why she married your father?"

"Because he always said she loved that place more than she loved him. And I believe him. They met at a party on a yacht moored off the north coast of Crete. He took her to his place the next day—it's not far from Knossos, and she'd never been there. She wanted to see the temple restoration, and she wanted to see Keftiu."

His voice cracked as he went on, "He—he told me once that he had never seen anything like the look she got on her face, the first time she saw his villa there. It really *is* beautiful, it's right on the coast and there are ruins all around it, and at night you can hear all these wild birds, and the wind on the water. But my father said that he had never seen anyone look as beautiful as my mother did when she first saw Keftiu. He said that from then on, all he wanted was to get her to look at him like that, just once."

I smiled, but when I glanced at Dylan I saw that his face was sad.

"And did she?" I asked softly.

"I don't know. My father never told me. He didn't like it out there as much as she did. There's no running water or air-conditioning, it's rather primitive. He never wanted to stay very long—he preferred our villa in Florence, or the Milan apartment.

"But Mom loved it. She never wanted to leave. But after he died there, and her father . . . she's only gone back a few times since then."

We turned and left the pool, walking down to the formal gardens, where swallowtails and tiny hairskipper butterflies fluttered everywhere, so that it looked as though someone had shaken all the rose petals from their beds. The air had a sweet, powdery smell. Beneath our feet the grass was lush and damp from hidden sprinklers. A woman held a baby out to admire a huge rose, and the baby laughed. For a long time we wandered in silence, Dylan stopping now and then to watch the butterflies on the roses, or bending to sniff delicately at a *dianthus* blossom like a fragrant pink spider.

At last I said, "How did they die? Or—never mind, you don't have to—"

"No, that's okay. It was a while ago. We were at Keftiu, my grandfather had come for the winter and they were out sailing, my father and him. It was kind of strange. My grandfather was this great sailor, and my father was too, he never had any trouble in the water. He used to take us sailing at night, in the middle of winter, anytime; but he was careful, he'd never go out if there was any danger, if there was a storm brewing or something. And he was very careful with my grandfather, because Grappa was so old—almost ninety.

"But anyway, they went out, just for a few hours. It was morning, a beautiful perfect clear day, there was nothing on the weather about a storm or anything. Then out of nowhere this gale came up—there were people out on the water who saw it happen, they said it was like these clouds just boiled over the horizon and overtook them and that was it. Their boat capsized, they couldn't get to their life jackets, and—"

He stopped. He was staring at the broken stalk of a yellow daylily, the flower's long petals wilted in the sun.

"Oh Dylan," I whispered. "I'm so sorry. I shouldn't have asked, I'm sorry—"

He turned to me and shook his head. "It just makes me sad, that's all. They never recovered the bodies. Some people—friends of my father, who never really liked my mother—they said it was like in *Rebecca*. That Hitchcock movie . . ."

I looked away, stunned, and pretended to examine the broken lily. It wasn't the notion that Angelica might have killed someone. I could imagine that; I could imagine almost anything of her. That golden faithless creature, beautiful and amoral as a fox, having another man act as father to Oliver's child (and had her husband ever known? had he even suspected? had Dylan?), dreaming her mad dreams of apocalypse in her million-dollar houses . . .

But killing her own *father*? One of the *Benandanti*?

"I—I—"

Suddenly Dylan grabbed me by the shoulders, so hard that I gasped.

"'*Rebecca? I hated Rebecca*!'" he hissed, then laughed sharply as he let me go, his face bright red. "Forget I ever said that! You must hate me, for having said that about—"

"No—really, of course not! It's—I should never have brought it up. It's none of my business, I don't even know you—"

"But I *want* you to know me," he said, with that same wistful earnestness. He took a deep breath, smoothed his hair from his face, and stared at his feet before looking up at me sideways. "I know this might sound strange. I know I just met you this morning and I know that you're—well, I know that you're older, okay? But—

"But this is *really weird*, Sweeney. I just have this amazing feeling about you. This incredible feeling that I *know* you. I mean, *really* know you." He tugged imploringly at my wrist, his eyes wide and beseeching. "Does that sound ridiculous?"

He sighed and gazed at the neatly clipped lawn, then shoved his hands disconsolately into his pockets. "Shit. I guess I should have gone to Nantucket."

I stared at him: his lanky body slung into its chinos and neat white shirt as into a prison uniform, the late afternoon sun glinting off that tiny constellation of gold and silver in one ear, his long hair slipping from its ponytail to spill across his shoulders. In the golden light he looked like someone who was melting, a wild boy poured into one careful upright mold but now slowly reverting to his true self. Not Angelica's Good Son, with his museum internship and Visa card and italicized list of contacts and places to go; but a wild boy, like Oliver himself had been. Maybe not truly crazy as Oliver was, but fey enough to be talking to me like this. Fey enough to sense the same eerie quality that had colored our afternoon together, that made me so reluctant to leave.

Unless, of course, it was all my imagination. Unless he was so much Angelica's child that she had put him up to this, to fit into some mad scheme of hers that I couldn't even begin to imagine.

But Dylan didn't look like he was playing a part. He looked stricken and lost, almost angry.

"No," I said at last. "You're supposed to be here, Dylan. I don't know why, but I feel it too. You—you remind me of someone I knew once, a long time ago. Someone I—somebody I was in love with."

"Oliver." The word was barely a whisper, but whatever anger had been welling inside of him spilled now into his eyes. "You just never got over him."

"Yes," I said, abashed. "How did you know?"

"Because my mother said that after he killed himself your life was ruined. And just now you had this look . . ."

"My life was *ruined*?"

". . . like maybe you were thinking about what it would have been like, not to have thrown your whole life away."

"*My* life? She said *my life* was ruined?"

"Well, you never got married. Dr. Dvorkin says you've been living alone in his carriage house for almost ten years—"

"*Eight* years! And I didn't *want* to get married. I mean, I could have married a lot of guys—"

"Oh yeah? Isn't that against the law?"

I stopped, my hands clenched at my sides, and realized that I was furious; that I was ready to pop him one. But then I looked up and saw him starting to laugh.

"Not *too* defensive, huh?" He shook his head. "*I* always thought it was romantic. I mean, nobody ever killed herself for *me*."

"He didn't kill himself for *me*, Dylan! He was crazy! Nowadays they'd probably have diagnosed him as some kind of latent schizophrenic. Back then we all just thought it was too much drugs."

"Well, still, no one ever carried a torch for *me* for twenty years—"

"Nineteen, kiddo. And give 'em time." I sighed in exasperation, but just then a woman in a white caftan strolled down between the rows of flowers, ringing a small brass bell.

"We're closing," she called in a low voice. "Five o'clock, we're closing." And passed on, her bell sending its cool clear notes into the greenery.

Like the hidden revelers in some Shakespearean romance, figures suddenly appeared from between stands of foxgloves, from beneath staked towers of delphiniums and the fragrant clouds of roses. We followed them to the main gate, and headed down the gravel drive to R Street.

At the gate the woman with the bell stood, smiling and nodding as we all filed out. When at last Dylan and I passed through she called a final, "Good evening." Then she pulled the gates closed. A lone guard locked the great curved iron arch. Dylan and I stood blinking in the golden sunlight of the street. I felt as though I had dreamed the entire afternoon: the honeyed light, the smell of roses and honeysuckle, Dylan himself. I yawned, rubbing my eyes. When I glanced around, all the other visitors had disappeared. We were once more alone.

"Well, I guess we could think about dinner now," I suggested. "Or cocktails. It's five."

"I'm not old enough to drink."

"But you do?"

He grinned. "On special occasions."

"Well, consider this a *very* special occasion—"

We walked down to Wisconsin Avenue and caught a cab to Mamma Desta's, a dinky little restaurant in a dicey part of town that had the best Ethiopian food in the city. The place was little more than a storefront with a handful of Formica tables lit by fluorescent lights, and two ceiling fans spinning dizzyingly fast overhead. We shoved into a corner table and Mamma Desta herself came out and took our orders, a tiny cheerful woman with frizzy greying hair and a bloodstained chef's apron. We ate with our fingers, food so hot we could watch beads of sweat pop out on our cheeks. T*ibs, zilzil wat*, bits of spiced meat and vegetable and sauce sopped up by spongy thick white pancakes that looked like foam insulation. We drank *tej*, sweet honey wine served in globular glasses like alembics. I had never been able to knock back more than one or two of these—too sweet, the taste of honey too unfamiliar—but that evening it went down like water, after all that hot food and the unsettling experience of meeting Dylan.

"My mother says that in ancient Crete they embalmed their dead in honey," he remarked, rolling a bit of *injera* between his fingers. "They'd curl up the corpses and put them into big clay jars and bury them."

"Ugh. Thanks for sharing, Dylan."

"And sometimes to torture a prisoner, they'd stick him in a vat of olive oil and leave him there, so eventually his flesh would just melt away. And they raised vipers, and used their venom as a hallucinogen—"

"*Dylan*. I am trying to *eat*."

"I thought you were an anthropologist. I thought you'd *like* to know these things."

"I'm an *armchair* anthropologist. I like to look at pictures of colorful peoples, I like to eat in exotic restaurants I can reach by cab from my home, I like to purchase my voodoo masks from The Artifactory and get my clothes at Banana Republic."

"So I guess watching dawn break over the Great Pyramid at Cheops is out, huh?"

"Dylan, I don't even have a passport. I've *never* had a passport. I mean, your mother—she leads the life I always wanted to lead. She's been to all these places, she's unearthed things in Crete and Italy and god knows where. And me, it's hard for me to find my shoes in the morning. She has all these theories about civilization, and *I'm* a civil servant."

I picked up my globe of *tej* and smiled bitterly. "I mean, I *wanted* to do the stuff she does, but somehow I never did. Sometimes I feel like the prince in one of those Russian fairy tales—you know, the guy whose soul is stolen by the witch, and he spends his life in a coma while Baba Yaga is out there watching dawn break at Cheops."

Dylan was silent. I thought I must have angered him, talking about Angelica like that; but suddenly I didn't care anymore. I was tired and drunk and probably had sunstroke, I was exhausted by the effort of trying to carry on a conversation with someone who not only didn't remember the day Kennedy died, he didn't remember the day Sid Vicious died. "I think it's time to call it a night, kiddo," I said, and motioned for the check.

Outside it was dusk, cars and passersby and crumbling buildings all cloaked in a blue-black haze. The sky was like one of those paintings on velvet, violet streaked with yellow and red, lurid yet also soft, and the smells of cumin and cayenne and coriander spilled out into the street with us, mingling with the putrid scents of rotting gingko fruit and stagnant water.

"We're going to have a hard time getting a cab here," I said, glancing down the street. "It's not a great neighborhood—"

"*I'll* get you a cab," Dylan said. He stepped to the curb, his effort at gallantry somewhat marred by his stumbling gait. I started to say something about walking over a few blocks, but he had already raised his arm.

As though he had summoned it from the underworld, a Yellow Cab came roaring up, its front wheel scoring the edge of the curb as Dylan and I jumped back.

"Step inside, step inside," called a rumbling voice.

Dylan looked at me and burst out laughing. "Wow! I'll have to try that in Rome sometime—" He yanked the cab door open and gestured extravagantly. *"Après-toi, mademoiselle."*

I slid into the cab, the seats warm as skin, the air smelling like Pine-Sol. Dylan sat beside me, so close our thighs touched. A broad-shouldered figure turned to look back at us, his hands resting lightly on the wheel.

"Where to, my man?"

I gasped.

"Where're we going, Sweeney?" asked Dylan. But I couldn't say anything, only stare at the cabdriver, his license dangling from the rearview mirror.

Yellow Cab Number 393, with its neatly patched seat backs and glove compartment cracked open ever-so-slightly, so that you could just make out the gleaming barrel of a gun inside, hidden in a nest of yellowing newspaper clippings covered with shadowy images of Cassius Clay and Sugar Ray and a square-jawed young black man beautiful enough to be a movie star.

"My man?" the driver repeated gently.

It was Handsome Brown.

"Uh—the Hill, we're going to 19 Ninth Street Northeast—"

"No—" Dylan suddenly leaned forward. "Take us down around the Washington Monument. Just drive around for a while; I've never been here before."

Handsome Brown looked at me, his eyebrows raised. "Is that what the lady wants?" he rumbled.

"Yes," Dylan said, before I could protest. He took my hands, pulled me gently but irresistibly to him. "So you never saw the pyramids," he said. "So we'll go look at an obelisk."

"Fine," I said hoarsely.

"Very good, very good. I'll have to charge you extra zones, my man, taking the grand tour like that."

"Whatever you say," said Dylan.

He took us through that warren of back streets and narrow alleys that only Handsome Brown had ever known, labyrinthine precincts of the city that I had seen years before, with Oliver dozing in the cab beside me and an unfinished bottle of Pernod in my lap. Embattled tenements behind their chain link fences; neat little row houses where old women sat fanning themselves with copies of *The Watchtower*; side streets rank with the gingko's shattered fruit.

Then we were cruising down Embassy Row, past mansions with battlements and minarets and towers, fake Tudor facades and Moorish splendors and crepe myrtles blooming everywhere in explosive bursts of magenta and rose. Handsome Brown said nothing, only turned up the radio. It was tuned to a station that played nothing but the lushest most soul-melting ballads, Al Green and Teddy Pendergrass and Prince wailing heartbreak like the world was going to end at midnight. Every now and then Handsome Brown's face would fill the rearview mirror as he glanced back at us, unsmiling but his eyes keen as blades.

I stared out my window, biting my lip and trying more than anything not to see him there beside me, though I could feel him and if the music died, I could hear his snores and his even breathing. There was a ghost there in the purple darkness, his long hair slipping around his shoulders like black rain and his white shirt undone at the throat, there were *two* ghosts—Oliver and myself, circling the city forever while outside the night deepened and distant laughter rose from the Tidal Basin—

The Beautiful Ones, they hurt you every time

I felt as though my heart would break, my eyes filled with tears even as I smiled bitterly—so this was what it was like to get old, you rode around in taxicabs and cried when you heard Prince on the radio . . .

"Sweeney," I heard a low voice whisper. *"I'll love you next time. I promise."*

And silently I wept. Because of course there would never be a next time. There had never even been a first time; and I moved closer to the window so that Dylan wouldn't see me crying.

After a minute or two I stopped. I wiped my eyes and hoped there wasn't mascara all over my face. We were downtown. Cab 393 slipped between the other cabs flowing past the White House, like caravels around a royal barge, then headed for the Mall.

"It's so beautiful," Dylan said softly. "And it's so *small.* Even the worst parts of it only go on for a few blocks."

"It's worse now than it used to be—now you've got all these crack houses, and gangs, people getting shot everywhere. It's just different now." I sighed. "I guess everything is different now."

The cab moved smoothly past the Monument, the museums in the distance and above all of it the Capitol, the City on the Hill. I could feel Dylan beside me, his warmth and the sweet soapy smell of his sweat. I stared resolutely out the window, pretending interest in the tourists in front of the Lincoln Memorial, gazing at the great sad giant entombed within.

"Maybe it's good that it's different," Dylan whispered. "Maybe it's better . . ."

He put his hand on my shoulder and gently turned me to him. For an instant I tried to resist, then gave up. I was staring into his sea blue eyes, his sunburned face spangled with green and crimson from the traffic lights outside. He wasn't smiling, there was nothing mocking in his gaze, nothing playful at all. He was staring at me as though he had never seen me before; he was looking at me as I imagined Angelica had looked upon Keftiu so long ago. As though he saw something in me long dreamed of, something he had hardly dared hope to find. I could feel his other hand on my thigh, his fingers burning through the coarse linen, his fingers trembling as they pulled the fabric taut, and then he drew me to him and I was gone. My fingers tangled in his long hair and I could feel him all around me, his arms pulling me close until I could hear the roaring of his heart as he kissed me and I wasn't thinking of Oliver anymore, I wasn't thinking how different we both were, how young he was or who his mother had been, I wasn't thinking of anything at all except for Dylan, Dylan, and how I would have waited another twenty years for him, a hundred, a thousand. I would wait forever for him, now that I knew he was there.

CHAPTER 18

A Meeting

Baby Joe met her in a Manhattan bar called Chumley Peckerwood's, a garishly lit franchised strip club where a visiting executive on an expense account could drop a grand for a steak and a few margaritas and a blond lap dancer from Massapequa named Tiffany Gayle.

"Hey, Annie," Baby Joe murmured, hugging her. "God, you feel good."

"Baby Joe . . ." She was surprised at how quickly the tears came; just as quickly she blinked them back. "I'm—I'm so sorry I missed Hasel's funeral. I was touring and I couldn't take off—I'm not big enough that I can get away with that—"

He made a dismissive gesture, slid into the booth, and sniffed her club soda. "Ugh." Grimacing, he beckoned a waitress. "Double vodka martini. And bring her one too."

Annie started to protest but he waved her off. "It'll put some hair on your head. So. Angie's found you."

Annie felt her chest contract. "How did you know?" She sank into her corner of the booth, shrinking like Alice into burgundy leather.

"'Cause you wouldn't be caught dead in a place like this, unless you were drunk or crazy or in very deep shit." He took his drink from the waitress, cast her an appraising look as she handed Annie her martini, then downed his in two gulps. "And I know you don't drink, and you didn't used to be crazy. So it's got to be mondo poo-poo. And I'm thinking it's got to be Angie."

Baby Joe slid his empty glass back onto the tray and glanced at the waitress. "Two more." He turned back to Annie. "I'm waiting."

"We-ell."

She took a deep breath. Every few months Baby Joe called her, but Annie hadn't actually *seen* him in years. He'd grown into an imposing figure: big and broad-shouldered, with a body that should have run to fat but so far had not. His hair hung to his shoulders, straight and very, very black. His deconstructed suit jacket was black, too, except for where the lining showed, as were his trousers and the T-shirt that read JELLY BISHOPS in tiny white letters. A pair of cheap plastic sunglasses was shoved into the thick hair above his forehead. He looked like a bellicose young *capo* in whatever the Filipino analog of the Mafia might be; though there was a weariness to his gaze she didn't recall, a sorrow she could see mapped in the lines around his dark eyes and mouth.

It's Hasel, thought Annie, and felt ashamed that she hadn't shown more grief over the death of their old friend. She stared at her untouched drink.

"Well, you're right," she said at last. "I *am* in trouble."

She gestured at the dark-paneled walls and crimson lighting behind them, the stage where a young woman in high heels and a peacock feather writhed to a synth-pop version of the theme from *Gigantor.* "This place, I heard about it from a girlfriend and I thought it'd be good cover for me."

Baby Joe's eyebrow arched. He reached for her martini and sipped it thoughtfully. "Trouble. Is it Angie?"

"I think so."

"Huh." He finished her first drink just as the waitress returned with his second. His expression remained impassive, but his eyes narrowed very slightly. "So. Our Lady of Perpetual Motion has decided to get in touch with all her old college chums."

Annie nodded.

Baby Joe reached into his pocket for a pack of cigarettes and tapped one out. "Tell me about it."

"There was a murder—two nights ago. In Provincetown—"

Baby Joe bared his teeth in a smile. "'The Eviscerator. ' I saw the file photos."

"I saw it in the flesh."

"You *saw* it?"

"I nearly *was* it. This rave out at Herring Cove. A bunch of Angelica's followers were there, performing some kind of ritual. And somebody must've slipped me something, 'cause it was like I was *someplace else*. Like I had some kind of out-of-body experience. I know for all you guys from the Divine, that would be, like, all in a day's work, but let me tell you, I was *freaked* . . .

"And then I turned around and saw *him*. This kid, laid out on the floor like a turkey on the day after Thanksgiving. And these geeks who killed *him*, they start coming after *me*, only this—well, somebody scared 'em off."

"You go to the cops?"

"No."

"How come?"

She shrugged, glancing around uneasily. "I don't know."

Baby Joe rolled his eyes. "You know, every movie I see, somebody witnesses a horrible murder, but they don't go to the cops. And I'm like, *Why don't they go to the cops!* So, why don't you—"

Annie started to slide from the booth, furious. "This is not a fucking *joke*, Baby Joe! If you're not gonna—"

"Hey! *Hija*, sit—" His hand clamped around hers and he pulled her into the seat beside him. "It was a rhetorical question. So you saw a bunch of Barbie's playmates waste this kid and you figure they'll pin it on you. Okay, I'll buy it. Hey, if Angie's involved, I'll buy *anything*. So now what?"

Annie glowered, her buzz cut sticking out in tiny spikes around her pale face. She looked even more like a feisty kid than she had back at the Divine. Feisty, but scared. When she didn't say anything Baby Joe tilted his head toward her second martini.

"Drink that. It's costing the paper thirty bucks."

Annie stared at him belligerently. Suddenly her hand shot out; she grabbed the glass and drank it, then gestured for the waitress to bring another.

"Okay," she said, her eyes watering. She turned sideways to face Baby Joe. "What do you remember about Oliver's death?"

"Oliver?" Baby Joe looked taken aback. "Oliver Crawford?"

"Yeah. Did you go to his funeral?"

"No."

"Know anybody who did?"

Baby Joe stared at her, brows furrowed. "No. Hasel and I wanted to go, but we got a call from Professor Warnick. He said the Crawfords didn't want anyone there but immediate family."

"Did you ever actually *meet* his immediate family?"

Baby Joe frowned. "Do you mean do I think they *exist*? I know they do, my brother was—"

"No—I meant, did you see any of them *then*. After Oliver supposedly jumped out the window of the hospital."

Baby Joe was silent. The waitress brought Annie's drink, disappeared into a flood of ruby light. Baby Joe looked at Annie holding her double martini in both hands, like a child drinking a glass of milk. "You think Angelica killed him?" he said at last.

"I don't know *what* I think." Annie sipped her martini, made a face. "This really costs thirty bucks?"

"Yeah."

"No wonder your newspaper's in trouble." She shuddered. "Listen. I want you to do me a favor."

Baby Joe raised an eyebrow.

"Labrys canceled the rest of my tour. Angelica called them. I don't know how she did it—like maybe she pulled Fiona from a flaming plane wreck once and I never knew about it. But Fiona called me a few nights ago and the tour's off. Angelica Furiano threatened them with a lawsuit, some bullshit about me making a statement to the press that Angelica was involved with that murder in P-town. Only I never *talked* to the press! I never talked to anyone except Helen and now you. But unless I go along with her, Labrys pulls the plug on me, MTV dumps my video, and the masters for my next album disappear somewhere between here and Iona Studios."

Baby Joe whistled. "Sounds like you're fucked, *hija*."

"Tell me about it. So I'm going underground for a little bit." She sighed and leaned back into the booth, her cheeks bright with a false rosy glow from the martini. "See, I'm thinking that maybe Angelica'll just kind of forget about me. Like maybe she just wanted to scare me; so *Whoo!* I'm scared." Annie fluttered her hands in front of her face, then cocked her head. "Think it'll work?"

"No." Baby Joe looked at the empty stage, his expression remote. When the music blared out again and another girl pranced onto the platform, he ducked his head to reach inside his jacket. "Here. You better read this."

It was Hasel's letter, and the worn obituary notices from the Charlottesville paper. Annie scanned them quickly.

"What *is* this?" Her face went dead white. "Baby Joe . . . ?"

"It's what happened to Hasel," he said softly.

"But—is it true? I mean, this stuff he wrote you about Angelica?"

"*I* think it's true, *hija*."

"B-but—but *why*?" Annie's voice broke and she looked away. "Why would she kill *Hasel*?"

"Why would Angelica kill anyone?" Before she could protest, he lit his cigarette and took a drag, leaned over and slid the pages from her hand. "You know what this is, *hija*?" He waved the papers at her and put them back inside his jacket.

Annie shook her head, hardly seeing him at all. "What?"

"This is some bad fucking fallout from the *Benandanti*."

"The *Benandanti*? But Angelica *hated* them, she told me! All that patriarchal shit—she was like, way ahead of the curve on that," Annie said, and in spite of herself smiled wryly. "She'd *never* go along with the *Benandanti*."

"I'm not saying she went *along* with them. I'm saying she's coming *back* at them. You ever read her books? No?" He looked surprised. "I would've thought you'd be into that shit—"

"Why? Because I'm a lesbian? Please." Annie's glare softened into curiosity. "So what about her books?"

"They're a fucking blueprint for a new religion, that's what. *Dios ka naman!* She's got women from here to Bombay, reading this stuff, making these *círculos*—" He inscribed a circle in the air, looking as though he'd spit into it. "—these, like, *covens. Talagang bruja!* When I first read her stuff, I couldn't believe it—I mean, I couldn't believe anyone would buy into it. Goddess rippers! Like Witchcraft 101. But now . . ."

His black eyes grew distant, unfocused; looking at him, Annie shivered. *The Benandanti*. For the first time in years she thought about Baby Joe being one of them. She swallowed, her mouth tasting bitterly of vermouth.

"Not any more, *hija*," he said softly. "I'm like Angie: I got out. But what she's doing—*Dios ko*, this is some serious shit! I been hearing about it for a while, at the paper. We get all the crazies, you know? Wife beaters, guys who want to stick it to little girls, but this is crazier even than *that*. These guys call us, saying their wives and girlfriends are into some kind of cult, you know—get together with the gals once a month over on the Upper East Side or wherever, and we should be writing about *that* instead of trade sanctions against Japan. Girlfriends dancing in the moonlight, snake handling, calling up demons, whatever. These guys talk about blood, they say the women're up to something weird. But you know—guys like *that*, they *always* think women are up to something weird. So who pays attention?

"But then I start to hear other stuff. Guy I know, covers homicide, starts talking about these ritual killings. Bones alongside the Major Deegan Expressway, this fire circle up by the Cloisters. A snuff video, with all these women and some guy who gets it at the end, only no one ever reports him missing. Stuff like that.

"Then some *bodies* start to show up. *Mutilated* bodies. No single MO, the killings are all over the map, but a lot of the victims are homeless men. Sometimes homeless women. And a *lot* of kids. I mean, like runaway boys who're hustling or whatever. Some people say it's *Santeria*; maybe even Anton LaVey's people. But then the *Santeria* folks say No way, this isn't them at all, and even the other guys, the *Satanists*, get pissed off! That's when *I* started to take a professional interest.

"Then I hear about something out West. One of Angelica's bodyguards is, like, *eaten by killer ants*! On Angie's ranch, with Angie supposedly asleep back in *la casa*. Then there's all these unsolved murders of runaways and homeless people out in Arizona and L.A. and Seattle, and your acid test up in Provincetown, some dumb kid on smart drugs ends up wearing his small intestine for a necktie. Now you look me in the eye and tell me there's not something weird going on."

She tried to look him in the eye, but Baby Joe only stared at the stage, where two women were embracing and simulating orgasm. Annie lowered her head into her hands and ran her fingers across her buzz-cut scalp.

"And you really think Angelica's behind it all?"

Baby Joe turned back to her. "Yeah," he said. "I do."

"But why? I mean, I know she's got *something* to do with it—I *saw* her, when I was hallucinating, or—well, whatever I was doing. But she can't be in all these places at once. Can she?" Annie added, a little desperately.

"'Let us placate her in advance by assuming the cannibalistic worst,'" recited Baby Joe softly.

"What?"

"Just something I read. Listen, Annie—"

He took her hand, her small fingers disappearing beneath his. "Something really strange is going on—I don't mean just with you, or me, or Hasel, but with everything. The whole world, maybe.

"You remember how Angie used to talk—all that goddess stuff, all those books Warnick gave her? Well, I read some of them too—back then, I mean. And I *saw* what happened at the Orphic Lodge that night, before—well, before Oliver jumped—"

"And?"

"And—well, what if something *really happened* to them? What if Angie *did* something—what if that night, her and Oliver *both* did something, and—well, what if they woke something. Something they shouldn't be screwing with."

"Something like—what?" Annie asked warily.

"Christ, Annie! You were at the Divine, you *know* there's a whole world of stuff out there that nobody else talks about! You weren't supposed to find out, and I walked away from it, and maybe Oliver killed himself because of it—but *it's still there*."

Annie tried to draw her hand away, but Baby Joe only clutched it tighter.

"It's still there, Annie! You know it is! Look what's happened to the world since that night at the Divine—only what, nineteen years ago? People always say how the past looks better than whatever we have now—but *Dios ko*, things really *have* gotten worse! There's all these horrible little wars, there's this horrible plague that's killing us and everyone's pretending not to notice. Things happen like Chernobyl and Three Mile Island, and we're supposed to just forget. Men go around hunting women and children like they were deer, and women fall on the men with knives. And on top of *that*, the whole fucking planet is just sort of *dying*. I mean, we got earthquakes, and fires, and floods, and droughts and blizzards and—well, *everything*! It's like the pregame show for the apocalypse!"

His voice rose as Annie continued to look at him with a stony expression. "Don't you see, Annie? This is *it*—and whatever it is, Angelica's not just *part* of it. Angelica *is* it. I mean, for two thousand years Christians have been talking about the Second Coming, about Jesus and the saints and all that shit . . . but what if there could be a *different* kind of Second Coming?"

"But why is she killing *us*?" Annie tried to keep her voice from quavering. "We were her friends! Why did Oliver have to die, and Hasel? Hasel would never hurt anyone! And me, they tried to kill *me*—"

"Maybe to her it's not like killing. I mean, if somehow this goddess has been reincarnated as Angelica." Baby Joe laughed, a soft ominous giggle. "Maybe she's trying to *save* us—keep us from seeing what comes next. Maybe she thinks she's doing her friends a *favor*."

For several minutes they sat without talking. Dancers walked on and off the stage behind them, sweat and glitter silvering the air in their wake. Finally Annie asked, "What about Sweeney? You're in touch with her—does she know?"

"I told her about Hasel. And she knows about Angelica—I mean she knows that Angelica's come back. She saw her on TV a week or so ago, some talk show."

"But this other stuff? These—" Annie raked her fingernails across the table's surface. "You know," she ended brokenly.

Baby Joe dropped his cigarette on the floor and let it burn there. "She knows some. Hasel's letter, and I faxed her some other things. Articles." Glitter and grey ash sifted over him; he waved it away and said, "I've tried calling her this week but she's never at the museum. Which is strange, 'cause I don't think she's taken a vacation in five years. When I call her at home I just keep getting her machine."

He fell silent. Annie couldn't meet his eyes: they were so black he looked stoned or crazy drunk, and ferociously intense. She turned instead to gaze at the stage, where two women caressed each other with luminous violet talons. The mirrored floor beneath them was streaked with sweat and god knows what else. One of them arched her back so that her blond mane swept the floor. Her spike heel impaled a twenty-dollar bill, and she laughed.

"Fucking shit." Annie swore beneath her breath and looked away. The sight of them sickened her, and the sound of the men watching, the way their drunken voices got husky and boyish at once. And their smell, that almost imperceptible musk of—what? Sweat and semen and whiskey-fueled hope, she guessed; then realized it was Baby Joe she could smell, the oily taint of vodka on his skin and pungent tobacco on his breath. Without wanting to Annie cringed, thinking of her old friend sitting beside her with an erection, his eyes fixed on the stage.

It almost makes you think they get what they deserve . . .

She recoiled in horror at the thought.

"What?" Baby Joe put a hand on her shoulder and started to his feet, looking around with that same fierce gaze. "You see someone, *hija?*"

At his touch she jumped, her skin prickling. But it was only Baby Joe. Sweet rude Baby Joe, with his Peter Lorre giggle and nicotine-stained fingers, his angry gaze directed at some imagined enemy out there in the strip club.

He's being protective, Annie thought with amazed tenderness, *protective of* me!

"N-nothing . . . She stared past him at the women onstage, their motions no longer grotesque or crude but merely pathetic, even childish. Suddenly she laughed.

"What?" Baby Joe demanded, but Annie could only point. *"What?"*

"Just the idea," she finally gasped through her laughter.

"*What* idea?" Baby Joe stared at her suspiciously.

"That Angelica could take over the world. That she could make us all afraid of each other—afraid enough to—"

She reached for his hand; but at that moment a shadow fell across the table. With a small cry Annie looked up. Baby Joe's back stiffened against the booth's leather seat, but then Annie exclaimed in relief.

"Justine! Jeez, you scared me."

"Ah-nee!" a lilting voice sang out. "I'm sorry I'm late."

"It's okay, Baby Joe." Annie scooted across the seat to make room. "This is Justine. She's a friend of mine. I asked her to meet us here."

Above them towered a six-and-a-half-foot Caribe beauty, her long black hair oiled and twisted into corkscrews, her full lips and high cheekbones dusted with silver powder. She wore a shocking pink sheath slit to her thighs, and over that a pink rubber girdle, and pink rubber platform shoes with tiny silver starfish embedded in them. A zircon studded one of her very white front teeth.

"Mr. Malabar. What a pleasure. I *enjoy* your writing in the *Beacon*." Her deep voice was French-inflected, luscious as fine chocolate. Her hand folded around Baby Joe's, larger and stronger than his, studded with rings and smelling of Obsession perfume. "Although you were very *unkind* to poor Miss Hyde Park last week, *cette femme maudite*! What can you have been thinking? I saw her show and it left me in tears. *Je pleurais."*

Justine dabbed an eye with a ruby-pointed finger, then smiled as she gently slapped Annie's cheek. "And *you*! I haven't seen you since Wigstock, except on TV. And now you have troubles with *voudon*?"

Annie glanced from Baby Joe to Justine, who were eyeing each other with polite wariness.

"Um, well . . ." Annie cleared her throat. Justine was really Helen's friend. Annie had only met her once before; she'd forgotten how imposing she was. "Justine, I need you to help me find someone. Someone special."

"In *here*?" Justine swept the room with a disdainful glare. "*Chérie,* you will need a Geiger counter to find someone special here."

"No, not here. I don't *know* where, exactly."

"Uh-huh." Justine rolled her eyes. She leaned over to pluck a cigarette from Baby Joe's pack, then slid into the booth beside Annie. "Girl problems, Annie?"

"Sort of." Annie looked at Baby Joe. "Now, I know this is going to sound crazy, but . . ."

She told them about the rave. Her vision—if that's what it was—of ritual sacrifice and the eerily beautiful demon in the boathouse, Angelica's role in the killing, the attempt to slay Annie herself, and then the phone call early the next morning, when Annie learned that Angelica had successfully derailed her tour. Finally, she told them of the woman who had saved her.

"And *that* freaked me as much as the rest of it. Maybe more." Annie leaned back in the booth and tugged at the collar of her tuxedo shirt. "God, I'm exhausted." She turned to Justine, who was listening with great seriousness, her dark eyes wide. "And I can't believe I'm *telling* you guys this. I'd think I hallucinated it all, except I know that kid is dead. And I know a strange woman brought flowers to me after my show that night. Patrick saw her, and Helen saw the flowers, and I recognized her—"

Baby Joe shook his head. "You *sure* about that, Annie?"

"No. I'm *not* sure. It was dark, I was scared to death, and messed up—I mean, they must have slipped me *something,* for me to see all that crazy shit! But I'm pretty certain. I got a good look, and . . ."

Her voice trailed off. She stared miserably down at the floor. "Maybe I'm just going nuts."

Justine shook her head. "Uh-uh. *I* believe you. Things like that, they happen to me all the time. Except for the black *gardon* with a face." She shuddered, wiping her mouth with a cocktail napkin and examining the lipstick stain as though it were an omen. "Now you said you have a photo for me? Because Justine knows a lot of people, but she is not *psychique*."

"Yeah. Sorry." From her knapsack Annie withdrew an envelope, opened it carefully, and removed a black-and-white photo, brown-stained and curling around the edges. "It's just an old Polaroid. But it's the only one I have."

"Hmmm." Justine squinted as Baby Joe peered over her shoulder, looking like he wanted to snatch the photo from her hand. "Well, you are right, it is not very good. But—"

"Who took that picture?" demanded Baby Joe.

Annie looked annoyed. "I don't remember. We were at a Halloween party. I had a life too, you know."

"Mes enfants!" Justine shook a finger at Baby Joe. She pursed her lips and stared at the photo for another moment, then slid it into a small plastic reticule hanging from her waist. "*Tant pis:* not someone I know, but we'll see. Now, I have to meet some friends of my own, so you will excuse me."

She stood, towering above the others. "Annie, you know how to call me? But it will be a while—"

"How long?"

Justine tilted her head, eyeing the girls onstage. "Bridge-and-tunnel *amateurs,*" she sniffed. "How long? A month . . ."

"A month! I can't wait a *month*—"

"You wait this long, you can wait a month. But I will start asking about your friend. Give Helen a kiss for me. And you—"

She ducked to kiss Baby Joe on the lips, letting her long fingernails tickle his throat. "Mr. Malabar! You need a date for one of your shows, you give me a call. Your friend has the number." Light sparked the zircon in her front tooth as Justine smiled and strode off through the club.

"That *puto*'s something else," observed Baby Joe.

"Helen knew Justine back when she was Jerome." Annie sighed. "Sometimes I think I've lived too interesting a life. Listen, Baby Joe—I hate to freak and run, but I'm so tired I feel sick, and *that*—"

She pointed at the remains of her vodka martini. "—that didn't help."

Baby Joe looked at her—the circles beneath her eyes that weren't smudged makeup, the sparks of silver-grey in her cropped hair. "Where you staying, *hija*?" he asked, reaching across the table for her hand.

"With friends."

"Where?"

Annie turned away. "I can't tell you. And I'm really not trying to be difficult," she insisted, when Baby Joe glowered. "But someone tried to *kill* me a few days ago, and—"

"And that's a good fucking reason to tell me where you'll be! Or come stay at my place—"

"No." Annie shook her head stubbornly. "Forget it, Baby Joe, don't even say it—just let me do this my way, okay? I promise, I'll call you if I hear anything from Justine—"

"Fuck that! You better call me tomorrow—"

"Friday, okay? I'll call you Friday, I promise—only don't tell anyone you saw me."

"What about Sweeney?"

Annie stood. She pulled a pair of sunglasses and a baseball cap from her knapsack and stepped out of the booth. With the cap slung on backward and the sunglasses riding on her snub nose, she looked about fourteen. "Sweeney? I don't think so. Look, Baby Joe—"

He met her in the aisle and threw an arm around her shoulder, hugged her close to him. "Look nothing! You better—"

"Shh." Annie stood on tiptoe and placed a finger on his lips. "I probably shouldn't even have told *you*. You're not going to write about this, are you?"

"Don't insult me." He walked her to the door, stood inside while she stepped out into the blazing late afternoon heat and shrieking tumult of midtown. "But you better call, *hija*."

Annie laughed. "Don't insult *me*! Friday—"

"I'll be waiting."

He stayed on at the strip joint after she left, checking his voice mail for messages, then leaving word at the paper that he'd be back late that night. He had a show to cover at Failté, a tiny downtown back room where a new band from Ireland would be playing after midnight. But there was a lot of ground to cover between now and then. It was almost one hundred degrees out on the pavement, and he'd already started a tab here. So he stayed.

Baby Joe hated places like this—too clean, too many suits, the dancers all commuters from Rutgers and SUNY Purchase working to pay off their student loans. Not to mention ten bucks for rail liquor and a DJ playing the Top Ten from the Jukebox in Hell. Still, he moved to a seat in front of the stage, knocked back a few more drinks and watched and thought about Annie and Sweeney and Oliver Crawford, about Hasel and Hasel's widow and Angelica Furiano. During a break, he talked with a dancer who was doing her thesis on the films of Ed Wood. Baby Joe bought her a seven-dollar ginger ale and gave her the name of a guy in Atlantic City who'd worked on *Glen or Glenda*.

After that he lost track of time. Outside the air took on that lowering orange-purple glare of city night, the sky between the high-rises colored like viscera. But inside all was rainbow light and smoke, the a/c cranked all the way down to sixty, so that he began to feel sorry for the dancers, their goose-pimpled flesh and the way they clutched at their cheap silk kimonos as they strode offstage. He'd actually started to fuzz out on the girls, lost in his own dreamscape. It was seeing Annie again, and thinking about Oliver and the others—something he'd been doing too much of since Hasel's death. He dipped his head to light another cigarette—he had myriad packs tucked into his pockets, like a hiker padded with trail mix—tossed the match on the floor, and swiped his long hair back from his eyes. And whistled.

At the edge of the stage, near the mirrored alley leading back to their dressing rooms, three girls stood watching him. Not the kind of girls you usually saw at places like this, either. They were far too young and brown, slender and restive as mink, their long dark hair pulled into topknots from which stray tendrils trailed like smoke. They reminded him of child prostitutes back in Manila, girls he'd seen washing in the runoff from hotel laundries. These three looked *way* underage, their bodies muscular and lean, small-breasted like young girls' bodies but with swelling hips. They were barefoot, and naked except for copper bracelets about their tiny wrists and ankles and silver necklaces upon their breasts. They stood side by side by side, staring at Baby Joe with narrow black eyes and smiling.

"Dios ko," he murmured. "New floor show."

He stared back at them and finished another drink. His mouth tasted burned from too many cigarettes, and the vodka was starting to give him a headache. He knew he should think about paying up and heading out to Failté, but he wanted to see what those girls were up to.

He didn't know how long he'd been watching them, but after a while he realized that the music had changed, from a monotonous downtown club standard to something he couldn't place. One of those eco-techno anthems, all soft percussives and breathy vocals in a language nobody could understand. Only in this music there was the rhythmic pulse of the sea and a faint hissing sound, steady and measured as his own breath.

"Hey," whispered Baby Joe. The girls didn't move. There was none of the usual chatter between performers, just those intense dark eyes boring into him. "Nice."

A moment later the girls took the stage. Not a replay of the same slow grinding dance he'd been watching all afternoon, but like circus acrobats vaulting into a ring. They leapt onto the raised platform, springing airy and careless as children through the smoke, their bare feet slapping the mirrored floor. Once there they seemed surprised: they stared giggling down at their reflections, pointing and hiding their faces behind their thin brown hands. Baby Joe glanced around to see if anyone else thought this was strange, but no one seemed to take any notice at all. The place had grown more crowded, but most of the clientele was jammed up against the bar. He turned back to the stage again.

One of the girls was listening to something—a cue, perhaps—poised like a Balinese *legong* dancer, her hand cupped around her ear like a curved leaf. With a cry she whirled on one heel and darted across the stage, stopping to raise her head. With murmured exclamations the other two raced after her, and began somersaulting and twirling, leaping to catch one another and racing apart again, like beads of mercury skimming across the floor.

Baby Joe watched them, breathless, his heart pounding. Their bracelets slid up and down, their anklets clattered as they danced and laughed, fingers brushing their girlish breasts and curling black hair tumbling about their shoulders. It was like watching the courtship of mayflies above a stream, all slender legs entwined amidst the ghosts of wings. In and out, up and down, until their steps assumed a pattern, the sound of their bare feet a muted *tantara* that was both summons and warning, and utterly hypnotic. And there was a voice as well, a woman's voice, so low and musical it might have been inside his head, whispering.

It is time. It is time . . .

Baby Joe jerked upright: where had he heard that before? He shuddered and fumbled at his jacket, searching for cigarettes. His mouth was dry; he needed another drink, but before he could signal the waitress one of the girls ran up to him and struck him under the chin, giggling, then darted off again.

"Dios mio."

Baby Joe began to sweat. It wasn't just her touch, those tiny fingers skimming above the loose collar of his T-shirt, or the way her hair had momentarily fallen across his face, warm and oddly tensile. He looked about, even more uneasy; as though he had remembered a dream from his childhood in another language, a garbled message he had not until this moment understood.

All around him the room looked the same—too bright, the men at the bar stupefied with drink or lust, the waitresses yawning and chatting with the other dancers. But when he turned at the stage again it was like he was in a different place. The mirrored floor broke into motes of silver and brown as the dancers whirled and leapt, feinting and dodging some unseen foe. There seemed to be other things in the air as well—flies maybe, or were they cockroaches?

No. They were butterflies, great violet-winged butterflies that floated between the girls, as though the dancers' soft cries had somehow been made carnate. Now and then a girl would leap as though to grasp one of the lovely creatures, but their slim fingers always closed on empty air. Then it seemed they would employ ropes to snare the butterflies: Baby Joe watched in dreamy amazement as thin brown cords whipped about the girls' heads as they pirouetted and struck at the swallowtails above them. And somehow even this bizarre capering was familiar to him; as was the smell of something burning, sweet and pungent like *katol* incense, and the echo of that insistent voice.

It is time.

"Fucking A, man." He forced himself to look away from the dancers, tried to stand but his legs gave way beneath him. With a grunt he crashed back into his chair. Laughing, the girls darted up to him. This time all three struck him, hard enough that he gasped, then ran off, calling out to one another in words he couldn't understand.

But if their words still made no sense, their motions did. It was like he was watching some bizarre shadow play: the three girls shades of someone else, someone he should remember, someone he knew—it should be *easy.* And why was it he couldn't get to his feet no matter how he tried, why couldn't he *escape* them? Because now, instead of striking at the butterflies, they struck *him,* their little hands much more forceful than you would think, their nails piercing him like tiny beaks. The cords they wielded like whips, and lashed—but gently—at his cheeks and shoulders. When he struggled to avoid their touch, they would only laugh the more, in high sweet voices. Then one might pluck at his jacket, while another would take his hand in hers and kiss it, her tongue sliding across the ball of his thumb before her sharp teeth sank into the flesh there and he cried aloud.

Baby Joe shut his eyes. His head throbbed, his heart hammered in his chest as though someone pounded him mercilessly.

"No!"

At the sound of his own anguish it all came back to him. The field, and Angelica weaving in and out among the trodden-down grasses, her bare legs streaked with dirt and sweat. He could see where her heels had left small indentations in the dust, and smell the sweetness of dried vetch and clover she had crushed in her passing. A few yards away from her the bull watched, stolid and unmoving as Baby Joe himself. But now Baby Joe knew, and understood, and surely the bull never had.

It is time.

A howl as he struggled to get to his feet. Again the girls laughed, but there was no mockery in their voices now. Instead they were gentle, even soothing, as though they had tired of their play and were ready now for some more serious pastime. They gathered round him, their hands surprisingly strong as they grasped his arms and drew him forward. He tried to shake them away but it was no use—they were too strong, he was too drunk, too exhausted to fight. About his head the butterflies weaved their own tipsy patterns in the air. A spicy scent surrounded him, something else remembered from his childhood. Crushed coriander seeds and sandalwood and *katol* incense, the bite of sour orange pulp in his mouth. He felt himself being lowered to the floor, the girls' hands everywhere upon his body—cheeks, forehead, arms, chest—their touch warm and smooth and dry. When he blinked the air seemed filled with snow, but then he saw that it was not snow but a sort of colored dust like pollen. His hands were coated with it. He brought a finger to his lips and tasted honey; looking down at the floor he saw that it was littered with the broken wings of butterflies, grey and colorless. Their scales filled the air, atoms of rust and violet, and settled like ash upon his cheeks.

Before him the girls knelt with arms extended. From their open hands dark cords slid to the floor, rustling. Their mouths were moving, he could not hear them but it didn't matter anymore; he knew he was dying. And suddenly he was no longer afraid: not of the girls, not of anything, not even of those thin brown ropes, which he now saw were moving, sliding between the girls' fingers and up along his legs. The sight should have terrified Baby Joe, but it did not. Instead he felt an odd exultation, a sense of imploding tension and release that was almost sexual. He knew he must be delirious.

Snakes, everywhere he looked there were snakes, slender brown vipers with triangular-shaped heads and tongues like split twigs dousing at the air. They slipped beneath the fabric of his trousers and flowed across his bare legs, and their touch was like the girls', warm and dry. As though desert sand was being poured onto him, slowly and with exquisite care, as though he was himself a serpent, sloughing away an old lifeless skin and wriggling through the dust.

The girls were still there, he could see them through slitted eyes. Only they no longer looked like bull-leapers or *legong* dancers but like people he knew. Angelica was there, which did not surprise him, but he felt no rancor toward her, no rage that she had somehow caused Hasel's death. Because Hasel was there, too, his ruddy face exploding into laughter when he saw Baby Joe—

Hey, man! What took you so long?!

—his embrace joyful as he reached for his friend. And there was someone else—Oliver, Baby Joe knew it must be Oliver though there was something different about him, he had changed somehow but it was all too much to take in, this mad exalted freedom, the sheer joy and unexpected *delight* of it all, nothing like what he had expected!

Hands were everywhere now, he could no longer see but he could feel them, pulling away his jacket and tearing open his T-shirt. Something bit at his left nipple; he shuddered and moaned at the sudden pain, and knew it must be one of the vipers. Its teeth piercing his flesh and then the slow surge of venom beneath the skin, like a wave building as it rushed through him. The pain came again at his left breast, but he was beyond that now. He was beyond them all, excepting only Hasel and the woman waiting behind him, her eyes laughing and her mouth forming his name as she took his hand and he knew at last what it was all about, there had been a mystery to it all along, serpents and bulls and a woman he had foolishly feared; but then he was lost in Her embrace, Her arms closing about him and his heart bursting with joy as She took him and he was Hers, Hers at last.

CHAPTER 19

Fire from the Middle Kingdom

On the patio at Huitaca Angelica stood. It was evening of a day so hot that all the small things of the desert had retreated to their lairs: rattlesnakes and Gila monsters and scorpions coiled beneath the burning stones like hidden treasure, with their gleaming black carapaces and jeweled eyes. Above the Devil's Clock lightning spiked the darkness. The bolts looked like cracks in the desert sky, but only Angelica knew what lay behind them.

She was alone now. Kendra and Martin had left earlier that week, Martin to return to California, Kendra to prepare for college in September. Kendra had never gotten over Cloud's death. Her relationship with Martin soured, she grew teary and slept too much and refused Angelica's offers to help her attend a grief workshop. Finally word came from Bennington that she would be able to start there as a freshman after all. The next day she told Angelica she was leaving, and the day after that she was gone. Martin split the following afternoon.

"You want me to, like, recommend someone to take my place?" He leaned across the hood of his Jeep, his white-blond hair falling into his eyes. "I mean, it's probably not so cool for you to be out here all by yourself, Angelica. That cougar could still be around—"

Angelica smiled. "Sunday will be here."

"Sunday!" Martin snorted. "Like *Sunday*'s gonna save you if something happens—"

"Nothing's going to happen, Martin," Angelica said soothingly. She tousled his hair and let her hand rest on his shoulder. He was so beautiful, beautiful things always made her yearn to possess them and it would be so easy, just a few moments alone and then . . .

Martin sighed. He took Angelica's hand in his and squeezed it, then grabbed her in a bear hug. "Well, I better go. But I'm gonna miss you, Angelica."

She laughed, her bronze hair falling across his. "Oh, you'll see me again, Martin. Don't worry."

She hadn't asked him to stay on. She knew he would refuse. The truth was that she no longer needed bodyguards. She no longer needed anyone. The house at Huitaca would be closed after tonight. Despite what Angelica had told Martin, Sunday would not go to Huitaca alone, so Angelica had given the housekeeper an envelope with a month's wages and a false promise that she would call her when she returned in the fall.

And that was that. She had already turned off the water and notified the electric and telephone companies that she was canceling their services. The oriental lilies and freesia that had been slowly deteriorating in their Waterford vases were gone, tossed into a patch of ocotillo outside. Before leaving, Sunday swept the floors clean of sand and cactus needles, folded Angelica's linen shifts and the embroidered camisoles of honey-colored silk, and set them inside drawers among little muslin bags of sandalwood and dried orange peel. Angelica had seen to the last bits of tidying up, putting back on the proper shelves the notebooks containing so much of her work. Translations of the Sybaris tablets that she had made at the National Museum in Naples, with their invocation of the Queen of the Underworld. The copy of the *Demæric Hymn to Othiym* from Keftiu, where night after night she had sat bowed over her desk, bathed in the light from a smoky clay lantern, its wick a calyx of false dittany floating in olive oil. One by one she had transcribed the cuneiform tablets, and returned them to their resting place in the tombs beneath the house. Hand-lettered sheets and Xeroxes of parchment pages, drawings she had copied from vases and rhytons and frescoes, from forgotten temples within the rain forest and subway platforms near the great necropolis in Paris: all of them would now be carefully interred at Huitaca, to be given over to whatever priestess next claimed them. For Angelica herself, they had no further use.

Looking over all her things for one last time, Angelica sighed. For nine days now she had been fasting, as the ritual commanded. She had grown so thin, and her skin had taken on an almost luminous translucence: as though her blood was already fleeing her, as though whatever strange raptures she had given herself to had purged her flesh of color and sinew and bone. When she gazed into the mirror her uncle had given her so long ago, the face that gazed back was no longer her own, but that of a caryatid or *kouroi*—beautiful, ageless, inhuman. For a long moment she stared at herself, touching the heavy mass of her bronze curls and seeking in vain for a grey hair. Letting her fingers brush against her cheeks, the skin smooth and cool as faience, unlined, unscarred. To look at her, one would never think that she was a grown woman with a grown son; but neither would one see anywhere within her the memory of the girl who once upon a time had astonished her friends with her explosive laugh.

"It was so long ago," she whispered, and set the mirror back amongst the curling photographs and antique silver frames, the papery nautilus and cowries and rose-colored sea urchin. As she removed her hand something fell. She heard the chime of breaking glass, and with a low cry reached to pluck a photo from a sad heap of shivered crystal.

It was a picture of herself and Baby Joe and Oliver, Baby Joe smiling for perhaps the only time in front of the camera, Angelica in the middle and Oliver at her other side. His arm was draped across her shoulder, his eyes were so bright they might have been lit from within by candles, like a jack-o'-lantern.

"Oliver." She bit her lip and blinked tears from her eyes. "Oh, Oliver . . ."

She thought of the poem that Sweeney Cassidy had liked to quote back at the Divine, drunk on cheap beer and sentiment—

When suddenly at the midnight hour
an invisible troupe is heard passing
with exquisite music, with shouts—
do not mourn in vain your fortune failing you now,
your works that have failed, the plans of your life
that have all turned out to be illusions . . .

Crazy drunken Sweeney, already seeing the end of things, but oh, Sweeney, if you only knew!—

As if long prepared for this, as if courageous,
as it becomes you who are worthy of such a city;
approach the window with firm step,
and listen with emotion, but not
with the entreaties and complaints of the coward,
as a last enjoyment listen to the sounds, the exquisite instruments of
the mystical troupe,
and bid her farewell, the Alexandria you are losing.

Angelica wept. Bowing her head and sobbing until her chest ached, she clutched their photos to her breast and wept for all of them. Oliver and Sweeney and Baby Joe and Hasel and Annie and Dylan, but for herself most of all: Angelica di Rienzi, like her poor dead friends given to the night.

It was twilight when she finally composed herself. No more time to waste. She wiped her eyes and brushed her hair, turned away forever from everything that might remind her of that other life and went to the bed where her clothes were laid out. There she readied herself for what was to come.

First she drank the *kykeon.* On her bookshelf was the recipe, garnered from a tablet she had found in the museum at Athens. Barley and honey and the crushed purple bracts and pink flowers of dittany of Crete, fermented in a vessel of fired clay; the same beverage the initiates had drunk at Eleusis millennia ago. It had a pleasant yeasty taste, the honey's sweetness offset by the dittany's raw earthiness. After drinking she wiped her mouth on a piece of cotton. She anointed herself with ground coriander and sandalwood, rubbed a fist-sized chunk of amber against the hollow of her throat until it released its musky resin. Then she drew over her head a simple shift of linen shot with gold thread, and piece by piece slipped on the sacred jewelry she had amassed over the years: bands of ivory and gold and sweet red sandalwood, rings shaped like serpents giving suck to children, bracelets heavy with steatite figures of women giving birth. Last of all she took the lunula. She turned to the window, raised the shining crescent to the eastern sky where the moon waited and cried out.

Nike Materon! Nike Materos obscura!

Victory to the Mothers. Victory to the Dark Mother. She slipped the lunula around her neck, and glanced around to see if she had forgotten anything.

The floor was swept clean, the gauze curtains had been drawn across the other windows. On her bed was an envelope containing a one-way ticket to Dulles Airport in Washington, D.C. It was dated the thirty-first of July, the eve of the ancient feast of Lammas.

But that festival had more names than Angelica had hairs on her head. In India it was called Kalipuja, by the worshipers at the Temple at Dakshineswarand and in Calcutta—the city whose name is actually Kali-Ghatt, "the steps of Kali." In Finland it had been the day of Kalma, "odor of corpses;" in the Antipodes that of Kalwadi, who devoured her own children and then gave them rebirth. On Coatepec—Snake Hill, in Mexico—there gathered followers of the serpent-skirted lunar goddess Coatlicue, she who wore upon her breast the moon and from whose girdle dangled dismembered hands and beating hearts, Coatlicue who danced upon the entrails of her son while wearing his flayed skin. Upon other hills, the sun-gilded mounds of Tuscany, the good fairy Turanna still brings children balloons and bells and Nintendo games, while her Etruscan companion Zirna strews the floor of their bedrooms with tiny sugared crescents.

But woe to those children whose windows are left open at summer's dying, because that is when Lilith comes and brings them fair dreams, then strangles them so that they die smiling; and woe to those who do not wear the new moon upon their breasts and so placate Lamasthu, whose bite leaves pestilence in the blood!

Upon the second day of the death of summer the silent poppy-goddess Spes walks. Spes whose mouth is red as poppies and whose skin is white, whose kiss is cold as alabaster. On that day, too, Aetna was worshiped, who disgorged her rage upon the city suckling at her breast; and the Haida goddess Dazalarhons, whose anger erupted when she saw that men were torturing the shining salmon in their streams instead of giving thanks for their plenty. In ancient Greece it had marked the transition to the time of the great women's festivals, culminating in the Thesmophoria, that greatest and most holy of all feasts, honoring Demeter's rescue of her ravished daughter from the lord of Hell. Everywhere that the moon shone, everywhere that people died and lamented, everywhere that infants failed to wake and grain turned to dust beneath the merciless sun, where women died in childbirth and their mothers and sisters keened in vain: in all these places, the dark goddess had been worshiped, and forgotten.

But now, in all these places and more, women had learned her name anew. Now, they called her Othiym. Now, her hour had come. Slowly she opened the doors leading onto the tiled patio, and stepped outside.

The dusk surrounded her like rumpled velvet, soft and warm and fragrant with the scent of crushed sage. Angelica breathed in deeply. Her heart was racing; a trickle of sweat traced its way across her rib cage. She tried to remember what Cloud had taught her about conserving energy in a marathon: breathe from the diaphragm, close your eyes, relax.

She began to pace across the patio, the heat from the tiles seeping through the soles of her feet and on up to her thighs. Compared to all that had come before—nearly two decades of work and study and sacrifice—there was really very little left to do. But the greatest sacrifice still remained. And only Angelica could perform that task.

In the course of the last year, she had instructed Elspeth and the other priestesses in the final rite of Waking the Moon. They, in turn, had gathered to them Circle upon Circle of women, radiating from Angelica outward to all the lost reaches of the world. It had taken years of patience for it to come to this, years of working alone and with small groups: waking first the women themselves, then encouraging them to teach their friends and neighbors.

But women work quickly once they are awakened. Angelica had learned that by watching television programs where women wept and fought and embraced; by reading the books that American women read, and the newspapers that told of their vengeance upon those who had harmed them; by visiting the tiny villages in Orisa and Bangladesh and Uttar, where girl children are aborted and wives are murdered for their dowries; by entering compounds in the countryside outside of Gracanica and Glamoc, where women were raped and forced to give up their babies to doctors and soldiers; by witnessing initiation ceremonies in Africa and New York, where girls were mutilated, and standing at the mass graves of nuns slaughtered in Central America and men and women and children in the jungles of Kampuchea. Everywhere, everywhere, she saw horror and death and brutality; everywhere she saw forgiveness, and ignorance, and endless cycles of poverty and servitude, women cringing before their masters and murmuring about love.

And everywhere she saw rage: rage that was twisted until, like an auger, it bored into the women themselves, and their children. Rage that like the desert creatures burrowed beneath the surface, waiting patiently for nightfall and moonrise.

"But it is time now," whispered Angelica. She raised her face to the Devil's Clock. Amethyst light danced across her brow, set the lunula aglow. "Oh Great Mother: *it is time*!"

She raised her arms, took another deep breath, and let her hands drop. Bracelets of bone and copper and gold slipped down about her wrists, and the linen shift fell from her shoulders, cascading around her waist and thighs in folds of white and gold to pool about her feet. Bare-breasted, naked save for her armillas and the lunula, she closed her eyes and sang.

From the purity of your blasted lands I come, Pure Queen of Those Below,
Of Hecate and Durga and the other Goddesses immortal.
For I claim that I too am of your blessed race.
I have flown out of the sorrowful weary Wheel.
I have passed with eager feet to the Circle desired.
I have entered into the bosom of Desponia, Queen of the Underworld.
I have passed with eager feet from the Circle desired.
O Blessed Othiym, thou shalt make me Goddess instead of mortal.
Haïyo Othiym! Othiym Lunarsa.

As she sang she began to move, swaying back and forth and stamping her bare feet upon the tiles. At each step dust rose beneath her, and tiny fragments of terracotta. Her dance inscribed a circle upon the ground, an orbit of dust and dried grass and the broken wings of moths. Her bare feet slapped the tiles, her heels grinding into them as though she were extinguishing small flames.

Out of the pure I come, Pure Queen of the Pure above,
Of Ashtaroth and Artemis and the other Goddesses and Daemons.
For I too, I cry to thee, am of your blessed race.
I have paid the penalty for deeds unrighteous
But now I come a suppliant to Holy Phersephoneia
That of her grace she receive me to the seats of the Hallowed.
Haïyo Othiym! Othiym Lunarsa.

Beneath her heels the tiles began to crack. Fissures ran from them toward the pool with its tranquil dark surface, and from the fissures reddish soil flowed, as though the earth beneath her was boiling. The soil stained her feet and ankles, but Angelica danced heedless, treading the red earth until it churned like wine or blood being poured in her wake.

Once on a time a youth was I, and I was a maiden,
A bush, a bird, and a serpent with scales that gleam in the moonlight.
But I turned from you, O Great Mother,
Like a bolt I fell, Othiym.
And in your sorrow you grew old and hungry,
In your sorrow you grew angry and pale.
In your sorrow you gave voice to anger.
You rose and began the sacred dance
And where your feet trod cities fell:
Knossos and Iraklion the fair, waves devoured the land

And Kalliste most beloved of all your children,
The sacred island consumed by flame.

Her voice rose to a wail, a lament for those green places burned by Othiym's anger, for the temples destroyed and the children buried when her rage erupted into streams of liquid fire and molten ash. She mourned for Kalliste and Keftiu, Aetna and Sumbawa and Pompeii; but most of all she mourned Kalliste, the island that had been her sacred jewel, her emerald eye, the center of all her worship. Kalliste, whose name meant "Most Beautiful," but which after its destruction was known as Thera: Fear.

For they turned from you, Great Mother,
The rhytons ran dry and you went hungry
Your thirst unappeased.
Your priestesses were seduced and then enslaved.
Your altars were dry and no blood given,
No marriage, no sons to slake your thirst.
For this I beg forgiveness.
I have paid the penalty for deeds unrighteous,
I have given you sons and daughters too.
Receive here the armor
Of Memory.
Angelica your daughter, by due rite grown to be a goddess.

Her face gleamed with sweat, sweat coursed down her throat and warmed the lunula until she felt as though a heated blade nudged between her breasts. Still she danced, her breath coming in sharp hard bursts that were counterpoint to her footsteps, and with each turn and stamp of her heels she drew nearer to the edge of the pool. Behind her now all the earth was broken, tiles shattered and stones as well, so that it looked as though some small but powerful machine had razed the patio. When she reached the edge of the pool she poised, shining like a glazed figure still cooling from the kiln, then without a sound dived beneath the surface.

The water was warm as new milk from a mother's breasts, so warm that her blood seemed to flow in and out of her veins, mixing with the quiescent darkness that surrounded her. Seven times she climbed from the pool, seven times returned to its depths; until at last she rose and stood upon the broken patio, the water sliding from her in pale ribbons.

Above the Devil's Clock the storm had spent itself. Now and then faint rumblings echoed from the distance, but otherwise the night was still. With the storm some of the evening's heat had passed. A chill breeze rustled the spiny ocotillo and the agave's heavy blade-shaped leaves, bringing with it the smell of rain and damp shale from the mountains far to the north, the first augury of summer's end. Angelica shivered a little in her nakedness, but the potent *kykeon* still burned inside her. She picked her way across the cracked tiles, nudging shards of terra-cotta out of her way. When she reached where the patio ended in a jumble of soil and broken pottery, she laughed and shook her head, her tangled curls flinging droplets into the air.

"Come then!" she called, opening her arms to the night. "I am ready—"

And they came: from every opening in the earth they scuttled and slithered and crept, hollow legs and shells rattling against the stones, scales rubbing together with a sound like sand running through the fingers, ponderous feet clawing for purchase upon terra-cotta. Gila monsters and elfin lizards, rattlesnakes and pit vipers, the tiny sacred scorpions of Innana that would be colorless were it not for the amber venom floating inside their arched tails, like retsina in a glass. Ancient tortoises pushed aside walls of earth and clambered up to gaze at the woman. Nestling spiders, and beetles that dwell within spheres of dung, and millipedes, whose legs whispered across the sand, and centipedes, with mandibles that clacked: all emerged from their sunken castles, to welcome her and give her homage.

But mostly, there were snakes. Docile rosy boas, western racers like wands of brushed steel, eyeless worm snakes so small a hundred of them would not fill a teacup. Puff adders, coachwhips, tiny ring-necked snakes that children could wear as glossy jewelry; lyre snakes, whose bite causes gongs to ring and clamor, and night snakes, whose rubbery fangs hold no more venom than a honeybee. As though they were being disgorged from the earth's very core, as though rivulets of magma spewed forth and then cooled into living coils and veins of serpents: in every direction the ground seethed with snakes.

"Children, children," murmured Angelica. The air was filled with a sound as of an entire forest of dried leaves taking flight. Still they came, forked tongues tasting the air, their supple bellies reading the stony earth, like so many fingers brushing across a loved one's face. As they passed the other creatures rustled and shivered, but did not flee.

At the very last the greatest of all the desert serpents appeared. Diamondbacks and rattlesnakes, the immense and terrible sidewinders. The ground shook beneath them, and the noise of their rattles was like that of sistrums and tambours and stones in a hollow gourd; the sound of the *krotalon,* the ancient Greek rattle from which they took their name. They surrounded Angelica, the stored-up warmth of their bodies making the violet air shimmer, and curled around her legs and ankles like kittens. As though they were kittens she stooped to pick them up, the largest ones as thick around as a man's arm, and strong enough to capture a young pig.

But to Angelica they did no harm. Instead they writhed and flung their coils about her wrists, their darkly patterned scales nearly lost among her clattering jewelry, and covered her until she seemed to be draped in a shadowy cloak set with winking gems. They gaped to display pale mouths and black tongues and fangs as long and curved as a hawk's talons. Had they struck her, their venom would have caused the tender flesh of her arms to swell and then decay as necrosis set in, with its subsequent hemorrhage and shock and renal failure.

They did not bite, and Angelica did not recoil at their touch. Thousands and thousands of years before, when the first woman poked at the African savanna in search of grubs and tubers, the snake befriended her, sharing with her its eggs, its young, its own sparse flesh in times of drought. From the snake she learned the patience to hunt, the wisdom of sleeping when one's belly is full and hiding when the inferno of midday raged. From the snake she learned that we can slough off our lives as easily as a dead skin, and that death need be no more terrifying than that empty sack. It warned her of earthquakes and devoured vermin. She read oracles in its sand tracks, and from its poison derived subtle visions as well as a cure for bites. Like the moon the snake renews itself; with the moon it became the first sacred thing.

And when the first woman's people migrated north, the snake went with them. In the Libyan desert it was worshiped as an avatar of the goddess. Still later it was the *uraeus,* the gold serpent that conferred power upon the crown of the Egyptian pharaohs, and wrapped its coils around the blessed *caduceus* of Innana and Hippocrates. Tame cobras slept in the palaces of the Indus queens, and nursed the godlings of the Aegean, and in Crete every house had its snake tubes, where the sacred adders and harmless vine snakes slept.

"And now you will serve me," whispered Angelica. "All of you . . ."

She lifted her arms. Above the Devil's Clock a crescent appeared, spare and pale as a crocus shoot. *"Othiym haïyo!"* Angelica cried. A ripple ran through the carpet of small things at her feet. "Oh Great Mother, it is begun."

Then:

"Go now," she said, and set the great sidewinders back upon the ground. "As Menat I command you, as Feronia and Pele and all those who rule the stones: wake the earth, free your children imprisoned there! So may we destroy the cities of men and reclaim what is ours."

And throwing their great coils across the shattered ground, the sidewinders departed, their rattles so loud they sent hollow echoes booming from the mesas.

"You, scorpions," she said next, "As Innana I command you, and Echidna and Walutahanga and all those who guard wives and concubines. Go now and hide beneath the beds of cruel and unfaithful lovers, and sting them with your tails!"

And the little scorpions raised their pincers and clacked them together like stones, then scattered across the desert in a great army.

"Tortoises now," she cried, and what had appeared to be a row of boulders lumbered toward her, their heads nodding wisely on withered necks. "In the name of the nymph Chelone I call you! She who was stoned when she refused to lay blossoms at the feet of Zeus. Go now to the lakes and seas and rivers, and wake there your sleeping sisters, the kraken and leviathan and Scylla of the gnashing waves! This I command in the name of Moroch, of all those who lay too long abed from fear."

On and on she went. Each creature she called to her by name, and in the name of each of their patronesses she commanded them: Melissa of the bees, Arachne's spiders, the patient ants and scarabs who had been waiting since Nefertari's death to receive their due. All the beasts she named, all those that crawl upon their bellies and more besides, wolves and shrikes and owls and bats, every creature maligned by men because it had once been sacred to Her. And all of them answered, all of them came; and into the darkness they all raced away, to bring to all the other creatures and places of the earth her bidding.

At last she seemed to be alone in the darkness. Above her the moon had risen into the soft summer sky, its crescent smiling down upon her and the lunula upon her breast smiling back. The air was strong with the acrid odor of ants and scorpions and the venom of rattlers, but there was another scent there too, something sweeter and yet more noisome to the woman. A faint noise sounded in the sharp spears of the ocotillo, and the dry leaves of the huisache rustled softly.

"Who is there?" Angelica called. She turned with fiery eyes to stare into the grove of trees. "Who has not answered me?"

There came no reply. But it seemed that a wind was stirring the huisache, though it was a wind Angelica did not feel; and then it seemed that upon the dry branches blossoms opened, blossoms pale and fragrant in the moonlight. Angelica drew her breath in sharply: the blossoms lifted from the trees, fluttered and circled the broken patio until they surrounded her, a silent rain of butterflies.

"No!" she cried, and stamped her bare foot upon the earth, so hard that the lunula shuddered upon her breast. "I did not call you, it is not time yet—"

"Oh, but it is," someone said in a low voice behind her.

Angelica whirled. *"No,"* she hissed.

In the shadows stood another figure—a tall woman with dark hair and deep-set eyes. Butterflies formed a halo above her, and momentarily lit upon her shoulders before wafting off once more. She was cloaked in purple and her face, though reserved, even sorrowing, was beautiful, as beautiful as Angelica's own.

"Well-met, Angelica," the woman said. She waved her hand, so lazily that a butterfly did not move from where it rested upon one finger like a topaz ring. "It's been too long." And though she did not smile, there seemed to be faint mockery, even laughter, in her voice.

"We have not met," said Angelica. But the wind that had not chilled her before, did so now.

"Oh no?"

The figure remained unmoving as Angelica took a step backward, her fingers covering the lunula. "Where have you come from?" she demanded.

The woman laughed softly, then recited,

> *"For years I roamed, far from the birch groves of Ida*
> *Until I lost myself among drifts of ice and the frozen steppes*
> *There I lamented in caves where ravaging beasts make their home."*

Angelica's fingers tightened upon the lunula. "You're lying," she said in a shaking voice. "I do not know you."

"No?" the woman replied.

> *"'But what shape is there I have not had'—"*

"No!" shrieked Angelica. "Why are you *here,* you *can't* be here—"

"The boy," the woman said simply. She slid her hands into the folds of her robe. "You're not to harm him."

"The boy is mine!"

The woman shook her head, just once. Her eyes glinted. "And mine."

"No," said Angelica. "Not yours. Never, *never* yours."

"A warning, Angelica," the dark-haired woman said in a low voice. "Don't hurt him."

Angelica laughed harshly. "You have no power here, sister," she said. She lifted her hands to the sky and glared. "Go, before my Mistress loses patience with you!"

"You should be more careful whom you bed, Angelica." The woman's voice was low and threatening. "Not everyone wants to embrace an asp—"

"Go!" screamed Angelica. Rage made a sibylline mask of her face, and her hair fell about her cheeks in tangled coils. "You—"

But the dark-haired woman was already gone. Only, on the ground where her bare feet had stood, a sheaf of flowers trembled, and stained the desert air with the scent of hyacinths.

CHAPTER 20

Threnody and Breakdown

Handsome Brown let us off in front of Dr. Dvorkin's house, solemnly accepting the wad of bills Dylan pressed into his hand.

"It's good to see you, my man," he said in his *basso* voice, and toasted us with a pint of Hennessy. "Take good care of the lady. *Always* take good care of the lady." Cab Number 393 lumbered off into the darkness, trailing the strains of Idris Mohammed.

Ninth Street was deserted, the streetlights casting their glow over the crepe myrtles and magnolias, the heaps of fallen petals that had drifted up against the curbstones. We stepped from the street and opened the wrought-iron gate that led into Dr. Dvorkin's front yard, the little lawn overgrown with myrtle and ivy and a single huge magnolia. The air was so warm and sweet it was like drowning to stand there and breathe it; but I could hardly breathe at all, my heart was pounding so fast, my mouth seemed filled with something thick and sweet and strong, honey wine or Handsome Brown's cognac. From the hidden garden echoed the burbling song of a mockingbird, so achingly beautiful it brought tears to my eyes.

"Sweeney." Dylan drew me to him, his long hair warm against my cheek. "What is it, Sweeney? You're crying—"

He held me gently against his chest, the two of us leaning against the magnolia. For all that his words were soft I could feel his heart pounding like my own. "Nothing," I whispered. I laughed, wiping my eyes. "It's just—god, I must be drunk or something, it's just all so beautiful, and—"

My voice caught. A warm breeze stirred the leaves of the magnolia. From its waxy blossoms scent poured like rain. "I'm—I'm just so happy," I said, and began to sob.

"Happy?" Dylan's voice was perplexed, and when I looked up his eyes were burning, flecked with gold from the streetlamps. Panic lanced through me: what was I *saying*? I tried to move away, but Dylan's arms tightened around my waist. "Happy? *I'll* show you happy—"

He kissed me again, pushing me against the tree, his hands stroking my face as I grabbed him and pulled him tight against me. I didn't care where we were, I didn't care who might see or hear. I couldn't hear anything, except for his heart and breath and the mockingbird singing blissfully somewhere in the green darkness. I thought I would faint: my head was roaring but all I could feel was Dylan's mouth and the taste of him, and everything about us hot and sweet and liquid.

"Sweeney," he whispered. "Oh, Sweeney . . ."

We made love there, the tree wound about with ivy that tangled with Dylan's hair and fingers, my skirt torn and scattered with bark as Dylan moved against me until he cried out and the two of us slid down, gasping, into the carpet of myrtle that blanketed the earth.

Nothing had changed. The night was soft and darkly golden as before. In its secret haven the mockingbird still sang. Overhead the sky was starless, but I could hear the first far-off stirrings of morning, subway cars moving into Union Station, the rush of distant wheels.

"We should go in," I said at last. I smoothed my ruined skirt, tried to stand, and slid down again helplessly, my legs were so weak. "Jesus! Where'd you learn to *do* that?"

Dylan pulled me up, grinning. "You liked it?"

I laughed and plucked a bit of vine from his hair. "It was okay," I said, and taking his hand started back toward the carriage house.

"Just okay?" His voice was plaintive. "Then maybe we should practice some more . . ."

And we did.

That was how Dylan missed his dinner with Dr. Dvorkin, as well as breakfast and any invitations for lunch that might have come to him. The next morning I called in sick, for the first time in almost two years. When Dylan wondered, somewhat nervously, if he should call in as well, I just laughed.

"Who do you think you'd call? *I'm* your boss, and *I* think you need to spend the day in bed . . ."

We made love until I ached all over, until I couldn't tell where my body ended and the damp warmth of the sheets and air and Dylan's skin began. He was so beautiful, I really did weep, watching him as he slept late that morning, his snores vying with the soft roar of a neighbor's lawn mower. I lay beside him and still couldn't keep my hands from him: his skin so warm and smooth it was like marble fitting into the curve of my palm, the swell of his narrow hips where I pressed my mouth so that I could feel the bone jutting beneath my tongue. I wanted to devour him, feel his soft skin break under my teeth like a pear's and my mouth fill with juice, sweet and hot. When I took him in my mouth again he groaned, his fingers pulled at my hair and once more we tangled together as he came, warmth spurting onto my breasts as he clutched me and cried my name aloud.

"I guess it's true," I said when we finally had both slept, and awakened to find ourselves bruised and soaked with sweat and wrapped in each other's arms. A fan moved lazily back and forth in front of a window, sending a faint coolness through the room.

"What?" Dylan mumbled.

"About guys reaching their sexual peak at nineteen."

"Yeah? Then you have something to look forward to." He rolled over and hugged me. "My birthday's not till August first."

"You're only *eighteen*?"

He sat up, grinning. "Yup. Wanna know something else?"

I fanned myself with yesterday's *Post*. "I don't know if my heart can stand any more."

"This is the first time I did it."

"Did what?"

"You know." He looked at me sheepishly, and I suddenly noticed he was blushing. *"It."*

"It?" I dropped the newspaper, shocked. "You mean, you're a—"

"A lot of people are," Dylan said defensively. "I mean, people *my* age. And—well, I never really *wanted* to before. Not much," he ended lamely, and stared out the window.

"Holy cow," I said, and collapsed onto a heap of pillows. "I think I need a drink."

I got up, padded downstairs, and got a nearly full bottle of chardonnay from the refrigerator. I found two wineglasses and some fruit that I put into a basket—a bunch of black grapes, a rather wizened orange, a couple of figs that I'd bought impulsively and at an outrageous price at Eastern Market a few days before.

"Here," I announced when I got back upstairs. I put the basket on the bed beside Dylan and poured some wine. "Nectar of the gods."

We lay next to each other and drank and ate. The sunlight didn't slant through the windows so much as flow, ripe with the carrion scents of wisteria and gingko fruit, burning charcoal and magnolia blossom and car exhaust: the sooty green smell that is summer in D.C.

"I love figs," said Dylan. He bit into one, exposing the tender pink flesh beneath the dark husk. "We had fig trees at Keftiu—my father always said they were the real fruit in the Bible—you know, with Adam and Eve. But my mother said it was pomegranates."

"Mmm," I said, sipping my wine. "So. You never had a girlfriend, huh?"

He finished his fig and tossed the gnarled remnant out the window. "Not really. I went away to school a lot—prep schools, you didn't really have a chance to meet girls. At least I never did, not in the States. Here I was like, Eurotrash, and over there I was the ugly American. And there was always my mother, you know?" He sighed and reached for his wineglass, stared into it for a long moment before going on. "My mother made me kind of paranoid about stuff."

"Stuff? You mean—uh, *sex?*" I caught myself. *Angelica* preaching abstinence? Anger warmed me along with the wine, but I bit my tongue and nodded. "How interesting."

"Yeah. I guess because I'm her only child. And AIDS, of course. And in Italy it's a little different from here. All those Catholics—"

A pang shot through me. It had been so long, and what with the *tej,* and the night—I hadn't even *thought* about AIDS. Or birth control. Or anything.

"Jesus, Dylan, you're not, uh—"

He looked at me with those brilliantly guileless blue eyes. "No. I never got tested for AIDS. I didn't need to."

"Me neither." I laughed, embarrassed, tried to cover for it by grabbing a handful of grapes. "I guess it's different now, huh?"

Dylan yawned. "I guess. But my mother always made such a big deal about my being pure. About *saving* myself. For some crazy sacred marriage." He stretched, his long lean body glistening with sweat, his hairless chest taut with muscle. I found my mouth getting dry, despite the grapes, and hastily drank some more wine.

"Saving yourself," I repeated stupidly. The idea was ludicrous. A child of Angelica's, saving himself for marriage?

"Not anymore." He leaned over and kissed me, then buried his face against my breasts. "Oh god, you smell so good—"

We kissed, too happily exhausted to do more, and then Dylan adjusted the fan so that its scant breeze coursed over us.

"I'm sorry—I'm probably the only person in D.C. who doesn't have air-conditioning."

He shook his head. "It doesn't bother me. It reminds me of—"

I laughed. "I know—Keftiu."

"I was going to say Venice. Crete is much hotter than this. Drier, too." He frowned and, with a swooping motion, pushed the hair from his face—a gesture that suddenly, heartbreakingly, made me think of Oliver. "Does it bother you? Talking about my mother?"

"No." The truth was, I'd somehow managed to forget about Angelica until he'd mentioned her—Oliver, too, until that moment. And it was strange, because being with Dylan suddenly made Oliver seem both more alive and more distant from me than he ever had. "No, it doesn't. It just seems weird. I never would have thought Angelica would consider—well, that she'd think marriage was sacred."

"My mother is very strange, Sweeney." I started to laugh again, but Dylan's expression was grim. "I'm not kidding. It's not that she thinks marriage is sacred—she doesn't. I still don't know why she married my father. I'm pretty sure she didn't love him. Not the way you're supposed to love someone. Not the way—"

He leaned over and let his lips graze mine. His hair fell across my eyes for a moment, and I felt dizzy, breathing in his scent; but then he drew back.

"Not the way I feel about you," he said in a soft voice, and any thought of laughing went right out of my head. He sat up again and sighed. "But she has this thing, about some sacred marriage—it's got to do with her goddamn cult. All those women . . ."

"You mean like Sun Myoung Moon, marrying off his followers in Madison Square Garden or something?"

"I don't know. It's a secret, to me at least. Maybe they're all going to marry each other. But I doubt it." He picked up his wineglass and stared into it. "Hey, look—a bug."

He tipped the glass toward the window, and I watched as a honeybee crawled out. Dylan blew on it; the bee somersaulted drunkenly across the windowsill, then disappeared outside.

"I know just how it feels," I said, and poured him the rest of the wine. "Listen, you don't have to talk about your mother if it—well, if it's weird for you."

"It's not weird for me." His voice took on an edgy, aloof tone, and for a moment I felt the same sharp panic that had seized me before.

Because crazy as it was—*and it was crazy!* I was twice this kid's age, I'd gone to school with his parents, if things had gone differently I might have *been* one of his parents, on top of which I'd only known him for twenty-four hours, during which we'd fucked six times and I had *called in sick to work!*—crazy as all this was, I knew I was falling for him. *Had* fallen for him. Me, Katherine Sweeney Cassidy, who'd spent almost twenty years in an emotional coma—

I. Was. In. Love.

". . . do you understand?"

I started. "Huh? I'm sorry, Dylan—"

He traced the line of my calf. "I was just saying that it's not weird for me to talk about my mother. It's that *she's* weird—*really* weird. I love her, I really do; but I don't really *know* her. I was always away at boarding schools, and she'd be off on all her digs, and even when she took me along there was always someone she paid to take care of me—tutors and stuff. She was always *nice* to me, it's not like she was mean or something, it's just—"

He stopped and sighed. I wanted to put my arms around him, I wanted to tell him I understood—that I knew what Angelica was like, that it was okay—but I was afraid to. I was afraid I'd seem too quick to comfort him, afraid I'd seem too *maternal.* So I just sat beside him on the bed and waited for him to go on.

"It's just that she's so fucking *intense,*" he said finally. Against his tan face his eyes burned like midnight blue flames. "She has all these bizarre ideas, these mad prophecies; but a lot of them come true."

"Like—what?" I asked guardedly.

"Like earthquakes. Remember that big quake in L.A.? Well, two days before it hits, out of nowhere she calls me at school and tells me that she's taking me with her to Minneapolis for a few days. Minneapolis! But I thought, okay, I'll check out the music scene there, which I did.

"But meanwhile, everything back in L.A. goes *fwooom*—"

He slapped the bed with his open palms, with such vehemence that I jumped.

"All our neighbors' houses slide into the canyon, but *our* house—*Mom's* house—it doesn't even *move.* Now you'd think my mother would be upset when she heard about this earthquake, right? That she'd be on the first plane back there to make sure everything's okay. But no—she takes her time, which is a good thing, considerng how violent all those aftershocks were. And when we finally get back to L.A., and get to the house—*nothing has moved.* I mean, *nothing.* All these rare statuettes and icons she brought from Crete and Italy, they haven't even shifted on their shelves. The books haven't moved. The dishes haven't moved. *Nada.* I asked her, I thought maybe she'd paid someone to come in and clean it up before she got back, but no. An earthquake has leveled the entire West Coast, except for my mother's house."

He fell silent, and stared fiercely out to where the wisteria leaves hung limply from their woody vines. I waited before saying anything. My mouth was dry, I felt chilled in spite of the torrid heat; but if it killed me I wasn't going to let Angelica and her weirdness into my carriage house.

"So she had a premonition," I said at last. "Well, thank god she did, or you might have been hurt, right?"

"Oh, sure," Dylan said bitterly. He shook his head, his long hair spilling across his shoulders. "A premonition! My mother has nothing *but* premonitions! Hurricane Andrew, Mount Pinatubo, some mudslide in Bangladesh—she's *always* got an inside track on natural disasters. This woman told me once that my mother had told some scientists—women scientists—to leave Finland, because there was going to be some kind of disaster, and it turned out she was right: it turned out she was talking about Chernobyl. Her and her followers, they're always on the first train out of town, a good twenty-four hours before the storm hits."

I took a deep breath. "So—what are you telling me, Dylan? Do you really think Angelica knew about all those things before they happened?"

Dylan turned those burning blue eyes on me. I saw a sort of desperation in him: that I didn't believe him, that I thought he was crazy. For the first time I could see how it might have been hard for him—despite his beauty, despite the gold earrings and Doc Martens and all the other trappings of flaming youth—to find a girlfriend. Hard maybe to make any friends at all.

"Yes," he said, daring me to argue. "She did."

I waited. Then, "I believe you, Dylan," I said softly. I reached to touch him on the shoulder, half-expecting him to flinch or turn away. But he didn't. He turned and took me in his arms. I could feel him trembling as he whispered, "She scares me sometimes, Sweeney. I know she's my mother, but she scares me . . ."

"Me too," I murmured, and stroked his tangled hair, the two of us holding each other so tightly that not even the golden air could slide between us.

"The way she talks," he went on in a low voice, like a child comforting himself. "All this crazy goddess stuff, but the way she goes on about it in her books and all, it almost makes sense. You can really see how these women fall for it. It's not just that she *knows* about these things. I can believe that. I mean, animals know when there's going to be an earthquake, right? But some of the people who're into all her New Age stuff, *they* think she *makes it happen*! Like in Hawaii they think there's this goddess Pele who makes the volcanoes blow up—these people think my mother can actually *do* that!"

He rubbed his forehead as though it pained him. "Sometimes, I think my mother believes it herself."

"Oh, she does, Dylan," I whispered, but he didn't hear me.

"You know what she's like?" he said at last. "This picture I saw when I was at Lawrenceville. An X ray of the inside of a nuclear blast, taken out at White Sands. Have you ever see that? Outside you can see all this smoke, this huge mushroom cloud and flames everywhere. But inside it's just all this fire, and then in the very middle, there's a black hollow core. Like there's all this destruction around it, but in the middle there's nothing there at all."

I shuddered and reached for my glass. "Maybe we should think about going out to get something to eat," I suggested, finishing my wine. "You hungry?"

Unexpectedly, Dylan laughed, as though we'd been talking of nothing more serious than the weather, then rolled over to slide his arms around my waist. "I could be," he said, nuzzling my throat. "Maybe. If I had the chance to work up an appetite—"

Later, we went out to eat.

When we returned that night, Dylan tried calling Dr. Dvorkin, to see about picking up his things from the main house. But Robert was out, no doubt caught up in selecting the new regent, or else with the Aditi or the Mall's Independence Day celebrations or any of the million other things that consumed his life. I finally gave Dylan my key, so he could get into the house and retrieve his things. He returned to the carriage house with a knapsack, a gym bag stuffed with clothes, a personal CD player, and a couple of paperbacks, *Shampoo Planet* and *Pylon* and a book about the Neanderthals.

"That's it?" I stared at the overflowing gym bag. "That's all you brought for the entire summer?"

Dylan shrugged. "My mom's coming out for my birthday. She'll get me some more clothes then."

We called in sick the next day, and the day after that. We stayed in my bedroom in the carriage house, with the wisteria trailing through the open window and the old fan in the belfry humming like a hornet's nest. At night we'd venture out onto the Hill, walking as in a trance through the blue-veined air, drunk on sex and heat and wine, both of us not a little stunned to find the city still around us, the sound of firecrackers and police cruisers crackling somewhere just out of sight. At twilight government workers filled the outdoor cafés, crowding the little round marble-topped tables. Street kids vied with each other along the southeast strip of Pennsylvania Avenue, kicking through spent blossoms and McDonald's wrappers and the frayed blackened tails of firecracker strings. At 3:00 A.M. the streets filled with revelers leaving the bars, and their laughter became part of our sleep and our lovemaking, laughter and the crash of bottles breaking against the curb, like surf pounding a far-off shore.

"I love you, Sweeney," Dylan would whisper, his hands warm against my breast.

Before I could fall asleep again, I would wait to hear his heavy breathing. I would wait, to make sure that he didn't disappear.

When I finally awoke, it was as though I had awakened to find myself in another city. The city I had first glimpsed years before, the city that Oliver had shown me, with its ghosts and transvestite hustlers and phantom cab drivers. Sometimes Dylan and I heard gunshots and far-off screams; more often the tired banter of lawyers and nannies, and college students walking home at 4:00 A.M. from tending bar and waiting tables on the Hill.

Best of all, early one evening, we saw a little family walking from Union Station: mother, small boy, father in military uniform, the exultant boy swinging between his parents and then suddenly bursting free, to run shouting into the empty traffic circle with its lines of American flags, arms raised as he yelled at the top of his lungs,

"ALREADY I LOVE IT!"

Dylan fell onto the sidewalk, laughing helplessly. I joined him, and we watched as the family raced gleefully toward the Capitol.

"Sweeney, this is a great place," said Dylan, wiping his eyes and turning to drape his arm around my shoulder. "Already I love it."

So that, too, he gave back to me: the city I had fallen in love with once, the city I thought I had lost forever—

Always you will arrive in this city. Do not hope for any other—

When at last we went to work again we walked with arms linked down Pennsylvania Avenue, disentangling ourselves when we reached the Mall and putting on our best sober faces when we got inside the museum. No one seemed surprised that I'd taken time off. Whenever I passed Dylan in the hall, whenever he ducked into my office, I felt as though wisps of smoke must hover above our heads like Pentecostal flames. But no one else seemed to notice at all, or if they did, no one cared.

Still, we tried to be discreet; at least I did. Dylan seemed immensely pleased to be carrying on an affair, and I suspected he was just waiting for someone to ask him so he could spill the beans.

"Don't," I cautioned him, almost daily. "I could get in trouble for this."

"How? We're consenting adults."

Well, one *of us is,* I thought. But I only said, "Dr. Dvorkin is very, very paranoid about this kind of thing, okay? This is government work, and there are big problems with sexual harassment in this city, and I just would rather we be discreet, all right?"

Dylan rolled his eyes and slung his hands into his pockets. "Of course. *Discreet.*"

Although I hadn't seen much of Dr. Dvorkin since Dylan arrived. He had greeted Dylan when we finally made it back to the museum. He seemed pleased enough to see him, and didn't appear to have taken note of the fact that neither of us had been in to work for some days, not to mention that Dylan was supposed to be staying in Dr. Dvorkin's guest room, rather than my bed.

"Your mother is well?" Dr. Dvorkin asked absently. He was even more preoccupied than he normally was. The phone in his office kept ringing, and his comments to whoever was on the other line were unusually terse. "Please give her my best, will you? Now then—"

He sighed and touched his brow with a handkerchief, and we followed him down the hall. "Katherine, I'll be out again all day. If you need me, talk to Laurie—"

"Has Dr. Dvorkin ever *met* your mother?" I asked, as Dylan and I stared after him.

"I don't know. He and my grandfather were good friends, I know that."

I glanced sideways at Dylan. He was wearing baggy khaki trousers and a white oxford cloth shirt, the sleeves rolled up loosely to expose smoothly muscled forearms and bony wrists, his tousled hair slipping from its ponytail. He leaned on the curved banister, staring rather mournfully down at Dr. Dvorkin's retreating figure. I wondered if Dylan knew about the *Benandanti*—it struck me that he should be a legacy of theirs, if anyone was. The thought was dispiriting, almost frightening, and I pushed it aside.

"Hey," I said, and turned away. "You got work to do."

"See you at lunch?"

I nodded and smiled. "Yeah. *Au revoir,* kiddo."

Summer was usually a slow time of year, despite the annual onslaught of tourists. While I'd been playing hooky with Dylan, only a few messages had come in on my machine—the usual inquiries for photos and videodiscs, a message from Jack Rogers, a few intelligently worded calls from Baby Joe in New York.

"Uh, yeah, hija, *what the fuck you doing? Call me."*

"Jeez, hija, *it's Thursday. Where the fuck are you?"*

There were several more variations on this theme. I played them back and grinned, wondering how Baby Joe would react when he learned I was fooling around with an intern. But the idea of telling him about Dylan himself, and Dylan's parentage, was just a little too much to contemplate. So I didn't call Baby Joe back right away. I figured I'd wait a couple of days, until I'd caught up with everything else.

It wasn't just me: that summer, *everything* was slightly skewed. The weather was strange—had been strange, for months and months, which made Dylan's comments about his mother even more unsettling. After a long and terrible winter, with its earthquakes and blizzards and record cold, there came a terrible spring—floods and mudslides, more earthquakes in places with unpronounceable names, unexpected volcanic eruptions in Indonesia that dumped a fine layer of ash into the atmosphere. That did not bode well for the coming winter, though scientists seemed to think we might be graced with a cooler summer.

But then summer came, and by the second week of July we were experiencing a record heat wave—a record even for D.C., which is really saying something. The temperature stayed up around a hundred, and scarcely dropped in the evening, when the streets and sidewalks would be covered with immense cockroaches and water bugs trying, like everyone else, to find some respite from the heat. At first the brownouts came weekly, then every few days; but I soon got used to hearing shouted curses and shrieks from odd corners of the museum, whenever the power cut and the computer network crashed.

Elsewhere it was worse. In the Midwest a drought ravaged crops. A biblical plague of locusts swept from Missouri to the Dakota Badlands, leaving dust and mounds of hollow carapaces in their wake. More flash fires devoured the West Coast, where people were still trying to rebuild from the earthquake. On the Baja Peninsula an outbreak of rodent-borne hantavirus caused a temporary quarantine to be set up. Up in Acadia National Park a devastating fire swept across Mount Desert, brought on by the hot weather and a careless hiker's match. In the Pacific Northwest a full-scale war broke out between loggers and environmentalists, with tree-spikers getting picked off with AK-47s and logging trucks blown up in the middle of Route 687. The locusts were blamed for at least one major airplane crash; in D.C., cockroaches literally smothered a child sleeping on a front porch swing.

"Jesus," I said when this last news item came over NPR, and switched stations.

There was the usual talk of apocalypse, of the coming millennium and the failure of schools, and god only knew what was going on in the Middle East. So yes, it was strange and disturbing and even frightening, but it was also so much business as usual—you know, Texas Cult Claims Entire Town. Bus Crashes in New Delhi, Thousands Die.

And I just didn't care, I just didn't want to think about it. I just didn't want to think about anything but Dylan. I bought some boric acid and a new fire extinguisher at Hechinger's, and laid in a case of decent chardonnay from the Mayflower. I stopped reading the front section of the *Post,* and started hanging out with Dylan at Tower Records and flipping through *Pulse.*

It was harder for me to ignore that something odd was going on in the museum, something that took up a great deal of Dr. Dvorkin's time. I saw him leaving his office at odd hours, always with a strained expression, often heavily laden with sheaves of papers, manila folders, even wooden boxes. When I went down to Laurie's desk to ask her about it, she only shrugged.

"I don't know, Katherine. It might be another one of those Native American things—"

I groaned. Like a number of museums across the country, we'd come under fire for having sacred objects in our collections. There'd been a few lawsuits, a few out-of-court settlements, a lot of unhappy-making press, and one of our Native American galleries closed for renovation when its permanent collection of *kachina* dolls turned out to be not so permanent after all. "Am I supposed to be doing something? Like, not talking to the press? Or talking to the press?"

Laurie jabbed at her computer with a paper clip. "Too late. Somebody from the *Post* was in already—oh, but you were out sick, weren't you? Well, anyway, there's supposed to be some big story coming out soon."

"More Indian stuff?"

"I don't know. I don't think so—I think it's something bigger than that. Something with Turkey, maybe."

"Turkey?"

"The country, Katherine." Laurie tossed the paper clip into a corner and looked at me suspiciously. "What's the matter with you, anyway? You still look a little out of it—"

I gestured feebly. "Nothing. A sinus infection. What's going on with Turkey?"

"I'm not sure. Robert hasn't told me, but everyone down in Paleo is having a cow. I think Robert's just trying to get some damage control going."

I tapped a handful of papers against my palm. "Guess I chose the wrong week to be out, huh?"

"Or the right one." The phone buzzed and she turned away. "See you later, Katherine. I'm glad you're feeling better."

I walked slowly back to my office. I wasn't terribly concerned about whatever might be happening in Paleolithic Europe, except insofar as it might cause me actually to think about my job instead of Dylan.

But whatever storm was brewing, it wasn't ready to break quite yet. The rest of that week was quiet—unusually quiet, even for the curatorial wing of the Museum of Natural History in mid-July. Dylan and I played hooky, coming in late, leaving early—the sort of thing that gives civil servants a bad name. I barely pretended to work. Instead I walked around in a Technicolor haze, feeling as though I'd somehow wandered from the world I knew into the Bombay Film Board's version of my life, the Mall outside magically transformed into an exotic festival complete with fireworks and sloe-eyed boys and girls, Hindi puppet shows, and little stalls selling bird cages and fighting kites and *puri.* The heat wasn't so bad, if you didn't actually have to move. Dylan and I took three-hour lunches, and I found that Jack Rogers had been as good as his word: Pink Pelican beer was now being sold at all Aditi food kiosks. I arranged to use up some of the million or so vacation days I'd accrued over the last eight years, and basically did what everyone else in D.C. did that summer: not a damn thing.

Dylan *did* get some work done. He cataloged photos for the Larkin Archive and gradually learned his way around the museum. For hours he'd wander through the Anthropology Wing by himself, poking into odd corners and storage bins, occasionally coming back by my office to show me something he'd found—a first edition of *The Origin of Species* shoved beneath the leg of an ancient rolltop desk; a cardboard folder holding original photo gravures of Edward Steichen's most famous works, the Flatiron Building and Central Park in the snow and half a dozen other images, all printed on tiny narrow bits of paper frail and lovely as dried violets; even one of Maggie's hissing cockroaches that had made its home near a collection of Malaysian spirit puppets in the Indonesian corner.

"Keep looking," I told him after he presented a German helmet from World War I to a bemused ornithologist. "Jimmy Hoffa's in there somewhere, and the guy who wrote *The Little Prince*."

Dylan grinned. "And Elvis?"

"Elvis is over in American History."

One week flowed into the next. I put off calling Baby Joe, just like I put off everything else. The heat wave showed no signs of abating. Perhaps as a result of that, the threatened *Post* article didn't appear. I was just starting to think that maybe, just maybe, I might get away with it. That maybe this was what it was all for—all those lost years, my exile from the Divine and the only people I had ever let myself love. That I had finally found a safe place; that I had finally found one of the Beautiful Ones. And he loved me.

Then Laurie Driscoll dropped by one morning with the latest issue of *Archaeology.*

"Here," she said. She opened the magazine and tossed it onto my desk. "This just came in. Check it out."

"What is it?"

"Just read."

Two brief articles crowded a page otherwise filled with ads for personalized cartouches and a bonded marble replica of Queen Hatshepsut's head. The first article noted that a prestigious Manhattan art dealer had agreed to return a collection of Middle Kingdom Minoan gold seal rings, ivory, necklaces, and faience sculptures, including two images of the so-called Cretan Snake Goddess, to the Greek National Museum in Athens. The collection was valued at over $2 million on the booming antiquities market, but before it could be transferred to Athens, the National Museum itself was slapped with a lawsuit by a feminist spiritualist group named Potnia, after the ancient Cretan mistress of the beasts.

"Oh, *great,*" I said under my breath. I glanced up at Laurie. "I guess you're not interested in talking about this nice ad for Mayaland Resorts, huh?" I asked wistfully.

"Read it."

I read that Potnia's attorney and spokeswoman, Rosanne Minerva, claimed that the collection should neither be in private hands nor in a museum. It was "the ancient spiritual legacy of women everywhere and, as such, should be given into the keeping of a sacred trust that will administer these objects, and others like them, for all womankind." In lieu of an expensive lawsuit, the Greek National Museum and the Manhattan art dealer agreed to donate the collection to Potnia, under Ms. Minerva's watchful eyes. It was presumed that both museum and gallery would reap substantial tax benefits from the transfer.

This article segued quite neatly into the second, which detailed how the well-known American businessman Michael Haring had agreed to donate his private collection of Neolithic artifacts, including a Celtic Bronze Age mummy, to Potnia. This was a timely decision on Haring's part, as there now seemed to be some question as to how he had come by many of these artifacts in the first place. Several governments, including those of Cyprus, Denmark, and Turkey, had threatened him with legal action, but the redoubtable Ms. Minerva seemed to wield a great deal of clout—more than I could easily fathom.

Until I got to the article's last sentence, which read,

> Potnia's actions toward retrieving "sacred womanist icons" is in large part underwritten by Dr. Angelica Furiano, the noted

archaeologist and author who has achieved fame through her best-selling works on women's spirituality.

"Ouch." I closed the magazine and pushed it away, pressed my fingers against my throbbing forehead. "Michael Haring, why is that name familiar?"

I looked up to see Laurie staring at me pointedly, her arms crossed.

"'Angelica Furiano, now why is that familiar?'" she said, mimicking me.

I opened my mouth, shut it again, turned to stare at my computer. "Am I missing something, Laurie? I'm serious. Who's Haring? I mean, besides being some capitalist tool?"

Laurie sighed and reached for the magazine. "Well, he's a regent of the National Museum of Natural History, for one thing."

My eyes widened. "No kidding?"

"No kidding."

"So you think this is what Robert's been dealing with? Some radical feminist group demanding he return their artifacts? No wonder he seems so depressed."

Laurie leaned against my desk, slipping her feet out of her espadrilles. "Are you telling me this is news to you, Katherine?"

"Well, yes," I said slowly. "I am. This is the first I've heard of it. I mean—well, Laurie, give me a break, okay?" I finally exploded. "I haven't been paying much attention lately, I'll admit it! But this stuff—"

I waved disparagingly at the magazine. "It's not my field, you know? And it sounds like all these cases are being settled out of court, so . . ."

Laurie stared at me as though I had suggested stomping a little bunny to death with her bare feet. "Pete Suthard said he heard they might have to shut down seven galleries."

"Seven! That's ridiculous! There can't be *one* gallery's worth of goddess stuff here—"

"I'm just telling you what I heard. He said these Potnia people have apparently joined up with an alliance of Native Americans' civil rights groups, some African-American groups, the Celtic Gay and Lesbian National Congress—"

She sighed and slid back into her shoes. "Well, anyway, I just thought you might have some inside track on this. Because of—well, because of Dylan."

"Dylan." I slumped farther down in my ergonomic chair. "Dylan?"

Laurie snorted. "What, you think nobody here's noticed you're shacking up with an intern?"

I rubbed my nose, then replied a little defensively, "Well, yes."

"Oh, please. Not that I care. I just thought, well, because of his mother—I thought you might know something about this other stuff."

"I don't."

"I believe you. It's just that whatever is going on seems to have Robert more worked up than I've ever seen him." Laurie looked uncomfortable, even somewhat pissed. "You know, if they bring the ombudsman in to check out whatever it is these Potnia people want, it's going to be a royal pain in the tush. At the *least.*"

"They won't bring the ombudsman in," I said, and tried to sound like I meant it. With Robert Dvorkin so preoccupied and the rest of the curators on vacation, I was just about the senior staff member. I had enough of a conscience to feel a vague sense of responsibility to the department, at least enough to make a cursory effort at reassuring our secretary that she wouldn't be out of a job anytime soon. "Relax, okay, Laurie?"

"I *am* relaxed. I'm going to Hatteras in a few weeks," she said smugly, and headed for the door. "I just thought *you* should know. Since with Robert so tied up, *you'll* pretty much be in charge of everything."

"Gee, thanks." I watched her go. For a moment I thought of chasing her down, to retrieve that magazine.

Then I decided I just wasn't going to think about it. For one thing, it wasn't any of my business. I didn't *want* it to be any of my business. I had invested almost my entire adult life into being a drone, a suit in Washington, a Videodisc Project Supervisor Grade 9, Step 4, and that's how I liked it. The museum wasn't paying me enough to think—that was Dr. Dvorkin's job. I didn't *want* to think, especially now. I wanted to believe this was all just some odd coincidence. I wanted to believe that Angelica had no reason to be thinking of me, or the museum, or even her own son, no reason at all beyond her own career concerns, whatever the hell *those* might be. I wanted Dylan, that was all. I wanted Dylan, and I didn't want to be reminded of anything strange in my past that might have led to his being here with me now.

And Dylan obviously didn't want to think about it, either. We had reached a sort of unspoken agreement about his mother. If he wanted to talk about Angelica, I'd listen; but I learned not to question him.

"Don't you think you should at least give her a call?" This was after we'd been together for a few weeks. I was on my way to Eastern Market to get some ribs for dinner. "I'll be out for a while, you could—"

"I already called her," Dylan said shortly. He was wearing tight frayed cutoffs and nothing else, sprawled on the old Castro Convertible with those impossibly long legs dangling over the sofa's edge. "She knows how to find me if she needs me."

"Fine," I said, and left.

I wondered about that. At Dr. Dvorkin's request, I'd been going over to the main house nearly every day after work, to water the orchids and feed the cats and gather up the mail. That evening my heart skipped: under the stacks of magazines and overseas correspondence I found an envelope with Dylan's name on it, written in Angelica's lovely handwriting with peacock blue ink. My hand shook a little as I picked it up, and the rest of the mail slid to the floor.

"You got a letter," I said when I got back to the carriage house, trying to sound nonchalant as I handed it to him. Dylan glanced at the envelope and tossed it aside. I went out onto the patio to check the grill. When I came inside again, the letter was gone—I know, because I looked for it when Dylan was in the bathroom. It finally appeared again a few days before Dylan's birthday, shoved beneath the kilim that covered the sofa. The envelope was still unopened. When I picked it up I could smell sandalwood, like incense clinging to the heavy paper—sandalwood and oranges and the odor of ground coriander seed.

Annie Harmon stared at the ranks of black and grey limousines lined up in front of the Javits Convention Center. Behind the soot-colored monolith, the Hudson moved sluggishly, streaked black and orange from where the sun was dipping behind the Jersey skyline. If she inhaled deeply enough, she could smell the river, rank with spilled gasoline and dead fish; but Annie didn't want to smell it. She didn't want to be there at all. The out-of-towners disgusted her, there wasn't a decent place to eat within ten blocks, and she didn't believe that Justine was going to show up in a limo with a very rich john.

Actually, Annie *could* believe that; she just preferred not to. If she looked closely at the vehicles pulled alongside the river, Annie could see heads bobbing up and down in most of them, TV and TS whores taking care of the tourists and bridge-and-tunnel regulars. But she didn't want to see that any more than she wanted to smell the garbage barge drifting past, with its clouds of gulls and blowflies; any more than she wanted to think about the message Justine had left on her hotel room's voice mail. So she sat on the convention center steps and tried not to think, that week's unread *Voice* balanced on her knees. Tried not to think at all.

It had been three weeks since Baby Joe's death. Pulmonary failure, said the coroner's report. Not as uncommon as you'd think at places like Chumley Peckerwood's; although at thirty-eight, José Malabar was still pretty young, even with the extra weight and cigarettes and peripatetic sleep habits. It made for a sordid little story nonetheless, a few inches of newsprint glorifying the death of a minor New York character in a strip club. The usual HEADLESS BODY IN TOPLESS BAR kind of stuff, a few halfhearted attempts at suspecting foul play; then someone from *Newsday* took over Baby Joe's column and that was the end of it. Annie had been afraid to go to the funeral in D.C. or even to call his family. Instead she'd had Helen send some flowers and a card with both their names on it. Later, after she'd gotten all this other screwed-up shit taken care of, she'd come up with a more fitting memorial for her murdered friend.

Because if Angelica di Rienzi didn't have something to do with Baby Joe's death, then she, Anne Marie Jeanne Harmon, was a Carmelite nun. And Carmelites don't hang out on the Manhattan riverfront, waiting to meet transsexual prostitutes early of a torrid July evening.

"Annie! I'm he-ere—"

Annie turned, and grinned in spite of herself. Justine had, indeed, arrived by limo. She watched as her leggy friend flowed from the back of an endless silvery vehicle, patting demurely at her carefully arranged coif and then striding across the street, skirting steaming puddles and rubbish-filled potholes with her size-thirteen platform shoes.

"Hi, Justine," said Annie. "Wanna go see *Cats?*"

"Uh." Justine swept up beside her and looked around disdainfully, adjusting a pair of gold-framed sunglasses on her aquiline nose. "I hate this place—*c'est a cochons*." She lifted her chin as someone on the other side of the street shouted her name and an epithet. "Eat *moi,* asshole! Girlfriend, you look terrible," she added, looking down at Annie.

Annie shrugged. A streetlamp clicked on, showering the steps with violent light and making Justine's shades glow taxi yellow. Annie could see herself in the lenses: her buzz cut growing out in sloppy tufts, her eyes shadowed and face blotched. No chance anyone would recognize her as last week's Heavy Rotation. "Yeah, I know," she sighed. "I look like shit. Pardon me—*merde*. So let's cut to the car crash. What did you find out?"

"I found your friend."

"You did." Annie took a deep breath, forgetting about the toxic air, and closed her eyes very tight. "I wasn't crazy. You really did." For a moment she thought she'd cry, from relief or exhaustion or maybe joy.

"She is in London—" Justine rummaged in her Day-Glo vinyl purse, spilling a wad of bills and Technicolor condoms onto the steps. "Ooops, wait—*here* it is—"

Justine stooped to sweep up the money in one hand, in the other flourished a piece of paper. "*Was* in London. Her roommate said the last time he saw her was several months ago. This is where she was until then. Sorry—there's no forwarding address."

Annie took the paper from Justine's enameled fingers and stared at it. A name she didn't recognize, an address on the Camden High Street. For a long time she said nothing. Justine stood above her and smoked a cigarette. The sun disappeared behind the river's western shore, the number of hired cars in front of the convention center dwindled to the occasional Yellow Cab or livery driver.

"Okay," Annie said at last. She folded the paper and put it carefully into her filofax. "Was there—was there anything else? I mean, do you know what she's been doing all this time?"

Justine took a final drag on her cigarette and tossed it away. She exhaled, then said, "She went to Southeast Asia. I think maybe Thailand, for a long time. No, wait—Taiwan, maybe? I don't remember. Her roommate said she had some problems with junk for a little while but she's clean now. Her doctor was there, Bangkok or someplace, that's why it took me so long to come up with anything for you—everyone I know sees someone here, or maybe in Stockholm. Not Taiwan."

"Bangkok's not in Taiwan," Annie said. "It's in Thailand."

Justine twisted her head and peered out above the rim of her sunglasses. Annie had a glimpse of kohl-rimmed eyes and pupils so dilated it was like staring into the empty sockets of a skull. "I will tell you something, *chérie*. Sometimes, people who do this don't want to be found—"

"No shit," Annie snapped, but Justine raised a hand warningly.

"I was *going* to say, *sometimes* they don't want to be found; but I think your friend *will* find you, Annie. She found you once already. She will again—"

"But—"

"But I have to go now, *chérie*." Justine stretched her arms and yawned loudly. "I have a date."

"Wait—" Annie stumbled to her feet, yanking her knapsack after her. "Look, Justine. I know you're a friend of Helen's and all, but I thought—well, I feel bad, you going to all this trouble. So—can I write you a check or something—something to reimburse you for your time?"

Justine dropped her arms, staring at Annie with those huge black eyes, and burst into laughter. "*Pay* me! No way, girl—"

"Aw, Justine, you made all those overseas phone calls! I *know* this was more trouble than you thought—"

Justine grabbed Annie by the chin. "*Chérie!* You and Helen are *both* my friends. Just remember me when you're rich and famous—*really* rich, and *really* famous.

"Besides," she said, letting go of Annie's chin and leaning down to kiss her noisily on the cheek, "I charged those calls to a client. And—"

She laughed again, swinging her vinyl bag through the hazy air. "You could never afford me, girlfriend."

"Justine . . ." Annie took her hand and squeezed it. "I can't thank you enough. Really."

Justine nodded. "I know." She clattered down the steps, stopped and looked back. "It is sad about José Malabar, uh? I will miss his columns in the *Beacon.*"

"Me too," Annie sighed. "Me fucking too."

Justine sauntered off, and Annie waved sadly after her. When the tall silhouette disappeared into the shadows at river's edge, Annie hitched her knapsack over her shoulder and began walking away from the Javits Center. At the corner she hailed a cab.

"Penn Station," she said, and slumped into the seat. As the taxi careened in and out of traffic she took out the paper Justine had given her and studied it again, finally put it aside and rummaged through her restaurant chits and airline stubs until she found a tattered Amtrak schedule.

TRAIN # 177 THE SENATOR DAILY/WEEKENDS
DEPART PENN STATION 9:45 P.M. ARRIVE UNION STATION, D.C. 1:13 A.M.

"Well," she said softly to herself. *Looks like old home week for the archangels.*

At Penn Station she paid for her ticket in cash—Helen had her credit cards—found a liquor store and bought a bottle of Pernod, because she remembered that was what her college friends used to drink. At 7:55 she boarded the train and collapsed into a seat. She took out a narrow sheaf of twenties—half of what remained of her cash—and stuck it in her right sneaker. Then she, Annie Harmon, who never, *ever* drank, spent the next few hours choking down Pernod until she finally passed out, somewhere around Wilmington, Delaware. She didn't wake up until they pulled into Union Station, an hour later than the Senator's scheduled arrival time and much too late for the Metro to still be running. The few other passengers trudged to where a handful of BMWs and Audis and Volvo wagons were waiting for them. Annie brought up the end of the parade, stumbling a little.

When she got outside she looked around blearily. It had been a few years since she'd been in D.C. It was like getting that first whiff of ocean air: just one deep breath and it all came back to her, the swampy heat and soot and honeysuckle, the sound of traffic a few blocks away in the old riot corridor and an ambulance wailing along North Capitol Street.

"Great," she muttered. At least they'd cleaned up Union Station.

A solitary cab was parked beside the curb in front of the station.

"I guess I need to find someplace that's still open," Annie announced thickly to the driver as she slid into the backseat. "I mean a hotel or something. There a Day's Inn around here?"

The engine started with a thrumming roar. "I'll take care of you, young lady, now don't you worry," the driver said in a deep, oddly comforting voice. Annie winced. She must sound like a hick. A *drunken* hick; this guy would never believe she'd lived here once. She stared defiantly at the back of his head, trying to remember the name of some other hotel, but her brain felt damp and empty. "Don't you worry at all."

"Yeah, okay." Annie glanced at his medallion, just in case he tried to overcharge her. Yellow Cab Number 393: easy enough to remember. "Maybe the Phoenix, then. Or the Tiber Creek . . ."

The taxi swung out into the empty traffic circle, with its carefully arranged plantings of red, white, and blue petunias. Annie thought of how she should have called Helen, let her know she was coming down here, but then Helen would just worry. Fuck it, Helen would worry no matter *what.* And Annie's lover was right, the cloak-and-dagger stuff was getting old. Their money was running low, people were starting to wonder where she was; Labrys had started calling about getting her back into the studio.

And it was probably a *really* stupid idea to come down here to D.C., especially since Annie didn't have a number or address or anything for Sweeney Cassidy. She wasn't even certain that Sweeney still lived here, although she was pretty sure Baby Joe had told her that she did; and even if she did find Sweeney, it might be too late to stop Angelica's little game of Ten Little College Friends . . .

Somehow, somewhere between Union Station and the Old Executive Office Building, Annie must have fallen asleep. Because the next thing she knew, she was being helped gently from the cab's backseat and led into the softly glowing lobby of the Hay-Adams, which was not anyplace she ordinarily would have been caught dead in, not to mention being a place neither she nor Labrys Music could possibly afford.

"Hey," Annie mumbled. "This is—maybe I just better—"

But before she could say anything else, or even really wake up, she was in an elevator, and then she was in a richly carpeted hallway, and stumbling into a room; and then she was lying on a bed fully clothed with a warm blanket pulled up around her chin against the arctic air-conditioning, and there were voices whispering, and someone saying, "Of course, we understand," and finally the sound of a door closing and blissful, peaceful silence.

When she woke up it was late morning. The phone was ringing to inform her that checkout time was noon.

"Unless you'll be staying another night?" The voice on the other end suggested.

Annie shook her head, dazed. "Huh? Oh—no, I mean, I think there's been a mistake. I—"

"Your bill's already been taken care of. Just leave your key at the front desk as you depart."

"What?" But the voice had already rung off.

She was still wearing the fatigues and sleeveless flannel shirt she'd had on last night; the same clothes she'd had on for several days, including her sneakers. She was too confused and hung over to feel panicky yet, but she figured she should get out of here fast, before someone figured out there'd been a mistake.

Although maybe there's time for a quick shower, she thought, gazing wistfully to where the bathroom door was cracked open. She tried to stand, had to pause and give her head a chance to stop reeling. *How do people* drink?

After her shower she felt better. She found her knapsack set carefully on a mahogany table, beside a brass lamp. Next to it was a message pad printed with a nice engraving of the Hay-Adams Hotel, circa 1923. She stared at the pad curiously, suddenly grabbed it.

"What the *hell?*"

Bold black letters marched across the paper where someone had written a message in Magic Marker. Annie's hands began to tremble as she read.

KATHERINE CASSIDY
19A NINTH STREET NE
547-8903

Compliments of a friend
and Handsome Brown.

So the summer passed. And in spite of the dreadful heat, the rumors of imminent disaster at the museum, and the usual threats of gang violence, random shootings, environmental cataclysm, and inflation, I was happier than I had ever been in my life.

If you had asked me what I was most afraid of, it wouldn't have been any of those awful things. It would have been that Dylan would wake up one morning and suddenly remember that he was only eighteen and I was thirty-eight; that it was his prerogative to be a fickle adolescent; that he had a whole other life to lead, with college and girls and god knows what, and I had Amex payments and the same dull job waiting for me that I'd held forever. My affair with Dylan shouldn't have meant anything to either of us; it should have been nothing but a summer fling. It seemed crazy, even irresponsible, for me to think otherwise.

But I did. Dylan and I had never really spoken about What Happened Next. The fall term at UCLA started before Labor Day, and September first I was supposed to go to Rochester to look over a collection that Kodak was thinking of selling to the museum. It seemed impossible that our relationship could outlast the summer; it seemed ridiculous that I should even dream of it doing so. Yet the mere thought of going on without Dylan, of returning home alone to the carriage house every day, was enough to reduce me to tears. But I was afraid to ask him to stay.

At night I lay beside him and listened to the mockingbird in the garden outside. Dylan's dark tousled hair spilled across the sheets, moonlight threw shadows across his chest and throat and I would be so flooded with love and desire that I would fall on him like a panther, biting softly at his throat, the skin there taut and tasting like a salted peach. Groaning, he would awaken and we'd fall onto the floor, Dylan clutching me as I straddled him, while outside the moon hung like another fruit in the sky.

"Oh, Sweeney, Sweeney . . ."

His voice broke as he hugged me to him and I cried, we both cried, from joy or exhaustion or unspoken fear, or perhaps just because it was so beautiful, so terribly, terribly beautiful there in the moonlit summer night with the smell of roses and wisteria perfuming our skin.

A few days before his birthday we went to Kelly's, the Irish bar next to the Dubliner. They knew me there and never raised an eyebrow when they saw me with Dylan, and never asked to see his ID. The ceiling fans turned desultorily overhead, but otherwise everyone seemed to have given in to the heat. Maureen the bartender had stripped down to a Wonderbra and a pair of men's plaid boxer shorts; the band was wearing much the same, minus the bra. Dylan drank black-and-tans and I sipped cognac. The band knocked back pints of Guinness and cooled off by spraying each other with bottles of Molson. When closing time came Maureen hopped over the bar, locked the door, and lowered the lights, so the rest of us could stay inside. We drank some more, yelling requests, and the band played everything from the Irish national anthem to "Purple Haze" and "Ghost on the Highway." Dylan took his shirt off and we danced by the unplugged jukebox, knocking over bottles and pint glasses and sliding in spilt beer. As the light in the windows turned the color of a steel penny, Dylan went up and gave Sean the lead singer a twenty-dollar-bill, and the band played their last song—

I never felt magic crazy as this
I never saw a moon knew the meaning of the sea
I never held emotion in the palm of my hand
Or felt sweet breezes in the top of a tree
But now you're here
To brighten my northern sky . . .

We stood and swayed in front of the tiny stage, and Dylan shouted drunkenly in my ear and pointed to where Sean listed in front of the microphone—

"Listen, Sweeney!"

—as Sean sang in his raw, Guinness-blurred tenor.

Would you love me for my money?
Would you love me for my head?

Would you love me through the winter?
Would you love me till I'm dead?
Oh if you would and you could
Come blow your horn on high . . .

"Would you, Sweeney?" Dylan pulled me to him until our noses bumped. His breath was warm and sweet and beery as his arms encircled me. "Would you?"

I looked at him, confused. "Would I—?"

"Stay with me? Marry me—forever?"

"*Marry* you?"

"Marry me!" Dylan shouted. He turned to the band and yelled drunkenly, "I just asked her to marry me!"

From behind the bar Maureen and her friends cheered, and the few others scattered at tables joined in. Sean laughed and yelled into the microphone, "And what did she say?"

Dylan looked at me. "What did you say?"

I stared up at him, at the grinning faces watching us from onstage and at Maureen and the expectant strangers behind the bar; then, laughing, I flung my arms out and shouted the only thing that seemed appropriate.

"Yes, I said—yes I will!—

"Yes."

That was how I decided to get married. The next morning neither Dylan nor I had changed our minds, although we didn't make any immediate plans to find a chapel. It was the thirty-first of July. Tomorrow Dylan would turn nineteen. Angelica was still supposed to be coming for his birthday, although I had no idea when she'd arrive or what arrangements, if any, she and Dylan had made. Now it felt even stranger to think about Angelica—my former friend and onetime lover was going to be my mother-in-law? I had no close friends of my own to confide in, certainly not anyone who would understand the inherent weirdness of the whole situation with Dylan and me. So I decided to concentrate on planning a private birthday celebration for just the two of us. Dinner at home, since otherwise we wouldn't be able to drink champagne. It was too hot to cook, so I thought we'd bring home a couple of boxes of sushi from a place on the Hill. I laid in three bottles of Taitinger and a pint of Ben & Jerry's. If Angelica decided to show up, well, I'd deal with that later.

I did want to tell *someone,* though. So when I got to the office I finally broke down and called Baby Joe. After three rings his machine clicked in and I heard an unfamiliar voice.

"You have reached Daniel Aquilante at the Arts Desk of the New York Beacon. *Please leave a message at the tone, or else call Reception at 8407."*

"That's weird." I frowned and dialed again, got the same recording. "Huh."

I double-checked the number in my computer, then tried Baby Joe at home.

"The number you have reached has been disconnected."

I dialed again and got the same playback. When I put the phone down I felt chilled. I walked over to my window and stared outside.

The Aditi had ended last weekend. Now the Mall looked like the aftermath of Woodstock or something worse—trash heaped in huge piles inside hurricane fencing, Park Police and orange-suited custodial engineers everywhere, bare scaffolding and dead grass where I had grown accustomed to seeing luminously colored kiosks and tents. That morning in the coffee room I'd overheard someone talking about an infestation of rats outside, drawn by the mountains of food left to rot in the heat. At the time I'd laughed, but now I felt distinctly uneasy. I turned back to my desk and dialed Manhattan information, then called the main number at the New York *Beacon.*

"I'm trying to reach José Malabar," I said when someone finally picked up the line.

Silence. "I'm a friend of his from college," I explained. "I was out of town for a while, and when I got back I had several messages from him on my machine—"

"Hold on, please."

A moment later someone else came on, a woman with a pleasant but reserved-sounding voice. "Who's calling, please?"

I took a deep breath. "My name is Katherine Cassidy. I'm with the National Museum in Washington and I had several messages to call José—"

"You said you were a friend of his?"

"Yes." My heart was pounding as I stammered, "Why?"

The woman sighed. "I'm not really supposed to do this, but—" She hesitated. "José passed away a few weeks ago."

I slumped back into my chair as she went on, "He had a heart attack—"

"A heart attack! But he couldn't—he's so young!"

"I know. I'm sorry." The woman's voice broke slightly. "I really am. It was a terrible thing, very unexpected. We're all really going to miss him around here . . ."

"Yes," I whispered. I wanted to ask more but suddenly I felt sick. "Th-thank you, thank you very much. I'll call somebody—I mean I'll call one of our friends . . ."

I hung up. For a moment I clung to the edge of my desk. Then it was too much, on top of cognac and a nearly sleepless night and everything else that had happened. I stumbled out of my office and down the hall, and fled into the ladies' room. I thought I'd throw up—I *wanted* to throw up—but I didn't. Instead I started choking with sobs, so violently that Laurie came running in from her cubicle around the corner.

"Katherine! What is it—"

She put her arm around me and I shook my head. "Here," she said in a softer voice, and turned on the tap. "Get some cold water on you—you're so hot! Is it heatstroke?"

"I'm okay—I'm okay," I gasped. "I just had some bad news—a friend of mine—a friend of mine died."

"Oh, Katherine—"

"I'll be all right. It's just—just so sudden," I said, and gulped back a sob.

Laurie nodded, her eyes wide with pity. "I'm *so* sorry. Do you want me to get Dylan?"

I shook my head. "N-no. It's—it's not anyone he knows, and tomorrow's his birthday and I don't want to upset him. I'll be okay, really. But thanks."

I stood over the sink with the cold water running, until finally I stopped crying. Then I went back to my office, hoping to hide until lunchtime.

But Dylan was already there. "Sweeney, I'm so sorry," he murmured, hugging me. "Who was it?"

"Just a—well, an old friend of mine. From school—from the Divine, I mean. I hadn't even seen him in a year or so, but we talked all the time, and he left me all these messages early in the month but I kept putting off calling him back. And then I—"

I bit my lip, trying to keep the tears back. "I called him this morning. To tell him about us. And someone at the *Beacon* told me he had a heart attack."

"Your friend Baby Joe?" Dismay flickered across Dylan's face as he made the connection.

I nodded. "Yeah. Oh god. I don't even know who to call—I mean, his family was from here, but I never met them or anything . . ."

"It's okay, Sweeney. It'll all be okay." Dylan soothed me, stroking my head. "Don't worry . . ."

I tried not to laugh bitterly. *Yeah, death sucks, man; but what the fuck does a kid like* you *know about it?*

But that was just mean. I looked up and could see how confused he looked, and also a little worried: was he doing this right, was this how you behaved when one of your girlfriend's friends died?

"I'll be okay," I said, and tried to sound like I meant it. "It's just so—unexpected. And I feel so fucking guilty. He left me all these messages, and I just blew him off. Because of—"

Because of you. I fought back the nasty thought, and ended, "Because I—I just didn't feel like talking. And now—he's *dead.*"

"How could he have a heart attack? I mean, if he's your age?"

I moved away from him. "I don't know. I—well, I don't know, that's all."

For the first time, I thought of Hasel: how had *he* died, really? That insane letter he'd sent to Baby Joe, about seeing Angelica bathing in a creek in Virginia; and the next thing I knew, he'd drowned.

What had Baby Joe been up to when *he* died?

I leaned against my desk. "You know," I said slowly, "I think I'm going to leave early today. I feel pretty awful—" I smiled ruefully. "No offense—it's just, you know, I'm kind of hung over and now this."

"It's okay." Dylan ran a hand through his hair. He hadn't showered that morning, and had dressed hastily, in wrinkled khakis and a blue cotton shirt that had seen better weeks. In the close hot room he still smelled like the smoke and beer from Kelly's. "I'd go too, but I told Laurie I'd help her with stuff downstairs."

"Okay." I felt relieved. I needed to be alone for a few hours, if nothing else just to sleep and take a cold shower. "Hey—"

I linked my hands behind his neck and kissed his chin. "You haven't changed your mind, have you? I mean about last night?"

He frowned. "Last night? Last night?—oh, you mean *that.*" He grinned. "Hell no. Have you?"

"Hell no." I pulled his face closer to mine and kissed him, his skin rough and hot where he hadn't shaved. "Never . . ."

Dylan half turned and reached for the door, closed and locked it. He turned back and gently pushed me until I was sitting on my desk. We made love with most of our clothes on, until the whole room smelled like sex and afterhours. When he came he bit my shoulder to keep from crying out, so hard he left a small bruise there beneath the silk. For a long time we sat on my desk curled in each other's arms, our hearts pounding, and when I drew away from him I knew that somehow things had changed. I knew that this was it: that there was no turning back now, for myself or Dylan. His skin and blood and memory were branded into me as surely as that little bruise on my shoulder, but I knew that none of those things would ever fade. He was mine now, he had always been mine, and nothing on earth would ever take him away from me.

"Sweeney," he whispered. "I love you so much. I always have."

"I know," I said, and gently pushed the long damp hair from his face. "I love you too, Dylan."

I left, not caring that my blouse was soaked with sweat as I walked unsteadily down the long curving marble stairs; not caring that I looked dazed and maybe even a little nuts, like someone who's survived a terrible accident; someone who had just watched everything she owned in the whole world go up in flames except what she loved most; someone who had seen all that, and just walked away with bruises.

I went home and took a cold shower and slept naked on our bed with the fan turned on me. When I woke it was after six o'clock—I could hear Dylan downstairs in the kitchen, watching the local news—and I felt much better. I had decided I'd call the *Beacon* again next week, after Dylan's birthday, to get the whole story. I could try to contact Annie Harmon, but that might be difficult. She was an up-and-coming star of sorts, and it seemed tacky to get in touch now, after such a long hiatus. Still, I figured if I got my nerve up, I could get her number from whoever had taken over Baby Joe's column.

And then there was Angelica, of course. The next day was Dylan's birthday, and while we'd made our own plans, he seemed to take it for granted that his mother was going to show up sometime. Maybe a few days late.

"But she'll call over at Dvorkin's," he'd assured me. "She gets caught up in her work, but she'll call."

"I hope so," I said. He still refused to let me buy him anything, and his wardrobe was looking pretty shabby. "You need some new clothes."

He rolled his eyes. "Clothes. Like you ever see me in *clothes.*"

"Good point." I left it at that.

Now I was hungry. I yawned and threw on a T-shirt and a pair of Dylan's cutoffs, then padded downstairs.

"Sweeney! Come here!"

"What?" I walked into the kitchen, to find him perched in a chair staring at the tiny Sony on the counter. "Is that *news?*" I asked darkly. "You know I hate news—"

"Just listen!"

He turned up the volume, so I could hear a correspondent in L.A. talking about how a previously unknown fungus had apparently been released from somewhere within the ground during the previous spring's earthquake. People all over southern California were getting sick, their symptoms alarmingly similar to those caused by biological warfare in Southeast Asia in the sixties.

"Isn't this great? First rats, now fungus!" Dylan shook his head and reached for an opened bag of tortilla chips. "My mother is right—we are going to hell in a clutch purse! Here—" He pushed the bag at me. "I got some salsa."

I grimaced. A list of symptoms was scrolling across the postcard-sized screen, along with information numbers for the Center for Disease Control and NIH. "Thanks, Dylan. Maybe later."

"Wait—don't go, there's supposed to be something about that man who boiled his kids in Trenton—"

"Dylan!"

I had started for the living room, when the screen switched from the L.A. correspondent to a woman standing in front of a huge sand-colored building.

"Hey," I said. "I know that—"

"*This morning, officials at the University of the Archangels and Saint John the Divine in Washington, D.C., confirmed that they had reached an agreement to transfer a collection of over three hundred ancient artifacts to the radical feminist group Potnia."*

"That's the Divine!" I grabbed Dylan's shoulder. "That's where—"

"Shh—I can't hear!"

"—as ongoing investigations continue at several museums in this country and abroad, amid rumors of a secret society from which women are barred, and even stranger allegations made by Potnia. We spoke to Professor Balthazar Warnick, Professor Emeritus at the University's Thaddeus College."

"Holy cow," I breathed. "I don't *believe* this—"

The screen showed a slight man in a three-piece suit, standing in a cavernous space. He was so thin as to appear almost wasted, but his hair was still dark, and his eyes were the same piercing eyes I had last seen years before at the Orphic Lodge.

"There has been absolutely no wrongdoing on the part of the University or any individuals associated with the institution," he said. At the sound of his voice—silken as ever it had been, with that same ironic undertone of menace and laughter—I hugged myself; as though someone had opened a window onto winter. "We have held these items—and numerous others of greater value, I should add—for many, *many* years. Centuries, some of them." He swept his hand upward to indicate the vaulted recesses of a ceiling high overhead, and I realized he was being taped somewhere in the recesses of the Shrine.

"*No one,* absolutely *no one,* at the University has ever gained any sort of financial benefit from these objects," he went on. For an instant I saw a glint of fire in his eyes. "I should also say that, considering the political climate in many of the countries where these artifacts have their origin, the University has done an *excellent* job of safekeeping—"

Abruptly the camera cut to an elegantly dressed young woman sitting behind an important-looking desk. She was even more diminutive than Professor Warnick, with straight jet black hair and white skin and black eyes. Her almost childlike beauty was belied by her suit, which probably cost what I made in a month, and the delicately drawn tattoo on her cheek.

The newscaster intoned, *"Rosanne Minerva, attorney and spokeswoman for Potnia, disagrees."*

"Some of these figurines, including the so-called 'Tahor Venus,' are literally *tens* of *thousands* of years *old,*" Rosanne Minerva said. Her tone was utterly self-assured. "For centuries this relatively small group of men—primarily American and European businessmen and scholars—has been hiding these treasures—these priceless religious artifacts that belong to women, and men, *everywhere*!"

When she said the word *men* it was with the sort of pity usually reserved for speaking of the terminally ill. The camera drew in for a close-up of her poised, aquiline face, and I got a better look at her tattoo. Without meaning to I gasped.

"What?" demanded Dylan.

The little cusp drawn so carefully upon her cheek was a perfect half-moon, incised with tiny swirled lines and meanders. The same lunar crescent that Angelica had worn: a lunula.

"What these men have done is nothing short of profanation," Rosanne Minerva said. Her hand rested lightly upon a stack of papers, but I could see how her fingers tensed. "It is a sin, and a crime, and it will be—it has been—stopped."

I continued to stare in disbelief even after the screen cut back to the newsroom.

"She's just a lawyer," Dylan said, reaching for another handful of chips. "I know who she is."

"You do?"

"Sure. Potnia—they're with my mother." He turned to look at me, a curtain of dark hair flopping over his eyes. "Haven't you ever heard of them?"

"Well, sort of. I read something about them. What—"

At that moment the door buzzer rang. Dylan stopped eating in mid-bite. I froze with one hand on the wall. *Nobody* rang that buzzer, except for UPS men and Seventh-Day Adventists.

"My mother!" whispered Dylan. He glanced nervously down at his shirt, then at me. "Uh-oh."

"You stay here," I commanded.

"Why?"

"I don't know!" I said, flustered. "It's my place, that's why, *I'll* open the door—"

"I live here too!" Dylan called after me plaintively, but he stayed in the kitchen.

I walked to the door in my bare feet, running a hand through my hair and cursing myself for not putting on makeup. Give it to Angelica to pull off something like this. After all these years, here she was coasting in with a little fanfare of related media coverage and not even a phone call to warn me. I could just make out a figure through the window, someone nearly hidden by wisteria. I stopped in front of the door, took a deep breath, and opened it.

"Surprise," someone rasped. It was Annie Harmon.

I was so stunned I could only gape. She had the same dun-colored hair, trimmed to a messy crew cut; the same recalcitrant cowlick, dusted now with grey; the same brown violet-tinged eyes and wanton voice. She was thinner than she had been, and it showed mostly in her face—puckish Annie had cheekbones now, and a small cleft in her chin, that obviously hadn't just been put there for her music video. She had lines too, around her eyes and mouth; her arms were thin and muscled, her hands worn and raw-looking. Her tiny feet were shoved into red tennis shoes—*expensive* red tennis shoes. She wore torn fatigues, a blue flannel shirt with the sleeves ripped out, a gold wedding band on her right hand. She looked absolutely beautiful.

"Annie." I fell back as she pushed past me into the room. "Uh—jeez, it's uh—it's great to see you."

"I'm underwhelmed," she said, and grabbed me in a hug. "Remember me? The girl least likely to succeed in a long-term heterosexual relationship?"

I laughed. "I dunno, Annie. I think I was in the running there for a while."

She dropped her knapsack to the floor. "So: you happy to see me, or is that a roll of pennies in your pocket?" She grinned, but her voice sounded strained. As though she was putting on an act for me, as though if she gave me the chance to think, I'd change my mind and push her right back out the door.

"Of course! Here—sit, sit," I urged, pointing her to the couch. "You want something to drink? No kidding, Annie, it really is great to see you. I mean it."

I hesitated, went on in a rush, "This is *so* weird. There was just something on the news about the Divine, and I've been thinking of calling you, but I didn't know how to find you. Did you hear about Baby Joe?"

She nodded, her expression guarded. "Yeah. I meant to call you when it happened." She sank onto the couch, tugging at her cowlick. "I know this is totally nutso, me just showing up like this—"

"No—I'm glad, Annie, really, I'm so happy you—"

"Well, you might not be so happy when you hear why I came." She sighed and leaned back into the couch. "God, I'm so exhausted. Can I crash here tonight?"

"Tonight? Sure, Annie, of course—" A little warning beeper went off in my head, reminding me that tomorrow was Dylan's birthday: I'd have to find some polite way of kicking Annie out by then. "You look beat. Don't you want something? I think there's some orange juice—"

"Orange juice sounds great. You know, I had some of that stuff on the train the other night—that Pernod shit you used to drink in school." Annie shook her head. "Now I know why you were always so nuts."

I hopped into the kitchen and got the juice. Dylan was finishing off the chips and salsa; before I could say anything he started into the other room. I hurried after him.

"Dylan—uh, wait a sec—"

Annie looked up just as the two of us came through the doorway. The blood drained from her face. For a moment I thought she was going to scream.

"Annie! This is Dylan—Dylan Furiano." I gestured weakly at Dylan with the glass of orange juice. "He's—he's Angelica's son," I went on breathlessly. "Annie is a friend of mine. We all went to college together. Your mom and Annie and I. Dylan's father was Angelica's husband in *Italy,*" I ended, willing Annie not to bring up Oliver's name.

"Hi," said Dylan politely. He smiled at Annie. She nodded—too fast, as though someone in a dark alley had just asked for her wallet.

"Yeah," she replied in a hoarse whisper. "I—Angelica? Angelica di Rienzi?"

"She's my mother." He peered more closely at Annie. "You look kind of familiar . . ."

I slapped my forehead: I was not handling this well *at all.* "Dylan, this is Annie Harmon—Annie Harmony, I guess you are now, huh?" I gave Annie an anxious look. I had the uneasy feeling that everyone in the room was covering for someone else, except for me. *I* was standing all alone out in the field, waiting to be plowed down.

"Annie Harmony?" Dylan tilted his head, suddenly exclaimed, "The singer?"

"Dylan," Annie was saying, her voice carefully modulated. "Angelica's son Dylan. And—"

I coughed loudly; I would have kicked her if I'd been a few inches closer. Annie whistled and gave me a sideways glance, her dark eyes narrowed so that she looked like an animal that's just been poked with a stick.

"*Sweeney Cassidy* and *Angelica's son Dylan,*" she said. "Dylan and Sweeney. Now I must have missed the pilot for this show, because I am *very* surprised to—"

Dylan stepped around Annie to stand awkwardly beside me. "I bet you girls have hair and fingernails to discuss, so maybe I'll go pick up something for dinner. Is that okay, Sweeney?"

"That'd be great, Dylan. Thanks."

He leaned down to brush his lips against my cheek. "See you later, Sweeney. Annie—"

Annie nodded, forced a smile so false I was glad Dylan was out the door before he could see it. I watched him go, then turned to Annie and said, "Well, hey, how about that orange juice."

Annie glared at me. Her face was dead white except for a fiery red spot on each cheek. "Yeah? Well hey, how about telling me who the *fuck* that is?"

I bit my lip. "Well, actually, Dylan is—"

"I know who he is! Anyone with half a brain can see who he is! The hell with Angie—that's *Oliver's* kid!"

She began to pace furiously across the room, punching the air with her fist. "Jesus Christ, Sweeney! I almost had a heart attack—I thought he *was* Oliver. *What* is he doing *here*? What are *you* doing—"

I shoved my hands into my cutoffs and glared back at her. "What am *I* doing? I *live* here—"

"What is *he* doing here?"

"*He* lives here! What are *you* doing here?"

Annie stopped and stared down at the harvest table. She reached for the sea urchin lamp, moving her fingers across its tiny raised nodes as though she were reading braille. Suddenly her expression changed. "I remember this," she said softly. "This was Angie's . . ."

I nodded. "She—she sent me that for Christmas, that first year . . ."

"That only year," Annie said, but there was no malice in her voice. "It always sort of gave me the creeps, this lamp. But it looks pretty in here." She sighed and turned, leaning against the table. "Man, it's hot. Where's that orange juice?"

I handed it to her, went and got the rest of the pitcher. "Here—" I poured her another glass. "Why don't you sit, Annie? It's too hot, and we don't have air-conditioning."

I could see her flinch when I said *we,* but she said nothing, just flopped onto the sofa and rested the glass against her forehead for a few minutes.

"Okay," she said at last. "I feel better now. At least I don't feel like I'm gonna run screaming out into the street and have fits."

I laughed. "Why not? Everyone on Capitol Hill has fits."

Annie sighed. "Right—Capitol Hill. Baby Joe said you lived on Capitol Hill."

I hesitated, then asked, "Is that—is that why you came here? To tell me about Baby Joe?"

Annie shook her head. "No. Not really. I mean, if I just wanted to tell you about Baby Joe, I would've called, probably. No, this is—well, this is a little more than that." She fixed me with a sharp glance. "A *lot* more."

"Oh, I don't know, Annie," I settled next to her on the couch, reached over to give her a tentative hug. "Try me. I'm more open-minded than I used to be."

She snorted. "No kidding. Open-minded Sweeney Cassidy, the girl with a hole in her head. I'm sorry—it's just a shock, you know? I haven't seen you in—what? Nineteen years?"

"Twenty, almost."

"Twenty years! And here I walk in and it's like a fucking time warp, you and Oliver . . ."

"Yeah, well, imagine how *I* felt."

Annie rested her elbows on her knees and looked at me, head cocked. "All right, girl. Shoot. Tell me how it felt."

I told her about Dylan. Everything about Dylan, up to and including about how the night before at Kelly's he'd asked me to marry him.

Annie cupped her chin in her hand. "And you said you'd wait for him to grow up, no matter how long it takes. How romantic."

"Fuck you, Harmon. I told him I'd marry him in a New York second."

"Wow." Annie looked at me with wide eyes. "Really? You said yes?"

"Of course I said yes! I'm in *love* with him, Annie." I tried to keep my voice from sounding desperate. "He's—he's everything I never thought I'd find. He's everything in the world to me," I said softly. "Everything."

I looked up, expecting to see Annie's mocking gaze or worse, her anger. Instead she was staring at me as though she'd somehow walked into a stranger's carriage house; which, I guess, she had.

"You said you'd marry him. Too much. And obviously he doesn't know who his real father is," she mused. "Which is probably for the best . . .

"Well. He sounds nice," she said after a long silence had passed. "Really, he does. I guess it's just that—well, some kind of intense stuff has happened to me in the last couple of months."

"Like what?"

She shifted uncomfortably on the couch, finally curled up into the corner facing me. "Well, like—like I guess maybe I'll have to wait a few minutes before getting into it. This is a lot to think about, after all this time. Right here—"

She gestured at me, then at the little room around us, with its ancient beams and slate floor and books and rose petals strewn everywhere.

"All this, and you, and him." She was quiet, and stared thoughtfully out the front window; then she asked in a low voice, "Don't take this the wrong way, Sweeney, but—well, are you sure it's Dylan you're in love with? I mean, you really used to bang your head against the wall over Oliver—"

"I'm sure," I said curtly. "I haven't thought about Oliver in years and years."

Which was a lie, of course. Annie didn't seem to believe it for an instant.

"Really? I have," she said, almost dreamily. "I thought about him, and you, and Angie, all the time. All the time. Especially Angie."

She pulled a pillow into her lap and kneaded it, and I was shocked to see her eyes were red. "I thought about Angie for years. Fucking years, girl. Did you know we slept together?"

I shook my head. "No," I said awkwardly. "But—well, I'm not surprised. You probably weren't the only one."

It was the wrong thing to say. Annie's face twisted, and she held the pillow so tightly her fingers were white.

"But I *wanted* to be the only one! I was so gone over her, I was *insane* for her. That time I found you in the room—I wanted to kill you, Sweeney, I mean, really kill you. It was like when I found out about what happened to my cousin Lisa—"

"But you know it didn't mean anything, Annie! I was drunk, that was such a horrible night, and she—"

"I know what she did. She did the same thing to you that she did to me, that she did to everyone. She *used* you, Sweeney. She used us all."

Annie's expression was so vehement, her eyes so black with rage that I moved a little closer to my end of the couch.

"Annie," I said gently, trying to be careful with my words, "I'm sure Angelica didn't mean to hurt you. I don't think she meant to hurt anyone. Things were different then, you remember what it was like—*lots* of people slept with their friends. We didn't know." It was like letting something go, that had been caged inside of me. "We were just kids, Annie. That was all. Besides—"

I pointed at the ring on her right hand. "You're a big star now. You can't be living alone."

"I'm not." Annie straightened, tilting her chin defiantly. "My lover, Helen—we've been together for almost eight years now. Shit," she added under her breath, "I think our anniversary's coming up, too, I got to remember that. But that's not what I meant, anyway."

"Then what *did* you mean?"

"I mean that she used us. *Really* used us—starting with me, and you, and Baby Joe, and Hasel, and then Oliver . . ."

My heart clenched, but I only nodded. "And Oliver."

"And I don't know who else, over the years." She pulled the pillow to her chest. "Have you been following Angelica, Sweeney?"

"You mean, watching her career?" I shook my head. "No. I never heard from her, after—after what happened. Until this summer, as a matter a fact. I saw her on TV about five or six weeks ago, I guess it was right before I met Dylan. But he's told me about her, so I know about her from him. Why?" I asked guardedly. "Have you been in touch with her?"

Annie let her breath out in a long low *whoosh.* "I have been doing everything on god's green earth *not* to be in touch with her."

She stood and crossed the room to stare at the sea urchin lamp. When she turned back to me she was pale but very calm.

"I don't know exactly *what* she is, Sweeney, but Angelica is dangerous. I mean *fatal.* She killed Baby Joe, and she killed Hasel; she's killed people we'll never know about, *hundreds* of them—thousands, maybe. Homeless people, runaways, people nobody would ever miss—you ever seen statistics on how many people just disappear, like that?"

She snapped her fingers and I jumped. "You know, I've known people who've seen snuff movies—movies where people literally get fucked to death, and someone's there behind the camera watching it all, and someone else is out there to market the stuff, and someone else is there to buy it . . . You like to think something that horrible could never happen, that it couldn't be real; but it is, Sweeney. It is."

Her eyes grew wide and unfocused. "It's like we spend our whole lives walking on this little rind that covers the world, this little crust that's got flowers on it, and dirt and houses and families and—and then one day, you break through, you just fall right through, and you see there's something else there. The *real* world, the world that was there a million years ago, the world you see when you're a kid alone in the dark; the world that fills your worst dreams until you can't even wake up screaming from it, you can't wake up at all . . .

"I've seen it, Sweeney," she whispered. I swallowed, thinking back to Balthazar Warnick's room at the Orphic Lodge, hobbled creatures whirling ecstatically around a single thin flame. "I've *seen* it, and you've seen it, Sweeney—that world is *real.* It's real, and Angelica's tapped into it. Whatever she is, whatever she's made herself into—she's found a way into that place. She's found a way to bring it here—"

Her hand slashed through the shadows. "To *make* it here. And she's doing it by feeding off all of us. It's like she set out to be some kind of crazy goddess of love, Ishtar or Mary Magdalene or whatever the hell she thought she was—but somehow she's really done it. She *has* turned into a goddess. She's got her bible, and her cult, she's got some kind of fucking black angels picking off kids from here to Seattle—"

"Annie!" I was shaking my head furiously. "*No*—"

"Listen to me, Sweeney!" She was kneeling in front of me, her hands on my knees. "She *killed* them! I *know* she killed them, because she tried to kill *me*—"

And then she told me about what she had seen: about the girls who would turn up at her shows, with their lunar tattoos and ominous chanting; about the sacrificial murder at Herring Cove, and the monstrously beautiful creature she had seen there; about the flowers left with Helen, and the strange woman who had saved her from becoming the next offering to Othiym. She told me that the same day he died, she had met Baby Joe alone at a strip club. But at that part of her story her voice faltered, and I knew she was keeping something from me.

Whatever it was, it could wait. My heart was racing; I felt as though the temperature had plummeted fifty degrees in five minutes.

"But why?" I said at last in a whisper. "If this is all true—"

"You don't believe me? Don't tell me that, Sweeney! I don't know what happened to Oliver at the Orphic Lodge that night, but you saw it—you and Hasel and Baby Joe, *you saw it*—"

"No," I said, pulling away from her. "I—I *do* believe you. Baby Joe sent me Hasel's letter, and an article about Angelica's bodyguard . . ."

I told what I had read about Potnia a few weeks before, and about the odd news item that evening, with Professor Warnick and the *Benandanti* seemingly under fire. Then, somewhat reticently, I told her what Dylan had said about his mother and the earthquake in Los Angeles, about the deaths of Rinaldo Furiano and Luciano di Rienzi in a freak storm in the Sea of Crete.

"But that's just—well, it's *got* to be coincidence," I finished. "I mean, *something's* got to be coincidence, right? We can't blame *everything* on Angelica."

I stood and went to the front door and looked outside, hugging my arms to my chest. I was surprised, almost unnerved, to see how quickly night had come. "It's dark already," I said mechanically. I felt almost calm now, as though I was dreaming.

"Not any cooler, though," Annie said softly.

"You know, the weather's been so horrible this summer that if D.C. had been a factory, OSHA would have shut it down."

Annie nodded. "Yeah. But it's not the heat. It's the humidity." She stepped up behind me and put her hand on my shoulder. "Sweeney. Listen to me—

"I'm glad for you, about Dylan. You deserve to be happy, Sweeney, you really do. I know we didn't know each other that well, and it was so long ago, but—you mattered to me anyway. You matter to me now."

"Even if I slept with Angelica that once?"

She grinned wryly. "Probably *especially* since you slept with Angelica. You mattered, and Baby Joe of course, and poor Hasel. Even Oliver . . . I guess what really used to bother me about Oliver, and about Angelica and that guy Francis, about all of them with their secret society or whatever the hell it is, was that even if they seemed to be like us—you know, just kids in college getting high or whatever—

well, they weren't. They could just do whatever they wanted and not get caught, not get hurt or anything. People like Lisa, or you—they just threw you away," she said bitterly. "The rest of them, though, they were always working with a net. No matter what they did up there, if they fell, somebody would catch them."

"Oliver fell, Annie," I whispered. "Oliver fell, and nobody caught him."

An odd look crossed her face and I thought she was going to tell me something, something about Oliver, but the moment passed.

"Well, Dylan sounds like a prize, at any rate. I guess if you get 'em that young, they're easier to train, huh?"

I couldn't keep from grinning. "Guess so."

"And if you love him—well, that's great, Sweeney. It's hard to find someone, to find anyone, and I hope it works out for you. I mean it."

Then, surprisingly, she took my chin in her hand. She turned my head, until I was looking down into her dark eyes. "But Sweeney—I came here because I was scared—for you, and me. And for Baby Joe, though it's too late for him—"

I swallowed. "And now?" I asked.

Annie tilted her head toward the soft darkness occluding the garden, the velvety chiaroscuro of leaves and brick and the first faint threads of lightning, like cracks in a lovely old fresco. "Now I'm scared worse than before."

"Because of Dylan?"

She nodded. Her gaze remained fixed on the sky, but her husky voice trembled. "And you, Sweeney. Especially you . . .

"Because if something really *has* happened to Angelica—if all this somehow *means* something—if she's turned herself into some kind of a, a goddess, or demon, or whatever the hell she is—well, what does that make Dylan?"

She turned and stared at me, her eyes emptied of anything but fear. "And Sweeney?—

"What does that make *you*?"

Dylan came home not long after that. He seemed quieter than usual, but I was too drained really to pay attention.

"Hey, Dylan, I'd like to hang with you some tomorrow. Maybe after work, okay?" Annie croaked as she came out of the shower. She walked over to the couch in her soaked T-shirt, leaving puddles on the slate floor. "I'm just too beat now to appreciate how wonderful you are. I think I'm gonna crash. That okay with you, Sweeney?"

"Sure." I leaned against Dylan, sighing, and he kneaded my shoulders. "I'm exhausted. You ready to turn in, kiddo?"

He smiled. "Sure."

We said good night to Annie, then crept up the creaking stairs to the tiny bedroom. We fell asleep immediately, despite the ungodly heat. Just before dawn we woke tangled in one another's arms, the sheets beneath us soft and damp as new green leaves, and made love without a sound, so as not to disturb Annie.

"Happy birthday, Dylan," I murmured, letting my fingers catch in his damp hair. I kissed him, my tongue lingering on his mouth so I could taste him, all sweat and my own salt honey. "Nineteen: it's all downhill from here."

Afterward we showered and dressed quickly. I left a note for Annie, telling her to call me at work so we could arrange to meet later. Just as the sun was rising, Dylan and I left for the museum. We stopped for bagels and iced coffee, then walked down Pennsylvania Avenue together. There were already a surprising number of joggers out on the Capitol grounds, like us trying to beat the heat, but it was hopeless. By seven-thirty the sky was the color of a spoiled egg yolk. An unbroken mass of clouds stretched from above the Hill out past the Tidal Basin, dark lowering clouds that seemed low enough to snag upon the drab blade of the Washington Monument. The air smelled awful, like kerosene and rotting vegetation. Inside the museum it wasn't much better. The air-conditioning was working fitfully, so it was cooler than outside, but even the upstairs curatorial wing reeked of a million sweaty tourists and greasy fast-food from the cafeteria.

"Listen," Dylan said, leaning into the door of my office. "I really need to finish up that Kroeber stuff today. So maybe you and your friend should just meet for lunch, and then you and me can leave early."

"Sounds good."

"You remember the champagne?"

"I remembered the champagne."

"So I'll come by around four, how's that?"

I stood on tiptoe to kiss his chin. "Sounds great. Later."

"*Ciao,* baby."

A few minutes after he left Annie called.

"I think I might just crash here today," she said. I could hear her gulping coffee. "If that's okay with you. It's so hot, and I'm kinda into keeping a low profile right now, if you know what I mean. I figured I'd sit out in the garden later. At least it *looks* cool there."

"Sure. Uh, listen, Annie—today's Dylan's birthday, and we had sort of planned an evening together—"

"Oops." A clink as her coffee mug knocked into the phone. "Say no more. I'll find something to do. Check out a movie. Maybe *The Sorrow and the Pity*'s playing at the Biograph."

"You don't mind?"

"Heck no."

"Thanks, Annie," I said, relieved. "I feel bad, but we had this all planned and—"

"Like, *no problemo,* Sweeney."

"Okay. We should be home by four-thirty or so. I'll give you a key and you can just let yourself in, then maybe tomorrow we can—"

Annie cut me off. "Sweeney?"

"Yeah?"

"Don't you have work to do?"

"Right. Later, Annie."

The problem was, I *didn't* have work to do. Because of the terrible weather and air quality both inside and out, the museum had put its Liberal Leave policy into effect; the place was almost deserted. With the Aditi gone, I couldn't even kill a few hours with some Pink Pelican, and I knew Dylan had been feeling guilty about not getting the Kroeber project wrapped up before now.

I really wished I could just go back home. But Annie was there, and Annie's arrival had me on edge. *Everything* had me on edge. I felt the way I did when Oliver and I used to drop acid: the same queasy mixture of terror and exhilaration, compounded when the drug started to kick in and everything got a little blurry around the edges. Only now it was a combination of not enough sleep, too much alcohol, too much heat, and far too many ghosts popping up. Like the end of a Restoration comedy, when all at once everyone shows up onstage, fools and diviners and soldiers and lovers and cuckolds, until you wonder whether the whole rickety platform will just collapse beneath them.

I wandered out into the corridor. Laurie wasn't at her desk, and I figured she'd probably just left early for Hatteras. I went by Robert Dvorkin's office, thinking I might grill him about what I'd seen on the news last night, but of course he wasn't in.

"Okay," I said out loud. There wasn't anyone around to hear me. "Time for Classics."

Classics was an expanse of brightly lit offices on the side of the museum abutting the dome. Fritz Kincaid was the chief of Hellenic Studies, a rosy-cheeked red-haired man of fifty who played squash on his lunch hour and lived in a houseboat tethered on the Potomac. I knew he'd be in because Fritz was *always* in. He was the kind of museum curator beloved of old movies and local news stations: photogenic, partial to polka-dot bow ties and cheerfully eccentric headgear, and most of all a terrific source of Strange but True (and often disgusting) Facts regarding the Ancients.

"Katherine Cassidy! Queen of the Interactive Video Display!" he crowed when he saw me peeking through the door. "What brings you to visit this old fossil?"

"You're the only old fossil here today," I said. "Actually, I saw the news last night, about all those artifacts at the University of the Archangels, and I thought of you."

Fritz rolled his eyes. "Oh, yes: Potnia. Just what we need in these troubled times, a revival of the ancient matristic societies of the Aegean." He turned and gave me a quizzical look. "Oh, but I forgot—your young friend Tristan—"

"Dylan."

"Yes, of course, I'm sorry—Dylan. His mother's the writer, isn't she? The one we have to thank for all this nice publicity."

He grimaced, then added, "Please, Katherine—come in, have a seat. Would you like some coffee?"

"No thanks. But are you busy? I wanted to pick your brain for a few minutes."

Fritz shook his head solemnly. "I am *never* too busy for lovely young ladies. *Entrez*—"

I walked around the perimeter of the long library table that took up most of his office. It held an exquisite scale model of the Acropolis and the Athenian Agora, constructed of paper and cardboard and balsa wood, with matchstick triremes in the distance that glowed against the painted sea. The model had been constructed for an exhibit dismantled years ago, but Fritz never had the heart to get rid of it. It made a nice backdrop when he was visited by local news crews, especially since he'd improved the Acropolis by adding several troll dolls and plastic velociraptors.

"So this group Potnia," I said. "Is that the name of a goddess?"

"In a manner of speaking. To be more accurate: it's *a* name of *the* goddess." Fritz cocked his head and raised gingery eyebrows, so that he looked like an intelligent Airedale. "Have you—taken an *interest* in this sort of thing, Katherine?"

I shrugged and tried to look noncommittal, although in truth my heart was racing. "Not really. Well, maybe a little."

He gave an understanding nod. "Probably young Dylan knows a great deal about it . . ."

I laughed. "Yeah—kids these days, with their wacky matristic cults! No, I was just kind of—intrigued. I saw that article in *Archaeology,* and I understand the museum might be hit with a lawsuit . . ."

Fritz shuddered. "God forbid—I'm sorry, *Goddess* forbid," he said quickly, raising his eyes to heaven. He picked up a piece of paper from his desk, holding it between thumb and forefinger and making a face as though it smelled bad. "Did you see this? No? It's Potnia's press release—they're timing all their little escapades by the old pagan calendar. Actually, this one is dated today, but they dropped it off yesterday."

"Today? What's today?"

Fritz made a great show of squinting as he held the release at arm's length and read aloud, " 'August First is Lammas, one of the great harvest festivals sacred to the blah blah blah.' " He grimaced, crumpled the page, and tossed it into a wastebasket. "So much for Potnia."

He turned to me and shook his head apologetically. "Oh! But I forgot, you asked about them—

"Well, Katherine, Potnia is a name found on various Linear A and Linear B tablets in Knossos and Mycenæ—you're familiar with those?"

"A little."

"Well, the tablets are some of the earliest records of our so-called Western Civilization, and Potnia is one of the oldest names found therein. It's been translated as one of the titles of the Great Mediterranean Goddess. *Atana Potnia,* she was called—*Atana* like Athena, do you see? Most of the Greek gods actually started out as Cretan gods—by Cretan I mean what we call the Minoan culture, from our old friend King Minos."

"The guy with the minotaur?"

"The guy with the minotaur. But these are very, *very* ancient gods, dating back millennia before the more well-known Greek gods. A lot of the place-names in that part of the Mediterranean are actually pre-Hellenic, completely different linguistically from Greek words. But the Greeks were so impressed by this culture that they ended up incorporating many of these names and words into their own language.

So a lot of words we think of as being classically Greek, like *theos* or *hieros* or *laburinthos,* actually belong to this earlier society."

I eased myself up onto the table beside the Agora. "Really? That's fascinating."

Fritz nodded, pleased. "It *is* fascinating. Because, you see, the Greeks did the same thing with their gods. They co-opted these more ancient deities for themselves—gods like Hyacinthus, who was sort of a proto-Apollo, although he was also associated with the death cults that the Greeks later attached to Adonis; and Posidas, who became Poseidon, and—"

He gave an effete wave. "—oh, you know a bunch of lesser deities. *But*—"

Fritz started pacing, carried away by his monologue. "Your feminist friends out there are onto something. Because in fact this entire Minoan/Mycenæan civilization probably grew up around the worship of *goddesses.* The gods were a much later addition, most of them we think brought in by Northern invaders. The goddess cults probably originated on the mainland—Turkey, Anatolia, that whole cauldron of Eastern European countries—and then were brought by colonists to Crete and its satellite islands. The Cyclades, Rhodes, Thera . . .

"These goddesses eventually took the form of our familiar Greek goddesses. But originally they had names that are very strange to us—I mean, they are linguistically very unusual, which makes the whole thing even more mysterious, don't you think?"

I nodded, not sure how many more mysterious things I could take. Fritz went on without missing a beat.

"*Wanasoi,*" he pronounced, gazing dreamily at the ceiling. "Those were the twin queens who may have become Demeter and her daughter Kore. *Sitopotiniya,* the Mistress of the Grain. *Erinu,* who also was a Demeter prototype, although her name sounds very like that of the Erinyes, "the Angry Ones" or Furies, who gave Orestes such a hard time. *Britomartis* or *Atemito,* who was probably Artemis. *Pasaya. Querasiyua,* the Huntress. *Inachus,* who was named for a sacred river. *Othiym* and her lover-son *Pade,* the sacred child—"

I gasped. "That name—"

Fritz looked at me sideways. "Which one?"

"Othiym—"

He nodded, smiling as though I had posed an intelligent question. "Ah yes: *Othiym Lunarsa.* The Woman in the Moon. Another garden-variety lunar deity, although some scholars translate her name as the Destroyer. You know, like the Hindu goddess Kali."

I swallowed. My mouth felt parched as I croaked, "And these goddesses—they all came from Crete?"

Fritz shrugged. "Who knows? Originally, no; but many of them were worshiped there. Crete was the center of the ancient Minoan civilization, which was an incredibly sophisticated and advanced civilization, even by our standards. Flush toilets, hot running water, and according to the frescoes and pottery they left, they had an absolutely *fantastic* sense of style. *And* they may have had optical lenses, for telescopes and spectacles, and wet-cell batteries—and this is four, five thousand years ago! Compared to the Minoans, the ancient Greeks were really just a bunch of pederastic misogynist thugs."

"But then what happened to them?"

Fritz looked wistful, almost sad. "That entire part of the Mediterranean was blown off the map by a gigantic volcanic eruption on Thera around 1628 B.C. *Ffft*—" He snapped his fingers. "Like that. Utterly destroyed, all in one day."

"But Crete wasn't destroyed," I broke in.

"It might as well have been. The island of Thera had been central to the Minoans, and Thera was completely obliterated—like Pompeii. So the Minoans lost one of their most important ports and cities. And their religion took a hit as well. The so-called labyrinth at Knossos, and all these other temples on Crete, had already sustained some pretty serious damage from earthquakes. They all had been rebuilt, but when Thera blew, that was pretty much the death knell for Minoa."

Fritz sighed. "All that beauty! Crete could have rivaled ancient Egypt—and we'll probably never know the extent of what we lost when we lost that culture."

"What were they like? Were they goddess-worshipers?"

"Ha!" exclaimed Fritz. "You *have* been listening to your young friend's mother! Yes, Virginia, they were goddess-worshipers, at least as far as we can tell. The Minoans left no literary accounts of their culture, but they did leave wonderful images: paintings, statues, temples, the entire marvelous temple-labyrinth at Knossos; and almost all of their religious images seem to be of goddesses or priestesses.

"The frescoes show that women were not only worshiped in Crete but probably also ruled there, and certainly played a major part in the political structure of the city-states. They seemed to have some sort of bull-worship, which was pretty common in the ancient world. It's very likely that the bull-worship as well as the goddess icons originally derived from central Europe, where we've found numerous similar icons and images."

"What about their religion—I mean, what did they *do*?"

He frowned. "What did they *do*?"

"You know, did they worship a golden calf, the Ark of the Covenant, stuff like that?"

"Who knows? The frescoes indicate they were real naturalists—there are beautiful, beautiful paintings of sea animals, of flowers and plants and trees. Sir Arthur Evans, who led much of the restoration at Knossos, liked to think they were flower children. You know, very airy-fairy, artsy-fartsy, wearing pretty clothes and jewelry, skirts for boys and girls and lots of makeup. A quote-unquote 'feminine' culture: fancy hairdos, ritual transvestism, lots of attractive young people doing aerobics in the stadia."

"Sounds like Dupont Circle."

Fritz smiled. "Well, Evans has been proved to be wrong, at least in part. It turns out that the Minoans, at least some of them, were actually more bloodthirsty than we first imagined. There is a famous fresco that shows women sharing communion in some kind of religious ritual—only women, which is interesting in itself—and some of the tablets we've deciphered in Linear B list as much as 14,000 liters of wine used in a single year at one major temple site."

"Mass alcohol consumption."

"To put it mildly. There's also evidence that opium was very widely used. Some people have said that the labyrinth—palace, really—at Knossos looks like it was designed by an architect under the influence."

Fritz laughed, somewhat grimly. "But some of them may have really *needed* a few drinks—

"Not long ago, archaeologists managed to decipher some of the script on one of the Linear A tablets that postdates the Thera eruption. It was a record of the *hieros gamos,* the so-called 'sacred marriage' that was supposed to appease the Great Goddess. Apparently these particular survivors believed that she had caused the volcanic eruption as punishment to them, for turning from her to these new young sky-gods from the north.

"But even before we learned *that,* we may have found evidence of the same ritual being performed. Back in 1979 another group of archaeologists discovered a small shrine overlooking Knossos—Anemospilia, on Mount Juktas. In addition to an arena where sacrifices were performed, and a sort of sacred rock—like those goddess-meteorites found in parts of old Europe—an altar was found, with the ossified remains of a seventeen-year-old boy on top of it. His legs were drawn up to his chest and might have been tied there, though of course we don't know that. What we *do* know is that he was murdered—sacrificed, there was a very ornate curved dagger in the shape of a crescent moon found next to the skeleton. A *lunula,* they call it. Bone analysis indicates that the blood had been completely drained from the upper portion of his body . . ."

I gasped, but Fritz wasn't finished.

"That's not all. It seems that this particular sacrifice was being carried out *at the exact moment* of the terrible earthquake that leveled Knossos in 1700 B.C. So when archaeologists searched the area further, they found the bodies of three *other* people who had been taking part in the sacrifice—skeletons of temple servants. One of them was holding a shattered rhyton with a bull painted on it. There was also a man, possibly a priest or priest-king—he was wearing a sacred ring—lying on his back in front of the altar. Probably the guy who used the knife. And finally the body of a woman, a priestess, who appears to have been anemic—so there may have been some kind of ritual bloodletting going on with her as well. The earthquake must have struck minutes after this boy was killed—the rhyton had traces of blood on it, and it had probably been full when the whole temple collapsed and buried them all. Nice, huh? Kind of makes you long for the good old days."

I stumbled down from the table and started for the door, my legs shaking so that I could hardly walk.

"What's the matter?" cried Fritz. "Katherine! Are you all right? Here, sit down, you look like you're going to pass out—"

"I can't," I whispered. At the door I turned and stammered, "Thanks, Fritz. I—I'm sorry, I don't feel well, I have to leave—"

"The Minoans really were a highly sophisticated people!" he called a little desperately, as I fled toward my office. "Caligula's Romans were much, *much* worse—"

But I turned the corner before I could hear any more.

The halls were empty, so there was no one to stare after me as I ran down the corridor, first to Dylan's office cubicle, which was empty, and then to the tiny room off the main library where he had been archiving the Kroeber collection.

He wasn't there. I stood for a moment, staring down at the digitizer and the neat stacks of photos, each appended with a number in Dylan's careful, European hand. I drew several shuddering breaths and tried to calm myself—he was probably in *my* office looking for me, he could have gone downstairs to get a soda, or to the bathroom—

His battered motorcycle jacket was tossed over a chair. It had been there for weeks, after Dylan had worn it against the rain one morning and then forgotten about it. I picked it up, holding it close to my face as I inhaled, the cracked leather rough against my fingers and his smell still clinging to it. After a moment I let it slide from my hand to the floor.

I forced myself to walk back to my office, fixing in my mind's eye just where he would be standing—there, by the window, his back to me as it was the first time I saw him—and how I would slip up behind him, slide my arms around his waist and pull him to me and whisper that we weren't going to wait till four o'clock, it was too hot, too scary, it was his birthday, we were going to leave *now* . . .

My office was empty, the video screens black and dead as when I had left them a few hours ago. My whole body shook as I approached the desk and saw the note there. A page torn from some anthropological journal, one corner damp from where it had been weighted with a coffee mug, and the ink smeared so that Dylan's careful hand looked rushed, almost frantic.

Dear Sweeney,

Guess what? My mother finally showed up. She was waiting at the guard's desk downstairs; they just called, so I'm going down now and I guess I'll go to her hotel or whatever. I told her you and I had plans for tonight and I had to leave by four so I'll just meet you back at the house. Keep the champagne cold—

"No!"

I pounded my fist against the desk, ripping the page so that no one else would ever read its final lines.

I love you, Sweeney. Don't worry!
I'll be RIGHT BACK—

Dylan.

CHAPTER 21

Waking the Moon

The car Angelica had hired was a Lincoln Town Car, pure white inside and out, with plush velvet seats and chromium fixtures. She could tell that Dylan thought it was tacky; it *was* tacky, but it was the only car she could find that had air-conditioning.

"Mmm, it's *so* nice to see you, sweetheart," she said, hugging him in front of the guard's desk in the museum.

"You too, Mom," said Dylan. She let her head rest upon his shoulder for a moment, then drew back to stare up at him.

"So what's this, you can't call your mother more than once a summer?" she teased. "I could have been worried, you know."

"But you weren't." Dylan let her slip her arm around him and together they walked outside. "I'm sorry, Mom—really, I am. I just—I've been kind of caught up in things."

Angelica nodded. She had dressed for the weather, in a sleeveless shift of ivory-colored crumpled silk, belted at the waist with a gold cord, and simple but very expensive Italian gladiator sandals. Her hair was pulled into a chignon, and she wore heavy gold earrings and bracelets of ivory and sandalwood. Around her neck she wore the lunula. The silver crescent should have been jarring with all that gold, but in fact it was hardly noticeable, like the moon seen during daylight.

"You look good, Dylan," Angelica said as they walked to the car. "I told you you'd like D.C."

"It's been great." He stopped at the curb and stared up at the sky. "Except for the weather," he added, frowning.

Overhead the liverish sky had grown even darker. Heavy brownish thunderclouds crept above the National Gallery and Regent's Castle and the Treasury Building. Everything had a strange greenish cast, as though he was seeing the world through a whorled glass. A hurricane sky, he thought.

But the first of August was too early to worry about hurricanes. Besides, he was with his mother.

"Hop in!" Angelica said cheerfully, pulling open the back door of the car. Cool air like water flowed into the street. "Your chariot has arrived."

Dylan looked at the town car and made a face. "Gee, Mom, is someone paying you to ride around in that?"

Angelica laughed. "Not yet. Come on, go easy on me—it's the only thing Elspeth could find that had air-conditioning."

Dylan slung his long legs into the car and slid inside. "Is Elspeth here?"

"No. I just implored her to take care of a few things for me—I've been *so* busy, and I didn't want to have to worry about anything on your birthday."

"Right." Dylan nodded, stared back out the window at the museum, its dome faded to grey in the glaucous light. He bit his lip, then said, "I know you came all this way to see me, but I have to be back here by four. I—I made plans for tonight. With a friend."

Angelica slipped onto the velvet-covered seat beside him, motioning to the driver. Without a sound the car eased onto Constitution Avenue and headed toward the Tidal Basin. "Plans? What kind of plans? Anyone I know?"

Dylan opened his mouth to reply, thought better of it. He shook his head. "Just some friends."

Angelica turned and stared at him. She plucked a stray tendril of hair from her forehead and pushed it aside. "I see," she said softly. Her voice was even, her emerald eyes unreadable. "Well, that still leaves us time for lunch, doesn't it?"

"Sure."

She leaned forward. "Don't you have something for me?" she asked playfully.

Dylan frowned. "Oh . . . yeah. Here—"

He handed her the fragment of the lunula he'd found in the museum. She took it and Dylan held his breath, waiting for her to say something else, but his mother seemed distracted. She looked out the window as the Mall slipped by, her mouth pursed, brow furrowed. He'd spoken to her a few times over the summer, usually calling her from the museum, but he hadn't told her about Sweeney. He hadn't told her about anything; he hadn't actually wanted to speak to her at all. But she *was* his mother, and this *was* his birthday. She'd come all the way here from Huitaca, though past experience had made it clear to Dylan that his mother usually visited him when there was some other business she could take care of at the same time—dress fittings in Milan, academic cronies in Princeton. This time it was probably some old friends in Congress and the diplomatic corps.

But here she was, cool and beautiful as always, sinking back and sighing luxuriously. "Isn't this air-conditoning *wonderful*? The flight here was a nightmare! Maybe we should just drive around for a few minutes and enjoy all this nice cold expensive air."

She smiled at Dylan, but her son noticed that she hadn't given any command to the driver: he was already headed for the Lincoln Memorial. Whatever she had planned, and wherever they were going, had all been decided long before Dylan came onto the scene.

"Sure. Just remember—four o'clock."

"Of course: Four o'clock!" Angelica repeated brightly. "Always time for tea!"

I raced downstairs to the guard's desk.

"Did someone come here looking for Dylan Furiano?" I asked breathlessly.

Captain Wyatt, the security chief, smiled. "You mean some sweet young thing pretending to be his mother?"

I gritted my teeth. "That would be her."

"Well, she came by, Katherine, but she didn't sign in. He came on down here and went on out with her—" He gestured over his shoulder at the Constitution Avenue exit, then looked at me with raised eyebrows. "What, they leave without you?"

"No—yes, I don't know," I cried, and turned away. "If you see Dylan, tell him I'm looking for him. Tell him I want to know *as soon* as he gets back."

Captain Wyatt nodded. As I left I could hear him saying, "I *knew* that wasn't his momma."

Once back in my office I called the carriage house. The line was busy. It stayed busy for nearly forty minutes, during which I thought alternately of jumping out the window or running home. But at last I got through, only to hear the answering machine kick in.

"Goddammit, somebody pick up!" I shouted when the recorded tape ended.

"Hey." Annie's voice came on, sounding a little sheepish. "I'm sorry, were you trying to call? I was talking to Helen—"

"Is Dylan there?"

"Dylan? No. Why?"

"You're sure?"

"I think I'm sure. Dylan?" I heard her calling his name as she carried the cordless phone outside. "Dylan? Nope. Sorry, Sweeney. Why? You guys have a fight or something?"

"A fight? No, we didn't have a *fight*—" I choked. Then I couldn't help it: I broke down. "He's—he's *gone,* Annie! She came and he's *gone*—"

"What do you *mean,* gone?"

I told her about the note, and in between sobs gasped out what I could remember of Fritz Kincaid's impromptu history lesson. When I finished I sat with the phone pressed up so hard against my ear, I felt as though I'd been punched.

"Oh, man. Sweeney, this is bad." I could only nod, my entire body trembling. "But let's think, let's think—"

I heard her crashing through the dried stalks of lilies by the front door. Then, "Okay. You're still at the museum, and he said he'd be back there by four, right?"

"Th-that's what his note said."

"So maybe he'll be back by four."

I drew a shuddering breath. "You really think so?"

"No. But I think we better wait at least until then. You can't file a missing persons report on someone who's gone to lunch with his mother."

"Okay." Hearing Annie's voice calmed me somewhat. "Okay—so, four o'clock. You'll call me if he comes in? If he calls or—"

"Of course, Sweeney," Annie said gently. "Of course."

I could hear her moving back across the little patio, clonking into deck chairs. "It's going to be all right, Sweeney. He'll be okay, don't worry. He'll be fine—"

Just like your cousin and Oliver and Hasel and Baby Joe, I thought, and clenched my hands. "Okay. Four o'clock—" I whispered.

And waited.

Inside her hired car, Angelica Furiano looked down upon the sleeping figure of her son, sprawled across the pristine seat with one hand against his cheek and the other drooping to touch the floor. His chest rose and fell easily, his mouth was slightly parted where his fist was pressed against it. The same way he had slept as a child, his knuckles digging into the soft hollow of his cheek, his lovely face calm and dreaming as the moon's.

Angelica sat—crouched, almost—in the corner of the seat farthest from her son. In front, the radio played softly as the driver hummed to himself. They were driving up Pennsylvania Avenue for the third time that afternoon, the car moving smoothly in and out of light traffic. But this time, when they reached Seventh Street, Angelica leaned forward and murmured, "Thank you, Bryant. I'd like you to take us to the University of Archangels now. It's quickest if you go by Edgewood—"

The driver nodded, and without a word steered the car onto the narrow cross street. Angelica turned her gaze back to Dylan. The seat beside him was littered with small crushed pods—the dried seed heads of *papaver somniferum,* opium poppies. On some you could still see where, days before, she had used the lunula to make the neat incisions that allowed the flower's blood to seep through and dry to a pale crust. Afterward she had carefully scraped off the opium paste, and with her hands formed it into a tiny cake. Kneading it carefully between her fingers, she added dittany of Crete and crushed roasted barley; then, in lieu of the sacred *mentha pulegium,* an aromatic mint that brings delirium, she added *salvia divinorum,* the diviner's sage that she herself had smuggled from the Sierra Mazateca to grow at Huitaca. At the last she flavored it with honey and dried orange peel, cardamom and coriander seed. Then she had wrapped the little square with gold tissue paper and a tiny white raffia ribbon, as a present.

"Here, sweetheart."

Dylan had gazed suspiciously at the gold-wrapped lozenge sitting in her palm.

"This isn't more jewelry, is it?" His mother was prone to giving him extravagant and unwearable gifts, ruby and emerald earring studs, a Rolex watch eminently unsuited for a college freshman.

"No, silly. Open it," she urged, leaning back in the seat. He peeled the tissue off with some difficulty, the paper catching on the sticky cake inside.

"Gee, Mom." Dylan stared at the gritty little cube. It looked like a caramel that had been dropped in the dirt. "You shouldn't have."

Angelica gave her rich throaty laugh. "Silly! It's a special herbal thingie I had the apothecary make up for you at the Body Shop. It's supposed to bring—well, you know, strength and long life and all that good stuff. For your birthday." She kissed him, tousling his hair. "And you better eat it, Dylan—it cost a *fortune.*"

Dylan rolled his eyes. "I bet." He grimaced, then popped the cube into his mouth. *"Bleagh—"*

"Oh, come on, it can't be *that* bad. It has honey and stuff in it."

"It tastes like *dirt,*" Dylan said thickly, chewing. "Ugh. Dirt and perfume." After a minute he swallowed, then reached for Angelica and gave her a kiss. "Well, thanks. I hope it works. But listen, Mom—next time, just give me a new car, okay?"

That had been over an hour ago. It hadn't taken long for the opium to have its effect. Just a few minutes, its power enhanced by the roasted barley and *salvia divinorum.*

"I think I'm getting carsick." Dylan had turned from the window to stare blearily at her, his face pale. He looked distinctly queasy; his eyes were glassy, his voice thick, childlike. "Mom . . . ?"

"Shhh. Lie back, darling. Put your head down and rest, you're just sleepy . . ."

Her voice soothed him; he lay across the seat and within minutes was snoring. Since then his breathing had grown softer as he plunged more deeply under the poppies' spell, though his face remained pale as new milk. Beside him Angelica sat and with one hand stroked his hair. Her other hand absently traced the silver curve upon her breast as she whispered,

My days are run. No servant I
Nor initiate; where Iakos lies
Upon the threshold I shall greet
You, having completed his red and bleeding feast.

I have held the Great Mother's mountain flame.
I am set free. I have given thee
Robes of pure white, libation of honey-cake, in anticipation
of the joy of the bright red fountains,
Hye kye! Beloved!
I come now unto the place allowed.

Dylan moaned. Angelica's hand lingered on his brow; then she leaned down to kiss him, very gently, on the lips.

You are the word unspoken:
Haïyo! Othiym Lunarsa.

She lifted her head to gaze outside. Overhead, the storm clouds hung so low that she could see threads of lightning racing across their undersides, like flames seeking purchase on damp wood. She could feel a faint throbbing at her temples; but Angelica felt no pain. She herself had eaten a cake similar to Dylan's, with *mentha pulegium* added to it. But for several weeks now she had been readying herself for this: each night swallowing a tiny spoonful of the aromatic paste, until now, while she could feel it flowing through her, the opium did not cloud her thoughts so much as color them, an antique palette of blues and soft golds and reds, like a crumbling *skyphos* . . .

The car made a quick turn. Angelica steadied herself, her fingers clutching at a brass handrail.

"Not many people here this time of year," the driver called back to her as the car shot onto North Capitol Street. Behind them the Capitol grew smaller and smaller, until it disappeared into the haze.

"We're almost there." Angelica rested one hand protectively upon Dylan's breast. "Dylan—"

And then in front of them, rising from the city's smoke and filth, the domes and minarets of the Shrine of the Archangels and Saint John the Divine came into view. Slowly, like varicolored dyes bleeding into a piece of linen, cobalt blue and saffron yellow, ruddy ocher and that pale silvery gold that she had only ever seen here, where the gilded stars marked out their own strange constellations on the lapis dome: slowly as in a dream, as though called from the thick haze by the sound of Angelica's voice, it all came back to her. Drooping oaks and elms, dun-colored grass that even the Divine's corps of gardeners had not been able to save from the terrible heat; the cornices and towers of all the gaunt Gothic buildings faded to bluish grey and bluish green in the suffering late afternoon light.

And above them all the Shrine, with its stained glass windows like sheets of hot copper, its triad of defiant angels with hands raised above the great oaken doors. Upon every turret and spire and building, angels; angels everywhere.

"Hah!" Angelica said triumphantly, her son forgotten. Her face grew taut as she stared out at the monstrous building, the few small figures walking slowly down the steps to the waiting tour buses. "At last."

"I'm sorry, ma'am?" the driver called.

Angelica started, looked at him and smiled. "Nothing, Bryant. I think if you pull up over there—"

She cocked her head to where a door stood open at the side of the Shrine.

"—right there, and if you don't mind waiting here a few minutes."

The driver brought the car up to where she had directed. "Man, I never knew a place for the kind of trouble we've had this summer. Guns and weather and everything else," he sighed, running his hand across his forehead. "And the thing is, it just keeps getting worse and worse, and nobody ever does anything about it."

Angelica nodded. *"Quis iniquæ tam patiens urbis, ut teneat se?"*

Bryant shook his head. "What's that?"

Angelica smiled. "Just something someone said a long time ago—

"Who can have the patience, in this wicked city, to restrain his indignation?"

"You can say that again," the driver agreed, and he reached to turn up the air-conditioning.

I thought I would go mad. Afraid to leave my office, because I might miss Dylan if he returned. Afraid to stay, because every minute that passed meant he was going farther and farther away, he was almost gone now, I was losing him, he was gone . . .

"Oh, *god,*" I cried, and laid my head on my desk. I stared at my watch, the numbers blurring: 3:45, 3:54, 3:57 . . .

Four o'clock.

No Dylan.

Four-fourteen; four-thirty; four thirty-five. I called Annie.

"He's not here," she said. She sounded as though she had been crying. "Sweeney. I think you better come home."

I have never felt anything like the air that afternoon: so moist and suffocating it was like being covered with hot wet plaster. The sky was the baleful color of lichen or tamarack. But dark as it was, the light stung my eyes, as though there was some subtle toxin in the haze, something that sapped the spirit and gave everything the livid bruised glow of a corpse. My nostrils burned; the air smelled of harsh smoke and something more organic, algae or decaying wood. I thought of the legendary swamp the city was said to have been built on—the buried River Tiber, somewhere below us the bones of people whose cemeteries had been covered over by cement and limestone and marble.

There were hardly any cars on the street. I paced nervously back and forth, looking for a cab, and had already started walking when one finally appeared.

"I'm going to Ninth Street, up by Eastern Market," I said, and flung myself into the seat.

"You live in Northeast?" the driver asked. She was a small grey-haired woman with a ring in her nose. "You know there's no power there, right?"

I shook my head. "No, I hadn't heard—"

She nodded. "No power. They had to shut down the Library of Congress and the Post Office. Some people got stuck in an elevator there, a guy had a heart attack. I guess the heat. Yeah, power's out all across Northeast. Metro's down, everything's off in Brookland, parts of Southeast, over in Maryland . . ."

The cab had no a/c, but I rolled up my window anyway. I couldn't stand to breathe that soupy air. I couldn't stand to think about what the driver was telling me; I couldn't stand anything.

"Yeah," the driver went on, wiping her face with a bandanna. "Me, I'm going home now, you're my last fare. They're talking about riots, you know? Power goes down, everybody takes to the street, you're looking at some trouble, sister. This whole place up in flames before you know it. You got a boyfriend?"

I tried to say something, but all that came out was a groan.

"'Cause you know, us ladies probably shouldn't be out alone if something like that comes down. All this heat, makes people crazy. That's why I'm going home now. You're my last fare . . ."

There were no people on the sidewalks. No one sitting on the stoops, no one hanging out on street corners. From far away I heard a siren, but I didn't see any police cars. I didn't see anyone. My chest felt heavy, crushed between my fear for Dylan and this new horror: was it really as simple as this? A few weeks of terrible weather, a gathering storm; then pull the plug on the air-conditioning and subway, and the city goes up in flames?

"Yeah, I was listening to WMAL, they got an emergency generator or something I guess. They said everybody should just *stay indoors.* Like if you got no air-conditioning and it's a hundred degrees out, you want to *stay indoors* . . ."

The woman gave a last harsh laugh and fell silent.

When we reached Dr. Dvorkin's house I shoved a handful of dollar bills into the driver's hand and stumbled from the cab. I shoved open the ramshackle door that led through the breezeway, my heart beating so hard it was as if it didn't belong to me anymore, it was like something trying to get *in.* Then I was running across the patio, and then I was at the carriage house.

Annie met me at the door. Her face was beet red and wet, from crying or from the heat I couldn't tell. "Sweeney. I tried to call but you'd already left your office . . ."

"Dylan?" I shouted, pushing her aside. *"Dylan—"*

Sitting on the couch, atop Annie's crumpled sheets and pillows, were two men. They wore faded khakis and their shirtsleeves were rolled, their heads bowed so at first I didn't recognize them.

Then the taller of the two looked up and saw me.

"Katherine," he said, starting to his feet. The man beside him looked up hesitantly; then he stood as well.

"This guy said he was your landlord," Annie said, cocking her thumb at Robert Dvorkin.

"He is," I said numbly, but I hardly glanced at him. My eyes were fixed on Balthazar Warnick.

"Sweeney," he said. "The time has come that we must ask for your help."

"Help?" I shook my head, dumfounded. "You want *my* help? Where's Dylan? What are you *doing* here?" My voice rose as my confusion boiled into anger. "What the hell is going on?"

"Please, Katherine." Dr. Dvorkin's tone was calm but edgy. "You must understand. We need you—"

I stared at him: so thin and worn-looking in his faded clothes, his eyes bright and desperate.

"No. Robert—you're not . . ."

But of course he was. This wasn't the Robert I had known and worked with all those years, not the neighbor and friend I had sat with in the hidden garden, drinking wine and talking of nothing at all. This was someone else entirely. This was one of the *Benandanti.*

"You're—you're one of them."

He nodded. "Yes. But surely you knew?"

"I—I guess I did," I said slowly. "I guess maybe I just didn't want to." I turned from him to Balthazar Warnick. "Why are you here? Where's Dylan?"

My hands bunched into fists; I started to move closer to them but Annie stopped me. "If you've hurt him—"

"We have not hurt him," said Balthazar Warnick quietly. "Angelica has taken her son."

"Why?" blurted Annie.

Balthazar's eyes remained fixed on me. "Sweeney. She will kill him—"

"No!"

"Yes. She is not the Angelica you knew, Sweeney. She hasn't been, for—for a long time."

For the first time since I arrived he took notice of Annie. "Tell her, Annie," he urged. "You saw—you know what happened to the others—"

Annie stared at him in disbelief. "You knew? All along, you knew what she was doing—and you didn't stop her? You let her kill Baby Joe, and Hasel—you almost let her kill *me*!" She looked as though she were about to grab Balthazar by the throat. "Why didn't you *stop* her—"

Balthazar stood his ground. "We couldn't—"

I broke in furiously. "You *couldn't*? *Why* couldn't you? *Why?* Where's your *Benandanti* magic now? Why don't you just stick Angelica through another door, Balthazar? Why don't you just go after her with a fucking *gun*?"

I lurched forward and grabbed Balthazar by the collar, no longer caring what happened to me. "What, all of a sudden you need my help? All of a sudden you need my *permission* to kill someone? You didn't bother asking when you killed Oliver—"

"We didn't kill Oliver!" Balthazar cried. "He—"

"You drove him to it! You had him locked up in that place, you knew he wasn't strong enough, you *knew* it! I thought you were supposed to help him, I thought you all had some special *plan* for him—"

"We had no plan, Katherine," Robert Dvorkin said softly. "All we ever knew of Oliver and Angelica was that they were Chosen. For some reason, they were Chosen. It's only now that we realize that *Dylan* must have been the reason—"

I shook my head. "Dylan?"

"He *must* be—else why would Angelica and Oliver have conceived him? He is the last great sacrifice Angelica must make, in order for her epiphany to be complete. Then she will truly be Othiym—"

"Then it will be as before," whispered Balthazar. "Have you forgotten, Sweeney?"

I flinched as Annie grabbed my arm. "What's he talking about, Sweeney?"

"Have you forgotten?" Balthazar took a step back and flung his hands upward. "Then remember *now*!"

Before us the room was rent apart. Where Balthazar and Robert had stood, there was utter darkness. From the wasteland came a freezing wind, its roar so deafening that I could not hear Annie's screams, only see her face contorted into mute horror. My sweat-soaked clothes grew stiff with rime as I grabbed her and pulled her to me, then crouched so as not to be borne into the abyss.

A terrible voice rang out. Balthazar's voice.

"Behold Her now!"

The darkness was sucked away, whirling into some vast fiery vortex whose center was an immense eye. An eye that was open yet at the same time without sensibility, like that of a stone idol. As the darkness coiled into that huge orb I could see that it was but part of a face, a face so horribly and inconceivably vast that I fell to my knees in awe and terror.

"Behold Othiym!"

It was Her—the same monstrous figure I had seen that night with Angelica so long ago. The sleeping goddess, the Woman in the Moon: Othiym Lunarsa. She wore upon her breast the lunula, but it was no longer a slender crescent of silver but the moon, the *real* moon. She was more beautiful and terrible than I could ever have imagined, her mouth parted like a dreaming child's—but it was Angelica's mouth, just as those dreaming eyes were Angelica's eyes, as the hair that was the very fabric of the night country was Angelica's hair . . .

With a shout of horror I drew my arm up over my face. Because that deathly wind, the wind that sucked all sound and color and life into the void—that wind was *her breath*. All life was being drawn into her, into the shining crescent that lay upon her white skin. It was so brilliant that I could not bear to look upon it, so bright that it would surely set aflame all who gazed upon it, all who dared to walk beneath it—

"Sweeney!"

Like a gong Balthazar's voice echoed across the wasteland. I lifted my head. As suddenly as it had appeared the night country was gone. I was kneeling on the slate floor of the carriage house, shuddering with cold. Beside me Annie moaned, then with a cry started to her feet.

"Sweeney—he's going to kill us!" She grabbed me, her eyes wild. "Come *on*—"

Before us stood Balthazar and Robert Dvorkin. Their hands hung limply at their sides and their eyes were wasted-looking. As I looked at them, Balthazar raised one hand and held it out to me.

"It is my fault, " he said, his voice so low I could scarcely hear him. "I thought Angelica was too young when the lunula came to her. I thought she could never be anything more than what Magda was—smart, ambitious, cunning. I thought—I thought she was just a girl. Just a woman . . .

"Even after that night at the Orphic Lodge—I never dreamed how powerful she might become. I never dreamed she would turn so completely from her father, from all of us—"

He looked at Annie. "From all of you," he said. "From her friends. And from her own son."

He fell silent. I thought I could hear my heart beating inside me, and in the stillness Annie's heart as well, and Balthazar's, and Robert's. I looked away from Balthazar and stared at the floor, trying to find some pattern there in the slate tile. Trying to find an answer; something to believe in.

"Sweeney." I raised my head and Balthazar was there, his hand still held out to me. "You are our last hope."

"You are Dylan's only hope," murmured Robert.

Annie yanked my wrist. "No, Sweeney, this is *insane*—"

With an effort I shook her from me. "No," I whispered. "Wait—"

The room was utterly still, save for the exhausted buzzing of a fly against the window. I could feel their eyes upon me—Balthazar's brilliant yet restrained gaze; Annie's fury and confusion; Dr. Dvorkin's pleading. I took a deep breath. Then I took Balthazar's hand.

"I will help you," I said in a low voice. "Not because I think you're any better than Angelica. I don't. You murdered Magda Kurtz and Oliver Crawford and god knows how many others. You stood by and did nothing while Angelica slaughtered my friends. You let her take Dylan, and—"

My voice began to shake. "—and you tossed *me* aside, like I was *nothing*! Like I had no place in your beautiful perfect world, your perfect Divine! Because I wasn't one of your golden children, one of your goddamn scholars. One of your fucking *chosen ones.*"

I tried to yank away from Balthazar, but he tightened his grip with one hand.

"No," he said. "You're wrong. All these years, here—"

He indicated the walls and ceiling of the carriage house, the garden outside. "All this time, Sweeney: you have been under our protection."

A chill ran through me. "No—"

"Yes." Beside him Robert Dvorkin nodded. "We have been taking care of you, Sweeney—"

"No—"

"Watching out for you. Protecting you . . ."

The blood was thrumming in my ears but I could only shake my head, saying *no, no, no* as he went on.

"All those years ago at the Divine, Sweeney—we were wrong. Or, at least, we were only partly right. We knew that Angelica and Oliver were part of the equation; later, we knew that Othiym was as well.

"But we did *not* understand that there might be someone who would love Angelica and Oliver both. Someone who would not just come between them, but who might, somehow, serve to bring them together again."

I groaned. *"No . . ."*

"And Dylan—We did not know that *he* was going to be born, that *he* would grow, perhaps, to become the real, the true Chosen One—

"We did not foresee that, Sweeney. And we did not foresee *you.*"

Silence. My legs buckled, but Balthazar pulled me to him, his hands surprisingly strong.

"Do you understand now?" he asked, his voice desperate. "Do you see, Sweeney? The pattern was there all along! It wasn't just Angelica and Oliver—it was *you* and Angelica and Oliver—*you* were there, all along—"

"But what can I do?" I cried. I could feel Annie next to me, her cold hands tight on one arm, Balthazar's on the other.

"You can save Dylan," Robert said. "If we haven't waited too long."

"But how—where is he?"

I pulled away from Balthazar, and pushed Annie aside. "Do you know? Is he hurt? Because if you hurt him—if *anyone* hurts him—I'll kill you with my bare hands. I swear to god by all that's holy, I will—"

Balthazar opened his mouth to speak. But before he could say anything, Annie erupted into laughter.

"What?" I shouted, whirling to face her. "What's so funny?"

"N-nothing," she gasped.

"Because I'm not kidding, I'll kill anyone—"

"That's what I *mean,*" Annie said, and wiped her eyes. "I think that's the point, Sweeney—"

She turned and stared at the two *Benandanti.* Then, to my surprise, she made a little bow. Her husky voice rang out as she announced, "Well, guys—whoever you really are, and whatever the hell you're doing—

"I *think* you finally got the right girl for the job."

I said nothing; what *could* I say? But at last Robert Dvorkin sighed and murmured, "We can't wait. Are you ready, Balthazar?"

Balthazar turned to me. I couldn't bear to look at him, so I stared at my feet and nodded. "I'm ready. But where is he? How are we going to find him?"

Balthazar took my hand. "This way, Sweeney," he said, and pointed at the front door of the carriage house. Abruptly Annie was there between us, shaking her head furiously.

"Hey! If you think you're taking her off somewhere—"

"No, Annie," I said. Adrenaline and dread and exhaustion had pumped me up so that I hardly even felt afraid anymore. "This is—well, I don't know *what* it is, but you better not come."

"Don't you *dare*—"

"Annie!"

"Let her go." Robert's calm voice cut through the anger. "One way or another, it won't matter."

Annie turned to him. "Oh, right, like *I* don't—"

I grabbed her. "Shut up, Annie. Balthazar, tell me what to do."

I looked into his eyes: those half-feral eyes, with their mockery and menace always waiting, waiting, like a patient wolf. I saw no mockery there now, or menace; but neither did I see any warmth. Only a cool, measuring regard, as though he were looking at a heated glass and wondering if it was strong enough not to shatter.

After a moment he nodded. "That way." Once again he pointed to the door.

I shook my head. "That's the front door of my house."

"That's right, Sweeney." A very small smile appeared on his face. "Go," he urged, and gave me a gentle push.

"But—"

"Go."

All the bravura I'd felt moments before was gone. I felt sick and numb with fear; but then I thought of Dylan. Somewhere, Angelica had Dylan; but where? I could only trust Balthazar now.

"Okay," I said. I walked toward the door, forgetting Annie stumbling behind me, forgetting Balthazar and Robert and even Angelica.

Dylan, Dylan, I thought, and reached until my hand pressed against the screen. *Oh, Dylan.*

The door bulged open, the bottom catching on the floor sill and groaning as I pushed. *Dylan. Dylan.* Then, with a sound like water bursting from a broken dam, the door gave way. Before me was a dazzling vista, gold and crimson and argent, nothing but radiance, and so brilliant I could not bear to gaze upon it. I closed my eyes and stepped forward. My hands flailed helplessly as I plunged. Before I could draw another breath I tumbled head over heels and struck the ground. I lay there for a moment, groaning.

I had walked through the *Benandanti*'s portal and left the carriage house behind, and it hadn't killed me. Yet. I took a deep breath and opened my eyes.

I was at the Divine.

"Sweeney—"

I stumbled to my feet as Annie staggered up beside me. "Sweeney—how did—are we—"

"Yes," I said, staring at the sky. "I think we are."

We were on the porch in front of Garvey House. Wherever I looked, everything seemed to be in motion. Immense oaks lashed back and forth like saplings, their leaves torn from them and sent spinning upward. All the air was charged with the sound of wind, a terrifying roar like a thousand engines racing. A power line whipped through the air, finally wrapped itself around a toppled pole. On the narrow path leading to the building, whirlwinds of dust and grit churned furiously. A chair went skidding across the porch to crash into the balustrade. I grabbed Annie to steady myself, then pulled her after me down the steps.

"Oh Annie," I breathed when we reached the bottom. "It's the end of the world."

Above us was a raging maelstrom like that I had glimpsed in my vision of Othiym. Only this was *real.* This was the *sky.* Like an endless sea of molten lead it flowed and boiled, iron-colored, streaked with waves of bruised green and violet. Lightning shot through the clouds, and as we watched a tree burst into blue flame, then, with a howl like a wounded leviathan, crashed to the ground.

"We have to go!" Annie shouted, pointing at the flaming wreckage. "Get off the hill!"

With a deafening boom the air exploded into white flame. I screamed and ducked, felt Annie pulling me down the path. Leaves and branches whipped my cheeks as I stumbled after her, until with a cry I looked up.

All the Divine was ablaze with lightning. Against this jagged splendor the Gothic buildings rose stark black, their towers and parapets rippling with phosphorescence, their angel guardians aglow. There were no people anywhere in sight, no lights on in any of the windows. I stared, speechless, half-deafened by thunder, like one of those stone figures brought to ground.

"What are we supposed to do?" yelled Annie.

I shook my head and shouted, "I don't know."

But I did. Because in all that raging tempest, only the Shrine was untouched. It loomed above the chaos of light and shadow, more the implacable sphinx than ever it had been: ponderous and silent, a behemoth waiting to give birth. Fox-fire flowed from its parapets, pooled like cyanic mist about its twisting stairs and the empty black eyes of its stained glass windows. The gilded stars burned a fiery gold against the lapis dome, and reflected within its curve was the most perfect white crescent of a moon, rising from volcanic clouds on the eastern horizon.

"In there." I pointed to the Shrine. "He's in there." Annie nodded mutely as I started to run. "Come on—"

Beneath our feet the grass kindled. Smoke billowed behind us and I choked on the scent of burning leaves. To either side rose the Piranesian citadels where for two hundred years the *Benandanti* had kept their treasures and lore intact, with their winged granite sentinels outside. I could feel their eyes upon me now, those same blank eyes that had greeted me on that first afternoon so long ago; could see them crouched on balusters and columns with wings arched as for flight, their hands drawn up before them prayerfully. I ran, wiping my eyes against the smoke and heat, while before me the Shrine seemed to swell ever more monstrous, and the impassive angels watched.

Suddenly Annie shrieked. I turned and saw her pointing wildly.

"Sweeney!—"

The sky was filled with angels: black and crimson angels with coppery wings. From towers and rooftops and steeples they flew, launching themselves with arms outflung, hair aflame and their wings spreading behind them in glorious arcs, and all the air thundered with their cries. Voices like bells and voices like the sea, children's voices and the groans of old men, exulting and lamenting and howling their triumph as they swooped from their pediments and made blazing Catherine wheels across the sky. I stared dumbfounded, too overcome by awe to feel afraid, until one careened through the air above me, so close that its fingers raked my scalp and I fell back screaming with pain.

"Fire—"

I covered my head, my palms scorched and the reek of singed hair filling my nostrils.

"Sweeney! Are you okay?" Annie shook me. "Sweeney!"

I bit my lip and nodded. "Can you still run, Annie?"

A grin broke through her ash-streaked face. "Hell," she shouted, "if I can't run *now*—" She raised her arms protectively as another shadow raced across us.

We ran, zigzagging among the trees, pursued by that yelping horde. Angels or demons, furies or divine escort, I never knew. Whether they were sent by the *Benandanti* to protect us, or by Angelica to hunt us, they followed Annie and me to the very foot of the Shrine. Only then did their whooping cries diminish. In twos and threes they flew to the uppermost rim of the Shrine and landed, wings spread, until the dome was ringed with them.

Beneath that watchful army Annie and I hesitated. Overhead storm clouds boiled. The sickle moon was a hooded eye within the tumult. Before us the great steps led up to the Shrine, the rosy sandstone given a lurid sheen by the storm. Dust eddied like smoke where the wind gathered it. I glanced to make sure Annie was beside me, and began to climb.

Nothing stopped our ascent; nothing was there to bar our way inside. The wind's roar seemed muted there, though its power was evident: a fallen column, a large concrete urn toppled and crushed like an acorn. Bitter smoke hung everywhere, and there was the funereal musk of another odor, myrrh and sandalwood incense.

"Look," whispered Annie.

Where the statues of the three archangels had once stood, there was now a single huge marble image, filigreed with smoke and flame. A young woman with huge staring eyes, her torso draped in heavy robes that parted to expose her chest. Only where her breasts should have been, there were mounded rows upon rows of teats, dozens of breasts like a dog's or sow's, like rows of monstrous eyes staring down upon us.

I tried to summon some thin veil of hope to cloak me when I walked through those doors. Nothing came. Only the thought of Dylan bore me on—but it was a distant and curiously detached thought, like the remnant of a dream quickly fading. My scalp ached dully, my mouth felt dry and chalky.

"Let's go." I pushed against the door, and we entered the Shrine.

The wind died. The ornate windows admitted no light from outside, and a pervasive grey haze clouded the air. Marble vessels that had once held holy water were now filled with glowing chunks of charcoal, from which rose thin columns of scented smoke. Blossoms carpeted the marble floor: crushed narcissus and purple hyacinth, tiny white rosebuds, anemones and cyclamen, wilted poppies and jonquils. There were figs, too, their black hearts bursting with pink juice; and small hard apples, and pomegranates big as gourds, their rinds cut away to reveal the moist seeds within like so many wine-stained teeth. And ears of corn no bigger than my hand, and barley sheaves and maize; clusters of grapes that oozed red and black where we trod upon them, and the swollen knobs of opium poppies whose blooms were spent. Everywhere we looked there were flowers and fruit wreathed in that dreamy haze.

I turned and saw Annie staring transfixed at a pile of grain.

"Look," she breathed. She reached to touch a single white kernel like a glistening pearl. "It's so—so perfect."

The mounded grain shimmered like fairy fruit. With an effort I turned away.

"Come on, Annie. We can't stay here."

I pulled her after me. She came reluctantly, glancing back as we walked from the bay into the nave of the Shrine.

"Oh," I gasped, and stopped.

All around us there were stones. Megaliths, I thought at first, or boulders; but then I saw that they were not stones at all. They were immense carven idols—the most ancient and holy of icons made huge and manifest, in anticipation of the epiphany that was to come. A bulbous-shaped woman who might have been molded of honey, so bedewed with moisture was she—eyeless, mouthless, her hands placed protectively over a swollen belly that flowed into huge jutting buttocks and plinthlike thighs. Behind her stretched rows of tall white figures like alabaster blades, their breasts mere jots upon their torsos, a knife-slit of vulva between their marble legs. There were simple basalt columns and stalactites, pregnant women carved of green serpentine and shining onyx; ivory figures twenty thousand years old, their smooth faces scrolled with indentations and meanders, their hair etched into elaborate braids and knots. Women with the curved beaks of ibises and women with the heads of bees; snake-women, bear-women, women bearing tusks and tails. Their necks were hung with ropes of blossoms, their mouths smeared with honey and wine. Bees crawled across their cheeks and nested in their parted thighs. On the floor the matted petals shivered as serpents made their way through the blossoms. The air steamed, as though the vegetation was already decaying. Sweat streamed down my body and soaked my shirt and bare legs. Mingled with the heady incense of sandalwood and myrrh was another smell, pungent and sweet and malty. Beer, and the unmistakable odor of crushed coriander seed, the fragrance of sandalwood and oranges.

As we approached the altar the stone figures gave way to forms of gold and silver and bronze. Queens in chariots borne by griffins, tiny girls cast in gold, with eyes of lapis lazuli and feathered crowns; a statuette of a monarch with her head thrown back, flanked by crouching lions. A goddess upon a mountaintop looking out to sea. Drowsy mothers nursing their young. A marble madonna holding the broken body of her son; the painted plaster image of a woman crowned with the moon and seven stars, a serpent coiled protectively about her ankle. Faint music sounded from the transepts. Flutes and tabors, a jangling sistrum.

And suddenly I was in that hot classroom again—the smells of chalk and wood polish, a faunlike man dancing across the floor with sistrum raised as a boy recited—

An Egyptian instrument used in the worship of Isis. Fourth Dynasty, I believe . . .

I started to fall, but Annie caught me.

"I'm okay," I said hoarsely. "Just dizzy . . ."

Chanting voices joined with the sound of bones and flutes. Women's voices—

Hail Hecate, Nemesis, Athena, Anahita! Hail Anat, Lyssa, Al-Lat, Kalika. Great Sow, Ravener of the Dead, Blind Owl and Ravening Justice. Hail Mouth of the World, Hail All-Sister, Othiym Lunarsa, haïyo! Othiym.

And now with them chimed the sweet piercing tones of boys or *castrati*—

Othiym, Anat, Innana.
Hail Artemis, Britomartis,
Ishtar, Astarte, Ashtaroth,
Bellona, More, Kali,
Durga, Khon-Ma, Kore.
Othiym Lunarsa, Othiym haïyo!

High overhead the vaulted dome arched, like a hand cupped above us. I knew its mosaic of semiprecious stones as well as I knew the lines of my palm: the sad somber face of Christ, haloed with chips of gold and jade, hands raised to display the stigmata.

That image was gone. Instead there was the sleeping visage of Othiym—her heavy-lidded eyes, her upturned mouth like the moon's spar. Within the streaming radiance of her hair a silver crescent was netted. The smell of sandalwood grew overpowering, the sweet odor of oranges so strong my mouth watered.

But I could not tear my eyes from the dreaming goddess. As I stared I realized this was no mosaic, no archaic fresco painted upon a crumbling facade. This was Othiym, and that was the Moon she held. Behind her I could glimpse the smoking towers and edifices of the city, the long shimmering stretch of turbid water that was the Potomac. As I stared the moon began to grow, swelling like a milky bubble that would burst and shower us all with bitter rain.

And then what would there be? When the moon goes black and cold, when Her fire is quenched and her hunger appeased: what becomes of us then?

An icy hand grabbed mine. In a daze I turned and saw Annie. She looked as dreamy as I felt, but I saw that she was pinching the inside of her arm, so hard that it bled.

"L-look," she said through gritted teeth. Her eyes teared with pain as she cocked her head. "I think we've found her."

In front of us was the altar. Its crimson carpeting was lost beneath the crushed pods and calyxes of fragrant plants. A life-size statue of a woman was there. She wore a pleated flounced skirt of many colors. Her broad hips narrowed to a small waist, cinched with a bodice that opened upon her breasts. Full and round and creamy as some lush fruit, her aureolae and nipples flushed red. Her hair was the color of amber, and fell in loose curls across her shoulders. Upon her brow was a silver crescent, and upon her breast. Her hands were raised. Clutched within them were two serpents that writhed and coiled.

This was not a statue. It was a woman, a priestess. It was Angelica.

"Haïyo!"

Her voice rang through the Shrine. Immediately those other voices answered—

"Othiym haïyo! Othiym Lunarsa!"

With a wordless cry Angelica brought her hands together. The snakes braided themselves around each other, their tails lashing at her wrists. And suddenly she no longer held them but instead an axe, a great double-bladed scythe of hammered bronze; but then that too was gone. Her hands were empty. With great reverence she let her fingers slide across the twin spars of the lunula upon her breast. Then she stepped forward and clapped, once.

Blessed, blessed are those who know the mysteries of the goddess.
Blessed is she who hallows her life in the worship of the goddess,
she whom the spirit of the goddess possesseth, who is one
with those who belong to the holy body of the goddess.

Her voice rose as she raised her hands to the vast face floating above us.

Blessed is he who is purified,
who has given himself in the holy place of the Lady.
Blessed is he who wears the crown of the ivy god.
Blessed, blessed is he!

A clattering noise. From the eastern transept stepped an ungainly form, its hooves cleaving flowers to strike at the marble below. A bull. About its neck loops of ivy were twined, and withered blossoms. It walked haltingly, as though it were exhausted, or drugged, its dark head hanging between its legs. In a low voice Angelica called out to it, in words I could not understand. The bull gave a soft moan, then walked toward her. Those same hidden voices sang out once more, their words counterpointed with the dry rattle of a tambour.

With reverence we welcome you
With tender caresses we stroke
the violent wand of the god!
Let the whirling dance begin!

With a soft laugh Angelica raised her hand, then struck the bull upon the muzzle. It shook its head distractedly, as though she were no more than a fly. She struck it again, harder, and yet again, with such force that I could hear the blows, as though she had struck a drum. The bull snorted, then bellowed loudly.

"Come now!" cried Angelica. She struck at the bull again and darted away, beckoning at the shadows. "Children!—"

The chanting voices grew louder. From the darkness of the western transept figures came, a slow procession of men and women—boys and girls, really, scarcely more than children. A sandy-haired boy and one blond as the sun; a girl with shaven head and a frayed pigtail running down her back. Seven and seven; and I remembered then the old story of Theseus sent to slay the minotaur, the monster given tribute every one hundred moons, of Athens's fairest children. Seven boys and seven girls, sacrificed to the bull . . .

But there was an older tale beneath that one: of a time when there were no gods, only men and children and bulls, and She who gave birth to all of them. She who must be worshiped and fed, She who must be appeased. The oldest tale of all, perhaps, and here it was now, before me.

Strabloe hathaneatidas druei tanaous kolabreusomena
Kirkotokous athroize te mani Grogopa Gnathoi ruseis itoa

Their voices intertwined, unpolished voices but sweetly poignant.

Gather your immortal sons, ready them for your wild dance
Harrow Circe's children beneath the binding Moon
Bare to them your dreadful face, inviolable Goddess, your clashing teeth

They walked to the bull, unafraid, and I saw that in their hands they held vines still wrapped about with leaves, and slender ropes.

All You have loved
All that is best
Is thine, O Beautiful One

They chanted, lashing the bull with ivy and hemp, their voices rising and falling in a cadence that kept time with my blood until I could feel their words inside me, and the whicking sound of the vines was one with the beating of my heart. I felt enthralled, no more capable of flight or thought than a stone . . .

All that is holy is thine
All that is meat
All that flowers and gives birth
All that is fecund.

Darkness is thine
The stealth of the hunter
That strikes in the field . . .

As one they turned from the bull, eyes raised to the sleeping moon overhead. I saw how deathly pale they were, their faces and bodies drained of blood and life. I knew then they were the chosen ones, those who had been given to Othiym—

"No!"

I flinched, turned to see Annie screaming.

"Joe! *Baby Joe—*"

She pointed to the last two in the line of the dead. Their skin faded to the color of oiled parchment, their hair bound with white fillet.

"Baby Joe!" Annie howled. "Hasel!—*here—*

I looked desperately among the others, trying to find Dylan among them, looking for his face, his beautiful eyes drained of all fire; but he was not there.

"Hasel!" Annie wailed. "Oh, no . . ."

They did not hear her. Instead they turned with the rest, and as slowly as they had entered they left the Shrine, arms hanging limply at their sides and ivy whips behind them.

"Oh god, get me out of here," sobbed Annie. "Please, oh please, let's go—"

I hugged her to me. I was alert now—seeing those walking corpses had made me feel the blood still pulsing in my own veins, made me taste rage like salt in my mouth.

"Angelica!" I shouted. I stepped away from Annie so that I stood in the center of the nave. "Angelica! Your son Dylan—where is he!"

She did not so much as glance at me. My voice echoed in the empty air; I might have been one of those basalt columns.

"Angelica!" I cried again. But this time there was desperation in my voice, and real fear.

On the altar Angelica stood beside the bull. She ran her hands across its back, soothing it. She tugged at the circlet of dried blossoms around its neck, breathed into its nostrils and stroked the hollow beneath its chin. Her bronzy hair spilled across its muzzle as she bent and kissed the smooth spot between its liquid eyes. With a gently lowing sound the bull knelt before her, its head moving back and forth, then rolled onto its side.

A soft echoing *boom* as it hit the floor and lay there, its sides heaving. For a moment Angelica stood above it. Her hair tumbled over her shoulders, her bare breasts gleamed with sweat. Above her the reflected face of Othiym stirred, mouth parting to show teeth like walls, the tip of a tongue red as blood.

Then, smoothing the layers of her flounced skirts, Angelica knelt beside the bull. She looked more beautiful than I had ever seen her, as serene as one of those faience images. Her eyes were brilliant, a flush spread from her breasts to her throat and cheeks. With sure hands she stroked the bull's side, all the while whispering to it; then very slowly she let one hand slide to where its groin was hidden in a thick mat of black hair.

I held my breath. One of its hind legs twitched; I glimpsed the dark flash of its hoof, large enough to crush a man's skull as though it were a bale of hay. Still Angelica kept murmuring. A shudder passed through the bull's entire body.

Angelica let her other hand slip beneath its leg and gave a quick satisfied smile. I sucked in my breath: she held its erect phallus between her hands, a thick dark column so big it was like watching a child put her fingers around a tree.

"Ugh—I'm going to be *sick*—"

Annie buried her head in her hands. I looked back at the altar, repulsed but also fascinated. It wasn't the idea of Angelica coupling with that huge creature—by now, I could imagine Angelica with *anything*. But she looked so frail and otherwordly, a woman spun of light and flowers; her glowing eyes green as elderflower, her lovely mouth mirroring the endless dreamy smile of the sleeping Othiym. If the bull were to move suddenly, it would crush her; its hooves would trample her carelessly as if she really were one of those scattered blossoms . . .

Rise up to heaven and arouse my son
after his sovereign mother.
Rise up to the abyss, and arouse the heart of this bull;
arouse the heart of Osiris after Isis;
arouse Othiym after the light;

arouse the heart of he whom I have borne. . .

It would not harm her. I stared in disbelief as Angelica stood, her hands still firmly wrapped around the animal's member. All about us the air grew warm and sweet, a cloying sweetness, like narcissus or a blood-soaked rag. The soft chanting and skirling that had been a constant undercurrent ceased. High, high above us the pale face of Othiym wavered, as if seen through smoke; then suddenly Her eyelids fluttered. I had a glimpse of a blackness so profound as to make the Shrine's cavernous space seem daylit. Her mouth opened in a yawn, wider, wider, wider; and my head reeled, seeing the void that lay within Her, that ever-hungering maw poised to engulf us all.

A susurrant sound, like a silk train being dragged across the floor. I looked down and saw an enormous sidewinder lazily throwing its coils across the floor. With a smile Angelica turned and gazed down upon it; then slowly she let her fingers slide from the bull's phallus. She drew her skirts up around her waist, those long slender legs honey-golden, her hips thrusting forward as though she would lower herself upon the bull.

I watched appalled. She would impale herself, she would be crushed and trampled into blood and pulp . . .

But then I saw that she had slid the lunula from her neck. Her skirts spilled behind her in folds of ocher and saffron and blue, the muscles in her thighs tensed as she held herself completely still. She gripped the necklace in both hands, its razored curve aimed at the bull's throat. A rumble shook the floor beneath me. I saw Othiym in the sky above us, Her eyes open now—Angelica's eyes, green as summer but uncomprehending and heavy with sleep, so huge that she would shed entire cities in a tear. Her expression mirrored Angelica's, rapt with desire but also avid, famished.

For an instant all was frozen in a grotesque tableau. The mute animal with its throat exposed for sacrifice; the priestess poised above it with her shining blade; and hovering above us all the moon, waiting, waiting . . .

Then with a cry Angelica fell upon the bull. Blood misted the air and spattered her face; there was a smell of dung and offal. With a howl it reared its head, then fell back upon the floor, its legs kicking uselessly. Angelica only smiled. She lifted her face and sang.

All that is beauty,
All that is bone

Is thine, Ravaging Mother
All You have loved
All that is best
Is thine, O Beautiful One.
Haïyo! Othiym!
Othiym Lunarsa

The bull stirred convulsively. From the transepts came the echo of triumphant voices. Beside me Annie crouched and refused to look up. But I could do nothing *but* look, though my whole body ached from the horror of it, as Angelica's hands tightened upon the lunula. With a single quick motion she moved to slash its throat.

"Ne Othiym anahta, Ne Othiym—praetorne*!"*

Through the sanctuary a shout rang out. A woman's voice, commanding, so loud that the stones trembled. As though a wind had risen from the night country, the hungering face above us shivered. With a cry Angelica stumbled backward.

"Who would profane this place?"

The other voice cried, *"Ne Othiym anahta, Ne Othiym*—praetorne*!"*

Annie looked up at me, her eyes wild.

"That's *Oliver*!"

I drew my hands to my breast. "Oliver's *dead*—"

"Angelica!" the voice commanded. Angelica froze. "Listen to me: You will not slay him!"

It was Oliver's voice. I whirled, trying to find him in the darkness, but there was only a woman there, tall and raven-haired. She wore a loose purple robe and her feet were bare. About her butterflies flew lazily, lighting upon her shoulders as though to feed.

"Go from here!" Angelica hissed.

The other woman shook her head. "Not yet. You have something of mine, Angelica." She stepped from the shadows and stretched out her hand.

For an instant I thought she was going to tear the lunula from Angelica. Instead she gestured at the bull. It snorted and gave a weird high-pitched wail; then it was as though it melted into the broken lattice of flowers upon the floor. I shouted in dismay and wonder.

Where the bull had been, Dylan sprawled on his back, naked, his arms flung protectively in front of him. From a gash on his collarbone blood welled and spilled down his chest. His hands clenched as his head moved blindly back and forth. There were streaks of black and red along his flanks and chest, and his hair fell in thick oiled curls about his shoulders.

"Dylan!"

He shook his head numbly.

"Dylan!" I shouted, and ran toward him. *"Dylan—"*

"Get back."

I screamed: it was as though I had been set aflame. My face and limbs burned, my bones blazed with the most acute pain I have ever felt. I stumbled to my knees and looked up helplessly.

"He is *my son*!" Angelica shrieked. She looked like a madwoman—her hair flung across her bloodstained face, bodice torn and skirts tangled behind her. *"Mine!"*

As though her voice were a match set to paper, rage leapt from Angelica to the Titan's head above us. The huge eyes narrowed, the mouth gaped open. Upon Othiym's brow the moon began to burn with a fierce black flame.

"And mine," the dark-haired woman said evenly. As though she were skirting a muddy curb she stepped across the mounded fruit and flowers, to where Dylan lay. *"Mine,"* she repeated.

It *was* Oliver—the same lustrous hair, the same fine cheekbones and strong chin, the same strong long-fingered hands. But it—she, he—was a woman, too, with rounded flesh and mouth, breasts and skin smooth and white as an eggshell.

A *woman.* My head roared. I could hear Baby Joe's voice, very faint as though recorded on faulty equipment, saying *Your goddess-worshipers . . . the priests would go into some kind of ecstatic frenzy and castrate themselves, then live like women, like priestesses . . .*

"Oliver?" I whispered.

But Oliver did not hear me. Oliver wasn't there. The dark woman was, and she was gazing upon her son for the first time, with the most intense yearning I had ever seen; with such raw love and pride and sorrow as to make my eyes grow hot with tears.

"Dylan," the woman said. She stooped and touched the place where the lunula had cut him. "Dylan, son of the wave. Here, get up."

My heart burst inside me. Because the gesture she made was Oliver's, pushing the long black hair from her face and smiling that crooked canine grin as Dylan stumbled to his feet. They stood and stared at each other, the dark woman with a sort of greed, Dylan with stoned incomprehension.

"What's—what's going on?" he asked, slurring his words. He looked around at the heaps of dead flowers and fruit with their heavy smells, the rows of silent icons. He held his hands out imploringly. "Where am I?"

"Dylan!" I lunged for him; but before I could grab his hand Angelica was there.

"No! He is mine—you are *nothing* to him, *nothing*!" Her voice rose to a shriek. "I will destroy you *all*—"

She raised the lunula above her. Her eyes closed as she let her head fall back, her mouth contorted as she opened herself to the waiting goddess and cried,

> *Strabloe hathaneatidas druei tanaous kolabreusomena*
> *Kirkotokous athroize te mani Grogopa Gnathoi ruseis itoa!*

From the emptiness above us came a roar, the sound of the last wave as it overtakes the shore. The sound grew louder and louder still, until I was deafened; until all about us I could hear the great stone idols shattering, an avalanche of ivory and granite and marble and bronze; and the sound of their destruction was that of a thousand prisons exploding into dust. Overhead the face of Othiym burgeoned until there was nothing in all the world but Her. She was the world, She *was* the Moon, Her eyes huge, no longer green but iridescent, all the colors of the spectrum streaming from them, lips curved into a vast and secret smile, Her hair a river of light coursing across the sky, the stars like silver dust upon Her cheeks. Her arms were upraised, only they were no longer arms but immense columns holding back the night. Her legs reared to either side of us, vaster than anything imaginable. When She moved the ground shook. On Her brow was a silver crescent, the hungry curve of the new moon like a mouth opening to feed. Beneath Her all the Earth was in shadow. But it was a moving darkness, a darkness that thrashed and flailed, a shadow that threw up first one leg like a continent and then another.

The darkness was a bull. It was *the* Bull, the great and eternal sacrifice, as she was *the* Woman, staggering to its feet and shaking its great black head, its horns the shadow of that blazing lunar crescent. The Woman in the Moon stared down at it, her mouth breaking into a smile.

And I knew Her. Her mouth the freezing maw of the abyss, her teeth like clashing knives, her tongue the flame that burned in the night country. Othiym the Devourer, Othiym the Mouth of the World—

Othiym Lunarsa! a million voices shouted. There was a smell of burning, of hyacinth and anemone and roses, of sandalwood and oranges. There was a smell of the sea. The chanting voices grew to a shout. The crescent in Othiym's hands burned brighter still, when with a sudden choking roar the bull staggered backward, tossing its head so that its horns were silhouetted against the blazing light—

And suddenly the vision of goddess and bull was gone. Suddenly all I saw was Dylan, and before him his mother, her eyes like scorched holes, her face a ravaged mask, and the lunula gripped in her hands like a scythe. On the floor behind her the dark woman lay, stirring weakly. Beside her Annie crouched.

"Oliver! Are you hurt—*oh*!"

"Now!" cried Angelica.

Before I knew it I was upon her. A searing pain as I wrenched the lunula from her raised hands; then a scream, whether my own or Angelica's I never knew. Then there was only light, light and sound, a vast echoing tumult. In my hands I clutched a flaming crescent.

"No, Sweeney!—please, you don't understand, you can't possibly—"

For one last instant I heard Angelica's voice, faint as the sound of rain dying into the wind. With both hands I raised the lunula before me. I had a flickering vision of eyes and mouths, of white throats raised in supplication and weeping women. With all my strength I broke the lunula upon my knee.

High above me Othiym threw Her head back and howled; then with a groan She stooped. Her monstrous hand closed around something on the ground—Angelica's doll-like figure. Othiym bore her upward. Her mouth opened, a yawning entrance to the abyss, and the moon upon Her brow glimmered fitfully as the tiny struggling figure was swallowed by that engulfing darkness. With a last howl of rage and hunger She was gone—and with Her, Angelica.

Every sense was riven from me. From very far away I heard a faint high *ping!*, a sound like the tiny crack that foretells the destruction of a prized vase. One moment I was numb; the next I was blinking as I looked around.

"Sweeney? Sweeney, it's me—"

I moaned. A few feet away Annie was still crouched over the dark woman. Beside me knelt Dylan. He was covered with blood, but the blood was cracked and drying, the slash along his collarbone already scabbing over.

"Dylan?" I grabbed him and began to sob. "Oh, Dylan—"

"It's okay, Sweeney," he murmured. "It's okay, it's okay . . ." He helped me to my feet.

"Is it—what happened?"

"Hush. Not now, Sweeney." He put his arm around me and we started toward the back of the Shrine. "Maybe not ever . . ."

The endless lines of goddesses were gone. Instead the same wooden pews stood there, rank upon rank, the same holy water fonts and Sunday Missalettes. There were dead leaves everywhere too, and mud—

Mud!

"Is it raining?" I asked thickly.

Dylan nodded, unexpectedly grinned. "Wait'll you see—"

We walked slowly till we came onto the Shrine's broad steps. Rain sluiced from the sky, rain so cold that within a minute I was shivering.

"It's broken!" somebody yelled. I turned, and saw Annie stomping in a puddle. "The heat wave's broken—"

A thunderclap boomed and I jumped, then laughed.

Across the campus of the Divine, lights were flickering on, one by one. Lights in turrets and paneled studies, streetlights and crimelights and lights in cars—

In *one* car, at least: Yellow Cab Number 393, idling at the base of the Shrine.

"Is that for us?" I croaked.

"Not this time." A diminutive figure slipped from behind Dylan, holding out some wadded clothing. "Here—put these on for now." He drew Dylan away from me.

"Professor Warnick." I raised my hand to my brow. "Angelica—where is she? What happened?"

"Hush," he said, and he sounded exactly like Dylan. "Later. Sweeney, I want you and the others to come with Robert and me."

"But Oliver!" I cried. "Where's Oliver?"

That was when I saw somone standing by the cab. A tall black man with barrel chest, an umbrella in his hand. He was holding the door open for a woman in a purple robe, a woman with long black hair that fell, wet and glistening, to her shoulders.

"Oliver!" I shouted. "Oliver—"

Handsome Brown raised the umbrella so the woman could step into the back of the cab.

"Oliver!"

The dark woman stopped, shaded her eyes, and looked up the steps to the Shrine.

"Sweeney," she said; although how could I hear her from that distance? She smiled, that beautiful crooked smile, and her voice rang out across the distance, across years and decades and maybe even centuries—

"I told you I'd be back."

Then there was the muted thump of a car door slamming shut. With a low rumble the cab pulled out of the parking circle and onto North Capitol Street. In a moment it was gone.

"Here, Professor Warnick. I can take over now."

Balthazar Warnick smiled slightly as Dylan pushed him aside. "You okay, Sweeney?" Dylan asked tenderly, drawing me close to him. "You okay?"

I stared at him openmouthed. He was wearing a clean, though damp, white oxford cloth shirt and chinos, and a pair of black leather wing tip shoes with no socks. One shirt cuff still bore the faded image, in blurred ballpoint ink, of a clock's face, the hands set to four. Always time for tea.

"Where—where did you get those clothes?" I stammered.

"From Professor Warnick." Dylan gestured to where the cab had been parked. "He said that woman told him to give them to me."

"That—that woman." I wiped my eyes and nodded. My throat was tight as I whispered, "They—they fit pretty good."

Dylan gave me a sad smile. "I know. It's weird, isn't it? Warnick said she was an old friend of—of my mother's." He plucked at his shirt. "He said she'd been holding on to these for a while, to give them to me. And she said to give you something, too—"

Behind him, Balthazar Warnick and Robert Dvorkin and Annie Harmon stood watching us.

"What's that?" I whispered.

"This," Dylan said. He bent to kiss my cheek, his warm breath smelling of honey and coriander. "And this—"

He handed me a flower: a small flower with violet-blue petals and brilliant yellow stamen, its scent faint as the fragrance of rain and sweeter than anything I had ever know.

Huakinthos. The flower of Adonis. A wood hyacinth.

There were lights burning in the carriage house when we returned. Balthazar and Robert Dvorkin stood on the sidewalk, waiting for us to go inside.

"I won't expect to see you in the office for several days," Robert said.

Annie rolled her eyes. "Gee, what a prince."

"Good-bye, Sweeney," said Balthazar. Again he had the barest hint of a smile. Unexpectedly he raised his hand and waggled his finger at me, just as he had that first night at Garvey House. "We'll be in touch."

Annie stared as the two *Benandanti* walked back to the main house. "Goody. Next time, why don't you just send a neutron bomb?" she muttered. Then we went inside.

Annie spent the night, and Dylan of course—I held him so tightly that more than once he woke, and I bit my lip to keep from crying out as he clutched me to his chest. When I finally slept I dreamed of the sun on blue waves, the warm fresh wind rushing down from a stony mountaintop and the smell of hyacinths perfuming the air.

Annie left the next morning, after having a *very* protracted telephone conversation with her lover. "Sorry, Sweeney. Helen is frantic and just about ready to come after me with a flaming sword, so I better go. But I'll be in touch," she added, grinning. "Just like everybody else. Now that I know how to find you."

She looked at me soberly for a minute, then said, "I have an idea, something I want to talk to you about after—after all this dies down. I'm thinking of taking some of the money I've made off that stupid song and endowing a scholarship at the Divine. In Baby Joe's and Hasel's names. Something for normal people, you know? For ordinary losers like you and me—"

I laughed and hugged her, trying my best to keep from crying. "I think that's a great idea, Annie. Call me—"

"Oh, I will." She hesitated at the door, shifted her knapsack from shoulder to shoulder. Finally she said, "Well. Bye, Dylan."

Dylan smiled. "Bye, Annie."

"*Ciao,* Sweeney." And she was gone.

That left only Dylan and me.

"Will—will you be going back to school?" I asked softly, late that night. Dylan lay beside me in the heated darkness, his breathing so slow and measured I thought he had fallen asleep.

"No," he said at last. He rolled over to look at me. "How can I go back there, after all this? I'm going to stay here. In D.C. And marry you, if it's still okay."

"Of course it's okay," I whispered, kissing him. "It's the most okay thing in the world. But what will you do?"

"I have a trust fund that my father set up for me. If my—if Angelica ever shows up, well, I guess I'll have to deal with her then."

He was silent. Then he said, "I talked to Dr. Dvorkin this morning."

"You did?" I was surprised and a little ashamed; I still hadn't called or gone over to see him.

"He said that he could arrange for me to go to the Divine, if I wanted to. I could start in September, get my transcripts sent out from UCLA. He says I won't have any trouble getting in—I'm a double legacy, whatever *that* is. I guess because of my mother and grandfather di Rienzi."

I said nothing, thinking of Oliver and the hyacinth, now wilted upon the harvest table downstairs.

"So I thought, if it was all right with you, maybe I might do that. We'd still have a few weeks before the fall term starts."

"And you won't mind living with someone who's older than most of your teachers?" I teased.

He shook his head. "No. Dr. Dvorkin said it's nobody's business, anyway—"

"Which it's not."

"—and he seems to think I'll do really well there. He says I'm sort of the ideal student for them, whatever that is. He says they've waited a long time for someone like me to come along."

"Oh, they have, Dylan," I murmured, drawing him close to me. "And so have I."

Coda

There is a woman in the moon.

Dylan and I see her, night after night, her face growing closer to ours until it fills the window, huge and round and white, and we can hear her singing to us in Angelica's voice. She has Angelica's face as well, but bleached of all color. Angelica's emerald eyes washed to grey, Angelica's hair streaming from her face like clouds, Angelica's hands the limbs of the willow tree tapping at the window. She is calling to us, she is waking us; she is willing us to follow her. Her hands reach through the window; the glass shatters as the moon engulfs our room and she is everywhere around us, the color of night, the color of milk, the color of bone.

We awaken in each other's arms. We are in bed, Dylan and I, in the carriage house—the place that Robert Dvorkin, and the *Benandanti,* have given us. Outside the late-night traffic on Capitol Hill murmurs past. A lone taxi trawls for passengers, two college girls call drunkenly to each other on the distant avenue.

With a groan Dylan turns to look out the window. The moon is full. It no longer has his mother's face, because he is awake now, and he remembers that his mother is gone. But something in the wind tapping at the glass reminds him of Angelica, I can tell, something in its low moaning makes him turn to hug me close to him, his arms tight around my stomach, his fingers moving restlessly, feeling what is there even though I have told him it is much too soon, it will be weeks, maybe months, before we will be able to feel the baby move.

But Dylan knows that she is there—his daughter, Oliver and Angelica's child as much as his and mine—just as he knows that Othiym is there too, somewhere beyond the rim of the sky and the racing ledge of clouds, someplace where the sky runs black and stars stream down the bowl of heaven like blood in a cauldron.

She is there now. She will be there for the rest of our lives, and our daughter's life, and perhaps beyond. That vast and dreaming form—sister, mother, daughter, wife—the eternal mystery, lover and destroyer. Othiym Lunarsa.

The woman in the moon.

Author's Notes

In the course of writing this novel I referred often to the works of many people, chief among them Carlo Ginzburg (whose studies of the benign and very real *benandanti* inspired the fictional *Benandanti*), Paul Faure, Marija Gimbutas, Camille Paglia, Riane Eisler, Robert Graves, Anne Baring and Jules Cashford, Yves Bonnefoy, Rodney Castleden, Charles Pellegrino, Clifford Geertz, Patricia Monaghan, Carl Kerényi, Merlin Stone, Christos Doumas, Sir Arthur Evans, and Jane Harrison, as well as to numerous primary sources from the ancient world. Whenever possible, I have tried not to wander too far from what is currently known or speculated about the various goddess cults of Old Europe and the Mediterranean; an exception is in my use of the Linear A script from the Minoan/Mycenæan cultures, which, insofar as I am aware, continues to confound translators. However, this is a work of *fiction,* an entertainment and improvisation on some classical themes. As the classicist M. P. Nilsson wrote, "gods also have their history and are subject to change." In no way should my pages be viewed as a critique, reflection, or interpretation of the works of those mentioned above. Any errors of fact contained herein are strictly my own.

Kudos to my wonderful agent, Martha Millard, for everything. Many thanks for all their help to my wonderful American and UK editors, Christopher Schelling and Jane Johnson; to Ellen Datlow, who read this manuscript in its nascent form; to Jennifer Hershey, whose insight contributed invaluably to this work; and to Jose Padua, who since 1975 has been feeding my head with poetry and music.

My love to Richard Grant, who introduced me to George Crumb's string quartet *Black Angels: Thirteen Images from the Dark Land*, from which some of *Waking the Moon*'s chapter titles have been drawn; and who proved himself to be the very model of a modern New Man by taking care of our children and household in the years it took to write this book.

Finally, to all of my old D.C. friends from CUA, NASM, and the Hamline—thanks. You really made it all Divine.